PENGUIN BOOKS

STORIES OF THE OLD WEST

John Seelye is Graduate Research Professor at the University of Florida, where he teaches American Studies, including courses on the West. He is the author of *Prophetic Waters: The River in Early American Life and Literature* (1977) and *Beautiful Machine: Rivers and the American Republic* (1991), as well as studies of Mark Twain and other aspects of the American West. He has also written fiction, including *The Kid* (1972, 1982), a Western.

# STORIES OF THE OLD WEST

## Tales of the Mining Camp, Cavalry Troop, & Cattle Ranch

Edited by
JOHN SEELYE

PENGUIN BOOKS

PENGUIN BOOKS
Published by the Penguin Group
Penguin Books USA Inc., 375 Hudson Street,
New York, New York 10014, U.S.A.
Penguin Books Ltd, 27 Wrights Lane,
London W8 5TZ, England
Penguin Books Australia Ltd, Ringwood,
Victoria, Australia
Penguin Books Canada Ltd, 10 Alcorn Avenue,
Toronto, Ontario, Canada M4V 3B2
Penguin Books (N.Z.) Ltd, 182–190 Wairau Road,
Auckland 10, New Zealand

Penguin Books Ltd, Registered Offices:
Harmondsworth, Middlesex, England

First published in Penguin Books 1994

1  3  5  7  9  10  8  6  4  2

LIBRARY OF CONGRESS CATALOGING IN PUBLICATION DATA
Stories of the old West : tales of the mining camp, cavalry troop, & cattle
ranch / edited by John Seelye.
p.  cm.
ISBN 0 14 01.4550 8
1. Western stories.  2. Frontier and pioneer life—West (U.S.)—
Fiction.  3. Gold mines and mining—West (U.S.)—Fiction.  4. Ranch
life—West (U.S.)—Fiction.  I. Seelye, John D.
PS648.W4S76  1994
813'.087408—dc20                    93-11941

Printed in the United States of America
Set in Century Expanded
Designed by Katy Riegel

# Contents

# Contents

# Introduction

The West, as a cardinal direction in America, has inspired considerable literature in the poetic vein, from Bishop George Berkeley's identification in 1728 of western regions with the movement of civilization and the Christian religion—"Westward the Course of Empire takes its way"—to the assertion of the popular versifier Arthur Chapman two centuries later that the West "begins" at that point on the map where skies are "bluer," friendship "truer," and handshakes and men are stronger. For Berkeley, the West held out hope for a Europe in moral decline, and for Chapman likewise those blue skies and strong handshakes bore implicit comparison with skies and men in the East, where such matters were paler, weaker, less pure. Horace Greeley, waist deep in the optimism of the nineteenth century, advised young men in search of opportunity to "Go West," and large numbers did so, often in the company of wives, children, and sundry livestock, inspiring the popular ballad about "Sweet Betsy from Pike." Indeed, it is difficult to find any sentiments concerning the American West, down to the turn of the last century into this, that do not give a long line of credit to that region, thought of as the direction of Empire and Full Employment.

But what lends a dimension of relativity to all those sentiments that piled up over the years is the extent to which the precise location of the West kept shifting in a westerly direction. The "Pike" from which Betsy and "her lover Ike" set out for California in the 1850s was a county in Missouri, which in 1776 was still territory controlled by Spain. And Greeley borrowed his famous line from a lesser-known journalist, John Babsone Lane Soule, who used it first (in 1851) in a Terre Haute newspaper, printed in a place that Bishop Berkeley, from his vantage point on the Rhode Island shore, would have thought rather much beyond the West *he* had in mind. By 1934, drawing his

conclusions from a long century of perspectives, Bernard De Voto
had opined that "the West begins where the average annual rainfall
drops below twenty inches," the hundredth meridian of longitude, a
definition that coordinates well with the backdrop to any number of
those kinds of movies called "westerns." Most Americans probably
still concur with De Voto, and think of the West as a region dry of
water if not whiskey, a place far different from the paradise Columbus
described when he returned from what he died thinking was not the
Far West but the Far East—China and India.

But if the location of the West has been fairly well established for
the past half-century, the values associated with it have continued to
change. From early on, the "Far West" in this country was associated
with that moving line called "the Frontier," whose implications continued to be debated long after Frederick Jackson Turner's epochal
announcement in 1893 that, with the disappearance of free land, the
frontier, which had for so long shaped the American character, had
closed and gone out of business. During the past decade especially,
thanks to a new breed of revisionist historian, typified by Patricia
Limerick and Richard Slotkin, the idea of the West, like earlier notions
of the East, has become filled with shadows other than those cast by
the empurpled sagebrush at sundown. The easy boomerism of Berkeley and Greeley and the self-assured sunshine of popular versifiers
like Chapman are now chiefly the province of Western politicians and
promoters. And when we come to consider what is meant by the term
*Old West*, a direction illuminated by flickering images on a screen, the
inherited iconography of Cowboys fighting Indians—especially when
translated into terms of Conquistadors and Aztecs—this also becomes
problematic. If *Old West* and *Far West* are synonymous, and I think
they are, then the dim imprint of prior Spanish mintage can be detected on that coin of the American realm. We have ended up where
we began, and must always start with the face of Columbus, as he
headed westward toward the East he never reached.

But as the profile of Columbus traditionally bears a Roman nose,
we must refer back to the classical world for our ur-etymology. The
word *west* is an Anglo-Saxon corruption of the Greek *hesperos*, meaning "evening," which, because it was associated with Hesper, the evening star, meant also "the west." *Hesperia*, "the Western Land," was
a place-name given by the Greeks to Italy and by ancient Italians—
Romans—to Spain, the place from which Columbus set sail for what
was to become once again "the Western Land." West for the ancient
world was the direction of empire—and of darkness. Once again we
may observe that what goes around comes around, and the halfway

route inscribed by Columbus on the globe has for some time now come full circle.

On a map that dates from the fourteenth century—less an example of cartography in the modern sense than a cosmograph, a diagram of the medieval world view—the cardinal directions we are familiar with are set askew, so that west is placed at the bottom, in the place where south is now located. East is at the top of the map, and is associated with the Holy Cross and heaven, but west is downward, toward death and hell, placed beyond the mouth of the Mediterranean Sea, past the Gates of Hercules, the navigational limits of the ancient (and heroic) world. It was that cosmographic conception that Columbus would challenge a century later as he set sail for what he assumed would be the Indies but turned out to be a continent entirely unknown to Europeans, whose discovery would give cardinal directions a radical reorientation. Over the next four centuries, as in Berkeley's poem, west would increasingly be the direction of hope, while east became associated with the Old World, with the despair inspired by the corruption of aristocracies and the ills of crowded cities. Moved to North America, the fourteenth-century diagram in time merged with the emerging realities—or at least the symbolisms—of the United States, and the South took on the resonances of what had been the West: now it was the great Mississippi River that gave way to hellground and death—a cosmography given particular point in 1852, with the publication of *Uncle Tom's Cabin.*

Moreover, by the middle of the nineteenth century the West had become compromised by nearly four centuries of exploration and settlement. What had been the direction of hope for Europeans had meant certain destruction and death to the native populations of the "new" world. Prosperity for white peoples meant impoverishment and worse for red. And, by 1852, the opening of Western territories that so excited Horace Greeley involved the extension westward of chattel slavery, yet another terrible price paid by many for the prosperity of a few. The opening of those territories also resulted in the injustices of the Mexican War, a display of naked imperialism that seized lands once claimed and settled by the Spanish so that the United States could extend its domain—now legitimized by the notion of Manifest Destiny—all the way to the Pacific Ocean. Henry David Thoreau, who refused to pay his taxes as a protest against that war, proclaimed that the woods of Maine were all the West he wanted, but what he got was the view through a window of the Concord jail.

Much as the French and Indian War had set in motion the forces that would result in the revolution, so the Mexican War was but a prelude to yet another, far greater conflict twenty years later, waged over the issues of national union and abolition but ignited by the heat generated during the debate concerning the spread of slavery into newly created Western states. Meanwhile, the spread of freeborn Americans pushed on toward the Pacific, and the direction of hope once again became the direction of death, as signaled by the graves distributed like mileposts along the California and Oregon Trail and by bones whitening under the Western sun, the remains of the buffalo whose extermination prefigured, even necessitated, the death and disappearance of entire tribes of Native Americans. The process was hastened by the completion of the Union Pacific after the end of the Civil War, and the final act of the imperial drama was presided over by a man named for the animal he had slaughtered in the name of progress, and who took advantage of the closing of the frontier by taking it on the road as "Buffalo Bill's Wild West Show."

By choosing the Columbian Exposition of 1892 as the site of his epochal announcement regarding the closing of the frontier, Turner gave a centennial period to the process initiated by Columbus. A century earlier, Joel Barlow had written an epic poem celebrating the glorious results of 1492, culminating with the American Revolution; and Turner's performance was likewise in a celebratory vein. Turner was of the opinion that the spirit of independence engendered by the frontier experience had been responsible for the spread of democratic institutions in the United States. He also maintained that the energies of the frontier would next be turned to other fields, like capitalist adventures and entrepreneurship. Turner was partly right on both scores, but he was also wrong, if only by omission, which subsequent historians have attempted to correct, with some measure of success.

As a consequence, the five hundredth anniversary of the arrival of Columbus was commemorated in the United States with something less than the self-congratulatory excesses of Barlow and Turner. The occasion was marked by exhibits giving graphic evidence of the terrible cost paid by non-Europeans for the frontier experience; and where such exhibits were lacking, demonstrations by Native Americans helped fill the void. Moreover, some historians, enlightened by the events of the past century, have refused to concede the closing of the frontier, pointing to the exercise of Anglo-American imperialism that continued long after 1892, indeed into quite recent years. A symbolically significant battle was fought in Cuba during the Spanish-American War of 1898 by a volunteer troop of (unmounted) cavalry made up of American cowboys and gentlemen ranchers led by Theodore Roosevelt, late secretary of the navy, cattle rancher, and deputy sheriff. The frontier, clearly, was still in business, conducted as usual by the force of arms (many of which, as in the battles with intransigent Apaches in the Far West, were carried by African-American soldiers), as the United States expanded its territorial purview. The frontier was a militant ideal kept alive by pulp fiction and motion pictures, and was revived in the sixties by the political rhetoric of John F. Kennedy, whose New Frontier gave us space exploration and, not incidentally, the Vietnam War, presided over by a general named Westmoreland.

Whereas in the Old World "frontiers" are more-or-less stable boundaries between nation states, in North America the idea of frontier is almost always etymologically intimate not only with movement (and, *vide* Turner, progress) but with the idea of a battlefront, conceived as the line between the forces of civilization and the ever-retreating wilderness. The United States, literally born of war, has a history, dating from colonial times, of constant armed struggle, a violent periodicity that gives point to our decadal chronology. We are a gun-bearing people, nursing a paranoia that may now be concentrated in urban centers but which can be traced straight to the conditions of frontier life. Fenimore Cooper's Leatherstocking, according to D. H. Lawrence, was a killer, and in him we can find the essential idea of that modern folk hero, the renegade detective. Steve McQueen was both Tom Horn and Bullitt.

From Powhatan to Geronimo, the Native American provided a worthy adversary in frontier battles, but antagonists were not always Indians, as the name we give to a century of conflict suggests: the French *and* Indian War involved European nation-states and conflicting religious dogmas as well as traditional rivalries between Hurons and Iroquois. The great historian of that conflict, Francis Parkman, Harvard-trained but schooled also in the novels of Scott and Cooper, regarded the war as the last and defining struggle between Normans and Anglo-Saxons, transplanted to American soil. Thus *Ivanhoe* and "Westward ho!" became conflated, and when General Custer commemorated the centennial of American Independence by his death at the hands of rebellious Sioux, the sound of his cavalry bugle resonated with echoes of Roland's horn at Roncevaux, imposing the ultimate sacrifice of chivalry upon the American scene.

Though identified first with Anglo-American then with United States energies, the "frontier spirit" engendered regional as well as international conflicts. During the period of interior expansion made possible by the Treaty of Paris in 1763, westering New Englanders moved into lands claimed by Pennsylvania, and the resulting hostilities between Yankees and "Pennamites" exploded as the Wyoming Massacre when in 1778 the regional struggle got caught up in the much larger war we call the revolution. A contemporary account of that tragic collision was written by Hector St. John de Crèvecoeur, a French physiocrat who as an "American Farmer" delighted in describing the rise of new farms in former wilderness areas, but who, having had trouble reconciling the bloody resolution of regional rivalries with the optimistic tenor of his *Letters*, did not include it in his published book. Crèvecoeur's *Letters from an American Farmer* contains sufficient troubling material as it is, and ends with the dispossession of a frontier settler by the outbreak of the revolution. Crèvecoeur, like Thomas Jefferson, saw slavery as the dark side of the pastoral ideal in North America and, more to the point here, had definitive reservations regarding the frontier process.

Though, also like Jefferson, Crèvecoeur praised the agrarian life which the frontier made possible, he regarded with distaste the kind of persons who formed the vanguard of civilization, the frontiersmen who made the first rude settlements in the wilderness. He defined the white hunter as a semi-savage, a once civilized man reduced by life in the woods (and a diet of wild meat) to barbarism. Eighteenth-century writers in general, perhaps because of the Enlightenment emphasis on rational balance and social harmony, brought to the wilderness a decidedly genteel sensibility, as in the case of Boston's Madame Knight, who looked down her westward-pointing nose at the rustic residents of Connecticut, or William Byrd, the Virginian wit and diary-keeper, whose westward-moving transit line, which determined the proper boundary between his colony and North Carolina, provided a diagram separating tidewater aristocrats from backwoods boors. It took a revolution in taste before Daniel Boone could be elevated to mythic stature as a nationalistic figure, whose hunting expeditions into Kentucky would be celebrated as the westward push of inexorable empire, equivalent to the Mosaic exodus.

Indian warfare, territorial battles between rival white settlers, the ridiculing by Eastern travelers of Western types, the constant movement of settlement westward, which gave opportunities alike for heroic deeds and for discontents—these repeated patterns would provide material for an emerging literature of the American West, which, like Crèvecoeur's *Letters*, would celebrate the frontier process while also revealing its problematic aspects. The captivity narrative, an "American" literary genre dating from the experiences of Captain John Smith, gave definitive form to the encounter between native and Anglo-American peoples. In the hands of Puritan authors, it gave a biblical resonance to the colonial experience, evoking the experience of the Israelites in the hands of the Babylonians. Captivity narratives also added drama to the jeremiads by which Puritans like Cotton Mather attempted to reform their fellow New Englanders. Here again, the frontier had its dark side: Native Americans were identified with the forces of Satan, and their white victims with the rampant expansion that Cotton Mather opposed as inimical to the original Puritan errand.

The literature of the "Old" West is very old indeed, dating in North America from the accounts of the earliest explorers; but *stories* of the Old West—that is, short fiction with sophisticated literary structures, as opposed to "true-life" adventures, however much edited for narrative (or ideological) effect—would have to wait until the short story genre emerged in the 1830s as a major literary form. The short story is generally credited as an American invention, which is to say it was an improvement upon an imported concept. Short narratives, or tales, are as old as literature itself, and emerged from an oral tradition during the first age of print in Europe. But like the famous stories told by the Canterbury Pilgrims, these are loosely framed structures, still rich with the cadences of oral delivery, and follow a leisurely, even random course of development. Carried to America, the tradition of tale-telling underwent some marvelous transformations, in large part because of the peculiar conditions of life in the young United States, including the emerging "Western" spirit of adventure, enterprise, and violence.

The invention of the modern short story is attributed to Poe and Hawthorne, and is associated with the rise in America of periodical literature in magazines that provided a ready market for writings that were brief and to the point—reading designed for Americans on the move. Both Poe and Hawthorne employed a certain exoticism, setting their stories in distant lands or in the Puritan past, appealing to their readers by a secondhand romanticism imported from Europe. The frontier—that is, the frontier of 1830–40—was not the subject or setting of those stories, despite the extent to which, as demonstrated by Edwin Fussell and others, it pervaded much of the literature of the American Renaissance by means of metaphor. In general, even the editors of Western magazines, published in Cincinnati and other commercial centers, saw themselves as purveyors and conveyors of Eastern, European-inspired culture, and their contributors, by and large, strove to prove that Westerners were as sophisticated and genteel as their Eastern counterparts. Only gradually did writers begin to accept the culture of the American West as separate, distinct, even praiseworthy, suitable for an emerging "Western" fiction—a phenomenon we can date from this side of the Civil War, not coincidentally associated with the rise of literary realism, with its emphasis on local color and regional distinctions.

This does not mean that the American West had no literary venue until the age of realism. Fenimore Cooper's *The Prairie* (1827), a historical romance set in the period of the Louisiana Purchase, in effect "invented" the West as a fictional zone, translating Scott's romantic Highland border into the grasslands of the trans-Mississippi region. But Cooper's romance did not bode well for Western fiction: the action begins with the heroic Leatherstocking, a buckskin-clad hero inspired in part by the myth of Daniel Boone, looming like a giant on the western horizon, glorious with the nimbus of a setting sun, but ends with the party of intended settlers retreating eastward and with the death of the old trapper, a demise that signals what was for Cooper and his contemporaries in 1827 the closing of the frontier. That termination was an illusion, promoted by the negative accounts of Western lands brought back by the Long Expeditions of 1820–21 and 1823—accounts that described the trans-Mississippi territory as the "Great American Desert," even as settlers were heading into that vast, unknown zone, families who would not follow the defeatist cue of Cooper's fictional pioneers.

But major American novelists did, and in the retreat of Cooper's frontiersmen we have in effect a signal to steer clear of the Far West as a fictional zone. In the 1830s, Washington Irving, recently returned from his long sojourn in Europe, went west in search of literary material, but the result, *A Tour on the Prairies* (1837), is an autobiographical account of his experiences, as is Caroline Kirkland's *A New Home—Who'll Follow* (1839) and Francis Parkman's *The Oregon Trail* (1849), with their very different perspectives on Western life. A possible exception is Melville's *The Confidence-Man* (1857), set on a Mississippi steamboat. The author's last extended work of fiction is savagely satiric of the optimistic "Western spirit," and contains a chapter on "Indian Hating" that casts a Swiftian glance at the frontier process.

Melville's satire may be read as an antidote to such exercises of Western boosterism as Timothy Flint's *Recollections of the Last Ten Years* (1825). Flint was a Massachusetts-born minister, educator, and missionary, who moved to St. Louis in 1815 and whose travels took him up and down the great river. He remained in the Western region, writing not only his *Recollections* and a geography of the Mississippi Valley but a series of romantic novels with settings heavily influenced by Chateaubriand's account of the American west in *Atala* (1801) and elsewhere. But Flint's fiction is decidedly of a second or lower rank, along with that of his contemporary, Judge James Hall, a Philadelphia-born lawyer who likewise identified himself with belles lettres in praise of his new Western home. Their works in turn provided material and inspiration for the Swiss émigré writer Karl Postl, who, as

Charles Sealsfield, wrote a number of popular novels about the frontiers-men of the Southwest—among them *The Cabin Book; or Sketches of Life in Texas* (1844)—many of which were translated from German into English and kept the tradition of Cooper alive, albeit in a minor key.

Flint and Hall deserve mention also because they were among the first writers to celebrate the exploits of the Mississippi river men, epitomized by the deeds of Mike Fink, the darkly heroic keelboater who was driven from the river by the coming of the steamboat. Where the post-revolutionary frontier was associated with Daniel Boone (and his literary shadow, Leatherstocking), whose adventures were elevated into myth by Eastern writers (including Timothy Flint), the expansion of the United States into the Mississippi Valley following the Louisiana Purchase signaled a burst of energy perfectly expressed by the brawny, brawling river man. Fink eventually followed the fur-trapping frontier up the Missouri, where his violent way of life led to his murder in 1822.

Another figure associated with the emerging literature of the trans-Mississippi frontier was Davy Crockett, a Tennessee congressman and renegade Jacksonian Democrat whose colorful manner and speech brought him a certain notoriety. Crockett's first literary appearance (in 1831) was as Colonel Nimrod Wildfire in a play by James Kirke Paulding, *The Lion of the West*; but the Tennessean soon published a collection of hunting anecdotes and then his "autobiography," *A Narrative of the Life of David Crockett* (1834), the exact authorship of which is in doubt but which is regarded as a minor masterpiece of vernacular narration. Where Fink was shot down by the friend of a man he had killed, Crockett died a hero's death at the Alamo, having moved to the Texas frontier after losing reelection to Congress, and he would increasingly displace Boone as a figure symbolic of imperial energies.

However, whereas Boone had a heroic, even epic, profile, Crockett was a figure inspiring laughter, and the works written or authorized by him during his lifetime were overwhelmingly comic in subject matter. After 1836, moreover, Crockett was given a bizarre immortality by annual comic almanacs that bore his name, in which he figured as the hero of short tales, often in the company of Mike Fink—a gratuitous association with no historical warrant. Wildly exaggerated accounts of violent encounters by Fink and Crockett with alligators, grizzly bears, Indians, Negroes, Mexicans, and sundry white inhabitants of the Mississippi Valley (including each other), these *Crockett Almanac* stories were accompanied by woodcut illustrations very much in the fantastic spirit of the fiction, the outlandishness of which gave the literary frontier a coloration it would never quite shed. The first four of the almanacs bore a fictitious Nashville imprint, and were regarded as a version of "folk" literature until recent scholarship revealed that they were written by relatively sophisticated Easterners whose Whig ideologies suggested imperfect sympathies with the Jacksonian "Western" spirit. Even during his lifetime, Crockett had let himself be exploited by Whig hacks, who were eager to follow the example of the Yankee humorist Seba Smith's "Major Jack Downing," a "common man" with a negative view of President Jackson.

Whatever the motives of the almanac humorists, their stories gave popular expression to regional and racial tensions, often bloodily resolved, and by the 1840s they espoused a consistent expansionist élan, especially concerning Mexico and Mexicans. They can be read as propaganda preparatory to the Mexican War, a conflict promoted chiefly by Democratic interests, not Whig. By that time, however, the mythic adventures of Davy Crockett had shed political overtones save in the most general sense; they had become humorous accoutrements to the westward march of empire. Still, the almanac tales are hardly flattering to Westerners, who are portrayed as loud and (in nineteenth-century terms) foul-mouthed louts, given to violent, even fatal encounters with one another and with the chance victims of their cantankerousness.

Virtually contemporaneous with this anonymous almanac tradition, and undoubtedly inspired by it, is the emergence of humorous short fiction written by identifiable Southwestern authors, such as Augustus Baldwin Longstreet, James G. Baldwin, George Washington Harris, and Johnson M. Hooper, Whig lawyers and journalists who betray considerable uneasiness toward the emerging Jacksonian "common man." Harris's Sut Lovingood and Hooper's Simon Suggs are cousins germane to the almanac "heroes," given to violent pranks and living in a decidedly equivocal moral zone. Somewhat more shapely than the almanac tales, these humorous stories show the clear marks of Eastern influence if not origins, and are clearly the residents of what Van Wyck Brooks called "the world of Washington Irving." For the long shadow of Irving's Ichabod Crane extends over much of this "Western" writing of the 1830s and 1840s: Irving, though he used a Hudson Valley setting, anticipated both the almanac writers and the Southwestern humorists in his use of regional rivalries and violent pranks as the subjects of short fiction. It was Irving's friend Paulding who first saw the literary potential in Davy Crockett, and it was Paulding, also, who in his *Letters from the South* (1817) in effect invented the rough-and-tumble fight which became a standard fixture in both the almanac tales and early Southwestern humor.

The literary West, in sum, was largely an Eastern invention, and because of Eastern uneasiness about "the Young Lion of the West," to use Paulding's epithet, the West in American literature was from the start an equivocal zone, part and parcel of that realm of death and damnation with which Western travelers have been threatened since the days of Christopher Columbus. No writer more clearly proves the argument than does Bret Harte, whose California tales signal the arrival in America of bona fide Western short stories evincing the mastery of a polished craftsman. A New York–born dilettante and Anglophile, who as a young man followed his mother to California after the gold rush, Harte may have had a brief experience in the mining camps, probably as a school teacher, and thenceforth made a career of writing Irvingesque stories with Gold Rush settings. The almanac Finks and Crocketts would have felt right at home in the rough-and-tumble life of California mining camps (in one almanac tradition, Crockett survives the Alamo only to be put to work in a Mexican silver mine!), which gave almost allegorical form to the rapacity associated with the frontier, but they have no equivalents among the tough-but-tender miners of Harte's fiction, who have a Dickensian capacity for large-heartedness.

We learn very little from Harte's stories about the day-to-day life in mining camps, which serve chiefly as atmospheric backdrops to theatrical, melodramatic plots in which the action turns on surprising revelations and sudden character transformations. Again, if Irving maintains an influential presence in Harte's fiction, especially in his nostalgic tales about California life before the gold rush, with its sleepy missions and indolent army posts, Dickens (himself indebted to Irving) is always "in camp." It was undoubtedly the gallant wastrel Sidney Carton in *Tale of Two Cities* who inspired Harte's noble-hearted gamblers Jack Hamlin and John Oakhurst, but whatever the source, Harte's card-playing heroes gave the speculative spirit of gold mining a human—and romantic—shape. His miners are brave and generous men, quick to rescue women and babies in distress, but they are also plebeians, whose lower-class origins are betrayed in their speech. Harte identified himself with his chivalric gamblers, whose mysterious backgrounds seem to involve educated if not high-born origins, and he lent them a subjective quality that transcends the tricks of mere literary formula.

The gambler, who in the reform literature of the day was portrayed as a shabby cardsharp and heartless swindler, would thenceforth join the heroic frontiersman in the emerging Western myth. We tend to associate his ambivalent figure with riverboat and cattle-town life, but in our literature, the gambler first appears in Bret Harte's short stories. Along with his generous whores and sentimental miners,

Harte's noble gamblers assist in converting the Old West into fairy-tale terrain, where we witness marvelous regenerations which assure us that beneath the roughest exteriors lurk tender feelings—a moral which is in all ways at odds with the lessons of the almanac tales but which would animate any number of heroes in subsequent stories (and movies) of the Old West. Washington Irving's tour of the prairies did not take him past the foothills of the Rockies, but through the agency of Bret Harte, Irving's genial and sentimental spirit, albeit with some help from Dickens, provided a definitive and transformational touch to Western fiction.

Among Harte's several contributions to American literature we may include Mark Twain, whose talents he early recognized and encouraged as editor of the influential *Californian*, a literary journal in which many of Twain's early sketches were published. The men were for a time close friends and literary collaborators, until Harte's habit of sponging off the Clemens family brought an end to the relationship. (Twain was seldom able to sort out his hostilities, and his eventual dismissal of Harte's "saintly whores and self-sacrificing sons-of-bitches" had something more than a literary basis.) Twain's own debt to Dickens, obvious in *The Gilded Age* and *The Adventures of Huckleberry Finn*, seldom influenced his Western stories, which mark a return to the Southwestern humor tradition of his Missouri youth. Twain's first published attempt at humor, "The Dandy Frightening the Squatter," written before he left for Nevada and California, is clearly in the vein of Johnson and Hooper, and his first and perhaps most famous Western story, "The Celebrated Jumping Frog of Calaveras County," depends upon the device of the practical joke, a hoaxing prank that was a standby of the Southwestern tradition—and of many of Twain's subsequent works of fiction. As in Harte's mining-camp stories, gambling is a central theme, but Twain's gamblers are boasting dupes and swindling rogues, not heroic, self-sacrificing sentimentalists. Like Harte, Twain used the device of a surprise ending, but to accelerate a pratfall instead of a sudden regeneration.

Although Mark Twain may have been more "honest" than Harte in depicting the realities of mining-camp life, his allegiance to the Southwestern tradition imposed a warp like that created by the other man's Irvingesque qualities. Twain also inherited a much older Eastern bias, which from Cotton Mather to Crèvecoeur stressed the uncertainties and dangers of frontier life; this gave a skeptical cast to his autobiographical *Roughing It*. Where Harte domesticated the mining camp by imposing a sentimental, child-oriented pattern, Twain emphasized the ruinous delusions associated with mining, playing off golden dreams against the bedrock of hard-bitten experience, a

Quixotism–versus–Sancho Panzaism that would characterize much of
his later fiction. For all their personal and artistic differences, however, Twain and Harte were alike in emphasizing the essentially masculine nature of frontier life. Whereas in the popular sentimental
literature of the day, women were essential to the process of regeneration, in his best-known stories Harte was true to the facts of the
mining camp in his insistence on a male hegemony. In his first published story, "M'liss," Harte created a charming tale of love between
a young teacher and one of his students, and in an early sketch, "A
Night at Wingdam," he provided a sympathetic portrait of a long-
suffering frontier wife; but increasingly women played at best equivocal roles in his Western fiction. One of his most effective early tales,
"Tennessee's Partner," concerns the strong male bond engendered,
even necessitated, by the conditions of mining-camp life.

Even when they play significant parts in his stories, Harte's
women fall into Dickensian stereotypes, from innocent virgins to
golden-hearted whores to cruel prudes and adulteresses. He is guilty
likewise of exploiting that well-worn Victorian cliché, the notion that
the "influence" of a woman (or a child) can have a transforming effect
upon a man steeped in vice. In *Roughing It*, Twain also devoted an
entire episode to the arrival in town of the "first woman" and its effect
upon the entirely male populace, a situation with an undoubted basis
in fact but susceptible, as in Harte's stories, to sentimental abuse, of
which Twain was never guilty. In 1859, in one of a series of semific-
tional tales about California life that undoubtedly influenced Bret
Harte, John W. Palmer—a doctor who witnessed the events of 1849
—described the arrival of the first woman in San Francisco, with pre-
dictable results:

> What was the spell that wrought these changes—that trans-
> muted the toads and lizards, and all the loathsome things of a
> dissolute and lawless community, into the very pearls and di-
> amonds of fairy tale—that by some wondrous cunning made, of
> a day of lust and rapine, and worse than Ishmael's rule, a lovely
> Age of Gold? The influence of a quiet eye, a graceful mien, a
> thousand pretty pleas for homage and protection—the power
> of woman, the potent restraint of her presence, the persuasive
> eloquence of her very silence, the flattery of her slightest ap-
> probation, the sufficing rebuke of her turned-away face—that
> dim religion of the heart which demands no costlier fame than
> the humblest roof-tree, no altar more formally consecrated than
> a cottage cradle, no deity more awful than that God of Love
> whose smile makes the wilderness blossom like the rose, and

the little hills skip like lambs. [*The New and the Old; or, California and India in Romantic Aspects*, pp. 80–81.]

But perhaps because of a souring marriage, Harte's California stories increasingly feature a scheming adulteress as a central figure, a foil for his noble-hearted gamblers. These tales are set not in mining camps but in towns and watering places, those "spas" which provide literary opportunity for affairs of the heart—and the heartless. Encouraged to expand "M'liss," Harte in 1873 introduced just such an equivocal figure, giving his sterling heroine a mother with a shadowy past. We must remember that Thackeray's *Vanity Fair* was published on the eve of the gold rush, and to the example of Dickens's redemptive sweethearts we must add the machinations of Becky Sharp, an ambitious adulteress who uses her sex to advance her fortunes—a literary type found also in Twain's *The Gilded Age* (1873), a story of disastrous railroad speculation with a decidedly Western coloration. "Fast" women were a Western staple, from Ada Menken to Lily Langtry, but historical facts do not warrant the allegorical prevalence of femmes fatales in Bret Harte's fiction with fairy-tale regularity.

Of course, it is a commonplace that until the advent of Henry James women occupy only stereotypical roles in American fiction written by men, with perhaps the single exception being Hawthorne's *The Scarlet Letter*, a pioneering instance of single motherhood that exemplifies family values. When male authors turned westward, the essential masculinity of their fiction intensified, because of the undeniable demographics of life on the frontier. In *The Prairie*, in order to fulfill the formula for historical romances made popular by Sir Walter Scott, Cooper packed a large and unlikely cast of characters into Western regions, providing not one but two sets of young lovers. Again, however, the retreat eastward of Cooper's settlers proved symbolic, in that they left the single and probably celibate figure of Leatherstocking still dominating the horizon, where he would enjoy a number of essentially male metamorphoses. It was not until Owen Wister's *The Virginian* (1902), perhaps the quintessential Western novel in American literature, that the influential and virtuous woman once again gained supremacy—but here Wister, like Cooper, was yielding to a formulaic necessity, in his desire to write a popular novel obeying market considerations.

In Wister's short stories, based on his actual experiences in the Far West, courtship and marriage are not important themes. If Wister can be credited with inventing the literary cowboy, in the flood of pulp fiction and formulaic movies to follow the hero in the ten-gallon hat generally survives as a Noah without a wife or children. Moreover, even in the literature of the grasslands frontier, the agricultural mid-region with which this anthology is not concerned, the necessary emphasis on domestic and family life is seldom one of balance and harmony. Significantly, in Willa Cather's *O Pioneers!* (1913), a novel whose title echoes Cooper's first Leatherstocking romance, the central figure is a heroic equivalent to his celibate frontiersman, the strong-willed Alexandra, who remains single (if hopeful) at story's end.

Of all the male figures generated by the literature of the Old West—including miners, soldiers, prospectors, sheep-drovers, gamblers, and lawmen—it is the cowboy who emerged as the most popular, universally mythic figure. Yet, like Davy Crockett (who in mythic terms is his sire), the cowboy is a compound of historical ironies. Although he is the regnant symbol of the Old West, his brief historical heyday (1875–85) was associated with the penultimate frontier, made possible by the paradoxical combination of an open range and the transcontinental railway, whose branch lines made the export of huge amounts of beef to Eastern markets practicable. But the same rail lines expedited the westward spread of agriculture, which, along with the privatizing (and fencing) of the range country, insured the diminishing heroic stature of the historical ranch hand. At novel's end, Wister's Virginian takes over an established ranch and stands to profit hugely from coal deposits on his own land. Wister's other marrying cowboy, Lin McLean, finds happiness in the arms of a female telegraph operator—a western union signaling the end of a footloose (and occasionally dissolute) career.

As an "American" icon, moreover, the cowboy is made up chiefly of articles of clothing and gear developed over the centuries by Mexican-American drovers, who herded cattle in the dominions which the Mexican War would make available to the beef barons of the post–Civil War years. As early as 1847, in *Evangeline*, Henry Wadsworth Longfellow (hardly thought of as a Western writer!) had foreseen the mythic importance of the cowboy. Longfellow's Acadian émigré, Basil Lajeunesse (a name taken by the poet from Frémont's account of his California expedition in 1843–44), having arrived in Louisiana, abandons his trade of blacksmithing and becomes a herder of cattle:

> *Just where the woodlands met the flowery surf of the prairie,*
> *Mounted upon his horse, with Spanish saddle and stirrups,*
> *Sat a herdsman, arrayed in gaiters and doublet of deerskin.*
> *Broad and brown was the face that from under the Spanish sombrero*
> *Gazed on the peaceful scene, with the lordly look of its master.*

Longfellow's embryonic version of the cowboy (a word which in 1847 had a negative association, "cowboys" having been Tory guerrillas who figure in Cooper's novel of the American Revolution, *The Spy*) bears significant witness to his Hispanic origins, a debt which was neglected by subsequent celebrants of the American West.

In an essay published in 1895, Wister acknowledged the Mexican priority, but only in grudging, even belittling terms—for he was anxious to assert Saxon supremacy as the dominant force in the western spread of empire. Notably, Lin McLean hails from Boston, and Wister's Virginian is from the state associated (by the author) with that archetype of Anglo-American heroism, George Washington. Like Harte, Wister was an Eastern snob: born in Philadelphia, educated at Harvard, and for a time ambitious to become a concert pianist, he joined the long line of "Western" writers who regarded the scene as through an opera glass. Following the lead of his friend and Harvard classmate Theodore Roosevelt (who, in terms of encouragement, must be accounted the Maecenas of the cowboy epic), Wister in 1885 made the first in a series of trips to Wyoming. Roosevelt had become a Dakota rancher the year before in a successful attempt to recover his health and mental stability after the death of his young wife; he would ever after draw upon his Western experiences for political and literary capital. The ostensible purpose of Wister's trips was to hunt the big game of the Rockies, but he too was in shaky mental shape, and would in time build a more than respectable literary career from material recorded in letters and diaries during his Western excursions.

Wister's literary models included Kipling and Stevenson, and like them he gave realistic backgrounds to situations essentially romantic in nature. His West is a decidedly amoral arena, peopled by rascally politicians and unscrupulous Indian traders, into whose midst the author characteristically introduces a strong male authority figure whose "influence" is generally associated with a revolver, not a feminine sensibility. Where in *The Virginian* the schoolteacher, Molly Wood, is instrumental in "civilizing" the cowboy-hero, women play disruptive roles in Wister's short stories, where they are elements of divisiveness, not domesticity. Moreover, in those tales that are distinct from the stories gathered together to form the novels *Lin McLean* (1898) and *The Virginian*, the cowboy gives way to the cavalryman as an avatar of sterling, incorruptible virtue, of which Specimen Jones, as his name suggests, is a representative sample. Like Harte's gamblers, and unlike the Virginian, who must be tutored by Molly to bring him up to an acceptable literary standard, Jones brings with him considerable culture but without a traceable past.

During the heyday of cattle ranching and cowboys, a book like

James Brisbin's *The Beef Bonanza; or, How to Get Rich on the Plains*
(1882) by its very title equated cattle with gold; nor were cattle barons
exempt from exploitive greed, as they revealed in the Johnson County
War (1892), when they employed violence in their struggle with encroaching homesteaders. But Wister, because of his social ties to big
ranchers, was never critical of them, no more than he was of the efforts of cavalrymen to rid the West of the Indian "menace." On the
contrary, Wister did for cattle rustlers what Horatio Alger did for
mortgage bankers, making of what were essentially populist renegades villains second only to white men who sold repeating rifles to
Indians. Besides, by the time Wister began to write his short stories,
in the mid-1890s, the easy profits of ranching and the way of life his
fiction records had disappeared, in large part because of the disastrous
blizzards of 1886 and 1887, which destroyed such large numbers of
livestock that recovery had been impossible for many ranchers. The
inexorable introduction of sheep to the range had likewise contributed
to the cattlemen's fall, along with the spread of agriculture and the
stringing of barbed wire across the once-open prairie.

As Wister noted in his introduction to *The Virginian*—a counter-
part to Turner's epochal notation, made ten years earlier, concerning
the closing of the frontier—his Western writing was an extended re-
quiem for a way of life no longer possible, a Virgilian commemoration
of a heroic past gone with the Indian from the land. The same may
be said of the work of Frederic Remington (another man encouraged
by Roosevelt), the artist who illustrated many of Wister's stories, and
who evoked in paint, often on a panoramic scale, the life of the cowboy
and cavalryman during the 1880s. Like Wister, Remington was an
Easterner, albeit from the wilder regions of upstate New York, and
had little real experience in the Western life he celebrated. With Wister and Roosevelt, he profited from a wave of nostalgia current during
the 1890s and afterward (indeed down to the present day in Texas)
for the simpler, pre-industrial life, in which individualism, not collec-
tivism, was the ruling principle—ironically identified with men on
horseback who were either soldiers or ranch hands, subject to the
regimentation of army or gang-labor life. Both Remington and Wister
were politically conservative, even racist, in their ideologies, Remington perhaps more so in his outspoken antagonism to modern democratic tendencies and to the influx of middle-European immigrants to
the United States.

Expression of these opinions, for the most part, were limited to
Remington's correspondence, and seldom appear in his published
writings—articles and stories written to create more opportunities for
his Western illustrations. At first taking the form of nonfiction pieces

based on his travels in the company of cavalry troops—including the African-Americans called "buffalo soldiers" by the Indians—Remington's writing eventually included short stories not much different in emphasis from Wister's. But where Wister's stories are carefully crafted in terms of plot, Remington's tend to hew more closely to the line of experience, and seldom move outside the delimiting frame of first-person narration. In a number of ways he played Mark Twain to Wister's Bret Harte, and had he not devoted so much time to the painterly and plastic arts, including the difficult lost-wax process by which he created his famous bronze horsemen, Remington might have become a better writer. His stories are still valuable as a record of life on the last frontier, especially in their treatment of Native Americans, whom they depict as worthy adversaries to the horse-mounted representatives of civilization.

Remington, himself something of a diamond in the rough, was attracted to the powerful lure of primitivism, and shared with Joseph Conrad a fascination with the results of exposing civilized men to the influences of a wilderness setting. Though he championed men of decisive action, he did not have Wister's faith in the power of single-handed authority, and saw the West as a much more complex mix of values than the other man's melodramatic arena. Typically, no single serial hero emerges to dominate Remington's tales, with the exception of the half-breed narrator Sun-Down Leflare, whose stories reflect the stoicism of the Indian, sustained by his faith in the power of his "medicine"—hardly an equivalent to the aria-singing Specimen Jones. Notably, Remington responded to *The Virginian* by writing a novel of his own, *John Ermine of the Yellowstone* (1902), in which a white man raised by Indians is destroyed, not redeemed, by his contact with a civilized woman—yet another example of the cruel, flirtatious type favored by Harte. In his writing as in his painting, Remington was true to what he thought to be the facts of Western life, and throughout his works he eschewed the cowboy operatics that characterize Wister's novelized West.

Remington's ally in this regard is Stephen Crane, whose several stories about the West—based on a short trip to Texas in 1896 on a journalistic errand—can also be read as attempts to debunk the myth of the cowboy that was emerging during that same period via Wister's magazine stories. In both "The Blue Hotel" and "The Bride Comes to Yellow Sky," Crane used the expressionistic, ironical mode of his most famous novel, *The Red Badge of Courage*, to portray Western life as a matter of exploded illusions. In "Blue Hotel," especially, Crane employed a number of trick devices, surprising turns of event recalling the fiction of Harte and Twain, as well as the sardonic stories of Ambrose Bierce, a Western writer best known for his tales of the Civil War. There is little of this in Wister or Remington, who regarded life in the West as a moral drama, in which surprises await the ignorant "pilgrim" but are always anticipated by the wisdom of experience. As Wister demonstrated in his first story about Specimen Jones, pranks can be serious business in the West, and as Remington attempts to show in much of his writing, cavalrymen familiar with the Indian's ways are always prepared for the unexpected.

We find similar lessons in the stories of Jack London and Frank Norris, writers whose view of frontier life corroborates Hobbes's definition of man living in a state of nature as being in a constant struggle for survival of an unremitting harshness. The comic spirit that suffuses so much Western writing, from the Crockett tales to Wister's wry parables, is pared down in the work of these naturalist writers to a grim thread of fatalistic irony. Jack London, schooled in Herbert Spencer's popularized Darwin and a reader of Nietzsche and Marx, found a perfect setting for his tangled ideology in the Klondike gold rush of 1896, a savage landscape that could hardly accommodate the sentimentalism of Harte's mining camps but was an ideal scene for stories illustrating a bloody and unremitting struggle to survive. Norris, whose privileged upbringing gave him a somewhat more balanced view, was capable of a certain grotesque comedy, perfectly exemplified in his expressionistic *McTeague* (1899), a novel about a San Francisco dentist driven mad by greed. Though a native and resident of California, London wrote only a very few short stories set in that region, which by 1900 had become far too settled and civilized for his violent muse. Though Norris was known as a California writer, his fame was earned through novels, such as the sprawling, epic *The Octopus* (1901), not short stories. Like other naturalist writers (with the exception of Stephen Crane), moreover, London and Norris avoided historical fiction, writing for the most part about their contemporary scene. By the turn of the century the Old West was becoming chiefly the province of pulp writers like Zane Grey and (in short order) of motion pictures. One of the first movies made in America was about a Western train robbery.

The cowboy stories of Stewart Edward White, a number of which were made into early motion pictures, provide a useful and very readable bridge in this regard. White, though a contemporary of Norris and London, was a celebrant of the "masculine" qualities of Western life associated with Wister and Remington. He began his career writing fiction about the lumber camps of northern Michigan, where he had worked as a youth; but in his subsequent stories of Arizona and California ranch life, he was a nostalgist of sorts, continuing to celebrate a way of life depicted by Remington and Wister, but with a significant difference. There is heroism in White's version of the Old West, but it is contained within a broadly comic frame, and the cowboy is given a reduced stature in keeping with his lowly place in the scheme of things. Though set forth in a grittily realistic manner, White's stories are nonetheless "literary," reflecting the influence of Wister, and perhaps relying on Roosevelt's *Ranch Life and the Hunting Trail* (1888) for details of Western life. Notably, the artist who illustrated White's cycle of cowboy stories, *Arizona Nights* (1907), was N. C. Wyeth, whose very brief Western experience was supplemented by his schooling at Howard Pyle's studio in techniques of historical accuracy, which became increasingly necessary as the ranching frontier receded into memory.

Still, White continued to write from firsthand experience, having worked as a boy on a California ranch. Most important, his self-conscious seeking out of primitive conditions at a time of increasing urbanization in the United States found a popular readership prepared by not only Wister and Remington but Jack London as well. Once again we find the hypermasculinity, the emphasis on male bonding, on violence, so characteristic of the fiction of the Old West, and in most of the stories we find plots turning on a surprise twist, whether pranks or tricks of fate. Like Mark Twain, to whom he is also indebted, White was a master of vernacular narration, and if his stories of men in action anticipate those of another writer associated with upstate Michigan, Ernest Hemingway, the essential comedy of his tales looks forward to the short fiction of William Faulkner, who reclaimed for the South the tradition of hoaxes and rascality that had for a time relocated in the Far West. A popular writer in his day, White was something more than an uneasy blend of literary influences; he can be seen as the quintessential Western writer, in that he removed the Eastern bias that shaped so much earlier fiction. His stories serve to encode and institutionalize the cowboy ideal without stooping to the hackneyed postures of pulp fiction, and in a number of his tales we catch quick glimpses of what will become cinema archetypes. In "The Two-Gun Man" we have a story in which we can envision the young Clint Eastwood playing opposite an aging John Wayne.

For a less heroic account of cowboys we can turn to a collection of stories published the same year as White's *Arizona Nights*, O. Henry's *Heart of the West*. William Sydney Porter's pen name is chiefly associated with fiction set in large eastern cities—specifically in New York—yet he wrote a considerable number of Western stories inspired by Porter's long residence in Texas, which included a stretch in prison. He brought to the Western experience the same word-rich style that characterizes so much of his fiction, a turbulent, slangy manner that resembles (indeed, often is) a salesman's or con man's pitch, clearly anticipating the urban dialect of Damon Runyon. Though senior to Norris, London, and White by a decade, O. Henry wrote of a somewhat more modern West than they, a scene contemporary with his own, in which the occasional introduction of an automobile is no anomaly. Before setting up shop as O. Henry, Porter worked as a bank clerk, not a cowboy, during his Texas years, and towns figure as importantly as the open range in his stories. He imposed on Western life the same sentimental devices that characterize the best-known of his city tales, in effect returning to the parables of Bret Harte and to the premise that it is goodness, not depravity, that is the common denominator in our fellow humans. But O. Henry departs from not only Harte but most Western writers of his time in his frequent if often wry celebration of the institution of marriage.

Where Wister in *Lin McLean* and *The Virginian* used marriage as a lamentable signal that the wild West was closing down—the bonds of matrimony being equivalent to the barbed wire that partitioned off the range—O. Henry displayed it as a necessary, even imperative rite, the alternative to which is an unbearable and sterile loneliness. While he often used courtship as a frame for comic routines, he presented marriage as a social inevitability; his brides are seldom those influential conveyors of Eastern and "civilized" manners found in Wister, but are honest working women or stalwart widows who share the slangy, energetic virtues of O. Henry's men. Whether older women in need of replacement spouses or young shopgirls, waitresses, and—occasionally—cowgirls, they do not differ much from their urban counterparts, but, because of their ebullient, outspoken character, they introduce a startling new note into the fiction of the Old West. Perhaps the closest prior instance is the sprightly telegraph operator who provides Lin McLean a more suitable match than the vulgar, bigamous waitress whose death frees him to remarry.

Surprisingly, given the number of his stories with a Texas setting, O. Henry is seldom thought of as a Western writer. Perhaps because his literary reputation has been in decline for decades, perhaps because he has been pegged as a writer of urban fiction, perhaps because his cowboy stories do not fit the heroic mold of Wister's, O. Henry's Texas tales have been largely ignored despite their richness and variety. Moreover, it is in those stories that the Old West begins to merge with the new, becoming domesticated in a positive vein, as the benign final assertions associated with his surprise endings turn the tables in an affirmatively comic way. Porter was Wister's contemporary, and shared with him a Southern heritage; but the West O. Henry wrote about was not a territory being fought over by cowboys and rustlers or cavalrymen and Indians, but a distinctly modern scene, in which the automobile was becoming as common a sight as the cow pony and the passenger train was convenient both as a means of transportation and a source of ready cash. Sentiment was certainly O. Henry's constant literary accessory, but nostalgia never was, and the sweetness of his endings is balanced by the pepper-and-salt of his dialogue. His stories belong to the twentieth century, not a belated nineteenth, and O. Henry is startlingly, when revisited, one of us.

He is, however, also one of "them." O. Henry's stories express, if only through their narrators, openly racist sentiments in keeping with the bigotry of other Western writers. They are consistent also in reinforcing the idea of male—as well as white—superiority. His women follow the pattern established by Molly Wood in *The Virginian*, their declarations of independence being mere preludes to the kind of marriage compact in which the balance of power is in the husband's hands. All of the Western fiction I have been discussing displays attitudes no longer acceptable in the United States: the Davy Crockett tales are violently racist; Harte's sentimentality does not extend to Indians and Mexicans (unless historically placed as aristocratic dons or priests); Twain's condescending attitude toward Native Americans inspired jokes no longer regarded as funny (though he shared with Harte a sympathy toward victimized Chinese); Wister and Remington portray Indian warriors as unredeemable savages, and their celebrations of "heroic" cavalry never acknowledge the imperial errand which those blue-clad horsemen were assigned to carry out. Even Stephen Crane, despite his modernity, insists on applying labels of national origin to his characters, and portrays Mexicans as oily, treacherous "Greasers." Also, as I have stated at the start of this introduction, misogyny is a constant in the fiction of the Old West (women in Crane's stories are mere shadows on a wall), coupled in an unholy marriage with the racist ideology essential to the imperial errand sustaining the Westward course of Americans.

In both these regards, the fiction of Mary Austin introduces a necessary corrective in this anthology, to which her Western stories provide a finale. No writer of her generation was more sympathetic to the American Indian than she. Austin followed the lead of Helen Hunt Jackson, whose *Ramona* (1888) was meant to be the *Uncle Tom's Cabin* of the Indian, calling attention to the plight of California tribes in the unscrupulous hands of Indian agents. Jackson's attempt miscarried, however; her novel was popular chiefly because of its nostalgic treatment of the region's Hispanic culture as it existed before the coming of Anglo-Americans. It reached an audience already prepared by Bret Harte's sentimental stories of two decades earlier. Joaquin Miller, a contemporary of Harte and Twain, had written sympathetically of the Modocs, a California tribe with which he lived for a time, and which was wretchedly used by white settlers seeking to displace the Indians from the land. But John Muir, the naturalist-writer, who in other ways influenced the work of Mary Austin, was condescendingly superior toward the Digger Indians of the Sierras, who somehow were exempt from his sympathy with the wilderness world. Austin shared none of Jackson's crusading spirit; while she was sympathetic to the Indians who struggled to survive in the California desert—to the point of mystic empathy with their attitude toward nature—she presented those very primitive people with an almost photographic clarity, and refused to sentimentalize their often brutal existence. If at times her description of the desert seems to anticipate the surreal paintings of Georgia O'Keeffe, her fiction shares with that of her contemporary Jack London an emphasis on the inevitability of violence in the natural world, so that her desert becomes an equivalent to his Yukon, a harsh backdrop to a ceaseless, often futile struggle to survive.

Unlike London, however, Austin did not write to illustrate the theories of Darwin or the dogma of Nietzsche, nor are her people mere victims of an indifferent wilderness. Whereas London's heroes are engaged in a struggle defined by the ancient dualism between humankind and the natural world, Austin's people are characters who emerge from and participate in the landscape, a mystical terrain that is infused with her own remarkable sensibility—if at times with an unfortunate tendency toward the anthropomorphic lapses of Emily Dickinson. Despite the sterility of the desert arena, Austin fits the pattern observed by Annette Kolodny in the nonfiction writings of pioneer women, for whom the raising of flower gardens was a means of asserting their domestic sensibilities. Austin's emphasis on the desert flora makes a garden of the world she describes, an affirmation of growth and display that redeems the otherwise deathly appearance of an arid landscape. Here again her descriptions evoke O'Keeffe's paintings, in which skulls bloom like flowers against desert hues.

If O. Henry is modern in his subject matter, Austin is virtually our contemporary in style; her literary manner is a miracle of clarity. Much of her fiction was derived from her experiences living in the Owens Valley, with its thin but resilient population of Indian shamans and basket-weavers, nomadic shepherds and quixotic prospectors—characters introduced into her stories with such verisimilitude that one is at a loss to know where the record ends and fiction begins. Though the endings of her stories can surprise an unwary reader,

Austin does not resort to the kinds of tricks so characteristic of much
Western fiction, but conveys her conclusions with an overwhelming
sense of inevitability—that concatenation of events we associate with
classical tragedy. In her first (and most famous) book, *The Land of
Little Rain* (1903), the narrative is dominated by autobiographical
matter, and the "stories" are seldom more than heightened episodes
or anecdotes, told in Austin's own voice, reminding us of her presence
throughout. A few of these sketches are self-consciously literary—
such as "Jimtown," written to "prove" that Bret Harte's sentimental
miners were authentic—and her description of the Mexican-American
community of Grapevine (like Harte's stories of Spanish California) is
reminiscent of Washington Irving's nostalgic treatment of the dis-
placed Dutch culture in the Hudson Valley.

It is in Austin's *Lost Borders* (1909), something of a sequel to *Land
of Little Rain*, that episodes cohere into fully realized short stories;
and though they are held together by the same autobiographical narrator, it is seldom as a participant witness. In two of the tales (of
which one, "The Readjustment," is included here), placed toward the
end of the volume, the first-person voice virtually disappears. These
two are, in effect, ghost stories, at once giving form to the omnipres-
ence of supernatural forces in Austin's created desert world and ne-
cessitating an element of self-removal so as to create distance between
the author and the narration. Most important, it is in *Lost Borders*
that Austin makes a clean break with the hitherto masculinist tradition of Western writing. A crusading feminist, Austin reveals in these
stories that her interest in marginalized human beings, be they Indians, prospectors, shepherds, or frontier housewives, is closely allied
to her own sense of artistic and personal displacement by the masculine presence in her life. Austin's mystical perception of the desert
as a living, anthropomorphic being, which lies at the heart of *The Land
of Little Rain*, receives particularly pointed expression in *Lost Borders*; here the desert is given a distinctly female identity, as a figu-
rative temptress of men and a rival to women, characterized as a
tawny, Sphinx-like giantess, indifferent to the lusts she inspires.

Austin's desert as femme fatale contradicts the extended metaphor
of nature found in so much Western writing by men, defined by Annette Kolodny as that of a voluptuous virgin, eager for the phallic
plow. Austin's goddess desert is not sterile but cruelly chaste, Diana-
like in her beauty and indifference to men's desires. Most of Austin's
stories, likewise, portray the borderlands as places in which the masculine ego is confounded, either by the desert itself or by the women
who live there, Native Americans and Anglo-Americans alike. Austin's fiction, like that of Henry James, is animated by a powerfully

erotic motive, a universal quality of yearning that gives her Western women roles with a meaning that powerfully transcends O. Henry's funny stories about cowboy (and cowgirl) courtships. Where for O. Henry matrimony is the solution to the essential loneliness of Western life, for Austin marriage often exacerbates the problem. Though pictured chiefly as victims, Austin's women exemplify Jane Tompkins's formula of the self-empowerment of female suffering, without ever evoking the Christian ideal of self-sacrifice that animates so much sentimental literature. Austin may join other women regionalists—such writers as Mary Wilkins Freeman and Sarah Orne Jewett—in giving her landscapes a female center, but the domestic nexus is not her emphasis. Like sentimental writers (including Bret Harte), Austin redeems the marginal elements of society, not by bringing them home to a hearth but by endowing them with the power of human love, a transcendent, not a tearful advent.

The importance of Austin's Western stories as corrective to a masculine hegemony in the literary region cannot be overemphasized. Though much recent discussion of her work has stressed its neurotic basis, on the grounds that the author spent her mature years asserting control over others by repeated bouts of mental and physical illness, the results, whatever the inspiration, are a remarkable contribution to the literature of the American West. Not only is Austin's a powerful lone female voice in the wilderness, her stories rate high in terms of craftsmanship and style, on a par with those of Wister and London, surely, and second only to Stephen Crane's. Indeed, in her sardonic display of the effects of male ego let loose upon the Western landscape, in her avoidance of sentimental postures, in her photographic clarity and freedom from formulaic responses to Western life, Austin merits comparison throughout her fiction to the spirit—if not the mastery—of Crane.

Theirs were minority voices. Not surprisingly, much of the fiction produced during the heyday of U.S. imperialism in the years following the Civil War shares the vices of the zeitgeist, a jingoistic, miscegenetic celebration of civilization's "advance" into Western regions—and beyond. But in pointing out the bad parts we should not neglect the good. Harte's parables of regeneration, like Dickens's, still awake within us our capacity for belief in the essential goodness of our fellow humans; Twain's tales of tricksters likewise appeal to a corresponding wariness of the covert motives of those same human beings, even while they inspire laughter at the expense of willing dupes; the cowboys and cavalrymen of Wister and Remington *are* heroic, whatever the contexts of their courage, and put forth a readiness for encounter in terms that still appeal; O. Henry flirts with postmodernism in his ornate delivery, and we recognize in his formulaic reverses the origins of modern situation comedy (the rights to dozens of his stories were secured for film and television years ago); and in White's garrulous cowboys and flinty-eyed gunslingers we detect a certain slant of light that transported high noon in Arizona to a hundred thousand matinees.

It is equally important to note that, unless we are to cut ourselves off entirely from our past, we must upon occasion set aside modern moral sensibilities, much as Coleridge recommended we suspend our disbelief when confronting literary works of art. True, we can read these stories as object lessons, as source material warranting the dismissive argument that the West as a national experience was chauvinistic, masculinist, racist, imperialist, exploitive: that the Old West was also the Bad West, a moral judgment from which no gun- or hash-slinger escapes. But it is also possible to regard the literary West as did so many of its writers (including Mary Austin), with a certain sense of humor. Here again, O. Henry provides a salutary example: By filtering ideologies through his innumerable tellers of tales, he obtains a certain obliqueness that, like his plots, gets it right by setting things at odds. It is not a matter of coincidence that the twist or surprise ending comes into its own in short stories of the West— turnabouts that exploit our moral as well as our clichéd expectations. As the readers who enter the fictional territory that lies beyond this introduction may discover, things are seldom what you expect they will be in the American West.

# STORIES OF
# THE OLD WEST

# BRET HARTE

## (1836–1902)

Born Francis Brett Harte in Albany, New York, he was the son of a
schoolteacher of Jewish-American origins. His father's turbulent career involved a number of relocations until his early death in 1850.
Harte's widowed mother followed the tide of Americans drawn to Gold
Rush California; she settled in San Francisco, where she remarried.
Young Bret, who had evinced some literary talent while still in school,
dropped out at the age of thirteen for a business career, but in 1854
he rejoined his mother and her new husband in California. Harte's
accounts of his Western years are untrustworthy, but he apparently
taught for a time in the mining country, then worked his way into
journalism by the usual route of the print shop. He eventually became
assistant editor of a small northern California paper, which he was
forced to leave for writing an article sympathetic to Indian victims of
white violence.

In 1857 he was back in San Francisco, setting type for the Golden
Era, a literary weekly sustained by local talents, including those of
Harte himself, who soon became a member of the city's literati. Per-
sonable and charming, he won his way to a sinecure at the U.S. Mint
in San Francisco; this made possible his marriage to Anna Griswold
in 1862, a match unsuitable to both parties. Harte continued to develop as a writer and in 1863 had a story about Spanish California
accepted by the prestigious Atlantic Monthly. In 1864, he became editor of a new literary weekly, The Californian, and added Mark Twain
to his circle of friends and contributors. In 1867, Harte's first book of
verse, The Lost Galleon, was published, as was his Condensed Novels,
parodies of popular books of the day; Harte's poetry is badly dated,
but his parodies are still quite funny to readers familiar with the
originals. Harte came into his own as the founding editor of the
Overland Monthly in 1868, to which he contributed the short stories

*that would make him famous with the publication of* The Luck of Roaring Camp *in 1870. His fame was enhanced by the appearance that same year of his dialect poem, "The Heathen Chinee," which quickly gained a faddish notoriety worldwide. In 1871, in order to capitalize on his newfound reputation, Harte and his family left for the East.*

*Harte was a slender, dapper, even dandyish man, with an ingratiating manner and quick wit. Though he was hardly the Forty-niner his Eastern fans expected, he quickly made influential friends and was given a lucrative contract by the* Atlantic Monthly *for a minimum of twelve stories over the next year. Never a writer who excelled under pressure, and always given to enjoying the good life, Harte satisfied the terms of the contract but lost the good opinion of the* Atlantic *editors. For the next seven years he remained in the East, writing stories that repeated the characters and situations established in* The Luck of Roaring Camp, *including a novel,* Gabriel Conroy—which *certified that his genius was for shorter forms—and two plays done in collaboration with Mark Twain, neither of which was the success the writers hoped for. With all his charm, Harte was something of a poseur and parasite, and Twain tired of both qualities. The partnership ended when Twain turned against his friend, and the rupture between the two was never mended.*

*Harte was helped in spending what money he made by his wife, who had expensive tastes. Having exhausted his sources of income in the United States, including an extensive lecture tour, Harte accepted a consulship in Prussia. In a break that was for all purposes final, he sailed for Europe without his wife and four children, though he continued to send home much of what he earned. Unhappy and lonely in Germany, Harte relieved his tedium by visits to England, where his literary reputation remained strong. In 1880, he was appointed to a consulate in Glasgow, which enabled him to exploit his British connections. This appointment was terminated by a change in administration in 1885, however, and Harte became dependent once again on his writing. Though his reputation in Great Britain never went into the decline it had suffered in the United States, most of his output during the last twenty years of his life amounted to pale imitations of the stories that had made him famous. In a literary equivalent to a time warp, Harte's California remained a land of red-shirted miners and "heathen" Chinese. His wife came to England in 1898, but the two maintained separate domiciles; Harte lived with a married couple in something of a ménage à trois, though the relationship was most likely free of sexual liaison. Harte's passion was largely concentered in his anglophilia, and he became a living caricature of a British clubman. He died of throat cancer, a miserable death that brought an end to an increasingly shabby existence.*

*Harte's biographer, George R. Stewart, Jr., has opined that the author attained his creative peak at the age of thirty-five, and that he thenceforth lived off the reputation gained during a marvelous five years of production, which ended with his return to the East in 1870. The stories written during those years are justly famous, and they established the formulas and conventions for much Western fiction written thereafter—including Harte's own. Virtually all of the writers in this collection, including Mary Austin, were in Harte's literary debt. Though he was not an original genius, Harte had a great gift for combining conventional formulas with original materials, as he synthesized elements from Irving and Dickens in what was perceived to be a new and quite different sort of work. It is not a coincidence that he also excelled at parody, since derivativeness was essential to his muse.*

# Muck-a-Muck

*A Modern Indian Novel*
*After Cooper*

## CHAPTER I

It was toward the close of a bright October day. The last rays of the setting sun were reflected from one of those sylvan lakes peculiar to the Sierras of California. On the right the curling smoke of an Indian village rose between the columns of the lofty pines, while to the left the log cottage of Judge Tompkins, embowered in buckeyes, completed the enchanting picture.

Although the exterior of the cottage was humble and unpretentious, and in keeping with the wildness of the landscape, its interior gave evidence of the cultivation and refinement of its inmates. An aquarium, containing goldfishes, stood on a marble centre-table at one end of the apartment, while a magnificent grand piano occupied the other. The floor was covered with a yielding tapestry carpet, and the walls were adorned with paintings from the pencils of Van Dyke, Rubens, Tintoretto, Michael Angelo, and the productions of the more modern Turner, Kensett, Church, and Bierstadt. Although Judge Tompkins had chosen the frontiers of civilization as his home, it was impossible for him to entirely forego the habits and tastes of his former life. He was seated in a luxurious armchair, writing at a mahogany escritoire, while his daughter, a lovely young girl of seventeen summers, plied her crotchet-needle on an ottoman beside him. A bright fire of pine logs flickered and flamed on the ample hearth.

Genevra Octavia Tompkins was Judge Tompkins's only child. Her mother had long since died on the Plains. Reared in affluence, no pains had been spared with the daughter's education. She was a graduate of one of the principal seminaries, and spoke French with a perfect Benicia accent. Peerlessly beautiful, she was dressed in a white moiré antique robe trimmed with tulle. That simple rosebud, with which most heroines exclusively decorate their hair, was all she wore in her raven locks.

The Judge was the first to break the silence.

"Genevra, the logs which compose yonder fire seem to have been incautiously chosen. The sibilation produced by the sap, which exudes copiously therefrom, is not conducive to composition."

"True, father, but I thought it would be preferable to the constant crepitation which is apt to attend the combustion of more seasoned ligneous fragments."

The Judge looked admiringly at the intellectual features of the graceful girl, and half forgot the slight annoyances of the green wood in the musical accents of his daughter. He was smoothing her hair tenderly, when the shadow of a tall figure, which suddenly darkened the doorway, caused him to look up.

## CHAPTER II

It needed but a glance at the new-comer to detect at once the form and features of the haughty aborigine,—the untaught and untrammeled son of the forest. Over one shoulder a blanket, negligently but gracefully thrown, disclosed a bare and powerful breast, decorated with a quantity of three-cent postage-stamps which he had despoiled from an Overland Mail stage a few weeks previous. A cast-off beaver of Judge Tompkins's, adorned by a simple feather, covered his erect head, from beneath which his straight locks descended. His right hand hung lightly by his side, while his left was engaged in holding on a pair of pantaloons, which the lawless grace and freedom of his lower limbs evidently could not brook.

"Why," said the Indian, in a low sweet tone,—"why does the Pale Face still follow the track of the Red Man? Why does he pursue him, even as O-kee chow, the wild cat, chases Ka-ka, the skunk? Why are the feet of Sorrel-top, the white chief, among the acorns of Muck-a-Muck, in the mountain forest? Why," he repeated, quietly but firmly abstracting a silver spoon from the table,—"why do you seek to drive him from the wigwams of his fathers? His brothers are already gone to the happy hunting-grounds. Will the Pale Face seek him there?" And, averting his face from the Judge, he hastily slipped a silver cake-basket beneath his blanket, to conceal his emotion.

"Muck-a-Muck has spoken," said Genevra softly. "Let him now listen. Are the acorns of the mountain sweeter than the esculent and nutritious bean of the Pale Face miner? Does my brother prize the edible qualities of the snail above that of the crisp and oleaginous bacon? Delicious are the grasshoppers that sport on the hillside,—are they better than the dried apples of the Pale Faces? Pleasant is the gurgle of the torrent, Kish-Kish, but is it better than the cluck-cluck of old Bourbon from the old stone bottle?"

"Ugh!" said the Indian,—"ugh! good. The White Rabbit is wise. Her words fall as the snow on Tootoonolo, and the rocky heart of Muck-a-Muck is hidden. What says my brother the Gray Gopher of Dutch Flat?"

"She has spoken, Muck-a-Muck," said the Judge, gazing fondly on his daughter. "It is well. Our treaty is concluded. No, thank you,— you need *not* dance the Dance of Snow-shoes, or the Moccasin Dance, the Dance of Green Corn, or the Treaty Dance. I would be alone. A strange sadness overpowers me."

"I go," said the Indian. "Tell your great chief in Washington, the Sachem Andy, that the Red Man is retiring before the footsteps of the adventurous pioneer. Inform him, if you please, that westward the star of empire takes its way, that the chiefs of the Pi-Ute nation are for Reconstruction to a man, and that Klamath will poll a heavy Republican vote in the fall."

And folding his blanket more tightly around him, Muck-a-Muck withdrew.

## CHAPTER III

Genevra Tompkins stood at the door of the log-cabin, looking after the retreating Overland Mail stage which conveyed her father to Virginia City. "He may never return again," sighed the young girl, as she glanced at the frightfully rolling vehicle and wildly careering horses, —"at least, with unbroken bones. Should he meet with an accident! I mind me now a fearful legend, familiar to my childhood. Can it be that the drivers on this line are privately instructed to dispatch all passengers maimed by accident, to prevent tedious litigation? No, no. But why this weight upon my heart?"

She seated herself at the piano and lightly passed her hand over the keys. Then, in a clear mezzo-soprano voice, she sang the first verse of one of the most popular Irish ballads:—

"O *Arrah ma dheelish*, the distant *dudheen*
Lies soft in the moonlight, *ma bouchal vourneen*:
The springing *gossoons* on the heather are still,
And the *caubeens* and *colleens* are heard on the hill."

But as the ravishing notes of her sweet voice died upon the air, her hands sank listlessly to her side. Music could not chase away the mysterious shadow from her heart. Again she rose. Putting on a white crape bonnet, and carefully drawing a pair of lemon-colored gloves over her taper fingers, she seized her parasol and plunged into the depths of the pine forest.

## CHAPTER IV

Genevra had not proceeded many miles before a weariness seized upon her fragile limbs, and she would fain seat herself upon the trunk of a prostrate pine, which she previously dusted with her handkerchief. The sun was just sinking below the horizon, and the scene was one of gorgeous and sylvan beauty. "How beautiful is nature!" murmured the innocent girl, as, reclining gracefully against the root of the tree, she gathered up her skirts and tied a handkerchief around her throat. But a low growl interrupted her meditation. Starting to her feet, her eyes met a sight which froze her blood with terror.

The only outlet to the forest was the narrow path, barely wide enough for a single person, hemmed in by trees and rocks, which she had just traversed. Down this path, in Indian file, came a monstrous grizzly, closely followed by a California lion, a wild cat, and a buffalo, the rear being brought up by a wild Spanish bull. The mouths of the three first animals were distended with frightful significance, the horns of the last were lowered as ominously. As Genevra was preparing to faint, she heard a low voice behind her.

"Eternally dog-gone my skin ef this ain't the puttiest chance yet!"

At the same moment, a long, shining barrel dropped lightly from behind her, and rested over her shoulder.

Genevra shuddered.

"Dern ye—don't move!"

Genevra became motionless.

The crack of a rifle rang through the woods. Three frightful yells were heard, and two sullen roars. Five animals bounded into the air and five lifeless bodies lay upon the plain. The well-aimed bullet had done its work. Entering the open throat of the grizzly it had traversed his body only to enter the throat of the California lion, and in like manner the catamount, until it passed through into the respective foreheads of the bull and the buffalo, and finally fell flattened from the rocky hillside.

Genevra turned quickly. "My preserver!" she shrieked, and fell into the arms of Natty Bumpo, the celebrated Pike Ranger of Donner Lake.

## CHAPTER V

The moon rose cheerfully above Donner Lake. On its placid bosom a dug-out canoe glided rapidly, containing Natty Bumpo and Genevra Tompkins.

Both were silent. The same thought possessed each, and perhaps there was sweet companionship even in the unbroken quiet. Genevra bit the handle of her parasol, and blushed. Natty Bumpo took a fresh chew of tobacco. At length Genevra said, as if in half-spoken reverie:—

"The soft shining of the moon and the peaceful ripple of the waves seem to say to us various things of an instructive and moral tendency."

"You may bet yer pile on that, miss," said her companion gravely. "It's all the preachin' and psalm-singin' I've heern since I was a boy."

"Noble being!" said Miss Tompkins to herself, glancing at the stately Pike as he bent over his paddle to conceal his emotion. "Reared in this wild seclusion, yet he has become penetrated with visible consciousness of a Great First Cause." Then, collecting herself, she said aloud: "Methinks 'twere pleasant to glide ever thus down the stream of life, hand in hand with the one being whom the soul claims as its affinity. But what am I saying?"—and the delicate-minded girl hid her face in her hands.

A long silence ensued, which was at length broken by her companion.

"Ef you mean you're on the marry," he said thoughtfully, "I ain't in no wise partikler."

"My husband!" faltered the blushing girl; and she fell into his arms.

In ten minutes more the loving couple had landed at Judge Tompkins's.

## CHAPTER VI

A year has passed away. Natty Bumpo was returning from Gold Hill, where he had been to purchase provisions. On his way to Donner Lake, rumors of an Indian uprising met his ears. "Dern their pesky skins, ef they dare to touch my Jenny," he muttered between his clenched teeth.

It was dark when he reached the borders of the lake. Around a glittering fire he dimly discerned dusky figures dancing. They were in war paint. Conspicuous among them was the renowned Muck-a-Muck. But why did the fingers of Natty Bumpo tighten convulsively around his rifle?

The chief held in his hand long tufts of raven hair. The heart of the pioneer sickened as he recognized the clustering curls of Genevra. In a moment his rifle was at his shoulder, and with a sharp "ping" Muck-a-Muck leaped into the air a corpse. To knock out the brains of the remaining savages, tear the tresses from the stiffening hand of Muck-a-Muck, and dash rapidly forward to the cottage of Judge Tompkins, was the work of a moment.

He burst open the door. Why did he stand transfixed with open mouth and distended eyeballs? Was the sight too horrible to be borne? On the contrary, before him, in her peerless beauty, stood Genevra Tompkins, leaning on her father's arm.

"Ye'r not scalped, then!" gasped her lover.

"No. I have no hesitation in saying that I am not; but why this abruptness?" responded Genevra.

Bumpo could not speak, but frantically produced the silken tresses. Genevra turned her face aside.

"Why, that's her waterfall!" said the Judge.

Bumpo sank fainting to the floor.

The famous Pike chieftain never recovered from the deceit, and refused to marry Genevra, who died, twenty years afterwards, of a broken heart. Judge Tompkins lost his fortune in Wild Cat. The stage passes twice a week the deserted cottage at Donner Lake. Thus was the death of Muck-a-Muck avenged.

# The Right Eye
# of the Commander

The year of grace 1797 passed away on the coast of California in a southwesterly gale. The little bay of San Carlos, albeit sheltered by the headlands of the Blessed Trinity, was rough and turbulent; its foam clung quivering to the seaward wall of the mission garden; the air was filled with flying sand and spume, and as the Señor Comandante, Hermenegildo Salvatierra, looked from the deep embrasured window of the presidio guardroom, he felt the salt breath of the distant sea buffet a color into his smoke-dried cheeks.

The commander, I have said, was gazing thoughtfully from the window of the guardroom. He may have been reviewing the events of the year now about to pass away. But, like the garrison at the Presidio, there was little to review. The year, like its predecessors, had been uneventful,—the days had slipped by in a delicious monotony of simple duties, unbroken by incident or interruption. The regularly recurring feasts and saints' days, the half-yearly courier from San Diego, the rare transport-ship and rarer foreign vessel, were the mere details of his patriarchal life. If there was no achievement, there was certainly no failure. Abundant harvests and patient industry amply supplied the wants of presidio and mission. Isolated from the family of nations, the wars which shook the world concerned them not so much as the last earthquake; the struggle that emancipated their sister colonies on the other side of the continent to them had no suggestiveness. In short, it was that glorious Indian summer of Californian history around which so much poetical haze still lingers,—that bland, indolent autumn of Spanish rule, so soon to be followed by the wintry storms of Mexican independence and the reviving spring of American conquest.

The commander turned from the window and walked toward the fire that burned brightly on the deep oven-like hearth. A pile of copy-

books, the work of the presidio school, lay on the table. As he turned
over the leaves with a paternal interest, and surveyed the fair round
Scripture text,—the first pious pothooks of the pupils of San Carlos,
an audible commentary fell from his lips: " 'Abimelech took her from
Abraham'—ah, little one, excellent!—'Jacob sent to see his brother'
—body of Christ! that up-stroke of thine, Paquita, is marvelous; the
governor shall see it!" A film of honest pride dimmed the commander's
left eye,—the right, alas! twenty years before had been sealed by an
Indian arrow. He rubbed it softly with the sleeve of his leather jacket,
and continued: " 'The Ishmaelites having arrived' "—

He stopped, for there was a step in the courtyard, a foot upon the
threshold, and a stranger entered. With the instinct of an old soldier,
the commander, after one glance at the intruder, turned quickly toward the wall, where his trusty Toledo hung, or should have been
hanging. But it was not there, and as he recalled that the last time he
had seen that weapon it was being ridden up and down the gallery by
Pepito, the infant son of Bautista, the tortilio-maker, he blushed, and
then contented himself with frowning upon the intruder.

But the stranger's air, though irreverent, was decidedly peaceful.
He was unarmed, and wore the ordinary cape of tarpaulin and sea-
boots of a mariner. Except a villainous smell of codfish, there was little
about him that was peculiar.

His name, as he informed the commander in Spanish that was more
fluent than elegant or precise,—his name was Peleg Scudder. He was
master of the schooner General Court, of the port of Salem, in Massachusetts, on a trading voyage to the South Seas, but now driven by
stress of weather into the bay of San Carlos. He begged permission
to ride out the gale under the headlands of the Blessed Trinity, and
no more. Water he did not need, having taken in a supply at Bodega.
He knew the strict surveillance of the Spanish port regulations in
regard to foreign vessels, and would do nothing against the severe
discipline and good order of the settlement. There was a slight tinge
of sarcasm in his tone as he glanced toward the desolate parade
ground of the presidio and the open unguarded gate. The fact was
that the sentry, Felipe Gomez, had discreetly retired to shelter at the
beginning of the storm, and was then sound asleep in the corridor.

The commander hesitated. The port regulations were severe, but
he was accustomed to exercise individual authority, and beyond an old
order issued ten years before, regarding the American ship Columbia,
there was no precedent to guide him. The storm was severe, and a
sentiment of humanity urged him to grant the stranger's request. It
is but just to the commander to say that his inability to enforce a
refusal did not weigh with his decision. He would have denied with

equal disregard of consequences that right to a seventy-four-gun ship
which he now yielded so gracefully to this Yankee trading schooner.
He stipulated only that there should be no communication between
the ship and shore. "For yourself, Señor Captain," he continued, "accept my hospitality. The fort is yours as long as you shall grace it with
your distinguished presence," and with old-fashioned courtesy he
made the semblance of withdrawing from the guardroom.

Master Peleg Scudder smiled as he thought of the half-dismantled
fort, the two mouldy brass cannon, cast in Manila a century previous,
and the shiftless garrison. A wild thought of accepting the commander's offer literally, conceived in the reckless spirit of a man who
never let slip an offer for trade, for a moment filled his brain, but a
timely reflection of the commercial unimportance of the transaction
checked him. He only took a capacious quid of tobacco, as the commander gravely drew a settle before the fire, and in honor of his guest
untied the black silk handkerchief that bound his grizzled brows.

What passed between Salvatierra and his guest that night it becomes me not, as a grave chronicler of the salient points of history, to
relate. I have said that Master Peleg Scudder was a fluent talker, and
under the influence of divers strong waters, furnished by his host, he
became still more loquacious. And think of a man with a twenty years'
budget of gossip! The commander learned, for the first time, how
Great Britain lost her colonies; of the French Revolution; of the great
Napoleon, whose achievements, perhaps, Peleg colored more highly
than the commander's superiors would have liked. And when Peleg
turned questioner, the commander was at his mercy. He gradually
made himself master of the gossip of the mission and presidio, the
"small beer" chronicles of that pastoral age, the conversion of the heathen, the presidio schools, and even asked the commander how he had
lost his eye. It is said that at this point of the conversation Master
Peleg produced from about his person divers small trinkets, kickshaws
and new-fangled trifles, and even forced some of them upon his host.
It is further alleged that under the malign influence of Peleg and several glasses of aguardiente the commander lost somewhat of his decorum, and behaved in a manner unseemly for one in his position,
reciting high-flown Spanish poetry, and even piping in a thin high
voice divers madrigals and heathen canzonets of an amorous complexion, chiefly in regard to a "little one" who was his, the commander's,
"soul." These allegations, perhaps unworthy the notice of a serious
chronicler, should be received with great caution, and are introduced
here as simple hearsay. That the commander, however, took a handkerchief and attempted to show his guest the mysteries of the sembi
cuacua, capering in an agile but indecorous manner about the apart-

ment, has been denied. Enough for the purposes of this narrative, that at midnight Peleg assisted his host to bed with many protestations of undying friendship, and then, as the gale had abated, took his leave of the presidio, and hurried aboard the General Court. When the day broke the ship was gone.

I know not if Peleg kept his word with his host. It is said that the holy Fathers at the mission that night heard a loud chanting in the plaza, as of the heathens singing psalms through their noses; that for many days after an odor of salt codfish prevailed in the settlement; that a dozen hard nutmegs, which were unfit for spice or seed, were found in the possession of the wife of the baker, and that several bushels of shoe-pegs, which bore a pleasing resemblance to oats, but were quite inadequate to the purposes of provender, were discovered in the stable of the blacksmith. But when the reader reflects upon the sacredness of a Yankee trader's word, the stringent discipline of the Spanish port regulations, and the proverbial indisposition of my countrymen to impose upon the confidence of a simple people, he will at once reject this part of the story.

A roll of drums, ushering in the year 1798, awoke the commander. The sun was shining brightly, and the storm had ceased. He sat up in bed, and through the force of habit rubbed his left eye. As the remembrance of the previous night came back to him, he jumped from his couch and ran to the window. There was no ship in the bay. A sudden thought seemed to strike him, and he rubbed both of his eyes. Not content with this, he consulted the metallic mirror which hung beside his crucifix. There was no mistake; the commander had a visible second eye,—a right one,—as good, save for the purposes of vision, as the left.

Whatever might have been the true secret of this transformation, but one opinion prevailed at San Carlos. It was one of those rare miracles vouchsafed a pious Catholic community as an evidence to the heathen, through the intercession of the blessed San Carlos himself. That their beloved commander, the temporal defender of the Faith, should be the recipient of this miraculous manifestation was most fit and seemly. The commander himself was reticent; he could not tell a falsehood,—he dared not tell the truth. After all, if the good folk of San Carlos believed that the powers of his right eye were actually restored, was it wise and discreet for him to undeceive them? For the first time in his life the commander thought of policy,—for the first time he quoted that text which has been the lure of so many well-meaning but easy Christians, of being "all things to all men." Infeliz Hermenegildo Salvatierra!

For by degrees an ominous whisper crept through the little settlement. The right eye of the commander, although miraculous, seemed to exercise a baleful effect upon the beholder. No one could look at it without winking. It was cold, hard, relentless, and unflinching. More than that, it seemed to be endowed with a dreadful prescience,—a faculty of seeing through and into the inarticulate thoughts of those it looked upon. The soldiers of the garrison obeyed the eye rather than the voice of their commander, and answered his glance rather than his lips in questioning. The servants could not evade the ever-watchful but cold attention that seemed to pursue them. The children of the presidio school smirched their copy-books under the awful supervision, and poor Paquita, the prize pupil, failed utterly in that marvelous up-stroke when her patron stood beside her. Gradually distrust, suspicion, self-accusation, and timidity took the place of trust, confidence, and security throughout San Carlos. Wherever the right eye of the commander fell, a shadow fell with it.

Nor was Salvatierra entirely free from the baleful influence of his miraculous acquisition. Unconscious of its effect upon others, he only saw in their actions evidence of certain things that the crafty Peleg had hinted on that eventful New Year's eve. His most trusty retainers stammered, blushed, and faltered before him. Self-accusations, confessions of minor faults and delinquencies, or extravagant excuses and apologies met his mildest inquiries. The very children that he loved —his pet pupil, Paquita—seemed to be conscious of some hidden sin. The result of this constant irritation showed itself more plainly. For the first half-year the commander's voice and eye were at variance. He was still kind, tender, and thoughtful in speech. Gradually, however, his voice took upon itself the hardness of his glance and its skeptical, impassive quality, and as the year again neared its close it was plain that the commander had fitted himself to the eye, and not the eye to the commander.

It may be surmised that these changes did not escape the watchful solicitude of the Fathers. Indeed, the few who were first to ascribe the right eye of Salvatierra to miraculous origin and the special grace of the blessed San Carlos, now talked openly of witchcraft and the agency of Luzbel, the evil one. It would have fared ill with Hermenegildo Salvatierra had he been aught but commander or amenable to local authority. But the reverend Father, Friar Manuel de Cortes, had no power over the political executive, and all attempts at spiritual advice failed signally. He retired baffled and confused from his first interview with the commander, who seemed now to take a grim satisfaction in the fateful power of his glance. The holy Father contradicted himself, exposed the fallacies of his own arguments, and even, it is asserted, committed himself to several undoubted heresies. When the commander stood up at mass, if the officiating priest caught that skeptical and searching eye, the service was inevitably ruined. Even the power of the Holy Church seemed to be lost, and the last hold upon the affections of the people and the good order of the settlement departed from San Carlos.

As the long dry summer passed, the low hills that surrounded the white walls of the presidio grew more and more to resemble in hue the leathern jacket of the commander, and Nature herself seemed to have borrowed his dry, hard glare. The earth was cracked and seamed with drought; a blight had fallen upon the orchards and vineyards, and the rain, long delayed and ardently prayed for, came not. The sky was as tearless as the right eye of the commander. Murmurs of discontent, insubordination, and plotting among the Indians reached his ear; he only set his teeth the more firmly, tightened the knot of his black silk handkerchief, and looked up at his Toledo.

The last day of the year 1798 found the commander sitting, at the hour of evening prayers, alone in the guardroom. He no longer attended the services of the Holy Church, but crept away at such times to some solitary spot, where he spent the interval in silent meditation. The firelight played upon the low beams and rafters, but left the bowed figure of Salvatierra in darkness. Sitting thus, he felt a small hand touch his arm, and, looking down, saw the figure of Paquita, his little Indian pupil, at his knee. "Ah! littlest of all," said the commander, with something of his old tenderness, lingering over the endearing diminutives of his native speech,—"sweet one, what doest thou here? Art thou not afraid of him whom every one shuns and fears?"

"No," said the little Indian readily, "not in the dark. I hear your voice,—the old voice; I feel your touch,—the old touch; but I see not your eye, Señor Comandante. That only I fear,—and that, O señor, O my father," said the child, lifting her little arms towards his,—"that I know is not thine own!"

The commander shuddered and turned away. Then, recovering himself, he kissed Paquita gravely on the forehead and bade her retire. A few hours later, when silence had fallen upon the presidio, he sought his own couch and slept peacefully.

At about the middle watch of the night a dusky figure crept through the low embrasure of the commander's apartment. Other figures were flitting through the parade-ground, which the commander might have seen had he not slept so quietly. The intruder stepped noiselessly to the couch and listened to the sleeper's deep-drawn respiration. Something glittered in the firelight as the savage lifted his arm; another moment and the sore perplexities of Hermenegildo Salvatierra would have been over, when suddenly the savage started and fell back in a paroxysm of terror. The commander slept peacefully, but his right eye, widely opened, fixed and unaltered, glared coldly on the would-be assassin. The man fell to the earth in a fit, and the noise awoke the sleeper.

To rise to his feet, grasp his sword, and deal blows thick and fast upon the mutinous savages who now thronged the room, was the work of a moment. Help opportunely arrived, and the undisciplined Indians were speedily driven beyond the walls; but in the scuffle the commander received a blow upon his right eye, and, lifting his hand to that mysterious organ, it was gone. Never again was it found, and never again, for bale or bliss, did it adorn the right orbit of the commander.

With it passed away the spell that had fallen upon San Carlos. The rain returned to invigorate the languid soil, harmony was restored between priest and soldier, the green grass presently waved over the sere hillsides, the children flocked again to the side of their martial preceptor, a Te Deum was sung in the mission church, and pastoral content once more smiled upon the gentle valleys of San Carlos. And far southward crept the General Court with its master, Peleg Scudder, trafficking in beads and peltries with the Indians, and offering glass eyes, wooden legs, and other Boston notions to the chiefs.

# The Luck
# of Roaring Camp

There was commotion in Roaring Camp. It could not have been a fight, for in 1850 that was not novel enough to have called together the entire settlement. The ditches and claims were not only deserted, but "Tuttle's grocery" had contributed its gamblers, who, it will be remembered, calmly continued their game the day that French Pete and Kanaka Joe shot each other to death over the bar in the front room. The whole camp was collected before a rude cabin on the outer edge of the clearing. Conversation was carried on in a low tone, but the name of a woman was frequently repeated. It was a name familiar enough in the camp,—"Cherokee Sal."

Perhaps the less said of her the better. She was a coarse and, it is to be feared, a very sinful woman. But at that time she was the only woman in Roaring Camp, and was just then lying in sore extremity, when she most needed the ministration of her own sex. Dissolute, abandoned, and irreclaimable, she was yet suffering a martyrdom hard enough to bear even when veiled by sympathizing womanhood, but now terrible in her loneliness. The primal curse had come to her in that original isolation which must have made the punishment of the first transgression so dreadful. It was, perhaps, part of the expiation of her sin that, at a moment when she most lacked her sex's intuitive tenderness and care, she met only the half-contemptuous faces of her masculine associates. Yet a few of the spectators were, I think, touched by her sufferings. Sandy Tipton thought it was "rough on Sal," and, in the contemplation of her condition, for a moment rose superior to the fact that he had an ace and two bowers in his sleeve.

It will be seen also that the situation was novel. Deaths were by no means uncommon in Roaring Camp, but a birth was a new thing. People had been dismissed from the camp effectively, finally, and with no possibility of return; but this was the first time that anybody had been introduced *ab initio*. Hence the excitement.

"You go in there, Stumpy," said a prominent citizen known as "Kentuck," addressing one of the loungers. "Go in there, and see what you kin do. You've had experience in them things."

Perhaps there was a fitness in the selection. Stumpy, in other climes, had been the putative head of two families; in fact, it was owing to some legal informality in these proceedings that Roaring Camp— a city of refuge—was indebted to his company. The crowd approved the choice, and Stumpy was wise enough to bow to the majority. The door closed on the extempore surgeon and midwife, and Roaring Camp sat down outside, smoked its pipe, and awaited the issue.

The assemblage numbered about a hundred men. One or two of these were actual fugitives from justice, some were criminal, and all were reckless. Physically they exhibited no indication of their past lives and character. The greatest scamp had a Raphael face, with a profusion of blonde hair; Oakhurst, a gambler, had the melancholy air and intellectual abstraction of a Hamlet; the coolest and most coura- geous man was scarcely over five feet in height, with a soft voice and an embarrassed, timid manner. The term "roughs" applied to them was a distinction rather than a definition. Perhaps in the minor details of fingers, toes, ears, etc., the camp may have been deficient, but these slight omissions did not detract from their aggregate force. The strongest man had but three fingers on his right hand; the best shot had but one eye.

Such was the physical aspect of the men that were dispersed around the cabin. The camp lay in a triangular valley between two hills and a river. The only outlet was a steep trail over the summit of a hill that faced the cabin, now illuminated by the rising moon. The suffering woman might have seen it from the rude bunk whereon she lay,—seen it winding like a silver thread until it was lost in the stars above.

A fire of withered pine boughs added sociability to the gathering. By degrees the natural levity of Roaring Camp returned. Bets were freely offered and taken regarding the result. Three to five that "Sal would get through with it;" even that the child would survive; side bets as to the sex and complexion of the coming stranger. In the midst of an excited discussion an exclamation came from those nearest the door, and the camp stopped to listen. Above the swaying and moaning of the pines, the swift rush of the river, and the crackling of the fire rose a sharp, querulous cry,—a cry unlike anything heard before in the camp. The pines stopped moaning, the river ceased to rush, and the fire to crackle. It seemed as if Nature had stopped to listen too.

The camp rose to its feet as one man! It was proposed to explode a barrel of gunpowder; but in consideration of the situation of the mother, better counsels prevailed, and only a few revolvers were discharged; for whether owing to the rude surgery of the camp, or some other reason, Cherokee Sal was sinking fast. Within an hour she had climbed, as it were, that rugged road that led to the stars, and so passed out of Roaring Camp, its sin and shame, forever. I do not think that the announcement disturbed them much, except in speculation as to the fate of the child. "Can he live now?" was asked of Stumpy. The answer was doubtful. The only other being of Cherokee Sal's sex and maternal condition in the settlement was an ass. There was some conjecture as to fitness, but the experiment was tried. It was less problematical than the ancient treatment of Romulus and Remus, and apparently as successful.

When these details were completed, which exhausted another hour, the door was opened, and the anxious crowd of men, who had already formed themselves into a queue, entered in single file. Beside the low bunk or shelf, on which the figure of the mother was starkly outlined below the blankets, stood a pine table. On this a candle-box was placed, and within it, swathed in staring red flannel, lay the last arrival at Roaring Camp. Beside the candle-box was placed a hat. Its use was soon indicated. "Gentlemen," said Stumpy, with a singular mixture of authority and *ex officio* complacency,—"gentlemen will please pass in at the front door, round the table, and out at the back door. Them as wishes to contribute anything toward the orphan will find a hat handy." The first man entered with his hat on; he uncovered, however, as he looked about him, and so unconsciously set an example to the next. In such communities good and bad actions are catching. As the procession filed in comments were audible,—criticisms addressed perhaps rather to Stumpy in the character of showman: "Is that him?" "Mighty small specimen;" "Hasn't more'n got the color;" "Ain't bigger nor a derringer." The contributions were as characteristic: A silver tobacco box; a doubloon; a navy revolver, silver mounted; a gold specimen; a very beautifully embroidered lady's handkerchief (from Oakhurst the gambler); a diamond breastpin; a diamond ring (suggested by the pin, with the remark from the giver that he "saw that pin and went two diamonds better"); a slung-shot; a Bible (contributor not detected); a golden spur; a silver teaspoon (the initials, I regret to say, were not the giver's); a pair of surgeon's shears; a lancet; a Bank of England note for £5; and about $200 in loose gold and silver coin. During these proceedings Stumpy maintained a silence as impassive as the dead on his left, a gravity as inscrutable as that of the newly born on his right. Only one incident

occurred to break the monotony of the curious procession. As Kentuck
bent over the candle-box half curiously, the child turned, and, in a
spasm of pain, caught at his groping finger, and held it fast for a
moment. Kentuck looked foolish and embarrassed. Something like
a blush tried to assert itself in his weather-beaten cheek. "The d——d
little cuss!" he said, as he extricated his finger, with perhaps more
tenderness and care than he might have been deemed capable of showing. He held that finger a little apart from its fellows as he went out,
and examined it curiously. The examination provoked the same original remark in regard to the child. In fact, he seemed to enjoy repeating it. "He rastled with my finger," he remarked to Tipton,
holding up the member, "the d——d little cuss!"

It was four o'clock before the camp sought repose. A light burnt
in the cabin where the watchers sat, for Stumpy did not go to bed
that night. Nor did Kentuck. He drank quite freely, and related with
great gusto his experience, invariably ending with his characteristic
condemnation of the newcomer. It seemed to relieve him of any unjust
implication of sentiment, and Kentuck had the weaknesses of the no-
bler sex. When everybody else had gone to bed, he walked down to
the river and whistled reflectingly. Then he walked up the gulch past
the cabin, still whistling with demonstrative unconcern. At a large
redwood-tree he paused and retraced his steps, and again passed the
cabin. Halfway down to the river's bank he again paused, and then
returned and knocked at the door. It was opened by Stumpy. "How
goes it?" said Kentuck, looking past Stumpy toward the candle-box.
"All serene!" replied Stumpy. "Anything up?" "Nothing." There was
a pause—an embarrassing one—Stumpy still holding the door. Then
Kentuck had recourse to his finger, which he held up to Stumpy. "Rastled with it,—the d——d little cuss," he said, and retired.

The next day Cherokee Sal had such rude sepulture as Roaring
Camp afforded. After her body had been committed to the hillside,
there was a formal meeting of the camp to discuss what should be
done with her infant. A resolution to adopt it was unanimous and
enthusiastic. But an animated discussion in regard to the manner and
feasibility of providing for its wants at once sprang up. It was remarkable that the argument partook of none of those fierce personalities with which discussions were usually conducted at Roaring
Camp. Tipton proposed that they should send the child to Red Dog,
—a distance of forty miles,—where female attention could be procured. But the unlucky suggestion met with fierce and unanimous
opposition. It was evident that no plan which entailed parting from
their new acquisition would for a moment be entertained. "Besides,"
said Tom Ryder, "them fellows at Red Dog would swap it, and ring

in somebody else on us." A disbelief in the honesty of other camps prevailed at Roaring Camp, as in other places.

The introduction of a female nurse in the camp also met with objection. It was argued that no decent woman could be prevailed to accept Roaring Camp as her home, and the speaker urged that "they didn't want any more of the other kind." This unkind allusion to the defunct mother, harsh as it may seem, was the first spasm of propriety,—the first symptom of the camp's regeneration. Stumpy advanced nothing. Perhaps he felt a certain delicacy in interfering with the selection of a possible successor in office. But when questioned, he averred stoutly that he and "Jinny"—the mammal before alluded to —could manage to rear the child. There was something original, independent, and heroic about the plan that pleased the camp. Stumpy was retained. Certain articles were sent for to Sacramento. "Mind," said the treasurer, as he pressed a bag of gold-dust into the expressman's hand, "the best that can be got,—lace, you know, and filigreework and frills,—d——n the cost!"

Strange to say, the child thrived. Perhaps the invigorating climate of the mountain camp was compensation for material deficiencies. Nature took the foundling to her broader breast. In that rare atmosphere of the Sierra foothills,—that air pungent with balsamic odor, that ethereal cordial at once bracing and exhilarating,—he may have found food and nourishment, or a subtle chemistry that transmuted ass's milk to lime and phosphorus. Stumpy inclined to the belief that it was the latter and good nursing. "Me and that ass," he would say, "has been father and mother to him! Don't you," he would add, apostrophizing the helpless bundle before him, "never go back on us."

By the time he was a month old the necessity of giving him a name became apparent. He had generally been known as "The Kid," "Stumpy's Boy," "The Coyote" (an allusion to his vocal powers), and even by Kentuck's endearing diminutive of "The d——d little cuss." But these were felt to be vague and unsatisfactory, and were at last dismissed under another influence. Gamblers and adventurers are generally superstitious, and Oakhurst one day declared that the baby had brought "the luck" to Roaring Camp. It was certain that of late they had been successful. "Luck" was the name agreed upon, with the prefix of Tommy for greater convenience. No allusion was made to the mother, and the father was unknown. "It's better," said the philosophical Oakhurst, "to take a fresh deal all round. Call him Luck, and start him fair." A day was accordingly set apart for the christening. What was meant by this ceremony the reader may imagine who has already gathered some idea of the reckless irreverence of Roaring Camp. The master of ceremonies was one "Boston," a noted wag, and

the occasion seemed to promise the greatest facetiousness. This ingenious satirist had spent two days in preparing a burlesque of the
Church service, with pointed local allusions. The choir was properly
trained, and Sandy Tipton was to stand godfather. But after the procession had marched to the grove with music and banners, and the
child had been deposited before a mock altar, Stumpy stepped before the expectant crowd. "It ain't my style to spoil fun, boys," said
the little man, stoutly eying the faces around him, "but it strikes me
that this thing ain't exactly on the squar. It's playing it pretty low
down on this yer baby to ring in fun on him that he ain't goin' to
understand. And ef there's goin' to be any godfathers round, I'd like
to see who's got any better rights than me." A silence followed
Stumpy's speech. To the credit of all humorists be it said that the first
man to acknowledge its justice was the satirist thus stopped of his
fun. "But," said Stumpy, quickly following up his advantage, "we're
here for a christening, and we'll have it. I proclaim you Thomas Luck,
according to the laws of the United States and the State of California,
so help me God." It was the first time that the name of the Deity had
been otherwise uttered than profanely in the camp. The form of christening was perhaps even more ludicrous than the satirist had conceived; but strangely enough, nobody saw it and nobody laughed.
"Tommy" was christened as seriously as he would have been under a
Christian roof, and cried and was comforted in as orthodox fashion.

And so the work of regeneration began in Roaring Camp. Almost
imperceptibly a change came over the settlement. The cabin assigned
to "Tommy Luck"—or "The Luck," as he was more frequently
called—first showed signs of improvement. It was kept scrupulously
clean and whitewashed. Then it was boarded, clothed, and papered.
The rosewood cradle, packed eighty miles by mule, had, in Stumpy's
way of putting it, "sorter killed the rest of the furniture." So the re-
habilitation of the cabin became a necessity. The men who were in the
habit of lounging in at Stumpy's to see "how 'The Luck' got on"
seemed to appreciate the change, and in self-defense the rival establishment of "Tuttle's grocery" bestirred itself and imported a carpet
and mirrors. The reflections of the latter on the appearance of Roaring
Camp tended to produce stricter habits of personal cleanliness. Again
Stumpy imposed a kind of quarantine upon those who aspired to the
honor and privilege of holding The Luck. It was a cruel mortification
to Kentuck—who, in the carelessness of a large nature and the habits
of frontier life, had begun to regard all garments as a second cuticle,
which, like a snake's, only sloughed off through decay—to be debarred
this privilege from certain prudential reasons. Yet such was the subtle
influence of innovation that he thereafter appeared regularly every

afternoon in a clean shirt and face still shining from his ablutions. Nor were moral and social sanitary laws neglected. "Tommy," who was supposed to spend his whole existence in a persistent attempt to repose, must not be disturbed by noise. The shouting and yelling, which had gained the camp its infelicitous title, were not permitted within hearing distance of Stumpy's. The men conversed in whispers or smoked with Indian gravity. Profanity was tacitly given up in these sacred precincts, and throughout the camp a popular form of expletive, known as "D——n the luck!" and "Curse the luck!" was abandoned, as having a new personal bearing. Vocal music was not interdicted, being supposed to have a soothing, tranquilizing quality; and one song, sung by "Man-o'-War Jack," an English sailor from her Majesty's Australian colonies, was quite popular as a lullaby. It was a lugubrious recital of the exploits of "the Arethusa, Seventy-four," in a muffled minor, ending with a prolonged dying fall at the burden of each verse, "On b-oo-o-ard of the Arethusa." It was a fine sight to see Jack holding The Luck, rocking from side to side as if with the motion of a ship, and crooning forth this naval ditty. Either through the peculiar rocking of Jack or the length of his song,—it contained ninety stanzas, and was continued with conscientious deliberation to the bitter end,—the lullaby generally had the desired effect. At such times the men would lie at full length under the trees in the soft summer twilight, smoking their pipes and drinking in the melodious utterances. An indistinct idea that this was pastoral happiness pervaded the camp. "This 'ere kind o' think," said the Cockney Simmons, meditatively reclining on his elbow, "is 'evingly." It reminded him of Greenwich.

On the long summer days The Luck was usually carried to the gulch from whence the golden store of Roaring Camp was taken. There, on a blanket spread over pine boughs, he would lie while the men were working in the ditches below. Latterly there was a rude attempt to decorate this bower with flowers and sweet-smelling shrubs, and generally some one would bring him a cluster of wild honeysuckles, azaleas, or the painted blossoms of Las Mariposas. The men had suddenly awakened to the fact that there were beauty and significance in these trifles, which they had so long trodden carelessly beneath their feet. A flake of glittering mica, a fragment of variegated quartz, a bright pebble from the bed of the creek, became beautiful to eyes thus cleared and strengthened, and were invariably put aside for The Luck. It was wonderful how many treasures the woods and hillsides yielded that "would do for Tommy." Surrounded by playthings such as never child out of fairyland had before, it is to be hoped that Tommy was content. He appeared to be serenely happy, albeit there was an infantine gravity about him, a contemplative light in his

round gray eyes, that sometimes worried Stumpy. He was always
tractable and quiet, and it is recorded that once, having crept
beyond his "corral,"—a hedge of tessellated pine boughs, which surrounded his bed,—he dropped over the bank on his head in the soft
earth, and remained with his mottled legs in the air in that position
for at least five minutes with unflinching gravity. He was extricated
without a murmur. I hesitate to record the many other instances of
his sagacity, which rest, unfortunately, upon the statements of prej-
udiced friends. Some of them were not without a tinge of superstition.
"I crep' up the bank just now," said Kentuck one day, in a breathless
state of excitement, "and dern my skin if he wasn't a-talking to a
jaybird as was a-sittin' on his lap. There they was, just as free and
sociable as anything you please, a-jawin' at each other just like two
cherrybums." Howbeit, whether creeping over the pine boughs or lying lazily on his back blinking at the leaves above him, to him the
birds sang, the squirrels chattered, and the flowers bloomed. Nature
was his nurse and playfellow. For him she would let slip between the
leaves golden shafts of sunlight that fell just within his grasp; she
would send wandering breezes to visit him with the balm of bay and
resinous gum; to him the tall redwoods nodded familiarly and sleepily,
the bumblebees buzzed, and the rooks cawed a slumbrous accompaniment.

Such was the golden summer of Roaring Camp. They were "flush
times," and the luck was with them. The claims had yielded enor-
mously. The camp was jealous of its privileges and looked suspiciously
on strangers. No encouragement was given to immigration, and, to
make their seclusion more perfect, the land on either side of the mountain wall that surrounded the camp they duly preëmpted. This, and a
reputation for singular proficiency with the revolver, kept the reserve
of Roaring Camp inviolate. The expressman—their only connecting
link with the surrounding world—sometimes told wonderful stories of
the camp. He would say, "They've a street up there in 'Roaring' that
would lay over any street in Red Dog. They've got vines and flowers
round their houses, and they wash themselves twice a day. But they're
mighty rough on strangers, and they worship an Ingin baby."

With the prosperity of the camp came a desire for further improvement. It was proposed to build a hotel in the following spring, and to
invite one or two decent families to reside there for the sake of The
Luck, who might perhaps profit by female companionship. The sacrifice that this concession to the sex cost these men, who were fiercely
skeptical in regard to its general virtue and usefulness, can only be
accounted for by their affection for Tommy. A few still held out. But
the resolve could not be carried into effect for three months, and the

minority meekly yielded in the hope that something might turn up to prevent it. And it did.

The winter of 1851 will long be remembered in the foothills. The snow lay deep on the Sierras, and every mountain creek became a river, and every river a lake. Each gorge and gulch was transformed into a tumultuous watercourse that descended the hillsides, tearing down giant trees and scattering its drift and débris along the plain. Red Dog had been twice under water, and Roaring Camp had been forewarned. "Water put the gold into them gulches," said Stumpy. "It's been here once and will be here again!" And that night the North Fork suddenly leaped over its banks and swept up the triangular valley of Roaring Camp.

In the confusion of rushing water, crashing trees, and crackling timber, and the darkness which seemed to flow with the water and blot out the fair valley, but little could be done to collect the scattered camp. When the morning broke, the cabin of Stumpy, nearest the river-bank, was gone. Higher up the gulch they found the body of its unlucky owner; but the pride, the hope, the joy, The Luck, of Roaring Camp had disappeared. They were returning with sad hearts when a shout from the bank recalled them.

It was a relief-boat from down the river. They had picked up, they said, a man and an infant, nearly exhausted, about two miles below. Did anybody know them, and did they belong here?

It needed but a glance to show them Kentuck lying there, cruelly crushed and bruised, but still holding The Luck of Roaring Camp in his arms. As they bent over the strangely assorted pair, they saw that the child was cold and pulseless. "He is dead," said one. Kentuck opened his eyes. "Dead?" he repeated feebly. "Yes, my man, and you are dying too." A smile lit the eyes of the expiring Kentuck. "Dying!" he repeated; "he's a-taking me with him. Tell the boys I've got The Luck with me now;" and the strong man, clinging to the frail babe as a drowning man is said to cling to a straw, drifted away into the shadowy river that flows forever to the unknown sea.

# The Outcasts of Poker Flat

As Mr. John Oakhurst, gambler, stepped into the main street of Poker Flat on the morning of the 23d of November, 1850, he was conscious of a change in its moral atmosphere since the preceding night. Two or three men, conversing earnestly together, ceased as he approached, and exchanged significant glances. There was a Sabbath lull in the air, which, in a settlement unused to Sabbath influences, looked ominous.

Mr. Oakhurst's calm, handsome face betrayed small concern in these indications. Whether he was conscious of any predisposing cause was another question. "I reckon they're after somebody," he reflected; "likely it's me." He returned to his pocket the handkerchief with which he had been whipping away the red dust of Poker Flat from his neat boots, and quietly discharged his mind of any further conjecture.

In point of fact, Poker Flat was "after somebody." It had lately suffered the loss of several thousand dollars, two valuable horses, and a prominent citizen. It was experiencing a spasm of virtuous reaction, quite as lawless and ungovernable as any of the acts that had provoked it. A secret committee had determined to rid the town of all improper persons. This was done permanently in regard of two men who were then hanging from the boughs of a sycamore in the gulch, and temporarily in the banishment of certain other objectionable characters. I regret to say that some of these were ladies. It is but due to the sex, however, to state that their impropriety was professional, and it was only in such easily established standards of evil that Poker Flat ventured to sit in judgment.

Mr. Oakhurst was right in supposing that he was included in this category. A few of the committee had urged hanging him as a possible example and a sure method of reimbursing themselves from his pockets of the sums he had won from them. "It's agin justice," said Jim Wheeler, "to let this yer young man from Roaring Camp—an entire stranger—carry away our money." But a crude sentiment of equity residing in the breasts of those who had been fortunate enough to win from Mr. Oakhurst overruled this narrower local prejudice.

Mr. Oakhurst received his sentence with philosophic calmness, none the less coolly that he was aware of the hesitation of his judges. He was too much of a gambler not to accept fate. With him life was at best an uncertain game, and he recognized the usual percentage in favor of the dealer.

A body of armed men accompanied the deported wickedness of Poker Flat to the outskirts of the settlement. Besides Mr. Oakhurst, who was known to be a coolly desperate man, and for whose intimidation the armed escort was intended, the expatriated party consisted of a young woman familiarly known as "The Duchess;" another who had won the title of "Mother Shipton;" and "Uncle Billy," a suspected sluice-robber and confirmed drunkard. The cavalcade provoked no comments from the spectators, nor was any word uttered by the escort. Only when the gulch which marked the uttermost limit of Poker Flat was reached, the leader spoke briefly and to the point. The exiles were forbidden to return at the peril of their lives.

As the escort disappeared, their pent-up feelings found vent in a few hysterical tears from the Duchess, some bad language from Mother Shipton, and a Parthian volley of expletives from Uncle Billy. The philosophic Oakhurst alone remained silent. He listened calmly to Mother Shipton's desire to cut somebody's heart out, to the repeated statements of the Duchess that she would die in the road, and to the alarming oaths that seemed to be bumped out of Uncle Billy as he rode forward. With the easy good humor characteristic of his class, he insisted upon exchanging his own riding-horse, "Five-Spot," for the sorry mule which the Duchess rode. But even this act did not draw the party into any closer sympathy. The young woman readjusted her somewhat draggled plumes with a feeble, faded coquetry; Mother Shipton eyed the possessor of "Five-Spot" with malevolence, and Uncle Billy included the whole party in one sweeping anathema.

The road to Sandy Bar—a camp that, not having as yet experienced the regenerating influences of Poker Flat, consequently seemed to offer some invitation to the emigrants—lay over a steep mountain range. It was distant a day's severe travel. In that advanced season the party soon passed out of the moist, temperate regions of the foothills into the dry, cold, bracing air of the Sierras. The trail was narrow and difficult. At noon the Duchess, rolling out of her saddle upon the ground, declared her intention of going no farther, and the party halted.

The spot was singularly wild and impressive. A wooded amphitheatre, surrounded on three sides by precipitous cliffs of naked granite, sloped gently toward the crest of another precipice that overlooked the valley. It was, undoubtedly, the most suitable spot for a camp, had camping been advisable. But Mr. Oakhurst knew that scarcely half the journey to Sandy Bar was accomplished, and the party were not equipped or provisioned for delay. This fact he pointed out to his companions curtly, with a philosophic commentary on the folly of "throwing up their hand before the game was played out." But they were furnished with liquor, which in this emergency stood them in place of food, fuel, rest, and prescience. In spite of his remonstrances, it was not long before they were more or less under its influence. Uncle Billy passed rapidly from a bellicose state into one of stupor, the Duchess became maudlin, and Mother Shipton snored. Mr. Oakhurst alone remained erect, leaning against a rock, calmly surveying them.

Mr. Oakhurst did not drink. It interfered with a profession which required coolness, impassiveness, and presence of mind, and, in his own language, he "couldn't afford it." As he gazed at his recumbent fellow exiles, the loneliness begotten of his pariah trade, his habits of life, his very vices, for the first time seriously oppressed him. He bestirred himself in dusting his black clothes, washing his hands and face, and other acts characteristic of his studiously neat habits, and for a moment forgot his annoyance. The thought of deserting his weaker and more pitiable companions never perhaps occurred to him. Yet he could not help feeling the want of that excitement which, singularly enough, was most conducive to that calm equanimity for which he was notorious. He looked at the gloomy walls that rose a thousand feet sheer above the circling pines around him, at the sky ominously clouded, at the valley below, already deepening into shadow; and, doing so, suddenly he heard his own name called.

A horseman slowly ascended the trail. In the fresh, open face of the newcomer Mr. Oakhurst recognized Tom Simson, otherwise known as "The Innocent," of Sandy Bar. He had met him some months before over a "little game," and had, with perfect equanimity, won the entire fortune—amounting to some forty dollars—of that guileless youth.

After the game was finished, Mr. Oakhurst drew the youthful speculator behind the door and thus addressed him: "Tommy, you're a good
little man, but you can't gamble worth a cent. Don't try it over again."
He then handed him his money back, pushed him gently from the
room, and so made a devoted slave of Tom Simson.

There was a remembrance of this in his boyish and enthusiastic greeting of Mr. Oakhurst. He had started, he said, to go to Poker Flat to
seek his fortune. "Alone?" No, not exactly alone; in fact (a giggle), he
had run away with Piney Woods. Didn't Mr. Oakhurst remember
Piney? She that used to wait on the table at the Temperance House?
They had been engaged a long time, but old Jake Woods had objected,
and so they had run away, and were going to Poker Flat to be married, and here they were. And they were tired out, and how lucky it
was they had found a place to camp, and company. All this the Innocent delivered rapidly, while Piney, a stout, comely damsel of fifteen,
emerged from behind the pine-tree, where she had been blushing unseen, and rode to the side of her lover.

Mr. Oakhurst seldom troubled himself with sentiment, still less
with propriety; but he had a vague idea that the situation was not
fortunate. He retained, however, his presence of mind sufficiently to
kick Uncle Billy, who was about to say something, and Uncle Billy
was sober enough to recognize in Mr. Oakhurst's kick a superior
power that would not bear trifling. He then endeavored to dissuade
Tom Simson from delaying further, but in vain. He even pointed out
the fact that there was no provision, nor means of making a camp.
But, unluckily, the Innocent met this objection by assuring the party
that he was provided with an extra mule loaded with provisions, and
by the discovery of a rude attempt at a log house near the trail. "Piney
can stay with Mrs. Oakhurst," said the Innocent, pointing to the Duchess, "and I can shift for myself."

Nothing but Mr. Oakhurst's admonishing foot saved Uncle Billy
from bursting into a roar of laughter. As it was, he felt compelled to
retire up the cañon until he could recover his gravity. There he confided the joke to the tall pine-trees, with many slaps of his leg, con-
tortions of his face, and the usual profanity. But when he returned to
the party, he found them seated by a fire—for the air had grown
strangely chill and the sky overcast—in apparently amicable conversation. Piney was actually talking in an impulsive girlish fashion to
the Duchess, who was listening with an interest and animation she
had not shown for many days. The Innocent was holding forth, apparently with equal effect, to Mr. Oakhurst and Mother Shipton, who

was actually relaxing into amiability. "Is this yer a d——d picnic?" said Uncle Billy, with inward scorn, as he surveyed the sylvan group, the glancing firelight, and the tethered animals in the foreground. Suddenly an idea mingled with the alcoholic fumes that disturbed his brain. It was apparently of a jocular nature, for he felt impelled to slap his leg again and cram his fist into his mouth.

As the shadows crept slowly up the mountain, a slight breeze rocked the tops of the pine-trees and moaned through their long and gloomy aisles. The ruined cabin, patched and covered with pine boughs, was set apart for the ladies. As the lovers parted, they unaffectedly exchanged a kiss, so honest and sincere that it might have been heard above the swaying pines. The frail Duchess and the malevolent Mother Shipton were probably too stunned to remark upon this last evidence of simplicity, and so turned without a word to the hut. The fire was replenished, the men lay down before the door, and in a few minutes were asleep.

Mr. Oakhurst was a light sleeper. Toward morning he awoke benumbed and cold. As he stirred the dying fire, the wind, which was now blowing strongly, brought to his cheek that which caused the blood to leave it,—snow!

He started to his feet with the intention of awakening the sleepers, for there was no time to lose. But turning to where Uncle Billy had been lying, he found him gone. A suspicion leaped to his brain, and a curse to his lips. He ran to the spot where the mules had been tethered—they were no longer there. The tracks were already rapidly disappearing in the snow.

The momentary excitement brought Mr. Oakhurst back to the fire with his usual calm. He did not waken the sleepers. The Innocent slumbered peacefully, with a smile on his good-humored, freckled face; the virgin Piney slept beside her frailer sisters as sweetly as though attended by celestial guardians; and Mr. Oakhurst, drawing his blanket over his shoulders, stroked his mustaches and waited for the dawn. It came slowly in a whirling mist of snowflakes that dazzled and confused the eye. What could be seen of the landscape appeared magically changed. He looked over the valley, and summed up the present and future in two words, "Snowed in!"

A careful inventory of the provisions, which, fortunately for the party, had been stored within the hut, and so escaped the felonious fingers of Uncle Billy, disclosed the fact that with care and prudence they might last ten days longer. "That is," said Mr. Oakhurst *sotto voce* to the Innocent, "if you're willing to board us. If you ain't—and perhaps you'd better not—you can wait till Uncle Billy gets back with provisions." For some occult reason, Mr. Oakhurst could not bring himself to disclose Uncle Billy's rascality, and so offered the hypothesis that he had wandered from the camp and had accidentally stampeded the animals. He dropped a warning to the Duchess and Mother Shipton, who of course knew the facts of their associate's defection. "They'll find out the truth about us *all* when they find out anything," he added significantly, "and there's no good frightening them now."

Tom Simson not only put all his worldly store at the disposal of Mr. Oakhurst, but seemed to enjoy the prospect of their enforced seclusion. "We'll have a good camp for a week, and then the snow'll melt, and we'll all go back together." The cheerful gayety of the young man and Mr. Oakhurst's calm infected the others. The Innocent, with the aid of pine boughs, extemporized a thatch for the roofless cabin, and the Duchess directed Piney in the rearrangement of the interior with a taste and tact that opened the blue eyes of that provincial maiden to their fullest extent. "I reckon now you're used to fine things at Poker Flat," said Piney. The Duchess turned away sharply to conceal something that reddened her cheeks through their professional tint, and Mother Shipton requested Piney not to "chatter." But when Mr. Oakhurst returned from a weary search for the trail, he heard the sound of happy laughter echoed from the rocks. He stopped in some alarm, and his thoughts first naturally reverted to the whiskey, which he had prudently cachéd. "And yet it don't somehow sound like whiskey," said the gambler. It was not until he caught sight of the blazing fire through the still blinding storm, and the group around it, that he settled to the conviction that it was "square fun."

Whether Mr. Oakhurst had cachéd his cards with the whiskey as something debarred the free access of the community, I cannot say. It was certain that, in Mother Shipton's words, he "didn't say 'cards' once" during that evening. Haply the time was beguiled by an accordion, produced somewhat ostentatiously by Tom Simson from his pack. Notwithstanding some difficulties attending the manipulation of this instrument, Piney Woods managed to pluck several reluctant melodies from its keys, to an accompaniment by the Innocent on a pair of bone castanets. But the crowning festivity of the evening was reached in a rude camp-meeting hymn, which the lovers, joining hands, sang with great earnestness and vociferation. I fear that a certain defiant tone and Covenanter's swing to its chorus, rather than any devotional quality, caused it speedily to infect the others, who at last joined in the refrain:—

*"I'm proud to live in the service of the Lord,*
*And I'm bound to die in His army."*

The pines rocked, the storm eddied and whirled above the miserable group, and the flames of their altar leaped heavenward, as if in token of the vow.

At midnight the storm abated, the rolling clouds parted, and the stars glittered keenly above the sleeping camp. Mr. Oakhurst, whose professional habits had enabled him to live on the smallest possible amount of sleep, in dividing the watch with Tom Simson somehow managed to take upon himself the greater part of that duty. He excused himself to the Innocent by saying that he had "often been a week without sleep." "Doing what?" asked Tom. "Poker!" replied Oakhurst sententiously. "When a man gets a streak of luck,—nigger-luck,—he don't get tired. The luck gives in first. Luck," continued the gambler reflectively, "is a mighty queer thing. All you know about it for certain is that it's bound to change. And it's finding out when it's going to change that makes you. We've had a streak of bad luck since we left Poker Flat,—you come along, and slap you get into it, too. If you can hold your cards right along you're all right. For," added the gambler, with cheerful irrelevance—

*" 'I'm proud to live in the service of the Lord,*
*And I'm bound to die in His army.' "*

The third day came, and the sun, looking through the white-curtained valley, saw the outcasts divide their slowly decreasing store of provisions for the morning meal. It was one of the peculiarities of that mountain climate that its rays diffused a kindly warmth over the wintry landscape, as if in regretful commiseration of the past. But it revealed drift on drift of snow piled high around the hut,—a hopeless, uncharted, trackless sea of white lying below the rocky shores to which the castaways still clung. Through the marvelously clear air the smoke of the pastoral village of Poker Flat rose miles away. Mother Shipton saw it, and from a remote pinnacle of her rocky fastness hurled in that direction a final malediction. It was her last vituperative attempt, and perhaps for that reason was invested with a certain degree of sublimity. It did her good, she privately informed the Duchess. "Just you go out there and cuss, and see." She then set herself to the task of amusing "the child," as she and the Duchess were pleased to call Piney. Piney was no chicken, but it was a soothing and original theory of the pair thus to account for the fact that she didn't swear and wasn't improper.

When night crept up again through the gorges, the reedy notes of the accordion rose and fell in fitful spasms and long-drawn gasps by the flickering campfire. But music failed to fill entirely the aching void left by insufficient food, and a new diversion was proposed by Piney, —storytelling. Neither Mr. Oakhurst nor his female companions caring to relate their personal experiences, this plan would have failed too, but for the Innocent. Some months before he had chanced upon a stray copy of Mr. Pope's ingenious translation of the Iliad. He now proposed to narrate the principal incidents of that poem—having thoroughly mastered the argument and fairly forgotten the words—in the current vernacular of Sandy Bar. And so for the rest of that night the Homeric demigods again walked the earth. Trojan bully and wily Greek wrestled in the winds, and the great pines in the cañon seemed to bow to the wrath of the son of Peleus. Mr. Oakhurst listened with quiet satisfaction. Most especially was he interested in the fate of "Ash-heels," as the Innocent persisted in denominating the "swift-footed Achilles."

So, with small food and much of Homer and the accordion, a week passed over the heads of the outcasts. The sun again forsook them, and again from leaden skies the snowflakes were sifted over the land. Day by day closer around them drew the snowy circle, until at last they looked from their prison over drifted walls of dazzling white, that towered twenty feet above their heads. It became more and more difficult to replenish their fires, even from the fallen trees beside them, now half hidden in the drifts. And yet no one complained. The lovers turned from the dreary prospect and looked into each other's eyes, and were happy. Mr. Oakhurst settled himself coolly to the losing game before him. The Duchess, more cheerful than she had been, assumed the care of Piney. Only Mother Shipton—once the strongest of the party—seemed to sicken and fade. At midnight on the tenth day she called Oakhurst to her side. "I'm going," she said, in a voice of querulous weakness, "but don't say anything about it. Don't waken the kids. Take the bundle from under my head, and open it." Mr. Oakhurst did so. It contained Mother Shipton's rations for the last week, untouched. "Give 'em to the child," she said, pointing to the sleeping Piney. "You've starved yourself," said the gambler. "That's what they call it," said the woman querulously, as she lay down again, and, turning her face to the wall, passed quietly away.

The accordion and the bones were put aside that day, and Homer was forgotten. When the body of Mother Shipton had been committed to the snow, Mr. Oakhurst took the Innocent aside, and showed him a pair of snowshoes, which he had fashioned from the old pack-saddle. "There's one chance in a hundred to save her yet," he said, pointing to Piney; "but it's there," he added, pointing toward Poker Flat. "If you can reach there in two days she's safe." "And you?" asked Tom Simson. "I'll stay here," was the curt reply.

The lovers parted with a long embrace. "You are not going, too?" said the Duchess, as she saw Mr. Oakhurst apparently waiting to accompany him. "As far as the cañon," he replied. He turned suddenly and kissed the Duchess, leaving her pallid face aflame, and her trembling limbs rigid with amazement.

Night came, but not Mr. Oakhurst. It brought the storm again and the whirling snow. Then the Duchess, feeding the fire, found that some one had quietly piled beside the hut enough fuel to last a few days longer. The tears rose to her eyes, but she hid them from Piney.

The women slept but little. In the morning, looking into each other's faces, they read their fate. Neither spoke, but Piney, accepting the position of the stronger, drew near and placed her arm around the Duchess's waist. They kept this attitude for the rest of the day. That night the storm reached its greatest fury, and, rending asunder the protecting vines, invaded the very hut.

Toward morning they found themselves unable to feed the fire, which gradually died away. As the embers slowly blackened, the Duchess crept closer to Piney, and broke the silence of many hours: "Piney, can you pray?" "No, dear," said Piney simply. The Duchess, without knowing exactly why, felt relieved, and, putting her head upon Piney's shoulder, spoke no more. And so reclining, the younger and purer pillowing the head of her soiled sister upon her virgin breast, they fell asleep.

The wind lulled as if it feared to waken them. Feathery drifts of snow, shaken from the long pine boughs, flew like white winged birds, and settled about them as they slept. The moon through the rifted clouds looked down upon what had been the camp. But all human stain, all trace of earthly travail, was hidden beneath the spotless mantle mercifully flung from above.

They slept all that day and the next, nor did they waken when voices and footsteps broke the silence of the camp. And when pitying fingers brushed the snow from their wan faces, you could scarcely have told from the equal peace that dwelt upon them which was she that had sinned. Even the law of Poker Flat recognized this, and turned away, leaving them still locked in each other's arms.

But at the head of the gulch, on one of the largest pine-trees, they found the deuce of clubs pinned to the bark with a bowie-knife. It bore the following, written in pencil in a firm hand:—

†
BENEATH THIS TREE
LIES THE BODY
OF
## JOHN OAKHURST,
WHO STRUCK A STREAK OF BAD LUCK
ON THE 23D OF NOVEMBER 1850,
AND
HANDED IN HIS CHECKS
ON THE 7TH DECEMBER, 1850.

☦

And pulseless and cold, with a Derringer by his side and a bullet in his heart, though still calm as in life, beneath the snow lay he who was at once the strongest and yet the weakest of the outcasts of Poker Flat.

# Tennessee's Partner

I do not think that we ever knew his real name. Our ignorance of it certainly never gave us any social inconvenience, for at Sandy Bar in 1854 most men were christened anew. Sometimes these appellatives were derived from some distinctiveness of dress, as in the case of "Dungaree Jack;" or from some peculiarity of habit, as shown in "Saleratus Bill," so called from an undue proportion of that chemical in his daily bread; or from some unlucky slip, as exhibited in "The Iron Pirate," a mild, inoffensive man, who earned that baleful title by his unfortunate mispronunciation of the term "iron pyrites." Perhaps this may have been the beginning of a rude heraldry; but I am constrained to think that it was because a man's real name in that day rested solely upon his own unsupported statement. "Call yourself Clifford, do you?" said Boston, addressing a timid newcomer with infinite scorn; "hell is full of such Cliffords!" He then introduced the unfortunate man, whose name happened to be really Clifford, as "Jaybird Charley,"—an unhallowed inspiration of the moment that clung to him ever after.

But to return to Tennessee's Partner, whom we never knew by any other than this relative title. That he had ever existed as a separate and distinct individuality we only learned later. It seems that in 1853 he left Poker Flat to go to San Francisco, ostensibly to procure a wife. He never got any farther than Stockton. At that place he was attracted by a young person who waited upon the table at the hotel where he took his meals. One morning he said something to her which caused her to smile not unkindly, to somewhat coquettishly break a plate of toast over his upturned, serious, simple face, and to retreat to the kitchen. He followed her, and emerged a few moments later, covered with more toast and victory. That day week they were married by a justice of the peace, and returned to Poker Flat. I am aware that something more might be made of this episode, but I prefer to tell it as it was current at Sandy Bar,—in the gulches and bar-rooms,—where all sentiment was modified by a strong sense of humor.

Of their married felicity but little is known, perhaps for the reason that Tennessee, then living with his partner, one day took occasion to say something to the bride on his own account, at which, it is said, she smiled not unkindly and chastely retreated,—this time as far as Marysville, where Tennessee followed her, and where they went to housekeeping without the aid of a justice of the peace. Tennessee's Partner took the loss of his wife simply and seriously, as was his fashion. But to everybody's surprise, when Tennessee one day returned from Marysville, without his partner's wife,—she having smiled and retreated with somebody else,—Tennessee's Partner was the first man to shake his hand and greet him with affection. The boys who had gathered in the cañon to see the shooting were naturally indignant. Their indignation might have found vent in sarcasm but for a certain look in Tennessee's Partner's eye that indicated a lack of humorous appreciation. In fact, he was a grave man, with a steady application to practical detail which was unpleasant in a difficulty.

Meanwhile a popular feeling against Tennessee had grown up on the Bar. He was known to be a gambler; he was suspected to be a thief. In these suspicions Tennessee's Partner was equally compromised; his continued intimacy with Tennessee after the affair above quoted could only be accounted for on the hypothesis of a copartnership of crime. At last Tennessee's guilt became flagrant. One day he overtook a stranger on his way to Red Dog. The stranger afterward related that Tennessee beguiled the time with interesting anecdote and reminiscence, but illogically concluded the interview in the following words: "And now, young man, I'll trouble you for your knife, your pistols, and your money. You see your weppings might get you into trouble at Red Dog, and your money's a temptation to the evilly disposed. I think you said your address was San Francisco. I shall endeavor to call." It may be stated here that Tennessee had a fine flow of humor, which no business preoccupation could wholly subdue.

This exploit was his last. Red Dog and Sandy Bar made common cause against the highwayman. Tennessee was hunted in very much the same fashion as his prototype, the grizzly. As the toils closed around him, he made a desperate dash through the Bar, emptying his revolver at the crowd before the Arcade Saloon, and so on up Grizzly Cañon; but at its farther extremity he was stopped by a small man on a gray horse. The men looked at each other a moment in silence.

Both were fearless, both self-possessed and independent, and both types of a civilization that in the seventeenth century would have been called heroic, but in the nineteenth simply "reckless."

"What have you got there?—I call," said Tennessee quietly.

"Two bowers and an ace," said the stranger as quietly, showing two revolvers and a bowie-knife.

"That takes me," returned Tennessee; and, with this gambler's epigram, he threw away his useless pistol and rode back with his captor.

It was a warm night. The cool breeze which usually sprang up with the going down of the sun behind the chaparral-crested mountain was that evening withheld from Sandy Bar. The little cañon was stifling with heated resinous odors, and the decaying driftwood on the Bar sent forth faint sickening exhalations. The feverishness of day and its fierce passions still filled the camp. Lights moved restlessly along the bank of the river, striking no answering reflection from its tawny current. Against the blackness of the pines the windows of the old loft above the express-office stood out staringly bright; and through their curtainless panes the loungers below could see the forms of those who were even then deciding the fate of Tennessee. And above all this, etched on the dark firmament, rose the Sierra, remote and passionless, crowned with remoter passionless stars.

The trial of Tennessee was conducted as fairly as was consistent with a judge and jury who felt themselves to some extent obliged to justify, in their verdict, the previous irregularities of arrest and indictment. The law of Sandy Bar was implacable, but not vengeful. The excitement and personal feeling of the chase were over; with Tennessee safe in their hands, they were ready to listen patiently to any defense, which they were already satisfied was insufficient. There being no doubt in their own minds, they were willing to give the prisoner the benefit of any that might exist. Secure in the hypothesis that he ought to be hanged on general principles, they indulged him with more latitude of defense than his reckless hardihood seemed to ask. The Judge appeared to be more anxious than the prisoner, who, otherwise unconcerned, evidently took a grim pleasure in the responsibility he had created. "I don't take any hand in this yer game," had been his invariable but good-humored reply to all questions. The Judge—who was also his captor—for a moment vaguely regretted that he had not shot him "on sight" that morning, but presently dismissed this human weakness as unworthy of the judicial mind. Nevertheless, when there was a tap at the door, and it was said that Tennessee's Partner was there on behalf of the prisoner, he was admitted at once without question. Perhaps the younger members of the jury, to whom the proceedings were becoming irksomely thoughtful, hailed him as a relief.

For he was not, certainly, an imposing figure. Short and stout, with a square face, sunburned into a preternatural redness, clad in a loose duck "jumper" and trousers streaked and splashed with red soil, his aspect under any circumstances would have been quaint, and was now even ridiculous. As he stooped to deposit at his feet a heavy carpetbag he was carrying, it became obvious, from partially developed legends and inscriptions, that the material with which his trousers had been patched had been originally intended for a less ambitious covering. Yet he advanced with great gravity, and after shaking the hand of each person in the room with labored cordiality, he wiped his serious perplexed face on a red bandana handkerchief, a shade lighter than his complexion, laid his powerful hand upon the table to steady himself, and thus addressed the Judge:—

"I was passin' by," he began, by way of apology, "and I thought I'd just step in and see how things was gittin' on with Tennessee thar,—my pardner. It's a hot night. I disremember any sich weather before on the Bar."

He paused a moment, but nobody volunteering any other meteorological recollection, he again had recourse to his pocket-handkerchief, and for some moments mopped his face diligently.

"Have you anything to say on behalf of the prisoner?" said the Judge finally.

"Thet's it," said Tennessee's Partner, in a tone of relief. "I come yar as Tennessee's pardner,—knowing him nigh on four year, off and on, wet and dry, in luck and out o' luck. His ways ain't aller my ways, but thar ain't any p'ints in that young man, thar ain't any liveliness as he's been up to, as I don't know. And you sez to me, sez you,—confidential-like, and between man and man,—sez you, 'Do you know anything in his behalf?' and I sez to you, sez I,—confidential-like, as between man and man,—'What should a man know of his pardner?' "

"Is this all you have to say?" asked the Judge impatiently, feeling, perhaps, that a dangerous sympathy of humor was beginning to humanize the court.

"Thet's so," continued Tennessee's Partner. "It ain't for me to say anything agin' him. And now, what's the case? Here's Tennessee wants money, wants it bad, and doesn't like to ask it of his old pardner. Well, what does Tennessee do? He lays for a stranger, and he fetches that stranger; and you lays for *him*, and you fetches *him*; and the honors is easy. And I put it to you, bein' a fa'r-minded man, and to you, gentlemen all, as fa'r-minded men, ef this isn't so."

"Prisoner," said the Judge, interrupting, "have you any questions to ask this man?"

"No! no!" continued Tennessee's Partner hastily. "I play this yer hand alone. To come down to the bed-rock, it's just this: Tennessee, thar, has played it pretty rough and expensive-like on a stranger, and on this yer camp. And now, what's the fair thing? Some would say more, some would say less. Here's seventeen hundred dollars in coarse gold and a watch,—it's about all my pile,—and call it square!" And before a hand could be raised to prevent him, he had emptied the contents of the carpetbag upon the table.

For a moment his life was in jeopardy. One or two men sprang to their feet, several hands groped for hidden weapons, and a suggestion to "throw him from the window" was only overridden by a gesture from the Judge. Tennessee laughed. And apparently oblivious of the excitement, Tennessee's Partner improved the opportunity to mop his face again with his handkerchief.

When order was restored, and the man was made to understand, by the use of forcible figures and rhetoric, that Tennessee's offense could not be condoned by money, his face took a more serious and sanguinary hue, and those who were nearest to him noticed that his rough hand trembled slightly on the table. He hesitated a moment as he slowly returned the gold to the carpetbag, as if he had not yet entirely caught the elevated sense of justice which swayed the tribunal, and was perplexed with the belief that he had not offered enough. Then he turned to the Judge, and saying, "This yer is a lone hand, played alone, and without my pardner," he bowed to the jury and was about to withdraw, when the Judge called him back:—

"If you have anything to say to Tennessee, you had better say it now."

For the first time that evening the eyes of the prisoner and his strange advocate met. Tennessee smiled, showed his white teeth, and saying, "Euchred, old man!" held out his hand. Tennessee's Partner took it in his own, and saying, "I just dropped in as I was passin' to see how things was gettin' on," let the hand passively fall, and adding that "it was a warm night," again mopped his face with his handkerchief, and without another word withdrew.

The two men never again met each other alive. For the unparalleled insult of a bribe offered to Judge Lynch—who, whether bigoted, weak, or narrow, was at least incorruptible—firmly fixed in the mind of that mythical personage any wavering determination of Tennessee's fate; and at the break of day he was marched, closely guarded, to meet it at the top of Marley's Hill.

How he met it, how cool he was, how he refused to say anything, how perfect were the arrangements of the committee, were all duly reported, with the addition of a warning moral and example to all future evil-doers, in the *Red Dog Clarion*, by its editor, who was present, and to whose vigorous English I cheerfully refer the reader. But the beauty of that midsummer morning, the blessed amity of earth and air and sky, the awakened life of the free woods and hills, the joyous renewal and promise of Nature, and above all, the infinite serenity that thrilled through each, was not reported, as not being a part of the social lesson. And yet, when the weak and foolish deed was done, and a life, with its possibilities and responsibilities, had passed out of the misshapen thing that dangled between earth and sky, the birds sang, the flowers bloomed, the sun shone, as cheerily as before; and possibly the *Red Dog Clarion* was right.

Tennessee's Partner was not in the group that surrounded the ominous tree. But as they turned to disperse, attention was drawn to the singular appearance of a motionless donkey-cart halted at the side of the road. As they approached, they at once recognized the venerable "Jenny" and the two-wheeled cart as the property of Tennessee's Partner, used by him in carrying dirt from his claim; and a few paces distant the owner of the equipage himself, sitting under a buckeye-tree, wiping the perspiration from his glowing face. In answer to an inquiry, he said he had come for the body of the "diseased," "if it was all the same to the committee." He didn't wish to "hurry anything;" he could "wait." He was not working that day; and when the gentlemen were done with the "diseased," he would take him. "Ef thar is any present," he added, in his simple, serious way, "as would care to jine in the fun'l, they kin come." Perhaps it was from a sense of humor, which I have already intimated was a feature of Sandy Bar,—perhaps it was from something even better than that, but two thirds of the loungers accepted the invitation at once.

It was noon when the body of Tennessee was delivered into the hands of his partner. As the cart drew up to the fatal tree, we noticed that it contained a rough oblong box,—apparently made from a section of sluicing,—and half filled with bark and the tassels of pine. The cart was further decorated with slips of willow and made fragrant with buckeye-blossoms. When the body was deposited in the box, Tennessee's Partner drew over it a piece of tarred canvas, and gravely mounting the narrow seat in front, with his feet upon the shafts, urged the little donkey forward. The equipage moved slowly on, at that decorous pace which was habitual with Jenny even under less solemn circumstances. The men—half curiously, half jestingly, but all good-humoredly—strolled along beside the cart, some in advance, some a little in the rear of the homely catafalque. But whether from the narrowing of the road or some present sense of decorum, as the cart passed on, the company fell to the rear in couples, keeping step, and otherwise assuming the external show of a formal procession. Jack Folinsbee, who had at the outset played a funeral march in dumb show upon an imaginary trombone, desisted from a lack of sympathy and appreciation,—not having, perhaps, your true humorist's capacity to be content with the enjoyment of his own fun.

The way led through Grizzly Cañon, by this time clothed in funereal drapery and shadows. The redwoods, burying their moccasined feet in the red soil, stood in Indian file along the track, trailing an uncouth benediction from their bending boughs upon the passing bier. A hare, surprised into helpless inactivity, sat upright and pulsating in the ferns by the roadside as the cortège went by. Squirrels hastened to gain a secure outlook from higher boughs; and the blue-jays, spreading their wings, fluttered before them like outriders, until the outskirts of Sandy Bar were reached, and the solitary cabin of Tennessee's Partner.

Viewed under more favorable circumstances, it would not have been a cheerful place. The unpicturesque site, the rude and unlovely outlines, the unsavory details, which distinguish the nest-building of the California miner, were all here with the dreariness of decay superadded. A few paces from the cabin there was a rough inclosure, which, in the brief days of Tennessee's Partner's matrimonial felicity, had been used as a garden, but was now overgrown with fern. As we approached it, we were surprised to find that what we had taken for a recent attempt at cultivation was the broken soil about an open grave.

The cart was halted before the inclosure, and rejecting the offers of assistance with the same air of simple self-reliance he had displayed throughout, Tennessee's Partner lifted the rough coffin on his back, and deposited it unaided within the shallow grave. He then nailed down the board which served as a lid, and mounting the little mound of earth beside it, took off his hat and slowly mopped his face with his handkerchief. This the crowd felt was a preliminary to speech, and they disposed themselves variously on stumps and boulders, and sat expectant.

"When a man," began Tennessee's Partner slowly, "has been running free all day, what's the natural thing for him to do? Why, to come home. And if he ain't in a condition to go home, what can his best friend do? Why, bring him home. And here's Tennessee has been running free, and we brings him home from his wandering." He paused and picked up a fragment of quartz, rubbed it thoughtfully on his sleeve, and went on: "It ain't the first time that I've packed him on my back, as you see'd me now. It ain't the first time that I brought him to this yer cabin when he couldn't help himself; it ain't the first time that I and Jinny have waited for him on yon hill, and picked him up and so fetched him home, when he couldn't speak and didn't know me. And now that it's the last time, why"—he paused and rubbed the quartz gently on his sleeve—"you see it's sort of rough on his pardner. And now, gentlemen," he added abruptly, picking up his long-handled shovel, "the fun'l's over; and my thanks, and Tennessee's thanks, to you for your trouble."

Resisting any proffers of assistance, he began to fill in the grave, turning his back upon the crowd, that after a few moments' hesitation gradually withdrew. As they crossed the little ridge that hid Sandy Bar from view, some, looking back, thought they could see Tennessee's Partner, his work done, sitting upon the grave, his shovel between his knees, and his face buried in his red bandana handkerchief. But it was argued by others that you couldn't tell his face from his handkerchief at that distance, and this point remained undecided.

In the reaction that followed the feverish excitement of that day, Tennessee's Partner was not forgotten. A secret investigation had cleared him of any complicity in Tennessee's guilt, and left only a suspicion of his general sanity. Sandy Bar made a point of calling on him, and proffering various uncouth but well-meant kindnesses. But from that day his rude health and great strength seemed visibly to decline; and when the rainy season fairly set in, and the tiny grass-blades were beginning to peep from the rocky mound above Tennessee's grave, he took to his bed.

One night, when the pines beside the cabin were swaying in the storm and trailing their slender fingers over the roof, and the roar and rush of the swollen river were heard below, Tennessee's Partner lifted his head from the pillow, saying, "It is time to go for Tennessee; I must put Jinny in the cart;" and would have risen from his bed but for the restraint of his attendant. Struggling, he still pursued his singular fancy: "There, now, steady, Jinny,—steady, old girl. How dark it is! Look out for the ruts,—and look out for him, too, old gal. Sometimes, you know, when he's blind drunk, he drops down right in the trail. Keep on straight up to the pine on the top of the hill. Thar! I told you so!—thar he is,—coming this way, too,—all by himself, sober, and his face a-shining. Tennessee! Pardner!"

And so they met.

# Brown
# of Calaveras

A subdued tone of conversation, and the absence of cigar-smoke and boot-heels at the windows of the Wingdam stagecoach, made it evident that one of the inside passengers was a woman. A disposition on the part of loungers at the stations to congregate before the window, and some concern in regard to the appearance of coats, hats, and collars, further indicated that she was lovely. All of which Mr. Jack Hamlin, on the box-seat, noted with the smile of cynical philosophy. Not that he depreciated the sex, but that he recognized therein a deceitful element, the pursuit of which sometimes drew mankind away from the equally uncertain blandishments of poker,—of which it may be remarked that Mr. Hamlin was a professional exponent.

So that, when he placed his narrow boot on the wheel and leaped down, he did not even glance at the window from which a green veil was fluttering, but lounged up and down with that listless and grave indifference of his class, which was, perhaps, the next thing to goodbreeding. With his closely buttoned figure and self-contained air he was a marked contrast to the other passengers, with their feverish restlessness and boisterous emotion; and even Bill Masters, a graduate of Harvard, with his slovenly dress, his overflowing vitality, his intense appreciation of lawlessness and barbarism, and his mouth filled with crackers and cheese, I fear cut but an unromantic figure beside this lonely calculator of chances, with his pale Greek face and Homeric gravity.

The driver called "All aboard!" and Mr. Hamlin returned to the coach. His foot was upon the wheel, and his face raised to the level of the open window, when, at the same moment, what appeared to him to be the finest eyes in the world suddenly met his. He quietly dropped down again, addressed a few words to one of the inside passengers, effected an exchange of seats, and as quietly took his place inside. Mr.

Hamlin never allowed his philosophy to interfere with decisive and prompt action.

I fear that this irruption of Jack cast some restraint upon the other passengers, particularly those who were making themselves most agreeable to the lady. One of them leaned forward, and apparently conveyed to her information regarding Mr. Hamlin's profession in a single epithet. Whether Mr. Hamlin heard it, or whether he recognized in the informant a distinguished jurist, from whom, but a few evenings before, he had won several thousand dollars, I cannot say. His colorless face betrayed no sign; his black eyes, quietly observant, glanced indifferently past the legal gentleman, and rested on the much more pleasing features of his neighbor. An Indian stoicism—said to be an inheritance from his maternal ancestor—stood him in good service, until the rolling wheels rattled upon the river gravel at Scott's Ferry, and the stage drew up at the International Hotel for dinner. The legal gentleman and a member of Congress leaped out, and stood ready to assist the descending goddess, while Colonel Starbottle of Siskiyou took charge of her parasol and shawl. In this multiplicity of attention there was a momentary confusion and delay. Jack Hamlin quietly opened the *opposite* door of the coach, took the lady's hand, with that decision and positiveness which a hesitating and undecided sex know how to admire, and in an instant had dexterously and gracefully swung her to the ground and again lifted her to the platform. An audible chuckle on the box, I fear, came from that other cynic, Yuba Bill, the driver. "Look keerfully arter that baggage, Kernel," said the expressman, with affected concern, as he looked after Colonel Starbottle, gloomily bringing up the rear of the triumphant procession to the waiting-room.

Mr. Hamlin did not stay for dinner. His horse was already saddled and awaiting him. He dashed over the ford, up the gravelly hill, and out into the dusty perspective of the Wingdam road, like one leaving an unpleasant fancy behind him. The inmates of dusty cabins by the roadside shaded their eyes with their hands and looked after him, recognizing the man by his horse, and speculating what "was up with Comanche Jack." Yet much of this interest centred in the horse, in a community where the time made by "French Pete's" mare, in his run from the Sheriff of Calaveras, eclipsed all concern in the ultimate fate of that worthy.

The sweating flanks of his gray at length recalled him to himself. He checked his speed, and turning into a byroad, sometimes used as a cut-off, trotted leisurely along, the reins hanging listlessly from his fingers. As he rode on, the character of the landscape changed and became more pastoral. Openings in groves of pine and sycamore disclosed some rude attempts at cultivation,—a flowering vine trailed over the porch of one cabin, and a woman rocked her cradled babe under the roses of another. A little farther on, Mr. Hamlin came upon some bare-legged children wading in the willowy creek, and so wrought upon them with a badinage peculiar to himself, that they were emboldened to climb up his horse's legs and over his saddle, until he was fain to develop an exaggerated ferocity of demeanor, and to escape, leaving behind some kisses and coin. And then, advancing deeper into the woods, where all signs of habitation failed, he began to sing, uplifting a tenor so singularly sweet, and shaded by a pathos so subdued and tender, that I wot the robins and linnets stopped to listen. Mr. Hamlin's voice was not cultivated; the subject of his song was some sentimental lunacy, borrowed from the negro minstrels; but there thrilled through all some occult quality of tone and expression that was unspeakably touching. Indeed, it was a wonderful sight to see this sentimental blackleg, with a pack of cards in his pocket and a revolver at his back, sending his voice before him through the dim woods with a plaint about his "Nelly's grave," in a way that overflowed the eyes of the listener. A sparrow-hawk, fresh from his sixth victim, possibly recognizing in Mr. Hamlin a kindred spirit, stared at him in surprise, and was fain to confess the superiority of man. With a superior predatory capacity *he* couldn't sing.

But Mr. Hamlin presently found himself again on the highroad and at his former pace. Ditches and banks of gravel, denuded hillsides, stumps, and decayed trunks of trees, took the place of woodland and ravine, and indicated his approach to civilization. Then a church-steeple came in sight, and he knew that he had reached home. In a few moments he was clattering down the single narrow street that lost itself in a chaotic ruin of races, ditches, and tailings at the foot of the hill, and dismounted before the gilded windows of the Magnolia saloon. Passing through the long bar-room, he pushed open a green-baize door, entered a dark passage, opened another door with a pass-key, and found himself in a dimly lighted room, whose furniture, though elegant and costly for the locality, showed signs of abuse. The inlaid centre-table was overlaid with stained disks that were not contemplated in the original design, the embroidered armchairs were discolored, and the green velvet lounge, on which Mr. Hamlin threw himself, was soiled at the foot with the red soil of Wingdam.

Mr. Hamlin did not sing in his cage. He lay still, looking at a highly colored painting above him, representing a young creature of opulent charms. It occurred to him then, for the first time, that he had never seen exactly that kind of a woman, and that, if he should, he would not, probably, fall in love with her. Perhaps he was thinking of another style of beauty. But just then some one knocked at the door. Without rising, he pulled a cord that apparently shot back a bolt, for the door swung open, and a man entered.

The new-comer was broad-shouldered and robust,—a vigor not borne out in the face, which, though handsome, was singularly weak and disfigured by dissipation. He appeared to be, also, under the influence of liquor, for he started on seeing Mr. Hamlin, and said, "I thought Kate was here;" stammered, and seemed confused and embarrassed.

Mr. Hamlin smiled the smile which he had before worn on the Wingdam coach, and sat up, quite refreshed and ready for business.

"You didn't come up on the stage," continued the new-comer, "did you?"

"No," replied Hamlin; "I left it at Scott's Ferry. It isn't due for half an hour yet. But how's luck, Brown?"

"D——d bad," said Brown, his face suddenly assuming an expression of weak despair. "I'm cleaned out again, Jack," he continued, in a whining tone, that formed a pitiable contrast to his bulky figure; "can't you help me with a hundred till to-morrow's clean-up? You see I've got to send money home to the old woman, and—you've won twenty times that amount from me."

The conclusion was, perhaps, not entirely logical, but Jack overlooked it, and handed the sum to his visitor. "The old-woman business is about played out, Brown," he added, by way of commentary; "why don't you say you want to buck ag'in' faro? You know you ain't married!"

"Fact, sir," said Brown, with a sudden gravity, as if the mere contact of the gold with the palm of the hand had imparted some dignity to his frame. "I've got a wife—a d——d good one, too, if I do say it —in the States. It's three years since I've seen her, and a year since I've writ to her. When things is about straight, and we get down to the lead, I'm going to send for her."

"And Kate?" queried Mr. Hamlin, with his previous smile.

Mr. Brown of Calaveras essayed an archness of glance to cover his confusion, which his weak face and whiskey-muddled intellect but poorly carried out, and said,—

"D——n it, Jack, a man must have a little liberty, you know. But come, what do you say to a little game? Give us a show to double this hundred."

Jack Hamlin looked curiously at his fatuous friend. Perhaps he knew that the man was predestined to lose the money, and preferred that it should flow back into his own coffers rather than any other. He nodded his head, and drew his chair toward the table. At the same moment there came a rap upon the door.

"It's Kate," said Mr. Brown.

Mr. Hamlin shot back the bolt and the door opened. But, for the first time in his life, he staggered to his feet utterly unnerved and abashed, and for the first time in his life the hot blood crimsoned his colorless cheeks to his forehead. For before him stood the lady he had lifted from the Wingdam coach, whom Brown, dropping his cards with a hysterical laugh, greeted as,—

"My old woman, by thunder!"

They say that Mrs. Brown burst into tears and reproaches of her husband. I saw her in 1857 at Marysville, and disbelieve the story. And the "Wingdam Chronicle" of the next week, under the head of "Touching Reunion," said: "One of those beautiful and touching incidents, peculiar to California life, occurred last week in our city. The wife of one of Wingdam's eminent pioneers, tired of the effete civilization of the East and its inhospitable climate, resolved to join her noble husband upon these golden shores. Without informing him of her intention, she undertook the long journey, and arrived last week. The joy of the husband may be easier imagined than described. The meeting is said to have been indescribably affecting. We trust her example may be followed."

Whether owing to Mrs. Brown's influence, or to some more successful speculations, Mr. Brown's financial fortune from that day steadily improved. He bought out his partners in the "Nip and Tuck" lead, with money which was said to have been won at poker a week or two after his wife's arrival, but which rumor, adopting Mrs. Brown's theory that Brown had forsworn the gaming-table, declared to have been furnished by Mr. Jack Hamlin. He built and furnished the Wingdam House, which pretty Mrs. Brown's great popularity kept overflowing with guests. He was elected to the Assembly, and gave largess to churches. A street in Wingdam was named in his honor.

Yet it was noted that in proportion as he waxed wealthy and fortunate, he grew pale, thin, and anxious. As his wife's popularity increased, he became fretful and impatient. The most uxorious of husbands, he was absurdly jealous. If he did not interfere with his wife's social liberty, it was because it was maliciously whispered that his first and only attempt was met by an outburst from Mrs. Brown that terrified him into silence. Much of this kind of gossip came from those of her own sex whom she had supplanted in the chivalrous at-

tentions of Wingdam, which, like most popular chivalry, was devoted
to an admiration of power, whether of masculine force or feminine
beauty. It should be remembered, too, in her extenuation, that, since
her arrival, she had been the unconscious priestess of a mythological
worship, perhaps not more ennobling to her womanhood than that
which distinguished an older Greek democracy. I think that Brown
was dimly conscious of this. But his only confidant was Jack Hamlin,
whose infelix reputation naturally precluded any open intimacy with
the family, and whose visits were infrequent.

It was midsummer and a moonlit night, and Mrs. Brown, very rosy,
large-eyed, and pretty, sat upon the piazza, enjoying the fresh incense
of the mountain breeze, and, it is to be feared, another incense which
was not so fresh nor quite as innocent. Beside her sat Colonel Starbottle and Judge Boompointer, and a later addition to her court in the
shape of a foreign tourist. She was in good spirits.

"What do you see down the road?" inquired the gallant Colonel,
who had been conscious, for the last few minutes, that Mrs. Brown's
attention was diverted.

"Dust," said Mrs. Brown, with a sigh. "Only Sister Anne's 'flock of
sheep.' "

The Colonel, whose literary recollections did not extend farther
back than last week's paper, took a more practical view. "It ain't
sheep," he continued; "it's a horseman. Judge, ain't that Jack Hamlin's
gray?"

But the Judge didn't know; and, as Mrs. Brown suggested the air
was growing too cold for further investigations, they retired to the
parlor.

Mr. Brown was in the stable, where he generally retired after dinner. Perhaps it was to show his contempt for his wife's companions;
perhaps, like other weak natures, he found pleasure in the exercise of
absolute power over inferior animals. He had a certain gratification in
the training of a chestnut mare, whom he could beat or caress as
pleased him, which he couldn't do with Mrs. Brown. It was here that
he recognized a certain gray horse which had just come in, and, looking a little farther on, found his rider. Brown's greeting was cordial
and hearty; Mr. Hamlin's somewhat restrained. But, at Brown's urgent request, he followed him up the back stairs to a narrow corridor,
and thence to a small room looking out upon the stable-yard. It was
plainly furnished with a bed, a table, a few chairs, and a rack for guns
and whips.

"This yer's my home, Jack," said Brown with a sigh, as he threw
himself upon the bed and motioned his companion to a chair. "Her
room's t' other end of the hall. It's more'n six months since we've lived

together, or met, except at meals. It's mighty rough papers on the head of the house, ain't it?" he said with a forced laugh. "But I'm glad to see you, Jack, d——d glad," and he reached from the bed, and again shook the unresponsive hand of Jack Hamlin.

"I brought ye up here, for I didn't want to talk in the stable; though, for the matter of that, it's all round town. Don't strike a light. We can talk here in the moonshine. Put up your feet on that winder and sit here beside me. Thar's whiskey in that jug."

Mr. Hamlin did not avail himself of the information. Brown of Calaveras turned his face to the wall, and continued,—

"If I didn't love the woman, Jack, I wouldn't mind. But it's loving her, and seeing her day arter day goin' on at this rate, and no one to put down the brake; that's what gits me! But I'm glad to see ye, Jack, d——d glad."

In the darkness he groped about until he had found and wrung his companion's hand again. He would have detained it, but Jack slipped it into the buttoned breast of his coat, and asked listlessly, "How long has this been going on?"

"Ever since she came here; ever since the day she walked into the Magnolia. I was a fool then; Jack, I'm a fool now; but I didn't know how much I loved her till then. And she hasn't been the same woman since.

"But that ain't all, Jack; and it's what I wanted to see you about, and I'm glad you've come. It ain't that she doesn't love me any more; it ain't that she fools with every chap that comes along; for perhaps I staked her love and lost it, as I did everything else at the Magnolia; and perhaps foolin' is nateral to some women, and thar ain't no great harm done, 'cept to the fools. But, Jack, I think,—I think she loves somebody else. Don't move, Jack! don't move; if your pistol hurts ye, take it off.

"It's been more'n six months now that she's seemed unhappy and lonesome, and kinder nervous and scared-like. And sometimes I've ketched her lookin' at me sort of timid and pitying. And she writes to somebody. And for the last week she's been gathering her own things,—trinkets, and furbelows, and jew'lry,—and, Jack, I think she's goin' off. I could stand all but that. To have her steal away like a thief!" He put his face downward to the pillow, and for a few moments there was no sound but the ticking of a clock on the mantel. Mr. Hamlin lit a cigar, and moved to the open window. The moon no longer shone into the room, and the bed and its occupant were in shadow. "What shall I do, Jack?" said the voice from the darkness.

The answer came promptly and clearly from the window-side, "Spot the man, and kill him on sight."

"But, Jack"—

"He's took the risk!"

"But will that bring *her* back?"

Jack did not reply, but moved from the window towards the door.

"Don't go yet, Jack; light the candle and sit by the table. It's a comfort to see ye, if nothin' else."

Jack hesitated and then complied. He drew a pack of cards from his pocket and shuffled them, glancing at the bed. But Brown's face was turned to the wall. When Mr. Hamlin had shuffled the cards, he cut them, and dealt one card on the opposite side of the table towards the bed, and another on his side of the table for himself. The first was a deuce; his own card a king. He then shuffled and cut again. This time "dummy" had a queen and himself a four-spot. Jack brightened up for the third deal. It brought his adversary a deuce and himself a king again. "Two out of three," said Jack audibly.

"What's that, Jack?" said Brown.

"Nothing."

Then Jack tried his hand with dice; but he always threw sixes and his imaginary opponent aces. The force of habit is sometimes confusing.

Meanwhile some magnetic influence in Mr. Hamlin's presence, or the anodyne of liquor, or both, brought surcease of sorrow, and Brown slept. Mr. Hamlin moved his chair to the window and looked out on the town of Wingdam, now sleeping peacefully, its harsh outlines softened and subdued, its glaring colors mellowed and sobered in the moonlight that flowed over all. In the hush he could hear the gurgling of water in the ditches and the sighing of the pines beyond the hill. Then he looked up at the firmament, and as he did so a star shot across the twinkling field. Presently another, and then another. The phenomenon suggested to Mr. Hamlin a fresh augury. If in another fifteen minutes another star should fall— He sat there, watch in hand, for twice that time, but the phenomenon was not repeated.

The clock struck two, and Brown still slept. Mr. Hamlin approached the table and took from his pocket a letter, which he read by the flickering candlelight. It contained only a single line, written in pencil, in a woman's hand,—

"Be at the corral with the buggy at three."

The sleeper moved uneasily and then awoke. "Are you there, Jack?"

"Yes."

"Don't go yet. I dreamed just now, Jack,—dreamed of old times. I thought that Sue and me was being married agin, and that the parson, Jack, was—who do you think?—you!"

The gambler laughed, and seated himself on the bed, the paper still in his hand.

"It's a good sign, ain't it?" queried Brown.

"I reckon! Say, old man, hadn't you better get up?"

The "old man," thus affectionately appealed to, rose, with the assistance of Hamlin's outstretched hand.

"Smoke?"

Brown mechanically took the proffered cigar.

"Light?"

Jack had twisted the letter into a spiral, lit it, and held it for his companion. He continued to hold it until it was consumed, and dropped the fragment—a fiery star—from the open window. He watched it as it fell, and then returned to his friend.

"Old man," he said, placing his hands upon Brown's shoulders, "in ten minutes I'll be on the road, and gone like that spark. We won't see each other agin; but, before I go, take a fool's advice: sell out all you've got, take your wife with you, and quit the country. It ain't no place for you nor her. Tell her she must go; make her go if she won't. Don't whine because you can't be a saint and she ain't an angel. Be a man, and treat her like a woman. Don't be a d——d fool. Good-by."

He tore himself from Brown's grasp and leaped down the stairs like a deer. At the stable-door he collared the half-sleeping hostler, and backed him against the wall. "Saddle my horse in two minutes, or I'll"— The ellipsis was frightfully suggestive.

"The missis said you was to have the buggy," stammered the man.

"D——n the buggy!"

The horse was saddled as fast as the nervous hands of the astounded hostler could manipulate buckle and strap.

"Is anything up, Mr. Hamlin?" said the man, who, like all his class, admired the élan of his fiery patron, and was really concerned in his welfare.

"Stand aside!"

The man fell back. With an oath, a bound, and clatter, Jack was into the road. In another moment, to the man's half-awakened eyes, he was but a moving cloud of dust in the distance, towards which a star just loosed from its brethren was trailing a stream of fire.

But early that morning the dwellers by the Wingdam turnpike, miles aways, heard a voice, pure as a sky-lark's, singing afield. They who were asleep turned over on their rude couches to dream of youth, and love, and olden days. Hard-faced men and anxious gold-seekers, already at work, ceased their labors and leaned upon their picks to listen to a romantic vagabond ambling away against the rosy sunrise.

# MARK TWAIN

## (Samuel Langhorne Clemens)

### (1835–1910)

Clemens was born in Florida, Missouri, son of a Whig lawyer who had emigrated from Virginia and a mother from Kentucky with ancestral claims to British aristocracy—a dual legacy which would haunt a man torn between faith in American progress and a deeply conservative nature. John Marshall Clemens was something of a dreamer, and kept his family moving from one promising prospect to another. When Sam was five, they moved to Hannibal, Missouri, where his father's sudden death in 1847 made it necessary that the boy leave school and work for his older brother, Orion, who ran a print shop and newspaper. In 1853, Clemens went on the road as a journeyman printer in eastern cities, but ended up back west in Keokuk, Iowa, once more working for his brother. In 1857, intending to set up as a coca planter in South America, Clemens again left the print shop; but while traveling down the Mississippi, he decided to apprentice himself to the more sensible (if glamorous) calling of riverboat pilot.

In this he was at least moderately successful, but the outbreak of the Civil War closed off river traffic. After a brief and abortive experience as a volunteer Confederate officer, Clemens once again joined Orion, who had been appointed secretary to the territorial governor of Nevada. The territory at that time was booming with a silver bonanza, and Clemens, attracted by the possibility of quick riches, next tried his luck at prospecting and speculating in mining stock, before he again resigned himself to a more practical course and became the editor of the Virginia City Enterprise. Using the pseudonym "Mark Twain" (a riverman's depth-sounding call for "safe water"), Clemens contributed stories and sketches crudely derived from the Southwestern tradition—but he had to leave town after he took too full an advantage of the scurrilous personal journalism then in fashion, nar-

*rowly escaping a duel. Moving to San Francisco in 1864, he continued as a reporter but also began to write humorous pieces for literary periodicals like the* Golden Era, *which brought him into contact with Bret Harte, who encouraged him to improve his craft. One of the first fruits of that encouragement was Twain's story about the jumping frog, which catapulted him into national prominence as a literary comedian, a reputation he cultivated by setting up as a comic lecturer. His journalistic career also prospered, and Clemens was commissioned to send travel letters back from Hawaii; this project in turn resulted in his signing aboard the* Quaker City *when that boat left New York with a group of pilgrims for Europe and the Holy Land.*

*From the humorous, satirical letters that resulted, Clemens—now Mark Twain—compiled his first full-length book,* Innocents Abroad *(1869). ("The Jumping Frog" had appeared with other sketches by Twain in 1867.) On the voyage, Clemens met the brother of the woman who would become his bride in 1870, Livy Langdon of Elmira, New York. Livy's wealthy father set Clemens up with a newspaper of his own, in Buffalo, but this brief arrangement ended in 1871, putting an end to Twain's journalistic career. Moving his family to Hartford— a town midway between the publishing centers of Boston and New York—Twain established himself as a professional author in an ostentatious mansion he helped design and which his newfound wealth made possible. For the next fifteen years he prospered, using his own life as the material for both nonfiction and fiction.* Roughing It *(1872) was derived from his Western experiences;* The Gilded Age *(1874), written with C. D. Warner, drew on his Missouri boyhood, as did* The Adventures of Tom Sawyer *(1878), his first book for children, and* The Adventures of Huckleberry Finn *(1884), a work of transcendent genius. Maintaining himself and his family in sumptuous style, lavishly entertaining any visitors who came to stay, Clemens sought to increase his wealth by inventions and investments—which only led to further expense, not income. He became his own publisher, and continued to compile popular travel books, including* Life on the Mississippi *(1883), the first part of which contained an account of his own pilot apprenticeship. After 1884, it must be said, Twain became a writing factory, churning out ephemeral publications in order to sustain his most visionary (but misconceived) project, the perfecting of the Page typesetting machine. The crankiness of Page's invention and the contemporary development of Linotype guaranteed failure, and bankruptcy followed. In order to pay off his debts and recoup his fortune, Twain traveled around the world delivering comic lectures, reviving his earlier fame as a literary comedian, much to his self-disgust.*

*His financial failure and consequent disillusionment began to color his writing. Having exhausted the rich mine of his personal experience, he became something of a fantast. In 1882, in part for the amusement of his three young daughters, Twain had written* The Prince and the Pauper, *another successful children's book, set in the time of Tudor England, using the ancient comic device of twins who switch identities to "expose" the social ills of that ancient time. Despite the success of* The Gilded Age, *during his prosperous years Twain was reluctant to address contemporary political matters in print, and channeled his discontent through indirect means, as in* Huckleberry Finn *and* Pudd'nhead Wilson *(1894), which addressed the hot issue of civil rights for African-Americans by attacking the no longer very relevant matter of slavery. In one of the greatest of the works of this later period,* A Connecticut Yankee in King Arthur's Court *(1889), he used the historical setting to attack once again his old enemy, the sentimental feudalism that had sustained the false chivalry of the Old South. But he managed also, intentionally or otherwise, to raise serious questions about the ultimate end of modern industrial technology.*

*In* Personal Recollections of Joan of Arc *(1896), Twain once again took refuge in history, this time without much relevance to contemporary matters, save the Victorian worship of virginal girlhood; the figure of the martyred Joan was modeled after his beloved daughter Susy, whose sudden death in 1895 (while Twain was traveling around the world to restore his wealth) was a shock from which Clemens and his wife would not recover. The couple never returned to the house in Hartford, which had been the scene of his literary triumphs and of the sort of hospitality only wealthy Southerners can extend, but lived in rented homes in New York and abroad. Livy died, after years of failing health, in 1904, and Clemens found a last refuge in a new mansion in the Berkshires, where, following the death of a second daughter, Jean, in 1909, he also died, a miserable and lonely old man whose ebullient sense of humor had long soured.*

*Much has been made of Twain's naïve genius, and of the adverse effects upon it of the Eastern culture, with its prudish attitude toward sexual matters—including "coarse" language—most notably as expressed by his wife, and by his friend and literary adviser, W. D. Howells. Twain's frontier spirit was seen as undergoing a conversion to respectability—equivalent to that of Owen Wister's Virginian at the hands of his wife, Molly—which turned him away from the open literary range toward the possibilities of manufacturing (including books) and technology. But as his fiction attests, Twain was never "easy" in the West, and hardly "free" of Eastern sensibilities which regarded it with disdain. Take away the marvelous voice of*

*Huck Finn—or regard that voice as a satiric mask—and you are left with a body of work that labors incessantly to maintain a posture of aristocratic distance, superior in execution but not much different from the efforts of those Whiggish lawyers who established the Southwestern school of humor to which Clemens served a youthful apprenticeship.*

*Yet Twain remains a writer whose greatness is invariably associated with the frontier, be it the river-centered turbulence of his Missouri boyhood or the rowdiness of the silver bonanza in Nevada. Symbolically, his fortunes took their severe downward turn about the time that Frederick Jackson Turner announced the closing of the frontier. By Twain's accounting, the West was a region large with the stuff of erroneous myth and vain ambition, and the chief purpose of his pen was to puncture that bubble—but one result of his consequent success was the inflating of his own personal bubble, which burst in concert with the disappearance of the West he had attacked. Ironically, he spent much of the time left to him raging in his diaries and in print against the extension of the U.S. frontier into Cuba and the Philippines.*

*Twain has been called "the Lincoln of our Literature," but that is a mistake. Where Lincoln truly drew his strength from his Midwestern origins and from the great Whig tradition of the West, with its emphasis on national union and the need of compromise to save that union, Twain's consciousness was deeply divided between the Whig faith in progress and his own deep-seated sense of aristocratic privilege—typically, he volunteered as a Confederate officer, suggesting the complexity of his subsequent attacks on the South. Similarly, he mined the West for his subject matter but, like so many miners, he was never at home there; and like Bret Harte, in other ways his antithesis, he left for the East as soon as he could. But that in many ways typifies the American West in literature, a place of recollection chiefly, already located in the past as the nation rushed on toward some other future, beyond the next range of western hills.*

# The Notorious Jumping Frog of Calaveras County

In compliance with the request of a friend of mine, who wrote me from the East, I called on good-natured, garrulous old Simon Wheeler, and inquired after my friend's friend, Leonidas W. Smiley, as requested to do, and I hereunto append the result. I have a lurking suspicion that *Leonidas W.* Smiley is a myth; that my friend never knew such a personage; and that he only conjectured that if I asked old Wheeler about him, it would remind him of his infamous *Jim* Smiley, and he would go to work and bore me to death with some exasperating reminiscence of him as long and as tedious as it should be useless to me. If that was the design, it succeeded.

I found Simon Wheeler dozing comfortably by the bar-room stove of the dilapidated tavern in the decayed mining camp of Angel's, and I noticed that he was fat and bald-headed, and had an expression of winning gentleness and simplicity upon his tranquil countenance. He roused up, and gave me good day. I told him that a friend of mine had commissioned me to make some inquiries about a cherished companion of his boyhood named *Leonidas W.* Smiley—*Rev. Leonidas W.* Smiley, a young minister of the Gospel, who he had heard was at one time a resident of Angel's Camp. I added that if Mr. Wheeler could tell me anything about this Rev. Leonidas W. Smiley, I would feel under many obligations to him.

Simon Wheeler backed me into a corner and blockaded me there with his chair, and then sat down and reeled off the monotonous narrative which follows this paragraph. He never smiled, he never frowned, he never changed his voice from the gentle-flowing key to which he tuned his initial sentence, he never betrayed the slightest suspicion of enthusiasm; but all through the interminable narrative there ran a vein of impressive earnestness and sincerity, which showed me plainly that, so far from his imagining that there was anything ridiculous or funny about his story, he regarded it as a really important matter, and admired its two heroes as men of transcendent genius in *finesse*. I let him go on in his own way, and never interrupted him once.

"Rev. Leonidas W. H'm, Reverend Le—well, there was a feller here once by the name of *Jim* Smiley, in the winter of '49—or maybe it was the spring of '50—I don't recollect exactly, somehow, though what makes me think it was one or the other is because I remember the big flume warn't finished when he first come to the camp; but anyway, he was the curiousest man about always betting on anything that turned up you ever see, if he could get anybody to bet on the other side; and if he couldn't he'd change sides. Any way that suited the other man would suit *him*—any way just so's he got a bet, *he* was satisfied. But still he was lucky, uncommon lucky; he most always come out winner. He was always ready and laying for a chance; there couldn't be no solit'ry thing mentioned but that feller'd offer to bet on it, and take ary side you please, as I was just telling you. If there was a horse-race, you'd find him flush or you'd find him busted at the end of it; if there was a dog-fight, he'd bet on it; if there was a cat-fight, he'd bet on it; if there was a chicken-fight, he'd bet on it; why, if there was two birds setting on a fence, he would bet you which one would fly first; or if there was a camp-meeting, he would be there reg'lar to bet on Parson Walker, which he judged to be the best exhorter about here, and so he was too, and a good man. If he even see a straddle-bug start to go anywheres, he would bet you how long it would take him to get to—to wherever he was going to, and if you took him up, he would foller that straddle-bug to Mexico but what he would find out where he was bound for and how long he was on the road. Lots of the boys here has seen that Smiley, and can tell you about him. Why, it never made no difference to *him*—he'd bet on *any* thing—the dangdest feller. Parson Walker's wife laid very sick once, for a good while, and it seemed as if they warn't going to save her; but one morning he come in, and Smiley up and asked him how she was, and he said she was considerable better—thank the Lord for his inf'nite mercy—and coming on so smart that with the blessing of Prov'dence she'd get well yet; and Smiley, before he thought, says, 'Well, I'll resk two-and-a-half she don't anyway.'

"Thish-yer Smiley had a mare—the boys called her the fifteen-minute nag, but that was only in fun, you know, because of course she was faster than that—and he used to win money on that horse, for all she was so slow and always had the asthma, or the distemper, or the consumption, or something of that kind. They used to give her two or three hundred yards' start, and then pass her under way; but always at the fag end of the race she'd get excited and desperate like, and come cavorting and straddling up, and scattering her legs around limber, sometimes in the air, and sometimes out to one side among the fences, and kicking up m-o-r-e dust and raising m-o-r-e racket with her coughing and sneezing and blowing her nose—and *always* fetch up at the stand just about a neck ahead, as near as you could cipher it down.

"And he had a little small bull-pup, that to look at him you'd think he warn't worth a cent but to set around and look ornery and lay for a chance to steal something. But as soon as money was up on him he was a different dog; his under-jaw'd begin to stick out like the fo'castle of a steamboat, and his teeth would uncover and shine like the furnaces. And a dog might tackle him and bully-rag him, and bite him, and throw him over his shoulder two or three times, and Andrew Jackson—which was the name of the pup—Andrew Jackson would never let on but what *he* was satisfied, and hadn't expected nothing else—and the bets being doubled and doubled on the other side all the time, till the money was all up; and then all of a sudden he would grab that other dog jest by the j'int of his hind leg and freeze to it— not chaw, you understand, but only just grip and hang on till they throwed up the sponge, if it was a year. Smiley always come out winner on that pup, till he harnessed a dog once that didn't have no hind legs, because they'd been sawed off in a circular saw, and when the thing had gone along far enough, and the money was all up, and he come to make a snatch for his pet holt, he see in a minute how he'd been imposed on, and how the other dog had him in the door, so to speak, and he 'peared surprised, and then he looked sorter discouraged-like, and didn't try no more to win the fight, and so he got shucked out bad. He give Smiley a look, as much as to say his heart was broke, and it was *his* fault, for putting up a dog that hadn't no hind legs for him to take holt of, which was his main dependence in a fight, and then he limped off a piece and laid down and died. It was a good pup, was that Andrew Jackson, and would have made a name for hisself if he'd lived, for the stuff was in him and he had genius—I know it, because he hadn't no opportunities to speak of, and it don't stand to reason that a dog could make such a fight as he could under them circumstances if he hadn't no talent. It always makes me feel sorry when I think of that last fight of his'n, and the way it turned out.

"Well, thish-yer Smiley had rat-tarriers, and chicken cocks, and tomcats and all them kind of things, till you couldn't rest, and you couldn't fetch nothing for him to bet on but he'd match you. He ketched a frog one day, and took him home, and said he cal'lated to educate him; and so he never done nothing for three months but set in his back yard and learn that frog to jump. And you bet you he *did* learn him, too. He'd give him a little punch behind, and the next minute you'd see that frog whirling in the air like a doughnut—see him turn one summerset, or maybe a couple, if he got a good start, and come down flat-footed and all right, like a cat. He got him up so in the matter of ketching flies, and kep' him in practice so constant, that he'd nail a fly every time as fur as he could see him. Smiley said all a frog wanted was education, and he could do 'most anything—and I believe him. Why, I've seen him set Dan'l Webster down here on this floor—Dan'l Webster was the name of the frog—and sing out, 'Flies, Dan'l, flies!' and quicker'n you could wink he'd spring straight up and snake a fly off'n the counter there, and flop down on the floor ag'in as solid as a gob of mud, and fall to scratching the side of his head with his hind foot as indifferent as if he hadn't no idea he'd been doin' any more'n any frog might do. You never see a frog so modest and straightfor'ard as he was, for all he was so gifted. And when it come to fair and square jumping on a dead level, he could get over more ground at one straddle than any animal of his breed you ever see. Jumping on a dead level was his strong suit, you understand; and when it come to that, Smiley would ante up money on him as long as he had a red. Smiley was monstrous proud of his frog, and well he might be, for fellers that had traveled and been everywheres all said he laid over any frog that ever *they* see.

"Well, Smiley kep' the beast in a little lattice box, and he used to fetch him down-town sometimes and lay for a bet. One day a feller—a stranger in the camp, he was—come acrost him with his box, and says:

" 'What might it be that you've got in the box?'

"And Smiley says, sorter indifferent-like, 'It might be a parrot, or it might be a canary, maybe, but it ain't—it's only just a frog.'

"And the feller took it, and looked at it careful, and turned it round this way and that, and says, 'H'm—so 'tis. Well, what's *he* good for?'

" 'Well,' Smiley says, easy and careless, 'he's good enough for *one* thing, I should judge—he can outjump any frog in Calaveras County.'

"The feller took the box again, and took another long, particular look, and give it back to Smiley, and says, very deliberate, 'Well,' he says, 'I don't see no p'ints about that frog that's any better'n any other frog.'

" 'Maybe you don't,' Smiley says. 'Maybe you understand frogs and maybe you don't understand 'em; maybe you've had experience, and maybe you ain't only a amature, as it were. Anyways, I've got *my* opinion, and I'll resk forty dollars that he can outjump any frog in Calaveras County.'

"And the feller studied a minute, and then says, kinder sad-like, 'Well, I'm only a stranger here, and I ain't got no frog; but if I had a frog, I'd bet you.'

"And then Smiley says, 'That's all right—that's all right—if you'll hold my box a minute, I'll go and get you a frog.' And so the feller took the box, and put up his forty dollars along with Smiley's, and set down to wait.

"So he set there a good while thinking and thinking to himself, and then he got the frog out and prized his mouth open and took a tea-spoon and filled him full of quail-shot—filled him pretty near up to his chin—and set him on the floor. Smiley he went to the swamp and slopped around in the mud for a long time, and finally he ketched a frog, and fetched him in, and give him to this feller, and says:

" 'Now, if you're ready, set him alongside of Dan'l, with his fore paws just even with Dan'l's, and I'll give the word.' Then he says, 'One—two—three—*git!*' and him and the feller touched up the frogs from behind, and the new frog hopped off lively, but Dan'l give a heave, and hysted up his shoulders—so—like a Frenchman, but it warn't no use—he couldn't budge; he was planted as solid as a church, and he couldn't no more stir than if he was anchored out. Smiley was a good deal surprised, and he was disgusted too, but he didn't have no idea what the matter was, of course.

"The feller took the money and started away; and when he was going out at the door, he sorter jerked his thumb over his shoulder—so—at Dan'l, and says again, very deliberate, 'Well,' he says, '*I* don't see no p'ints about that frog that's any better'n any other frog.'

"Smiley he stood scratching his head and looking down at Dan'l a long time, and at last he says, 'I do wonder what in the nation that frog throw'd off for—I wonder if there ain't something the matter with him—he 'pears to look mighty baggy, somehow.' And he ketched Dan'l by the nap of the neck, and hefted him, and says, 'Why blame my cats if he don't weigh five pound!' and turned him upside down and he belched out a double handful of shot. And then he see how it was, and he was the maddest man—he set the frog down and took out after that feller, but he never ketched him. And—"

[Here Simon Wheeler heard his name called from the front yard, and got up to see what was wanted.] And turning to me as he moved away, he said: "Just set where you are, stranger, and rest easy—I ain't going to be gone a second."

But, by your leave, I did not think that a continuation of the history of the enterprising vagabond *Jim* Smiley would be likely to afford me much information concerning the Rev. *Leonidas W.* Smiley, and so I started away.

At the door I met the sociable Wheeler returning, and he button-holed me and recommenced:

"Well, thish-yer Smiley had a yaller one-eyed cow that didn't have no tail, only just a short stump like a bannanner, and—"

However, lacking both time and inclination, I did not wait to hear about the afflicted cow, but took my leave.

# Jim Blaine and
# His Grandfather's Ram

Every now and then, in these days, the boys used to tell me I ought
to get one Jim Blaine to tell me the stirring story of his grandfather's
old ram—but they always added that I must not mention the matter
unless Jim was drunk at the time—just comfortably and sociably
drunk. They kept this up until my curiosity was on the rack to hear
the story. I got to haunting Blaine; but it was of no use, the boys
always found fault with his condition; he was often moderately but
never satisfactorily drunk. I never watched a man's condition with
such absorbing interest, such anxious solicitude; I never so pined to
see a man uncompromisingly drunk before. At last, one evening I hurried to his cabin, for I learned that this time his situation was such
that even the most fastidious could find no fault with it—he was tranquilly, serenely, symmetrically drunk—not a hiccup to mar his voice,
not a cloud upon his brain thick enough to obscure his memory. As I
entered, he was sitting upon an empty powder-keg, with a clay pipe
in one hand and the other raised to command silence. His face was
round, red, and very serious; his throat was bare and his hair tumbled;
in general appearance and costume he was a stalwart miner of the
period. On the pine table stood a candle, and its dim light revealed
"the boys" sitting here and there on bunks, candle-boxes, powder-
kegs, etc. They said:

"Sh—! Don't speak—he's going to commence."

## THE STORY OF THE OLD RAM

I found a seat at once, and Blaine said:

"I don't reckon them times will ever come again. There never was
a more bullier old ram than what he was. Grandfather fetched him
from Illinois—got him of a man by the name of Yates—Bill Yates—

maybe you might have heard of him; his father was a deacon—
Baptist—and he was a rustler, too; a man had to get up ruther early
to get the start of old Thankful Yates; it was him that put the Greens
up to j'ining teams with my grandfather when he moved west. Seth
Green was prob'ly the pick of the flock; he married a Wilkerson—
Sarah Wilkerson—good cretur, she was—one of the likeliest heifers
that was ever raised in old Stoddard, everybody said that knowed
her. She could heft a bar'l of flour as easy as I can flirt a flapjack. And
spin? Don't mention it! Independent? Humph! When Sile Hawkins
come a-browsing around her, she let him know that for all his tin he
couldn't trot in harness alongside of *her*. You see, Sile Hawkins was
—no, it warn't Sile Hawkins, after all—it was a galoot by the name
of Filkins—I disremember his first name; but he *was* a stump—come
into pra'r-meeting drunk, one night, hooraying for Nixon, becuz he
thought it was a primary; and old Deacon Ferguson up and scooted
him through the window and he lit on old Miss Jefferson's head, poor
old filly. She was a good soul—had a glass eye and used to lend it to
old Miss Wagner, that hadn't any, to receive company in; it warn't big
enough, and when Miss Wagner warn't noticing, it would get twisted
around in the socket, and look up, maybe, or out to one side, and every
which way, while t'other one was looking as straight ahead as a spyglass. Grown people didn't mind it, but it 'most always made the children cry, it was so sort of scary. She tried packing it in raw cotton,
but it wouldn't work, somehow—the cotton would get loose and stick
out and look so kind of awful that the children couldn't stand it no
way. She was always dropping it out, and turning up her old deadlight
on the company empty, and making them oncomfortable, becuz *she*
never could tell when it hopped out, being blind on that side, you see.
So somebody would have to hunch her and say, 'Your game eye has
fetched loose, Miss Wagner, dear'—and then all of them would have
to sit and wait till she jammed it in again—wrong side before, as a
general thing, and green as a bird's egg, being a bashful cretur and
easy sot back before company. But being wrong side before warn't
much difference, anyway, becuz her own eye was sky-blue and the
glass one was yaller on the front side, so whichever way she turned
it it didn't match nohow. Old Miss Wagner was considerable on the
borrow, she was. When she had a quilting, or Dorcas S'iety at her
house she gen'ally borrowed Miss Higgins's wooden leg to stump
around on; it was considerable shorter than her other pin, but much
*she* minded that. She said she couldn't abide crutches when she had
company, becuz they were so slow; said when she had company and
things had to be done, she wanted to get up and hump herself. She

was as bald as a jug, and so she used to borrow Miss Jacops's wig—
Miss Jacops was the coffin-peddler's wife—a ratty old buzzard, he
was, that used to go roosting around where people was sick, waiting
for 'em; and there that old rip would sit all day, in the shade, on a
coffin that he judged would fit the can'idate; and if it was a slow cus-
tomer and kind of uncertain, he'd fetch his rations and a blanket along
and sleep in the coffin nights. He was anchored out that way, in frosty
weather, for about three weeks, once, before old Robbins's place, waiting for him; and after that, for as much as two years, Jacops was not
on speaking terms with the old man, on account of his disapp'inting
him. He got one of his feet froze, and lost money, too, becuz old Robbins took a favorable turn and got well. The next time Robbins got
sick, Jacops tried to make up with him, and varnished up the same
old coffin and fetched it along; but old Robbins was too many for him;
he had him in, and 'peared to be powerful weak; he bought the coffin
for ten dollars and Jacops was to pay it back and twenty-five more
besides if Robbins didn't like the coffin after he'd tried it. And then
Robbins died, and at the funeral he bursted off the lid and riz up in
his shroud and told the parson to let up on the performances, becuz
he could *not* stand such a coffin as that. You see he had been in a
trance once before, when he was young, and he took the chances on
another, cal'lating that if he made the trip it was money in his pocket,
and if he missed fire he couldn't lose a cent. And, by George, he sued
Jacops for the rhino and got judgment; and he set up the coffin in his
back parlor and said he 'lowed to take his time, now. It was always
an aggravation to Jacops, the way that miserable old thing acted. He
moved back to Indiany pretty soon—went to Wellsville—Wellsville
was the place the Hogadorns was from. Mighty fine family. Old Mary-
land stock. Old Squire Hogadorn could carry around more mixed
licker, and cuss better than 'most any man I ever see. His second wife
was the Widder Billings—she that was Becky Martin; her dam was
Deacon Dunlap's first wife. Her oldest child, Maria, married a missionary and died in grace—et up by the savages. They et *him*, too,
poor feller—biled him. It warn't the custom, so they say, but they
explained to friends of his'n that went down there to bring away his
things, that they'd tried missionaries every other way and never could
get any good out of 'em—and so it annoyed all his relations to find
out that that man's life was fooled away just out of a dern'd experiment, so to speak. But mind you, there ain't anything ever reely lost;
everything that people can't understand and don't see the reason of
does good if you only hold on and give it a fair shake; Prov'dence don't
fire no blank ca'tridges, boys. That there missionary's substance, un-

beknowns to himself, actu'ly converted every last one of them heathens that took a chance at the barbecue. Nothing ever fetched them
but that. Don't tell *me* it was an accident that he was biled. There
ain't no such a thing as an accident. When my Uncle Lem was leaning
up agin a scaffolding once, sick, or drunk, or suthin, an Irishman with
a hod full of bricks fell on him out of the third story and broke the
old man's back in two places. People said it was an accident. Much
accident there was about that. He didn't know what he was there for,
but he was there for a good object. If he hadn't been there the Irishman would have been killed. Nobody can ever make me believe anything different from that. Uncle Lem's dog was there. Why didn't the
Irishman fall on the dog? Becuz the dog would 'a' seen him a-coming
and stood from under. That's the reason the dog warn't app'inted. A
dog can't be depended on to carry out a special prov'dence. Mark my
words, it was a put-up thing. Accidents don't happen, boys. Uncle
Lem's dog—I wish you could 'a' seen that dog. He was a reg'lar
shepherd—or ruther he was part bull and part shepherd—splendid
animal; belonged to Parson Hagar before Uncle Lem got him. Parson
Hagar belonged to the Western Reserve Hagars; prime family; his
mother was a Watson; one of his sisters married a Wheeler; they settled in Morgan County, and he got nipped by the machinery in a carpet
factory and went through in less than a quarter of a minute; his widder
bought the piece of carpet that had his remains wove in, and people
come a hundred mile to 'tend the funeral. There was fourteen yards
in the piece. She wouldn't let them roll him up, but planted him just
so—full length. The church was middling small where they preached
the funeral, and they had to let one end of the coffin stick out of the
window. They didn't bury him—they planted one end, and let him
stand up, same as a monument. And they nailed a sign on it and put
—put on—put on it—sacred to—the m-e-m-o-r-y—of fourteen
y-a-r-d-s—of three-ply—car - - - pet—containing all that was—
m-o-r-t-a-l—of—of—W-i-l-l-i-a-m—W-h-e—"

Jim Blaine had been growing gradually drowsy and drowsier—his
head nodded, once, twice, three times—dropped peacefully upon his
breast, and he fell tranquilly asleep. The tears were running down the
boys' cheeks—they were suffocating with suppressed laughter—and
had been from the start, though I had never noticed it. I perceived
that I was "sold." I learned then that Jim Blaine's peculiarity was that
whenever he reached a certain stage of intoxication, no human power
could keep him from setting out, with impressive unction, to tell about
a wonderful adventure which he had once had with his grandfather's
old ram—and the mention of the ram in the first sentence was as far

as any man had ever heard him get, concerning it. He always maundered off, interminably, from one thing to another, till his whisky got the best of him, and he fell asleep. What the thing was that happened to him and his grandfather's old ram is a dark mystery to this day, for nobody has ever yet found out.

# Scotty Briggs
# and the Parson

Somebody has said that in order to know a community, one must observe the style of its funerals and know what manner of men they bury with most ceremony. I cannot say which class we buried with most éclat in our "flush times," the distinguished public benefactor or the distinguished rough—possibly the two chief grades or grand divisions of society honored their illustrious dead about equally; and hence, no doubt, the philosopher I have quoted from would have needed to see two representative funerals in Virginia before forming his estimate of the people.

There was a grand time over Buck Fanshaw when he died. He was a representative citizen. He had "killed his man"—not in his own quarrel, it is true, but in defense of a stranger unfairly beset by numbers. He had kept a sumptuous saloon. He had been the proprietor of a dashing helpmeet whom he could have discarded without the formality of a divorce. He had held a high position in the fire department and been a very Warwick in politics. When he died there was great lamentation throughout the town, but especially in the vast bottom-stratum of society.

On the inquest it was shown that Buck Fanshaw, in the delirium of a wasting typhoid fever, had taken arsenic, shot himself through the body, cut his throat, and jumped out of a four-story window and broken his neck—and after due deliberation, the jury, sad and tearful, but with intelligence unblinded by its sorrow, brought in a verdict of death "by the visitation of God." What could the world do without juries?

Prodigious preparations were made for the funeral. All the vehicles in town were hired, all the saloons put in mourning, all the municipal and fire-company flags hung at half-mast, and all the firemen ordered to muster in uniform and bring their machines duly draped in black.

Now—let us remark in parentheses—as all the peoples of the earth had representative adventurers in the Silverland, and as each adventurer had brought the slang of his nation or his locality with him, the combination made the slang of Nevada the richest and the most infinitely varied and copious that had ever existed anywhere in the world, perhaps, except in the mines of California in the "early days." Slang was the language of Nevada. It was hard to preach a sermon without it, and be understood. Such phrases as "You bet!" "Oh, no, I reckon not!" "No Irish need apply," and a hundred others, became so common as to fall from the lips of a speaker unconsciously—and very often when they did not touch the subject under discussion and consequently failed to mean anything.

After Buck Fanshaw's inquest, a meeting of the short-haired brotherhood was held, for nothing can be done on the Pacific coast without a public meeting and an expression of sentiment. Regretful resolutions were passed and various committees appointed; among others, a committee of one was deputed to call on the minister, a fragile, gentle, spirituel new fledgling from an Eastern theological seminary, and as yet unacquainted with the ways of the mines. The committeeman, "Scotty" Briggs, made his visit; and in after days it was worth something to hear the minister tell about it. Scotty was a stalwart rough, whose customary suit, when on weighty official business, like committee work, was a fire-helmet, flaming red flannel shirt, patent-leather belt with spanner and revolver attached, coat hung over arm, and pants stuffed into boot-tops. He formed something of a contrast to the pale theological student. It is fair to say of Scotty, however, in passing, that he had a warm heart, and a strong love for his friends, and never entered into a quarrel when he could reasonably keep out of it. Indeed, it was commonly said that whenever one of Scotty's fights was investigated, it always turned out that it had originally been no affair of his, but that out of native good-heartedness he had dropped in of his own accord to help the man who was getting the worst of it. He and Buck Fanshaw were bosom friends, for years, and had often taken adventurous "pot-luck" together. On one occasion, they had thrown off their coats and taken the weaker side in a fight among strangers, and after gaining a hard-earned victory, turned and found that the men they were helping had deserted early, and not only that, but had stolen their coats and made off with them! But to return to Scotty's visit to the minister. He was on a sorrowful mission, now, and his face was the picture of woe. Being admitted to the presence he sat down before the clergyman, placed his fire-hat on an unfinished manuscript sermon under the minister's nose, took from it a red silk handkerchief, wiped his brow and heaved a sigh of dismal

impressiveness, explanatory of his business. He choked, and even shed
tears; but with an effort he mastered his voice and said in lugubrious
tones:

"Are you the duck that runs the gospel-mill next door?"

"Am I the—pardon me, I believe I do not understand?"

With another sigh and a half-sob, Scotty rejoined:

"Why you see we are in a bit of trouble, and the boys thought
maybe you would give us a lift, if we'd tackle you—that is, if I've got
the rights of it and you are the head clerk of the doxology-works next
door."

"I am the shepherd in charge of the flock whose fold is next door."

"The which?"

"The spiritual adviser of the little company of believers whose
sanctuary adjoins these premises."

Scotty scratched his head, reflected a moment, and then said:

"You ruther hold over me, pard. I reckon I can't call that hand.
Ante and pass the buck."

"How? I beg pardon. What did I understand you to say?"

"Well, you've ruther got the bulge on me. Or maybe we've both
got the bulge, somehow. You don't smoke me and I don't smoke you.
You see, one of the boys has passed in his checks, and we want to
give him a good send-off, and so the thing I'm on now is to roust out
somebody to jerk a little chin-music for us and waltz him through
handsome."

"My friend, I seem to grow more and more bewildered. Your observations are wholly incomprehensible to me. Cannot you simplify
them in some way? At first I thought perhaps I understood you, but
I grope now. Would it not expedite matters if you restricted yourself
to categorical statements of fact unencumbered with obstructing ac-
cumulations of metaphor and allegory?"

Another pause, and more reflection. Then, said Scotty:

"I'll have to pass, I judge."

"How?"

"You've raised me out, pard."

"I still fail to catch your meaning."

"Why, that last lead of yourn is too many for me—that's the idea.
I can't neither trump nor follow suit."

The clergyman sank back in his chair perplexed. Scotty leaned his
head on his hand and gave himself up to thought. Presently his face
came up, sorrowful but confident.

"I've got it now, so's you can savvy," he said. "What we want is a
gospel-sharp. See?"

"A what?"

"Gospel-sharp. Parson."

"Oh! Why did you not say so before? I am a clergyman—a parson."

"Now you talk! You see my blind and straddle it like a man. Put it there!"—extending a brawny paw, which closed over the minister's small hand and gave it a shake indicative of fraternal sympathy and fervent gratification.

"Now we're all right, pard. Let's start fresh. Don't you mind my snuffling a little—becuz we're in a power of trouble. You see, one of the boys has gone up the flume—"

"Gone where?"

"Up the flume—throwed up the sponge, you understand."

"Thrown up the sponge?"

"Yes—kicked the bucket—"

"Ah—has departed to that mysterious country from whose bourne no traveler returns."

"Return! I reckon not. Why, pard, he's *dead!*"

"Yes, I understand."

"Oh, you do? Well I thought maybe you might be getting tangled some more. Yes, you see he's dead again—"

"*Again!* Why, has he ever been dead before?"

"Dead before? No! Do you reckon a man has got as many lives as a cat? But you bet you he's awful dead now, poor old boy, and I wish I'd never seen this day. I don't want no better friend than Buck Fanshaw. I knowed him by the back; and when I know a man and like him, I freeze to him—you hear *me*. Take him all round, pard, there never was a bullier man in the mines. No man ever knowed Buck Fanshaw to go back on a friend. But it's all up, you know, it's all up. It ain't no use. They've scooped him."

"Scooped him?"

"Yes—death has. Well, well, well, we've got to give him up. Yes, indeed. It's a kind of a hard world, after all, *ain't* it? But pard, he was a rustler! You ought to seen him get started once. He was a bully boy with a glass eye! Just spit in his face and give him room according to his strength, and it was just beautiful to see him peel and go in. He was the worst son of a thief that ever drawed breath. Pard, he was *on* it! He was on it bigger than an Injun!"

"On it? On what?"

"On the shoot. On the shoulder. On the fight, you understand. *He* didn't give a continental for *any*body. *Beg* your pardon, friend, for coming so near saying a cuss-word—but you see I'm on an awful strain, in this palaver, on account of having to cramp down and draw everything so mild. But we've got to give him up. There ain't any getting around that, I don't reckon. Now if we can get you to help plant him—"

"Preach the funeral discourse? Assist at the obsequies?"

"Obs'quies is good. Yes. That's it—that's our little game. We are going to get the thing up regardless, you know. He was always nifty himself, and so you bet you his funeral ain't going to be no slouch—solid-silver door-plate on his coffin, six plumes on the hearse, and a nigger on the box in a biled shirt and a plug hat—how's that for high? And we'll take care of *you*, pard. We'll fix you all right. There'll be a kerridge for you; and whatever you want, you just 'scape out and we'll 'tend to it. We've got a shebang fixed up for you to stand behind, in No. 1's house, and don't you be afraid. Just go in and toot your horn, if you don't sell a clam. Put Buck through as bully as you can, pard, for anybody that knowed him will tell you that he was one of the whitest men that was ever in the mines. You can't draw it too strong. He never could stand it to see things going wrong. He's done more to make this town quiet and peaceable than any man in it. I've seen him lick four Greasers in eleven minutes, myself. If a thing wanted regulating, *he* warn't a man to go browsing around after somebody to do it, but he would prance in and regulate it himself. He warn't a Catholic. Scasely. He was down on 'em. His word was, 'No Irish need apply!' But it didn't make no difference about that when it came down to what a man's rights was—and so, when some roughs jumped the Catholic boneyard and started in to stake out town lots in it he *went* for 'em! And he *cleaned* 'em, too! I was there, pard, and I seen it myself."

"That was very well indeed—at least the impulse was—whether the act was strictly defensible or not. Had deceased any religious convictions? That is to say, did he feel a dependence upon, or acknowledge allegiance to a higher power?"

More reflection.

"I reckon you've stumped me again, pard. Could you say it over once more, and say it slow?"

"Well, to simplify it somewhat, was he, or rather had he ever been connected with any organization sequestered from secular concerns and devoted to self-sacrifice in the interests of morality?"

"All down but nine—set 'em up on the other alley, pard."

"What did I understand you to say?"

"Why, you're most too many for me, you know. When you get in with your left I hunt grass every time. Every time you draw, you fill; but I don't seem to have any luck. Let's have a new deal."

"How? Begin again?"

"That's it."

"Very well. Was he a good man, and—"

"There—I see that; don't put up another chip till I look at my hand. A good man, says you? Pard, it ain't no name for it. He was the best man that ever—pard, you would have doted on that man. He could lam any galoot of his inches in America. It was him that put down the riot last election before it got a start; and everybody said he was the only man that could have done it. He waltzed in with a spanner in one hand and a trumpet in the other, and sent fourteen men home on a shutter in less than three minutes. He had that riot all broke up and prevented nice before anybody ever got a chance to strike a blow. He was always for peace, and he would *have* peace—he could not stand disturbances. Pard, he was a great loss to this town. It would please the boys if you could chip in something like that and do him justice. Here once when the Micks got to throwing stones through the Methodis' Sunday-school windows, Buck Fanshaw, all of his own notion, shut up his saloon and took a couple of six-shooters and mounted guard over the Sunday-school. Says he, 'No Irish need apply!' And they didn't. He was the bulliest man in the mountains, pard! He could run faster, jump higher, hit harder, and hold more tanglefoot whisky without spilling it than any man in seventeen counties. Put that in, pard—it'll please the boys more than anything you could say. And you can say, pard, that he never shook his mother."

"Never shook his mother?"

"That's it—any of the boys will tell you so."

"Well, but why *should* he shake her?"

"That's what *I* say—but some people does."

"Not people of any repute?"

"Well, some that averages pretty so-so."

"In my opinion the man that would offer personal violence to his own mother, ought to—"

"Cheese it, pard; you've banked your ball clean outside the string. What I was a drivin' at, was, that he never *throwed off* on his mother—don't you see? No indeedy. He give her a house to live in, and town lots, and plenty of money; and he looked after her and took care of her all the time; and when she was down with the smallpox I'm d——d if he didn't set up nights and nuss her himself! *Beg* your pardon for saying it, but it hopped out too quick for yours truly. You've treated me like a gentleman, pard, and I ain't the man to hurt your feelings intentional. I think you're white. I think you're a square man, pard. I like you, and I'll lick any man that don't. I'll lick him till he can't tell himself from a last year's corpse! Put it *there*!" [Another fraternal hand-shake—and exit.]

The obsequies were all that "the boys" could desire. Such a marvel of funeral pomp had never been seen in Virginia. The plumed hearse, the dirge-breathing brass-bands, the closed marts of business, the flags drooping at half-mast, the long, plodding procession of uniformed secret societies, military battalions and fire companies, draped engines, carriages of officials, and citizens in vehicles and on foot, attracted multitudes of spectators to the sidewalks, roofs, and windows; and for years afterward, the degree of grandeur attained by any civic display in Virginia was determined by comparison with Buck Fanshaw's funeral.

Scotty Briggs, as a pall-bearer and a mourner, occupied a prominent place at the funeral, and when the sermon was finished and the last sentence of the prayer for the dead man's soul ascended, he responded, in a low voice, but with feeling:

"AMEN. No Irish need apply."

As the bulk of the response was without apparent relevancy, it was probably nothing more than a humble tribute to the memory of the friend that was gone; for, as Scotty had once said, it was "his word."

Scotty Briggs, in after days, achieved the distinction of becoming the only convert to religion that was ever gathered from the Virginia roughs; and it transpired that the man who had it in him to espouse the quarrel of the weak out of inborn nobility of spirit was no mean timber whereof to construct a Christian. The making him one did not warp his generosity or diminish his courage; on the contrary it gave intelligent direction to the one and a broader field to the other. If his Sunday-school class progressed faster than the other classes, was it matter for wonder? I think not. He talked to his pioneer small-fry in a language they understood! It was my large privilege, a month before he died, to hear him tell the beautiful story of Joseph and his brethren to his class "without looking at the book." I leave it to the reader to fancy what it was like, as it fell, riddled with slang, from the lips of that grave, earnest teacher, and was listened to by his little learners with a consuming interest that showed that they were as unconscious as he was that any violence was being done to the sacred proprieties!

# What Stumped the Bluejays
# (Jim Baker's Bluejay Yarn)

Animals talk to each other, of course. There can be no question about
that; but I suppose there are very few people who can understand
them. I never knew but one man who could. I knew he could, however,
because he told me so himself. He was a middle-aged, simple-hearted
miner who had lived in a lonely corner of California, among the woods
and mountains, a good many years, and had studied the ways of his
only neighbors, the beasts and the birds, until he believed he could
accurately translate any remark which they made. This was Jim
Baker. According to Jim Baker, some animals have only a limited education, and use only very simple words, and scarcely ever a comparison or a flowery figure; whereas, certain other animals have a large
vocabulary, a fine command of language and a ready and fluent delivery; consequently these latter talk a great deal; they like it; they are
conscious of their talent, and they enjoy "showing off." Baker said,
that after long and careful observation, he had come to the conclusion
that the bluejays were the best talkers he had found among birds and
beasts. Said he:

"There's more *to* a bluejay than any other creature. He has got
more moods, and more different kinds of feelings than other creatures;
and, mind you, whatever a bluejay feels, he can put into language.
And no mere commonplace language, either, but rattling, out-and-out
book-talk—and bristling with metaphor, too—just bristling! And as
for command of language—why *you* never see a bluejay get stuck for
a word. No man ever did. They just boil out of him! And another thing:
I've noticed a good deal, and there's no bird, or cow, or anything that
uses as good grammar as a bluejay. You may say a cat uses good
grammar. Well, a cat does—but you let a cat get excited once; you
let a cat get to pulling fur with another cat on a shed, nights, and
you'll hear grammar that will give you the lockjaw. Ignorant people

think it's the *noise* which fighting cats make that is so aggravating, but it ain't so; it's the sickening grammar they use. Now I've never heard a jay use bad grammar but very seldom; and when they do, they are as ashamed as a human; they shut right down and leave.

"You may call a jay a bird. Well, so he is, in a measure—because he's got feathers on him, and don't belong to no church, perhaps; but otherwise he is just as much a human as you be. And I'll tell you for why. A jay's gifts, and instincts, and feelings, and interests, cover the whole ground. A jay hasn't got any more principle than a Congressman. A jay will lie, a jay will steal, a jay will deceive, a jay will betray; and four times out of five, a jay will go back on his solemnest promise. The sacredness of an obligation is a thing which you can't cram into no bluejay's head. Now, on top of all this, there's another thing; a jay can outswear any gentleman in the mines. You think a cat can swear. Well, a cat can; but you give a bluejay a subject that calls for his reserve-powers, and where is your cat? Don't talk to *me*—I know too much about this thing. And there's yet another thing; in the one little particular of scolding—just good, clean, out-and-out scolding—a bluejay can lay over anything, human or divine. Yes, sir, a jay is everything that a man is. A jay can cry, a jay can laugh, a jay can feel shame, a jay can reason and plan and discuss, a jay likes gossip and scandal, a jay has got a sense of humor, a jay knows when he is an ass just as well as you do—maybe better. If a jay ain't human, he better take in his sign, that's all. Now I'm going to tell you a perfectly true fact about some bluejays.

"When I first begun to understand jay language correctly, there was a little incident happened here. Seven years ago, the last man in this region but me moved away. There stands his house—been empty ever since; a log house, with a plank roof—just one big room, and no more; no ceiling—nothing between the rafters and the floor. Well, one Sunday morning I was sitting out here in front of my cabin, with my cat, taking the sun, and looking at the blue hills, and listening to the leaves rustling so lonely in the trees, and thinking of the home away yonder in the states, that I hadn't heard from in thirteen years, when a bluejay lit on that house, with an acorn in his mouth, and says, 'Hello, I reckon I've struck something.' When he spoke, the acorn dropped out of his mouth and rolled down the roof, of course, but he didn't care; his mind was all on the thing he had struck. It was a knot-hole in the roof. He cocked his head to one side, shut one eye and put the other one to the hole, like a possum looking down a jug; then he glanced up with his bright eyes, gave a wink or two with his wings—which signifies gratification, you understand—and says, 'It looks like a hole, it's located like a hole—blamed if I don't believe it *is* a hole!'

"Then he cocked his head down and took another look; he glances up perfectly joyful, this time; winks his wings and his tail both, and says, 'Oh, no, this ain't no fat thing, I reckon! If I ain't in luck!—why it's a perfectly elegant hole!' So he flew down and got that acorn, and fetched it up and dropped it in, and was just tilting his head back, with the heavenliest smile on his face, when all of a sudden he was paralyzed into a listening attitude and that smile faded gradually out of his countenance like breath off'n a razor, and the queerest look of surprise took its place. Then he says, 'Why, I didn't hear it fall!' He cocked his eye at the hole again, and took a long look; raised up and shook his head; stepped around to the other side of the hole and took another look from that side; shook his head again. He studied a while, then he just went into the *de*tails—walked round and round the hole and spied into it from every point of the compass. No use. Now he took a thinking attitude on the comb of the roof and scratched the back of his head with his right foot a minute, and finally says, 'Well, it's too many for *me*, that's certain; must be a mighty long hole; however, I ain't got no time to fool around here, I got to 'tend to business; I reckon it's all right—chance it, anyway.'

"So he flew off and fetched another acorn and dropped it in, and tried to flirt his eye to the hole quick enough to see what become of it, but he was too late. He held his eye there as much as a minute; then he raised up and sighed, and says, 'Confound it, I don't seem to understand this thing, no way; however, I'll tackle her again.' He fetched another acorn, and done his level best to see what become of it, but he couldn't. He says, 'Well, *I* never struck no such a hole as this before; I'm of the opinion it's a totally new kind of a hole.' Then he begun to get mad. He held in for a spell, walking up and down the comb of the roof and shaking his head and muttering to himself; but his feelings got the upper hand of him, presently, and he broke loose and cussed himself black in the face. I never see a bird take on so about a little thing. When he got through he walks to the hole and looks in again for half a minute; then he says, 'Well, you're a long hole, and a deep hole, and a mighty singular hole altogether—but I've started in to fill you, and I'm d——d if I *don't* fill you, if it takes a hundred years!'

"And with that, away he went. You never see a bird work so since you was born. He laid into his work like a nigger, and the way he hove acorns into that hole for about two hours and a half was one of the most exciting and astonishing spectacles I ever struck. He never stopped to take a look any more—he just hove 'em in and went for more. Well, at last he could hardly flop his wings, he was so tuckered out. He comes a-drooping down, once more, sweating like an ice-

pitcher, drops his acorn in and says, 'Now I guess I've got the bulge
on you by this time!' So he bent down for a look. If you'll believe me,
when his head come up again he was just pale with rage. He says,
'I've shoveled acorns enough in there to keep the family thirty years,
and if I can see a sign of one of 'em I wish I may land in a museum
with a belly full of sawdust in two minutes!'

"He just had strength enough to crawl up on to the comb and lean
his back agin the chimbly, and then he collected his impressions and
begun to free his mind. I see in a second that what I had mistook for
profanity in the mines was only just the rudiments, as you may say.·

"Another jay was going by, and heard him doing his devotions, and
stops to inquire what was up. The sufferer told him the whole circumstance, and says, 'Now yonder's the hole, and if you don't believe me,
go and look for yourself.' So this fellow went and looked, and comes
back and says, 'How many did you say you put in there?' 'Not any
less than two tons,' says the sufferer. The other jay went and looked
again. He couldn't seem to make it out, so he raised a yell, and three
more jays come. They all examined the hole, they all made the sufferer
tell it over again, then they all discussed it, and got off as many
leather-headed opinions about it as an average crowd of humans could
have done.

"They called in more jays; then more and more, till pretty soon
this whole region 'peared to have a blue flush about it. There must
have been five thousand of them; and such another jawing and dis-
puting and ripping and cussing, you never heard. Every jay in the
whole lot put his eye to the hole and delivered a more chuckle-headed
opinion about the mystery than the jay that went there before him.
They examined the house all over, too. The door was standing half
open, and at last one old jay happened to go and light on it and look
in. Of course, that knocked the mystery galley-west in a second. There
lay the acorns, scattered all over the floor. He flopped his wings and
raised a whoop. 'Come here!' he says, 'Come here, everybody; hang'd
if this fool hasn't been trying to fill up a house with acorns!' They all
came a-swooping down like a blue cloud, and as each fellow lit on the
door and took a glance, the whole absurdity of the contract that that
first jay had tackled hit him home and he fell over backward suffocating with laughter, and the next jay took his place and done the
same.

"Well, sir, they roosted around here on the housetop and the trees
for an hour, and guffawed over that thing like human beings. It ain't
any use to tell me a bluejay hasn't got a sense of humor, because I
know better. And memory, too. They brought jays here from all over

the United States to look down that hole, every summer for three years. Other birds, too. And they could all see the point, except an owl that come from Nova Scotia to visit the Yo Semite, and he took this thing in on his way back. He said he couldn't see anything funny in it. But then he was a good deal disappointed about Yo Semite, too."

# The Californian's Tale

Thirty-five years ago I was out prospecting on the Stanislaus, tramping all day long with pick and pan and horn, and washing a hatful of dirt here and there, always expecting to make a rich strike, and never doing it. It was a lovely region, woodsy, balmy, delicious, and had once been populous, long years before, but now the people had vanished and the charming paradise was a solitude. They went away when the surface diggings gave out. In one place, where a busy little city with banks and newspapers and fire companies and a mayor and aldermen had been, was nothing but a wide expanse of emerald turf, with not even the faintest sign that human life had ever been present there. This was down toward Tuttletown. In the country neighborhood thereabouts, along the dusty roads, one found at intervals the prettiest little cottage homes, snug and cozy, and so cobwebbed with vines snowed thick with roses that the doors and windows were wholly hidden from sight—sign that these were deserted homes, forsaken years ago by defeated and disappointed families who could neither sell them nor give them away. Now and then, half an hour apart, one came across solitary log cabins of the earliest mining days, built by the first gold-miners, the predecessors of the cottage-builders. In some few cases these cabins were still occupied; and when this was so, you could depend upon it that the occupant was the very pioneer who had built the cabin; and you could depend on another thing, too—that he was there because he had once had his opportunity to go home to the States rich, and had not done it; had rather lost his wealth, and had then in his humiliation resolved to sever all communication with his home relatives and friends, and be to them thenceforth as one dead. Round about California in that day were scattered a host of these living dead men—pride-smitten poor fellows, grizzled and old at forty, whose secret thoughts were made all of regrets and longings—regrets for their wasted lives, and longings to be out of the struggle and done with it all.

It was a lonesome land! Not a sound in all those peaceful expanses of grass and woods but the drowsy hum of insects; no glimpse of man or beast; nothing to keep up your spirits and make you glad to be alive. And so, at last, in the early part of the afternoon, when I caught sight of a human creature, I felt a most grateful uplift. This person was a man about forty-five years old, and he was standing at the gate of one of those cozy little rose-clad cottages of the sort already referred to. However, this one hadn't a deserted look; it had the look of being lived in and petted and cared for and looked after; and so had its front yard, which was a garden of flowers, abundant, gay, and flourishing. I was invited in, of course, and required to make myself at home—it was the custom of the country.

It was delightful to be in such a place, after long weeks of daily and nightly familiarity with miners' cabins—with all which this implies of dirt floor, never-made beds, tin plates and cups, bacon and beans and black coffee, and nothing of ornament but war pictures from the Eastern illustrated papers tacked to the log walls. That was all hard, cheerless, materialistic desolation, but here was a nest which had aspects to rest the tired eye and refresh that something in one's nature which, after long fasting, recognizes, when confronted by the belongings of art, howsoever cheap and modest they may be, that it has unconsciously been famishing and now has found nourishment. I could not have believed that a rag carpet could feast me so, and so content me; or that there could be such solace to the soul in wallpaper and framed lithographs, and bright-colored tidies and lampmats, and Windsor chairs, and varnished what-nots, with sea-shells and books and china vases on them, and the score of little unclassifiable tricks and touches that a woman's hand distributes about a home, which one sees without knowing he sees them, yet would miss in a moment if they were taken away. The delight that was in my heart showed in my face, and the man saw it and was pleased; saw it so plainly that he answered it as if it had been spoken.

"All her work," he said, caressingly; "she did it all herself—every bit," and he took the room in with a glance which was full of affectionate worship. One of those soft Japanese fabrics with which women drape with careful negligence the upper part of a picture-frame was out of adjustment. He noticed it, and rearranged it with cautious pains, stepping back several times to gauge the effect before he got it to suit him. Then he gave it a light finishing pat or two with his hand, and said: "She always does that. You can't tell just what it lacks, but it does lack something until you've done that—you can see it yourself after it's done, but that is all you know; you can't find out the law of it. It's like the finishing pats a mother gives the child's hair after she's got it combed and brushed, I reckon. I've seen her fix all these things so much that I can do them all just her way, though I don't know the law of any of them. But she knows the law. She knows the why and the how both; but I don't know the why; I only know the how."

He took me into a bedroom so that I might wash my hands; such a bedroom as I had not seen for years: white counterpane, white pillows, carpeted floor, papered walls, pictures, dressing-table, with mirror and pin-cushion and dainty toilet things; and in the corner a wash-stand, with real china-ware bowl and pitcher, and with soap in a china dish, and on a rack more than a dozen towels—towels too clean and white for one out of practice to use without some vague sense of profanation. So my face spoke again, and he answered with gratified words:

"All her work; she did it all herself—every bit. Nothing here that hasn't felt the touch of her hand. Now you would think— But I mustn't talk so much."

By this time I was wiping my hands and glancing from detail to detail of the room's belongings, as one is apt to do when he is in a new place, where everything he sees is a comfort to his eye and his spirit; and I became conscious, in one of those unaccountable ways, you know, that there was something there somewhere that the man wanted me to discover for myself. I knew it perfectly, and I knew he was trying to help me by furtive indications with his eye, so I tried hard to get on the right track, being eager to gratify him. I failed several times, as I could see out of the corner of my eye without being told; but at last I knew I must be looking straight at the thing—knew it from the pleasure issuing in invisible waves from him. He broke into a happy laugh, and rubbed his hands together, and cried out:

"That's it! You've found it. I knew you would. It's her picture."

I went to the little black-walnut bracket on the farther wall, and did find there what I had not yet noticed—a daguerreotype-case. It contained the sweetest girlish face, and the most beautiful, as it seemed to me, that I had ever seen. The man drank the admiration from my face, and was fully satisfied.

"Nineteen her last birthday," he said, as he put the picture back; "and that was the day we were married. When you see her—ah, just wait till you see her!"

"Where is she? When will she be in?"

"Oh, she's away now. She's gone to see her people. They live forty or fifty miles from here. She's been gone two weeks to-day."

"When do you expect her back?"

"This is Wednesday. She'll be back Saturday, in the evening—about nine o'clock, likely."

I felt a sharp sense of disappointment.

"I'm sorry, because I'll be gone then," I said, regretfully.

"Gone? No—why should you go? Don't go. She'll be so disappointed."

She would be disappointed—that beautiful creature! If she had said the words herself they could hardly have blessed me more. I was feeling a deep, strong longing to see her—a longing so supplicating, so insistent, that it made me afraid. I said to myself: "I will go straight away from this place, for my peace of mind's sake."

"You see, she likes to have people come and stop with us—people who know things, and can talk—people like you. She delights in it; for she knows—oh, she knows nearly everything herself, and can talk, oh, like a bird—and the books she reads, why, you would be astonished. Don't go; it's only a little while, you know, and she'll be so disappointed."

I heard the words, but hardly noticed them, I was so deep in my thinkings and strugglings. He left me, but I didn't know. Presently he was back, with the picture-case in his hand, and he held it open before me and said:

"There, now, tell her to her face you could have stayed to see her, and you wouldn't."

That second glimpse broke down my good resolution. I would stay and take the risk. That night we smoked the tranquil pipe, and talked till late about various things, but mainly about her; and certainly I had had no such pleasant and restful time for many a day. The Thursday followed and slipped comfortably away. Toward twilight a big miner from three miles away came—one of the grizzled, stranded pioneers—and gave us warm salutation, clothed in grave and sober speech. Then he said:

"I only just dropped over to ask about the little madam, and when is she coming home. Any news from her?"

"Oh yes, a letter. Would you like to hear it, Tom?"

"Well, I should think I would, if you don't mind, Henry!"

Henry got the letter out of his wallet, and said he would skip some of the private phrases, if we were willing; then he went on and read the bulk of it—a loving, sedate, and altogether charming and gracious piece of handiwork, with a postscript full of affectionate regards and messages to Tom, and Joe, and Charley, and other close friends and neighbors.

As the reader finished, he glanced at Tom, and cried out:

"Oho, you're at it again! Take your hands away, and let me see your eyes. You always do that when I read a letter from her. I will write and tell her."

"Oh no, you mustn't, Henry. I'm getting old, you know, and any little disappointment makes me want to cry. I thought she'd be here herself, and now you've got only a letter."

"Well, now, what put that in your head? I thought everybody knew she wasn't coming till Saturday."

"Saturday! Why, come to think, I did know it. I wonder what's the matter with me lately? Certainly I knew it. Ain't we all getting ready for her? Well, I must be going now. But I'll be on hand when she comes, old man!"

Late Friday afternoon another gray veteran tramped over from his cabin a mile or so away, and said the boys wanted to have a little gaiety and a good time Saturday night, if Henry thought she wouldn't be too tired after her journey to be kept up.

"Tired? She tired! Oh, hear the man! Joe, *you* know she'd sit up six weeks to please any one of you!"

When Joe heard that there was a letter, he asked to have it read, and the loving messages in it for him broke the old fellow all up; but he said he was such an old wreck that *that* would happen to him if she only just mentioned his name. "Lord, we miss her so!" he said.

Saturday afternoon I found I was taking out my watch pretty often. Henry noticed it, and said, with a startled look:

"You don't think she ought to be here so soon, do you?"

I felt caught, and a little embarrassed; but I laughed, and said it was a habit of mine when I was in a state of expectancy. But he didn't seem quite satisfied; and from that time on he began to show uneasiness. Four times he walked me up the road to a point whence we could see a long distance; and there he would stand, shading his eyes with his hand, and looking. Several times he said:

"I'm getting worried, I'm getting right down worried. I know she's not due till about nine o'clock, and yet something seems to be trying to warn me that something's happened. You don't think anything has happened, do you?"

I began to get pretty thoroughly ashamed of him for his childishness; and at last, when he repeated that imploring question still another time, I lost my patience for the moment, and spoke pretty brutally to him. It seemed to shrivel him up and cow him; and he looked so wounded and so humble after that, that I detested myself for having done the cruel and unnecessary thing. And so I was glad when Charley, another veteran, arrived toward the edge of the evening, and nestled up to Henry to hear the letter read, and talked over the preparations for the welcome. Charley fetched out one hearty speech after another, and did his best to drive away his friend's bodings and apprehensions.

"Anything *happened* to her? Henry, that's pure nonsense. There isn't anything going to happen to her; just make your mind easy as to that. What did the letter say? Said she was well, didn't it? And said she'd be here by nine o'clock, didn't it? Did you ever know her to fail of her word? Why, you know you never did. Well, then, don't you fret; she'll *be* here, and that's absolutely certain, and as sure as you are born. Come, now, let's get to decorating—not much time left."

Pretty soon Tom and Joe arrived, and then all hands set about adorning the house with flowers. Toward nine the three miners said that as they had brought their instruments they might as well tune up, for the boys and girls would soon be arriving now, and hungry for a good, old-fashioned break-down. A fiddle, a banjo, and a clarinet— these were the instruments. The trio took their places side by side, and began to play some rattling dance-music, and beat time with their big boots.

It was getting very close to nine. Henry was standing in the door with his eyes directed up the road, his body swaying to the torture of his mental distress. He had been made to drink his wife's health and safety several times, and now Tom shouted:

"All hands stand by! One more drink, and she's here!"

Joe brought the glasses on a waiter, and served the party. I reached for one of the two remaining glasses, but Joe growled, under his breath:

"Drop that! Take the other."

Which I did. Henry was served last. He had hardly swallowed his drink when the clock began to strike. He listened till it finished, his face growing pale and paler; then he said:

"Boys, I'm sick with fear. Help me—I want to lie down!"

They helped him to the sofa. He began to nestle and drowse, but presently spoke like one talking in his sleep, and said: "Did I hear horses' feet? Have they come?"

One of the veterans answered, close to his ear: "It was Jimmy Parrish come to say the party got delayed, but they're right up the road a piece, and coming along. Her horse is lame, but she'll be here in half an hour."

"Oh, I'm *so* thankful nothing has happened!"

He was asleep almost before the words were out of his mouth. In a moment those handy men had his clothes off, and had tucked him into his bed in the chamber where I had washed my hands. They closed the door and came back. Then they seemed preparing to leave;

but I said: "Please don't go, gentlemen. She won't know me; I am a stranger."

They glanced at each other. Then Joe said:

"She? Poor thing, she's been dead nineteen years!"

"Dead?"

"That or worse. She went to see her folks half a year after she was married, and on her way back, on a Saturday evening, the Indians captured her within five miles of this place, and she's never been heard of since."

"And he lost his mind in consequence?"

"Never has been sane an hour since. But he only gets bad when that time of the year comes round. Then we begin to drop in here, three days before she's due, to encourage him up, and ask if he's heard from her, and Saturday we all come and fix up the house with flowers, and get everything ready for a dance. We've done it every year for nineteen years. The first Saturday there was twenty-seven of us, without counting the girls; there's only three of us now, and the girls are all gone. We drug him to sleep, or he would go wild; then he's all right for another year—thinks she's with him till the last three or four days come round; then he begins to look for her, and gets out his poor old letter, and we come and ask him to read it to us. Lord, she was a darling!"

# AMBROSE BIERCE

*(1842–1914?)*

*Born Ambrose Gwinett Bierce in Ohio of parents who had come there
from New England, and raised on a farm which he loathed—along
with his parents and most of his siblings—Bierce found paradoxical
refuge in the army, first in the Kentucky Military Institute then in
regular service during the Civil War. Enlisting as a drummer boy,
he rose to the rank of brevet major, and fought in a number of campaigns, including the battle of Kenesaw Mountain, where he was
wounded. Sent with General Hazen to the west coast on an inspection
tour, Bierce reunited with his favorite brother, Albert, in San Francisco, and resigned from the army in order to remain with him. Ob-
taining a sinecure with the U.S. Mint, Bierce interested himself in
local politics, first as an anonymous cartoonist, but soon enough as
a journalist, thereby launching a literary career which, with a five-
year interlude in Great Britain (1871–76), was chiefly identified with
the rich and turbulent artists' community in the San Francisco area.
Respected and feared for his scathing wit—he wrote regular columns
in the* Argonaut, *edited the* Wasp, *and contributed stories to* Overland
Magazine—*Bierce became the literary eminence of the city that Bret
Harte and Mark Twain had left for Eastern centers. His career
reached its peak in 1887, when he became a columnist for William
Randolph Hearst's* Examiner. *Bierce had long been estranged from
his wife (whom he had married in 1871) when, in 1889, his older son
was killed in a shoot-out with another young man over a woman; in
1901, Bierce's other son died of alcoholism. In 1896, Hearst sent Bierce
to Washington, D.C., as correspondent to the New York* American, *in
a move that resulted for Bierce in a permanent break—except for a
brief visit toward the end of his life—with the San Francisco literary
scene in which he had played such an important role. Bitter and de-
spondent, his satiric talents having soured into cynicism, Bierce dis-*

*appeared into revolution-torn Mexico in 1914 and was not heard from*
*again.*

*Much of what he wrote was contemporary satire and has not sur-*
*vived as literature, despite Bierce's efforts to preserve it in the twelve*
*volumes of his* Collected Works *(1909–12). He is best known, ironi-*
*cally, for his stories of the Civil War, gathered in* Tales of Soldiers
and Civilians *(1891), especially "Occurrence at Owl Creek Bridge,"*
*rather than for his California tales, many of which only incidentally*
*involve a San Francisco setting. A fantast in the tradition of Edgar*
*Allan Poe, Bierce was no regionalist-realist, but used his considerable*
*powers of imagination in developing complicated plots with surprise*
*—or twist—endings that emphasize the cruel coincidences of fate.*
*Characteristically, he imposed a gothic mood in his stories with*
*mining-camp settings, which he generally depicted as deserted, ram-*
*shackle relics of once-bustling communities. Where Harte and Twain*
*celebrated the mining frontier at its most rambunctious, Bierce's*
*camps are haunted by past crimes, including genocidal murder; yet*
*he too was a humorist, albeit a grim one, and took sardonic satisfac-*
*tion from the grotesque dealings of fate, signaled by the deadly twist*
*of a final surprise.*

*Along with* Tales of Soldiers and Civilians, *republished in 1898*
*(and in his* Collected Works*) as* In the Midst of Life *(a title with the*
*proper air of memento mori), Bierce's best work is represented by the*
*stories gathered in* Can Such Things Be? *(1893) and by the poetry in*
Black Beetles in Amber *(1892). A meticulous craftsman with a bril-*
*liant command of the language, Bierce is justly famed for his* The
Devil's Dictionary *(1906).*

# A Holy Terror

There was an entire lack of interest in the latest arrival at Hurdy-Gurdy. He was not even christened with the picturesquely descriptive nick-name which is so frequently a mining camp's word of welcome to the newcomer. In almost any other camp thereabout this circumstance would of itself have secured him some such appellation as "The White-headed Conundrum," or "No Sarvey"—an expression naïvely supposed to suggest to quick intelligences the Spanish *quien sabe*. He came without provoking a ripple of concern upon the social surface of Hurdy-Gurdy—a place which to the general Californian contempt of men's personal history superadded a local indifference of its own. The time was long past when it was of any importance who came there, or if anybody came. No one was living at Hurdy-Gurdy.

Two years before, the camp had boasted a stirring population of two or three thousand males and not fewer than a dozen females. A majority of the former had done a few weeks' earnest work in demonstrating, to the disgust of the latter, the singularly mendacious character of the person whose ingenious tales of rich gold deposits had lured them thither—work, by the way, in which there was as little mental satisfaction as pecuniary profit; for a bullet from the pistol of a public-spirited citizen had put that imaginative gentleman beyond the reach of aspersion on the third day of the camp's existence. Still, his fiction had a certain foundation in fact, and many had lingered a considerable time in and about Hurdy-Gurdy, though now all had been long gone.

But they had left ample evidence of their sojourn. From the point where Injun Creek falls into the Rio San Juan Smith, up along both banks of the former into the cañon whence it emerges, extended a double row of forlorn shanties that seemed about to fall upon one another's neck to bewail their desolation; while about an equal number appeared to have straggled up the slope on either hand and perched themselves upon commanding eminences, whence they craned forward to get a good view of the affecting scene. Most of these habitations were emaciated as by famine to the condition of mere skeletons, about which clung unlovely tatters of what might have been skin, but was really canvas. The little valley itself, torn and gashed by pick and shovel, was unhandsome with long, bending lines of decaying flume resting here and there upon the summits of sharp ridges, and stilting awkwardly across the intervals upon unhewn poles. The whole place presented that raw and forbidding aspect of arrested development which is a new country's substitute for the solemn grace of ruin wrought by time. Wherever there remained a patch of the original soil a rank overgrowth of weeds and brambles had spread upon the scene, and from its dank, unwholesome shades the visitor curious in such matters might have obtained numberless souvenirs of the camp's former glory—fellowless boots mantled with green mould and plethoric of rotting leaves; an occasional old felt hat; desultory remnants of a flannel shirt; sardine boxes inhumanly mutilated and a surprising profusion of black bottles distributed with a truly catholic impartiality, everywhere.

## II

The man who had now rediscovered Hurdy-Gurdy was evidently not curious as to its archaeology. Nor, as he looked about him upon the dismal evidences of wasted work and broken hopes, their dispiriting significance accentuated by the ironical pomp of a cheap gilding by the rising sun, did he supplement his sigh of weariness by one of sensibility. He simply removed from the back of his tired burro a miner's outfit a trifle larger than the animal itself, picketed that creature and selecting a hatchet from his kit moved off at once across the dry bed of Injun Creek to the top of a low, gravelly hill beyond.

Stepping across a prostrate fence of brush and boards he picked up one of the latter, split it into five parts and sharpened them at one end. He then began a kind of search, occasionally stooping to examine something with close attention. At last his patient scrutiny appeared to be rewarded with success, for he suddenly erected his figure to its full height, made a gesture of satisfaction, pronounced the word "Scarry" and at once strode away with long, equal steps, which he counted. Then he stopped and drove one of his stakes into the earth. He then looked carefully about him, measured off a number of paces over a singularly uneven ground and hammered in another. Pacing off twice the distance at a right angle to his former course he drove down a third, and repeating the process sank home the fourth, and then a fifth. This he split at the top and in the cleft inserted an old letter envelope covered with an intricate system of pencil tracks. In short, he staked off a hill claim in strict accordance with the local mining laws of Hurdy-Gurdy and put up the customary notice.

It is necessary to explain that one of the adjuncts to Hurdy-Gurdy—one to which that metropolis became afterward itself an adjunct—was a cemetery. In the first week of the camp's existence this had been thoughtfully laid out by a committee of citizens. The day after had been signalized by a debate between two members of the committee, with reference to a more eligible site, and on the third day the necropolis was inaugurated by a double funeral. As the camp had waned the cemetery had waxed; and long before the ultimate inhabitant, victorious alike over the insidious malaria and the forthright revolver, had turned the tail of his pack-ass upon Injun Creek the outlying settlement had become a populous if not popular suburb. And now, when the town was fallen into the sere and yellow leaf of an unlovely senility, the graveyard—though somewhat marred by time and circumstance, and not altogether exempt from innovations in grammar and experiments in orthography, to say nothing of the devastating coyote—answered the humble needs of its denizens with reasonable completeness. It comprised a generous two acres of ground, which with commendable thrift but needless care had been selected for its mineral unworth, contained two or three skeleton trees (one of which had a stout lateral branch from which a weather-wasted rope still significantly dangled), half a hundred gravelly mounds, a score of rude headboards displaying the literary peculiarities above mentioned and a struggling colony of prickly pears. Altogether, God's Location, as with characteristic reverence it had been called, could justly boast of an indubitably superior quality of desolation. It was in the most thickly settled part of this interesting demesne that Mr. Jefferson Doman staked off his claim. If in the prosecution of his design he should deem it expedient to remove any of the dead they would have the right to be suitably re-interred.

### III

This Mr. Jefferson Doman was from Elizabethtown, New Jersey, where six years before he had left his heart in the keeping of a golden-haired, demure-mannered young woman named Mary Matthews, as collateral security for his return to claim her hand.

"I just *know* you'll never get back alive—you never do succeed in anything," was the remark which illustrated Miss Matthews's notion

of what constituted success and, inferentially, her view of the nature
of encouragement. She added: "If you don't I'll go to California too. I
can put the coins in little bags as you dig them out."

This characteristically feminine theory of auriferous deposits did
not commend itself to the masculine intelligence: it was Mr. Doman's
belief that gold was found in a liquid state. He deprecated her intent
with considerable enthusiasm, suppressed her sobs with a light hand
upon her mouth, laughed in her eyes as he kissed away her tears, and
with a cheerful "Ta-ta" went to California to labor for her through the
long, loveless years, with a strong heart, an alert hope and a steadfast
fidelity that never for a moment forgot what it was about. In the mean
time, Miss Matthews had granted a monopoly of her humble talent for
sacking up coins to Mr. Jo. Seeman, of New York, gambler, by whom
it was better appreciated than her commanding genius for unsacking
and bestowing them upon his local rivals. Of this latter aptitude, indeed, he manifested his disapproval by an act which secured him the
position of clerk of the laundry in the State prison, and for her the
*sobriquet* of "Split-faced Moll." At about this time she wrote to Mr.
Doman a touching letter of renunciation, inclosing her photograph to
prove that she had no longer a right to indulge the dream of becoming
Mrs. Doman, and recounting so graphically her fall from a horse that
the staid "plug" upon which Mr. Doman had ridden into Red Dog to
get the letter made vicarious atonement under the spur all the way
back to camp. The letter failed in a signal way to accomplish its object;
the fidelity which had before been to Mr. Doman a matter of love and
duty was thenceforth a matter of honor also; and the photograph,
showing the once pretty face sadly disfigured as by the slash of a knife,
was duly instated in his affections and its more comely predecessor
treated with contumelious neglect. On being informed of this, Miss
Matthews, it is only fair to say, appeared less surprised than from the
apparently low estimate of Mr. Doman's generosity which the tone of
her former letter attested one would naturally have expected her to
be. Soon after, however, her letters grew infrequent, and then ceased
altogether.

But Mr. Doman had another correspondent, Mr. Barney Bree, of
Hurdy-Gurdy, formerly of Red Dog. This gentleman, although a notable figure among miners, was not a miner. His knowledge of mining
consisted mainly in a marvelous command of its slang, to which he
made copious contributions, enriching its vocabulary with a wealth of
uncommon phrases more remarkable for their aptness than their refinement, and which impressed the unlearned "tenderfoot" with a
lively sense of the profundity of their inventor's acquirements. When
not entertaining a circle of admiring auditors from San Francisco or

the East he could commonly be found pursuing the comparatively obscure industry of sweeping out the various dance houses and purifying
the cuspidors.

Barney had apparently but two passions in life—love of Jefferson
Doman, who had once been of some service to him, and love of whisky,
which certainly had not. He had been among the first in the rush to
Hurdy-Gurdy, but had not prospered, and had sunk by degrees to the
position of grave digger. This was not a vocation, but Barney in a
desultory way turned his trembling hand to it whenever some local
misunderstanding at the card table and his own partial recovery from
a prolonged debauch occurred coincidently in point of time. One day
Mr. Doman received, at Red Dog, a letter with the simple postmark,
"Hurdy, Cal.," and being occupied with another matter, carelessly
thrust it into a chink of his cabin for future perusal. Some two years
later it was accidentally dislodged and he read it. It ran as follows:—

HURDY, June 6.

FRIEND JEFF: I've hit her hard in the boneyard. She's blind
and lousy. I'm on the divvy—that's me, and mum's my lay till
you toot. Yours,

BARNEY

P.S.—I've clayed her with Scarry.

With some knowledge of the general mining camp *argot* and of Mr.
Bree's private system for the communication of ideas Mr. Doman had
no difficulty in understanding by this uncommon epistle that Barney
while performing his duty as grave digger had uncovered a quartz
ledge with no outcroppings; that it was visibly rich in free gold; that,
moved by considerations of friendship, he was willing to accept Mr.
Doman as a partner and awaiting that gentleman's declaration of his
will in the matter would discreetly keep the discovery a secret. From
the postscript it was plainly inferable that in order to conceal the
treasure he had buried above it the mortal part of a person named
Scarry.

From subsequent events, as related to Mr. Doman at Red Dog, it
would appear that before taking this precaution Mr. Bree must have
had the thrift to remove a modest competency of the gold; at any rate,
it was at about that time that he entered upon that memorable series
of potations and treatings which is still one of the cherished traditions
of the San Juan Smith country, and is spoken of with respect as far
away as Ghost Rock and Lone Hand. At its conclusion some former

citizens of Hurdy-Gurdy, for whom he had performed the last kindly office at the cemetery, made room for him among them, and he rested well.

## IV

Having finished staking off his claim Mr. Doman walked back to the centre of it and stood again at the spot where his search among the graves had expired in the exclamation, "Scarry." He bent again over the headboard that bore that name and as if to reinforce the senses of sight and hearing ran his forefinger along the rudely carved letters. Re-erecting himself he appended orally to the simple inscription the shockingly forthright epitaph, "She was a holy terror!"

Had Mr. Doman been required to make these words good with proof—as, considering their somewhat censorious character, he doubtless should have been—he would have found himself embarrassed by the absence of reputable witnesses, and hearsay evidence would have been the best he could command. At the time when Scarry had been prevalent in the mining camps thereabout—when, as the editor of the *Hurdy Herald* would have phrased it, she was "in the plenitude of her power"—Mr. Doman's fortunes had been at a low ebb, and he had led the vagrantly laborious life of a prospector. His time had been mostly spent in the mountains, now with one companion, now with another. It was from the admiring recitals of these casual partners, fresh from the various camps, that his judgment of Scarry had been made up; he himself had never had the doubtful advantage of her acquaintance and the precarious distinction of her favor. And when, finally, on the termination of her perverse career at Hurdy-Gurdy he had read in a chance copy of the *Herald* her column-long obituary (written by the local humorist of that lively sheet in the highest style of his art) Doman had paid to her memory and to her historiographer's genius the tribute of a smile and chivalrously forgotten her. Standing now at the grave-side of this mountain Messalina he recalled the leading events of her turbulent career, as he had heard them celebrated at his several camp-fires, and perhaps with an unconscious attempt at self-justification repeated that she was a holy terror, and sank his pick into her grave up to the handle. At that moment a raven, which had silently settled upon a branch of the blasted tree above his head, solemnly snapped its beak and uttered its mind about the matter with an approving croak.

Pursuing his discovery of free gold with great zeal, which he probably credited to his conscience as a grave digger, Mr. Barney Bree had made an unusually deep sepulcher, and it was near sunset before

Mr. Doman, laboring with the leisurely deliberation of one who has "a dead sure thing" and no fear of an adverse claimant's enforcement of a prior right, reached the coffin and uncovered it. When he had done so he was confronted by a difficulty for which he had made no provision; the coffin—a mere flat shell of not very well-preserved redwood boards, apparently—had no handles, and it filled the entire bottom of the excavation. The best he could do without violating the decent sanctities of the situation was to make the excavation sufficiently longer to enable him to stand at the head of the casket and getting his powerful hands underneath erect it upon its narrower end; and this he proceeded to do. The approach of night quickened his efforts. He had no thought of abandoning his task at this stage to resume it on the morrow under more advantageous conditions. The feverish stimulation of cupidity and the fascination of terror held him to his dismal work with an iron authority. He no longer idled, but wrought with a terrible zeal. His head uncovered, his outer garments discarded, his shirt opened at the neck and thrown back from his breast, down which ran sinuous rills of perspiration, this hardy and impenitent gold-getter and grave-robber toiled with a giant energy that almost dignified the character of his horrible purpose; and when the sun fringes had burned themselves out along the crest line of the western hills, and the full moon had climbed out of the shadows that lay along the purple plain, he had erected the coffin upon its foot, where it stood propped against the end of the open grave. Then, standing up to his neck in the earth at the opposite extreme of the excavation, as he looked at the coffin upon which the moonlight now fell with a full illumination he was thrilled with a sudden terror to observe upon it the startling apparition of a dark human head—the shadow of his own. For a moment this simple and natural circumstance unnerved him. The noise of his labored breathing frightened him, and he tried to still it, but his bursting lungs would not be denied. Then, laughing half-audibly and wholly without spirit, he began making movements of his head from side to side, in order to compel the apparition to repeat them. He found a comforting reassurance in asserting his command over his own shadow. He was temporizing, making, with unconscious prudence, a dilatory opposition to an impending catastrophe. He felt that invisible forces of evil were closing in upon him, and he parleyed for time with the Inevitable.

He now observed in succession several unusual circumstances. The surface of the coffin upon which his eyes were fastened was not flat; it presented two distinct ridges, one longitudinal and the other transverse. Where these intersected at the widest part there was a corroded metallic plate that reflected the moonlight with a dismal lustre.

Along the outer edges of the coffin, at long intervals, were rust-eaten heads of nails. This frail product of the carpenter's art had been put into the grave the wrong side up!

Perhaps it was one of the humors of the camp—a practical manifestation of the facetious spirit that had found literary expression in the topsy-turvy obituary notice from the pen of Hurdy-Gurdy's great humorist. Perhaps it had some occult personal signification impenetrable to understandings uninstructed in local traditions. A more charitable hypothesis is that it was owing to a misadventure on the part of Mr. Barney Bree, who, making the interment unassisted (either by choice for the conservation of his golden secret, or through public apathy), had committed a blunder which he was afterward unable or unconcerned to rectify. However it had come about, poor Scarry had indubitably been put into the earth face downward.

When terror and absurdity make alliance, the effect is frightful. This strong-hearted and daring man, this hardy night worker among the dead, this defiant antagonist of darkness and desolation, succumbed to a ridiculous surprise. He was smitten with a thrilling chill —shivered, and shook his massive shoulders as if to throw off an icy hand. He no longer breathed, and the blood in his veins, unable to abate its impetus, surged hotly beneath his cold skin. Unleavened with oxygen, it mounted to his head and congested his brain. His physical functions had gone over to the enemy; his very heart was arrayed against him. He did not move; he could not have cried out. He needed but a coffin to be dead—as dead as the death that confronted him with only the length of an open grave and the thickness of a rotting plank between.

Then, one by one, his senses returned; the tide of terror that had overwhelmed his faculties began to recede. But with the return of his senses he became singularly unconscious of the object of his fear. He saw the moonlight gilding the coffin, but no longer the coffin that it gilded. Raising his eyes and turning his head, he noted, curiously and with surprise, the black branches of the dead tree, and tried to estimate the length of the weather-worn rope that dangled from its ghostly hand. The monotonous barking of distant coyotes affected him as something he had heard years ago in a dream. An owl flapped awkwardly above him on noiseless wings, and he tried to forecast the direction of its flight when it should encounter the cliff that reared its illuminated front a mile away. His hearing took account of a gopher's stealthy tread in the shadow of the cactus. He was intensely observant; his senses were all alert; but he saw not the coffin. As one can gaze at the sun until it looks black and then vanishes, so his mind, having exhausted its capacities of dread, was no longer conscious of the separate existence of anything dreadful. The Assassin was cloaking the sword.

It was during this lull in the battle that he became sensible of a faint, sickening odor. At first he thought it was that of a rattlesnake, and involuntarily tried to look about his feet. They were nearly invisible in the gloom of the grave. A hoarse, gurgling sound, like the death-rattle in a human throat, seemed to come out of the sky, and a moment later a great, black, angular shadow, like the same sound made visible, dropped curving from the topmost branch of the spectral tree, fluttered for an instant before his face and sailed fiercely away into the mist along the creek. It was the raven. The incident recalled him to a sense of the situation, and again his eyes sought the upright coffin, now illuminated by the moon for half its length. He saw the gleam of the metallic plate and tried without moving to decipher the inscription. Then he fell to speculating upon what was behind it. His creative imagination presented him a vivid picture. The planks no longer seemed an obstacle to his vision and he saw the livid corpse of the dead woman, standing in grave-clothes, and staring vacantly at him, with lidless, shrunken eyes. The lower jaw was fallen, the upper lip drawn away from the uncovered teeth. He could make out a mottled pattern on the hollow cheeks—the maculations of decay. By some mysterious process his mind reverted for the first time that day to the photograph of Mary Matthews. He contrasted its blonde beauty with the forbidding aspect of this dead face—the most beloved object that he knew with the most hideous that he could conceive.

The Assassin now advanced and displaying the blade laid it against the victim's throat. That is to say, the man became at first dimly, then definitely, aware of an impressive coincidence—a relation—a parallel between the face on the card and the name on the headboard. The one was disfigured, the other described a disfiguration. The thought took hold of him and shook him. It transformed the face that his imagination had created behind the coffin lid; the contrast became a resemblance; the resemblance grew to identity. Remembering the many descriptions of Scarry's personal appearance that he had heard from the gossips of his camp-fire he tried with imperfect success to recall the exact nature of the disfiguration that had given the woman her ugly name; and what was lacking in his memory fancy supplied, stamping it with the validity of conviction. In the maddening attempt to recall such scraps of the woman's history as he had heard, the muscles of his arms and hands were strained to a painful tension, as by an effort to lift a great weight. His body writhed and twisted with the exertion. The tendons of his neck stood out as tense as whip-cords, and his breath came in short, sharp gasps. The catastrophe could not be much longer delayed, or the agony of anticipation would leave nothing to be done by the *coup de grâce* of verification. The scarred face behind the lid would slay him through the wood.

A movement of the coffin diverted his thought. It came forward to within a foot of his face, growing visibly larger as it approached. The rusted metallic plate, with an inscription illegible in the moonlight, looked him steadily in the eye. Determined not to shrink, he tried to brace his shoulders more firmly against the end of the excavation, and nearly fell backward in the attempt. There was nothing to support him; he had unconsciously moved upon his enemy, clutching the heavy knife that he had drawn from his belt. The coffin had not advanced and he smiled to think it could not retreat. Lifting his knife he struck the heavy hilt against the metal plate with all his power. There was a sharp, ringing percussion, and with a dull clatter the whole decayed coffin lid broke in pieces and came away, falling about his feet. The quick and the dead were face to face—the frenzied, shrieking man— the woman standing tranquil in her silences. She was a holy terror!

## V

Some months later a party of men and women belonging to the highest social circles of San Francisco passed through Hurdy-Gurdy on their way to the Yosemite Valley by a new trail. They halted for dinner and during its preparation explored the desolate camp. One of the party had been at Hurdy-Gurdy in the days of its glory. He had, indeed, been one of its prominent citizens; and it used to be said that more money passed over his faro table in any one night than over those of all his competitors in a week; but being now a millionaire engaged in greater enterprises, he did not deem these early successes of sufficient importance to merit the distinction of remark. His invalid wife, a lady famous in San Francisco for the costly nature of her entertainments and her exacting rigor with regard to the social position and "antecedents" of those who attended them, accompanied the expedition. During a stroll among the shanties of the abandoned camp Mr. Porfer directed the attention of his wife and friends to a dead tree on a low hill beyond Injun Creek.

"As I told you," he said, "I passed through this camp in 1852, and was told that no fewer than five men had been hanged here by vigilantes at different times, and all on that tree. If I am not mistaken, a rope is dangling from it yet. Let us go over and see the place."

Mr. Porfer did not add that the rope in question was perhaps the very one from whose fatal embrace his own neck had once had an escape so narrow that an hour's delay in taking himself out of that region would have spanned it.

Proceeding leisurely down the creek to a convenient crossing, the party came upon the cleanly picked skeleton of an animal which Mr. Porfer after due examination pronounced to be that of an ass. The distinguishing ears were gone, but much of the inedible head had been spared by the beasts and birds, and the stout bridle of horsehair was intact, as was the riata, of similar material, connecting it with a picket pin still firmly sunken in the earth. The wooden and metallic elements of a miner's kit lay near by. The customary remarks were made, cynical on the part of the men, sentimental and refined by the lady. A little later they stood by the tree in the cemetery and Mr. Porfer sufficiently unbent from his dignity to place himself beneath the rotten rope and confidently lay a coil of it about his neck, somewhat, it appeared, to his own satisfaction, but greatly to the horror of his wife, to whose sensibilities the performance gave a smart shock.

An exclamation from one of the party gathered them all about an open grave, at the bottom of which they saw a confused mass of human bones and the broken remnants of a coffin. Coyotes and buzzards had performed the last sad rites for pretty much all else. Two skulls were visible and in order to investigate this somewhat unusual redundancy one of the younger men had the hardihood to spring into the grave and hand them up to another before Mrs. Porfer could indicate her marked disapproval of so shocking an act, which, nevertheless, she did with considerable feeling and in very choice words. Pursuing his search among the dismal débris at the bottom of the grave the young man next handed up a rusted coffin plate, with a rudely cut inscription, which with difficulty Mr. Porfer deciphered and read aloud with an earnest and not altogether unsuccessful attempt at the dramatic effect which he deemed befitting to the occasion and his rhetorical abilities:

MANUELITA MURPHY.
Born at the Mission San Pedro—Died in
Hurdy-Gurdy,
Aged 47.
Hell's full of such.

In deference to the piety of the reader and the nerves of Mrs. Porfer's fastidious sisterhood of both sexes let us not touch upon the painful impression produced by this uncommon inscription, further than to say that the elocutionary powers of Mr. Porfer had never before met with so spontaneous and overwhelming recognition.

The next morsel that rewarded the ghoul in the grave was a long tangle of black hair defiled with clay: but this was such an anti-climax that it received little attention. Suddenly, with a short exclamation and a gesture of excitement, the young man unearthed a fragment of grayish rock, and after a hurried inspection handed it up to Mr. Porfer. As the sunlight fell upon it it glittered with a yellow luster—it was thickly studded with gleaming points. Mr. Porfer snatched it, bent his head over it a moment and threw it lightly away with the simple remark:

"Iron pyrites—fool's gold."

The young man in the discovery shaft was a trifle disconcerted, apparently.

Meanwhile, Mrs. Porfer, unable longer to endure the disagreeable business, had walked back to the tree and seated herself at its root. While rearranging a tress of golden hair which had slipped from its confinement she was attracted by what appeared to be and really was the fragment of an old coat. Looking about to assure herself that so unladylike an act was not observed, she thrust her jeweled hand into the exposed breast pocket and drew out a mouldy pocket-book. Its contents were as follows:

One bundle of letters, postmarked "Elizabethtown, New Jersey."

One circle of blonde hair tied with a ribbon.

One photograph of a beautiful girl.

One ditto of same, singularly disfigured.

One name on back of photograph—"Jefferson Doman."

A few moments later a group of anxious gentlemen surrounded Mrs. Porfer as she sat motionless at the foot of the tree, her head dropped forward, her fingers clutching a crushed photograph. Her husband raised her head, exposing a face ghastly white, except the long, deforming cicatrice, familiar to all her friends, which no art could ever hide, and which now traversed the pallor of her countenance like a visible curse.

Mary Matthews Porfer had the bad luck to be dead.

# The Secret of
# Macarger's Gulch

Northwestwardly from Indian Hill, about nine miles as the crow flies, is Macarger's Gulch. It is not much of a gulch—a mere depression between two wooded ridges of inconsiderable height. From its mouth up to its head—for gulches, like rivers, have an anatomy of their own—the distance does not exceed two miles, and the width at bottom is at only one place more than a dozen yards; for most of the distance on either side of the little brook which drains it in winter, and goes dry in the early spring, there is no level ground at all; the steep slopes of the hills, covered with an almost impenetrable growth of manzanita and chemisal, are parted by nothing but the width of the water course. No one but an occasional enterprising hunter of the vicinity ever goes into Macarger's Gulch, and five miles away it is unknown, even by name. Within that distance in any direction are far more conspicuous topographical features without names, and one might try in vain to ascertain by local inquiry the origin of the name of this one.

About midway between the head and the mouth of Macarger's Gulch, the hill on the right as you ascend is cloven by another gulch, a short dry one, and at the junction of the two is a level space of two or three acres, and there a few years ago stood an old board house containing one small room. How the component parts of the house, few and simple as they were, had been assembled at that almost inaccessible point is a problem in the solution of which there would be greater satisfaction than advantage. Possibly the creek bed is a reformed road. It is certain that the gulch was at one time pretty thoroughly prospected by miners, who must have had some means of getting in with at least pack animals carrying tools and supplies; their profits, apparently, were not such as would have justified any considerable outlay to connect Macarger's Gulch with any center of civilization enjoying the distinction of a sawmill. The house, however, was there, most of it. It lacked a door and a window frame, and the chimney of mud and stones had fallen into an unlovely heap, overgrown with rank weeds. Such humble furniture as there may once have been and much of the lower weatherboarding, had served as fuel in the camp fires of hunters; as had also, probably, the curbing of an old well, which at the time I write of existed in the form of a rather wide but not very deep depression near by.

One afternoon in the summer of 1874, I passed up Macarger's Gulch from the narrow valley into which it opens, by following the dry bed of the brook. I was quail-shooting and had made a bag of about a dozen birds by the time I had reached the house described, of whose existence I was until then unaware. After rather carelessly inspecting the ruin I resumed my sport, and having fairly good success prolonged it until near sunset, when it occurred to me that I was a long way from any human habitation—too far to reach one by nightfall. But in my game bag was food, and the old house would afford shelter, if shelter were needed on a warm and dewless night in the foothills of the Sierra Nevada, where one may sleep in comfort on the pine needles, without covering. I am fond of solitude and love the night, so my resolution to "camp out" was soon taken, and by the time that it was dark I had made my bed of boughs and grasses in a corner of the room and was roasting a quail at a fire that I had kindled on the hearth. The smoke escaped out of the ruined chimney, the light illuminated the room with a kindly glow, and as I ate my simple meal of plain bird and drank the remains of a bottle of red wine which had served me all the afternoon in place of the water, which the region did not supply, I experienced a sense of comfort which better fare and accommodations do not always give.

Nevertheless, there was something lacking. I had a sense of comfort, but not of security. I detected myself staring more frequently at the open doorway and blank window than I could find warrant for doing. Outside these apertures all was black, and I was unable to repress a certain feeling of apprehension as my fancy pictured the outer world and filled it with unfriendly entities, natural and supernatural—chief among which, in their respective classes, were the grizzly bear, which I knew was occasionally still seen in that region, and the ghost, which I had reason to think was not. Unfortunately, our feelings do not always respect the law of probabilities, and to me that evening, the possible and the impossible were equally disquieting.

Everyone who has had experience in the matter must have observed that one confronts the actual and imaginary perils of the night with far less apprehension in the open air than in a house with an open doorway. I felt this now as I lay on my leafy couch in a corner of the room next to the chimney and permitted my fire to die out. So strong became my sense of the presence of something malign and menacing in the place, that I found myself almost unable to withdraw my eyes from the opening, as in the deepening darkness it became more and more indistinct. And when the last little flame flickered and went out I grasped the shotgun which I had laid at my side and actually turned the muzzle in the direction of the now invisible entrance, my thumb on one of the hammers, ready to cock the piece, my breath suspended, my muscles rigid and tense. But later I laid down the weapon with a sense of shame and mortification. What did I fear, and why?—I, to whom the night had been

> *a more familiar face*
> *Than that of man—*

I, in whom that element of hereditary superstition from which none of us is altogether free had given to solitude and darkness and silence only a more alluring interest and charm! I was unable to comprehend my folly, and losing in the conjecture the thing conjectured of, I fell asleep. And then I dreamed.

I was in a great city in a foreign land—a city whose people were of my own race, with minor differences of speech and costume; yet precisely what these were I could not say; my sense of them was indistinct. The city was dominated by a great castle upon an overlooking height whose name I knew, but could not speak. I walked through many streets, some broad and straight with high, modern buildings, some narrow, gloomy, and tortuous, between the gables of quaint old houses whose overhanging stories, elaborately ornamented with carvings in wood and stone, almost met above my head.

I sought someone whom I had never seen, yet knew that I should recognize when found. My quest was not aimless and fortuitous; it had a definite method. I turned from one street into another without hesitation and threaded a maze of intricate passages, devoid of the fear of losing my way.

Presently I stopped before a low door in a plain stone house which might have been the dwelling of an artisan of the better sort, and without announcing myself, entered. The room, rather sparely furnished, and lighted by a single window with small diamond-shaped panes, had but two occupants; a man and a woman. They took no notice of my intrusion, a circumstance which, in the manner of dreams, appeared entirely natural. They were not conversing; they sat apart, unoccupied and sullen.

The woman was young and rather stout, with fine large eyes and a certain grave beauty; my memory of her expression is exceedingly vivid, but in dreams one does not observe the details of faces. About her shoulders was a plaid shawl. The man was older, dark, with an evil face made more forbidding by a long scar extending from near the left temple diagonally downward into the black mustache; though in my dreams it seemed rather to haunt the face as a thing apart—I can express it no otherwise—than to belong to it. The moment that I found the man and woman I knew them to be husband and wife.

What followed, I remember indistinctly; all was confused and inconsistent—made so, I think, by gleams of consciousness. It was as if two pictures, the scene of my dream, and my actual surroundings, had been blended, one overlying the other, until the former, gradually fading, disappeared, and I was broad awake in the deserted cabin, entirely and tranquilly conscious of my situation.

My foolish fear was gone, and opening my eyes I saw that my fire, not altogether burned out, had revived by the falling of a stick and was again lighting the room. I had probably slept only a few minutes, but my commonplace dream had somehow so strongly impressed me that I was no longer drowsy; and after a little while I rose, pushed the embers of my fire together, and lighting my pipe proceeded in a rather ludicrously methodical way to meditate upon my vision.

It would have puzzled me then to say in what respect it was worth attention. In the first moment of serious thought that I gave to the matter I recognized the city of my dream as Edinburgh, where I had never been; so if the dream was a memory it was a memory of pictures and description. The recognition somehow deeply impressed me; it was as if something in my mind insisted rebelliously against will and reason on the importance of all this. And that faculty, whatever it was, asserted also a control of my speech. "Surely," I said aloud, quite involuntarily, "the MacGregors must have come here from Edinburgh."

At the moment, neither the substance of this remark nor the fact of my making it, surprised me in the least; it seemed entirely natural that I should know the name of my dreamfolk and something of their history. But the absurdity of it all soon dawned upon me: I laughed aloud, knocked the ashes from my pipe and again stretched myself upon my bed of boughs and grass, where I lay staring absently into my failing fire, with no further thought of either my dream or my surroundings. Suddenly the single remaining flame crouched for a moment, then, springing upward, lifted itself clear of its embers and expired in air. The darkness was absolute.

At that instant—almost, it seemed, before the gleam of the blaze had faded from my eyes—there was a dull, dead sound, as of some heavy body falling upon the floor, which shook beneath me as I lay. I sprang to a sitting posture and groped at my side for my gun; my notion was that some wild beast had leaped in through the open window. While the flimsy structure was still shaking from the impact I heard the sound of blows, the scuffling of feet upon the floor, and then—it seemed to come from almost within reach of my hand, the sharp shrieking of a woman in mortal agony. So horrible a cry I had never heard nor conceived; it utterly unnerved me; I was conscious for a moment of nothing but my own terror! Fortunately my hand now found the weapon of which it was in search, and the familiar touch somewhat restored me. I leaped to my feet, straining my eyes to pierce the darkness. The violent sounds had ceased, but more terrible than these, I heard, at what seemed long intervals, the faint intermittent gasping of some living, dying thing!

As my eyes grew accustomed to the dim light of the coals in the fireplace, I saw first the shapes of the door and window, looking blacker than the black of the walls. Next, the distinction between wall and floor became discernible, and at last I was sensible to the form and full expanse of the floor from end to end and side to side. Nothing was visible and the silence was unbroken.

With a hand that shook a little, the other still grasping my gun, I restored my fire and made a critical examination of the place. There was nowhere any sign that the cabin had been entered. My own tracks were visible in the dust covering the floor, but there were no others. I relit my pipe, provided fresh fuel by ripping a thin board or two from the inside of the house—I did not care to go into the darkness out of doors—and passed the rest of the night smoking and thinking, and feeding my fire; not for added years of life would I have permitted that little flame to expire again.


Some years afterward I met in Sacramento a man named Morgan, to whom I had a note of introduction from a friend in San Francisco. Dining with him one evening at his home I observed various "trophies" upon the wall, indicating that he was fond of shooting. It turned out that he was, and in relating some of his feats he mentioned having been in the region of my adventure.

"Mr. Morgan," I asked abruptly, "do you know a place up there called Macarger's Gulch?"

"I have good reason to," he replied; "it was I who gave to the newspapers, last year, the accounts of the finding of the skeleton there."

I had not heard of it; the accounts had been published, it appeared, while I was absent in the East.

"By the way," said Morgan, "the name of the gulch is a corruption; it should have been called 'MacGregor's.' My dear," he added, speaking to his wife, "Mr. Elderson has upset his wine."

That was hardly accurate—I had simply dropped it, glass and all.

"There was an old shanty once in the gulch," Morgan resumed when the ruin wrought by my awkwardness had been repaired, "but just previously to my visit it had been blown down, or rather blown away, for its *débris* was scattered all about, the very floor being parted, plank from plank. Between two of the sleepers still in position I and my companion observed the remnant of a plaid shawl, and examining it found that it was wrapped about the shoulders of the body of a woman, of which but little remained besides the bones, partly covered with fragments of clothing, and brown dry skin. But we will spare Mrs. Morgan," he added with a smile. The lady had indeed exhibited signs of disgust rather than sympathy.

"It is necessary to say, however," he went on, "that the skull was fractured in several places, as by blows of some blunt instrument; and that instrument itself—a pick-handle, still stained with blood—lay under the boards near by."

Mr. Morgan turned to his wife. "Pardon me, my dear," he said with affected solemnity, "for mentioning these disagreeable particulars, the natural though regrettable incidents of a conjugal quarrel—resulting, doubtless, from the luckless wife's insubordination."

"I ought to be able to overlook it," the lady replied with composure; "you have so many times asked me to in those very words."

I thought he seemed rather glad to go on with his story.

"From these and other circumstances," he said, "the coroner's jury found that the deceased, Janet MacGregor, came to her death from blows inflicted by some person to the jury unknown; but it was added that the evidence pointed strongly to her husband, Thomas MacGregor, as the guilty person. But Thomas MacGregor has never been found nor heard of. It was learned that the couple came from Edinburgh, but not—my dear, do you not observe that Mr. Elderson's boneplate has water in it?"

I had deposited a chicken bone in my finger bowl.

"In a little cupboard I found a photograph of MacGregor, but it did not lead to his capture."

"Will you let me see it?" I said.

The picture showed a dark man with an evil face made more forbidding by a long scar extending from near the temple diagonally downward into the black mustache.

"By the way, Mr. Elderson," said my affable host, "may I know why you asked about 'Macarger's Gulch'?"

"I lost a mule near there once," I replied, "and the mischance has—has quite—upset me."

"My dear," said Mr. Morgan, with the mechanical intonation of an interpreter translating, "the loss of Mr. Elderson's mule has peppered his coffee."

# The Night-Doings at "Deadman's"

## A Story That Is Untrue

It was a singularly sharp night, and clear as the heart of a diamond. Clear nights have a trick of being keen. In darkness you may be cold and not know it; when you see, you suffer. This night was bright enough to bite like a serpent. The moon was moving mysteriously along behind the giant pines crowning the South Mountain, striking a cold sparkle from the crusted snow, and bringing out against the black west the ghostly outlines of the Coast Range, beyond which lay the invisible Pacific. The snow had piled itself, in the open spaces along the bottom of the gulch, into long ridges that seemed to heave, and into hills that appeared to toss and scatter spray. The spray was sunlight, twice reflected: dashed once from the moon, once from the snow.

In this snow many of the shanties of the abandoned mining camp were obliterated (a sailor might have said they had gone down), and at irregular intervals it had overtopped the tall trestles which had once supported a river called a flume; for, of course, "flume" is *flumen*. Among the advantages of which the mountains cannot deprive the gold-hunter is the privilege of speaking Latin. He says of his dead neighbor, "He has gone up the flume." This is not a bad way to say, "His life has returned to the Fountain of Life."

While putting on its armor against the assaults of the wind, this snow had neglected no coign of vantage. Snow pursued by the wind is not wholly unlike a retreating army. In the open field it ranges itself in ranks and battalions; where it can get a foothold it makes a stand; where it can take cover it does so. You may see whole platoons of snow cowering behind a bit of broken wall. The devious old road, hewn out of the mountain-side, was full of it. Squadron upon squadron had struggled to escape by this line, when suddenly pursuit had ceased. A more desolate and dreary spot than Deadman's Gulch in a winter midnight it is impossible to imagine. Yet Mr. Hiram Beeson elected to live there, the sole inhabitant.

Away up the side of the North Mountain his little pine-log shanty projected from its single pane of glass a long, thin beam of light, and looked not altogether unlike a black beetle fastened to the hillside with a bright new pin. Within it sat Mr. Beeson himself, before a roaring fire, staring into its hot heart as if he had never before seen such a thing in all his life. He was not a comely man. He was gray; he was ragged and slovenly in his attire; his face was wan and haggard; his eyes were too bright. As to his age, if one had attempted to guess it, one might have said forty-seven, then corrected himself and said seventy-four. He was really twenty-eight. Emaciated he was; as much, perhaps, as he dared be, with a needy undertaker at Bentley's Flat and a new and enterprising coroner at Sonora. Poverty and zeal are an upper and a nether millstone. It is dangerous to make a third in that kind of sandwich.

As Mr. Beeson sat there, with his ragged elbows on his ragged knees, his lean jaws buried in his lean hands, and with no apparent intention of going to bed, he looked as if the slightest movement would tumble him to pieces. Yet during the last hour he had winked no fewer than three times.

There was a sharp rapping at the door. A rap at that time of night and in that weather might have surprised an ordinary mortal who had dwelt two years in the gulch without seeing a human face, and could not fail to know that the country was impassable; but Mr. Beeson did not so much as pull his eyes out of the coals. And even when the door was pushed open he only shrugged a little more closely into himself, as one does who is expecting something that he would rather not see. You may observe this movement in women when, in a mortuary chapel, the coffin is borne up the aisle behind them.

But when a long old man in a blanket overcoat, his head tied up in a handkerchief and nearly his entire face in a muffler, wearing green goggles and with a complexion of glittering whiteness where it could be seen, strode silently into the room, laying a hard, gloved hand on Mr. Beeson's shoulder, the latter so far forgot himself as to look up with an appearance of no small astonishment; whomever he may have been expecting, he had evidently not counted on meeting anyone like this. Nevertheless, the sight of this unexpected guest produced in Mr. Beeson the following sequence: a feeling of astonishment; a sense of gratification; a sentiment of profound good will. Rising from his seat, he took the knotty hand from his shoulder, and shook it up and down with a fervor quite unaccountable; for in the old man's aspect was

nothing to attract, much to repel. However, attraction is too general
a property for repulsion to be without it. The most attractive object
in the world is the face we instinctively cover with a cloth. When it
becomes still more attractive—fascinating—we put seven feet of
earth above it.

"Sir," said Mr. Beeson, releasing the old man's hand, which fell
passively against his thigh with a quiet clack, "it is an extremely disagreeable night. Pray be seated; I am very glad to see you."

Mr. Beeson spoke with an easy good breeding that one would
hardly have expected, considering all things. Indeed, the contrast between his appearance and his manner was sufficiently surprising to
be one of the commonest of social phenomena in the mines. The old
man advanced a step toward the fire, glowing cavernously in the green
goggles. Mr. Beeson resumed:

"You bet your life I am!"

Mr. Beeson's elegance was not too refined; it had made reasonable
concessions to local taste. He paused a moment, letting his eyes drop
from the muffled head of his guest, down along the row of moldy
buttons confining the blanket overcoat, to the greenish cowhide boots
powdered with snow, which had begun to melt and run along the floor
in little rills. He took an inventory of his guest, and appeared satisfied.
Who would not have been? Then he continued:

"The cheer I can offer you is, unfortunately, in keeping with my
surroundings; but I shall esteem myself highly favored if it is your
pleasure to partake of it, rather than seek better at Bentley's Flat."

With a singular refinement of hospitable humility Mr. Beeson
spoke as if a sojourn in his warm cabin on such a night, as compared
with walking fourteen miles up to the throat in snow with a cutting
crust, would be an intolerable hardship. By way of reply, his guest
unbuttoned the blanket overcoat. The host laid fresh fuel on the fire,
swept the hearth with the tail of a wolf, and added:

"But *I* think you'd better skedaddle."

The old man took a seat by the fire, spreading his broad soles to
the heat without removing his hat. In the mines the hat is seldom
removed except when the boots are. Without further remark Mr. Beeson also seated himself in a chair which had been a barrel, and which,
retaining much of its original character, seemed to have been designed
with a view to preserving his dust if it should please him to crumble.
For a moment there was silence; then, from somewhere among the
pines, came the snarling yelp of a coyote; and simultaneously the door
rattled in its frame. There was no other connection between the two
incidents than that the coyote has an aversion to storms, and the wind
was rising; yet there seemed somehow a kind of supernatural con-

spiracy between the two, and Mr. Beeson shuddered with a vague sense of terror. He recovered himself in a moment and again addressed his guest.

"There are strange doings here. I will tell you everything, and then if you decide to go I shall hope to accompany you over the worst of the way; as far as where Baldy Peterson shot Ben Hike—I dare say you know the place."

The old man nodded emphatically, as intimating not merely that he did, but that he did indeed.

"Two years ago," began Mr. Beeson, "I, with two companions, occupied this house; but when the rush to the Flat occurred we left, along with the rest. In ten hours the Gulch was deserted. That evening, however, I discovered I had left behind me a valuable pistol (that is it) and returned for it, passing the night here alone, as I have passed every night since. I must explain that a few days before we left, our Chinese domestic had the misfortune to die while the ground was frozen so hard that it was impossible to dig a grave in the usual way. So, on the day of our hasty departure, we cut through the floor there, and gave him such burial as we could. But before putting him down I had the extremely bad taste to cut off his pigtail and spike it to that beam above his grave, where you may see it at this moment, or, preferably, when warmth has given you leisure for observation.

"I stated, did I not, that the Chinaman came to his death from natural causes? I had, of course, nothing to do with that, and returned through no irresistible attraction, or morbid fascination, but only because I had forgotten a pistol. This is clear to you, is it not, sir?"

The visitor nodded gravely. He appeared to be a man of few words, if any. Mr. Beeson continued:

"According to the Chinese faith, a man is like a kite: he cannot go to heaven without a tail. Well, to shorten this tedious story—which, however, I thought it my duty to relate—on that night, while I was here alone and thinking of anything but him, that Chinaman came back for his pigtail.

"He did not get it."

At this point Mr. Beeson relapsed into blank silence. Perhaps he was fatigued by the unwonted exercise of speaking; perhaps he had conjured up a memory that demanded his undivided attention. The wind was now fairly abroad, and the pines along the mountain-side sang with singular distinctness. The narrator continued:

"You say you do not see much in that, and I must confess I do not myself.

"But he keeps coming!"

There was another long silence, during which both stared into the fire without the movement of a limb. Then Mr. Beeson broke out, almost fiercely, fixing his eyes on what he could see of the impassive face of his auditor:

"Give it him? Sir, in this matter I have no intention of troubling anyone for advice. You will pardon me, I am sure"—here he became singularly persuasive—"but I have ventured to nail that pigtail fast, and have assumed the somewhat onerous obligation of guarding it. So it is quite impossible to act on your considerate suggestion.

"Do you play me for a Modoc?"

Nothing could exceed the sudden ferocity with which he thrust this indignant remonstrance into the ear of his guest. It was as if he had struck him on the side of the head with a steel gauntlet. It was a protest, but it was a challenge. To be mistaken for a coward—to be played for a Modoc: these two expressions are one. Sometimes it is a Chinaman. Do you play me for a Chinaman? is a question frequently addressed to the ear of the suddenly dead.

Mr. Beeson's buffet produced no effect, and after a moment's pause, during which the wind thundered in the chimney like the sound of clods upon a coffin, he resumed:

"But, as you say, it is wearing me out. I feel that the life of the last two years has been a mistake—a mistake that corrects itself; you see how. The grave! No; there is no one to dig it. The ground is frozen, too. But you are very welcome. You may say at Bentley's—but that is not important. It was very tough to cut: they braid silk into their pigtails. Kwaagh."

Mr. Beeson was speaking with his eyes shut, and he wandered. His last word was a snore. A moment later he drew a long breath, opened his eyes with an effort, made a single remark, and fell into a deep sleep. What he said was this:

"They are swiping my dust!"

Then the aged stranger, who had not uttered one word since his arrival, arose from his seat and deliberately laid off his outer clothing, looking as angular in his flannels as the late Signorina Festorazzi, an Irish woman, six feet in height, and weighing fifty-six pounds, who used to exhibit herself in her chemise to the people of San Francisco. He then crept into one of the "bunks," having first placed a revolver in easy reach, according to the custom of the country. This revolver he took from a shelf, and it was the one which Mr. Beeson had mentioned as that for which he had returned to the Gulch two years before.

In a few moments Mr. Beeson awoke, and seeing that his guest had retired he did likewise. But before doing so he approached the long, plaited wisp of pagan hair and gave it a powerful tug, to assure himself that it was fast and firm. The two beds—mere shelves covered with blankets not overclean—faced each other from opposite sides of the room, the little square trapdoor that had given access to the Chinaman's grave being midway between. This, by the way, was crossed by a double row of spike-heads. In his resistance to the supernatural, Mr. Beeson had not disdained the use of material precautions.

The fire was now low, the flames burning bluely and petulantly, with occasional flashes, projecting spectral shadows on the walls— shadows that moved mysteriously about, now dividing, now uniting. The shadow of the pendent queue, however, kept moodily apart, near the roof at the further end of the room, looking like a note of admiration. The song of the pines outside had now risen to the dignity of a triumphal hymn. In the pauses the silence was dreadful.

It was during one of these intervals that the trap in the floor began to lift. Slowly and steadily it rose, and slowly and steadily rose the swaddled head of the old man in the bunk to observe it. Then, with a clap that shook the house to its foundation, it was thrown clean back, where it lay with its unsightly spikes pointing threateningly upward. Mr. Beeson awoke, and without rising, pressed his fingers into his eyes. He shuddered; his teeth chattered. His guest was now reclining on one elbow, watching the proceedings with the goggles that glowed like lamps.

Suddenly a howling gust of wind swooped down the chimney, scattering ashes and smoke in all directions, for a moment obscuring everything. When the firelight again illuminated the room there was seen, sitting gingerly on the edge of a stool by the hearthside, a swarthy little man of prepossessing appearance and dressed with faultless taste, nodding to the old man with a friendly and engaging smile. "From San Francisco, evidently," thought Mr. Beeson, who having somewhat recovered from his fright was groping his way to a solution of the evening's events.

But now another actor appeared upon the scene. Out of the square black hole in the middle of the floor protruded the head of the departed Chinaman, his glassy eyes turned upward in their angular slits and fastened on the dangling queue above with a look of yearning unspeakable. Mr. Beeson groaned, and again spread his hands upon his face. A mild odor of opium pervaded the place. The phantom, clad only in a short blue tunic quilted and silken but covered with grave-mold, rose slowly, as if pushed by a weak spiral spring. Its knees were at the level of the floor, when with a quick upward impulse like the silent leaping of a flame it grasped the queue with both hands, drew up its body and took the tip in its horrible yellow teeth. To this it clung in a seeming frenzy, grimacing ghastly, surging and plunging from side to side in its efforts to disengage its property from the beam, but uttering no sound. It was like a corpse artificially convulsed by means of a galvanic battery. The contrast between its superhuman activity and its silence was no less than hideous!

Mr. Beeson cowered in his bed. The swarthy little gentleman uncrossed his legs, beat an impatient tattoo with the toe of his boot and consulted a heavy gold watch. The old man sat erect and quietly laid hold of the revolver.

Bang!

Like a body cut from the gallows the Chinaman plumped into the black hole below, carrying his tail in his teeth. The trapdoor turned over, shutting down with a snap. The swarthy little gentleman from San Francisco sprang nimbly from his perch, caught something in the air with his hat, as a boy catches a butterfly, and vanished into the chimney as if drawn up by suction.

From away somewhere in the outer darkness floated in through the open door a faint, far cry—a long, sobbing wail, as of a child death-strangled in the desert, or a lost soul borne away by the Adversary. It may have been the coyote.

In the early days of the following spring a party of miners on their way to new diggings passed along the Gulch, and straying through the deserted shanties found in one of them the body of Hiram Beeson, stretched upon a bunk, with a bullet hole through the heart. The ball had evidently been fired from the opposite side of the room, for in one of the oaken beams overhead was a shallow blue dint, where it had struck a knot and been deflected downward to the breast of its victim. Strongly attached to the same beam was what appeared to be an end of a rope of braided horsehair, which had been cut by the bullet in its passage to the knot. Nothing else of interest was noted, excepting a suit of moldy and incongruous clothing, several articles of which were afterward identified by respectable witnesses as those in which certain deceased citizens of Deadman's had been buried years before. But it is not easy to understand how that could be, unless, indeed, the garments had been worn as a disguise by Death himself—which is hardly credible.

# The Stranger

A man stepped out of the darkness into the little illuminated circle about our failing campfire and seated himself upon a rock.

"You are not the first to explore this region," he said, gravely.

Nobody controverted his statement; he was himself proof of its truth, for he was not of our party and must have been somewhere near when we camped. Moreover, he must have companions not far away; it was not a place where one would be living or traveling alone. For more than a week we had seen, besides ourselves and our animals, only such living things as rattlesnakes and horned toads. In an Arizona desert one does not long coexist with only such creatures as these: one must have pack animals, supplies, arms—"an outfit." And all these imply comrades. It was perhaps a doubt as to what manner of men this unceremonious stranger's comrades might be, together with something in his words interpretable as a challenge, that caused every man of our half-dozen "gentlemen adventurers" to rise to a sitting posture and lay his hand upon a weapon—an act signifying, in that time and place, a policy of expectation. The stranger gave the matter no attention and began again to speak in the same deliberate, uninflected monotone in which he had delivered his first sentence:

"Thirty years ago Ramon Gallegos, William Shaw, George W. Kent and Berry Davis, all of Tucson, crossed the Santa Catalina mountains and traveled due west, as nearly as the configuration of the country permitted. We were prospecting and it was our intention, if we found nothing, to push through to the Gila river at some point near Big Bend, where we understood there was a settlement. We had a good outfit but no guide—just Ramon Gallegos, William Shaw, George W. Kent and Berry Davis."

The man repeated the names slowly and distinctly, as if to fix them in the memories of his audience, every member of which was now attentively observing him, but with a slackened apprehension regarding his possible companions somewhere in the darkness that seemed to enclose us like a black wall; in the manner of this volunteer historian was no suggestion of an unfriendly purpose. His act was rather that of a harmless lunatic than an enemy. We were not so new to the country as not to know that the solitary life of many a plainsman had a tendency to develop eccentricities of conduct and character not always easily distinguishable from mental aberration. A man is like a tree: in a forest of his fellows he will grow as straight as his generic and individual nature permits; alone in the open, he yields to the deforming stresses and tortions that environ him. Some such thoughts were in my mind as I watched the man from the shadow of my hat, pulled low to shut out the firelight. A witless fellow, no doubt, but what could he be doing there in the heart of a desert?

Having undertaken to tell this story, I wish that I could describe the man's appearance; that would be a natural thing to do. Unfortunately, and somewhat strangely, I find myself unable to do so with any degree of confidence, for afterward no two of us agreed as to what he wore and how he looked; and when I try to set down my own impressions they elude me. Anyone can tell some kind of story; narration is one of the elemental powers of the race. But the talent for description is a gift.

Nobody having broken silence the visitor went on to say:

"This country was not then what it is now. There was not a ranch between the Gila and the Gulf. There was a little game here and there in the mountains, and near the infrequent water-holes grass enough to keep our animals from starvation. If we should be so fortunate as to encounter no Indians we might get through. But within a week the purpose of the expedition had altered from discovery of wealth to preservation of life. We had gone too far to go back, for what was ahead could be no worse than what was behind; so we pushed on, riding by night to avoid Indians and the intolerable heat, and concealing ourselves by day as best we could. Sometimes, having exhausted our supply of wild meat and emptied our casks, we were days without food or drink; then a water-hole or a shallow pool in the bottom of an *arroyo* so restored our strength and sanity that we were able to shoot some of the wild animals that sought it also. Sometimes it was a bear, sometimes an antelope, a coyote, a cougar—that was as God pleased; all were food.

"One morning as we skirted a mountain range, seeking a practicable pass, we were attacked by a band of Apaches who had followed our trail up a gulch—it is not far from here. Knowing that they out-

numbered us ten to one, they took none of their usual cowardly precautions, but dashed upon us at a gallop, firing and yelling. Fighting
was out of the question: we urged our feeble animals up the gulch as
far as there was footing for a hoof, then threw ourselves out of our
saddles and took to the *chaparral* on one of the slopes, abandoning
our entire outfit to the enemy. But we retained our rifles, every
man—Ramon Gallegos, William Shaw, George W. Kent and Berry
Davis."

"Same old crowd," said the humorist of our party. He was an Eastern man, unfamiliar with the decent observances of social intercourse.
A gesture of disapproval from our leader silenced him and the
stranger proceeded with his tale:

"The savages dismounted also, and some of them ran up the gulch
beyond the point at which we had left it, cutting off further retreat
in that direction and forcing us on up the side. Unfortunately the
*chaparral* extended only a short distance up the slope, and as we came
into the open ground above we took the fire of a dozen rifles; but
Apaches shoot badly when in a hurry, and God so willed it that none
of us fell. Twenty yards up the slope, beyond the edge of the brush,
were vertical cliffs, in which, directly in front of us, was a narrow
opening. Into that we ran, finding ourselves in a cavern about as large
as an ordinary room in a house. Here for a time we were safe: a single
man with a repeating rifle could defend the entrance against all the
Apaches in the land. But against hunger and thirst we had no defense.
Courage we still had, but hope was a memory.

"Not one of those Indians did we afterward see, but by the smoke
and glare of their fires in the gulch we knew that by day and by night
they watched with ready rifles in the edge of the bush—knew that if
we made a sortie not a man of us would live to take three steps into
the open. For three days, watching in turn, we held out before our
suffering became insupportable. Then—it was the morning of the
fourth day—Ramon Gallegos said:

" 'Señores, I know not well of the good God and what please him.
I have live without religion, and I am not acquaint with that of you.
Pardon, señores, if I shock you, but for me the time is come to beat
the game of the Apache.'

"He knelt upon the rock floor of the cave and pressed his pistol
against his temple. 'Madre de Dios,' he said, 'comes now the soul of
Ramon Gallegos.'

"And so he left us—William Shaw, George W. Kent and Berry
Davis.

"I was the leader: it was for me to speak.

" 'He was a brave man,' I said—'he knew when to die, and how. It is foolish to go mad from thirst and fall by Apache bullets, or be skinned alive—it is in bad taste. Let us join Ramon Gallegos.'

" 'That is right,' said William Shaw.

" 'That is right,' said George W. Kent.

"I straightened the limbs of Ramon Gallegos and put a handkerchief over his face. Then William Shaw said: 'I should like to look like that—a little while.'

"And George W. Kent said that he felt that way, too.

" 'It shall be so,' I said: 'the red devils will wait a week. William Shaw and George W. Kent, draw and kneel.'

"They did so and I stood before them.

" 'Almighty God, our Father,' said I.

" 'Almighty God, our Father,' said William Shaw.

" 'Almighty God, our Father,' said George W. Kent.

" 'Forgive us our sins,' said I.

" 'Forgive us our sins,' said they.

" 'And receive our souls.'

" 'And receive our souls.'

" 'Amen!'

" 'Amen!'

"I laid them beside Ramon Gallegos and covered their faces."

There was a quick commotion on the opposite side of the campfire: one of our party had sprung to his feet, pistol in hand.

"And you!" he shouted—"*you* dared to escape?—you dare to be alive? You cowardly hound, I'll send you to join them if I hang for it!"

But with the leap of a panther the captain was upon him, grasping his wrist. "Hold it in, Sam Yountsey, hold it in!"

We were now all upon our feet—except the stranger, who sat motionless and apparently inattentive. Some one seized Yountsey's other arm.

"Captain," I said, "there is something wrong here. This fellow is either a lunatic or merely a liar—just a plain, every-day liar whom Yountsey has no call to kill. If this man was of that party it had five members, one of whom—probably himself—he has not named."

"Yes," said the captain, releasing the insurgent, who sat down, "there is something—unusual. Years ago four dead bodies of white men, scalped and shamefully mutilated, were found about the mouth of that cave. They are buried there; I have seen the graves—we shall all see them to-morrow."

The stranger rose, standing tall in the light of the expiring fire, which in our breathless attention to his story we had neglected to keep going.

"There were four," he said—"Ramon Gallegos, William Shaw, George W. Kent and Berry Davis."

With this reiterated roll-call of the dead he walked into the darkness and we saw him no more.

At that moment one of our party, who had been on guard, strode in among us, rifle in hand and somewhat excited.

"Captain," he said, "for the last half-hour three men have been standing out there on the *mesa*." He pointed in the direction taken by the stranger. "I could see them distinctly, for the moon is up, but as they had no guns and I had them covered with mine I thought it was their move. They have made none, but, damn it! they have got on to my nerves."

"Go back to your post, and stay till you see them again," said the captain. "The rest of you lie down again, or I'll kick you all into the fire."

The sentinel obediently withdrew, swearing, and did not return. As we were arranging our blankets the fiery Yountsey said: "I beg your pardon, Captain, but who the devil do you take them to be?"

"Ramon Gallegos, William Shaw and George W. Kent."

"But how about Berry Davis? I ought to have shot him."

"Quite needless; you couldn't have made him any deader. Go to sleep."

# OWEN WISTER

## (1860–1938)

Born in Philadelphia to a physician father and a mother who was the
daughter of British actress Fanny Kemble and her planter-husband
Pierce Butler, Wister enjoyed a privileged and cultured childhood. He
was educated at exclusive private schools and at Harvard, where he
early demonstrated literary talent inherited from his mother, a published poet who kept a salon attended by notable writers of the day.
But Wister was ambitious to excel in music, and over his father's
objections, he spent two years in Paris studying piano and composing.
He was encouraged by Franz Liszt, and his interest in music would
be lifelong. Nevertheless, a combination of paternal pressure and his
own uncertainty resulted in Wister's return in 1884 to the United
States, where he obtained a clerkship in a Philadelphia bank vault.
He returned to writing fiction, but W. D. Howells, a friend of his
mother, advised him not to publish his first novel. This discourage-
ment helped bring on a "nervous" disorder. Seeking to restore his
health, Wister spent a summer on a ranch in Wyoming; thereafter, he
became a regular seasonal visitor to Wyoming. In the fall of 1885, he
entered Harvard Law School, and three years later was admitted to
the Philadelphia bar.
  Wister entered the practice of law, but it was not a satisfying career
for someone of his creative drives; another bout of mental illness sent
him on his fifth summer trip to Wyoming in 1891. Wister kept a diary
recording his experiences during these sojourns, and in 1891 he had
his first Western story, "Hank's Woman," published in Harper's
Weekly. This was shortly followed by his second, in Harper's Monthly,
"How Lin McLean Went East," which became the first of a series of
stories that would form Lin McLean (1898), a novel about a naïve
young cowboy and the troubles that befall him. (McLean figures also
in Hank's Woman, but would later be supplanted in that story by the

*Virginian.) These tales, and many that followed, were illustrated by
Frederic Remington, and the two men shared a long friendship. At
Harvard, Wister had been close with Theodore Roosevelt, and their
common Western interests strengthened that bond; Roosevelt encouraged Wister to become "the Kipling of the West." Through the influence
of his mother and grandmother, Wister became an intimate of many
talented persons, not the least of whom was Henry James, Jr., whose
ornate prose style would influence some of Wister's later stories. Despite his links with Remington and Roosevelt, Wister was an unlikely
celebrant of the cowboy.*

*In 1898, he married Mary Channing, of the Boston Unitarian
Channings, an ardent feminist and volunteer charity worker, and at
least in part the model for the heroine of Wister's most famous Western novel,* The Virginian *(1902). Like* Lin McLean, *Wister's second
cowboy novel was a composite of stories previously published in* Harper's Monthly—*others were gathered in collections like* Red Men and
White *(1895) and* The JimmyJohn Boss *(1900)—and the story has a
highly episodic quality with some resulting problems of narration.
But Wister's shrewd addition of a love story to an essentially masculine sequence of tales earned the book quick and enduring popularity; Henry James was apparently alone in his stated wish that the
Virginian had died young and unmarried. Wister's accomplishment
was nonetheless great, for he had lifted the cowboy out of the dime-
novel fiction of the day and transplanted him into a novel with considerable literary pretensions—as James also acknowledged.*

*Still, as a celebration of the cowboy, Wister's story was somewhat
lacking in specifics of bunkhouse and cattle-drive life. His Western
travels had put him in the company of ranch owners and cavalry
officers—the aristocracy of the frontier—and these associations not
only reinforced his deep-seated snobbery but cut him off from any
real contact with the cowboys and horse soldiers about whom he wrote.
Significantly, the model for the Virginian (if any one man qualified)
was Wister's cowboy guide on his many hunting trips, whose relationship to Wister was one of servant to master, not one of equals.
Wister's elitism is reflected in the Virginian himself, who rises from
cowhand to partnership with his former employer in the course of the
novel. Like Wister's much-admired George Washington, the Virginian
is a natural leader of men, courageous and decisive, who avoids hasty
action in favor of carefully planned strategies—as in his dealings
with a bunch of mutinous cowboys on a cattle train. As a foil to his
hero, Wister wove through the novel the misadventures of a foolish
cowboy called Shorty, an inept victim of other men's greed. Like Mark*

*Twain and Howells, Wister gave his fiction a strong moral basis, and his readers were somewhat scandalized to discover that the Virginian had had sexual experiences prior to his courtship of Molly Wood. Though Molly's influence (and some Indian arrows) brings him around, the heroic cowboy still does not surrender his male authority, but remains firmly in charge at novel's end.*

*Wister had capped his Western stories with* The Virginian, *and thereafter, ignoring appeals to continue in that vein, he turned his talents to attacks on aspects of "modern" America he disliked—including the influx of European immigrants, labor agitation, and the urging of civil rights for African-Americans. His most Jamesian concoction,* Lady Baltimore *(1906), was a celebration of the spirit of the old South as represented by life in Charleston, South Carolina, and contained such an explicit defense of the "color line," maintaining the "natural" inferiority of Negroes, that it caused Theodore Roosevelt to explode in epistolary (but private) anger, in startling contrast to the praise he had heaped on Wister's cowboy fiction. For the time, Wister abandoned the subject of race, but with the advent of the First World War, which closely followed the early death of his wife in 1913, he returned to the glories of the Anglo-Saxons, and, by contrast, the arrogant claims of Prussians to superiority, which Wister angrily refuted in* The Pentecost of Calamity *(1915). An elegantly handsome man, Wister had considerable public impact through his speeches and writings, but his politics became increasingly reactionary as he aged. Born on the eve of the Civil War, he lived to see the forces gathering that would erupt as the Second World War, but the currents of change left him stranded, rather much like Kipling, whose stories of empire Wister admired and attempted to emulate with his tales of the Far West.*

*Very little that he wrote after* The Virginian *has endured as literature, but that book was a sufficient accomplishment, and his hero was given further life through a series of motion picture versions, culminating in the one starring Gary Cooper, which Wister lived to see. In 1928, Wister published a final, valedictorian collection of western stories,* When West was West, *most notable perhaps for a tale about the degeneration of a cowboy who is a titled Englishman, "The Right Honorable the Strawberries," an apparent rejection of the myth of "Saxon" superiority and a recantation of his Anglophilia. It is of interest also that he warmly encouraged the talents of a young writer and admirer of his stories, Ernest Hemingway. In his final years, Wister—by that time a museum piece himself—served as a source of anecdotal information about literary friends long dead for the histo-*

*rian Van Wyck Brooks. He went to his grave an outraged opponent
of the policies of Franklin D. Roosevelt. If Wister was the man who
invented the literary cowboy, and he surely was, the paternity was
conservative to the core, nor has any notable attempt been made subsequently to alter the image—no more than any cowboy has been
depicted riding a cow.*

# Specimen Jones

Ephraim, the proprietor of Twenty Mile, had wasted his day in burying a man. He did not know the man. He had found him, or what the
Apaches had left of him, sprawled among some charred sticks just
outside the Cañon del Oro. It was a useful discovery in its way, for
otherwise Ephraim might have gone on hunting his strayed horses
near the cañon, and ended among charred sticks himself. Very likely
the Indians were far away by this time, but he returned to Twenty
Mile with the man tied to his saddle, and his pony nervously snorting.
And now the day was done, and the man lay in the earth, and they
had even built a fence around him; for the hole was pretty shallow,
and coyotes have a way of smelling this sort of thing a long way off
when they are hungry, and the man was not in a coffin. They were
always short of coffins in Arizona.

Day was done at Twenty Mile, and the customary activity prevailed inside that flat-roofed cube of mud. Sounds of singing, shooting,
dancing, and Mexican tunes on the concertina came out of the windows, to float and die among the hills. A limber, pretty boy, who might
be nineteen, was dancing energetically, while a grave old gentleman,
with tobacco running down his beard, pointed a pistol at the boy's
heels, and shot a hole in the earth now and then to show that the
weapon was really loaded. Everybody was quite used to all of this—
excepting the boy. He was an Eastern new-comer, passing his first
evening at a place of entertainment.

Night in and night out every guest at Twenty Mile was either
happy and full of whisky, or else his friends were making arrangements for his funeral. There was water at Twenty Mile—the only
water for twoscore of miles. Consequently it was an important station
on the road between the southern country and Old Camp Grant, and
the new mines north of the Mescal Range. The stunt, liquor-perfumed

adobe cabin lay on the gray floor of the desert like an isolated slab of chocolate. Near it a corral, two desolate stable-sheds, and the slowly turning windmill completed the establishment. Here Ephraim and one or two helpers abode, armed against Indians, and selling whisky. Variety in their vocation of drinking and killing was brought them by the travellers. These passed and passed through the glaring vacant months—some days only one ragged fortune-hunter, riding a pony; again by twos and threes, with high-loaded burros; and sometimes they came in companies, walking beside their clanking freight-wagons. Some were young, and some were old, and all drank whisky, and wore knives and guns to keep each other civil. Most of them were bound for the mines, and some of them were seen again. No man trusted the next man, and their names, when they had any, would be O'Rafferty, Angus, Schwartzmeyer, José Maria, and Smith. All stopped for one night; some longer, remaining drunk and profitable to Ephraim; now and then one stayed permanently, and had a fence built round him. Whoever came, and whatever befell them, Twenty Mile was chronically hilarious after sundown—a dot of riot in the dumb Arizona night.

On this particular evening they had a tenderfoot. The boy, being new in Arizona, still trusted his neighbor. Such people turned up occasionally. This one had paid for everybody's drink several times, because he felt friendly, and never noticed that nobody ever paid for his. They had played cards with him, stolen his spurs, and now they were making him dance. It was an ancient pastime; yet two or three were glad to stand round and watch it, because it was some time since they had been to the opera. Now the tenderfoot had misunderstood these friends at the beginning, supposing himself to be among good fellows, and they therefore naturally set him down as a fool. But even while dancing you may learn much, and suddenly. The boy, besides being limber, had good tough black hair, and it was not in fear, but with a cold blue eye, that he looked at the old gentleman. The trouble had been that his own revolver had somehow hitched, so he could not pull it from the holster at the necessary moment.

"Tried to draw on me, did yer?" said the old gentleman. "Step higher! Step, now, or I'll crack open yer kneepans, ye robin's egg."

"Thinks he's having a bad time," remarked Ephraim. "Wonder how he'd like to have been that man the Injuns had sport with?"

"Weren't his ear funny?" said one who had helped bury the man.

"Ear?" said Ephraim. "You boys ought to been along when I found him, and seen the way they'd fixed up his mouth." Ephraim explained the details simply, and the listeners shivered. But Ephraim was a humorist. "Wonder how it feels," he continued, "to have—"

Here the boy sickened at his comments and the loud laughter. Yet a few hours earlier these same half-drunken jesters had laid the man to rest with decent humanity. The boy was taking his first dose of Arizona. By no means was everybody looking at his jig. They had seen tenderfeet so often. There was a Mexican game of cards; there was a concertina; and over in the corner sat Specimen Jones, with his back to the company, singing to himself. Nothing had been said or done that entertained him in the least. He had seen everything quite often.

"Higher! skip higher, you elegant calf," remarked the old gentleman to the tenderfoot. "High-yer!" And he placidly fired a fourth shot that scraped the boy's boot at the ankle and threw earth over the clock, so that you could not tell the minute from the hour hand.

" 'Drink to me only with thine eyes,' " sang Specimen Jones, softly. They did not care much for his songs in Arizona. These lyrics were all, or nearly all, that he retained of the days when he was twenty, although he was but twenty-six now.

The boy was cutting pigeon-wings, the concertina played "Matamoras," Jones continued his lyric, when two Mexicans leaped at each other, and the concertina stopped with a quack.

"Quit it!" said Ephraim from behind the bar, covering the two with his weapon. "I don't want any greasers scrapping round here to-night. We've just got cleaned up."

It had been cards, but the Mexicans made peace, to the regret of Specimen Jones. He had looked round with some hopes of a crisis, and now for the first time he noticed the boy.

"Blamed if he ain't neat," he said. But interest faded from his eye, and he turned again to the wall. " 'Lieb Vaterland magst ruhig sein,' " he melodiously observed. His repertory was wide and refined. When he sang he was always grammatical.

"Ye kin stop, kid," said the old gentleman, not unkindly, and he shoved his pistol into his belt.

The boy ceased. He had been thinking matters over. Being lithe and strong, he was not tired nor much out of breath, but he was trembling with the plan and the prospect he had laid out for himself. "Set 'em up," he said to Ephraim. "Set 'em up again all round."

His voice caused Specimen Jones to turn and look once more, while the old gentleman, still benevolent, said, "Yer langwidge means pleasanter than it sounds, kid." He glanced at the boy's holster, and knew he need not keep a very sharp watch as to that. Its owner had bungled over it once already. All the old gentleman did was to place himself next the boy on the off side from the holster; any move the tenderfoot's hand might make for it would be green and unskilful, and easily anticipated. The company lined up along the bar, and the bottle slid from glass to glass. The boy and his tormentor stood together in the middle of the line, and the tormentor, always with half a thought for the holster, handled his drink on the wet counter, waiting till all should be filled and ready to swallow simultaneously, as befits good manners.

"Well, my regards," he said, seeing the boy raise his glass; and as the old gentleman's arm lifted in unison, exposing his waist, the boy reached down a lightning hand, caught the old gentleman's own pistol, and jammed it in his face.

"Now you'll dance," said he.

"Whoop!" exclaimed Specimen Jones, delighted. "*Blamed* if he ain't neat!" And Jones's handsome face lighted keenly.

"Hold on!" the boy sang out, for the amazed old gentleman was mechanically drinking his whisky out of sheer fright. The rest had forgotten their drinks. "Not one swallow," the boy continued. "No, you'll not put it down either. You'll keep hold of it, and you'll dance all round this place. Around and around. And don't you spill any. And I'll be thinking what you'll do after that."

Specimen Jones eyed the boy with growing esteem. "Why, he ain't bigger than a pint of cider," said he.

"Prance away!" commanded the tenderfoot, and fired a shot between the old gentleman's not widely straddled legs.

"You hev the floor, Mr. Adams," Jones observed, respectfully, at the old gentleman's agile leap. "I'll let no man here interrupt you." So the capering began, and the company stood back to make room. "I've saw juicy things in this Territory," continued Specimen Jones, aloud, to himself, "but this combination fills my bill."

He shook his head sagely, following the black-haired boy with his eye. That youth was steering Mr. Adams round the room with the pistol, proud as a ring-master. Yet not altogether. He was only nineteen, and though his heart beat stoutly, it was beating alone in a strange country. He had come straight to this from hunting squirrels along the Susquehanna, with his mother keeping supper warm for him in the stone farm-house among the trees. He had read books in which hardy heroes saw life, and always triumphed with precision on the last page, but he remembered no receipt for this particular situation. Being good game American blood, he did not think now about the Susquehanna, but he did long with all his might to know what he ought to do next to prove himself a man. His buoyant rage, being glutted with the old gentleman's fervent skipping, had cooled, and a stress of reaction was falling hard on his brave young nerves. He imagined everybody against him. He had no notion that there was another American wanderer there, whose reserved and whimsical nature he had touched to the heart.

The fickle audience was with him, of course, for the moment, since he was upper dog and it was a good show; but one in that room was distinctly against him. The old gentleman was dancing with an ugly eye; he had glanced down to see just where his knife hung at his side, and he had made some calculations. He had fired four shots; the boy had fired one. "Four and one hez always made five," the old gentleman told himself with much secret pleasure, and pretended that he was going to stop his double shuffle. It was an excellent trap, and the boy fell straight into it. He squandered his last precious bullet on the spittoon near which Mr. Adams happened to be at the moment, and the next moment Mr. Adams had him by the throat. They swayed and gulped for breath, grooving the earth with sharp heels; they rolled to the floor and floundered with legs tight tangled, the boy in his inexperience blindly striking at Mr. Adams with the pistol butt, instead of its barrel, and the audience drawing closer to lose nothing, when the bright knife flashed suddenly. It poised, and flew across the room, harmless; for a foot had driven into Mr. Adams's arm, and he felt a cold circle pressing his temple. It was the smooth, chilly muzzle of Specimen Jones's six-shooter.

"That's enough," said Jones. "More than enough."

Mr. Adams, being mature in judgment, rose instantly, like a good old sheep, and put his knife back obedient to orders. But in the brain of the overstrained, bewildered boy universal destruction was whirling. With a face stricken lean with ferocity, he staggered to his feet, plucking at his holster, and glaring for a foe. His eye fell first on his deliverer, leaning easily against the bar watching him, while the more and more curious audience scattered, and held themselves ready to murder the boy if he should point his pistol their way. He was dragging at it clumsily, and at last it came. Specimen Jones sprang like a cat, and held the barrel vertical and gripped the boy's wrist.

"Go easy, son," said he.

The boy had been wrenching to get a shot at Jones, and now the quietness of the man's voice reached his brain, and he looked at Specimen Jones. He felt a potent brotherhood in the eyes that were considering him, and he began to fear he had been a fool. There was his dwarf Eastern revolver, slack in his inefficient fist, and the singular person still holding its barrel and tapping one derisive finger over the end, careless of the risk to his first joint.

"Why, you little yearling," said Specimen Jones, caressingly, to the hypnotized youth, "if you was to pop that squirt off at me, I'd turn you up and spank y'u. Set 'em up, Ephraim."

But the commercial Ephraim hesitated, and Jones remembered. His last cent was gone. It was his third day at Ephraim's. He had stopped, having a little money, on his way to Tucson, where a friend

had a job for him, and was waiting. He was far too experienced a
character ever to sell his horse or his saddle on these occasions, and
go on drinking. He looked as if he might, but he never did; and this
was what disappointed business men like Ephraim in Specimen Jones.

But now, here was this tenderfoot he had undertaken to see
through, and Ephraim reminding him that he had no more of the
wherewithal. "Why, so I haven't," he said, with a short laugh, and his
face flushed. "I guess," he continued, hastily, "this is worth a dollar
or two." He drew a chain up from below his flannel shirt-collar and
over his head. He drew it a little slowly. It had not been taken off for
a number of years—not, indeed, since it had been placed there originally. "It ain't brass," he added lightly, and strewed it along the
counter without looking at it. Ephraim did look at it, and, being satisfied, began to uncork a new bottle, while the punctual audience came
up for its drink.

"Won't you please let me treat?" said the boy, unsteadily. "I ain't
likely to meet you again, sir." Reaction was giving him trouble inside.

"Where are you bound, kid?"

"Oh, just a ways up the country," answered the boy, keeping a
grip on his voice.

"Well, you *may* get there. Where did you pick up that—that thing?
Your pistol, I mean."

"It's a present from a friend," replied the tenderfoot, with dignity.

"Farewell gift, wasn't it, kid? Yes; I thought so. Now I'd hate to
get an affair like that from a friend. It would start me wondering if
he liked me as well as I'd always thought he did. Put up that money,
kid. You're drinking with me. Say, what's yer name?"

"Cumnor—J. Cumnor."

"Well, J. Cumnor, I'm glad to know y'u. Ephraim, let me make you
acquainted with Mr. Cumnor. Mr. Adams, if you're rested from your
quadrille, you can shake hands with my friend. Step around, you Miguels and Serapios and Cristobals, whatever y'u claim your names are.
This is Mr. J. Cumnor."

The Mexicans did not understand either the letter or the spirit of
these American words, but they drank their drink, and the concertina
resumed its acrid melody. The boy had taken himself off without being
noticed.

"Say, Spec," said Ephraim to Jones, "I'm no hog. Here's yer chain.
You'll be along again."

"Keep it till I'm along again," said the owner.

"Just as you say, Spec," answered Ephraim, smoothly, and he hung
the pledge over an advertisement chromo of a nude cream-colored
lady with bright straw hair holding out a bottle of somebody's cham-

pagne. Specimen Jones sang no more songs, but smoked, and leaned in silence on the bar. The company were talking of bed, and Ephraim plunged his glasses into a bucket to clean them for the morrow.

"Know anything about that kid?" inquired Jones, abruptly.

Ephraim shook his head as he washed.

"Travelling alone, ain't he?"

Ephraim nodded.

"Where did y'u say y'u found that fellow layin' the Injuns got?"

"Mile this side the cañon. 'Mong them sand-humps."

"How long had he been there, do y'u figure?"

"Three days, anyway."

Jones watched Ephraim finish his cleansing. "Your clock needs wiping," he remarked. "A man might suppose it was nine, to see that thing the way the dirt hides the hands. Look again in half an hour and it'll say three. That's the kind of clock gives a man the jams. Sends him crazy."

"Well, that ain't a bad thing to be in this country," said Ephraim, rubbing the glass case and restoring identity to the hands. "If that man had been crazy he'd been livin' right now. Injuns'll never touch lunatics."

"That band have passed here and gone north," Jones said. "I saw a smoke among the foot-hills as I came along day before yesterday. I guess they're aiming to cross the Santa Catalina. Most likely they're that band from round the San Carlos that were reported as raiding down in Sonora."

"I seen well enough," said Ephraim, "when I found him that they wasn't going to trouble us any, or they'd have been around by then."

He was quite right, but Specimen Jones was thinking of something else. He went out to the corral, feeling disturbed and doubtful. He saw the tall white freight-wagon of the Mexicans, looming and silent, and a little way off the new fence where the dead man lay. An odd sound startled him, though he knew it was no Indians at this hour, and he looked down into a little dry ditch. It was the boy, hidden away flat on his stomach among the stones, sobbing.

"Oh, snakes!" whispered Specimen Jones, and stepped back. The Latin races embrace and weep, and all goes well; but among Saxons tears are a horrid event. Jones never knew what to do when it was a woman, but this was truly disgusting. He was well seasoned by the frontier, had tried a little of everything: town and country, ranches, saloons, stage-driving, marriage occasionally, and latterly mines. He had sundry claims staked out, and always carried pieces of stone in his pockets, discoursing upon their mineral-bearing capacity, which was apt to be very slight. That is why he was called Specimen Jones.

He had exhausted all the important sensations, and did not care much for anything any more. Perfect health and strength kept him from discovering that he was a saddened, drifting man. He wished to kick the boy for his baby performance, and yet he stepped carefully away from the ditch so the boy should not suspect his presence. He found himself standing still, looking at the dim, broken desert.

"Why, hell," complained Specimen Jones, "he played the little man to start with. He did so. He scared that old horse-thief, Adams, just about dead. Then he went to kill me, that kep' him from bein' buried early to-morrow. I've been wild that way myself, and wantin' to shoot up the whole outfit." Jones looked at the place where his middle finger used to be, before a certain evening in Tombstone. "But I never—" He glanced towards the ditch, perplexed. "What's that mean? Why in the world does he git to cryin' for *now*, do you suppose?" Jones took to singing without knowing it. " 'Ye shepherds, tell me, have you seen my Flora pass this way?' " he murmured. Then a thought struck him. "Hello, kid!" he called out. There was no answer. "Of course," said Jones. "Now he's ashamed to hev me see him come out of there." He walked with elaborate slowness round the corral and behind a shed. "Hello, you kid!" he called again.

"I was thinking of going to sleep," said the boy, appearing quite suddenly. "I—I'm not used to riding all day. I'll get used to it, you know," he hastened to add.

" 'Ha-ve you seen my Flo'— Say, kid, where y'u bound, anyway?"

"San Carlos."

"San Carlos? Oh. Ah. 'Flo-ra pass this way?' "

"Is it far, sir?"

"Awful far, sometimes. It's always liable to be far through the Arivaypa Cañon."

"I didn't expect to make it between meals," remarked Cumnor.

"No. Sure. What made you come this route?"

"A man told me."

"A man? Oh. Well, it *is* kind o' difficult, I admit, for an Arizonan not to lie to a stranger. But I think I'd have told you to go by Tres Alamos and Point of Mountain. It's the road the man that told you would choose himself every time. Do you like Injuns, kid?"

Cumnor snapped eagerly.

"Of course y'u do. And you've never saw one in the whole minute-and-a-half you've been alive. I know all about it."

"I'm not afraid," said the boy.

"Not afraid? Of course y'u ain't. What's your idea in going to Carlos? Got town lots there?"

"No," said the literal youth, to the huge internal diversion of Jones.

"There's a man there I used to know back home. He's in the cavalry. What sort of a town is it for sport?" asked Cumnor, in a gay Lothario tone.

"*Town?*" Specimen Jones caught hold of the top rail of the corral. "*Sport?* Now I'll tell y'u what sort of a town it is. There ain't no streets. There ain't no houses. There ain't any land and water in the usual meaning of them words. There's Mount Turnbull. It's pretty near a usual mountain, but y'u don't want to go there. The Creator didn't make San Carlos. It's a heap older than Him. When He got around to it after slickin' up Paradise and them fruit-trees, He just left it to be as He found it, as a sample of the way they done business before He come along. He ain't done any work around the spot at all, He ain't. Mix up a barrel of sand and ashes and thorns, and jam scorpions and rattlesnakes along in, and dump the outfit on stones, and heat yer stones red-hot, and set the United States army loose over the place chasin' Apaches, and you've got San Carlos."

Cumnor was silent for a moment. "I don't care," he said. "I want to chase Apaches."

"Did you see that man Ephraim found by the cañon?" Jones inquired.

"Didn't get here in time."

"Well, there was a hole in his chest made by an arrow. But there's no harm in that if you die at wunst. That chap didn't, y'u see. You heard Ephraim tell about it. They'd done a number of things to the man before he could die. Roastin' was only one of 'em. Now your road takes you through the mountains where these Injuns hev gone. Kid, come along to Tucson with me," urged Jones, suddenly.

Again Cumnor was silent. "Is my road different from other people's?" he said, finally.

"Not to Grant, it ain't. These Mexicans are hauling freight to Grant. But what's the matter with your coming to Tucson with me?"

"I started to go to San Carlos, and I'm going," said Cumnor.

"You're a poor chuckle-headed fool!" burst out Jones, in a rage. "And y'u can go, for all I care—you and your Christmas-tree pistol. Like as not you won't find your cavalry friend at San Carlos. They've killed a lot of them soldiers huntin' Injuns this season. Good-night."

Specimen Jones was gone. Cumnor walked to his blanket-roll, where his saddle was slung under the shed. The various doings of the evening had bruised his nerves. He spread his blankets among the dry cattle-dung and sat down, taking off a few clothes slowly. He lumped his coat and overalls under his head for a pillow, and, putting the despised pistol alongside, lay between the blankets. No object showed in the night but the tall freight-wagon. The tenderfoot thought he had made altogether a fool of himself upon the first trial trip of his manhood, alone on the open sea of Arizona. No man, not even Jones now, was his friend. A stranger, who could have had nothing against him but his inexperience, had taken the trouble to direct him on the wrong road. He did not mind definite enemies. He had punched the heads of those in Pennsylvania, and would not object to shooting them here; but this impersonal, surrounding hostility of the unknown was new and bitter: the cruel, assassinating, cowardly Southwest, where prospered those jail-birds whom the vigilantes had driven from California. He thought of the nameless human carcass that lay near, buried that day, and of the jokes about its mutilations. Cumnor was not an innocent boy, either in principles or in practice, but this laughter about a dead body had burned into his young, unhardened soul. He lay watching with hot, dogged eyes the brilliant stars. A passing wind turned the windmill, which creaked a forlorn minute, and ceased. He must have gone to sleep and slept soundly, for the next he knew it was the cold air of dawn that made him open his eyes. A numb silence lay over all things, and the tenderfoot had that moment of curiosity as to where he was now which comes to those who have journeyed for many days. The Mexicans had already departed with their freight-wagon. It was not entirely light, and the embers where these early starters had cooked their breakfast lay glowing in the sand across the road. The boy remembered seeing a wagon where now he saw only chill, distant peaks, and while he lay quiet and warm, shunning full consciousness, there was a stir in the cabin, and at Ephraim's voice reality broke upon his drowsiness, and he recollected Arizona and the keen stress of shifting for himself. He noted the gray paling round the grave. Indians? He would catch up with the Mexicans, and travel in their company to Grant. Freighters made but fifteen miles in the day, and he could start after breakfast and be with them before they stopped at noon. Six men need not worry about Apaches, Cumnor thought. The voice of Specimen Jones came from the cabin, and sounds of lighting the stove, and the growling conversation of men getting up. Cumnor, lying in his blankets, tried to overhear what Jones was saying, for no better reason than this was the only man he had met lately who seemed to care whether he were alive or dead. There was the clink of Ephraim's whisky-bottles, and the cheerful tones of old Mr. Adams, saying, "It's better'n brushin' yer teeth"; and then further clinking, and an inquiry from Specimen Jones.

"Whose spurs?" said he.

"Mine." This came from Mr. Adams.

"How long have they been yourn?"

"Since I got 'em, I guess."

"Well, you've enjoyed them spurs long enough." The voice of Specimen Jones now altered in quality. "And you'll give 'em back to that kid."

Muttering followed that the boy could not catch. "You'll give 'em back," repeated Jones. "I seen y'u lift 'em from under that chair when I was in the corner."

"That's straight, Mr. Adams," said Ephraim. "I noticed it myself, though I had no objections, of course. But Mr. Jones has pointed out—"

"Since when have you growed so honest, Jones?" cackled Mr. Adams, seeing that he must lose his little booty. "And why didn't you raise yer objections when you seen me do it?"

"I didn't know the kid," Jones explained. "And if it don't strike you that game blood deserves respect, why it does strike me."

Hearing this, the tenderfoot, outside in his shed, thought better of mankind and life in general, arose from his nest, and began preening himself. He had all the correct trappings for the frontier, and his toilet in the shed gave him pleasure. The sun came up, and with a stroke struck the world to crystal. The near sand-hills went into rose, the crabbed yucca and the mesquite turned transparent, with lances and pale films of green, like drapery graciously veiling the desert's face, and the distant violet peaks and edges framed the vast enchantment beneath the liquid exhalations of the sky. The smell of bacon and coffee from open windows filled the heart with bravery and yearning, and Ephraim, putting his head round the corner, called to Cumnor that he had better come in and eat. Jones, already at table, gave him the briefest nod; but the spurs were there, replaced as Cumnor had left them under a chair in the corner. In Arizona they do not say much at any meal, and at breakfast nothing at all; and as Cumnor swallowed and meditated, he noticed the cream-colored lady and the chain, and he made up his mind he should assert his identity with regard to that business, though how and when was not clear to him. He was in no great haste to take up his journey. The society of the Mexicans whom he must sooner or later overtake did not tempt him. When breakfast was done he idled in the cabin, like the other guests, while Ephraim and his assistant busied about the premises. But the morning grew on, and the guests, tilted back against the wall, after a season of smoking and silence, shook themselves and their effects together, saddled, and were lost among the waste thorny hills. Twenty Mile became hot and torpid. Jones lay on three consecutive chairs, occasionally singing, and old Mr. Adams had not gone away either, but watched him, with more tobacco running down his beard.

"Well," said Cumnor, "I'll be going."

"Nobody's stopping y'u," remarked Jones.

"You're going to Tucson?" the boy said, with the chain problem still unsolved in his mind. "Good-bye, Mr. Jones. I hope I'll—we'll—"

"That'll do," said Jones; and the tenderfoot, thrown back by this severity, went to get his saddle-horse and his burro.

Presently Mr. Jones remarked to Mr. Adams that he wondered what Ephraim was doing, and went out. The old gentleman was left alone in the room, and he swiftly noticed that the belt and pistol of Specimen Jones were left alone with him. The accoutrement lay by the chair its owner had been lounging in. It is an easy thing to remove cartridges from the chambers of a revolver, and replace the weapon in its holster so that everything looks quite natural. The old gentleman was entertained with the notion that somewhere in Tucson Specimen Jones might have a surprise, and he did not take a minute to prepare this, drop the belt as it lay before, and saunter innocently out of the saloon. Ephraim and Jones were criticizing the tenderfoot's property as he packed his burro.

"Do y'u make it a rule to travel with ice-cream?" Jones was inquiring.

"They're for water," Cumnor said. "They told me at Tucson I'd need to carry water for three days on some trails."

It was two good-sized milk-cans that he had, and they bounced about on the little burro's pack, giving him as much amazement as a jackass can feel. Jones and Ephraim were hilarious.

"Don't go without your spurs, Mr. Cumnor," said the voice of old Mr. Adams, as he approached the group. His tone was particularly civil.

The tenderfoot had, indeed, forgotten his spurs, and he ran back to get them. The cream-colored lady still had the chain hanging upon her, and Cumnor's problem was suddenly solved. He put the chain in his pocket, and laid the price of one round of drinks for last night's company on the shelf below the chromo. He returned with his spurs on, and tightened the cinches; but the chain was now in the saddle-bag of Specimen Jones, mixed up with some tobacco, stale bread, a box of matches, and a hunk of fat bacon. The men at Twenty Mile said good-day to the tenderfoot, with monosyllables and indifference, and watched him depart into the heated desert. Wishing for a last look at Jones, he turned once, and saw the three standing, and the chocolate brick of the cabin, and the windmill white and idle in the sun.

"He'll be gutted by night," remarked Mr. Adams.

"I ain't buryin' him, then," said Ephraim.

"Nor I," said Specimen Jones. "Well, it's time I was getting to Tucson."

He went to the saloon, strapped on his pistol, saddled, and rode away. Ephraim and Mr. Adams returned to the cabin; and here is the final conclusion they came to after three hours of discussion as to who took the chain and who had it just then:

*Ephraim.* Jones, he hadn't no cash.

*Mr. Adams.* The kid, he hadn't no sense.

*Ephraim.* The kid, he lent the cash to Jones.

*Mr. Adams.* Jones, he goes off with his chain.

*Both.* What damn fools everybody is, anyway!

And they went to dinner. But Mr. Adams did not mention his doings with Jones's pistol. Let it be said, in extenuation of that performance, that Mr. Adams supposed Jones was going to Tucson, where he said he was going, and where a job and a salary were awaiting him. In Tucson an unloaded pistol in the holster of so handy a man on the drop as was Specimen would keep people civil, because they would not know, any more than the owner, that it was unloaded; and the mere possession of it would be sufficient in nine chances out of ten— though it was undoubtedly for the tenth that Mr. Adams had a sneaking hope. But Specimen Jones was not going to Tucson. A contention in his mind as to whether he would do what was good for himself, or what was good for another, had kept him sullen ever since he got up. Now it was settled, and Jones in serene humor again. Of course he had started on the Tucson road, for the benefit of Ephraim and Mr. Adams.

The tenderfoot rode along. The Arizona sun beat down upon the deadly silence, and the world was no longer of crystal, but a mesa, dull and gray and hot. The pony's hoofs grated in the gravel, and after a time the road dived down and up among lumpy hills of stone and cactus, always nearer the fierce glaring Sierra Santa Catalina. It dipped so abruptly in and out of the shallow sudden ravines that, on coming up from one of these into sight of the country again, the tenderfoot's heart jumped at the close apparition of another rider quickly bearing in upon him from gullies where he had been moving unseen. But it was only Specimen Jones.

"Hello!" said he, joining Cumnor. "Hot, ain't it?"

"Where are you going?" inquired Cumnor.

"Up here a ways." And Jones jerked his finger generally towards the Sierra, where they were heading.

"Thought you had a job in Tucson."

"That's what I have."

Specimen Jones had no more to say, and they rode for a while, their ponies' hoofs always grating in the gravel, and the milk-cans lightly clanking on the burro's pack. The bunched blades of the yuccas bristled steel-stiff, and as far as you could see it was a gray waste of mounds and ridges sharp and blunt, up to the forbidding boundary walls of the Tortilita one way and the Santa Catalina the other. Cumnor wondered if Jones had found the chain. Jones was capable of not finding it for several weeks, or of finding it at once and saying nothing.

"You'll excuse my meddling with your business?" the boy hazarded.

Jones looked inquiring.

"Something's wrong with your saddle-pocket."

Specimen saw nothing apparently wrong with it, but perceiving Cumnor was grinning, unbuckled the pouch. He looked at the boy rapidly, and looked away again, and as he rode, still in silence, he put the chain back round his neck below the flannel shirt-collar.

"Say, kid," he remarked, after some time, "what does J stand for?"

"J? Oh, my name! Jock."

"Well, Jock, will y'u explain to me as a friend how y'u ever come to be such a fool as to leave yer home—wherever and whatever it was—in exchange for this here God-forsaken and iniquitous hole?"

"If you'll explain to me," said the boy, greatly heartened, "how you come to be ridin' in the company of a fool, instead of going to your job at Tucson."

The explanation was furnished before Specimen Jones had framed his reply. A burning freight-wagon and five dismembered human stumps lay in the road. This was what had happened to the Miguels and Serapios and the concertina. Jones and Cumnor, in their dodging and struggles to exclude all expressions of growing mutual esteem from their speech, had forgotten their journey, and a sudden bend among the rocks where the road had now brought them revealed the blood and fire staring them in the face. The plundered wagon was three parts empty; its splintered, blazing boards slid down as they burned into the fiery heap on the ground; packages of soda and groceries and medicines slid with them, bursting into chemical spots of green and crimson flame; a wheel crushed in and sank, spilling more packages that flickered and hissed; the garbage of combat and murder littered the earth, and in the air hung an odor that Cumnor knew, though he had never smelled it before. Morsels of dropped booty up among the rocks showed where the Indians had gone, and one horse remained, groaning, with an accidental arrow in his belly.

"We'll just kill him," said Jones; and his pistol snapped idly, and snapped again, as his eye caught a motion—a something—two hundred yards up among the bowlders on the hill. He whirled round. The enemy was behind them also. There was no retreat. "Yourn's no good!" yelled Jones, fiercely, for Cumnor was getting out his little foolish revolver. "Oh, what a trick to play on a man! Drop off yer horse, kid; drop, and do like me. Shootin's no good here, even if I was loaded. *They* shot, and look at them now. God bless them ice-cream freezers of yourn, kid! Did y'u ever see a crazy man? If you ain't, *make it up as y'u go along!*"

More objects moved up among the bowlders. Specimen Jones ripped off the burro's pack, and the milk-cans rolled on the ground. The burro began grazing quietly, with now and then a step towards new patches of grass. The horses stood where their riders had left them, their reins over their heads, hanging and dragging. From two hundred yards on the hill the ambushed Apaches showed, their dark, scattered figures appearing cautiously one by one, watching with suspicion. Specimen Jones seized up one milk-can, and Cumnor obediently did the same.

"You kin dance, kid, and I kin sing, and we'll go to it," said Jones. He rambled in a wavering loop, and diving eccentrically at Cumnor, clashed the milk-cans together. " 'Es schallt ein Ruf wie Donnerhall,' " he bawled, beginning the song of "Die Wacht am Rhein." "Why don't you dance?" he shouted, sternly. The boy saw the terrible earnestness of his face, and, clashing his milk-cans in turn, he shuffled a sort of jig. The two went over the sand in loops, toe and heel; the donkey continued his quiet grazing, and the flames rose hot and yellow from the freight-wagon. And all the while the stately German hymn pealed among the rocks, and the Apaches crept down nearer the bowing, scraping men. The sun shone bright, and their bodies poured with sweat. Jones flung off his shirt; his damp, matted hair was half in ridges and half glued to his forehead, and the delicate gold chain swung and struck his broad, naked breast. The Apaches drew nearer again, their bows and arrows held uncertainly. They came down the hill, fifteen or twenty, taking a long time, and stopping every few yards. The milk-cans clashed, and Jones thought he felt the boy's strokes weakening. "Die Wacht am Rhein" was finished, and now it was "Ha-ve you seen my Flora pass this way?" "Y'u mustn't play out, kid," said Jones, very gently. "Indeed y'u mustn't"; and he at once resumed his song. The silent Apaches had now reached the bottom of the hill. They stood some twenty yards away, and Cumnor had a good chance to see his first Indians. He saw them move, and the color and slim shape of their bodies, their thin arms, and their long, black hair. It went through his mind that if he had no more clothes on than that, dancing would come easier. His boots were growing heavy to lift, and his overalls seemed to wrap his sinews in wet, strangling thongs. He wondered how long he had been keeping this up. The legs of the Apaches were free, with light moccasins only half-way to the thigh, slenderly held up by strings from the waist. Cumnor envied their unencumbered steps as he saw them again walk nearer to where he was dancing. It was long since he had eaten, and he noticed a singing dullness in his brain, and became frightened at his thoughts, which were running and melting into one fixed idea. This idea was to take off his boots, and offer to trade them for a pair of moccasins. It terrified him—this endless, molten rush of thoughts; he could see them coming in different shapes from different places in his head, but they all joined immediately, and always formed the same fixed idea. He ground his teeth to master this encroaching inebriation of his will and judgment. He clashed his can more loudly to wake him to reality, which he still could recognize and appreciate. For a time he found it a good plan to listen to what Specimen Jones was singing, and tell himself the name of the song, if he knew it. At present it was "Yankee Doodle," to which Jones was fitting words of his own. These ran, "Now I'm going to try a bluff, And mind you do what I do"; and then again, over and over. Cumnor waited for the word "bluff"; for it was hard and heavy, and fell into his thoughts, and stopped them for a moment. The dance was so long now he had forgotten about that. A numbness had been spreading through his legs, and he was glad to feel a sharp pain in the sole of his foot. It was a piece of gravel that had somehow worked its way in, and was rubbing through the skin into the flesh. "That's good," he said, aloud. The pebble was eating the numbness away, and Cumnor drove it hard against the raw spot, and relished the tonic of its burning friction. The Apaches had drawn into a circle. Standing at some interval apart, they entirely surrounded the arena. Shrewd, half convinced, and yet with awe, they watched the dancers, who clashed their cans slowly now in rhythm to Jones's hoarse, parched singing. He was quite master of himself, and led the jig round the still blazing wreck of the wagon, and circled in figures of eight between the corpses of the Mexicans, clashing the milk-cans above each one. Then, knowing his strength was coming to an end, he approached an Indian whose splendid fillet and trappings denoted him as a chief of consequence; and Jones was near shouting with relief when the Indian shrank backward. Suddenly he saw Cumnor let his can drop, and without stopping to see why, he caught it up, and, slowly rattling both, approached each Indian in turn with tortuous steps. The circle that had never uttered a sound till now receded, chanting almost in a whisper some exorcising song which the man with the fillet had begun. They gathered round him, retreating always, and the strain, with its rapid muttered words, rose and fell softly among them. Jones had supposed the boy was overcome by faintness, and looked to see where he lay. But it was not faintness. Cumnor, with his boots off, came by and walked after the Indians in a trance. They saw him, and quickened their pace, often turning to be sure he was not overtaking them. He called to them unintelligibly, stumbling up the sharp hill, and pointing to the boots. Finally he sat down. They continued ascending the mountain, herding close round the man with the feathers, until the rocks and the filmy tangles screened them from sight; and like a wind that hums uncertainly in grass, their chanting died away.

The sun was half behind the western range when Jones next moved. He called, and, getting no answer, he crawled painfully to where the boy lay on the hill. Cumnor was sleeping heavily; his head was hot, and he moaned. So Jones crawled down, and fetched blankets and the canteen of water. He spread the blankets over the boy, wet a handkerchief and laid it on his forehead; then he lay down himself.

The earth was again magically smitten to crystal. Again the sharp cactus and the sand turned beautiful, and violet floated among the mountains, and rose-colored orange in the sky above them.

"Jock," said Specimen at length.

The boy opened his eyes.

"Your foot is awful, Jock. Can y'u eat?"

"Not with my foot."

"Ah, God bless y'u, Jock! Y'u ain't turruble sick. But *can* y'u eat?"

Cumnor shook his head.

"Eatin's what y'u need, though. Well, here." Specimen poured a judicious mixture of whisky and water down the boy's throat, and wrapped the awful foot in his own flannel shirt. "They'll fix y'u over to Grant. It's maybe twelve miles through the cañon. It ain't a town any more than Carlos is, but the soldiers'll be good to us. As soon as night comes you and me must somehow git out of this."

Somehow they did, Jones walking and leading his horse and the imperturbable little burro, and also holding Cumnor in the saddle. And when Cumnor was getting well in the military hospital at Grant, he listened to Jones recounting to all that chose to hear how useful a weapon an ice-cream freezer can be, and how if you'll only chase Apaches in your stocking feet they are sure to run away. And then Jones and Cumnor both enlisted; and I suppose Jones's friend is still expecting him in Tucson.

# The Serenade
# at Siskiyou

Unskilled at murder and without training in running away, one of the two Healy boys had been caught with ease soon after their crime. What they had done may be best learned in the following extract from a certain official report:

"The stage was within five miles of its destination when it was confronted by the usual apparition of a masked man levelling a double-barrelled shot-gun at the driver, and the order to 'Pull up, and throw out the express box.' The driver promptly complied. Meanwhile the guard, Buck Montgomery, who occupied a seat inside, from which he caught a glimpse of what was going on, opened fire at the robber, who dropped to his knees at the first shot, but a moment later discharged both barrels of his gun at the stage. The driver dropped from his seat to the foot-board with five buckshot in his right leg near the knee, and two in his left leg; a passenger by his side also dropped with three or four buckshot in his legs. Before the guard could reload, two shots came from behind the bushes back of the exposed robber, and Buck fell to the bottom of the stage mortally wounded—shot through the back. The whole murderous sally occupied but a few seconds, and the order came to 'Drive on.' Officers and citizens quickly started in pursuit, and the next day one of the robbers, a well-known young man of that vicinity, son of a respectable farmer in Fresno County, was overtaken and arrested."

Feeling had run high in the streets of Siskiyou when the prisoner was brought into town, and the wretch's life had come near a violent end at the hands of the mob, for Buck Montgomery had many friends. But the steadier citizens preserved the peace, and the murderer was in the prison awaiting his trial by formal law. It was now some weeks since the tragedy, and Judge Campbell sat at breakfast reading his paper.

"Why, that is excellent!" he suddenly exclaimed.

"May I ask what is excellent, Judge?" inquired his wife. She had a big nose.

"They've caught the other one, Amanda. Got him last evening in a restaurant at Woodland." The judge read the paragraph to Mrs. Campbell, who listened severely. "And so," he concluded, "when to-night's train gets up, we'll have them both safe in jail."

Mrs. Campbell dallied over her eggs, shaking her head. Presently she sighed. But as Amanda often did this, her husband finished his own eggs and took some more. "Poor boy!" said the lady, pensively. "Only twenty-three last 12th of October. What a cruel fate!"

Now the judge supposed she referred to the murdered man. "Yes," he said. "Vile. You've got him romantically young, my dear. I understood he was thirty-five."

"I know his age perfectly, Judge Campbell. I made it my business to find out. And to think his brother might actually have been lynched!"

"I never knew that either. You seem to have found out about the family, Amanda. What were they going to lynch the brother for?"

The ample lady folded her fat, middle-aged hands on the edge of the table, and eyed her husband with bland displeasure. "Judge Campbell!" she uttered, and her lips shut wide and firm. She would restrain herself, if possible.

"Well, my dear?"

"You ask me that. You pretend ignorance of that disgraceful scene. Who was it said to me right in the street that he disapproved of lynching? I ask you, Judge, who was it right there at the jail—"

"Oh!" said the enlightened judge.

"—Right at the left-hand side of the door of the jail in this town of Siskiyou, who was it got that trembling boy safe inside from those yelling fiends and talked to the crowd on a barrel of number ten nails and made those wicked men stop and go home?"

"Amanda, I believe I recognize myself."

"I should think you did, Judge Campbell. And now they've caught the other one, and he'll be up with the sheriff on to-night's train, and I suppose they'll lynch *him* now!"

"There's not the slightest danger," said the judge. "The town wants them to have a fair trial. It was natural that immediately after such an atrocious act—"

"Those poor boys had never murdered anybody before in their lives," interrupted Amanda.

"But they did murder Montgomery, you will admit."

"Oh yes!" said Mrs. Campbell, with impatience. "I saw the hole in

his back. You needn't tell me all that again. If he'd thrown out the
express box quicker they wouldn't have hurt a hair of his head. Wells
Fargo's messengers know that perfectly. It was his own fault. Those
boys had no employment and they only wanted money. They did not
seek human blood, and you needn't tell me they did."

"They shed it, however, Amanda. Quite a lot of it. Stage-driver
and a passenger too."

"Yes, you keep going back to that as if they'd all been murdered
instead of only one, and you don't care about those two poor boys
locked in a dungeon, and their gray-haired father down in Fresno
County who never did anything wrong at all, and he sixty-one in
December."

"The county isn't thinking of hanging the old gentleman," said the
judge.

"That will do, Judge Campbell," said his lady, rising. "I shall say
no more. Total silence for the present is best for you and best for me.
Much best. I will leave you to think of your speech, which was by no
means silver. Not even life with you for twenty-five years this coming
10th of July has inured me to insult. I am capable of understanding
whom they think of hanging, and your speaking to me as if I did not
does you little credit; for it was a mere refuge from a woman's just
accusation of heartlessness which you felt, and like a man would not
acknowledge; and therefore it is that I say no more but leave you to
go down the street to the Ladies' Lyceum where I shall find companions with some spark of humanity in their bosoms and milk of human
kindness for those whose hasty youth has plunged them in misery and
delivered them to the hands of those who treat them as if they were
stones and sticks full of nothing but monstrosity instead of breathing
men like themselves to be shielded by brotherhood and hope and not
dashed down by cruelty and despair."

It had begun stately as a dome, with symmetry and punctuation,
but the climax was untrammelled by a single comma. The orator swept
from the room, put on her bonnet and shawl, and the judge, still sitting
with his eggs, heard the front door close behind her. She was president of the Ladies' Reform and Literary Lyceum, and she now trod
thitherward through Siskiyou.

"I think Amanda will find companions there," mused the judge.
"But her notions of sympathy beat me." The judge had a small, wise
blue eye, and he liked his wife more than well. She was sincerely good,
and had been very courageous in their young days of poverty. She
loved their son, and she loved him. Only, when she took to talking, he
turned up a mental coat-collar and waited. But if the male sex did not
appreciate her powers of eloquence her sister citizens did; and Mrs.

Campbell, besides presiding at the Ladies' Reform and Literary Lyceum in Siskiyou, often addressed female meetings in Ashland, Yreka,
and even as far away as Tehama and Redding. She found companions
this morning.

"To think of it!" they exclaimed, at her news of the capture, for
none had read the paper. They had been too busy talking of the next
debate, which was upon the question, "Ought we to pray for rain?"
But now they instantly forgot the wide spiritual issues raised by this
inquiry, and plunged into the fascinations of crime, reciting once more
to each other the details of the recent tragedy. The room hired for
the Lyceum was in a second story above the apothecary and book
shop—a combined enterprise in Siskiyou—and was furnished with
fourteen rocking-chairs. Pictures of Mount Shasta and Lucretia Mott
ornamented the wall, with a photograph from an old master representing Leda and the Swan. This typified the Lyceum's approval of
Art, and had been presented by one of the husbands upon returning
from a three days' business trip to San Francisco.

"Dear! dear!" said Mrs. Parsons, after they had all shuddered anew
over the shooting and the blood. "With so much suffering in the world,
how fulsome seems that gay music!" She referred to the Siskiyou
brass-band, which was rehearsing the march from "Fatinitza" in an
adjacent room in the building. Mrs. Parsons had large mournful eyes,
a poetic vocabulary, and wanted to be president of the Lyceum
herself.

"Melody has its sphere, Gertrude," said Mrs. Campbell, in a wholesome voice. "We must not be morbid. But this I say to you, one and
all: Since the men of Siskiyou refuse, it is for the women to vindicate
the town's humanity, and show some sympathy for the captive who
arrives to-night."

They all thought so too.

"I do not criticize," continued their president, magnanimously, "nor
do I complain of any one. Each in this world has his or her mission,
and the most sacred is woman's own—to console!"

"True, true!" murmured Mrs. Slocum.

"We must do something for the prisoner, to show him we do not
desert him in his hour of need," Mrs. Campbell continued.

"We'll go and meet the train!" Mrs. Slocum exclaimed, eagerly.
"I've never seen a real murderer."

"A bunch of flowers for him," said Mrs. Parsons, closing her mournful eyes. "Roses." And she smiled faintly.

"Oh, lilies!" cried little Mrs. Day, with rapture. "Lilies would look
*real* nice."

"Don't you think," said Miss Sissons, who had not spoken before, and sat a little apart from the close-drawn clump of talkers, "that we might send the widow some flowers too, some time?" Miss Sissons was a pretty girl, with neat hair. She was engaged to the captain of Siskiyou's baseball nine.

"The widow?" Mrs. Campbell looked vague.

"Mrs. Montgomery, I mean—the murdered man's wife. I—I went to see if I could do anything, for she has some children; but she wouldn't see me," said Miss Sissons. "She said she couldn't talk to anybody."

"Poor thing!" said Mrs. Campbell. "I dare say it was a dreadful shock to her. Yes, dear, we'll attend to her after a while. We'll have her with us right along, you know, whereas these unhappy boys may—may be—may soon meet a cruel death on the scaffold." Mrs. Campbell evaded the phrase "may be hanged" rather skilfully. To her trained oratorical sense it had seemed to lack dignity.

"So young!" said Mrs. Day.

"And both so full of promise, to be cut off!" said Mrs. Parsons.

"Why, they can't hang them both, I should think," said Miss Sissons. "I thought only one killed Mr. Montgomery."

"My dear Louise," said Mrs. Campbell, "they can do anything they want, and they will. Shall I ever forget those ruffians who wanted to lynch the first one? They'll be on the jury!"

The clump returned to their discussion of the flowers, and Miss Sissons presently mentioned she had some errands to do, and departed.

"Would that that girl had more soul!" said Mrs. Parsons.

"She has plenty of soul," replied Mrs. Campbell, "but she's under the influence of a man. Well, as I was saying, roses and lilies are too big."

"Oh, *why?*" said Mrs. Day. "They would *please* him so."

"He couldn't carry them, Mrs. Day. I've thought it all out. He'll be walked to the jail between strong men. We must have some small bokay to pin on his coat, for his hands will be shackled."

"You don't say!" cried Mrs. Slocum. "How awful! I must get to that train. I've never seen a man in shackles in my life."

So violets were selected; Mrs. Campbell brought some in the afternoon from her own borders, and Mrs. Parsons furnished a large pin. She claimed also the right to affix the decoration upon the prisoner's breast because she had suggested the idea of flowers; but the other ladies protested, and the president seemed to think that they all should draw lots. It fell to Mrs. Day.

"Now I declare!" twittered the little matron. "I do believe I'll never dare."

"You must say something to him," said Amanda; "something fitting and choice."

"Oh dear no, Mrs. Campbell. Why, I never—my gracious! Why, if I'd known I was expected—Really, I couldn't think—I'll let *you* do it!"

"We can't hash up the ceremony that way, Mrs. Day," said Amanda, severely. And as they all fell arguing, the whistle blew.

"There!" said Mrs. Slocum. "Now you've made me late, and I'll miss the shackles and everything."

She flew down-stairs, and immediately the town of Siskiyou saw twelve members of the Ladies' Reform and Literary Lyceum follow her in a hasty phalanx across the square to the station. The train approached slowly up the grade, and by the time the wide smoke-stack of the locomotive was puffing its wood smoke in clouds along the platform, Amanda had marshalled her company there.

"Where's the gals all goin', Bill?" inquired a large citizen in boots of the ticket-agent.

"Nowheres, I guess, Abe," the agent replied. "Leastways, they ain't bought any tickets off me."

"Maybe they're for stealin' a ride," said Abe.

The mail and baggage cars had passed, and the women watched the smoking-car that drew up opposite them. Mrs. Campbell had informed her friends that the sheriff always went in the smoker; but on this occasion, for some reason, he had brought his prisoner in the Pullman sleeper at the rear, some way down the track, and Amanda's vigilant eye suddenly caught the group, already descended and walking away. The platoon of sympathy set off, and rapidly came up with the sheriff, while Bill, Abe, the train conductor, the Pullman conductor, the engineer, and the fireman abandoned their duty, and stared, in company with the brakeman and many passengers. There was perfect silence but for the pumping of the air-brake on the engine. The sheriff, not understanding what was coming, had half drawn his pistol; but now, surrounded by universal petticoats, he pulled off his hat and grinned doubtfully. The friend with him also stood bareheaded and grinning. He was young Jim Hornbrook, the muscular betrothed of Miss Sissons. The prisoner could not remove his hat, or he would have done so. Miss Sissons, who had come to the train to meet her lover, was laughing extremely in the middle of the road.

"Take these violets," faltered Mrs. Day, and held out the bunch, backing away slightly at the same time.

"Nonsense," said Amanda, stepping forward and grasping the flowers. "The women of Siskiyou are with you," she said, "as we are with all the afflicted." Then she pinned the violets firmly to the prisoner's flannel shirt. His face, at first amazed as the sheriff's and Hornbrook's, smoothed into cunning and vanity, while Hornbrook's turned an angry red, and the sheriff stopped grinning.

"Them flowers would look better on Buck Montgomery's grave, madam," said the officer. "Maybe you'll let us pass now." They went on to the jail.

"Waal," said Abe, on the platform, "that's the most disgustin' fool thing I ever did see."

"All aboard!" said the conductor, and the long train continued its way to Portland.

The platoon, well content, dispersed homeward to supper, and Jim Hornbrook walked home with his girl.

"For Lord's sake, Louise," he said, "who started that move?"

She told him the history of the morning.

"Well," he said, "you tell Mrs. Campbell, with my respects, that she's just playing with fire. A good woman like her ought to have more sense. Those men are going to have a fair trial."

"She wouldn't listen to me, Jim, not a bit. And, do you know, she really didn't seem to feel sorry—except just for a minute—about that poor woman."

"Louise, why don't you quit her outfit?"

"Resign from the Lyceum? That's so silly of you, Jim. We're not all crazy there; and that," said Miss Sissons, demurely, "is what makes a girl like me so valuable!"

"Well, I'm not stuck on having you travel with that lot."

"They speak better English than you do, Jim dear. Don't! in the street!"

"Sho! It's dark now," said Jim. "And it's been three whole days since—" But Miss Sissons escaped inside her gate and rang the bell. "Now see here, Louise," he called after her, "when I say they're playing with fire I mean it. That woman will make trouble in this town."

"She's not afraid," said Miss Sissons. "Don't you know enough about us yet to know we can't be threatened?"

"You!" said the young man. "I wasn't thinking of you." And so they separated.

Mrs. Campbell sat opposite the judge at supper, and he saw at once from her complacent reticence that she had achieved some triumph against his principles. She chatted about topics of the day in terms that were ingeniously trite. Then a letter came from their son in Denver, and she forgot her rôle somewhat, and read the letter aloud to the judge, and wondered wistfully who in Denver attended to the boy's buttons and socks; but she made no reference whatever to Siskiyou jail or those inside it. Next morning, however, it was the judge's turn to be angry.

"Amanda," he said, over the paper again, "you had better stick to socks, and leave criminals alone."

Amanda gazed at space with a calm smile.

"And I'll tell you one thing, my dear," her husband said, more incisively, "it don't look well that I should represent the law while my wife figures" (he shook the morning paper) "as a public nuisance. And one thing more: *Look out!* For if I know this community, and I think I do, you may raise something you don't bargain for."

"I can take care of myself, Judge," said Amanda, always smiling. These two never were angry both at once, and to-day it was the judge that sailed out of the house. Amanda pounced instantly upon the paper. The article was headed "Sweet Violets." But the editorial satire only spurred the lady to higher efforts. She proceeded to the Lyceum, and found that "Sweet Violets" had been there before her. Every woman held a copy, and the fourteen rocking-chairs were swooping up and down like things in a factory. In the presence of this blizzard, Mount Shasta, Lucretia Mott, and even Leda and the Swan looked singularly serene on their wall, although on the other side of the wall the "Fatinitza" march was booming brilliantly. But Amanda quieted the storm. It was her gift to be calm when others were not, and soon the rocking-chairs were merely rippling.

"The way my boys scolded me—" began Mrs. Day.

"For men I care not," said Mrs. Parsons. "But when my own sister upbraids me in a public place—" The lady's voice ceased, and she raised her mournful eyes. It seemed she had encountered her unnatural relative at the post-office. Everybody had a tale similar. Siskiyou had denounced their humane act.

"Let them act ugly," said Mrs. Slocum. "We will not swerve."

"I sent roses this morning," said Mrs. Parsons.

"*Did* you, dear?" said Mrs. Day. "My lilies shall go this afternoon."

"Here is a letter from the prisoner," said Amanda, producing the treasure; and they huddled to hear it. It was very affecting. It mentioned the violets blooming beside the hard couch, and spoke of prayer.

"He had lovely hair," said Mrs. Slocum.

"*So* brown!" said Mrs. Day.

"Black, my dear, and curly."

"Light brown. I was a good deal closer, Susan—"

"Never mind about his hair," said Amanda. "We are here not to flinch. We must act. Our course is chosen, and well chosen. The prison fare is a sin, and a beefsteak goes to them both at noon from my house."

"Oh, why didn't we ever think of that before?" cried the ladies, in an ecstasy, and fell to planning a series of lunches in spite of what Siskiyou might say or do. Siskiyou did not say very much; but it looked; and the ladies waxed more enthusiastic, luxuriating in a sense of martyrdom because now the prisoners were stopped writing any more letters to them. This was doubtless a high-handed step, and it set certain pulpits preaching about love. The day set for the trial was approaching; Amanda and her flock were going. Prayer-meetings were held, food and flowers for the two in jail increased in volume, and every day saw some of the Lyceum waiting below the prisoners' barred windows till the men inside would thrust a hand through and wave to them; then they would shake a handkerchief in reply, and go away thrilled to talk it over at the Lyceum. And Siskiyou looked on all the while, darker and darker.

Then finally Amanda had a great thought. Listening to "Fatinitza" one morning, she suddenly arose and visited Herr Schwartz, the band-master. Herr Schwartz was a wise and well-educated German. They had a lengthy conference.

"I don't pelief dot vill be very goot," said the band-master.

But at that Amanda talked a good deal; and the worthy Teuton was soon bewildered, and at last gave a dubious consent, "since it would blease de ladies."

The president of the Lyceum arranged the coming event after her own heart. The voice of Woman should speak in Siskiyou. The helpless victims of male prejudice and the law of the land were to be flanked with consolation and encouragement upon the eve of their ordeal in court. In their lonely cell they were to feel that there were those outside whose hearts beat with theirs. The floral tribute was to be sumptuous, and Amanda had sent to San Francisco for pound-cake. The special quality she desired could not be achieved by the Siskiyou confectioner.

Miss Sissons was not a party to this enterprise, and she told its various details to Jim Hornbrook, half in anger, half in derision. He listened without comment, and his face frightened her a little.

"Jim, what's the matter?" said she.

"Are you going to be at that circus?" he inquired.

"I thought I might just look on, you know," said Miss Sissons. "Mrs. Campbell and a brass-band—"

"You'll stay in the house that night, Louise."

"Why, the ring isn't even on my finger yet," laughed the girl, "the fatal promise of obedience—" But she stopped, perceiving her joke was not a good one. "Of course, Jim, if you feel that way," she finished. "Only I'm grown up, and I like reasons."

"Well—that's all right too."

"Ho, ho! All right! Thank you, sir. Dear me!"

"Why, it ain't to please me, Louise; indeed it ain't. I can't swear everything won't be nice and all right and what a woman could be mixed up in, but—well, how should you know what men are, anyway, when they've been a good long time getting mad, and are mad all through? That's what this town is to-day, Louise."

"I don't know," said Miss Sissons, "and I'm sure I'd rather not know." And so she gave her promise. "But I shouldn't suppose," she added, "that the men of Siskiyou, mad or not, would forget that women are women."

Jim laughed. "Oh no," he said, "they ain't going to forget that."

The appointed day came; and the train came, several hours late, bearing the box of confectionery, addressed to the Ladies' Reform and Literary Lyceum. Bill, the ticket-agent, held his lantern over it on the platform.

"That's the cake," said he.

"What cake?" Abe inquired.

Bill told him the rumor.

"Cake?" repeated Abe. "Fer them?" and he tilted his head towards the jail. "Will you say that again, friend? I ain't clear about it. *Cake*, did ye say?"

"Pound-cake," said Bill. "Ordered special from San Francisco."

Now pound-cake for adults is considered harmless. But it is curious how unwholesome a harmless thing can be if administered at the wrong time. The gaunt, savage-looking Californian went up to the box slowly. Then he kicked it lightly with his big boot, seeming to listen to its reverberation. Then he read the address. Then he sat down on the box to take a think. After a time he began speaking aloud. "They hold up a stage," he said, slowly. "They lay up a passenger fer a month. And they lame Bob Griffiths fer life. And then they do up Buck. Shoot a hole through his spine. And I helped bury him; fer I liked Buck." The speaker paused, and looked at the box. Then he got up. "I hain't attended their prayer-meetin's," said he, "and I hain't smelt their flowers. Such perfume's liable to make me throw up. But I guess I'll hev a look at their cake."

He went to the baggage-room and brought an axe. The axe descended, and a splintered slat flew across the platform. "There's a lot of cake," said Abe. The top of the packing-case crashed on the railroad track, and three new men gathered to look on. "It's fresh cake too," remarked the destroyer. The box now fell to pieces, and the tattered

paper wrapping was ripped away. "Step up, boys," said Abe, for a
little crowd was there now. "Soft, ain't it?" They slung the cake about
and tramped it in the grime and oil, and the boards of the box were
torn apart and whirled away. There was a singular and growing impulse about all this. No one said anything; they were very quiet; yet
the crowd grew quickly, as if called together by something in the air.
One voice said, "Don't forgit we're all relyin' on yer serenade, Mark,"
and this raised a strange united laugh that broke brief and loud, and
stopped, leaving the silence deeper than before. Mark and three more
left, and walked towards the Lyceum. They were members of the
Siskiyou band, and as they went one said that the town would see an
interesting trial in the morning. Soon after they had gone the crowd
moved from the station, compact and swift.

Meanwhile the Lyceum had been having disappointments. When
the train was known to be late, Amanda had abandoned bestowing
the cake until morning. But now a horrid thing had happened: the
Siskiyou band refused its services! The rocking-chairs were plying
strenuously; but Amanda strode up and down in front of Mount Shasta
and Lucretia Mott.

Herr Schwartz entered. "It's all right, madam," said he. "My trombone haf come back, und—"

"You'll play?" demanded the president.

"We blay for de ladies."

The rocking-chairs were abandoned; the Lyceum put on its bonnet
and shawl, and marshalled downstairs with the band.

"Ready," said Amanda.

"Ready," said Herr Schwartz to his musicians. "Go a leedle easy
mit der Allegro, or we bust 'Fatinitza.' "

The spirited strains were lifted in Siskiyou, and the procession was
soon at the jail in excellent order. They came round the corner with
the trombone going as well as possible. Two jerking bodies dangled
at the end of ropes, above the flare of torches. Amanda and her flock
were shrieking.

"So!" exclaimed Herr Schwartz. "Dot was dose Healy boys we haf
come to gif serenade." He signed to stop the music.

"No you don't," said two of the masked crowd, closing in with
pistols. "You'll play fer them fellers till you're told to quit."

"Cerdainly," said the philosophical Teuton. "Only dey gif brobably
very leedle attention to our Allegro."

So "Fatinitza" trumpeted on while the two on the ropes twisted,
and grew still by-and-by. Then the masked men let the band go home.
The Lyceum had scattered and fled long since, and many days passed
before it revived again to civic usefulness, nor did its members find

comfort from their men. Herr Schwartz gave a parting look at the bodies of the lynched murderers. "My," said he, "das Ewigweibliche haf draw them apove sure enough."

Miss Sissons next day was walking and talking off her shock and excitement with her lover. "And oh, Jim," she concluded, after they had said a good many things, "you hadn't anything to do with it, had you?" The young man did not reply, and catching a certain expression on his face, she hastily exclaimed: "Never mind! I don't want to know—ever!"

So James Hornbrook kissed his sweetheart for saying that, and they continued their walk among the pleasant hills.

# The Second
# Missouri Compromise

## I

The Legislature had sat up all night, much absorbed, having taken off its coat because of the stove. This was the fortieth and final day of its first session under an order of things not new only, but novel. It sat with the retrospect of forty days' duty done, and the prospect of forty days' consequent pay to come. Sleepy it was not, but wide and wider awake over a progressing crisis. Hungry it had been until after a breakfast fetched to it from the Overland at seven, three hours ago. It had taken no intermission to wash its face, nor was there just now any apparatus for this, as the tin pitcher commonly used stood not in the basin in the corner, but on the floor by the Governor's chair; so the eyes of the Legislature, though earnest, were dilapidated. Last night the pressure of public business had seemed over, and no turning back the hands of the clock likely to be necessary. Besides Governor Ballard, Mr. Hewley, Secretary and Treasurer, was sitting up too, small, iron-gray, in feature and bearing every inch the capable, dignified official, but his necktie had slipped off during the night. The bearded Councillors had the best of it, seeming after their vigil less stale in the face than the member from Silver City, for instance, whose day-old growth blurred his dingy chin, or the member from Big Camas, whose scantier red crop bristled on his cheeks in sparse wandering arrangements, like spikes on the barrel of a musical box. For comfort, most of the pistols were on the table with the Statutes of the United States. Secretary and Treasurer Hewley's lay on his strong-box immediately behind him. The Governor's was a light one, and always hung in the armhole of his waistcoat. The graveyard of Boisé City this year had twenty-seven tenants, two brought there by meningitis, and twenty-five by difference of opinion. Many denizens of the Territory were miners, and the unsettling element of gold-dust hung in the air, breeding argument. The early, thin, bright morning steadily

mellowed against the windows distant from the stove; the panes
melted clear until they ran, steamed faintly, and dried, this fresh May
day, after the night's untimely cold; while still the Legislature sat in
its shirt-sleeves, and several statesmen had removed their boots.
Even had appearances counted, the session was invisible from the
street. Unlike a good number of houses in the town, the State-House
(as they called it from old habit) was not all on the ground-floor for
outsiders to stare into, but up a flight of wood steps to a wood gallery.
From this, to be sure, the interior could be watched from several
windows on both sides; but the journey up the steps was precisely
enough to disincline the idle, and this was counted a sensible thing by
the law-makers. They took the ground that shaping any government
for a raw wilderness community needed seclusion, and they set a high
value upon unworried privacy.

The sun had set upon a concentrated Council, but it rose upon faces
that looked momentous. Only the Governor's and Treasurer's were
impassive, and they concealed something even graver than the matter
in hand.

"I'll take a hun'red mo', Gove'nuh," said the member from Silver
City, softly, his eyes on space. His name was Powhattan Wingo.

The Governor counted out the blue, white, and red chips to
Wingo, pencilled some figures on a thickly ciphered and cancelled paper that bore in print the words "Territory of Idaho, Council Chamber," and then filled up his glass from the tin pitcher, adding a little
sugar.

"And I'll trouble you fo' the toddy," Wingo added, always softly,
and his eyes always on space. "Raise you ten, suh." This was to the
Treasurer. Only the two were playing at present. The Governor was
kindly acting as bank; the others were looking on.

"And ten," said the Treasurer.

"And ten," said Wingo.

"And twenty," said the Treasurer.

"And fifty," said Wingo, gently bestowing his chips in the middle
of the table.

The Treasurer called.

The member from Silver City showed down five high hearts, and
a light rustle went over the Legislature when the Treasurer displayed three twos and a pair of threes, and gathered in his harvest.
He had drawn two cards, Wingo one; and losing to the lowest hand
that could have beaten you is under such circumstances truly hard
luck. Moreover, it was almost the only sort of luck that had attended
Wingo since about half after three that morning. Seven hours of cards
just a little lower than your neighbor's is searching to the nerves.

"Gove'nuh, I'll take a hun'red mo'," said Wingo; and once again the Legislature rustled lightly, and the new deal began.

Treasurer Hewley's winnings flanked his right, a pillared fortress on the table, built chiefly of Wingo's misfortunes. Hewley had not counted them, and his architecture was for neatness and not ostentation; yet the Legislature watched him arrange his gains with sullen eyes. It would have pleased him now to lose; it would have more than pleased him to be able to go to bed quite a long time ago. But winners cannot easily go to bed. The thoughtful Treasurer bet his money and deplored this luck. It seemed likely to trap himself and the Governor in a predicament they had not foreseen. All had taken a hand at first, and played for several hours, until Fortune's wheel ran into a rut deeper than usual. Wingo slowly became the loser to several, then Hewley had forged ahead, winner from everybody. One by one they had dropped out, each meaning to go home, and all lingering to see the luck turn. It was an extraordinary run, a rare specimen, a breaker of records, something to refer to in the future as a standard of measure and an embellishment of reminiscence; quite enough to keep the Idaho Legislature up all night. And then it was their friend who was losing. The only speaking in the room was the brief card talk of the two players.

"Five better," said Hewley, winner again four times in the last five.

"Ten," said Wingo.

"And twenty," said the Secretary and Treasurer.

"Call you."

"Three kings."

"They are good, suh. Gove'nuh, I'll take a hun'red mo'."

Upon this the wealthy and weary Treasurer made a try for liberty and bed. How would it do, he suggested, to have a round of jack-pots, say ten—or twenty, if the member from Silver City preferred—and then stop? It would do excellently, the member said, so softly that the Governor looked at him. But Wingo's large countenance remained inexpressive, his black eyes still impersonally fixed on space. He sat thus till his chips were counted to him, and then the eyes moved to watch the cards fall. The Governor hoped he might win now, under the jack-pot system. At noon he should have a disclosure to make; something that would need the most cheerful and contented feelings in Wingo and the Legislature to be received with any sort of calm. Wingo was behind the game to the tune of—the Governor gave up adding as he ran his eye over the figures of the bank's erased and tormented record, and he shook his head to himself. This was inadvert.ent

"May I inquah who yo're shakin' yoh head at, suh?" said Wingo, wheeling upon the surprised Governor.

"Certainly," answered that official. "You." He was never surprised for very long. In 1867 it did not do to remain surprised in Idaho.

"And have I done anything which meets yoh disapprobation?" pursued the member from Silver City, enunciating with care.

"You have met my disapprobation."

Wingo's eyes were on the Governor, and now his friends drew a little together, and as a unit sent a glance of suspicion at the lone bank.

"You will gratify me by being explicit, suh," said Wingo to the bank.

"Well, you've emptied the toddy."

"Ha-ha, Gove'nuh! I rose, suh, to yoh little fly. We'll awduh some mo'."

"Time enough when he comes for the breakfast things," said Governor Ballard, easily.

"As yuh say, suh. I'll open for five dolluhs." Wingo turned back to the game. He was winning, and as his luck continued his voice ceased to be soft, and became a shade truculent. The Governor's ears caught this change, and he also noted the lurking triumph in the faces of Wingo's fellow-statesmen. Cheerfulness and content were scarcely reigning yet in the Council Chamber of Idaho as Ballard sat watching the friendly game. He was beginning to fear that he must leave the Treasurer alone and take some precautions outside. But he would have to be separated for some time from his ally, cut off from giving him any hints. Once the Treasurer looked at him, and he immediately winked reassuringly, but the Treasurer failed to respond. Hewley might be able to wink after everything was over, but he could not find it in his serious heart to do so now. He was wondering what would happen if this game should last till noon with the company in its present mood. Noon was the time fixed for paying the Legislative Assembly the compensation due for its services during this session; and the Governor and the Treasurer had put their heads together and arranged a surprise for the Legislative Assembly. They were not going to pay them.

A knock sounded at the door, and on seeing the waiter from the Overland enter, the Governor was seized with an idea. Perhaps precaution could be taken from the inside. "Take this pitcher," said he, "and have it refilled with the same. Joseph knows my mixture." But Joseph was night bar-tender, and now long in his happy bed, with a day successor in the saloon, and this one did not know the mixture.

Ballard had foreseen this when he spoke, and that his writing a note of directions would seem quite natural.

"The receipt is as long as the drink," said a legislator, watching the Governor's pencil fly.

"He don't know where my private stock is located," explained Ballard. The waiter departed with the breakfast things and the note, and while the jack-pots continued the Governor's mind went carefully over the situation.

Until lately the Western citizen has known one every-day experience that no dweller in our thirteen original colonies has had for two hundred years. In Massachusetts they have not seen it since 1641; in Virginia not since 1628. It is that of belonging to a community of which every adult was born somewhere else. When you come to think of this a little it is dislocating to many of your conventions. Let a citizen of Salem, for instance, or a well-established Philadelphia Quaker, try to imagine his chief-justice fresh from Louisiana, his mayor from Arkansas, his tax-collector from South Carolina, and himself recently arrived in a wagon from a thousand-mile drive. To be governor of such a community Ballard had travelled in a wagon from one quarter of the horizon; from another quarter Wingo had arrived on a mule. People reached Boisé in three ways: by rail to a little west of the Missouri, after which it was wagon, saddle, or walk for the remaining fifteen hundred miles; from California it was shorter; and from Portland, Oregon, only about five hundred miles, and some of these more agreeable, by water up the Columbia. Thus it happened that salt often sold for its weight in gold-dust. A miner in the Bannock Basin would meet a freight teamster coming in with the staples of life, having journeyed perhaps sixty consecutive days through the desert, and valuing his salt highly. The two accordingly bartered in scales, white powder against yellow, and both parties content. Some in Boisé to-day can remember these bargains. After all, they were struck but thirty years ago. Governor Ballard and Treasurer Hewley did not come from the same place, but they constituted a minority of two in Territorial politics because they hailed from north of Mason and Dixon's line. Powhattan Wingo and the rest of the Council were from Pike County, Missouri. They had been Secessionists, some of them Knights of the Golden Circle; they had belonged to Price's Left Wing, and they flocked together. They were seven—two lying unwell at the Overland, five now present in the State-House with the Governor and Treasurer. Wingo, Gascon Claiborne, Gratiot des Pères, Pete Cawthon, and F. Jackson Gilet were their names. Besides this Council of seven were thirteen members of the Idaho House of Representatives, mostly of the same political feather with the Council, and they too would be

present at noon to receive their pay. How Ballard and Hewley came
to be a minority of two is a simple matter. Only twenty-five months
had gone since Appomattox Court-House. That surrender was presently followed by Johnston's to Sherman, at Durhams Station, and
following this the various Confederate armies in Alabama, or across
the Mississippi, or wherever they happened to be, had successively
surrendered,—but not Price's Left Wing. There was the wide open
West under its nose, and no Grant or Sherman infesting that void.
Why surrender? Wingos, Claibornes, and all, they melted away.
Price's Left Wing sailed into the prairie and passed below the horizon.
To know what it next did you must, like Ballard or Hewley, pass below
the horizon yourself, clean out of sight of the dome at Washington to
remote, untracked Idaho. There, besides wild red men in quantities,
would you find not very tame white ones, gentlemen of the ripest
Southwestern persuasion, and a Legislature to fit. And if, like Ballard
or Hewley, you were a Union man, and the President of the United
States had appointed you Governor or Secretary of such a place, your
days would be full of awkwardness, though your difference in creed
might not hinder you from playing draw-poker with the unrecon-
structed. These Missourians were whole-souled, ample-natured males
in many ways, but born with a habit of hasty shooting. The Governor,
on setting foot in Idaho, had begun to study pistolship, but acquired
thus in middle life it could never be with him that spontaneous art
which it was with Price's Left Wing. Not that the weapons now lying
loose about the State-House were brought for use there. Everybody
always went armed in Boisé, as the grave-stones impliedly testified.
Still, the thought of the bad quarter of an hour which it might come
to at noon did cross Ballard's mind, raising the image of a column in
the morrow's paper: "An unfortunate occurrence has ended relations
between esteemed gentlemen hitherto the warmest personal friends.
. . . They will be laid to rest at 3 p.m. . . . As a last token of respect
for our lamented Governor the troops from Boisé Barracks. . . ." The
Governor trusted that if his friends at the post were to do him any
service it would not be a funeral one.

The new pitcher of toddy came from the Overland, the jack-pots
continued, were nearing a finish, and Ballard began to wonder if anything had befallen a part of his note to the bar-tender, an enclosure
addressed to another person.

"Ha, suh!" said Wingo to Hewley. "My pot again, I declah." The
chips had been crossing the table his way, and he was now loser but
six hundred dollars.

"Ye ain't goin' to whip Mizzooruh all night an' all day, ez a rule,"
observed Pete Cawthon, Councillor from Lost Leg.

" 'Tis a long road that has no turnin', Gove'nuh," said F. Jackson Gilet, more urbanely. He had been in public life in Missouri, and was now President of the Council in Idaho. He, too, had arrived on a mule, but could at will summon a rhetoric dating from Cicero, and preserved by many luxuriant orators until after the middle of the present century.

"True," said the Governor, politely. "But here sits the long-suffering bank, whichever way the road turns. I'm sleepy."

"You sacrifice yo'self in the good cause," replied Gilet, pointing to the poker game. "Oneasy lies the head that wahs an office, suh." And Gilet bowed over his compliment.

The Governor thought so indeed. He looked at the Treasurer's strong-box, where lay the appropriation lately made by Congress to pay the Idaho Legislature for its services; and he looked at the Treasurer, in whose pocket lay the key of the strong-box. He was accountable to the Treasury at Washington for all money dispersed for Territorial expenses.

"Eleven-twenty," said Wingo, "and only two hands mo' to play."

The Governor slid out his own watch.

"I'll scahsely recoup," said Wingo.

They dealt and played the hand, and the Governor strolled to the window.

"Three aces," Wingo announced, winning again handsomely. "I struck my luck too late," he commented to the on-lookers. While losing he had been able to sustain a smooth reticence; now he gave his thoughts freely to the company, and continually moved and fingered his increasing chips. The Governor was still looking out of the window, where he could see far up the street, when Wingo won the last hand, which was small. "That ends it, suh, I suppose?" he said to Hewley, letting the pack of cards linger in his grasp.

"I wouldn't let him off yet," said Ballard to Wingo from the window, with sudden joviality, and he came back to the players. "I'd make him throw five cold hands with me."

"Ah, Gove'nuh, that's yoh spo'tin' blood! Will you do it, Mistuh Hewley—a hun'red a hand?"

Mr. Hewley did it; and winning the first, he lost the second, third and fourth in the space of an eager minute, while the Councillors drew their chairs close.

"Let me see," said Wingo, calculating, "if I lose this—why still—" He lost. "But I'll not have to ask you to accept my papuh, suh. Wingo liquidates. Fo'ty days at six dolluhs a day makes six times fo' is twenty-fo'—two hun'red an' fo'ty dolluhs spot cash in hand at noon, without computation of mileage to and from Silver City at fo' dolluhs

every twenty miles, estimated according to the nearest usually travelled route." He was reciting part of the statute providing mileage for
Idaho legislators. He had never served the public before, and he knew
all the laws concerning compensation by heart. "You'll not have to
wait fo' yoh money, suh," he concluded.

"Well, Mr. Wingo," said Governor Ballard, "it depends on yourself
whether your pay comes to you or not." He spoke cheerfully. "If you
don't see things my way, our Treasurer will have to wait for his
money." He had not expected to break the news just so, but it made
as easy a beginning as any.

"See things yoh way, suh?"

"Yes. As it stands at present I cannot take the responsibility of
paying you."

"The United States pays me, suh. My compensation is provided by
act of Congress."

"I confess I am unable to discern your responsibility, Gove'nuh,"
said F. Jackson Gilet. "Mr. Wingo has faithfully attended the session,
and is, like every gentleman present, legally entitled to his emoluments."

"You can all readily become entitled—"

"All? Am I—are my friends—included in this new depa'tyuh?"

"The difficulty applies generally, Mr. Gilet."

"Do I understand the Gove'nuh to insinuate—nay, gentlemen, do
not rise! Be seated, I beg." For the Councillors had leaped to their
feet.

"Whar's our money?" said Pete Cawthon. "Our money was put in
thet yere box."

Ballard flushed angrily, but a knock at the door stopped him, and
he merely said, "Come in."

A trooper, a corporal, stood at the entrance, and the disordered
Council endeavored to look usual in a stranger's presence. They resumed their seats, but it was not easy to look usual on such short
notice.

"Captain Paisley's compliments," said the officer, mechanically,
"and will Governor Ballard take supper with him this evening?"

"Thank Captain Paisley," said the Governor (his tone was quite
usual), "and say that official business connected with the end of the
session makes it imperative for me to be at the State-House. Imperative."

The trooper withdrew. He was a heavy-built, handsome fellow,
with black mustache and black eyes that watched through two
straight, narrow slits beneath straight black brows. His expression in
the council chamber had been of the regulation military indifference,

and as he went down the steps he irrelevantly sang an old English tune:

> " *'Since first I saw your face I resolved*
> *To honor and re—'*

I guess," he interrupted himself as he unhitched his horse, "parrot and monkey hev broke loose."

The Legislature, always in its shirt-sleeves, the cards on the table, and the toddy on the floor, sat calm a moment, cooled by this brief pause from the first heat of its surprise, while the clatter of Corporal Jones's galloping shrank quickly into silence.

## II

Captain Paisley walked slowly from the adjutant's office at Boisé Barracks to his quarters, and his orderly walked behind him. The captain carried a letter in his hand, and the orderly, though distant a respectful ten paces, could hear him swearing plain as day. When he reached his front door Mrs. Paisley met him.

"Jim," cried she, "two more chickens froze in the night." And the delighted orderly heard the captain so plainly that he had to blow his nose or burst.

The lady, merely remarking "My goodness, Jim," retired immediately to the kitchen, where she had a soldier cook baking, and feared he was not quite sober enough to do it alone. The captain had paid eighty dollars for forty hens this year at Boisé, and twenty-nine had passed away, victims to the climate. His wise wife perceived his extreme language not to have been all on account of hens, however; but he never allowed her to share in his professional worries, so she stayed safe with the baking, and he sat in the front room with a cigar in his mouth.

Boisé was a two-company post without a major, and Paisley, being senior captain, was in command, an office to which he did not object. But his duties so far this month of May had not pleased him in the least. Theoretically, you can have at a two-company post the following responsible people: one major, two captains, four lieutenants, a doctor, and a chaplain. The major has been spoken of; it is almost needless to say that the chaplain was on leave, and had never been seen at Boisé by any of the present garrison; two of the lieutenants were also on leave, and two on surveying details—they had influence at Washington; the other captain was on a scout with General Crook somewhere near the Malheur Agency, and the doctor had only arrived this week.

There had resulted a period when Captain Paisley was his own adjutant, quartermaster, and post surgeon, with not even an efficient sergeant to rely upon; and during this period his wife had stayed a good deal in the kitchen. Happily the doctor's coming had given relief to the hospital steward and several patients, and to the captain not only an equal, but an old friend, with whom to pour out his disgust; and together every evening they freely expressed their opinion of the War Department and its treatment of the Western army.

There were steps at the door, and Paisley hurried out. "Only you!" he exclaimed, with such frank vexation that the doctor laughed loudly. "Come in, man, come in," Paisley continued, leading him strongly by the arm, sitting him down, and giving him a cigar. "Here's a pretty how de do!"

"More Indians?" inquired Dr. Tuck.

"Bother! they're nothing. It's Senators—Councillors—whatever the Territorial devils call themselves."

"Gone on the war-path?" the doctor said, quite ignorant how nearly he had touched the Council.

"Precisely, man. War-path. Here's the Governor writing me they'll be scalping him in the State-House at twelve o'clock. It's past 11:30. They'll be whetting knives about now." And the captain roared.

"I know you haven't gone crazy," said the doctor, "but who has?"

"The lot of them. Ballard's a good man, and—what's his name?—the little Secretary. The balance are just mad dogs—mad dogs. Look here: 'Dear Captain'—that's Ballard to me. I just got it—'I find myself unexpectedly hampered this morning. The South shows signs of being too solid. Unless I am supported, my plan for bringing our Legislature to terms will have to be postponed. Hewley and I are more likely to be brought to terms ourselves—a bad precedent to establish in Idaho. Noon is the hour for drawing salaries. Ask me to supper as quick as you can, and act on my reply.' I've asked him," continued Paisley, "but I haven't told Mrs. Paisley to cook anything extra yet." The captain paused to roar again, shaking Tuck's shoulder for sympathy. Then he explained the situation in Idaho to the justly bewildered doctor. Ballard had confided many of his difficulties lately to Paisley.

"He means you're to send troops?" Tuck inquired.

"What else should the poor man mean?"

"Are you sure it's constitutional?"

"Hang constitutional! What do I know about their legal quibbles at Washington?"

"But, Paisley—"

"They're unsurrendered rebels, I tell you. Never signed a parole."

"But the general amnesty—"

"Bother general amnesty! Ballard represents the Federal government in this territory, and Uncle Sam's army is here to protect the Federal government. If Ballard calls on the army it's our business to obey, and if there's any mistake in judgment it's Ballard's, not mine." Which was sound soldier common-sense, and happened to be equally good law. This is not always the case.

"You haven't got any force to send," said Tuck.

This was true. General Crook had taken with him both Captain Sinclair's infantry and the troop (or company, as cavalry was also then called) of the First.

"A detail of five or six with a reliable non-commissioned officer will do to remind them it's the United States they're bucking against," said Paisley. "There's a deal in the moral of these things. Crook—" Paisley broke off and ran to the door. "Hold his horse!" he called out to the orderly; for he had heard the hoofs, and was out of the house before Corporal Jones had fairly arrived. So Jones sprang off and hurried up, saluting. He delivered his message.

"Um—umpra—what's that? Is it *imperative* you mean?" suggested Paisley.

"Yes, sir," said Jones, reforming his pronunciation of that unaccustomed word. "He said it twiced."

"What were they doing?"

"Blamed if I—beg the captain's pardon—they looked like they was waitin' fer me to git out."

"Go on—go on. How many were there?"

"Seven, sir. There was Governor Ballard and Mr. Hewley and—well, them's all the names I know. But," Jones hastened on with eagerness, "I've saw them five other fellows before at a—at—" The corporal's voice failed, and he stood looking at the captain.

"Well? Where?"

"At a cock-fight, sir," murmured Jones, casting his eyes down.

A slight sound came from the room where Tuck was seated, listening, and Paisley's round gray eyes rolled once, then steadied themselves fiercely upon Jones.

"Did you notice anything further unusual, corporal?"

"No, sir, except they was excited in there. Looked like they might be goin' to hev considerable rough house—a fuss, I mean, sir. Two was in their socks. I counted four guns on a table."

"Take five men and go at once to the State-House. If the Governor needs assistance you will give it, but do nothing hasty. Stop trouble, and make none. You've got twenty minutes."

"Captain—if anybody needs arrestin'—"

"You must be judge of that." Paisley went into the house. There was no time for particulars.

"Snakes!" remarked Jones. He jumped on his horse and dashed down the slope to the men's quarters.

"Crook may be here any day or any hour," said Paisley, returning to the doctor. "With two companies in the background, I think Price's Left Wing will subside this morning."

"Supposing they don't?"

"I'll go myself; and when it gets to Washington that the commanding officer at Boisé personally interfered with the Legislature of Idaho, it'll shock 'em to that extent that the government will have to pay for a special commission of investigation and two tons of red tape. I've got to trust to that corporal's good sense. I haven't another man at the post."

Corporal Jones had three-quarters of a mile to go, and it was ten minutes before noon, so he started his five men at a run. His plan was to walk and look quiet as soon as he reached the town, and thus excite no curiosity. The citizens were accustomed to the sight of passing soldiers. Jones had thought out several things, and he was not going to order bayonets fixed until the final necessary moment. "Stop trouble and make none" was firm in his mind. He had not long been a corporal. It was still his first enlistment. His habits were by no means exemplary; and his frontier personality, strongly developed by six years of vagabonding before he enlisted, was scarcely yet disciplined into the military machine of the regulation pattern that it should and must become before he could be counted a model soldier. His captain had promoted him to steady him, if that could be, and to give his better qualities a chance. Since then he had never been drunk at the wrong time. Two years ago it would not have entered his free-lance heart to be reticent with any man, high or low, about any pleasure in which he saw fit to indulge; to-day he had been shy over confessing to the commanding officer his leaning to cock-fights—a sign of his approach to the correct mental attitude of the enlisted man. Being corporal had wakened in him a new instinct, and this State-House affair was the first chance he had had to show himself. He gave the order to proceed at a walk in such a tone that one of the troopers whispered to another, "Specimen ain't going to forget he's wearing a chevron."

## III

The brief silence that Jones and his invitation to supper had caused among the Councillors was first broken by F. Jackson Gilet.

"Gentlemen," he said, "as President of the Council I rejoice in an interruption that has given pause to our haste and saved us from ill-considered expressions of opinion. The Gove'nuh has, I confess, surprised me. Befo' examining the legal aspect of our case I will ask the Gove'nuh if he is familiar with the sundry statutes applicable."

"I think so," Ballard replied, pleasantly.

"I had supposed," continued the President of the Council—"nay, I had congratulated myself that our weightiuh tasks of law-making and so fo'th were consummated yesterday, our thirty-ninth day, and that our friendly game of last night would be, as it were, the finis that crowned with pleashuh the work of a session memorable for its harmony."

This was not wholly accurate, but near enough. The Governor had vetoed several bills, but Price's Left Wing had had much more than the required two-thirds vote of both Houses to make these bills laws over the Governor's head. This may be called harmony in a manner. Gilet now went on to say that any doubts which the Governor entertained concerning the legality of his paying any salaries could easily be settled without entering upon discussion. Discussion at such a juncture could not but tend towards informality. The President of the Council could well remember most unfortunate discussions in Missouri between the years 1856 and 1860, in some of which he had had the honor to take part—*minima pars*, gentlemen! Here he digressed elegantly upon civil dissensions, and Ballard, listening to him and marking the slow, sure progress of the hour, told himself that never before had Gilet's oratory seemed more welcome or less lengthy. A plan had come to him, the orator next announced, a way out of the present dilemma, simple and regular in every aspect. Let some gentleman present now kindly draft a bill setting forth in its preamble the acts of Congress providing for the Legislature's compensation, and let this bill in conclusion provide that all members immediately receive the full amount due for their services. At noon both Houses would convene; they would push back the clock, and pass this bill before the term of their session should expire.

"Then, Gove'nuh," said Gilet, "you can amply vindicate yo'self by a veto, which, together with our votes on reconsideration of yoh objections, will be reco'ded in the journal of our proceedings, and copies transmitted to Washington within thirty days as required by law. Thus, suh, will you become absolved from all responsibility."

The orator's face, while he explained this simple and regular way out of the dilemma, beamed with acumen and statesmanship. Here they would make a law, and the Governor must obey the law!

Nothing could have been more to Ballard's mind as he calculated the fleeting minutes than this peaceful, pompous farce. "Draw your bill, gentlemen," he said. "I would not object if I could."

The Statutes of the United States were procured from among the pistols and opened at the proper page. Gascon Claiborne, upon another sheet of paper headed "Territory of Idaho, Council Chamber," set about formulating some phrases which began "Whereas," and Gratiot des Pères read aloud to him from the statutes. Ballard conversed apart with Hewley; in fact, there was much conversing aside.

" 'Third March, 1863, c. 117, s. 8, v. 12, p. 811,' " dictated Des Pères.

"Skip the chaptuhs and sections," said Claiborne. "We only require the date."

" 'Third March, 1863. The sessions of the Legislative Assemblies of the several Territories of the United States shall be limited to forty days' duration.' "

"Wise provision that," whispered Ballard. "No telling how long a poker game might last."

But Hewley could not take anything in this spirit. "Genuine business was not got through till yesterday," he said.

" 'The members of each branch of the Legislature,' " read Des Pères, " 'shall receive a compensation of six dollars per day during the sessions herein provided for, and they shall receive such mileage as now provided by law: *Provided*, that the President of the Council and the Speaker of the House of Representatives shall each receive a compensation of ten dollars a day.' "

At this the President of the Council waved a deprecatory hand to signify that it was a principle, not profit, for which he battled. They had completed their *Whereases*, incorporating the language of the several sections as to how the appropriation should be made, who disbursed such money, mileage, and, in short, all things pertinent to their bill, when Pete Cawthon made a suggestion.

"Ain't there anything 'bout how much the Gove'nuh gits?" he asked.

"And the Secretary?" added Wingo.

"Oh, you can leave us out," said Ballard.

"Pardon me, Gove'nuh," said Gilet. "You stated that yoh difficulty was not confined to Mr. Wingo or any individual gentleman, but was general. Does it not apply to yo'self, suh? Do you not need any bill?"

"Oh, no," said Ballard, laughing. "I don't need any bill."

"And why not?" said Cawthon. "You've jist ez much earned yoh money ez us fellers."

"Quite as much," said Ballard. "But we're not alike—at present."

Gilet grew very stately. "Except certain differences in political opinions, suh, I am not awah of how we differ in merit as public servants of this Territory."

"The difference is of your own making, Mr. Gilet, and no bill you could frame would cure it or destroy my responsibility. You cannot make any law contrary to a law of the United States."

"Contrary to a law of the United States? And what, suh, has the United States to say about my pay I have earned in Idaho?"

"Mr. Gilet, there has been but one government in this country since April, 1865, and as friends you and I have often agreed to differ as to how many there were before then. That government has a law compelling people like you and me to go through a formality, which I have done, and you and your friends have refused to do each time it has been suggested to you. I have raised no point until now, having my reasons, which were mainly that it would make less trouble now for the Territory of which I have been appointed Governor. I am held accountable to the Secretary of the Treasury semiannually for the manner in which the appropriation has been expended. If you will kindly hand me that book—"

Gilet, more and more stately, handed Ballard the Statutes, which he had taken from Des Pères. The others were watching Ballard with gathering sullenness, as they had watched Hewley while he was winning Wingo's money, only now the sullenness was of a more decided complexion.

Ballard turned the pages. " 'Second July, 1862. Every person elected or appointed to any office of honor or profit, either in the civil, military, or naval service, . . . shall, before entering upon the duties of such office, and before being entitled to any salary or other emoluments thereof, take and subscribe the following oath: I—' "

"What does this mean, suh?" said Gilet.

"It means there is no difference in our positions as to what preliminaries the law requires of us, no matter how we may vary in convictions. I as Governor have taken the oath of allegiance to the United States, and you as Councillor must do the same before you can get your pay. Look at the book."

"I decline, suh. I repudiate yoh proposition. There is a wide difference in our positions."

"What do you understand it to be, Mr. Gilet?" Ballard's temper was rising.

"If you have chosen to take an oath that did not go against yoh convictions—"

"Oh, Mr. Gilet!" said Ballard, smiling. "Look at the book." He would not risk losing his temper through further discussion. He would stick to the law as it lay open before them.

But the Northern smile sent Missouri logic to the winds. "In what are you superior to me, suh, that I cannot choose? Who are you that I and these gentlemen must take oaths befo' you?"

"Not before me. Look at the book."

"I'll look at no book, suh. Do you mean to tell me you have seen me day aftuh day and meditated this treacherous attempt?"

"There is no attempt and no treachery, Mr. Gilet. You could have taken the oath long ago, like other officials. You can take it to-day—or take the consequences."

"What? You threaten me, suh? Do I understand you to threaten me? Gentlemen of the Council, it seems Idaho will be less free than Missouri unless we look to it." The President of the Council had risen in his indignant oratorical might, and his more and more restless friends glared admiration at him. "When was the time that Price's Left Wing surrendered?" asked the orator. "Nevuh! Others have, be it said to their shame. We have not toiled these thousand miles fo' that! Others have crooked the pliant hinges of the knee that thrift might follow fawning. As fo' myself, two grandfathers who fought fo' our libuhties rest in the soil of Virginia, and two uncles who fought in the Revolution sleep in the land of the Dark and Bloody Ground. With such blood in my veins I will nevuh, nevuh, nevuh submit to Northern rule and dictation. I will risk all to be with the Southern people, and if defeated I can, with a patriot of old, exclaim,

" *'More true joy an exile feels*
*Than Cæsuh with a Senate at his heels.'*

Aye, gentlemen! And we will not be defeated! Our rights are here and are ours." He stretched his arm towards the Treasurer's strong-box, and his enthusiastic audience rose at the rhetoric. "Contain yo'-selves, gentlemen," said the orator. "Twelve o'clock and our bill!"

"I've said my say," said Ballard, remaining seated.

"An' what'll ye do?" inquired Pete Cawthon from the agitated group.

"I forbid you to touch that!" shouted Ballard. He saw Wingo moving towards the box.

"Gentlemen, do not resort—" began Gilet.

But small, iron-gray Hewley snatched his pistol from the box, and sat down astraddle of it, guarding his charge. At this hostile movement the others precipitated themselves towards the table where lay their weapons, and Governor Ballard, whipping his own from his arm-hole, said, as he covered the table: "Go easy, gentlemen! Don't hurt our Treasurer!"

"Don't nobody hurt anybody," said Specimen Jones, opening the door.

This prudent corporal had been looking in at a window and hearing plainly for the past two minutes, and he had his men posted. Each member of the Council stopped as he stood, his pistol not quite yet attained; Ballard restored his own to its armhole and sat in his chair; little Hewley sat on his box; and F. Jackson Gilet towered haughtily, gazing at the intruding blue uniform of the United States.

"I'll hev to take you to the commanding officer," said Jones, briefly, to Hewley. "You and yer box."

"Oh, my stars and stripes, but that's a keen move!" rejoiced Ballard to himself. "He's arresting *us*."

In Jones's judgment, after he had taken in the situation, this had seemed the only possible way to stop trouble without making any, and therefore, even now, bayonets were not fixed. Best not ruffle Price's Left Wing just now, if you could avoid it. For a new corporal it was well thought and done. But it was high noon, the clock not pushed back, and punctual Representatives strolling innocently towards their expected pay. There must be no time for a gathering and possible reaction. "I'll hev to clear this State-House out," Jones decided. "We're makin' an arrest," he said aloud, "and we want a little room." The outside bystanders stood back obediently, but the Councillors de-layed. Their pistols were, with Ballard's and Hewley's, of course, in custody. "Here," said Jones, restoring them. "Go home now. The com-manding officer's waitin' fer the prisoner. Put yer boots on, sir, and leave," he added to Pete Cawthon, who still stood in his stockings. "I don't want to hev to disperse anybody more'n what I've done."

Disconcerted Price's Left Wing now saw file out between armed soldiers the Treasurer and his strong-box; and thus guarded they were brought to Boisé Barracks, whence they did not reappear. The Governor also went to the post.

After delivering Hewley and his treasure to the commanding of-ficer, Jones with his five troopers went to the sutler's store and took a drink at Jones's expense. Then one of them asked the corporal to have another. But Jones refused. "If a man drinks much of that," said he (and the whisky certainly was of a livid, unlikely flavor), "he's liable to go home and steal his own pants." He walked away to his quarters, and as he went they heard him thoughtfully humming his most invet-erate song, "Ye shepherds tell me have you seen my Flora pass this way."

But poisonous whisky was not the inner reason for his moderation. He felt very much like a responsible corporal to-day, and the troopers knew it. "Jones has done himself a good turn in this fuss," they said. "He'll be changing his chevron."

That afternoon the Legislature sat in the State-House and read to itself in the Statutes all about oaths. It is not believed that any of them sat up another night; sleeping on a problem is often much better. Next morning the commanding officer and Governor Ballard were called upon by F. Jackson Gilet and the Speaker of the House. Everyone was civil and hearty as possible. Gilet pronounced the captain's whisky "equal to any at the Southern, Saint Louey," and conversed for some time about the cold season, General Crook's remarkable astuteness in dealing with Indians, and other topics of public interest. "And concernin' yoh difficulty yesterday, Gove'nuh," said he, "I've been consulting the laws, suh, and I perceive yoh construction is entahley correct."

And so the Legislature signed that form of oath prescribed for participants in the late Rebellion, and Hewley did not have to wait for his poker money. He and Wingo played many subsequent games; for, as they all said in referring to the matter, "A little thing like that should nevuh stand between friends."

Thus was accomplished by Ballard, Paisley—and Jones—the Second Missouri Compromise, at Boisé City, Idaho, 1867—an eccentric moment in the eccentric years of our development westward; and historic also. That it has gone unrecorded until now is because of Ballard's modesty, Paisley's preference for the sword, and Jones's hatred of the pen. He was never known to write except, later, in the pages of his company roster and such unavoidable official places; for the troopers were prophetic. In not many months there was no longer a Corporal Jones, but a person widely known as Sergeant Jones of Company A; called also the "Singing Sergeant"; but still familiar to his intimate friends as "Specimen."

# Sharon's Choice

Under Providence, a man may achieve the making of many things—ships, books, fortunes, himself even, quite often enough to encourage others; but let him beware of creating a town. Towns mostly happen. No real-estate operator decided that Rome should be. Sharon was an intended town; a one man's piece of deliberate manufacture; his whim, his pet, his monument, his device for immortally continuing above ground. He planned its avenues, gave it his middle name, fed it with his railroad. But he had reckoned without the inhabitants (to say nothing of nature), and one day they displeased him. Whenever you wish, you can see Sharon and what it has come to, as I saw it when, as a visitor without local prejudices, they asked me to serve with the telegraph-operator and the ticket-agent and the hotel-manager on the literary committee of judges at the school festival. There would be a stage, and flags, and elocution, and parents assembled, and afterwards ice-cream with strawberries from El Paso.

"Have you ever awarded prizes for school speaking?" inquired the telegraph-operator, Stuart.

"Yes," I told him. "At Concord in New Hampshire."

"Ever have a chat afterwards with a mother whose girl did not get the prize?"

"It was boys," I replied. "And parents had no say in it."

"It's boys and girls in Sharon," said he. "Parents have no say in it here, either. But that don't seem to occur to them at the moment. We'll all stick together, of course."

"I think I had best resign," said I. "You would find me no hand at pacifying a mother."

"There are fathers also," said Stuart. "But individual parents are small trouble compared with a big split in public opinion. We've missed that so far, though."

"Then why have judges? Why not a popular vote?" I inquired.

"Don't go back on us," said Stuart. "We are so few here. And you know education can't be democratic, or where will good taste find itself? Eastman knows that much, at least." And Stuart explained that Eastman was the head of the school and chairman of our committee. "He is from Massachusetts, and his taste is good, but he is total abstinence. Won't allow any literature with the least smell of a drink in it, not even in the singing-class. Would not have 'Here's a health to King Charles' inside the door. Narrowing, that; as many of the finest classics speak of wine freely. Eastman is useful, but a crank. Now take 'Lochinvar.' We are to have it on strawberry night; but say! Eastman kicked about it. Told the kid to speak something else. Kid came to me, and I—"

A smile lurked for one instant in the corner of Stuart's eye, and disappeared again. Then he drew his arm through mine as we walked.

"You have never seen anything in your days like Sharon," said he. "You could not sit down by yourself and make such a thing up. Shakespeare might have, but he would have strained himself doing it. Well, Eastman says 'Lochinvar' will go in my expurgated version. Too bad Sir Walter cannot know. Ever read his *Familiar Letters*? Great grief! but he was a good man. Eastman stuck about that mention of wine. Remember?

'So now am I come with this lost love of mine
To lead but one measure, drink one cup of wine.'

'Well,' thought I, 'Eastman would agree to water. Water and daughter would go, but is frequently used, and spoils the metre.' So I fiddled with my pencil down in the telegraph-office, and I fixed the thing up. How's this?

'So now am I come with this beautiful maid
To lead but one measure, drink one lemonade.'

Eastman accepts that. Says it's purer. Oh, it's not all sadness here!"

"How did you come to be in Sharon?" I asked my exotic acquaintance.

"Ah, how did I? How did all our crowd at the railroad? Somebody has got to sell tickets, somebody has got to run that hotel, and telegraphs have got to exist here. That's how we foreigners came. Many travellers change cars here, and one train usually misses the other, because the two companies do not love each other. You hear lots of language, especially in December. Eastern consumptives bound for

southern California get left here, and drummers are also thick. Remarks range from 'How provoking!' to things I would not even say
myself. So that big hotel and depot has to be kept running, and we
fellows get a laugh now and then. Our lot is better than these people's." He made a general gesture at Sharon.

"I should have thought it was worse," said I.

"No, for we'll be transferred some day. These poor folks are ship-
wrecked. Though it is their own foolishness, all this."

Again my eye followed as he indicated the town with a sweep of
his hand; and from the town I looked to the four quarters of heaven.
I may have seen across into Old Mexico. No sign labels the boundary;
the vacuum of continent goes on, you might think, to Patagonia. Symptoms of neighboring Mexico basked on the sand heaps along Sharon's
spacious avenues—little torpid, indecent gnomes in sashes and open
rags, with crowning-steeple straw hats, and murder dozing in their
small black eyes. They might have crawled from holes in the sand, or
hatched out of brown cracked pods on some weeds that trailed
through the broken bottles, the old shoes, and the wire fences. Outside
these ramparts began the vacuum, white, gray, indigo, florescent,
where all the year the sun shines. Not the semblance of any tree
dances in the heat; only rocks and lumps of higher sand waver and
dissolve and reappear in the shaking crystal of mirage. Not the scar
of any river-bed furrows the void. A river there is, flowing somewhere
out of the shiny violet mountains to the North, but it dies subterra-
neously on its way to Sharon, misses the town, and emerges thirty
miles south across the sunlight in a shallow, futile lake, a *cienega*,
called Las Palomas. Then it evaporates into the ceaseless blue sky.

The water you get in Sharon is dragged by a herd of wind-wheels
from the bowels of the sand. Over the town they turn and turn—
Sharon's upper story—a filmy colony of slats. In some of the homes
beneath them you may go up-stairs—in the American homes, not in
the adobe Mexican caves of song, woman, and knives; and brick and
stone edifices occur. Monuments of perished trade, these rise among
their flatter neighbors cubical and stark; under-shirts, fire-arms, and
groceries for sale in the ground-floor, blind dust-windows above. Most
of the mansions, however, squat ephemerally upon the soil, no cellar
to them, and no stair-case, the total fragile box ready to bounce and
caracole should the wind drive hard enough. Inside them, eating,
mending, the newspaper, and more babies, eke out the twelvemonth;
outside, the citizens loiter to their errands along the brief wide avenues of Sharon that empty into space. Men, women, and children move
about in the town, sparse and casual, and over their heads in a white
tribe the wind-wheels on their rudders veer to the breeze and indo-

lently revolve above the gaping obsoleteness. Through the dumb town the locomotive bell tolls pervadingly when a train of freight or passengers trundles in from the horizon or out along the dwindling fence of telegraph poles. No matter where you are, you can hear it come and go, leaving Sharon behind, an airy carcass, bleached and ventilated, setting on the sand, with the sun and the hot wind pouring through its bones.

This town was the magnate's child, the thing that was to keep his memory green; and as I took it in on that first walk of discovery, Stuart told me its story: how the magnate had decreed the railroad shops should be here; how, at that, corner lots grew in a night; how horsemen galloped the streets, shooting for joy, and the hasty tents rose while the houses were hammered together; how they had song, dance, cards, whisky, license, murder, marriage, opera—the whole usual thing—regular as the clock in our West, in Australia, in Africa, in every virgin corner of the world where the Anglo-Saxon rushes to spend his animal spirits—regular as the clock, and in Sharon's case about fifteen minutes long. For they became greedy, the corner-lot people. They ran up prices for land which the railroad, the breath of their nostrils, wanted. They grew ugly, forgetting they were dealing with a magnate, and that a railroad from ocean to ocean can take its shops somewhere else with appalling ease. Thus did the corner lots become sand again in a night. "And in the words of the poet," concluded Stuart, "Sharon has an immense future behind it."

Our talk was changed by the sight of a lady leaning and calling over a fence.

"Mrs. Jeffries," said she. "Oh, Mrs. Jeffries!"

"Well?" called a voice next door.

"I want to send Leola and Arvasita into your yard."

"Well?" the voice repeated.

"Our tool-house blew over into your yard last night. It's jammed behind your tank."

"Oh, indeed!"

A window in the next house was opened, a head put out, and this occasioned my presentation to both ladies. They were Mrs. Mattern and Mrs. Jeffries, and they fell instantly into a stiff caution of deportment; but they speedily found I was not worth being cautious over. Stuart whispered to me that they were widows of high standing, and mothers of competing favorites for the elocution prize; and I hastened to court their esteem. Mrs. Mattern was in body more ample, standing high and yellow and fluffy; but Mrs. Jeffries was smooth and small, and behind her spectacles she had an eye.

"You must not let us interrupt you, ladies," said I, after some civilities. "Did I understand that something was to be carried somewhere?"

"You did," said Mrs. Jeffries (she had come out of her house); "and I am pleased to notice no damage has been done to our fence—this time."

"It would have been fixed right up at my expense, as always, Mrs. Jeffries," retorted her neighbor, and started to keep abreast of Mrs. Jeffries as that lady walked and inspected the fence. Thus the two marched parallel along the frontier to the rear of their respective territories.

"You'll not resign?" said Stuart to me. "It is 'yours till death,' ain't it?"

I told him that it was.

"About once a month I can expect this," said Mrs. Jeffries, returning along her frontier.

"Well, it's not the only case in Sharon, Mrs. Jeffries," said Mrs. Mattern. "I'll remind you of them three coops when you kept poultry, and they got away across the railroad, along with the barber's shop."

"But cannot we help you get it out?" said I, with a zealous wish for peace.

"You are very accommodating, sir," said Mrs. Mattern.

"One of the prize-awarding committee," said Stuart. "An elegant judge of oratory. Has decided many contests at Concord, the home of Emerson."

"Concord, New Hampshire," I corrected; but neither lady heard me.

"How splendid for Leola!" cried Mrs. Mattern, instantly. "Leola! Oh, Leola! Come right out here!"

Mrs. Jeffries had been more prompt. She was already in her house, and now came from it, bringing a pleasant-looking boy of sixteen, it might be. The youth grinned at me as he stood awkwardly, brought in shirt-sleeves from the performance of some household work.

"This is Guy," said his mother. "Guy took the prize last year. Guy hopes—"

"Shut up, mother," said Guy, with entire sweetness. "I don't hope twice—"

"Twice or a dozen times should raise no hard feelings if my son is Sharon's best speaker," cried Mrs. Jeffries, and looked across the fence viciously.

"Shut up, mother; I ain't," said Guy.

"He is a master of humor recitations," his mother now said to me. "Perhaps you know, or perhaps you do not know, how high up that is reckoned."

"Why, mother, Leola can speak all around me. She can," Guy added to me, nodding his head confidentially.

I did not believe him, I think because I preferred his name to that of Leola.

"Leola will study in Paris, France," announced Mrs. Mattern, arriving with her child. "She has no advantages here. This is the gentleman, Leola."

But before I had more than noted a dark-eyed maiden who would not look at me, but stood in skirts too young for her figure, black stockings, and a dangle of hair that should have been up, her large parent had thrust into my hand a scrap-book.

"Here is what the Santa Fé *Observer* says"; and when I would have read, she read aloud for me. "The next is the Los Angeles *Christian Home*. And here's what they wrote about her in El Paso: 'Her histrionic genius for one so young'—it commences below that picture. That's Leola." I now recognized the black stockings and the hair. "Here's what a literary lady in Lordsburg thinks," pursued Mrs. Mattern.

"Never mind that," murmured Leola.

"I shall." And the mother read the letter to me. "Leola has spoke in five cultured cities," she went on. "Arvasita can depict how she was oncored at Albuquerque last Easter-Monday."

"Yes, sir, three recalls," said Arvasita, arriving at our group by the fence. An elder sister, she was, evidently. "Are you acquainted with 'Camill'?" she asked me, with a trifle of sternness; and upon my hesitating, "the celebrated French drayma of 'Camill,' " she repeated, with a trifle more of sternness. " 'Camill' is the lady in it who dies of consumption. Leola recites the letter-and-coughing scene, Act Third. Mr. Patterson of Coloraydo Springs pronounces it superior to Modjeska."

"That is Leola again," said Mrs. Mattern, showing me another newspaper cut—hair, stockings, and a candle this time.

"Sleep-walking scene, 'Macbeth,' " said Arvasita. "Leola's great night at the church fair and bazar, El Paso, in Shakespeare's acknowledged masterpiece. Leola's repetwar likewise includes 'Catherine the Queen before her Judges,' 'Quality of Mercy is not Strained,' 'Death of Little Nell,' 'Death of Paul Dombey,' 'Death of the Old Year,' 'Burial of Sir John Moore,' and other standard gems suitable for ladies."

"Leola," said her mother, "recite 'When the British Warrior Queen' to the gentleman."

"No, momma, please not," said Leola, and her voice made me look at her; something of appeal sounded in it.

"Leola is that young you must excuse her," said her mother—and I thought the girl winced.

"Come away, Guy," suddenly snapped little Mrs. Jeffries. "We are wasting the gentleman's time. You are no infant prodigy, and we have no pictures of your calves to show him in the papers."

"Why, mother!" cried the boy, and he gave a brotherly look to Leola.

But the girl, scarlet and upset, now ran inside the house.

"As for wasting time, madam," said I, with indignation, "you are wasting yours in attempting to prejudice the judges."

"There!" said Guy.

"And, Mrs. Mattern," I continued, "if I may say so without offence, the age (real or imaginary) of the speakers may make a difference in Albuquerque, but with our committee not the slightest."

"Thank you, I'm sure," said Mrs. Mattern, bridling.

"Eastern ideas are ever welcome in Sharon," said Mrs. Jeffries. "Good-morning." And she removed Guy and herself into her house, while Mrs. Mattern and Arvasita, stiffly ignoring me, passed into their own door.

"Come have a drink," said Stuart to me. "I am glad you said it. Old Mother Mattern will let down those prodigy skirts. The poor girl has been ashamed of them these two years, but momma has bulldozed her into staying young for stage effect. The girl's not conceited, for a wonder, and she speaks well. It is even betting which of the two widows you have made the maddest."

Close by the saloon we were impeded by a rush of small boys. They ran before and behind us suddenly from barrels and unforeseen places, and wedging and bumping between us, they shouted: "Chicken-legs! Ah, look at the chicken-legs!"

For a sensitive moment I feared they were speaking of me; but the folding slat-doors of the saloon burst open outward, and a giant barkeeper came among the boys and caught and shook them to silence.

"You want to behave," was his single remark; and they dispersed like spray from an atomizer.

I did not see why they should thus describe him. He stood and nodded to us, and jerked a big thumb towards the departing flock. "Funny how a boy will never think," said he, with amiability. "But they'll grow up to be about as good as the rest of us, I guess. Don't you let them monkey with you, Josey!" he called.

"Naw, I won't," said a voice. I turned and saw, by a barrel, a youth in knee-breeches glowering down the street at his routed enemies. He was possibly eight, and one hand was bound in a grimy rag. This was Chicken-legs.

"Did they harm you, Josey?" asked the giant.

"Naw, they didn't."

"Not troubled your hand any?"

"Naw, they didn't."

"Well, don't you let them touch you. We'll see you through." And as we followed him in towards our drink through his folding slat-doors he continued discoursing to me, the newcomer. "I am against interfering with kids. I like to leave 'em fight and fool just as much as they see fit. Now them boys ain't malicious, but they're young, you see, they're young, and misfortune don't appeal to them. Josey lost his father last spring, and his mother died last month. Last week he played with a freight-car and left two of his fingers with it. Now you might think that was enough hardship."

"Indeed yes," I answered.

"But the little stake he inherited was gambled away by his stinking old aunt."

"Well!" I cried.

"So we're seeing him through."

"You bet," said a citizen in boots and pistol, who was playing billiards.

"This town is not going to permit any man to fool with Josey," stated his opponent in the game.

"Or women either," added a lounger by the bar, shaggy-bearded and also with a pistol.

"Mr. Abe Hanson," said the barkeeper, presenting me to him. "Josey's father's partner. He's took the boy from the aunt and is going to see him through."

"How 'r' ye?" said Mr. Hanson, hoarsely, and without enthusiasm.

"A member of the prize-awarding committee," explained Stuart, and waved a hand at me.

They all brightened up and came round me.

"Heard my boy speak?" inquired one. "Reub Gadsden's his name."

I told him I had heard no speaker thus far; and I mentioned Leola and Guy.

"Hope the boy'll give us 'The Jumping Frog' again," said one. "I near bust."

"What's the heifer speakin' this trip?" another inquired.

"Huh! Her!" said a third.

"You'll talk different, maybe, this time," retorted the other.

"Not agin 'The Jumping Frog,' he won't," the first insisted. "I near bust," he repeated.

"I'd like for you to know my boy Reub," said Mr. Gadsden to me, insinuatingly.

"Quit fixin' the judge, Al," said Leola's backer. "Reub forgets his words, an' says 'em over, an' balks, an' mires down, an' backs out, an' starts fresh, an' it's confusin' to foller him."

"I'm glad to see you take so much interest, gentlemen," said I.

"Yes, we're apt to see it through," said the barkeeper. And Stuart and I bade them a good-morning.

As we neared the school-master's house, where Stuart was next taking me, we came again upon the boys with Josey, and no barkeeper at hand to "see him through." But Josey made it needless. At the word "Chicken-legs" he flew in a limber manner upon the nearest, and knocking him immediately flat, turned with spirit upon a second and kicked him. At this they set up a screeching and fell all together, and the school-master came out of his door.

"Boys, boys!" said he. "And the Sabbath, too!"

As this did not immediately affect them, Mr. Eastman made a charge, and they fled from him then. A long stocking of Josey's was torn, and hung in two streamers round his ankles; and his dangling shoe-laces were trodden to fringe.

"If you want your hand to get well for strawberry night—" began Mr. Eastman.

"Ah, bother strawberry night!" said Josey, and hopped at one of his playmates. But Mr. Eastman caught him skilfully by the collar.

"I am glad his misfortunes have not crushed him altogether," said I.

"Josey Yeatts is an anxious case, sir," returned the teacher. "Several influences threaten his welfare. Yesterday I found tobacco on him. Chewing, sir."

"Just you hurt me," said Josey, "and I'll tell Abe."

"Abe!" exclaimed Mr. Eastman, lifting his brow. "He means a man old enough to be his father, sir. I endeavor to instill him with some few notions of respect, but the town spoils him. Indulges him completely, I may say. And when Sharon's sympathies are stirred, sir, it will espouse a cause very warmly— Give me that!" broke off the school-master, and there followed a brief wrestle. "Chewing again to-day, sir," he added to me.

"Abe lemme have it," shrieked Josey. "Lemme go, or he'll come over and fix you."

But the calm, chilly Eastman had ground the tobacco under his heel. "You can understand how my hands are tied," he said to me.

"Readily," I answered.

"The men give Josey his way in everything. He has a—I may say an unworthy aunt."

"Yes," said I. "So I have gathered."

At this point Josey ducked and slid free, and the united flock vanished with jeers at us. Josey forgot they had insulted him, they forgot he had beaten them; against a common enemy was their friendship cemented.

"You spoke of Sharon's warm way of espousing causes," said I to Eastman.

"I did, sir. No one could live here long without noticing it."

"Sharon is a quiet town, but sudden," remarked Stuart. "Apt to be sudden. They're beginning about strawberry night," he said to Eastman. "Wanted to know about things down in the saloon."

"How does their taste in elocution chiefly lie?" I inquired.

Eastman smiled. He was young, totally bald, the moral dome of his skull rising white above visionary eyes and a serious auburn beard. He was clothed in a bleak, smooth slate-gray suit, and at any climax of emphasis he lifted slightly upon his toes and relaxed again, shutting his lips tight on the finished sentence. "Your question," said he, "has often perplexed me. Sometimes they seem to prefer verse; sometimes prose stirs them greatly. We shall have a liberal crop of both this year. I am proud to tell you I have augmented our number of strawberry speakers by nearly fifty per cent."

"How many will there be?" said I.

"Eleven. You might wish some could be excused. But I let them speak to stimulate their interest in culture. Will you not take dinner with me, gentlemen? I was just sitting down when little Josey Yeatts brought me out."

We were glad to do this, and he opened another can of corned beef for us. "I cannot offer you wine, sir," said he to me, "though I am aware it is a general habit in luxurious homes." And he tightened his lips.

"General habit wherever they don't prefer whisky," said Stuart.

"I fear so," the school-master replied, smiling. "That poison shall never enter my house, gentlemen, any more than tobacco. And as I cannot reform the adults of Sharon, I am doing what I can for their children. Little Hugh Straight is going to say his 'Lochinvar' very pleasingly, Mr. Stuart. I went over it with him last night. I like them to be word perfect," he continued to me, "as failures on exhibition night elicit unfavorable comment."

"And are we to expect failures also?" I inquired.

"Reuben Gadsden is likely to mortify us. He is an earnest boy, but nervous; and one or two others. But I have limited their length. Reuben Gadsden's father declined to have his boy cut short, and he will give us a speech of Burke's; but I hope for the best. It narrows down, it narrows down. Guy Jeffries and Leola Mattern are the two."

"The parents seem to take keen interest," said I.

Mr. Eastman smiled at Stuart. "We have no reason to suppose they have changed since last year," said he. "Why, sir," he suddenly exclaimed, "if I did not feel I was doing something for the young generation here, I should leave Sharon to-morrow! One is not appreciated, not appreciated."

He spoke fervently of various local enterprises, his failures, his hopes, his achievements; and I left his house honoring him, but amazed—his heart was so wide and his head so narrow; a man who would purify with simultaneous austerity the morals of Lochinvar and of Sharon.

"About once a month," said Stuart, "I run against a new side he is blind on. Take his puzzlement as to whether they prefer verse or prose. Queer and dumb of him that, you see. Sharon does not know the difference between verse and prose."

"That's going too far," said I.

"They don't," he repeated, "when it comes to strawberry night. If the piece is about something they understand, rhymes do not help or hinder. And of course sex is apt to settle the question."

"Then I should have thought Leola—" I began.

"Not the sex of the speaker. It's the listeners. Now you take women. Women generally prefer something that will give them a good cry. We men want to laugh mostly."

"Yes," said I; "I would rather laugh myself, I think."

"You'd know you'd rather if you had to live in Sharon. The laugh is one of the big differences between women and men, and I would give you my views about it, only my Sunday-off time is up, and I've got to go to telegraphing."

"Our ways are together," said I. "I'm going back to the railroad hotel."

"There's Guy," continued Stuart. "He took the prize on 'The Jumping Frog.' Spoke better than Leola, anyhow. She spoke 'The Wreck of the Hesperus.' But Guy had the back benches—that's where the men sit—pretty well useless. Guess if there had been a fire, some of the fellows would have been scorched before they'd have got strength sufficient to run out. But the ladies did not laugh much. Said they saw nothing much in jumping a frog. And if Leola had made 'em cry good and hard that night, the committee's decision would have kicked up more of a fuss than it did. As it was, Mrs. Mattern got me alone; but I worked us around to where Mrs. Jeffries was having her ice-cream, and I left them to argue it out."

"Let us adhere to that policy," I said to Stuart; and he replied nothing, but into the corner of his eye wandered that lurking smile which revealed that life brought him compensations.

He went to telegraphing, and I to reverie concerning strawberry night. I found myself wishing now that there could have been two prizes; I desired both Leola and Guy to be happy; and presently I found the matter would be very close, so far at least as my judgment went. For boy and girl both brought me their selections, begging I would coach them, and this I had plenty of leisure to do. I preferred Guy's choice—the story of that blue-jay who dropped nuts through the hole in a roof, expecting to fill it, and his friends came to look on and discovered the hole went into the entire house. It is better even than "The Jumping Frog"—better than anything, I think—and young Guy told it well. But Leola brought a potent rival on the tearful side of things. "The Death of Paul Dombey" is plated pathos, not wholly sterling; but Sharon could not know this; and while Leola most prettily recited it to me I would lose my recent opinion in favor of Guy, and acknowledge the value of her performance. Guy might have the men strong for him, but this time the women were going to cry. I got also a certain other sort of entertainment out of the competing mothers. Mrs. Jeffries and Mrs. Mattern had a way of being in the hotel office at hours when I passed through to meals. They never came together, and always were taken by surprise at meeting me.

"Leola is ever so grateful to you," Mrs. Mattern would say.

"Oh," I would answer, "do not speak of it. Have you ever heard Guy's 'Blue-Jay' story?"

"Well, if it's anything like that frog business, I don't want to." And the lady would leave me.

"Guy tells me you are helping him so kindly," said Mrs. Jeffries.

"Oh, yes, I'm severe," I answered, brightly. "I let nothing pass. I only wish I was as careful with Leola. But as soon as she begins 'Paul had never risen from his little bed,' I just lose myself listening to her."

On the whole, there were also compensations for me in these mothers, and I thought it as well to secure them in advance.

When the train arrived from El Paso, and I saw our strawberries and our ice-cream taken out, I felt the hour to be at hand, and that whatever our decision, no bias could be laid to me. According to his prudent habit, Eastman had the speakers follow each other alphabetically. This happened to place Leola after Guy, and perhaps might give her the last word, as it were, with the people; but our committee was there, and superior to such accidents. The flags and the bunting hung gay around the draped stage. While the audience rustled or resoundingly trod to its chairs, and seated neighbors conferred solemnly together over the programme, Stuart, behind the bunting, played "Silver Threads among the Gold" upon a melodeon.

"Pretty good this," he said to me, pumping his feet.

"What?" I said.

"Tune. Sharon is for free silver."

"Do you think they will catch your allusion?" I asked him.

"No. But I have a way of enjoying a thing by myself." And he pumped away, playing with tasteful variations until the hall was full and the singing-class assembled in gloves and ribbons.

They opened the ceremonies for us by rendering "Sweet and Low" very happily; and I trusted it was an omen.

Sharon was hearty, and we had "Sweet and Low" twice. Then the speaking began, and the speakers were welcomed, coming and going, with mild and friendly demonstrations. Nothing that one would especially mark went wrong until Reuben Gadsden. He strode to the middle of the boards, and they creaked beneath his tread. He stood a moment in large glittering boots and with hair flat and prominently watered. As he straightened from his bow his suspender-buttons came into view, and remained so for some singular internal reason, while he sent his right hand down into the nearest pocket and began his oratory:

"It is sixteen or seventeen years since I saw the Queen of France," he said, impressively, and stopped.

We waited, and presently he resumed:

"It is sixteen or seventeen years since I saw the Queen of France." He took the right hand out and put the left hand in.

"It is sixteen or seventeen years," said he, and stared frowning at his boots.

I found the silence was getting on my nerves. I felt as if it were myself who was drifting to idiocy, and tremulous empty sensations began to occur in my stomach. Had I been able to recall the next sentence, I should have prompted him.

"It is sixteen or seventeen years since I saw the Queen of France," said the orator, rapidly.

And down deep back among the men came a voice, "Well, I guess it must be, Reub."

This snapped the tension. I saw Reuben's boots march away; Mr. Eastman came from behind the bunting and spoke (I suppose) words of protest. I could not hear them, but in a minute, or perhaps two, we grew calm, and the speaking continued.

There was no question what they thought of Guy and Leola. He conquered the back of the room. They called his name, they blessed him with endearing audible oaths, and even the ladies smiled at his pleasant, honest face—the ladies, except Mrs. Mattern. She sat near Mrs. Jeffries, and throughout Guy's "Blue-Jay" fanned herself, exhibiting a well-sustained inattention. She might have foreseen that Mrs.

Jeffries would have her turn. When "The Death of Paul Dombey" came, and handkerchiefs began to twinkle out among the audience, and various noises of grief were rising around us, and the men themselves murmured in sympathy, Mrs. Jeffries not only preserved a suppressed-hilarity countenance, but managed to cough twice with a cough that visibly bit into Mrs. Mattern's soul.

But Leola's appealing cadences moved me also. When Paul was dead, she made her pretty little bow, and we sat spellbound, then gave her applause surpassing Guy's. Unexpectedly I found embarrassment of choice dazing me, and I sat without attending to the later speakers. Was not successful humor more difficult than pathos? Were not tears more cheaply raised than laughter? Yet, on the other hand, Guy had one prize, and where merit was so even—I sat, I say, forgetful of the rest of the speakers, when suddenly I was aware of louder shouts of welcome, and I awaked to Joseph Yeatts bowing at us.

"Spit it out, Josey!" a large encouraging voice was crying in the back of the hall. "We'll see you through."

"Don't be scared, Josey!" yelled another.

Then Josey opened his mouth and rhythmically rattled the following:

> *"I love little pussy her coat is so warm*
> *And if I don't hurt her she'll do me no harm*
> *I'll sit by the fi-yer and give her some food*
> *And pussy will love me because I am good."*

That was all. It had come without falter or pause, even for breath. Josey stood, and the room rose to him.

"Again! again!" they roared. "He ain't a bit scared!" "Go it, Josey!" "You don't forget yer piece!" And a great deal more, while they pounded with their boots.

> *"I love little pussy,"*

began Josey.

"Poor darling!" said a lady next me. "No mother."

> *"I'll sit by the fi-yer,"*

Josey was continuing. But nobody heard him finish. The room was a babel.

"Look at his little hand!" "Only three fingers inside them rags!" "Nobody to mend his clothes any more." They all talked to each other, and clapped and cheered, while Josey stood, one leg slightly advanced and proudly stiff, somewhat after the manner of those military engravings where some general is seen erect upon an eminence at the moment of victory.

Mr. Eastman again appeared from the bunting, and was telling us, I have no doubt, something of importance; but the giant barkeeper now shouted above the din, "Who says Josey Yeatts ain't the speaker for this night?"

At that striking of the common chord I saw them heave, promiscuous and unanimous, up the steps to the stage. Josey was set upon Abe Hanson's shoulder, while ladies wept around him. What the literary committee might have done I do not know, for we had not the time even to resign. Guy and Leola now appeared, bearing the prize between them—a picture of Washington handing the Bible out of clouds to Abraham Lincoln—and very immediately I found myself part of a procession. Men and women we were, marching about Sharon. The barkeeper led; four of Sharon's fathers followed him, escorting Josey borne aloft on Abe Hanson's shoulder, and rigid and military in his bearing. Leola and Guy followed with the picture; Stuart walked with me, whistling melodies of the war—Dixie and others. Eastman was not with us. When the ladies found themselves conducted to the saloon, they discreetly withdrew back to the entertainment we had broken out from. Josey saw them go, and shrilly spoke his first word:

"Ain't I going to have any ice-cream?"

This presently caused us to return to the ladies, and we finished the evening with entire unity of sentiment. Eastman alone took the incident to heart; inquired how he was to accomplish anything with hands tied, and murmured his constant burden once more: "One is not appreciated, not appreciated."

I do not stop over in Sharon any more. My ranch friend, whose presence there brought me to visit him, is gone away. But such was my virgin experience of the place; and in later days fate led me to be concerned with two more local competitions—one military and one civil—which greatly stirred the population. So that I never pass Sharon on my long travels without affectionately surveying the sandy, quivering, bleached town, unshaded by its twinkling forest of windwheels. Surely the heart always remembers a spot where it has been merry! And one thing I should like to know—shall know, perhaps: what sort of citizen in our republic Josey will grow to be. For whom will he vote? May he not himself come to sit in Washington and make laws for us? Universal suffrage holds so many possibilities.

# FREDERIC REMINGTON

## (1861–1909)

Born in Canton, New York, near the Canadian border, Remington grew up in a near-wilderness region, and became an avid hunter and horseman. His father, a Republican newspaper publisher and politician, had been an officer in the Civil War, and thereby cast a heroic shadow which Remington strove to match. The boy was no lover of academic studies, and because of modest artistic abilities, after he had struggled through public, private, and military schools, he elected to enter the School of Arts at Yale in 1878, where he excelled more at sports than in painting, playing football under the captaincy of the famous Walter Camp. The artistic training he received during the two years at Yale helped move him out of the amateur ranks; still, it would be the life he led thereafter that provided Remington his material.

Called back home in 1880 by the death of his father, Remington was given a minor position in the state capital through the influence of an uncle. A year later, having been refused the hand of the woman who would eventually become his wife, Remington left in a huff for the far West. Unlike Wister, he did not go as a tourist and dude-rancher, but like him Remington found his calling. A brief encounter with a wagon freighter was, as he later recalled, akin to a religious experience: the West, he was told by the man as they sat by their campfire, was gone, and Remington resolved, like Wister a few years later, to preserve the old heroic West through his art. His money exhausted, Remington returned home, and after working in another unpromising patronage job in Albany, and having at twenty-one received his patrimony, he left again for the West. Inspired by "bonanza" propaganda, Remington thought to make his fortune by becoming a stockman in Kansas, but his venture in ranch ownership met with little success. Selling out, he returned briefly to Canton in

*1884, was again refused the hand of his intended, then set out for
Arizona and New Mexico, with the intention of fulfilling his resolve
of turning out pictures of the Western scene for money.*

*Returning to Kansas City with the paintings that resulted from
this trip, Remington invested the remains of his estate in a saloon,
thinking to earn therefrom sufficient income to live on while pursuing
his artistic career. He managed to dispose of the crude paintings, but
without much return, and soon discovered that he had been swindled
by the other owners of the saloon. This left him with nothing. Returning east again, Remington was finally successful in winning the hand
of his bride, Eva Caton, taking her back with him to Kansas City,
where her presence gave his life a long needed stability. Having placed
in 1882 a Western sketch with* Harper's Weekly, *Remington continued
to try that market, with little success. When Eva returned home for
an extended visit, her husband rode west into the Arizona Territory
in 1885 in search of more material. In a positive turn of luck, he
encountered the campaign of the U.S. cavalry against the Apaches of
Geronimo, which was getting much attention in the East. Throwing
in his lot with the "buffalo soldiers," Remington submersed himself
in a rugged and extremely arduous life, and gained considerable experience in the elusiveness of Native Americans on the run and the
tenacity of cavalrymen in pursuit. Returning east to New York City
with a bulging portfolio, Remington discovered that the editor of* Outing Magazine *was his fellow student at Yale, Poultney Bigelow. His
troubles were over. Not only was Bigelow enthusiastic about his Western drawings, but Bigelow's encouragement sent Remington to the
offices of* Harper's Weekly, *this time with positive results. Commenc-
ing in January, 1886, his work began appearing regularly in that
popular journal.*

*It never stopped. Eva soon joined him in New York, and in 1887
Remington returned to Arizona in a search for Indians that was now
somewhat different from the one pursued by the U.S. cavalry he once
rode with; now he sought to capture their essence in pictures and,
increasingly, in prose descriptions. In the course of repeated returns
to the West, he developed a complex attitude toward the Native American, one of admiration qualified by a conviction that a vast distance
separated primitive from civilized people. Like Cooper before him, he
celebrated the exploits of a doomed way of life, and in so doing, assisted in the preservation of that frontier whose closing Frederick
Jackson Turner was about to commemorate. Riding a wave of nostalgia, Remington found his work in sudden demand, and as his fame
as a Western artist grew, he received requests for book illustrations,
one of the first being for pictures to accompany the serialized publi-*

*cation in* Century Magazine *of Roosevelt's* Ranch Life and the Hunting Trail *(1888), which brought him the friendship of that proponent of the "strenuous life." He drew the illustrations for Wister's first two cowboy tales, for* Harper's *in 1891, and soon began illustrating his own essays and stories for* Century *and* Harper's.

*In 1888, also, Remington had exhibited a Western watercolor in a competition in New York, and a year later, his ambitious painting of Custer's last stand received a silver medal at the Paris Exposition. These successes started him in yet another artistic direction. During the next decade he was busy with Western trips to seek material, with working up essays, stories, and illustrations drawn from those trips, and with painting and exhibiting the heroic canvases that were becoming in great demand. In 1892, he traveled to Russia and North Africa with Bigelow in search of other exotic subjects—the colorful and ferocious Cossack and Bedouin horsemen—and a layover in Germany during this trip resulted in some amusing depictions of posturing Prussian officers as well. Still, Remington's career would be identified chiefly with the American West, including the illustrations he did for an 1892 edition of Parkman's* Oregon Trail, *as well as the many that accompanied Wister's stories in* Harper's.

*In 1898, Remington was sent to Cuba to cover the Spanish-American War, that jingoistic conflict that attracted many artists and writers of the day, but the overweight New Yorker found conditions in the field not at all to his liking; he preferred the comforts of the Navy gunboats offshore. Increasingly, Remington became a studio artist, turning out immense canvases and experimenting with the horseman bronzes that would make him famous as a sculptor. His illustrated short stories and essays were gathered in several volumes—*Pony Tracks *(1895),* Crooked Trails *(1898), and* Men With the Bark On *(1900)—and his Western drawings were published in 1902 in* Done in the Open, *with an admiring introduction and verses contributed by Wister. But the publication of Wister's* The Virginian *that same year aroused Remington's ire over his friend's pasteurized West, with its convenient, sentimental ending. Remington's stories, based on his long and hard experience with the cavalry on the march, belonged to the Mark Twain tradition of unsentimental realism, and though (like Twain) he could portray tearful situations, they generally involved the deaths and sacrifices of brave soldiers well clear of the influence of women, and they were always close to the facts of Western life—as had been the stories by Wister that he had illustrated. Remington in reaction dashed off a remarkable novel,* John Ermine of the Yellowstone, *writing so quickly that the book appeared the same year as Wister's. In effect, the story fulfilled Henry James's desires* *regarding the fate of Wister's hero, that he had died young and unmarried. John Ermine is a white boy raised by Indians, who becomes thereby a savage; his subsequent tutoring in civilized ways by a white man, a humpbacked hermit who has fled the ridicule of society for the wilderness, only applies a veneer to the young man's character. Searching to reclaim his white inheritance, John Ermine becomes a cavalry scout, and falls in love with the flirtatious daughter of an army major. Having already promised herself to a young officer, she first encourages then spurns him. In a fit of jealous rage, Ermine sets out to kill his rival, but before he can carry out his plan, he is killed himself by an Indian whom he had earlier insulted. Though clearly the stuff of melodrama, and hardly a considerable challenge to Wister (Remington's novel was never a popular success), John Ermine is a fascinating study of primitivism, and establishes themes and situations that transcend the easy generalities of Wister's text. No American writer of the West before Remington attempted to get inside the Indian character, and in his* The Way of an Indian *(1906) and the humorous stories told by Sun-Down Leflare, he was perhaps more successful than any white man before him in grasping the essence of primitive life.*

*Remington died suddenly in his studio home in New Rochelle, New York, from the effects of appendicitis. It is doubtful that he would have done much more with his writing, as his experiments with oils inspired by French Impressionism had taken him in an exciting new direction, and his work with bronzes continued to make great demands on his time. But his writings remain a fascinating and idiosyncratic contribution to the literature of the West, a vital expression of a vernacular sensibility, whose rough good nature and slangy personal style are in all ways a contrast to the snobbish and polished manner of his friend and associate Wister. Like Wister, Remington was a bigot; his sympathy with Indians did not extend to other ethnic groups, and he was hostile to the immigration to the United States of Middle Europeans, which he viewed as a threat to the Anglo-Saxon hegemony. These expressions are largely limited to his letters, however, nor do they differ much from the feelings of many of his generation, for whom the Europeanization of America was a terrifying phenomenon. This was in part responsible for the contemporary nostalgia for an earlier time, when moral issues were supposed to have been simple and could be settled summarily with a gun. The result was the myth of the cowboy, with his inevitable horse and invariable Colt, a myth which Remington perhaps more even than Wister was responsible for fixing in vivid and memorable images forever.*

# A Sergeant of
# the Orphan Troop

While it is undisputed that Captain Dodd's troop of the Third Cavalry is not an orphan, and is, moreover, quite as far from it as any troop of cavalry in the world, all this occurred many years ago, when it was, at any rate, so called. There was nothing so very unfortunate about it, from what I can gather, since it seems to have fought well on its own hook, quite up to all expectations, if not beyond. No officer at that time seemed to care to connect his name with such a rioting, nose-breaking band of desperado cavalrymen, unless it was temporarily, and that was always in the field, and never in garrison. However, in this case it did not have even an officer in the field. But let me go on to my sergeant.

This one was a Southern gentleman, or rather a boy, when he refugeed out of Fredericksburg with his family, before the Federal advance, in a wagon belonging to a Mississippi rifle regiment; but nevertheless, some years later he got to be a gentleman, and passed through the Virginia Military Institute with honor. The desire to be a soldier consumed him, but the vicissitudes of the times compelled him, if he wanted to be a soldier, to be a private one, which he became by duly enlisting in the Third Cavalry. He struck the Orphan Troop.

Physically, Nature had slobbered all over Carter Johnson; she had lavished on him her very last charm. His skin was pink, albeit the years of Arizona sun had heightened it to a dangerous red; his mustache was yellow and ideally military; while his pure Virginia accent, fired in terse and jerky form at friend and enemy alike, relieved his natural force of character by a shade of humor. He was thumped and bucked and pounded into what was in the seventies considered a proper frontier soldier, for in those days the nursery idea had not been lugged into the army. If a sergeant bade a soldier "go" or "do," he instantly "went" or "did"—otherwise the sergeant belted him over the head with his six-shooter, and had him taken off in a cart. On pay-days, too, when men who did not care to get drunk went to bed in barracks, they slept under their bunks and not in them, which was conducive to longevity and a good night's rest. When buffalo were scarce they ate the army rations in those wild days; they had a fight often enough to earn thirteen dollars, and at times a good deal more. This was the way with all men at that time, but it was rough on recruits.

So my friend Carter Johnson wore through some years, rose to be a corporal, finally a sergeant, and did many daring deeds. An atavism from "the old border riders" of Scotland shone through the boy, and he took on quickly. He could act the others off the stage and sing them out of the theatre in his chosen profession.

There was fighting all day long around Fort Robinson, Nebraska —a bushwhacking with Dull-Knife's band of the Northern Cheyennes, the Spartans of the plains. It was January; the snow lay deep on the ground, and the cold was knifelike as it thrust at the fingers and toes of the Orphan Troop. Sergeant Johnson with a squad of twenty men, after having been in the saddle all night, was in at the post drawing rations for the troop. As they were packing them up for transport, a detachment of F Troop came galloping by, led by the sergeant's friend, Corporal Thornton. They pulled up.

"Come on, Carter—go with us. I have just heard that some troops have got a bunch of Injuns corralled out in the hills. They can't get 'em down. Let's go help 'em. It's a chance for the fight of your life. Come on."

Carter hesitated for a moment. He had drawn the rations for his troop, which was in sore need of them. It might mean a court martial and the loss of his chevrons—but a fight! Carter struck his spurred heels, saying, "Come on, boys; get your horses; we will go."

The line of cavalry was half lost in the flying snow as it cantered away over the white flats. The dry powder crunched under the thud-ding hoofs, the carbines banged about, the overcoat capes blew and twisted in the rushing air, the horses grunted and threw up their heads as the spurs went into their bellies, while the men's faces were serious with the interest in store. Mile after mile rushed the little column, until it came to some bluffs, where it drew rein and stood gazing across the valley to the other hills.

Down in the bottoms they espied an officer and two men sitting quietly on their horses, and on riding up found a lieutenant gazing at the opposite bluffs through a glass. Far away behind the bluffs a sharp ear could detect the reports of guns.

"We have been fighting the Indians all day here," said the officer, putting down his glass and turning to the two "non-coms." "The command has gone around the bluffs. I have just seen Indians up there on the rim-rocks. I have sent for troops, in the hope that we might get up there. Sergeant, deploy as skirmishers, and we will try."

At a gallop the men fanned out, then forward at a sharp trot across the flats, over the little hills, and into the scrub pine. The valley gradually narrowed until it forced the skirmishers into a solid body, when the lieutenant took the lead, with the command tailing out in single file. The signs of the Indians grew thicker and thicker—a skirmisher's nest here behind a scrub-pine bush, and there by the side of a rock. Kettles and robes lay about in the snow, with three "bucks" and some women and children sprawling about, frozen as they had died; but all was silent except the crunch of the snow and the low whispers of the men as they pointed to the telltales of the morning's battle.

As the column approached the precipitous rim-rock the officer halted, had the horses assembled in a side cañon, putting Corporal Thornton in charge. He ordered Sergeant Johnson to again advance his skirmish-line, in which formation the men moved forward, taking cover behind the pine scrub and rocks, until they came to an open space of about sixty paces, while above it towered the cliff for twenty feet in the sheer. There the Indians had been last seen. The soldiers lay tight in the snow, and no man's valor impelled him on. To the casual glance the rim-rock was impassable. The men were discouraged and the officer nonplussed. A hundred rifles might be covering the rock fort for all they knew. On closer examination a cutting was found in the face of the rock which was a rude attempt at steps, doubtless made long ago by the Indians. Caught on a bush above, hanging down the steps, was a lariat, which, at the bottom, was twisted around the shoulders of a dead warrior. They had evidently tried to take him up while wounded, but he had died and had been abandoned.

After cogitating, the officer concluded not to order his men forward, but he himself stepped boldly out into the open and climbed up. Sergeant Johnson immediately followed, while an old Swedish soldier by the name of Otto Bordeson fell in behind them. They walked briskly up the hill, and placing their backs against the wall of rock, stood gazing at the Indian.

With a grin the officer directed the men to advance. The sergeant, seeing that he realized their serious predicament, said,

"I think, lieutenant, you had better leave them where they are; we are holding this rock up pretty hard."

They stood there and looked at each other. "We's in a fix," said Otto.

"I want volunteers to climb this rock," finally demanded the officer.

The sergeant looked up the steps, pulled at the lariat, and commented: "Only one man can go at a time; if there are Indians up there, an old squaw can kill this command with a hatchet; and if there are no Indians, we can all go up."

The impatient officer started up, but the sergeant grabbed him by the belt. He turned, saying, "If I haven't got men to go, I will climb myself."

"Stop, lieutenant. It wouldn't look right for the officer to go. I have noticed a pine-tree the branches of which spread over the top of the rock," and the sergeant pointed to it. "If you will make the men cover the top of the rim-rock with their rifles, Bordeson and I will go up;" and turning to the Swede, "Will you go, Otto?"

"I will go anywhere the sergeant does," came his gallant reply.

"Take your choice, then, of the steps or the pine-tree," continued the Virginian; and after a rather short but sharp calculation the Swede declared for the tree, although both were death if the Indians were on the rim-rock. He immediately began sidling along the rock to the tree, and slowly commenced the ascent. The Sergeant took a few steps up the cutting, holding on by the rope. The officer stood out and smiled quizzically. Jeers came from behind the soldiers' bushes—"Go it, Otto! Go it, Johnson! Your feet are loaded! If a snow-bird flies, you will drop dead! Do you need any help? You'd make a hell of a sailor!" and other gibes.

The gray clouds stretched away monotonously over the waste of snow, and it was cold. The two men climbed slowly, anon stopping to look at each other and smile. They were monkeying with death.

At last the sergeant drew himself up, slowly raised his head, and saw snow and broken rock. Otto lifted himself likewise, and he too saw nothing. Rifle-shots came clearly to their ears from far in front—many at one time, and scattering at others. Now the soldiers came briskly forward, dragging up the cliff in single file. The dull noises of the fight came through the wilderness. The skirmish-line drew quickly forward and passed into the pine woods, but the Indian trails scattered. Dividing into sets of four, they followed on the tracks of small parties, wandering on until night threatened. At length the main trail of the fugitive band ran across their front, bringing the command together. It was too late for the officer to get his horses before dark, nor could he follow with his exhausted men, so he turned to the sergeant and asked him to pick some men and follow on the trail. The sergeant picked Otto Bordeson, who still affirmed that he would go anywhere that Johnson went, and they started. They were old hunting companions, having confidence in each other's sense and shooting. They ploughed through the snow, deeper and deeper into the pines, then on down a cañon where the light was failing. The sergeant was sweating freely; he raised his hand to press his fur cap backward from his forehead. He drew it quickly away; he stopped and started, caught Otto by the sleeve, and drew a long breath. Still holding his companion, he put his glove again to his nose, sniffed at it again, and with a mighty tug brought the startled Swede to his knees, whispering, "I smell Indians; I can sure smell 'em, Otto—can you?"

Otto sniffed, and whispered back, "Yes, plain!"

"We are ambushed! Drop!" and the two soldiers sunk in the snow. A few feet in front of them lay a dark thing; crawling to it, they found a large calico rag, covered with blood.

"Let's do something, Carter; we's in a fix."

"If we go down, Otto, we are gone; if we go back, we are gone; let's go forward," hissed the sergeant.

Slowly they crawled from tree to tree.

"Don't you see the Injuns?" said the Swede, as he pointed to the rocks in front, where lay their dark forms. The still air gave no sound. The cathedral of nature, with its dark pine trunks starting from gray snow to support gray sky, was dead. Only human hearts raged, for the forms which held them lay like black bowlders.

"Egah—lelah washatah," yelled the sergeant.

Two rifle-shots rang and reverberated down the cañon; two more replied instantly from the soldiers. One Indian sunk, and his carbine went clanging down the rocks, burying itself in the snow. Another warrior rose slightly, took aim, but Johnson's six-shooter cracked again, and the Indian settled slowly down without firing. A squaw moved slowly in the half-light to where the buck lay. Bordeson drew a bead with his carbine.

"Don't shoot the woman, Otto. Keep that hole covered; the place is alive with Indians;" and both lay still.

A buck rose quickly, looked at the sergeant, and dropped back. The latter could see that he had him located, for he slowly poked his rifle up without showing his head. Johnson rolled swiftly to one side, aiming with his deadly revolver. Up popped the Indian's head, crack went the six-shooter; the head turned slowly, leaving the top exposed. Crack again went the alert gun of the soldier, the ball striking the head just below the scalp-lock and instantly jerking the body into a kneeling position.

Then all was quiet in the gloomy woods.

After a time the sergeant addressed his voice to the lonely place in Sioux, telling the women to come out and surrender—to leave the bucks, etc.

An old squaw rose sharply to her feet, slapped her breast, shouted

"Lela washatah," and gathering up a little girl and a bundle, she strode forward to the soldiers. Three other women followed, two of them in the same blanket.

"Are there any more bucks?" roared the sergeant, in Sioux.

"No more alive," said the old squaw, in the same tongue.

"Keep your rifle on the hole between the rocks; watch these people; I will go up," directed the sergeant as he slowly mounted to the ledge, and with levelled six-shooter peered slowly over. He stepped in and stood looking down on the dead warriors.

A yelling in broken English smote the startled sergeant. "Tro up your hands, you d—— Injun! I'll blow the top off you!" came through the quiet. The sergeant sprang down to see the Swede standing with carbine levelled at a young buck confronting him with a drawn knife in his hands, while his blanket lay back on the snow.

"He's a buck—he ain't no squaw; he tried to creep on me with a knife. I'm going to kill him," shouted the excited Bordeson.

"No, no, don't kill him. Otto, don't you kill him," expostulated Johnson, as the Swede's finger clutched nervously at the trigger, and turning, he roared, "Throw away that knife, you d—— Indian!"

The detachment now came charging in through the snow, and gathered around excitedly. A late arrival came up, breathing heavily, dropped his gun, and springing up and down, yelled, "Be jabbers, I have got among om at last!" A general laugh went up, and the circle of men broke into a straggling line for the return. The sergeant took the little girl up in his arms. She grabbed him fiercely by the throat like a wild-cat, screaming. While nearly choking, he yet tried to mollify her, while her mother, seeing no harm was intended, pacified her in the soft gutturals of the race. She relaxed her grip, and the brave Virginian packed her down the mountain, wrapped in his soldier cloak. The horses were reached in time, and the prisoners put on double behind the soldiers, who fed them crackers as they marched. At 2 o'clock in the morning the little command rode into Fort Robinson and dismounted at the guard-house. The little girl, who was asleep and half frozen in Johnson's overcoat, would not go to her mother: poor little cat, she had found a nest. The sergeant took her into the guard-house, where it was warm. She soon fell asleep, and slowly he undid her, delivering her to her mother.

On the following morning he came early to the guard-house, loaded with trifles for his little Indian girl. He had expended all his credit at the post-trader's, but he could carry sentiment no further, for "To horse!" was sounding, and he joined the Orphan Troop to again ride on the Dull-Knife trail. The brave Cheyennes were running through the frosty hills, and the cavalry horses pressed hotly after. For ten days the troops surrounded the Indians by day, and stood guard in the snow by night, but coming day found the ghostly warriors gone and their rifle-pits empty. They were cut off and slaughtered daily, but the gallant warriors were fighting to their last nerve. Toward the end they were cooped in a gully on War-Bonnatt Creek, where they fortified: but two six-pounders had been hauled out, and were turned on their works. The four troops of cavalry stood to horse on the plains all day, waiting for the poor wretches to come out, while the guns roared, ploughing the frozen dirt and snow over their little stronghold; but they did not come out. It was known that all the provisions they had was the dead horse of a corporal of E Troop, which had been shot within twenty paces of their rifle-pits.

So, too, the soldiers were starving, and the poor Orphans had only crackers to eat. They were freezing also, and murmuring to be led to "the charge," that they might end it there, but they were an orphan troop, and must wait for others to say. The sergeant even asked an officer to let them go, but was peremptorily told to get back in the ranks.

The guns ceased at night, while the troops drew off to build fires, warm their rigid fingers, thaw out their buffalo moccasins, and munch crackers, leaving a strong guard around the Cheyennes. In the night there was a shooting—the Indians had charged through and had gone.

The day following they were again surrounded on some bluffs, and the battle waged until night. Next day there was a weak fire from the Indian position on the impregnable bluffs, and presently it ceased entirely. The place was approached with care and trepidation, but was empty. Two Indian boys, with their feet frozen, had been left as decoys, and after standing off four troops of cavalry for hours, they too had in some mysterious way departed.

But the pursuit was relentless; on, on over the rolling hills swept the famishing troopers, and again the Spartan band turned at bay, firmly intrenched on a bluff as before. This was the last stand—nature was exhausted. The soldiers surrounded them, and Major Wessells turned the handle of the human vise. The command gathered closer about the doomed pits—they crawled on their bellies from one stack of sage-brush to the next. They were freezing. The order to charge came to the Orphan Troop, and yelling his command, Sergeant Johnson ran forward. Up from the sage-brush floundered the stiffened troopers, following on. They ran over three Indians, who lay sheltered in a little cut, and these killed three soldiers together with an old frontier sergeant who wore long hair, but they were destroyed in turn. While the Orphans swarmed under the hill, a rattling discharge poured from the rifle-pits; but the troop had gotten under the fire, and

it all passed over their heads. On they pressed, their blood now quickened by excitement, crawling up the steep, while volley on volley
poured over them. Within nine feet of the pits was a rim-rock ledge
over which the Indian bullets swept, and here the charge was stopped.
It now became a duel. Every time a head showed on either side, it
drew fire like a flue-hole. Suddenly our Virginian sprang on the ledge,
and like a trill on a piano poured a six-shooter into the intrenchment,
and dropped back.

Major Wessells, who was commanding the whole force, crawled to
the position of the Orphan Troop, saying, "Doing fine work, boys. Sergeant, I would advise you to take off that red scarf"—when a bullet
cut the major across the breast, whirling him around and throwing
him. A soldier, one Lannon, sprang to him and pulled him down the
bluff, the major protesting that he was not wounded, which proved to
be true, the bullet having passed through his heavy clothes.

The troops had drawn up on the other sides, and a perfect storm
of bullets whirled over the intrenchments. The powder blackened the
faces of the men, and they took off their caps or had them shot off.
To raise the head for more than a fraction of a second meant death.

Johnson had exchanged five shots with a fine-looking Cheyenne,
and every time he raised his eye to a level with the rock, White Antelope's gun winked at him.

"You will get killed directly," yelled Lannon to Johnson; "they
have you spotted."

The smoke blew and eddied over them; again Johnson rose, and
again White Antelope's pistol cracked an accompaniment to his own;
but with movement like lightning the sergeant sprang through the
smoke, and fairly shoving his carbine to White Antelope's breast, he
pulled the trigger. A 50-calibre gun boomed in Johnson's face, and a
volley roared from the pits, but he fell backward into cover. His comrades set him up to see if any red stains came through the grime, but
he was unhurt.

The firing grew; a blue haze hung over the hill. Johnson again
looked across the glacis, but again his eye met the savage glare of
White Antelope.

"I haven't got him yet, Lannon, but I will;" and Sergeant Johnson
again slowly reloaded his pistol and carbine.

"Now, men, give them a volley!" ordered the enraged man, and as
volley answered volley, through the smoke sprang the daring soldier,
and standing over White Antelope as the smoke swirled and almost
hid him, he poured his six balls into his enemy, and thus died one
brave man at the hands of another in fair battle. The sergeant leaped
back and lay down among the men, stunned by the concussions. He

said he would do no more. His mercurial temperament had undergone a change, or, to put it better, he conceived it to be outrageous to fight these poor people, five against one. He characterized it as "a d—— infantry fight," and rising, talked in Sioux to the enemy—asked them to surrender, or they must otherwise die. A young girl answered him, and said they would like to. An old woman sprang on her and cut her throat with a dull knife, yelling meanwhile to the soldiers that "they would never surrender alive," and saying what she had done.

Many soldiers were being killed, and the fire from the pits grew weaker. The men were beside themselves with rage. "Charge!" rang through the now still air from some strong voice, and, with a volley, over the works poured the troops, with six-shooters going, and clubbed carbines. Yells, explosions, and amid a whirlwind of smoke the soldiers and Indians swayed about, now more slowly and quieter, until the smoke eddied away. Men stood still, peering about with wild open eyes through blackened faces. They held desperately to their weapons. An old bunch of buckskin rags rose slowly and fired a carbine aimlessly. Twenty bullets rolled and tumbled it along the ground, and again the smoke drifted off the mount. This time the air grew clear. Buffalo-robes lay all about, blood spotted everywhere. The dead bodies of thirty-two Cheyennes lay, writhed and twisted, on the packed snow, and among them many women and children, cut and furrowed with lead. In a corner was a pile of wounded squaws, half covered with dirt swept over them by the storm of bullets. One broken creature half raised herself from the bunch. A maddened trumpeter threw up his gun to shoot, but Sergeant Johnson leaped and kicked his gun out of his hands high into the air, saying, "This fight is over."

# Sun-Down Leflare's
# Warm Spot

Towards mid-day the steady brilliancy of the sun had satiated my color sense, and the dust kicked up in an irritating way, while the chug-a-chug, chug-a-chug, of the ponies began to bore me. I wished for something to happen.

We had picked wild plums, which had subdued my six-hour appetite, but the unremitting walk-along of our march had gotten on my nerves. A proper man should not have such fussy things—but I have them, more is the pity. The pony was going beautifully: I could not quarrel with him. The high plains do things in such a set way, so far as weather is concerned, and it is a day's march before you change views. I began to long for a few rocks—a few rails and some ragged trees—a pool of water with some reflections—in short, anything but the horizontal monotony of our surroundings.

To add to this complaining, it could not be expected that these wild men would ever stop until they got there, wherever "there" might happen to be this day. I evidently do not have their purpose, which is "big game," close to my heart. The chickens in this creek-bottom which we are following up would suit me as well.

These people will not be diverted, though I must, so I set my self-considering eye on Sun-Down Leflare. He will answer, for he is a strange man, with his curious English and his weird past. He is a tall person of great physical power, and must in his youth have been a handsome vagabond. Born and raised with the buffalo Indians, still there was white man enough about him for a point of view which I could understand. His great head, almost Roman, was not Indian, for it was too fine; nor was it French; it answered to none of those requirements. His character was so fine a balance between the two, when one considered his environment, that I never was at a loss to place the inflections. And yet he was an exotic, and could never bore a man who had read a little history.

Sombreroed and moccasined, Sun-Down pattered along on his roan pinto, talking seven languages at the pack-ponies, and I drew alongside. I knew he never contributed to the sum of human knowledge gratuitously; it had to be irritated out of him with delicacy. I wondered if he ever had a romance. I knew if he ever had, it would be curious. We bumped along for a time doggedly, and I said,

"Where you living now, Sun-Down?"

Instantly came the reply, "Leevin' here." He yelled at a packhorse; but, turning with a benignant smile, added, "Well, I weare leeve on dees pony, er een de blanket on de white pack-horse."

"No tepee?" I asked.

"No—no tepee," came rather solemnly for Sun-Down, who was not solemn by nature, having rather too much variety for that.

"I suppose you are a married man?"

"No—no—me not marry," came the heavy response.

"Had no woman, hey?" I said, as I gave up the subject.

"Oh, yees! woman—had seex woman," came the rather overwhelming information.

"Children too, I suppose?"

"Oh, dam, yees! whole tribe. Why, I was have boy old as you aire. He up Canada way; hees mudder he Blackfoot woman. Dat was 'way, 'way back yondair, when I was firs' come Rocky Mountain. I weare a boy."

I asked where the woman was now.

"Dead—long, long time. She got keel by buffalo. She was try for skin buffalo what was not dead 'nough for skin. Buffalo was skin her," and Sun-Down grinned quickly at his pleasantry; but it somehow did not appeal to my humor so much as to my imagination, and it revealed an undomesticated mind.

"Did you never have one woman whom you loved more than all the others?" I went on.

"Yees; twenty year 'go I had Gros Ventre woman. She was fine woman—bes' woman I evair have. I pay twenty-five pony for her. She was dress de robe un paint eet bettair, un I was mak heap of money on her. But she was keel by de Sioux while she was one day pick de wil' plum, un I lose de twenty-five pony een leetle ovair a year I have her. Sacré!

"Eef man was hab seex woman lak dat een dose day, he was not ask de odds of any reech man. He could sell de robe plenty;" and Sun-Down heaved a downright sigh.

I charged him with being an old trader, who always bought his women and his horses; and Sun-Down turned his head to me with the chin raised, while there was the wild animal in his eye.

"Buy my woman! What de 'ell you know I buy my woman?"

And then I could see my fine work. I gave him a contemptuous laugh.

Then his voice came high-pitched: "You ask me de oddar night eef I weare evair cole. Do you tink I was evair cole now? You say I buy my woman. Now I weel tell you I deed not always buy my woman."

And I knew that he would soon vindicate his gallantry, so I said, softly, "I will have to believe what you tell me about it."

"I don' wan' for dat agent to know 'bout all dees woman beesness. He was good frien' of mine, but he pretty good man back Eas'—maybeso he not lak me eef he know more 'bout me;" and Sun-Down regained his composure.

"Oh, don't you fret—I won't say a word," I assured him. And here I find myself violating his confidence in print; but it won't matter. Neither Sun-Down nor the agent will ever read it.

" 'Way back yondair, maybeso you 'bout dees high"—and he leaned down from his pony, spreading his palm about two feet and a half above the buffalo-grass—"I was work for Meestar MacDonnail, what hab trade-pos' on Missouri Reever. I was go out to de Enjun camp, un was try for mak 'em come to Meestar MacDonnail for trade skin. Well, all right. I was play de card for dose Enjun, un was manage for geet some skin myself for trade Meestar MacDonnail. I was know dose Enjun varrie well. I was play de card, was run de buffalo, un was trap de skin.

"I was all same Enjun—fringe, bead, long hair—but I was wear de hat. I was hab de bes' pony een de country, un I was hab de firs' breech-loadair een de country. Ah, I was reech! Well, I young man, un de squaw she was good frien' for me, but Snow-Owl hab young woman, un he tink terreble lot 'bout her—was watch her all time. Out of de side of her eye she was watch me, un I was watch her out of de side of my eye—we was both watch each oddar, but we deed not speak. She was look fine, by gar! You see no woman at Billings Fair what would speet even wid her. I tink she not straight-bred Enjun woman—I tink she 'bout much Enjun as I be. All time we watch each oddar. I know eet no use for try trade Snow-Owl out of her, so I tink I win her wid de cards. Den I was deal de skin game for Snow-Owl, un was hab heem broke—was geet all hees pony, all hees robe, was geet hees gun; but eet no use. Snow-Owl she not put de woman on de blanket. I tell heem, 'You put de woman on de blanket, by gar I put twenty pony un forty robe on de blanket.'

"No, he sais he weel not put de woman on de blanket. He nevair mind de robe un de pony. He go to de Alsaroke un steal more pony, un he have de robe plenty by come snow.

"Well, he tak some young man un he go off to Alsaroke to steal horse, un I seet roun' un watch dat woman. She watch me. Pretty soon camp was hunt de buffalo, un I was hunt Snow-Owl's woman. Every one was excite, un dey don' tak no 'count of me. I see de woman go up leetle coulie for stray horse, un I follar her. I sais: 'How do? You come be my woman. We run off to Meestar MacDonnail's trade-house.'

"She sais she afraid. I tole her: 'Your buck no good; he got no robe, no pony; he go leave you to live on de camp. I am reech. Come wid me.' And den I walk up un steek my knife eento de ribs of de old camp pony what she was ride. He was go hough! hough! un was drop down. She was say she weel go wid me, un I was tie her hand un feet, all same cowboy she rope de steer down, un I was leave her dair on de grass. I was ride out een de plain for geet my horse-ban', un was tell my moccasin-boy I was wan' heem go do dees ting, go do dat ting—I was forget now.

"Well, den back I go wid de horse-ban' to de woman, un was put her on good strong pony, but I was tak off hees lariat un was tie her feet undar hees belly. I tink maybeso she skin out. Den we mak trail for Meestar MacDonnail, un eet was geet night. I was ask her eef she be my squaw. She sais she will be my squaw; but by gar she was my squaw, anyhow, eef I not tak off de rawhide." Sun-Down here gave himself up to a little merriment, which called crocodiles and hyenas to my mind.

"I was tell you not for doubt I mak dat horse-ban' burn de air dat night. I knew eef dose Enjun peek up dat trail, dey run me to a stan'-steel. Eet was two day to Meestar MacDonnail, un I got dair 'bout dark, un Meestar MacDonnail she sais, 'When dose Enjun was come een?' I sais, 'Dey come pretty queek, I guess.'

"I was glad for geet een dat log fence. My pony she could go no more. Well, I was res' up, un maybeso eet four day when up come de 'vance-guard of dose Enjun, un dey was mad as wolf. Deedn't have nothin' on but de moccasin un de red paint. Dey was crazy. Meestar MacDonnail he not let 'em een de log fence. Den he was say, 'What een hell de mattair, Leflare?' I sais, 'Guess dey los' someting.'

"Meestar MacDonnail was geet up on de beeg gate, un was say, 'What you Enjun want?' Dey was say, 'Leflare; he stole chief's wife.' Dey was want heem for geeve me up. Den Meestar MacDonnail he got crazy, un he dam me terreble. He sais I was no beesness steal woman un come to hees house; but I was tol' heem I have no oddar plass for go but hees house. He sais, 'Why you tak woman, anyhow?' I was shrug my shouldair.

"Dose Enjun dey was set roun' on dair ham-bone un watch dat plass, un den pretty soon was come de village—dog, baby, dry meat —whole outfeet. Well, Leflare he was up in a tree, for dey was mak camp all roun' dat log fence. Meestar MacDonnail he was geet on de gate, de Enjun dey was set on de grass, un dey was talk a heap—dey was talk steady for two day. De Enjun was have me or dey was burn de pos'. Meestar MacDonnail sais he was geeve up de woman. De Enjun was say, dam de woman—was want me. I was say I was not geeve up de woman. Dat was fine woman, un I was say eef dey geet dat woman, dey must geet Leflare firs'.

"All night dar was more talk, un de Enjun dey was yell. Meestar MacDonnail was want me for mak run een de night-time, but I was not tink I geet troo. 'Well, den,' he sais, 'you geeve yourself to dose Enjun.' I was laugh at heem, un cock my breech-loadair, un say, 'You cannot mak me.'

"De Enjun dey was shoot dar gun at de log fence, un de white man he was shoot een de air. Eet was war.

"All right. Pretty soon dey was mak de peace sign, un was talk some more. Snow-Owl had come.

"Den I got on de gate un I yell at dem. I was call dem all de dog, all de woman een de worl'. I was say Snow-Owl he dam ole sage-hen. He lose hees robe, hees pony, hees woman, un I leek heem een de bargain eef he not run lak deer when he hear my voice. Den I was yell, bah!" which Sun-Down did, putting all the prairie-dogs into their holes for our day's march.

"Den dey was talk.

"Well, I sais, eef Snow-Owl he any good, let us fight for de woman. Let dose Enjun sen' two beeg chief eento de log fence, un I weel go out eento de plain un fight Snow-Owl for de woman. Eef I leek, dose Enjun was have go 'way; un eef dar was any one strike me but Snow-Owl, de two chief mus' die. Meestar MacDonnail he say de two chief mus' die. De Enjun was talk heap. Was say 'fraid of my gun. I was say eef I not tak my gun, den Snow-Owl mus' not tak hees bow-arrow. Den dey send de two chief eento de log house. We was fight wid de lance un de skin-knife.

"Eet was noon, un was hot. I was sharp my knife, was tie up my bes' pony tail, un was tak off my clothes, but was wear my hat for keep de sun out of my eye. Den I was geet on my pony un go out troo de gate. I was yell, 'Come on, Snow-Owl; I teach you new game;' un I was laugh at dem.

"Dose Enjun weare not to come within rifle-shot of de pos', or de chief mus' die.

"All right. Out come Snow-Owl. He was pretty man—pretty good man, I guess. Oh, eet was long time 'go. I tink he was brav' man, but he was tink too much of dat woman. He was on pinto pony, un was have not a ting on heem but de breech-clout un de bull-hide shiel'. Den we leek our pony, un we went for fight. I dun'no' jes what eet all weare;" and Sun-Down began to undo his shirt, hauling it back to show me a big livid scar through the right breast, high up by the shoulder.

"De pony go pat, pat, pat, un lak de light in de mornin' she trabel 'cross de plain we come togaddar. Hees beeg buffalo-lance she go clean troo my shouldar, un br'ak off de blade, un trow me off my pony. Snow-Owl she stop hees pony chuck, chunck, chinck, un was come roun' for run me down. I peeked up a stone un trow eet at heem. You bet my medicine she good; eet heet heem een de back of de head.

"Snow-Owl she go wobble, wobble, un she slide off de pony slow lak, un I was run up for heem. When I was geet dair he was geet on hees feet, un we was go at eet wid de knife. Snow-Owl was bes' man wid de lance, but I was bes' man wid de knife, un hees head was not come back to heem from de stone, for I keel heem, un I took hees hair; all de time de lance she steek out of my shouldar. I was go to de trade-pos', un dose Enjun was yell terreble; but Meestar Mac-Donnail she was geet on de gate un say dey mus' go 'way or de chief mus' die.

"Nex' morning dey was all go 'way; un Leflare he go 'way too. Meestar MacDonnail he did not tink I was buy all my squaw. Sacré!

"Oh, de squaw—well, I sol' her for one hundred dollar to white man on de Yellowstone. 'Twas t'ree year aftair dat fight;" and Sun-Down made a détour into the brushy bottom to head back the kitchen-mare, while I rode along, musing.

This rough plains wanderer is an old man now, and he may have forgotten his tender feelings of long ago. He had never examined himself for anything but wounds of the flesh and nature had laid rough roads in his path, but still he sold the squaw for whom he had been willing to give his life. How can I reconcile this romance to its positively fatal termination?

Back came Sun-Down presently, and spurring up the cut bank, he sang out, "You tink I always buy my squaw, hey?—what you tink 'bout eet now?"

Oh, you old land-loper, I do not know what to think about you, was what came into my head; but I said, "Sun-Down, you are a raw dog," and we both laughed.

So over the long day's ride we bobbed along together, with no more romance than hungry men are apt to feel before the evening meal. We toiled up the hills, driving the pack-horses, while the disappearing sun made the red sand-rocks glitter with light on our left, and about us the air and the grass were cold. Presently we made camp in the canyon, and what with laying our bedding, cooking our supper, and smoking, the darkness had come. Our companions had turned into their blankets, leaving Sun-Down and me gazing into the fire. The dance of the flames was all that occupied my mind until Sun-Down said, "I want for go Buford dees wintair."

"Why don't you go?" I chipped in.

"Oh—leetle baby—so long," and he showed me by spreading his hands about eighteen inches.

"Your baby, Sun-Down?"

"Yees—my little baby," he replied, meditatively.

"Why can't you go to Buford?" I hazarded.

"Leetle baby she no stan' de trip. Eet varrie late een de fall—maybeso snow—leetle baby she no stand dat."

"Why don't you go by railroad?" I pressed; but, bless me, I knew that was a foolish question, since Sun-Down Leflare did not belong to the railroad period, and could not even contemplate going anywhere that way.

"I got de wagon un de pony, but de baby she too leetle. Maybeso I go nex' year eef baby she all right. I got white woman up at agency for tak care of de baby, un eet cos' me t'ree dollar a week. You s'pose I put dat baby een a dam Enjun tepee?" And his voice rose truculently.

As I had not supposed anything concerning it, I was embarrassed somewhat, and said, "Of course not—but where was the mother of the child?"

"Oh, her mudder—well, she was no Enjun. Don' know where she ees now. When de leetle baby was born, her mudder was run off on de dam railroad;" and we turned in for the night.

My romance had arrived.

# Sun-Down's Higher Self

I sat in the growing dusk of my room at the agency, before a fire, and was somewhat lonesome. My stay was about concluded, and I dreaded the long ride home on the railroad—an institution which I wish from the bottom of my heart had never been invented.

The front door opened quietly, and shut. The grating or sand-paper sound of moccasined feet came down the hall, my door opened, and Sun-Down Leflare stole in.

"Maybeso you wan' some coal on dees fire—hey?" he observed, looking in at the top of the stove.

"No, thank you—sit down," I replied, which he did, performing forthwith the instinctive act of making a cigarette.

"Sun-Down, I am going home tomorrow."

"Where you was go home?" came the guttural response.

"Back East."

"Ah, yees. I come back Eas' myself—I was born back Eas'. I was come out here long, long time 'go, when I was boy."

"And what part of the East did you come from?"

"Well—Pembina Reever—I was born een dat plass, un I was geet be good chunk of boy een dat plass—un, by gar, I wish I geet be dead man een dat plass. Maybeso I weel."

"You think you will go back some day?" I ventured.

"Oh, yees—I tink eet weel all come out dat way. Some day dat leetle baby he geet ole for mak de travel, un I go slow back dat plass. I mak dat baby grow up where dar ees de white woman un de pries'. I mak heem 'ave de farm, un not go run roun' deese heel on de dam pony." Sun-Down threw away his cigarette, and leaned forward on his hands.

"You are a Roman Catholic?" I asked.

"Yees, I am Roman Catholic. Dose pries' ees de only peop' what care de one dam 'bout de poor half-breed Enjun. You good man, but you not so good man lak de pries'. You go run roun' wid de soldier, go paint up deese Enjun, un den go back Eas'; maybeso nevair see you 'gain. Pries' he stay where we stay, un he not all de while wan' hear how I raise de hell ober de country. He keep say, 'You be good man, Sun-Down'; un, by gar, he keep tell me how for be good man.

"I be pretty good man now: maybeso eet 'cause I too ole for be bad man;" and Sun-Down's cynicism had asserted itself, whereat we laughed.

It occurred to me that time had fought for the priest and against the medicine-man in these parts, and I so inquired.

"Yees, dey spleet even nowday. Pries' he bes' man for half-breed; but he be white man, un course he not know great many ting what dose Enjun know."

"Why, doesn't he know as much as the medicine-man?" came my infantlike question.

"Oh, well, pries' he good peop'; all time he varrie good for poor Sun-Down; but I keep tell you he ees white man. All time wan' tak care of me when I die. Well, all right, dees Enjun medicine-man she tak care of me when I was leeve sometime. You s'pose I wan' die all time? No; I wan' leeve; un I got de medicine ober een my tepee— varrie good medicine. Eet tak me troo good many plass where I not geet troo maybeso."

"What is your medicine, Sun-Down?"

"Ah, you nevair min' what my medicine ees. You white man; what you know 'bout medicine? I see you 'fraid dat fores' fire out dair een dose mountain. You ask de question how dose canyon run. Well, you not be so 'fraid you 'ave de medicine. De medicine she tak care dose fire.

"White man she leeve een de house; she walk een de road; she nevair go half-mile out of hees one plass; un I guess all de medicine he care 'bout he geet een hees pocket.

"I see deese soldier stan' up, geet keel, geet freeze all up; don' 'pear care much. He die pretty easy, un de pries' he all time talk 'bout die, un dey don't care much 'bout leeve. All time deese die: eet mak me seeck. Enjun she wan' leeve, un, by gar, she look out pretty sharp 'bout eet too.

"Maybeso white man she don' need medicine. White man she don' 'pear know enough see speeret. Humph! white man can't see wagon-track on de grass; don't know how he see wagon-track on de cloud. Enjun he go all ober de snow; he lie een de dark; he leeve wid de win', de tunder—well, he leeve all time out on de grass—night-time— daytime—all de time."

"Yes, yes—certainly, Sun-Down. It is all very strange to me, but how can you prove to me that good comes to you which is due to your medicine alone?"

"Ah-h—my medicine—when weare she evair do me any good? Ah-h, firs' time I evair geet my medicine she save my life—what? She do me great deal good, I tell you. Eef dose pries' be dair, she tell me, 'You geet ready for die'; but I no wan' die.

"Well, fellar name Wauchihong un me was trap de bevair ovair by de Souris Reever, un we weare not geet to dat reever one night, un weare lay down for go sleep. We weare not know where we weare. We weare wak up een de middle of dat night, un de plain she all great beeg grass fire. De win' she weare blow hard, un de fire she come 'whew-o-o-o!' We say, where we run? My medicine she tell me run off lef' han', un Wauchihong hees medicine tell heem you run off right-hau' way. I weare say my medicine she good; he weare say hees medicine varrie ole—have done de great ting—weare nevair fail. We follow our medicine, un so we weare part. I run varrie fas', un leetle while I fall een de Souris Reever, un den I know dose fire she not geet Leflare. My medicine was good.

"Nex' day I fin' Wauchihong dead. All burn—all black. He was burn up een dose fire what catch heem on de plain. De win' she drove de fire so fas' he could do not'ing, un hees medicine she lie to heem.

"You s'pose de pries' he tole me wheech way for run dat night? No; she tell me behave myself, un geet ready for die right dair. Now what you tink?"

Revelations and truths of this sort were overpowering, and no desire to change a man of Sun-Down's age and rarity came to my mind; but in hopes I said, "Did it ever so happen that your medicine failed you?"

"My medicine she always good, but medicine ees not so good one time as nodder time. Do you s'pose I geet dat soldier order to Buford eef my medicine bad? But de medicine she was not ac' varrie well dat time.

"Deed you evair lie down alone een de bottom of de Black Canyon for pass de night? I s'pose you tink dair not'ing but bear een dat canyon; but I 'ave 'ear dem speerets dance troo dat canyon, un I 'ave see dem shoot troo dem pine-tree when I was set on de rim-rock. Deed you evair see de top of dose reever een de moonlight? What you know 'bout what ees een dat reever? White man he don't know so much he tink he know. Guess de speeret don' come een de board house, but she howl roun' de tepee een de wintair night. Enjun see de speerets dance un talk plenty een de lodge fire; white man he see not'ing but de coffee boil.

"White man mak de wagon, un de seelver dollar, un de dam railroad, un he tink dat ees all dair ees een de country;" and Sun-Down left off with a guttural "humph," which was the midship shot of disaster for me.

"But you don't tell the priest about this medicine?"

"No—what ees de use for tell de pries'?—he ees white man."

I asked Sun-Down what was the greatest medicine he ever knew, and he did not answer until, fired by my doubts, he continued, slowly, "My medicine ees de great medicine."

A critic must be without fear, since he can never fully comprehend the intent of other minds, so I saw that fortune must favor my investigations, for I knew not how to proceed; but knowing that action is life, I walked quickly to my grip-sack and took out my silver pocket-flask, saying: "You know, Sun-Down, very well, that it is dead against the rule to give a redskin a drink on a United States agency, but I am going to give you one if you will promise me not to go out and talk about it in this collection of huts. Are you with me?"

"Long-Spur—we pretty good frien'—hey? I weel say not a ting."

Then the conventionalities were gone through with, and they are doubtless familiar to many of my readers.

"Now I tole you dees ting—what was de great medicine—but I don' wan' you for go out here een de village un talk no more dan I talk—are you me?"

"I am you," and we forgathered.

"Now le's see; I weel tole you 'bout de bigges' medicine," and he made a cigarette.

"You aire young man—I guess maybeso you not born when I was be medicine-man; but eet was bad medicine for Absaroke, un you mus' not say a ting 'bout dees to dem. I am good frien' here now, but een dose day I was good frien' of de Piegan, un dey wan' come down here to de Absaroke un steal de pony. De party was geet ready—eet was ten men, un we come on de foot. We come 'long slow troo de mountain un was hunt for de grub. Aftair long time we was fin' de beeg Crow camp—we was see eet from de top of de Pryor Mountain. Den we go 'way back up head of de canyon, 'way een dat plass where de timber she varrie tick, un we buil' de leetle log fort, 'bout as beeg as t'ree step 'cross de meddle. We was wan' one plass for keep de dry meat; we weare not wan' any one for see our fire; un we weare put up de beeg fight dair eef de Absaroke she roun' us up.

"Een dose day de Enjun he not come een de mountain varrie much—dey was hunt de buffalo on de flat, but maybeso she come een de mountain, un we watch out varrie sharp. Every night, jus' sun-down, we go out—each man by hees self, un we watch dat beeg camp un de horse ban's. Eet was 'way out on de plain great many mile. White man lak you he see not'ing, but de Enjun he mak out de tepee un de pony. I was always see much bettair dan de odder Enjun— varrie much bettair—un when we come back to de log fort for smoke de pipe, I was tole dose Enjun jus' how de country lay, un where de bes' plass for catch dem pony."

I think one who has ever looked at the Western landscape from a mountain-top will understand what Sun-Down intended by this extensive view. If one has never seen it, words will hardly tell him how it stretches away, red, yellow, blue, in a prismatic way, shaded by cloud forms and ending among them—a sort of topographical map. I can think of nothing else, except that it is an unreal thing to look at.

"Well, for begeen wid, one man she always go alone; nex' night noddair man go. Firs' man she 'ave de bes' chance, un eet geet varrie bad for las' man, 'cause dose Enjun dey catch on to de game un watch un go roun' for cut de trail. But de Enjun horse-t'ief he mak de trail lak de snake—eet varrie hard for peek up.

"I was 'ave de idea I geet be medicine-man, un I tole dem dey don' know not'ing 'cause dey cannot see, un I tole dem I see everyting; see right troo de cloud. I say each dose Enjun now you do jus' what I tole you, den you fin' de pony.

"So de firs' man he was start off een de afternoon, un we see heem no more. When de man was geet de horse, un maybeso de scalp, he skin out for de Piegan camp.

"Nex' night noddair man she go start off late een de afternoon, un I go wid heem, un I sais, 'You stay here, pull your robe ovair your head, un I go een de brush un mak de medicine for tell where ees good plass for heem to go.' When I was mak de medicine I come back, un we set dair on de mountain, un I tell heem where he go 'way out dair on de plain. I sais: 'You go down dees canyon un follow de creek down, un twenty-five mile out dair you fin' de horse ban'. You can sleep one night een de plass where I was point heem out—den you geet de pony. Eef you not fin' eet so, I am not medicine-man.'

"So dees man was go. One man she go every night, un I was set een de log fort all 'lone las' night. I was say eef deese Enjun she do what I tole heem, I be beeg great medicine-man dees time. Den I geet varrie much scare, for I was las' man, un dose Absaroke dey sure begin see our trail, un I put out de fire een de log fort, un I go off down de mountain for geet 'way from de trail what deese Enjun she mak. I was wan' mak de fire on dees mountain, 'cause she jus' 'live wid dose grizzily-bear. I varrie much 'fraid—I sleep een de tree dat night, un jus' come day I was go down de creek een de canyon. I was walk een de water un walk on de rocks. I was geet big bau' elk to run ovair my trail. I was walk long de rim-rock, un was geet pretty well down een de plain. I was sleep dat night een de old bear-cave, un I was see dees camp pretty well. Eet was good plass, 'bout ten mile out een de uppair valley of de Beeg-Horn Reever, but I was 'ave be careful, for dose Enjun dey weare run all ovair de country hunt deese horse-t'ief tracks. Oh, I see dem varrie well. I see Enjun come up my canyon un pass by me so near I hear dem talk. I was scare.

"Jus' come dark I crawl up on de rim-rock, un eet was rain hard. Enjun she no lak de rain, so I sais: 'I go down now. I keep out een de heel, for I see varrie much bettair dan de Absaroke, un eef I tink dey see me I drop een de sage-bush.' " And here Sun-Down laughed, but I did not think such hide-and-seek was very funny.

"Eet geet varrie dark, un I walk up to dees camp, not more dan ten step from de tepee. I tak de dry meat off de pole un trow eet to dose dog for mak dem keep still while I was hear de Absaroke laugh un talk. De dog he bark not so much at de Enjun as eef I be de white man; jus' same de white man dog he bite de dam leg off de Enjun.

"I cut de rope two fine pony what was tie up near de lodge, un I know deese weare war-pony or de strong buffalo-horse. I lead dem out of dose camp. Eet was no use for try geet more as de two pony, for I could not run dem een de dark night. I feel dem all ovair for see dey all right. I could not see much. Den I ride off."

"You got home all right, I suppose?"

"Eef I not geet home all right, by gar, I nevair geet home 'tall. Dey chasse me, I guess, but I 'ave de good long start, un I leave varrie bad trail, I tink. Man wid de led horse he can leave blind trail more def'rent dan when he drive de pony.

"When I geet to dat Piegan camp I was fin' all dose Enjun 'cept one: he was nevair come back. Un I sais my medicine she ees good; she see where no one can see. Dey all sais my medicine she varrie strong for steal de pony. I was know ting what no man she see. Dey was all fin' de camp jus' as I say so. I was geet be strong een dat camp, un dey all say I see bes' jus' at sun-down, un dey always call me de sun-down medicine."

I asked, "How did it happen that you could see so much better than the others; was it your medicine which made it possible?"

"No. I was fool dose Enjun. I was 'ave a new pair of de fiel'-glass what I was buy from a white man, un I was not let dose Enjun see dem—dat ees how."

"So, you old fraud, it was not your medicine, but the field-glasses?" and I jeered him.

"Ah, dam white man, she nevair understan' de medicine. De medicine not 'ave anyting to do wid de fiel'-glass; but how you know what happen to me een dat canyon on dat black night? How you know dat? Eef eet not for my medicine, maybeso I not be here. I see dose speeret—dey was come all roun' me—but my medicine she strong, un dey not touch me."

"Have a drink, Sun-Down," I said, and we again forgathered. The wild man smacked his lips.

"I say, Sun-Down, I have always treated you well; I want you to tell me just what that medicine is like, over there in your tepee."

"Ah, dat medicine. Well, she ees leetle bagful of de bird claw, de wolf tooth, t'ree arrow-head, un two bullet what 'ave go troo my body."

"Is that all?"

"Ah, you white man!"

# When a Document
# Is Official

William or "Billy" Burling had for these last four years worn three yellow stripes on his coat sleeve with credit to the insignia. Leading up to this distinction were two years when he had only worn two, and back of that were yet other annums when his blue blouse had been severely plain except for five brass buttons down the front. This matter was of no consequence in all the world to any one except Burling, but the nine freezing, grilling, famishing years which he had so successfully contributed to the cavalry service of the United States were the "clean-up" of his assets. He had gained distinction in several pounding finishes with the Indians; he was liked in barracks and respected on the line; and he had wrestled so sturdily with the books that when his name came up for promotion to an officer's commission he had passed the examinations. On the very morning of which I speak, a lieutenant of his company had quietly said to him: "You need not say anything about it, but I heard this morning that your commission had been signed and is now on the way from Washington. I want to congratulate you."

"Thank you," replied William Burling as the officer passed on. The sergeant sat down on his bunk and said, mentally, "It was a damn long time coming."

There is nothing so strong in human nature as the observance of custom, especially when all humanity practises it, and the best men in America and Europe, living or dead, have approved of this one. It has, in cases like the sergeant's, been called "wetting a new commission." I suppose in Mohammedan Asia they buy a new wife. Something outrageous must be done when a military man celebrates his "step"; but be that as it may, William Burling was oppressed by a desire to blow off steam. Here is where the four years of the three stripes stood by this hesitating mortal and overpowered the exposed human nature.

Discipline had nearly throttled custom, and before this last could catch its breath again the orderly came in to tell Burling that the colonel wanted him up at headquarters.

It was early winter at Fort Adobe, and the lonely plains were white with a new snow. It certainly looked lonely enough out beyond the last buildings, but in those days one could not trust the plains to be as lonely as they looked. Mr. Sitting-Bull or Mr. Crazy-Horse might pop out of any *coulee* with a goodly following, and then life would not be worth living for a wayfarer. Some of these high-flavored romanticists had but lately removed the hair from sundry buffalo-hunters in Adobe's vicinity, and troops were out in the field trying to "kill, capture, or destroy" them, according to the ancient and honorable form. All this was well known to Sergeant Burling when he stiffened up before the colonel.

"Sergeant, all my scouts are out with the commands, and I am short of officers in post. I have an order here for Captain Morestead, whom I suppose to be at the juncture of Old Womans Fork and Lightning Creek, and I want you to deliver it. You can easily find their trail. The order is important, and must go through. How many men do you want?"

Burling had not put in nine years on the plains without knowing a scout's answer to that question. "Colonel, I prefer to go alone." There was yet another reason than "he travels the fastest who travels alone" in Burling's mind. He knew it would be a very desirable thing if he could take that new commission into the officers' mess with the prestige of soldierly devotion upon it. Then, too, nothing short of twenty-five men could hope to stand off a band of Indians.

Burling had flipped a mental coin. It came down heads for him, for the colonel said: "All right, sergeant. Dress warm and travel nights. There is a moon. Destroy that order if you have bad luck. Understand?"

"Very well, sir," and he took the order from the colonel's hand.

The old man noticed the figure of the young cavalryman, and felt proud to command such a man. He knew Burling was an officer, and he thought he knew that Burling did not know it. He did not like to send him out in such weather through such a country, but needs must.

As a man Burling was at the ripe age of thirty, which is the middle distance of usefulness for one who rides a government horse. He was a light man, trim in his figure, quiet in manner, serious in mind. His nose, eyes, and mouth denoted strong character, and also that there had been little laughter in his life. He had a mustache, and beyond this nothing can be said, because cavalrymen are primitive men, weighing no more than one hundred and sixty pounds. The horse is responsible for this, because he cannot carry more, and that weight even then must be pretty much on the same ancient lines. You never see long, short, or odd curves on top of a cavalry horse—not with nine years of field service.

Marching down to the stables, he gave his good bay horse quite as many oats as were good for him. Then going to his quarters, he dressed himself warmly in buffalo coat, buffalo moccasins, fur cap and gloves, and he made one saddle pocket bulge with coffee, sugar, crackers, and bacon, intending to fill the opposite side with grain for his horse. Borrowing an extra six-shooter from Sergeant McAvoy, he returned to the stables and saddled up. He felt all over his person for a place to put the precious order, but the regulations are dead set against pockets in soldiers' clothes. He concluded that the upper side of the saddle-bags, where the extra horseshoes go, was a fit place. Strapping it down, he mounted, waved his hand at the fellow-soldiers, and trotted off up the road.

It was getting toward evening, there was a fine brisk air, and his horse was going strong and free. There was no danger until he passed the Frenchman's ranch where the buffalo-hunters lived; and he had timed to leave there after dark and be well out before the moon should discover him to any Indians who might be viewing that log house with little schemes of murder in expectance.

He got there in the failing light, and tying his horse to the rail in front of the long log house, he entered the big room where the buffalo-hunters ate, drank, and exchanged the results of their hard labor with each other as the pasteboards should indicate. There were about fifteen men in the room, some inviting the bar, but mostly at various tables guessing at cards. The room was hot, full of tobacco smoke and many democratic smells, while the voices of the men were as hard as the pounding of two boards together. What they said, for the most part, can never be put in your library, neither would it interest if it was. Men with the bark on do not say things in their lighter moods which go for much; but when these were behind a sage-bush handling a Sharps, or skinning among the tailing buffaloes on a strong pony, what grunts were got out of them had meaning!

Buffalo-hunters were men of iron endeavor for gain. They were adventurers; they were not nice. Three buckets of blood was four dollars to them. They had thews, strong-smelling bodies, and eager minds. Life was red on the buffalo-range in its day. There was an intellectual life—a scientific turn—but it related to flying lead, wolfish knowledge of animals, and methods of hide-stripping.

The sergeant knew many of them, and was greeted accordingly.

He was feeling well. The new commission, the dangerous errand, the fine air, and the ride had set his blood bounding through a healthy frame. A young man with an increased heart action is going to do something besides standing on one foot leaning against a wall: nature arranged that long ago.

Without saying what he meant, which was "let us wet the new commission," he sang out: "Have a drink on the army. Kem up, all you hide-jerkers," and they rallied around the young soldier and "wet." He talked with them a few minutes, and then stepped out into the air—partly to look at his horse, and partly to escape the encores which were sure to follow. The horse stood quietly. Instinctively he started to unbuckle the saddle pocket. He wanted to see how the "official document" was riding, that being the only thing that oppressed Burling's mind. But the pocket was unbuckled, and a glance showed that the paper was gone.

His bowels were in tremolo. His heart lost three beats; and then, as though to adjust matters, it sent a gust of blood into his head. He pawed at his saddle-bags; he unbuttoned his coat and searched with nervous fingers everywhere through his clothes; and then he stood still, looking with fixed eyes at the nigh front foot of the cavalry horse. He did not stand mooning long; but he thought through those nine years, every day of them, every minute of them; he thought of the disgrace both at home and in the army; he thought of the lost commission, which would only go back the same route it came. He took off his overcoat and threw it across the saddle. He untied his horse and threw the loose rein over a post. He tugged at a big sheath-knife until it came from the back side of his belt to the front side, then he drew two big army revolvers and looked at the cylinders—they were full of gray lead. He cocked both, laid them across his left arm, and stepped quickly to the door of the Frenchman's log house. As he backed into the room he turned the key in the lock and put it under his belt. Raising the revolvers breast-high in front of him, he shouted, "Attention!" after the loud, harsh habit of the army. An officer might talk to a battalion on parade that way.

No one had paid any attention to him as he entered. They had not noticed him, in the preoccupation of the room, but every one quickly turned at the strange word.

"Throw up your hands instantly, every man in the room!" and with added vigor, "Don't move!"

Slowly, in a surprised way, each man began to elevate his hands —some more slowly than others. In settled communities this order would make men act like a covey of quail, but at that time at Fort

Adobe the six-shooter was understood both in theory and in practice.

"You there, bartender, be quick! I'm watching you." And the bartender exalted his hands like a practised saint.

"Now, gentlemen," began the soldier, "the first man that bats an eye or twitches a finger or moves a boot in this room will get shot just that second. Sabe?"

"What's the matter, Mr. Soldier? Be you *loco?*" sang out one.

"No, I am not *loco*. I'll tell you why I am not." Turning one gun slightly to the left, he went on: "You fellow with the long red hair over there, you sit still if you are not hunting for what's in this gun. I rode up to this shack, tied my horse outside the door, came in here, and bought the drinks. While I was in here some one stepped out and stole a paper—official document—from my saddle pockets, and unless that paper is returned to me, I am going to turn both of these guns loose on this crowd. I know you will kill me, but unless I get the paper I want to be killed. So, gentlemen, you keep your hands up. You can talk it over: but remember, if that paper is not handed me in a few minutes, I shall begin to shoot." Thus having delivered himself, the sergeant stood by the door with his guns levelled. A hum of voices filled the room.

"The soldier is right," said some one.

"Don't point that gun at me; I hain't got any paper, pardner. I can't even read paper, pard. Take it off; you might git narvous."

"That sojer's out fer blood. Don't hold his paper out on him."

"Yes, give him the paper," answered others. "The man what took that paper wants to fork it over. This soldier means business. Be quick."

"Who's got the paper?" sang a dozen voices. The bartender expostulated with the determined man—argued a mistake—but from the compressed lips of desperation came the word "Remember!"

From a near table a big man with a gray beard said: "Sergeant, I am going to stand up and make a speech. Don't shoot. I am with you." And he rose quietly, keeping an inquisitive eye on the Burling guns, and began:

"This soldier is going to kill a bunch of people here; any one can see that. That paper ain't of no account. What ever did any fool want to steal it for? I have been a soldier myself, and I know what an officer's paper means to a despatch-bearer. Now, men, I say, after we get through with this mess, what men is alive ought to take the dog-gone paper-thief, stake the feller out, and build a slow fire on him, if he can be ridden down. If the man what took the paper will hand it up, we all agree not to do anything about it. Is that agreed?"

"Yes, yes, that's agreed," sang the chorus.

"Say, boss, can't I put my arms down?" asked a man who had become weary.

"If you do, it will be forever," came the simple reply.

Said one man, who had assembled his logistics: "There was some stompin' around yar after we had that drink on the sojer. Whoever went out that door is the feller what got yer document; and ef he'd a-tooken yer horse, I wouldn't think much—I'd be lookin' fer that play, stranger. But to go *cincha* a piece of paper! Well, I think you must be plumb *loco* to shoot up a lot of men like we be fer that yar."

"Say," remarked a natural observer—one of those minds which would in other places have been a head waiter or some other highly sensitive plant—"I reckon that Injun over thar went out of this room. I seen him go out."

A little French half-breed on Burling's right said, "Maybe as you keel de man what 'ave 'and you de papier—hey?"

"No, on my word I will not," was the promise, and with that the half-breed continued: "Well, de papier ees een ma pocket. Don't shoot."

The sergeant walked over to the abomination of a man, and putting one pistol to his left ear, said, "Give it up to me with one fist only—mind, now!" But the half-breed had no need to be admonished, and he handed the paper to Burling, who gathered it into the grip of his pistol hand, crushing it against the butt.

Sidling to the door, the soldier said, "Now I am going out, and I will shoot any one who follows me." He returned one gun to its holster, and while covering the crowd, fumbled for the key-hole, which he found. He backed out into the night, keeping one gun at the crack of the door until the last, when with a quick spring he dodged to the right, slamming the door.

The room was filled with a thunderous roar, and a dozen balls crashed through the door.

He untied his horse, mounted quickly with the overcoat underneath him, and galloped away. The hoof-beats reassured the buffalo-hunters; they ran outside and blazed and popped away at the fast-receding horseman, but to no purpose. Then there was a scurrying for ponies, and a pursuit was instituted, but the grain-fed cavalry horse was soon lost in the darkness. And this was the real end of Sergeant William Burling.

The buffalo-hunters followed the trail next day. All night long galloped and trotted the trooper over the crunching snow, and there was no sound except when the moon-stricken wolves barked at his horse from the gray distance.

The sergeant thought of the recent occurrence. The reaction weak-ened him. His face flushed with disgrace; but he knew the commission was safe, and did not worry about the vengeance of the buffalo-hunters, which was sure to come.

At daylight he rested in a thick timbered bottom, near a cut bank, which in plains strategy was a proper place to make a fight. He fed himself and his horse, and tried to straighten and smooth the crumpled order on his knee, and wondered if the people at Adobe would hear of the unfortunate occurrence. His mind troubled him as he sat gazing at the official envelope; he was in a brown study. He could not get the little sleep he needed, even after three hours' halt. Being thus preoccupied, he did not notice that his picketed horse from time to time raised his head and pricked his ears toward his back track. But finally, with a start and a loud snort, the horse stood eagerly watching the bushes across the little opening through which he had come.

Burling got on his feet, and untying his lariat, led his horse directly under the cut bank in some thick brush. As he was in the act of crawling up the bank to have a look at the flat plains beyond, a couple of rifles cracked and a ball passed through the soldier's hips. He dropped and rolled down the bank, and then dragged himself into the brush.

From all sides apparently came Indians' "Ki-yis," and "coyote yelps." The cavalry horse trembled and stood snorting, but did not know which way to run. A great silence settled over the snow, lasting for minutes. The Sioux crawled closer, and presently saw a bright little flare of fire from the courier's position, and they poured in their bullets, and again there was quiet. This the buffalo-hunters knew later by the "sign" on the trail. To an old hunter there is no book so plain to read as footprints in the snow.

And long afterwards, in telling about it, an old Indian declared to me that when they reached the dead body they found the ashes of some paper which the soldier had burned, and which had revealed his position. "Was it his medicine which had gone back on him?"

"No," I explained, "it wasn't his medicine, but the great medicine of the white man, which bothered the soldier so."

"Hump! The great Washington medicine maybeso. It make dam fool of soldiers lots of time I know 'bout," concluded "Bear-in-the-Night," as he hitched up his blanket around his waist.

# Billy's
# Tearless Woe

Mr. Bolette, ranch-man, sat with me on the corral fence looking away
at the yellow meadows—seeing them through our squinted eyelids, as
they rolled one plain into another—growing pink and more cold, losing
themselves in blue hills, until one had to squint the more to distinguish
what was finally land and what was cloud form. When a mortal looks
on these things he ceases to think—it does him so little good. As a
mental proposition it is too exhausting. Like the ocean lying quiet at
mid-day, it is only fit for brown study.

Presently our vision came back to the vicinity of the corral fence,
where was passing a cow-puncher on a pony with a small basket on
his arm.

"Good-by, Billy," sung out Bolette.

The individual addressed simply turned his solemn brown face to
us, and broke away into a gentle lope.

"That basket is full of pie," exclaimed the ranch owner.

"Pie?"

"Yes; it's the only bait that will draw Billy off the range, 'cept
medicine for a dog."

"Medicine for a dog?"

"Oh, yes; Billy's all snarled up with a Scotch stag-hound. He just
is naturally in love with the beast—won't let us put out wolf poison
on account of him."

The receding Billy was a handsome figure on a horse; bronzed,
saturnine, silent. This might in no way distinguish him among his kind,
except that it did. He was pronouncedly more so than others. His
mission with the Coon Skin outfit was horse-wrangler and rider of the
western fence. He lived in a tent miles away in a small horse pasture
on the banks of the Little Big Horn, and only came up to the ranch
buildings at long intervals to report matters, and petition for pie. One

of Billy's few weaknesses lay strong on the fat pastries fabricated by the Coon Skin chef. He rarely stayed longer than was necessary to tell Mr. Bolette that "Brindle Legs" got cut up in some wire which had been carried down by the flood, that "Sloppy Weather" had a sore back, and to recommend the selling of "Magpie" before time set too strong against him, and to acquire the pie.

As Billy grew smaller on the rolling grass, Mr. Bolette observed: "That puncher don't come here often, and he don't stay long, but his dog is sick now, and he can't stay at all. It beats all how that boy hooks up to that dog. He don't appear to care for anything or anybody in the world but Keno. I don't believe that Billy has a brand on anything but that pup. Most of these punchers and line-riders tie up a little to some of the Pocahontases from the agency, but I never saw one around Billy's camp. If they ever are there, they hunt brush when they see me cleaving the air. Maybe it's a good thing for me. Most of these punchers have got a bad case of the gypsies, and that dog seems to hold Billy level. Now the dog is sick. He is getting thinner and thinner—won't eat, and I don't know what's the matter with him. Dogs don't round up much in cow-outfits. Do you know anything about a dog? Can you feel a dog's pulse and figure out what is going on under his belt?"

I admitted my helplessness in the matter.

"Taps, chaps, and ladigo straps—if that dog don't get well my horses can look after themselves, and if he dies, Billy will make the Big Red Medicine. I lose anyway," and Mr. Bolette slid off the fence.

"I reckon we had better go over to Billy's pasture to-morrow, and shove some drugs into Keno. If it don't do any good it may help bring things to a head—so that's what we'll do."

On the morrow, late in the afternoon, we took down the bars in front of Billy's lonely tent on the banks of the Little Big Horn.

On a bright Navajo blanket in the tent lay a big, black, Scotch stag-hound—the sick Keno—Billy's idol. He raised his eyelids at us, but closed them again wearily.

"Don't touch him," sharply said Bolette. "I wouldn't touch him with a shovel in his grave when Billy wasn't around. He's a holy terror. When one of these Injuns about here wants to dine with Billy, he gets off on that hill and sings bass at Billy, till Billy comes out in front and rides the peace-sign; otherwise he wouldn't come into camp at all. An Injun would just as soon go against a ghost as this dog. Keno never did like anything about Injuns except the taste, and it's a good thing for a line-rider to have some safeguard on his mess-box. These Injuns calculate that a cow-puncher is a pretty close relation, and Injuns don't let little matters like grub stand between kinfolks. Then again there are white men who cut this range that need watching, and Keno never played favorites. He was always willing to hook onto anybody that showed up, and say, when that dog was in good health you wouldn't want to mix up with him much."

Over the hills from the south came a speck—a horseman—Billy himself, as the ranch-man said. Slowly the figure drew on—now going out of sight in the wavy plains—moving steadily toward the tent by the river. He dismounted at the bars with the stiff drop peculiar to his species, and, coming in, began to untackle his horse.

He never bowed to us, nor did he greet us. He never cast his eyes on us sitting there so far from any other people in that world of his. In the guild of riders politeness in any form is not an essential— indeed, it is almost a sign of weakness to their minds, because it must necessarily display emotion of a rather tender sort. Odds Fish! Zounds! Away with it. It is not of us. Suffice it to Billy that he could see us for the last three miles sitting there, and equally we were seeing him. What more?

Untying two Arctic hares from his saddle, he straddled on his horseman's legs to Keno's bed and patted him on the head. Keno looked up and licked his hand, and then his face, as he bent toward him. For a little time they looked at each other, while Bolette and I pared softly at two sticks with our jack-knives.

Then Billy got up, came out, and began to skin his rabbits. As he slit one down, he said: "I had to work for these two jacks. When Keno was well he thinned them out round here. Whenever he got after a rabbit it was all day with him. I'm going to make some soup for him. He won't stand for no tin grub," said Billy, as he skinned away.

"Have you any idea what's the matter with the dog?" was asked.

"No, I don't savvy his misery. I'd give up good if there was a doctor within wagon-shot of this place. I'd bring him out here if I had to steal him. I'm afraid the dog has got 'to Chicago.'* He can't eat, and he's got to eat to live, I reckon. I've fixed up all kinds of hash for him— more kinds than Riley's Chinaman can make over to the station, and Keno won't even give it a smell. I lay out to shoot a little rabbit soup into him about once a day, but it's like fillin' ole ca'tridge shells. Been sort of hopin' he might take a notion to come again. Seen a man once that far gone that the boys built a box for him. And that man is a- ridin' somewhere in the world to-day."

Billy made his soup, and we put aconite and cowtownie whiskey in it. The troubled puncher poured it down Keno's resisting throat with a teaspoon until the patient fell back on the blanket exhausted.

* To die.

After this the poor fellow went around to the far side of the tent, and, sitting down, gazed vacantly into the woods across the Big Horn. A passing word from us met with no response. The man himself would not show his emotions, though the listless melancholy was an emotion, but the puncher did not recognize it as such. The fierce and lonely mind was being chastened, but so long as we were the other side of the canvas there could be no weakness; at least he would not have permitted that—not for an instant—had he known.

Night came on, and, with supper finished, we turned into our blankets. My eyes were opened several times during the night by the flashes of a light, and I could distinguish that it was Billy with a candle, looking over his dog.

In the morning Bolette and I rode the range in pursuit of his details of business management—fences and washouts, the new Texan two-year-olds, and the sizing up of the beef steers fit for Chicago, and then back to Billy's on the second day.

As we jogged up the river, we saw several Indians trailing about in the brush by the river—weird and highly colored figures—leading their ponies and going slowly. They were looking for a lost object, a trail possibly.

"What are they doing?" I asked.

"Don't you put in your time worrying what Injuns are doing," said Bolette. "When they are doing anything, it's worse than when they ain't doing anything. An Injun is all right when he is doing nothing. I like him laying down better than standing up."

"Oh! I say, old 'One Feather,' what you do, hey?" shouted Bolette, and "One Feather," thus addressed, came slowly forward to us.

"Ugh—Billy's dog he cow-eek—he go die—get fi' dollar mabeso we find um."

Bolette turned in his saddle to me, and with a wide, open-eyed wonderment slowly told off the words, "Billy's—kettle—is full—of mud," and I savvied.

This time we approached the camp from down the river, through a brush trail, and Bolette pulled up his horse on the fringe, pointing and saying in a whisper, "Look at Billy."

Sure enough, by the tent on a box sat the bent-over form of the puncher who despised his own emotions. His head was face downward in his hands. He was drawing on the reserve of his feelings, no doubt.

We rode up, and Bolette sang out: "Hello, Billy; hear Keno's passed it up. Sorry 'bout that, Billy. Had to go, though, I suppose. That's life, Billy. We'll all go that way, sooner or later. Don't see any use of worrying."

Billy got up quickly, saying: "Sure thing. Didn't see anything of the pup, did you?" His face was dry and drawn.

"No. Why?"

"Oh, d——n him, he pulled out on me!" and Billy started for his picketed horse.

In chorus we asked, "What do you mean—he pulled out on you?"

Turning quickly, raising his chin, and with the only arm gesture I ever saw him make, he said quickly: "He left me—he went away from me—he pulled out—savvy? Now what do you suppose he wanted to do that for? To me!"

We explained that it was a habit of animals to take themselves off on the approach of death—that they seem to want to die alone; but the idea took no grip on Billy's mind, for he still stood facing us, saying: "But he shouldn't have gone away from me—I would never have deserted him. If I was going to die for it I wouldn't have left him."

Saddling his horse, he took a pan of cooked food and started away down the river, returning after some hours with the empty tin. "I put out fresh grub every day so Keno can get something to eat if he finds it. I put little caches of corn-beef every few rods along the river, enough to give him strength to get back to me. He may be weak, and he may be lost. It's no use to tell me that Keno wouldn't come back to me if he could get back. I don't give a d——n what dogs do when they die. Keno wouldn't do what any ordinary dog would."

We sat about under the shadow of the great trouble, knowing better than to offer weak words to one whose rugged nature would find nothing but insult in them, when an Indian trotted up, and, leaning over his horse's neck, said, "Billy, I find him dog—he in de river—drown—you follar me."

In due time we trotted in single file after the blanketed form of Know-Coose. For five miles down the Little Big Horn we wended our way, and the sun was down on the western hills when the Indian turned abruptly into some long sedge-grass and stopped his horse, pointing.

We dismounted, and, sure enough, there lay Keno—not a lovely thing to look at after two days of water and buzzards and sun.

"He must have gone to the river and fallen in from weakness," was ventured.

"No, there was water in the tent," snapped the surly cow-boy in response, for this implied a lack of attention on his part. As there was clearly no use for human comfort in Billy's case, we desisted.

The cow-puncher and the Indian went back on the dry ground, and, with their gloved hands and knives, dug a shallow grave. The puncher took a fine Navajo blanket from his saddle, and in it the carefully wrapped remains of Keno were deposited in the hole. A fifty-dollar blanket was all that Billy could render up to Keno now, excepting the interment in due form, and the rigid repression of all unseemly emotion.

"I wouldn't have pulled out on him. I don't see what he wanted to go pull out on me for," Billy said softly, as we again mounted and took up our backward march.

When we reached camp there was no Billy. After supper he did not come, and for hours there was no Billy, and in the morning there was no Billy.

"I have got it put up," soliloquized Bolette, "that Billy is making medicine over in Riley's saloon at the station, and I reckon I can get a new horse-wrangler, because if I understand the curves of that puncher's mental get-up, New Mexico or Arizona will see William Fling about ten days from now, or some country as far from Keno as he can travel on what money Riley don't get."

So it was that Keno and Billy passed without tears from the knowledge of men.

# STEPHEN CRANE

## (1871–1900)

Crane was born in Newark, New Jersey, to a Methodist minister and his pious wife. During Crane's early years, his father's calling occasioned numerous moves, ending in Port Jervis, New York, where the minister died in 1880. Young Crane was educated in a private school, and spent two years consecutively at Lafayette College and Syracuse University, working his way as a correspondent for the New York Tribune but devoting much of his time and energy competing in college baseball. At eighteen, he lost his mother, and, dropping out of college, headed for New York City, where he continued to work for newspapers but planned to become a writer of fiction. As a free-lancer, he made little money and was often hungry; his impoverished circumstances forced him to live in the Bowery, where he witnessed the scenes of violence and degradation that inspired his first novel, Maggie: A Girl of the Streets (1892), which was so grimly realistic that he was forced to publish it himself with money borrowed from his brother. The book had few sales, but it called attention to Crane's talents, and was admired by influential critics like W. D. Howells and Hamlin Garland, the pioneering realist.

Crane's career took a turn for the better with the publication of The Red Badge of Courage (1895), which brought him recognition as a writer of genius and which remains one of the classics of American literature, but which made him little money. Though a remarkably realistic account of warfare, it was something of a historical novel, since the Civil War, which was its subject, had ended five years before Crane was born. Crane's newfound reputation brought him a journalistic assignment, to travel to Texas and Mexico and send back an account of his experiences; this journey would provide material for a number of Crane's finest short stories. On his return, he was assigned by the New York Journal to cover the Greco-Turkish War, ironically because of his skill in describing the battles of a war he knew only secondhand. He next planned to cover the filibustering activities in Cuba, and set out from Florida in an ill-fated voyage that resulted in shipwreck—providing the material for perhaps his greatest short story, "The Open Boat," a naturalist tour de force.

In Jacksonville, Florida, Crane had met Cora Taylor, who kept a house of convenience for prostitutes, and who helped nurse him back to health after his rescue. In 1898 they traveled to England and were married. Their relationship inspired considerable malicious gossip, which also seized on his frequent bouts of illness—the onset of tuberculosis—as a sign of alcoholism and narcotics abuse. In England, Crane met Joseph Conrad, who gave him friendship and literary encouragement; but his efforts to write were hampered by his good-natured hospitality, as his house was overrun with parasitic acquaintances who took advantage of the intimacy to spread further gossip. Crane was relieved when he was sent by the New York World to cover the war in Cuba—where he was an exhilarated witness to battles that verified the realism of his accounts in Red Badge—but the arduousness of the experience aggravated his illness. He found mean gossip awaiting him in New York, and fled back to rural England, where he drove himself literally to death by writing for his living. His lungs hemorrhaged, and he was taken to a health spa in Germany, but too late. He died there at the age of twenty-eight.

Save for Keats, perhaps, no writer of greater genius has been lost so young. In the years following the publication of Red Badge, Crane turned out ten volumes of writing—novels and short stories chiefly, but also two books of poetry, powerful, experimental verse inspired by the recently discovered manuscripts of Emily Dickinson. Because of financial need, and because of his increasing ill health, not all of Crane's work is without faults, but at his best he is the match of any writer of his day. Perhaps because of his early interest in sports, he excelled in the description of action, to which he brought a visceral vicariousness comparable to that of Robert Louis Stevenson at his most masterful—nor was Conrad much Crane's superior in this regard. Perhaps because like Stevenson, Crane was tubercular, his writings vibrate with hectic energy; but, unlike Stevenson, he was no lapsed romantic, no refugee in exotic or historical fictions. His work is grimly naturalistic—it is set, with the mighty exception of Red Badge, in a modern moment, and even that bloody classic is relatively bare of historical detail—and framed with irony in both circumstance and style.

Like Ambrose Bierce, Crane remains best known as a writer of the Civil War, and his novel and stories about the war resemble (and

*perhaps are indebted to) Bierce's in their concentration on the grotes-
queries of combat. But where Bierce's Western tales are not the
writer's best work, but are a kind of curiosity shop of little horrors
extrapolated from Poe, the handful of short stories Crane derived
from his brief tour of the West are among the best of their kind, and
helped lift the subject matter higher than it had been lifted before,
debunking the myth of the "heroic" West even as it was being born.
In all that he wrote about the West, Crane catapulted the scene into
a modern moment, with a vividness of description and characteriza-
tion than even now has nothing of the antique. Had he chosen to work
his Western sojourn into the fabric of a novel, it would no doubt have
overshadowed Wister's* The Virginian *and Remington's* John Ermine;
*one can only wonder what the subsequent course of Western fiction
might have been.*

# A Man
# and Some Others

Dark mesquit spread from horizon to horizon. There was no house or
horseman from which a mind could evolve a city or a crowd. The world
was declared to be a desert and unpeopled. Sometimes, however, on
days when no heat-mist arose, a blue shape, dim, of the substance of
a specter's veil, appeared in the southwest, and a pondering sheep-
herder might remember that there were mountains.

In the silence of these plains the sudden and childish banging of a
tin pan could have made an iron-nerved man leap into the air. The sky
was ever flawless; the manœuvering of clouds was an unknown pageant; but at times a sheep-herder could see, miles away, the long,
white streamers of dust rising from the feet of another's flock, and
the interest became intense.

Bill was arduously cooking his dinner, bending over the fire, and
toiling like a blacksmith. A movement, a flash of strange color, perhaps, off in the bushes, caused him suddenly to turn his head. Presently he arose, and, shading his eyes with his hand, stood motionless
and gazing. He perceived at last a Mexican sheep-herder winding
through the brush toward his camp.

"Hello!" shouted Bill.

The Mexican made no answer, but came steadily forward until he
was within some twenty yards. There he paused, and, folding his arms,
drew himself up in the manner affected by the villain in the play. His
serape muffled the lower part of his face, and his great sombrero
shaded his brow. Being unexpected and also silent, he had something
of the quality of an apparition; moreover, it was clearly his intention
to be mysterious and devilish.

The American's pipe, sticking carelessly in the corner of his mouth,
was twisted until the wrong side was uppermost, and he held his
frying-pan poised in the air. He surveyed with evident surprise this

apparition in the mesquit. "Hello, José!" he said; "what's the matter?"

The Mexican spoke with the solemnity of funeral tollings: "Beel, you mus' geet off range. We want you geet off range. We no like. Un'erstan'? We no like."

"What you talking about?" said Bill. "No like what?"

"We no like you here. Un'erstan'? Too mooch. You mus' geet out. We no like. Un'erstan'?"

"Understand? No; I don't know what the blazes you're gittin' at." Bill's eyes wavered in bewilderment, and his jaw fell. "I must git out? I must git off the range? What you givin' us?"

The Mexican unfolded his serape with his small yellow hand. Upon his face was then to be seen a smile that was gently, almost caressingly murderous. "Beel," he said, "geet out!"

Bill's arm dropped until the frying-pan was at his knee. Finally he turned again toward the fire. "Go on, you dog-gone little yaller rat!" he said over his shoulder. "You fellers can't chase me off this range. I got as much right here as anybody."

"Beel," answered the other in a vibrant tone, thrusting his head forward and moving one foot, "you geet out or we keel you."

"Who will?" said Bill.

"I—and the others." The Mexican tapped his breast gracefully.

Bill reflected for a time, and then he said: "You ain't got no manner of license to warn me off'n this range, and I won't move a rod. Understand? I've got rights, and I suppose if I don't see 'em through, no one is likely to give me a good hand and help me lick you fellers, since I'm the only white man in half a day's ride. Now, look; if you fellers try to rush this camp, I'm goin' to plug about fifty per cent of the gentlemen present, sure. I'm goin' in for trouble, an' I'll git a lot of you. 'Nuther thing: if I was a fine valuable caballero like you, I'd stay in the rear till the shootin' was done, because I'm goin' to make a particular p'int of shootin' you through the chest." He grinned affably, and made a gesture of dismissal.

As for the Mexican, he waved his hands in a consummate expression of indifference. "Oh, all right," he said. Then, in a tone of deep menace and glee, he added: "We will keel you eef you no geet. They have decide'."

"They have, have they?" said Bill. "Well, you tell them to go to the devil!"

## II

Bill had been a mine-owner in Wyoming, a great man, an aristocrat, one who possessed unlimited credit in the saloons down the gulch. He had the social weight that could interrupt a lynching or advise a bad man of the particular merits of a remote geographical point. However, the fates exploded the toy balloon with which they had amused Bill, and on the evening of the same day he was a professional gambler with ill fortune dealing him unspeakable irritation in the shape of three big cards whenever another fellow stood pat. It is well here to inform the world that Bill considered his calamities of life all dwarfs in comparison with the excitement of one particular evening, when three kings came to him with criminal regularity against a man who always filled a straight. Later he became a cow-boy, more weirdly abandoned than if he had never been an aristocrat. By this time all that remained of his former splendor was his pride, or his vanity, which was one thing which need not have remained. He killed the foreman of the ranch over an inconsequent matter as to which of them was a liar, and the midnight train carried him eastward. He became a brakeman on the Union Pacific, and really gained high honors in the hobo war that for many years has devastated the beautiful railroads of our country. A creature of ill fortune himself, he practised all the ordinary cruelties upon these other creatures of ill fortune. He was of so fierce a mien that tramps usually surrendered at once whatever coin or tobacco they had in their possession; and if afterward he kicked them from the train, it was only because this was a recognized treachery of the war upon the hoboes. In a famous battle fought in Nebraska in 1879, he would have achieved a lasting distinction if it had not been for a deserter from the United States army. He was at the head of a heroic and sweeping charge, which really broke the power of the hoboes in that county for three months; he had already worsted four tramps with his own coupling-stick, when a stone thrown by the ex-third baseman of F Troop's nine laid him flat on the prairie, and later enforced a stay in the hospital in Omaha. After his recovery he engaged with other railroads, and shuffled cars in countless yards. An order to strike came upon him in Michigan, and afterward the vengeance of the railroad pursued him until he assumed a name. This mask is like the darkness in which the burglar chooses to move. It destroys many of the healthy fears. It is a small thing, but it eats that which we call our conscience. The conductor of No. 419 stood in the caboose within two feet of Bill's nose, and called him a liar. Bill requested him to use a milder term. He had not bored the foreman of Tin Can Ranch with any such request, but had killed him with expedition. The conductor seemed to insist, and so Bill let the matter drop.

He became the bouncer of a saloon on the Bowery in New York. Here most of his fights were as successful as had been his brushes with the hoboes in the West. He gained the complete admiration of the four clean bartenders who stood behind the great and glittering bar. He was an honored man. He nearly killed Bad Hennessy, who, as a matter of fact, had more reputation than ability, and his fame moved up the Bowery and down the Bowery.

But let a man adopt fighting as his business, and the thought grows constantly within him that it is his business to fight. These phrases became mixed in Bill's mind precisely as they are here mixed; and let a man get this idea in his mind, and defeat begins to move toward him over the unknown ways of circumstances. One summer night three sailors from the U.S.S. *Seattle* sat in the saloon drinking and attending to other people's affairs in an amiable fashion. Bill was a proud man since he had thrashed so many citizens, and it suddenly occurred to him that the loud talk of the sailors was very offensive. So he swaggered upon their attention, and warned them that the saloon was the flowery abode of peace and gentle silence. They glanced at him in surprise, and without a moment's pause consigned him to a worse place than any stoker of them knew. Whereupon he flung one of them through the side door before the others could prevent it. On the sidewalk there was a short struggle, with many hoarse epithets in the air, and then Bill slid into the saloon again. A frown of false rage was upon his brow, and he strutted like a savage king. He took a long yellow night-stick from behind the lunch-counter, and started importantly toward the main doors to see that the incensed seamen did not again enter.

The ways of sailormen are without speech, and, together in the street, the three sailors exchanged no word, but they moved at once. Landsmen would have required two years of discussion to gain such unanimity. In silence, and immediately, they seized a long piece of scantling that lay handily. With one forward to guide the battering-ram, and with two behind him to furnish the power, they made a beautiful curve, and came down like the Assyrians on the front door of that saloon.

Strange and still strange are the laws of fate. Bill, with his kingly frown and his long night-stick, appeared at precisely that moment in the doorway. He stood like a statue of victory; his pride was at its zenith; and in the same second this atrocious piece of scantling punched him in the bulwarks of his stomach, and he vanished like a mist. Opinions differed as to where the end of the scantling landed him, but it was ultimately clear that it landed him in southwestern Texas, where he became a sheep-herder.

The sailors charged three times upon the plate-glass front of the saloon, and when they had finished, it looked as if it had been the victim of a rural fire company's success in saving it from the flames.

As the proprietor of the place surveyed the ruins, he remarked that Bill was a very zealous guardian of property. As the ambulance surgeon surveyed Bill, he remarked that the wound was really an excavation.

### III

As his Mexican friend tripped blithely away, Bill turned with a thoughtful face to his frying-pan and his fire. After dinner he drew his revolver from its scarred old holster, and examined every part of it. It was the revolver that had dealt death to the foreman, and it had also been in free fights in which it had dealt death to several or none. Bill loved it because its allegiance was more than that of man, horse, or dog. It questioned neither social nor moral position; it obeyed alike the saint and the assassin. It was the claw of the eagle, the tooth of the lion, the poison of the snake; and when he swept it from its holster, this minion smote where he listed, even to the battering of a far penny. Wherefore it was his dearest possession, and was not to be exchanged in southwestern Texas for a handful of rubies, nor even the shame and homage of the conductor of No. 419.

During the afternoon he moved through his monotony of work and leisure with the same air of deep meditation. The smoke of his supper-time fire was curling across the shadowy sea of mesquit when the instinct of the plainsman warned him that the stillness, the desolation, was again invaded. He saw a motionless horseman in black outline against the pallid sky. The silhouette displayed serape and sombrero, and even the Mexican spurs as large as pies. When this black figure began to move toward the camp, Bill's hand dropped to his revolver.

The horseman approached until Bill was enabled to see pronounced American features, and a skin too red to grow on a Mexican face. Bill released his grip on his revolver.

"Hello!" called the horseman.

"Hello!" answered Bill.

The horseman cantered forward. "Good evening," he said, as he again drew rein.

"Good evenin'," answered Bill, without committing himself by too much courtesy.

For a moment the two men scanned each other in a way that is not ill-mannered on the plains, where one is in danger of meeting horse-thieves or tourists.

Bill saw a type which did not belong in the mesquit. The young fellow had invested in some Mexican trappings of an expensive kind.

Bill's eyes searched the outfit for some sign of craft, but there was none. Even with his local regalia, it was clear that the young man was of a far, black Northern city. He had discarded the enormous stirrups of his Mexican saddle; he used the small English stirrup, and his feet were thrust forward until the steel tightly gripped his ankles. As Bill's eyes traveled over the stranger, they lighted suddenly upon the stirrups and the thrust feet, and immediately he smiled in a friendly way. No dark purpose could dwell in the innocent heart of a man who rode thus on the plains.

As for the stranger, he saw a tattered individual with a tangle of hair and beard, and with a complexion turned brick-color from the sun and whisky. He saw a pair of eyes that at first looked at him as the wolf looks at the wolf, and then became childlike, almost timid, in their glance. Here was evidently a man who had often stormed the iron walls of the city of success, and who now sometimes valued himself as the rabbit values his prowess.

The stranger smiled genially, and sprang from his horse. "Well, sir, I suppose you will let me camp here with you to-night?"

"Eh?" said Bill.

"I suppose you will let me camp here with you to-night?"

Bill for a time seemed too astonished for words. "Well,"—he answered, scowling in inhospitable annoyance—"well, I don't believe this here is a good place to camp to-night, mister."

The stranger turned quickly from his saddle-girth.

"What?" he said in surprise. "You don't want me here? You don't want me to camp here?"

Bill's feet scuffled awkwardly, and he looked steadily at a cactus-plant. "Well, you see, mister," he said, "I'd like your company well enough, but—you see, some of these here greasers are goin' to chase me off the range to-night; and while I might like a man's company all right, I couldn't let him in for no such game when he ain't got nothin' to do with the trouble."

"Going to chase you off the range?" cried the stranger.

"Well, they said they were goin' to do it," said Bill.

"And—great heavens! will they kill you, do you think?"

"Don't know. Can't tell till afterwards. You see, they take some feller that's alone like me, and then they rush his camp when he ain't quite ready for 'em, and ginerally plug 'im with a sawed-off shot-gun load before he has a chance to git at 'em. They lay around and wait for their chance, and it comes soon enough. Of course a feller alone like me has got to let up watching some time. Maybe they ketch 'im asleep. Maybe the feller gits tired waiting, and goes out in broad day, and kills two or three just to make the whole crowd pile on him and settle the thing. I heard of a case like that once. It's awful hard on a man's mind—to git a gang after him."

"And so they're going to rush your camp to-night?" cried the stranger. "How do you know? Who told you?"

"Feller come and told me."

"And what are you going to do? Fight?"

"Don't see nothin' else to do," answered Bill, gloomily, still staring at the cactus-plant.

There was a silence. Finally the stranger burst out in an amazed cry. "Well, I never heard of such a thing in my life! How many of them are there?"

"Eight," answered Bill. "And now look-a-here; you ain't got no manner of business foolin' around here just now, and you might better lope off before dark. I don't ask no help in this here row. I know your happening along here just now don't give me no call on you, and you better hit the trail."

"Well, why in the name of wonder don't you go get the sheriff?" cried the stranger.

"Oh, h——!" said Bill.

## IV

Long, smoldering clouds spread in the western sky, and to the east silver mists lay on the purple gloom of the wilderness.

Finally, when the great moon climbed the heavens and cast its ghastly radiance upon the bushes, it made a new and more brilliant crimson of the camp-fire, where the flames capered merrily through its mesquit branches, filling the silence with the fire chorus, an ancient melody which surely bears a message of the inconsequence of individual tragedy—a message that is in the boom of the sea, the sliver of the wind through the grass-blades, the silken clash of hemlock boughs.

No figures moved in the rosy space of the camp, and the search of the moonbeams failed to disclose a living thing in the bushes. There was no owl-faced clock to chant the weariness of the long silence that brooded upon the plain.

The dew gave the darkness under the mesquit a velvet quality that made air seem nearer to water, and no eye could have seen through it the black things that moved like monster lizards toward the camp. The branches, the leaves, that are fain to cry out when death approaches in the wilds, were frustrated by these uncanny bodies gliding with the finesse of the escaping serpent. They crept forward to the last point where assuredly no frantic attempt of the fire could discover them, and there they paused to locate the prey. A romance relates the tale of the black cell hidden deep in the earth, where, upon entering, one sees only the little eyes of snakes fixing him in menaces. If a man could have approached a certain spot in the bushes, he would not have found it romantically necessary to have his hair rise. There would have been a sufficient expression of horror in the feeling of the death-hand at the nape of his neck and in his rubber knee-joints.

Two of these bodies finally moved toward each other until for each there grew out of the darkness a face placidly smiling with tender dreams of assassination. "The fool is asleep by the fire, God be praised!" The lips of the other widened in a grin of affectionate appreciation of the fool and his plight. There was some signaling in the gloom, and then began a series of subtle rustlings, interjected often with pauses, during which no sound arose but the sound of faint breathing.

A bush stood like a rock in the stream of firelight, sending its long shadow backward. With painful caution the little company traveled along this shadow, and finally arrived at the rear of the bush. Through its branches they surveyed for a moment of comfortable satisfaction a form in a gray blanket extended on the ground near the fire. The smile of joyful anticipation fled quickly, to give place to a quiet air of business. Two men lifted shot-guns with much of the barrels gone, and sighting these weapons through the branches, pulled trigger together.

The noise of the explosions roared over the lonely mesquit as if these guns wished to inform the entire world; and as the gray smoke fled, the dodging company back of the bush saw the blanketed form twitching. Whereupon they burst out in chorus in a laugh, and arose as merry as a lot of banqueters. They gleefully gestured congratulations, and strode bravely into the light of the fire.

Then suddenly a new laugh rang from some unknown spot in the darkness. It was a fearsome laugh of ridicule, hatred, ferocity. It might have been demoniac. It smote them motionless in their gleeful prowl, as the stern voice from the sky smites the legendary malefactor. They might have been a weird group in wax, the light of the dying fire on their yellow faces, and shining athwart their eyes turned toward the darkness whence might come the unknown and the terrible.

The thing in the gray blanket no longer twitched; but if the knives in their hands had been thrust toward it, each knife was now drawn back, and its owner's elbow was thrown upward, as if he expected death from the clouds.

This laugh had so chained their reason that for a moment they had no wit to flee. They were prisoners to their terror. Then suddenly the

belated decision arrived, and with bubbling cries they turned to run;
but at that instant there was a long flash of red in the darkness, and
with the report one of the men shouted a bitter shout, spun once, and
tumbled headlong. The thick bushes failed to impede the rout of the
others.

The silence returned to the wilderness. The tired flames faintly
illumined the blanketed thing and the flung corse of the marauder,
and sang the fire chorus, the ancient melody which bears the message
of the inconsequence of human tragedy.

## V

"Now you are worse off than ever," said the young man, dry-voiced
and awed.

"No, I ain't," said Bill, rebelliously. "I'm one ahead."

After reflection, the stranger remarked, "Well, there's seven
more."

They were cautiously and slowly approaching the camp. The sun
was flaring its first warming rays over the gray wilderness. Upreared
twigs, prominent branches, shone with golden light, while the shadows
under the mesquit were heavily blue.

Suddenly the stranger uttered a frightened cry. He had arrived at
a point whence he had, through openings in the thicket, a clear view
of a dead face.

"Gosh!" said Bill, who at the next instant had seen the thing; "I
thought at first it was that there José. That would have been queer,
after what I told 'im yesterday."

They continued their way, the stranger wincing in his walk, and
Bill exhibiting considerable curiosity.

The yellow beams of the new sun were touching the grim hues of
the dead Mexican's face, and creating there an inhuman effect, which
made his countenance more like a mask of dulled brass. One hand,
grown curiously thinner, had been flung out regardlessly to a cactus
bush.

Bill walked forward and stood looking respectfully at the body. "I
know that feller; his name is Miguel. He—"

The stranger's nerves might have been in that condition when
there is no backbone to the body, only a long groove. "Good heavens!"
he exclaimed, much agitated; "don't speak that way!"

"What way?" said Bill. "I only said his name was Miguel."

After a pause the stranger said:

"Oh, I know; but—" He waved his hand. "Lower your voice, or

something. I don't know. This part of the business rattles me, don't you see?"

"Oh, all right," replied Bill, bowing to the other's mysterious mood. But in a moment he burst out violently and loud in the most extraordinary profanity, the oaths winging from him as the sparks go from the funnel.

He had been examining the contents of the bundled gray blanket, and he had brought forth, among other things, his frying-pan. It was now only a rim with a handle; the Mexican volley had centered upon it. A Mexican shot-gun of the abbreviated description is ordinarily loaded with flat-irons, stove-lids, lead pipe, old horseshoes, sections of chain, window weights, railroad sleepers and spikes, dumb-bells, and any other junk which may be at hand. When one of these loads encounters a man vitally, it is likely to make an impression upon him, and a cooking-utensil may be supposed to subside before such an assault of curiosities.

Bill held high his desecrated frying-pan, turning it this way and that way. He swore until he happened to note the absence of the stranger. A moment later he saw him leading his horse from the bushes. In silence and sullenly the young man went about saddling the animal. Bill said, "Well, goin' to pull out?"

The stranger's hands fumbled uncertainly at the throat-latch. Once he exclaimed irritably, blaming the buckle for the trembling of his fingers. Once he turned to look at the dead face with the light of the morning sun upon it. At last he cried, "Oh, I know the whole thing was all square enough—couldn't be squarer—but—somehow or other, that man there takes the heart out of me." He turned his troubled face for another look. "He seems to be all the time calling me a—he makes me feel like a murderer."

"But," said Bill, puzzling, "you didn't shoot him, mister; I shot him."

"I know; but I feel that way, somehow. I can't get rid of it."

Bill considered for a time; then he said diffidently, "Mister, you're a' eddycated man, ain't you?"

"What?"

"You're what they call a'—a' eddycated man, ain't you?"

The young man, perplexed, evidently had a question upon his lips, when there was a roar of guns, bright flashes, and in the air such hooting and whistling as would come from a swift flock of steam-boilers. The stranger's horse gave a mighty, convulsive spring, snorting wildly in its sudden anguish, fell upon its knees, scrambled afoot again, and was away in the uncanny death run known to men who have seen the finish of brave horses.

"This comes from discussin' things," cried Bill, angrily.

He had thrown himself flat on the ground facing the thicket whence had come the firing. He could see the smoke winding over the bush-tops. He lifted his revolver, and the weapon came slowly up from the ground and poised like the glittering crest of a snake. Somewhere on his face there was a kind of smile, cynical, wicked, deadly, of a ferocity which at the same time had brought a deep flush to his face, and had caused two upright lines to glow in his eyes.

"Hello, José!" he called, amiable for satire's sake. "Got your old blunderbusses loaded up again yet?"

The stillness had returned to the plain. The sun's brilliant rays swept over the sea of mesquit, painting the far mists of the west with faint rosy light, and high in the air some great bird fled toward the south.

"You come out here," called Bill, again addressing the landscape, "and I'll give you some shootin' lessons. That ain't the way to shoot." Receiving no reply, he began to invent epithets and yell them at the thicket. He was something of a master of insult, and, moreover, he dived into his memory to bring forth imprecations tarnished with age, unused since fluent Bowery days. The occupation amused him, and sometimes he laughed so that it was uncomfortable for his chest to be against the ground.

Finally the stranger, prostrate near him, said wearily, "Oh, they've gone."

"Don't you believe it," replied Bill, sobering swiftly. "They're there yet—every man of 'em."

"How do you know?"

"Because I do. They won't shake us so soon. Don't put your head up, or they'll get you, sure."

Bill's eyes, meanwhile, had not wavered from their scrutiny of the thicket in front. "They're there, all right; don't you forget it. Now you listen." So he called out: "José! Ojo, José! Speak up, *hombre!* I want have talk. Speak up, you yaller cuss, you!"

Whereupon a mocking voice from off in the bushes said, "Señor?"

"There," said Bill to his ally; "didn't I tell you? The whole batch." Again he lifted his voice. "José—look—ain't you gittin' kinder tired? You better go home, you fellers, and git some rest."

The answer was a sudden furious chatter of Spanish, eloquent with hatred, calling down upon Bill all the calamities which life holds. It was as if some one had suddenly enraged a cageful of wildcats. The spirits of all the revenges which they had imagined were loosened at this time, and filled the air.

"They're in a holler," said Bill, chuckling, "or there'd be shootin'."
Presently he began to grow angry. His hidden enemies called him
nine kinds of coward, a man who could fight only in the dark, a baby
who would run from the shadows of such noble Mexican gentlemen, a
dog that sneaked. They described the affair of the previous night, and
informed him of the base advantage he had taken of their friend. In
fact, they in all sincerity endowed him with every quality which he no
less earnestly believed them to possess. One could have seen the
phrases bite him as he lay there on the ground fingering his revolver.

## VI

It is sometimes taught that men do the furious and desperate thing
from an emotion that is as even and placid as the thoughts of a village
clergyman on Sunday afternoon. Usually, however, it is to be believed
that a panther is at the time born in the heart, and that the subject
does not resemble a man picking mulberries.

"B' G——!" said Bill, speaking as from a throat filled with dust,
"I'll go after 'em in a minute."

"Don't you budge an inch!" cried the stranger, sternly. "Don't you
budge!"

"Well," said Bill, glaring at the bushes—"well—"

"Put your head down!" suddenly screamed the stranger, in white
alarm. As the guns roared, Bill uttered a loud grunt, and for a moment
leaned panting on his elbow, while his arm shook like a twig. Then he
upreared like a great and bloody spirit of vengeance, his face lighted
with the blaze of his last passion. The Mexicans came swiftly and in
silence.

The lightning action of the next few moments was of the fabric of
dreams to the stranger. The muscular struggle may not be real to the
drowning man. His mind may be fixed on the far, straight shadows
back of the stars, and the terror of them. And so the fight, and his
part in it, had to the stranger only the quality of a picture half drawn.
The rush of feet, the spatter of shots, the cries, the swollen faces seen
like masks on the smoke, resembled a happening of the night.

And yet afterward certain lines, forms, lived out so strongly from
the incoherence that they were always in his memory.

He killed a man, and the thought went swiftly by him, like the
feather on the gale, that it was easy to kill a man.

Moreover, he suddenly felt for Bill, this grimy sheep-herder, some
deep form of idolatry. Bill was dying, and the dignity of last defeat,

the superiority of him who stands in his grave, was in the pose of the lost sheep-herder.

The stranger sat on the ground idly mopping the sweat and powder-stain from his brow. He wore the gentle idiot smile of an aged beggar as he watched three Mexicans limping and staggering in the distance. He noted at this time that one who still possessed a serape had from it none of the grandeur of the cloaked Spaniard, but that against the sky the silhouette resembled a cornucopia of childhood's Christmas.

They turned to look at him, and he lifted his weary arm to menace them with his revolver. They stood for a moment banded together, and hooted curses at him.

Finally he arose, and, walking some paces, stooped to loosen Bill's gray hands from a throat. Swaying as if slightly drunk, he stood looking down into the still face.

Struck suddenly with a thought, he went about with dulled eyes on the ground, until he plucked his gaudy blanket from where it lay dirty from trampling feet. He dusted it carefully, and then returned and laid it over Bill's form. There he again stood motionless, his mouth just agape and the same stupid glance in his eyes, when all at once he made a gesture of fright and looked wildly about him.

He had almost reached the thicket when he stopped, smitten with alarm. A body contorted, with one arm stiff in the air, lay in his path. Slowly and warily he moved around it, and in a moment the bushes, nodding and whispering, their leaf-faces turned toward the scene behind him, swung and swung again into stillness and the peace of the wilderness.

# The Bride Comes
# to Yellow Sky

## I

The great Pullman was whirling onward with such dignity of motion
that a glance from the window seemed simply to prove that the plains
of Texas were pouring eastward. Vast flats of green grass, dull-hued
spaces of mesquite and cactus, little groups of frame houses, woods of
light and tender trees, all were sweeping into the east, sweeping over
the horizon, a precipice.

A newly married pair had boarded this coach at San Antonio. The
man's face was reddened from many days in the wind and sun, and a
direct result of his new black clothes was that his brick-colored hands
were constantly performing in a most conscious fashion. From time to
time he looked down respectfully at his attire. He sat with a hand on
each knee, like a man waiting in a barber's shop. The glances he devoted to other passengers were furtive and shy.

The bride was not pretty, nor was she very young. She wore a
dress of blue cashmere, with small reservations of velvet here and
there and with steel buttons abounding. She continually twisted her
head to regard her puff sleeves, very stiff, straight, and high. They
embarrassed her. It was quite apparent that she had cooked, and that
she expected to cook, dutifully. The blushes caused by the careless
scrutiny of some passengers as she had entered the car were strange
to see upon this plain, under-class countenance, which was drawn in
placid, almost emotionless lines.

They were evidently very happy. "Ever been in a parlor-car before?" he asked, smiling with delight.

"No," she answered. "I never was. It's fine, ain't it?"

"Great! And then after a while we'll go forward to the diner and
get a big lay-out. Finest meal in the world. Charge a dollar."

"Oh, do they?" cried the bride. "Charge a dollar? Why, that's too
much—for us—ain't it, Jack?"

"Not this trip, anyhow," he answered bravely. "We're going to go the whole thing."

Later, he explained to her about the trains. "You see, it's a thousand miles from one end of Texas to the other, and this train runs right across it and never stops but four times." He had the pride of an owner. He pointed out to her the dazzling fittings of the coach, and in truth her eyes opened wider as she contemplated the sea-green figured velvet, the shining brass, silver, and glass, the wood that gleamed as darkly brilliant as the surface of a pool of oil. At one end a bronze figure sturdily held a support for a separated chamber, and at convenient places on the ceiling were frescoes in olive and silver.

To the minds of the pair, their surroundings reflected the glory of their marriage that morning in San Antonio. This was the environment of their new estate, and the man's face in particular beamed with an elation that made him appear ridiculous to the negro porter. This individual at times surveyed them from afar with an amused and superior grin. On other occasions he bullied them with skill in ways that did not make it exactly plain to them that they were being bullied. He subtly used all the manners of the most unconquerable kind of snobbery. He oppressed them, but of this oppression they had small knowledge, and they speedily forgot that infrequently a number of travelers covered them with stares of derisive enjoyment. Historically there was supposed to be something infinitely humorous in their situation.

"We are due in Yellow Sky at 3:42," he said, looking tenderly into her eyes.

"Oh, are we?" she said, as if she had not been aware of it. To evince surprise at her husband's statement was part of her wifely amiability. She took from a pocket a little silver watch, and as she held it before her and stared at it with a frown of attention, the new husband's face shone.

"I bought it in San Anton' from a friend of mine," he told her gleefully.

"It's seventeen minutes past twelve," she said, looking up at him with a kind of shy and clumsy coquetry. A passenger, noting this play, grew excessively sardonic, and winked at himself in one of the numerous mirrors.

At last they went to the dining-car. Two rows of negro waiters in glowing white suits surveyed their entrance with the interest and also the equanimity of men who had been forewarned. The pair fell to the lot of a waiter who happened to feel pleasure in steering them through their meal. He viewed them with the manner of a fatherly pilot, his countenance radiant with benevolence. The patronage entwined with the ordinary deference was not plain to them. And yet as they returned to their coach they showed in their faces a sense of escape.

To the left, miles down a long purple slope, was a little ribbon of mist where moved the keening Rio Grande. The train was approaching it at an angle, and the apex was Yellow Sky. Presently it was apparent that as the distance from Yellow Sky grew shorter, the husband became commensurately restless. His brick-red hands were more insistent in their prominence. Occasionally he was even rather absent-minded and far-away when the bride leaned forward and addressed him.

As a matter of truth, Jack Potter was beginning to find the shadow of a deed weigh upon him like a leaden slab. He, the town marshal of Yellow Sky, a man known, liked, and feared in his corner, a prominent person, had gone to San Antonio to meet a girl he believed he loved, and there, after the usual prayers, had actually induced her to marry him, without consulting Yellow Sky for any part of the transaction. He was now bringing his bride before an innocent and unsuspecting community.

Of course, people in Yellow Sky married as it pleased them in accordance with a general custom; but such was Potter's thought of his duty to his friends, or of their idea of his duty, or of an unspoken form which does not control men in these matters, that he felt he was heinous. He had committed an extraordinary crime. Face to face with this girl in San Antonio, and spurred by his sharp impulse, he had gone headlong over all the social hedges. At San Antonio he was like a man hidden in the dark. A knife to sever any friendly duty, any form, was easy to his hand in that remote city. But the hour of Yellow Sky, the hour of daylight, was approaching.

He knew full well that his marriage was an important thing to his town. It could only be exceeded by the burning of the new hotel. His friends would not forgive him. Frequently he had reflected on the advisability of telling them by telegraph, but a new cowardice had been upon him. He feared to do it. And now the train was hurrying him toward a scene of amazement, glee, reproach. He glanced out of the window at the line of haze swinging slowly in toward the train.

Yellow Sky had a kind of brass band which played painfully to the delight of the populace. He laughed without heart as he thought of it. If the citizens could dream of his prospective arrival with his bride, they would parade the band at the station and escort them, amid cheers and laughing congratulations, to his adobe home.

He resolved that he would use all the devices of speed and plainscraft in making the journey from the station to his house. Once within that safe citadel, he could issue some sort of a vocal bulletin, and then not go among the citizens until they had time to wear off a little of their enthusiasm.

The bride looked anxiously at him. "What's worrying you, Jack?"

He laughed again. "I'm not worrying, girl. I'm only thinking of Yellow Sky."

She flushed in comprehension.

A sense of mutual guilt invaded their minds and developed a finer tenderness. They looked at each other with eyes softly aglow. But Potter often laughed the same nervous laugh. The flush upon the bride's face seemed quite permanent.

The traitor to the feelings of Yellow Sky narrowly watched the speeding landscape. "We're nearly there," he said.

Presently the porter came and announced the proximity of Potter's home. He held a brush in his hand and, with all his airy superiority gone, he brushed Potter's new clothes as the latter slowly turned this way and that way. Potter fumbled out a coin and gave it to the porter as he had seen others do. It was a heavy and muscle-bound business, as that of a man shoeing his first horse.

The porter took their bag, and as the train began to slow they moved forward to the hooded platform of the car. Presently the two engines and their long string of coaches rushed into the station of Yellow Sky.

"They have to take water here," said Potter, from a constricted throat and in mournful cadence as one announcing death. Before the train stopped his eye had swept the length of the platform, and he was glad and astonished to see there was none upon it but the station-agent, who, with a slightly hurried and anxious air, was walking toward the water-tanks. When the train had halted, the porter alighted first and placed in position a little temporary step.

"Come on, girl," said Potter hoarsely. As he helped her down they each laughed on a false note. He took the bag from the negro, and bade his wife cling to his arm. As they slunk rapidly away, his hang-dog glance perceived that they were unloading the two trunks, and also that the station-agent far ahead near the baggage-car had turned and was running toward him, making gestures. He laughed, and groaned as he laughed, when he noted the first effect of his marital bliss upon Yellow Sky. He gripped his wife's arm firmly to his side, and they fled. Behind them the porter stood chuckling fatuously.

## II

The California Express on the Southern Railway was due at Yellow Sky in twenty-one minutes. There were six men at the bar of the

Weary Gentleman saloon. One was a drummer who talked a great deal and rapidly; three were Texans who did not care to talk at that time; and two were Mexican sheep-herders who did not talk as a general practice in the Weary Gentleman saloon. The bar-keeper's dog lay on the board-walk that crossed in front of the door. His head was on his paws, and he glanced drowsily here and there with the constant vigilance of a dog that is kicked on occasion. Across the sandy street were some vivid green grass plots, so wonderful in appearance amid the sands that burned near them in a blazing sun that they caused a doubt in the mind. They exactly resembled the grass mats used to represent lawns on the stage. At the cooler end of the railway station a man without a coat sat in a tilted chair and smoked his pipe. The fresh-cut bank of the Rio Grande circled near the town, and there could be seen beyond it a great plum-colored plain of mesquite.

Save for the busy drummer and his companions in the saloon, Yellow Sky was dozing. The new-comer leaned gracefully upon the bar, and recited many tales with the confidence of a bard who has come upon a new field.

"—and at the moment that the old man fell down stairs with the bureau in his arms, the old woman was coming up with two scuttles of coal, and, of course—"

The drummer's tale was interrupted by a young man who suddenly appeared in the open door. He cried: "Scratchy Wilson's drunk, and has turned loose with both hands." The two Mexicans at once set down their glasses and faded out of the rear entrance of the saloon.

The drummer, innocent and jocular, answered: "All right, old man. S'pose he has. Come in and have a drink, anyhow."

But the information had made such an obvious cleft in every skull in the room that the drummer was obliged to see its importance. All had become instantly morose. "Say," said he, mystified, "what is this?" His three companions made the introductory gesture of eloquent speech, but the young man at the door forestalled them.

"It means, my friend," he answered, as he came into the saloon, "that for the next two hours this town won't be a health resort."

The bar-keeper went to the door and locked and barred it. Reaching out of the window, he pulled in heavy wooden shutters and barred them. Immediately a solemn, chapel-like gloom was upon the place. The drummer was looking from one to another.

"But say," he cried, "what is this, anyhow? You don't mean there is going to be a gun-fight?"

"Don't know whether there'll be a fight or not," answered one man grimly. "But there'll be some shootin'—some good shootin'."

The young man who had warned them waved his hand. "Oh,

there'll be a fight fast enough, if anyone wants it. Anybody can get a fight out there in the street. There's a fight just waiting."

The drummer seemed to be swayed between the interest of a foreigner and a perception of personal danger.

"What did you say his name was?" he asked.

"Scratchy Wilson," they answered in chorus.

"And will he kill anybody? What are you going to do? Does this happen often? Does he rampage around like this once a week or so? Can he break in that door?"

"No, he can't break down that door," replied the bar-keeper. "He's tried it three times. But when he comes you'd better lay down on the floor, stranger. He's dead sure to shoot at it, and a bullet may come through."

Thereafter the drummer kept a strict eye upon the door. The time had not yet been called for him to hug the floor, but as a minor precaution he sidled near to the wall. "Will he kill anybody?" he said again.

The men laughed low and scornfully at the question.

"He's out to shoot, and he's out for trouble. Don't see any good in experimentin' with him."

"But what do you do in a case like this? What do you do?"

A man responded: "Why, he and Jack Potter—"

But, in chorus, the other men interrupted: "Jack Potter's in San Anton'."

"Well, who is he? What's he got to do with it?"

"Oh, he's the town marshal. He goes out and fights Scratchy when he gets on one of these tears."

"Wow," said the drummer, mopping his brow. "Nice job he's got."

The voices had toned away to mere whisperings. The drummer wished to ask further questions which were born of an increasing anxiety and bewilderment; but when he attempted them, the men merely looked at him in irritation and motioned him to remain silent. A tense waiting hush was upon them. In the deep shadows of the room their eyes shone as they listened for sounds from the street. One man made three gestures at the bar-keeper, and the latter, moving like a ghost, handed him a glass and a bottle. The man poured a full glass of whisky, and set down the bottle noiselessly. He gulped the whisky in a swallow, and turned again toward the door in immovable silence. The drummer saw that the bar-keeper, without a sound, had taken a Winchester from beneath the bar. Later he saw this individual beckoning to him, so he tiptoed across the room.

"You better come with me back of the bar."

"No, thanks," said the drummer, perspiring. "I'd rather be where I can make a break for the back door."

Whereupon the man of bottles made a kindly but peremptory gesture. The drummer obeyed it, and finding himself seated on a box with his head below the level of the bar, balm was laid upon his soul at sight of various zinc and copper fittings that bore a resemblance to armor-plate. The bar-keeper took a seat comfortably upon an adjacent box.

"You see," he whispered, "this here Scratchy Wilson is a wonder with a gun—a perfect wonder—and when he goes on the war trail, we hunt our holes—naturally. He's about the last one of the old gang that used to hang out along the river here. He's a terror when he's drunk. When he's sober he's all right—kind of simple—wouldn't hurt a fly—nicest fellow in town. But when he's drunk—whoo!"

There were periods of stillness. "I wish Jack Potter was back from San Anton'," said the bar-keeper. "He shot Wilson up once—in the leg—and he would sail in and pull out the kinks in this thing."

Presently they heard from a distance the sound of a shot, followed by three wild yowls. It instantly removed a bond from the men in the darkened saloon. There was a shuffling of feet. They looked at each other. "Here he comes," they said.

### III

A man in a maroon-colored flannel shirt, which had been purchased for purposes of decoration and made, principally, by some Jewish women on the east side of New York, rounded a corner and walked into the middle of the main street of Yellow Sky. In either hand the man held a long, heavy blue-black revolver. Often he yelled, and these cries rang through a semblance of a deserted village, shrilly flying over the roofs in a volume that seemed to have no relation to the ordinary vocal strength of a man. It was as if the surrounding stillness formed the arch of a tomb over him. These cries of ferocious challenge rang against walls of silence. And his boots had red tops with gilded imprints, of the kind beloved in winter by little sledding boys on the hillsides of New England.

The man's face flamed in a rage begot of whisky. His eyes, rolling and yet keen for ambush, hunted the still door-ways and windows. He walked with the creeping movement of the midnight cat. As it occurred to him, he roared menacing information. The long revolvers in his hands were as easy as straws; they were moved with an electric swiftness. The little fingers of each hand played sometimes in a musician's way. Plain from the low collar of the shirt, the cords of his neck straightened and sank, straightened and sank, as passion moved him. The only sounds were his terrible invitations. The calm adobes preserved their demeanor at the passing of this small thing in the middle of the street.

There was no offer of fight; no offer of fight. The man called to the sky. There were no attractions. He bellowed and fumed and swayed his revolvers here and everywhere.

The dog of the bar-keeper of the Weary Gentleman saloon had not appreciated the advance of events. He yet lay dozing in front of his master's door. At sight of the dog, the man paused and raised his revolver humorously. At sight of the man, the dog sprang up and walked diagonally away, with a sullen head and growling. The man yelled, and the dog broke into a gallop. As it was about to enter an alley, there was a loud noise, a whistling, and something spat the ground directly before it. The dog screamed, and, wheeling in terror, galloped headlong in a new direction. Again there was a noise, a whistling, and sand was kicked viciously before it. Fear-stricken, the dog turned and flurried like an animal in a pen. The man stood laughing, his weapons at his hips.

Ultimately the man was attracted by the closed door of the Weary Gentleman saloon. He went to it, and hammering with a revolver, demanded drink.

The door remaining imperturbable, he picked a bit of paper from the walk and nailed it to the framework with a knife. He then turned his back contemptuously upon this popular resort, and walking to the opposite side of the street, and spinning there on his heel quickly and lithely, fired at the bit of paper. He missed it by a half inch. He swore at himself, and went away. Later, he comfortably fusilladed the windows of his most intimate friend. The man was playing with this town. It was a toy for him.

But still there was no offer of fight. The name of Jack Potter, his ancient antagonist, entered his mind, and he concluded that it would be a glad thing if he should go to Potter's house and by bombardment induce him to come out and fight. He moved in the direction of his desire, chanting Apache scalp-music.

When he arrived at it, Potter's house presented the same still, calm front as had the other adobes. Taking up a strategic position, the man howled a challenge. But this house regarded him as might a great stone god. It gave no sign. After a decent wait, the man howled further challenges, mingling with them wonderful epithets.

Presently there came the spectacle of a man churning himself into deepest rage over the immobility of a house. He fumed at it as the winter wind attacks a prairie cabin in the North. To the distance there should have gone the sound of a tumult like the fighting of two hundred Mexicans. As necessity bade him, he paused for breath or to reload his revolvers.

## IV

Potter and his bride walked sheepishly and with speed. Sometimes they laughed together shamefacedly and low.

"Next corner, dear," he said finally.

They put forth the efforts of a pair walking bowed against a strong wind. Potter was about to raise a finger to point the first appearance of the new home when, as they circled the corner, they came face to face with a man in a maroon-colored shirt who was feverishly pushing cartridges into a large revolver. Upon the instant the man dropped this revolver to the ground, and, like lightning, whipped another from its holster. The second weapon was aimed at the bridegroom's chest.

There was a silence. Potter's mouth seemed to be merely a grave for his tongue. He exhibited an instinct to at once loosen his arm from the woman's grip, and he dropped the bag to the sand. As for the bride, her face had gone as yellow as old cloth. She was a slave to hideous rites gazing at the apparitional snake.

The two men faced each other at a distance of three paces. He of the revolver smiled with a new and quiet ferocity. "Tried to sneak up on me," he said. "Tried to sneak up on me!" His eyes grew more baleful. As Potter made a slight movement, the man thrust his revolver venomously forward. "No, don't you do it, Jack Potter. Don't you move a finger toward a gun just yet. Don't you move an eyelash. The time has come for me to settle with you, and I'm goin' to do it my own way and loaf along with no interferin'. So if you don't want a gun bent on you, just mind what I tell you."

Potter looked at his enemy. "I ain't got a gun on me, Scratchy," he said. "Honest, I ain't." He was stiffening and steadying, but yet somewhere at the back of his mind a vision of the Pullman floated, the sea-green figured velvet, the shining brass, silver, and glass, the wood that gleamed as darkly brilliant as the surface of a pool of oil—all the glory of the marriage, the environment of the new estate. "You know I fight when it comes to fighting, Scratchy Wilson, but I ain't got a gun on me. You'll have to do all the shootin' yourself."

His enemy's face went livid. He stepped forward and lashed his weapon to and fro before Potter's chest. "Don't you tell me you ain't got no gun on you, you whelp. Don't tell me no lie like that. There ain't a man in Texas ever seen you without no gun. Don't take me for no kid." His eyes blazed with light, and his throat worked like a pump.

"I ain't takin' you for no kid," answered Potter. His heels had not moved an inch backward. "I'm takin' you for a—fool. I tell you I ain't got a gun, and I ain't. If you're goin' to shoot me up, you better begin now. You'll never get a chance like this again."

So much enforced reasoning had told on Wilson's rage. He was calmer. "If you ain't got a gun, why ain't you got a gun?" he sneered. "Been to Sunday-school?"

"I ain't got a gun because I've just come from San Anton' with my wife. I'm married," said Potter. "And if I'd thought there was going to be any galoots like you prowling around when I brought my wife home, I'd had a gun, and don't you forget it."

"Married!" said Scratchy, not at all comprehending.

"Yes, married. I'm married," said Potter distinctly.

"Married?" said Scratchy. Seemingly for the first time he saw the drooping drowning woman at the other man's side. "No!" he said. He was like a creature allowed a glimpse of another world. He moved a pace backward, and his arm with the revolver dropped to his side. "Is this—is this the lady?" he asked.

"Yes, this is the lady," answered Potter.

There was another period of silence.

"Well," said Wilson at last, slowly, "I s'pose it's all off now."

"It's all off if you say so, Scratchy. You know I didn't make the trouble." Potter lifted his valise.

"Well, I 'low it's off, Jack," said Wilson. He was looking at the ground. "Married!" He was not a student of chivalry; it was merely that in the presence of this foreign condition he was a simple child of the earlier plains. He picked up his starboard revolver, and placing both weapons in their holsters, he went away. His feet made funnel-shaped tracks in the heavy sand.

# Twelve O'Clock

"Where were you at twelve o'clock, noon, on the 9th of June, 1875?"
—*Question on intelligent cross-examination*

## I

Excuse *me*," said Ben Roddle with graphic gestures to a group of citizens in Nantucket's store. "Excuse *me*. When them fellers in leather pants an' six-shooters ride in, I go home an' set in th' cellar. That's what I do. When you see me pirooting through the streets at th' same time an' occasion as them punchers, you kin put me down fer bein' crazy. Excuse *me*."

"Why, Ben," drawled old Nantucket, "you ain't never really seen 'em turned loose. Why, I kin remember—in th' old days—when—"

"Oh, damn yer old days!" retorted Roddle. Fixing Nantucket with the eye of scorn and contempt, he said: "I suppose you'll be sayin' in a minute that in th' old days you used to kill Injuns, won't you?"

There was some laughter, and Roddle was left free to expand his ideas on the periodic visits of cowboys to the town. "Mason Rickets, he had ten big punkins a-sittin' in front of his store, an' them fellers from the Upside-down-F ranch shot 'em up—shot 'em all up—an' Rickets lyin' on his belly in th' store a-callin' fer 'em to quit it. An' what did they do! Why, they *laughed* at 'im!—just *laughed* at 'im! That don't do a town no good. Now, how would an eastern capiterlist"—(it was the town's humor to be always gassing of phantom investors who were likely to come any moment and pay a thousand prices for everything)—"how would an eastern capiterlist like that? Why, you couldn't see 'im fer th' dust on his trail. Then he'd tell all his friends that 'their town may be all right, but ther's too much loose-handed shootin' fer my money.' An' he'd be right, too. Them rich fellers, they don't make no bad breaks with their money. They watch it all th' time b'cause they know blame well there ain't hardly room fer their feet fer th' pikers an' tin-horns an' thimble-riggers what are layin' fer 'em. I tell you, one puncher racin' his cow-pony hell-bent-fer-election down Main Street an' yellin' an' shootin' an' nothin' at all done about it, would scare away a whole herd of capiterlists. An' it ain't right. It oughter be stopped."

A pessimistic voice asked: "How you goin' to stop it, Ben?"

"Organize," replied Roddle pompously. "Organize: that's the only way to make these fellers lay down. I—"

From the street sounded a quick scudding of pony hoofs, and a party of cowboys swept past the door. One man, however, was seen to draw rein and dismount. He came clanking into the store. "Mornin', gentlemen," he said, civilly.

"Mornin'," they answered in subdued voices.

He stepped to the counter and said, "Give me a paper of fine cut, please." The group of citizens contemplated him in silence. He certainly did not look threatening. He appeared to be a young man of twenty-five years, with a tan from wind and sun, with a remarkably clear eye from perhaps a period of enforced temperance, a quiet young man who wanted to buy some tobacco. A six-shooter swung low on his hip, but at the moment it looked more decorative than warlike; it seemed merely a part of his odd gala dress—his sombrero with its band of rattlesnake skin, his great flaming neckerchief, his belt of embroidered Mexican leather, his high-heeled boots, his huge spurs. And, above all, his hair had been watered and brushed until it lay as close to his head as the fur lays to a wet cat. Paying for his tobacco, he withdrew.

Ben Roddle resumed his harangue. "Well, there you are! Looks like a calm man now, but in less'n half an hour he'll be as drunk as three bucks an' a squaw, an' then. . . . excuse *me*!"


## II

On this day the men of two outfits had come into town, but Ben Roddle's ominous words were not justified at once. The punchers spent most of the morning in an attack on whiskey which was too earnest to be noisy.

At five minutes of eleven, a tall, lank, brick-colored cowboy strode over to Placer's Hotel. Placer's Hotel was a notable place. It was the best hotel within two hundred miles. Its office was filled with armchairs and brown papier-maché receptacles. At one end of the room was a wooden counter painted a bright pink, and on this morning a man was behind the counter writing in a ledger. He was the proprietor of the hotel, but his customary humor was so sullen that all strangers immediately wondered why in life he had chosen to play the part of mine host. Near his left hand, double doors opened into the dining-room, which in warm weather was always kept darkened in order to discourage the flies, which was not compassed at all.

Placer, writing in his ledger, did not look up when the tall cowboy entered.

"Mornin', mister," said the latter. "I've come to see if you kin grub-stake th' hull crowd of us fer dinner t'day."

Placer did not then raise his eyes, but with a certain churlishness, as if it annoyed him that his hotel was patronized, he asked: "How many?"

"Oh, about thirty," replied the cowboy. "An' we want th' best dinner you kin raise an' scrape. Everything th' best. We don't care what it costs s'long as we git a good square meal. We'll pay a dollar a head: by God, we will! We won't kick on nothin' in the bill if you do it up fine. If you ain't got it in th' house, russle th' hull town fer it. That's our gait. So you just tear loose, an' we'll—"

At this moment the machinery of a cuckoo-clock on the wall began to whirr, little doors flew open, and a wooden bird appeared and cried, "Cuckoo!" And this was repeated until eleven o'clock had been announced, while the cowboy, stupefied, glassy-eyed, stood with his red throat gulping. At the end he wheeled upon Placer and demanded: *"What in hell is that?"*

Placer revealed by his manner that he had been asked this question too many times. "It's a clock," he answered shortly.

"I know it's a clock," gasped the cowboy; "but what *kind* of a clock?"

"A cuckoo-clock. Can't you see?"

The cowboy, recovering his self-possession by a violent effort, suddenly went shouting into the street. "Boys! Say, boys! Com' 'ere a minute!"

His comrades, comfortably inhabiting a near-by saloon, heard his stentorian calls, but they merely said to one another: "What's th' matter with Jake?—he's off his nut again."

But Jake burst in upon them with violence. "Boys," he yelled, "come over to th' hotel! They got a clock with a bird inside it, an' when it's eleven o'clock or anything like that, th' bird comes out an' says, '*toot*-toot, *toot*-toot!'" that way, as many times as whatever time of day it is. It's immense! Come on over!"

The roars of laughter which greeted his proclamation were of two qualities; some men laughing because they knew all about cuckoo-clocks, and other men laughing because they had concluded that the eccentric Jake had been victimized by some wise child of civilization.

Old Man Crumford, a venerable ruffian who probably had been born in a corral, was particularly offensive with his loud guffaws of contempt. "Bird a-comin' out of a clock an' a-tellin' ye th' time! Haw-haw-haw!" He swallowed his whiskey. "A bird! a-tellin' ye th' time! Haw-haw! Jake, you ben up agin some new drink. You ben drinkin' lonely an' got up agin some snake-medicine licker. A bird a-tellin' ye th' time! Haw-haw!"

The shrill voice of one of the younger cowboys piped from the background. "Brace up, Jake. Don't let 'em laugh at ye. Bring 'em that salt cod-fish of yourn what kin pick out th' ace."

"Oh, he's only kiddin' us. Don't pay no 'tention to 'im. He thinks he's smart."

A cowboy whose mother had a cuckoo-clock in her house in Philadelphia spoke with solemnity. "Jake's a liar. There's no such clock in the world. What? a bird inside a clock to tell the time? Change your drink, Jake."

Jake was furious, but his fury took a very icy form. He bent a withering glance upon the last speaker. "I don't mean a *live* bird," he said, with terrible dignity. "It's a wooden bird, an'—"

"A wooden bird!" shouted Old Man Crumford. "Wooden bird a-tellin' ye th' time! Haw-haw!"

But Jake still paid his frigid attention to the Philadelphian. "An' if yer sober enough to walk, it ain't such a blame long ways from here to th' hotel, an' I'll bet my pile agin yours if you only got two bits."

"I don't want your money, Jake," said the Philadelphian. "Somebody's been stringin' you—that's all. I wouldn't take your money." He cleverly appeared to pity the other's innocence.

"You couldn't *git* my money," cried Jake, in sudden hot anger. "You couldn't git it. Now—since yer so fresh—let's see how much you got." He clattered some large gold pieces noisily upon the bar.

The Philadelphian shrugged his shoulders and walked away. Jake was triumphant. "Any more bluffers 'round here?" he demanded. "Any more? Any more bluffers? Where's all these here hot sports? Let 'em step up. Here's my money—come an' git it."

But they had ended by being afraid. To some of them his tale was absurd, but still one must be circumspect when a man throws forty-five dollars in gold upon the bar and bids the world come and win it. The general feeling was expressed by Old Man Crumford, when with deference he asked: "Well, this here bird, Jake—what kinder lookin' bird is it?"

"It's a little brown thing," said Jake briefly. Apparently he almost disdained to answer.

"Well—how does it work?" asked the old man meekly.

"Why in blazes don't you go an' look at it?" yelled Jake. "Want me to paint it in iles fer you? Go an' look!"

## III

Placer was writing in his ledger. He heard a great trample of feet and clink of spurs on the porch, and there entered quietly the band of cowboys, some of them swaying a trifle, and these last being the most painfully decorous of all. Jake was in advance. He waved his hand toward the clock. "There she is," he said laconically. The cowboys drew up and stared. There was some giggling, but a serious voice said half-audibly, "I don't see no bird."

Jake politely addressed the landlord. "Mister, I've fetched these here friends of mine in here to see yer clock—"

Placer looked up suddenly. "Well, they can see it, can't they?" he asked in sarcasm. Jake, abashed, retreated to his fellows.

There was a period of silence. From time to time the men shifted their feet. Finally, Old Man Crumford leaned toward Jake, and in a penetrating whisper demanded, "Where's th' bird?" Some frolicsome spirits on the outskirts began to call "Bird! Bird!" as men at a political meeting call for a particular speaker.

Jake removed his big hat and nervously mopped his brow.

The young cowboy with the shrill voice again spoke from the skirts of the crowd. "Jake, is ther' sure-'nough a bird in that thing?"

"Yes. Didn't I tell you once?"

"Then," said the shrill-voiced man, in a tone of conviction, "it ain't a clock at all. It's a bird-cage."

"I tell you it's a clock," cried the maddened Jake, but his retort could hardly be heard above the howls of glee and derision which greeted the words of him of the shrill voice.

Old Man Crumford was again rampant. "Wooden bird a-tellin' ye th' time! Haw-haw!"

Amid the confusion Jake went again to Placer. He spoke almost in supplication. "Say, mister, what time does this here thing go off agin?"

Placer lifted his head, looked at the clock, and said: "Noon."

There was a stir near the door, and Big Watson of the Square-X outfit, and at this time very drunk indeed, came shouldering his way through the crowd and cursing everybody. The men gave him much room, for he was notorious as a quarrelsome person when drunk. He paused in front of Jake, and spoke as through a wet blanket. "What's all this—monkeyin' about?"

Jake was already wild at being made a butt for everybody, and he did not give backward. "None a' your damn business, Watson."

"Huh?" growled Watson, with the surprise of a challenged bull.

"I said," repeated Jake distinctly, "it's none a' your damn business."

Watson whipped his revolver half out of its holster. "I'll make it m' business, then, you—"

But Jake had backed a step away, and was holding his left-hand palm outward toward Watson, while in his right he held his six-shooter, its muzzle pointing at the floor. He was shouting in a frenzy,—"No—don't you try it, Watson! Don't you dare try it, or, by Gawd, I'll kill you, sure—*sure!*"

He was aware of a torment of cries about him from fearful men; from men who protested, from men who cried out because they cried out. But he kept his eyes on Watson, and those two glared murder at each other, neither seeming to breathe, fixed like statues.

A loud new voice suddenly rang out: "Hol' on a minute!" All spectators who had not stampeded turned quickly, and saw Placer standing behind his bright pink counter, with an aimed revolver in each hand.

"Cheese it!" he said. "I won't have no fightin' here. If you want to fight, git out in the street."

Big Watson laughed, and, speeding up his six-shooter like a flash of blue light, he shot Placer through the throat—shot the man as he stood behind his absurd pink counter with his two aimed revolvers in his incompetent hands. With a yell of rage and despair, Jake smote Watson on the pate with his heavy weapon, and knocked him sprawling and bloody. Somewhere a woman shrieked like windy, midnight death. Placer fell behind the counter, and down upon him came his ledger and his inkstand, so that one could not have told blood from ink.

The cowboys did not seem to hear, see, or feel, until they saw numbers of citizens with Winchesters running wildly upon them. Old Man Crumford threw high a passionate hand. "Don't shoot! We'll not fight ye fer 'im."

Nevertheless two or three shots rang, and a cowboy who had been about to gallop off suddenly slumped over on his pony's neck, where he held for a moment like an old sack, and then slid to the ground, while his pony, with flapping rein, fled to the prairie.

"In God's name, don't shoot!" trumpeted Old Man Crumford. "We'll not fight ye fer 'im!"

"It's murder," bawled Ben Roddle.

In the chaotic street it seemed for a moment as if everybody would kill everybody. "Where's the man what done it?" These hot cries seemed to declare a war which would result in an absolute annihilation of one side. But the cowboys were singing out against it. They would fight for nothing—yes—they often fought for nothing—but they would not fight for this dark something.

At last, when a flimsy truce had been made between the inflamed men, all parties went to the hotel. Placer, in some dying whim, had made his way out from behind the pink counter, and, leaving a horrible trail, had travelled to the centre of the room, where he had pitched headlong over the body of Big Watson.

The men lifted the corpse and laid it at the side.

"Who done it?" asked a white, stern man.

A cowboy pointed at Big Watson. "That's him," he said huskily.

There was a curious grim silence, and then suddenly, in the death-chamber, there sounded the loud whirring of the clock's works, little doors flew open, a tiny wooden bird appeared and cried "Cuckoo"—twelve times.

# Moonlight
# on the Snow

## I

The town of War Post had an evil name for three hundred miles in every direction. It radiated like the shine from some stupendous light. The citizens of the place had been for years grotesquely proud of their fame as a collection of hard-shooting gentlemen who invariably "got" the men who came up against them. When a citizen went abroad in the land he said, "I'm f'm War Post." And it was as if he had said, "I am the devil himself."

But ultimately it became known to War Post that the serene-browed angel of peace was in the vicinity. The angel was full of projects for taking comparatively useless bits of prairie and sawing them up into town lots, and making chaste and beautiful maps of his handi-work which shook the souls of people who had never been in the West. He commonly traveled here and there in a light wagon, from the tail-board of which he made orations which soared into the empyrean regions of true hydrogen gas. Towns far and near listened to his voice and followed him singing, until in all that territory you couldn't throw a stone at a jack-rabbit without hitting the site of a projected mammoth hotel; estimated cost, fifteen thousand dollars. The stern and lonely buttes were given titles like grim veterans awarded tawdry patents of nobility—Cedar Mountain, Red Cliffs, Lookout Peak. And from the East came both the sane and the insane with hope, with courage, with hoarded savings, with cold decks, with Bibles, with knives in boots, with humility and fear, with bland impudence. Most came with their own money; some came with money gained during a moment of inattention on the part of somebody in the East. And high in the air was the serene-browed angel of peace, with his endless gabble and his pretty maps. It was curious to walk out of an evening to the edge of a vast silent sea of prairie, and to reflect that the angel had parceled this infinity into building lots.

But no change had come to War Post. War Post sat with her reputation for bloodshed pressed proudly to her bosom and saw her mean neighbors leap into being as cities. She saw drunken old reprobates selling acres of red-hot dust and becoming wealthy men of affairs, who congratulated themselves on their shrewdness in holding land which, before the boom, they would have sold for enough to buy a treat all 'round in the Straight Flush Saloon—only nobody would have given it.

War Post saw dollars rolling into the coffers of a lot of contemptible men who couldn't shoot straight. She was amazed and indignant. She saw her standard of excellence, her creed, her reason for being great, all tumbling about her ears, and after the preliminary gasps she sat down to think it out.

The first man to voice a conclusion was Bob Hether, the popular barkeeper in Stevenson's Crystal Palace. "It's this here gun-fighter business," he said, leaning on his bar, and, with the gentle, serious eyes of a child, surveying a group of prominent citizens who had come in to drink at the expense of Tom Larpent, a gambler. They solemnly nodded assent. They stood in silence, holding their glasses and thinking.

Larpent was a chief factor in the life of the town. His gambling-house was the biggest institution in War Post. Moreover, he had been educated somewhere, and his slow speech had a certain mordant quality which was apt to puzzle War Post, and men heeded him for the reason that they were not always certain as to what he was saying. "Yes, Bob," he drawled, "I think you are right. The value of human life has to be established before there can be theatres, water-works, street cars, women and babies."

The other men were rather aghast at this cryptic speech, but somebody managed to snigger appreciatively and the tension was eased.

Smith Hanham, who whirled roulette for Larpent, then gave his opinion.

"Well, when all this here coin is floatin' 'round, it 'pears to me we orter git our hooks on some of it. Them little tin-horns over at Crowdger's Corners are up to their necks in it, an' we ain't yit seen a centavo. Not a centavetto. That ain't right. It's all well enough to sit 'round takin' money away from innercent cow-punchers s'long's ther's nothin' better; but when these here speculators come 'long flashin' rolls as big as water-buckets, it's up to us to whirl in an' git some of it."

This became the view of the town, and, since the main stipulation was virtue, War Post resolved to be virtuous. A great meeting was held, at which it was decreed that no man should kill another man under penalty of being at once hanged by the populace. All the influential citizens were present, and asserted their determination to deal out a swift punishment which would take no note of an acquaintance or friendship with the guilty man. Bob Hether made a loud, long speech, in which he declared that he for one would help hang his "own brother" if his "own brother" transgressed this law which now, for the good of the community, must be forever held sacred. Everybody was enthusiastic save a few Mexicans, who did not quite understand; but as they were more than likely to be the victims of any affray in which they were engaged, their silence was not considered ominous.

At half-past ten on the next morning Larpent shot and killed a man who had accused him of cheating at a game. Larpent had then taken a chair by the window.

## II

Larpent grew tired of sitting in the chair by the window. He went to his bedroom, which opened off the gambling hall. On the table was a bottle of rye whiskey, of a brand which he specially and secretly imported from the East. He took a long drink; he changed his coat after laving his hands and brushing his hair. He sat down to read, his hand falling familiarly upon an old copy of Scott's "Fair Maid of Perth."

In time he heard the slow trample of many men coming up the stairs. The sound certainly did not indicate haste; in fact, it declared all kinds of hesitation. The crowd poured into the gambling hall; there was low talk; a silence; more low talk. Ultimately somebody rapped diffidently on the door of the bedroom. "Come in," said Larpent. The door swung back and disclosed War Post with a delegation of its best men in the front, and at the rear men who stood on their toes and craned their necks. There was no noise. Larpent looked up casually into the eyes of Bob Hether. "So you've come up to the scratch all right, eh, Bobbie?" he asked kindly. "I was wondering if you would weaken on the blood-curdling speech you made yesterday."

Hether first turned deadly pale and then flushed beet red. His six-shooter was in his hand, and it appeared for a moment as if his weak fingers would drop it to the floor. "Oh, never mind," said Larpent in the same tone of kindly patronage. "The community must and shall hold this law forever sacred; and your own brother lives in Connecticut, doesn't he?" He laid down his book and arose. He unbuckled his revolver belt and tossed it on the bed. A look of impatience had come suddenly upon his face. "Well, you don't want me to be master of ceremonies at my own hanging, do you? Why don't somebody say something or do something? You stand around like a lot of bottles.

Where's your tree, for instance? You know there isn't a tree between here and the river. Damned little jack-rabbit town hasn't even got a tree for its hanging. Hello, Coats, you live in Crowdger's Corners, don't you? Well, you keep out of this thing, then. The Corners has had its boom, and this is a speculation in real estate which is the business solely of the citizens of War Post."

The behavior of the crowd became extraordinary. Men began to back away; eye did not meet eye; they were victims of an inexplicable influence; it was as if they had heard sinister laughter from a gloom. "I know," said Larpent considerately, "that this isn't as if you were going to hang a comparative stranger. In a sense, this is an intimate affair. I know full well you could go out and jerk a comparative stranger into kingdom come and make a sort of festal occasion of it. But when it comes to performing the same office for an old friend, even the ferocious Bobbie Hether stands around on one leg like a damned white-livered coward. In short, my milk-fed patriots, you seem fat-headed enough to believe that I am going to hang myself if you wait long enough; but unfortunately I am going to allow you to conduct your own real-estate speculations. It seems to me there should be enough men here who understand the value of corner lots in a safe and godly town, and hence should be anxious to hurry this business."

The icy tones had ceased, and the crowd breathed a great sigh, as if it had been freed of a physical pain. But still no one seemed to know where to reach for the scruff of this weird situation. Finally there was some jostling on the outskirts of the crowd, and some men were seen to be pushing old Billie Simpson forward amid some protests. Simpson was, on occasion, the voice of the town. Somewhere in his past he had been a Baptist preacher. He had fallen far, very far, and the only remnant of his former dignity was a fatal facility of speech when half drunk. War Post used him on those state occasions when it became bitten with a desire to "do the thing up in style." So the citizens pushed the blear-eyed old ruffian forward until he stood hemming and hawing in front of Larpent. It was evident at once that he was brutally sober, and hence wholly unfitted for whatever task had been planned for him. A dozen times he croaked like a frog, meanwhile wiping the back of his hand rapidly across his mouth. At last he managed to stammer, "Mister Larpent—"

In some indescribable manner Larpent made his attitude of respectful attention to be grossly contemptuous and insulting. "Yes, Mister Simpson?"

"Er—now—Mister Larpent," began the old man hoarsely, "we wanted to know—" Then obviously feeling that there was a detail

which he had forgotten, he turned to the crowd and whispered,
"Where is it?" Many men precipitately cleared themselves out of the
way, and down this lane Larpent had an unobstructed view of the
body of the man he had slain. Old Simpson again began to croak like
a frog, "Mister Larpent."

"Yes, Mister Simpson."

"Do you—er—do you—admit—"

"Oh, certainly," said the gambler good-humoredly. "There can be
no doubt of it, Mister Simpson, although, with your well-known ability
to fog things, you may later possibly prove that you did it yourself. I
shot him because he was too officious. Not quite enough men are shot
on that account, Mister Simpson. As one fitted in every way by nature
to be consummately officious, I hope you will agree with me, Mister
Simpson."

Men were plucking old Simpson by the sleeve and giving him directions. One could hear him say, "What?" "Yes." "All right." "What?"
"All right." In the end he turned hurriedly upon Larpent and blurted
out, "Well, I guess we're goin' to hang you."

Larpent bowed. "I had a suspicion that you would," he said in a
pleasant voice. "There has been an air of determination about the
entire proceeding, Mister Simpson."

There was an awkward moment. "Well—well—well, come
ahead—"

Larpent courteously relieved a general embarrassment. "Why, of
course. We must be moving. Clergy first, Mister Simpson. I'll take my
old friend, Bobbie Hether, on my right hand, and we'll march soberly
to the business, thus lending a certain dignity to this outing of real-
estate speculators."

"Tom," quavered Bob Hether, "for Gawd's sake, keep your mout'
shut."

"He invokes the deity," remarked Larpent placidly. "But, no; my
last few minutes I am resolved to devote to inquiries as to the welfare
of my friends. Now, you, for instance, my dear Bobbie, present to-day
the lamentable appearance of a rattlesnake that has been four times
killed and then left in the sun to rot. It is the effect of friendship upon
a highly delicate system. You suffer? It is cruel. Never mind; you will
feel better presently."

## III

War Post had always risen superior to her lack of a tree by making
use of a fixed wooden crane which appeared over a second-story window on the front of Pigrim's general store. This crane had a long tackle

always ready for hoisting merchandise to the store's loft. Larpent, coming in the midst of a slow-moving throng, cocked a bright bird-like eye at this crane.

"Mm—yes," he said.

Men began to work frantically. They called each to each in voices strenuous but low. They were in a panic to have the thing finished. Larpent's cold ironical survey drove them mad, and it entered the minds of some that it would be felicitous to hang him before he could talk more. But he occupied the time in pleasant discourse. "I see that Smith Hanham is not here. Perhaps some undue tenderness of sentiment keeps him away. Such feelings are entirely unnecessary. Don't you think so, Bobbie? Note the feverish industry with which the renegade parson works at the rope. You will never be hung, Simpson. You will be shot for fooling too near a petticoat which doesn't belong to you—the same old habit which got you flung out of the Church, you red-eyed old satyr. Ah, the Cross Trail stage coach approaches. What a situation!" The crowd turned uneasily to follow his glance, and saw, truly enough, the dusty rickety old vehicle coming at the gallop of four lean horses. Ike Boston was driving the coach, and far away he had seen and defined the throng in front of Pigrim's store. First calling out excited information to his passengers, who were all inside, he began to lash his horses and yell. As a result he rattled wildly up to the scene just as they were arranging the rope around Larpent's neck.

"Whoa!" said he to his horses.

The inhabitants of War Post peered at the windows of the coach and saw therein six pale, horror-stricken faces. The men at the rope stood hesitating. Larpent smiled blandly. There was a silence. At last a broken voice cried from the coach: "Driver! Driver! What is it? What is it?"

Ike Boston spat between the wheel horses and mumbled that he s'posed anybody could see, less'n they were blind. The door of the coach opened and out stepped a beautiful young lady. She was followed by two little girls hand clasped in hand, and a white-haired old gentleman with a venerable and peaceful face. And the rough West stood in naked immorality before the eyes of the gentle East. The leather-faced men of War Post had never imagined such perfection of feminine charm, such radiance; and as the illumined eyes of the girl wandered doubtfully, fearfully, toward the man with the rope around his neck, a certain majority of the practiced ruffians tried to look as if they were having nothing to do with the proceedings.

"Oh," she said, in a low voice, "what are you going to do?"

At first none made reply; but ultimately a hero managed to break the harrowing stillness by stammering out, "Nothin'!" And then, as if aghast at his own prominence, he shied behind the shoulders of a big neighbor.

"Oh, I know," she said, "but it's wicked. Don't you see how wicked it is? Papa, do say something to them."

The clear, deliberate tones of Tom Larpent suddenly made every one stiffen. During the early part of the interruption he had seated himself upon the steps of Pigrim's store, in which position he had maintained a slightly bored air. He now was standing with the rope around his neck and bowing. He looked handsome and distinguished and—a devil. A devil as cold as moonlight upon the ice. "You are quite right, miss. They are going to hang me, but I can give you my word that the affair is perfectly regular. I killed a man this morning, and you see these people here who look like a fine collection of premier scoundrels are really engaged in forcing a real-estate boom. In short, they are speculators, land barons, and not the children of infamy which you no doubt took them for at first."

"O—oh!" she said, and shuddered.

Her father now spoke haughtily. "What has this man done? Why do you hang him without a trial, even if you have fair proofs?"

The crowd had been afraid to speak to the young lady, but a dozen voices answered her father. "Why, he admits it." "Didn't ye hear?" "There ain't no doubt about it." "No!" "He *sez* he did."

The old man looked at the smiling gambler. "Do you admit that you committed murder?"

Larpent answered slowly. "For the first question in a temporary acquaintance that is a fairly strong beginning. Do you wish me to speak as man to man, or to one who has some kind of official authority to meddle in a thing that is none of his affair?"

"I—ah—I," stuttered the other. "Ah—man to man."

"Then," said Larpent, "I have to inform you that this morning, at about 10:30, a man was shot and killed in my gambling house. He was engaged in the exciting business of trying to grab some money out of which he claimed I had swindled him. The details are not interesting."

The old gentleman waved his arm in a gesture of terror and despair and tottered toward the coach; the young lady fainted; the two little girls wailed. Larpent sat on the steps with the rope around his neck.

## IV

The chief function of War Post was to prey upon the bands of cowboys who, when they had been paid, rode gayly into town to look for sin.

To this end there were in War Post many thugs and thieves. There was treachery and obscenity and merciless greed in every direction. Even Mexico was levied upon to furnish a kind of ruffian which appears infrequently in the northern races. War Post was not good; it was not tender; it was not chivalrous; but—

But—

There was a quality to the situation in front of Pigrim's store which made War Post wish to stampede. There were the two children, their angelic faces turned toward the sky, weeping in the last anguish of fear; there was the beautiful form of the young lady prostrate in the dust of the road, with her trembling father bending over her; on the steps sat Larpent, waiting, with a derisive smile, while from time to time he turned his head in the rope to make a forked-tongued remark as to the character and bearing of some acquaintance. All the simplicity of a mere lynching was gone from this thing. Through some bewildering inner power of its own it had carried out of the hands of its inaugurators and was marching along like a great drama and they were only spectators. To them it was ungovernable; they could do no more than stand on one foot and wonder.

Some were heartily sick of everything and wished to run away. Some were so interested in the new aspect that they had forgotten why they had originally come to the front of Pigrim's store. These were the poets. A large practical class wished to establish at once the identity of the new comers. Who were they? Where did they come from? Where were they going to? It was truthfully argued that they were the parson for the new church at Crowdger's Corners, with his family.

And a fourth class—a dark-browed, muttering class—wished to go at once to the root of all disturbance by killing Ike Boston for trundling up his old omnibus and dumping out upon their ordinary lynching party such a load of tears and inexperience and sentimental argument. In low tones they addressed vitriolic reproaches.

"But how'd I know?" he protested, almost with tears. "How'd I know ther'd be all this here kick up?"

But Larpent suddenly created a great stir. He stood up, and his face was inspired with a new, strong resolution. "Look here, boys," he said decisively, "you hang me to-morrow. Or, anyhow, later on to-day. We can't keep frightening the young lady and these two poor babies out of their wits. Ease off on the rope, Simpson, you blackguard! Frightening women and children is your game, but I'm not going to stand it. Ike Boston, take your passengers on to Crowdger's Corners, and tell the young lady that, owing to her influence, the boys changed their minds about making me swing. Somebody lift the rope where it's caught under my ear, will you? Boys, when you want me you'll find me in the Crystal Palace."

His tone was so authoritative that some obeyed him at once involuntarily; but, as a matter of fact, his plan met with general approval. War Post heaved a great sigh of relief. Why had nobody thought earlier of so easy a way out of all these here tears?

## V

Larpent went to the Crystal Palace, where he took his comfort like a gentleman, conversing with his friends and drinking. At nightfall two men rode into town, flung their bridles over a convenient post and clanked into the Crystal Palace. War Post knew them in a glance. Talk ceased and there was a watchful squaring back.

The foremost was Jack Potter, a famous town marshal of Yellow Sky, but now sheriff of the county; the other was Scratchy Wilson, once a no less famous desperado. They were both two-handed men of terrific prowess and courage, but War Post could hardly believe her eyes at view of this daring invasion. It was unprecedented.

Potter went straight to the bar, behind which frowned Bobbie Hether.

"You know a man by the name of Larpent?"

"Supposin' I do?" said Bobbie sourly.

"Well, I want him. Is he in the saloon?"

"Maybe he is an' maybe he isn't," said Bobbie.

Potter went back among the glinting eyes of the citizens. "Gentlemen, I want a man named Larpent. Is he here?"

War Post was sullen, but Larpent answered lazily for himself. "Why, you must mean me. My name is Larpent. What do you want?"

"I've got a warrant for your arrest."

There was a movement all over the room as if a puff of wind had come. The swing of a hand would have brought on a murderous mêlée. But after an instant the rigidity was broken by Larpent's laughter.

"Why, you're sold, sheriff!" he cried. "I've got a previous engagement. The boys are going to hang me to-night."

If Potter was surprised he betrayed nothing.

"The boys won't hang you to-night, Larpent," he said calmly, "because I'm goin' to take you in to Yellow Sky."

Larpent was looking at the warrant. "Only grand larceny," he observed. "But still, you know, I've promised these people to appear at their performance."

"You're goin' in with me," said the impassive sheriff.

"You bet he is, sheriff!" cried an enthusiastic voice, and it belonged to Bobbie Hether. The barkeeper moved down inside his rail, and, inspired like a prophet, he began a harangue to the citizens of War Post. "Now, look here, boys, that's jest what we want, ain't it? Here we were goin' to hang Tom Larpent jest for the reputation of the town, like. 'Long comes Sheriff Potter, the reg-u-lerly cons-ti-tuted officer of the law, an' he says, 'No; the man's mine.' Now, we want to make the reputation of the town as a law-abidin' place, so what do we say to Sheriff Potter? We says, 'A-a-ll right, sheriff; you're reg'lar; we ain't; he's your man.' But supposin' we go to fightin' over it? Then what becomes of the reputation of the town which we was goin' to swing Tom Larpent for?"

The immediate opposition to these views came from a source which a stranger might have difficulty in imagining. Men's foreheads grew thick with lines of obstinacy and disapproval. They were perfectly willing to hang Larpent yesterday, to-day, or to-morrow as a detail in a set of circumstances at War Post; but when some outsider from the alien town of Yellow Sky came into the sacred precincts of War Post and proclaimed the intention of extracting a citizen for cause, any citizen for any cause, the stomach of War Post was fed with a clan's blood, and her children gathered under one invisible banner, prepared to fight as few people in few ages were enabled to fight for their— points of view. There was a guttural murmuring.

"No; hold on!" screamed Bobbie, flinging up his hands. "He'll come clear all right. Tom," he appealed wildly to Larpent, "you never committed no—— ——low-down grand larceny?"

"No," said Larpent coldly.

"But how was it? Can't you tell us how it was?"

Larpent answered with plain reluctance. He waved his hand to indicate that it was all of little consequence. "Well, he was a tenderfoot, and he played poker with me, and he couldn't play quite good enough. But he thought he could; he could play extremely well, he thought. So he lost his money. I thought he'd squeal."

"Boys," begged Bobbie, "let the sheriff take him."

Some answered at once, "Yes!" Others continued to mutter. The sheriff had held his hand because, like all quiet and honest men, he did not wish to perturb any progress toward a peaceful solution; but now he decided to take the scene by the nose and make it obey him.

"Gentlemen," he said formally, "this man is comin' with me. Larpent, get up and come along."

This might have been the beginning, but it was practically the end. The two opinions in the minds of War Post fought in the air and, like a snow-squall, discouraged all action. Amid general confusion Jack

Potter and Scratchy Wilson moved to the door with their prisoner. The last thing seen by the men in the Crystal Palace was the bronze countenance of Jack Potter as he backed from the place.

A man filled with belated thought suddenly cried out, "Well, they'll hang him fer this here shootin' game, anyhow."

Bobbie Hether looked disdain upon the speaker.

"Will they! An' where'll they get their witnesses? From here, do y' think? No; not a single one. All he's up against is a case of grand larceny; and—even supposin' he done it—what in hell does grand larceny amount to?"

# JACK LONDON

## (1876–1916)

London was born in San Francisco, the illegitimate child of an itinerant Irish astrologer named Chaney and Flora Wellman, an eccentric but strong-willed woman from Wisconsin farming parentage. Flora soon afterward married Pennsylvania-born John London, who gave his name and a precarious existence to young Jack, supporting his family by means of a grocery store, a boardinghouse, and finally a chicken farm. Although London in later life tended to overemphasize the hardships of his youth, he was never hungry or poorly clothed. He early discovered the delights of reading and was a regular visitor to the public library in Oakland, headed by the poet Ina Coolbrith, who took an interest in the boy, as she would later encourage the literary talents of Mary Austin. To help with the family income, London worked peddling newspapers and at a number of jobs requiring manual labor, and had considerable experience with the sufferings of the working class—of which he was never a member. Again, his own account of his early life was gauged to enhance his literary reputation as a naturalist, but he seems for a time to have worked as an oyster "pirate" in San Francisco Bay, then turned against his former fellow thieves and worked for the police.

On something of a lark, London joined the army of unemployed men who were moving across the country toward Washington under the leadership of the wealthy James S. Coxey, riding in freight cars and in general having a good time until he was arrested for vagrancy and thrown into the Erie County Penitentiary. There he was brought into direct contact with the dregs of society, an experience that occasioned in him something akin to a religious conversion, which instilled in him a social, not a pious, resolve. Resolving never to allow himself to be dragged down by economic adversity, London began also to develop a social consciousness, which was deepened by his reading

*in popularized versions the ideas of Marx and Darwin. Though he
became associated with the Socialist party, he was never entirely committed to the cause, and a later exposure to the writings of Nietzsche,
along with Darwin's theory of the survival of the fittest, made something of a protofascist of him, in his identification of himself with the
Nietzschean Superman, the "Blond Beast" he increasingly cast himself (and his created heroes) as.*

*Having dropped out of school as a boy, London resolved to improve
himself intellectually; he enrolled as a high school freshman at the
age of nineteen, and later managed to be accepted by the university
across the bay, but his college career was brief. As Melville declared
that his Harvard and Yale was a whaling ship, so London received
his definitive education in the Klondike, where the discovery of gold
in 1896 drew a human flood into the northern wastes. London spent
less than a year in the Yukon, and never did discover any gold, but
the experiences of that brief stay provided the material for the novels
and stories that would result in his eventual fame. Along with life in
the Canadian wilds, London depended for material on his seagoing
experiences on a sealer in northern waters, where he began the heavy
drinking that would eventually put an end to his career.*

*With Kipling and Stevenson as his literary models, London began
to conceive of himself as a writer. The results of his initial efforts
would have discouraged another person; but his short stories eventually began to appear in local magazines, and in 1899 the prestigious*
Atlantic Monthly *published a longish story, "An Odyssey of the
North," and at about the same time London was given a contract by
Houghton Mifflin (then affiliated with the magazine) for a book of
short stories,* The Son of the Wolf *(1900). His career was underway
with extraordinary swiftness, and was accelerated by the publication
in 1903 of* The Call of the Wild, *into whose anthropomorphic sled-dog,
Buck, London poured all of his eclectic and subjective thought. Animated by similarly Darwinian considerations, in 1901 London
married Bessie Maddern, chosen for her physical attributes as an
ideal mother to his children—but such considerations proved not to
be a solid basis for matrimony, and the couple were soon estranged.
In 1904 he married his "mate," Charmian Kittredge, who helped sustain his self-image as the absolutely self-reliant male, and whose sympathetic companionship was in part responsible for the appearance of
a kinder, gentler London, as witnessed by the happy ending of* White
Fang *(1905), the companion volume to his story of the dog who succumbed to the wilderness's call.*

*Like so many of the writers anthologized here, London parlayed
his booming literary reputation into journalistic errands. Too late for*

*the Spanish-American War, he set off to cover the Boer War in 1902, but ended up stranded in London; then in 1904 he was sent by Hearst to report on the Russo-Japanese War. But the conflict with which he was chiefly concerned was social, and his experiences while stuck in London resulted in his militantly angry* The People of the Abyss *(1903). In the following year appeared* The Sea Wolf, *a semiautobiographical but highly imaginative account of a Nietzschean sea captain, serialized first in* Century Magazine. *London's literary career thenceforth drew heavily upon the facts (and myths) of his own life, and he increasingly engineered events to generate material, as when at great expense he had built an experimental sloop, the* Lark, *on which he and Charmain set out for the South Pacific—a disastrous voyage, but with considerable literary consequences. While on the cruise, he wrote the autobiographical* Martin Eden *(1909); and his encounter with the people of the South Pacific provided material for a number of stories with settings in the Solomon Islands and Hawaii.*

*Much of the time remaining to London was spent establishing a utopian ranch in northern California, into which he poured much of his energy and all of his money. He became reliant on various narcotic remedies for illnesses real and imagined, and this sapped such strength as had survived his earlier career in alcoholism. The ranch project was centered in an ambitiously conceived dwelling, Wolf House, which was destroyed in a fire set by a disgruntled employee on the eve of its completion. London's last years were devoted to a ceaseless (but hardly tireless) outpouring of writings of decreasing literary value, which were often pale imitations of his earlier successes. He died of causes variously attributed to uremic poisoning and suicide by morphine, leaving his ravaged literary reputation in the capable hands of his widow, who saw to it that the myth he had carefully cultivated would be sustained for yet another generation.*

*London was not a writer of the Old or Far West, but of that territory to the north which in so many ways replicated the older frontier, particularly the bonanza years celebrated by Harte and Twain. He did write about California, but his was a newer West, the agricultural region that had replaced the older mining frontier. But his dreams and the directions in which he expended his energies were most definitely the children of the old Western myths, of self-reliance, of courage, and of sudden and great wealth awaiting the man who was ready to seize the main chance at the proper time. Of the many stories he wrote delineating the hazards that await adventurers into the wilderness zone, only one has what can be called a setting in an earlier time: "All Gold Canyon," a California story that is idiosyncratic within the London canon for another reason, namely in that its protagonist survives and succeeds in deriving great riches from the ground. Curious also is London's detailed account of the prospector's technology, as he tirelessly samples the soil for indicators of the mother lode, the "pocket" of pure gold he is looking for. In contrast to many of his stories, in which nature is depicted as a terrific and un-relenting adversary, the emphasis here is on the devastating effects left by the prospector when he abandons his mine. This is a note not found in any other of the stories gathered here, not even in the nature-sensitive tales of Mary Austin.*

# All Gold Canyon

It was the green heart of the canyon, where the walls swerved back from the rigid plan and relieved their harshness of line by making a little sheltered nook and filling it to the brim with sweetness and roundness and softness. Here all things rested. Even the narrow stream ceased its turbulent down-rush long enough to form a quiet pool. Knee-deep in the water, with drooping head and half-shut eyes, drowsed a red-coated, many-antlered buck.

On one side, beginning at the very lip of the pool, was a tiny meadow, a cool, resilient surface of green that extended to the base of the frowning wall. Beyond the pool a gentle slope of earth ran up and up to meet the opposing wall. Fine grass covered the slope—grass that was spangled with flowers, with here and there patches of color, orange and purple and golden. Below, the canyon was shut in. There was no view. The walls leaned together abruptly and the canyon ended in a chaos of rocks, moss-covered and hidden by a green screen of vines and creepers and boughs of trees. Up the canyon rose far hills and peaks, the big foothills, pine-covered and remote. And far beyond, like clouds upon the border of the sky, towered minarets of white, where the Sierra's eternal snows flashed austerely the blazes of the sun.

There was no dust in the canyon. The leaves and flowers were clean and virginal. The grass was young velvet. Over the pool three cottonwoods sent their snowy fluffs fluttering down the quiet air. On the slope the blossoms of the wine-wooded manzanita filled the air with springtime odors, while the leaves, wise with experience, were already beginning their vertical twist against the coming aridity of summer. In the open spaces on the slope, beyond the farthest shadow-reach of the manzanita, poised the mariposa lilies, like so many flights of jewelled moths suddenly arrested and on the verge of trembling into flight again. Here and there that woods harlequin, the madrone, permitting itself to be caught in the act of changing its pea-green trunk to madder-red, breathed its fragrance into the air from great clusters of waxen bells. Creamy white were these bells, shaped like lilies-of-the-valley, with the sweetness of perfume that is of the springtime.

There was not a sigh of wind. The air was drowsy with its weight of perfume. It was a sweetness that would have been cloying had the air been heavy and humid. But the air was sharp and thin. It was as starlight transmuted into atmosphere, shot through and warmed by sunshine, and flower-drenched with sweetness.

An occasional butterfly drifted in and out through the patches of light and shade. And from all about rose the low and sleepy hum of mountain bees—feasting Sybarites that jostled one another good-naturedly at the board, nor found time for rough discourtesy. So quietly did the little stream drip and ripple its way through the canyon that it spoke only in faint and occasional gurgles. The voice of the stream was as a drowsy whisper, ever interrupted by dozings and silences, ever lifted again in the awakenings.

The motion of all things was a drifting in the heart of the canyon. Sunshine and butterflies drifted in and out among the trees. The hum of the bees and the whisper of the stream were a drifting of sound. And the drifting sound and drifting color seemed to weave together in the making of a delicate and intangible fabric which was the spirit of the place. It was a spirit of peace that was not of death, but of smooth-pulsing life, of quietude that was not silence, of movement that was not action, of repose that was quick with existence without being violent with struggle and travail. The spirit of the place was the spirit of the peace of the living, somnolent with the easement and content of prosperity, and undisturbed by rumors of far wars.

The red-coated, many-antlered buck acknowledged the lordship of the spirit of the place and dozed knee-deep in the cool, shaded pool. There seemed no flies to vex him and he was languid with rest. Sometimes his ears moved when the stream awoke and whispered; but they moved lazily, with foreknowledge that it was merely the stream grown garrulous at discovery that it had slept.

But there came a time when the buck's ears lifted and tensed with swift eagerness for sound. His head was turned down the canyon. His sensitive, quivering nostrils scented the air. His eyes could not pierce the green screen through which the stream rippled away, but to his ears came the voice of a man. It was a steady, monotonous, singsong voice. Once the buck heard the harsh clash of metal upon rock. At the sound he snorted with a sudden start that jerked him through the air from water to meadow, and his feet sank into the young velvet, while he pricked his ears and again scented the air. Then he stole across the tiny meadow, pausing once and again to listen, and faded away out of the canyon like a wraith, soft-footed and without sound.

The clash of steel-shod soles against the rocks began to be heard, and the man's voice grew louder. It was raised in a sort of chant and became distinct with nearness, so that the words could be heard:

> *"Tu'n around an' tu'n yo' face*
> *Untoe them sweet hills of grace*
> *(D' pow'rs of sin yo' am scornin'!).*
> *Look about an' look aroun',*
> *Fling yo' sin-pack on d' groun'*
> *(Yo' will meet wid d' Lord in d' mornin'!)."*

A sound of scrambling accompanied the song, and the spirit of the place fled away on the heels of the red-coated buck. The green screen was burst asunder, and a man peered out at the meadow and the pool and the sloping side-hill. He was a deliberate sort of man. He took in the scene with one embracing glance, then ran his eyes over the details to verify the general impression. Then, and not until then, did he open his mouth in vivid and solemn approval:

"Smoke of life an' snakes of purgatory! Will you just look at that! Wood an' water an' grass an' a side-hill! A pocket-hunter's delight an' a cayuse's paradise! Cool green for tired eyes! Pink pills for pale people ain't in it. A secret pasture for prospectors and a resting-place for tired burros, by damn!"

He was a sandy-complexioned man in whose face geniality and humor seemed the salient characteristics. It was a mobile face, quick-changing to inward mood and thought. Thinking was in him a visible process. Ideas chased across his face like wind-flaws across the surface of a lake. His hair, sparse and unkempt of growth, was as indeterminate and colorless as his complexion. It would seem that all the color of his frame had gone into his eyes, for they were startlingly blue. Also, they were laughing and merry eyes, within them much of the naïveté and wonder of the child; and yet, in an unassertive way, they contained much of calm self-reliance and strength of purpose founded upon self-experience and experience of the world.

From out the screen of vines and creepers he flung ahead of him a miner's pick and shovel and gold-pan. Then he crawled out himself into the open. He was clad in faded overalls and black cotton shirt, with hobnailed brogans on his feet, and on his head a hat whose shapelessness and stains advertised the rough usage of wind and rain and sun and camp-smoke. He stood erect, seeing wide-eyed the secrecy of the scene and sensuously inhaling the warm, sweet breath of the canyon-garden through nostrils that dilated and quivered with delight. His eyes narrowed to laughing slits of blue, his face wreathed itself in joy, and his mouth curled in a smile as he cried aloud:

"Jumping dandelions and happy hollyhocks, but that smells good to me! Talk about your attar o' roses an' cologne factories! They ain't in it!"

He had the habit of soliloquy. His quick-changing facial expressions might tell every thought and mood, but the tongue, perforce, ran hard after, repeating, like a second Boswell.

The man lay down on the lip of the pool and drank long and deep of its water. "Tastes good to me," he murmured, lifting his head and gazing across the pool at the side-hill, while he wiped his mouth with the back of his hand. The side-hill attracted his attention. Still lying on his stomach, he studied the hill formation long and carefully. It was a practised eye that travelled up the slope to the crumbling canyon-wall and back and down again to the edge of the pool. He scrambled to his feet and favored the side-hill with a second survey.

"Looks good to me," he concluded, picking up his pick and shovel and gold-pan.

He crossed the stream below the pool, stepping agilely from stone to stone. Where the side-hill touched the water he dug up a shovelful of dirt and put it into the gold-pan. He squatted down, holding the pan in his two hands, and partly immersing it in the stream. Then he imparted to the pan a deft circular motion that sent the water sluicing in and out through the dirt and gravel. The larger and the lighter particles worked to the surface, and these, by a skilful dipping movement of the pan, he spilled out and over the edge. Occasionally, to expedite matters, he rested the pan and with his fingers raked out the large pebbles and pieces of rock.

The contents of the pan diminished rapidly until only fine dirt and the smallest bits of gravel remained. At this stage he began to work very deliberately and carefully. It was fine washing, and he washed fine and finer, with a keen scrutiny and delicate and fastidious touch. At last the pan seemed empty of everything but water; but with a quick semicircular flirt that sent the water flying over the shallow rim into the stream, he disclosed a layer of black sand on the bottom of the pan. So thin was this layer that it was like a streak of paint. He examined it closely. In the midst of it was a tiny golden speck. He dribbled a little water in over the depressed edge of the pan. With a quick flirt he sent the water sluicing across the bottom, turning the grains of black sand over and over. A second tiny golden speck rewarded his effort.

The washing had now become very fine—fine beyond all need of ordinary placer-mining. He worked the black sand, a small portion at a time, up the shallow rim of the pan. Each small portion he examined sharply, so that his eyes saw every grain of it before he allowed it to slide over the edge and away. Jealously, bit by bit, he let the black sand slip away. A golden speck, no larger than a pin-point, appeared on the rim, and by his manipulation of the water it returned to the bottom of the pan. And in such fashion another speck was disclosed, and another. Great was his care of them. Like a shepherd he herded his flock of golden specks so that not one should be lost. At last, of the pan of dirt nothing remained but his golden herd. He counted it, and then, after all his labor, sent it flying out of the pan with one final swirl of water.

But his blue eyes were shining with desire as he rose to his feet. "Seven," he muttered aloud, asserting the sum of the specks for which he had toiled so hard and which he had so wantonly thrown away. "Seven," he repeated, with the emphasis of one trying to impress a number on his memory.

He stood still a long while, surveying the hillside. In his eyes was a curiosity, new-aroused and burning. There was an exultance about his bearing and a keenness like that of a hunting animal catching the fresh scent of game.

He moved down the stream a few steps and took a second panful of dirt.

Again came the careful washing, the jealous herding of the golden specks, and the wantonness with which he sent them flying into the stream when he had counted their number.

"Five," he muttered, and repeated, "five."

He could not forbear another survey of the hill before filling the pan farther down the stream. His golden herds diminished. "Four, three, two, two, one," were his memory-tabulations as he moved down the stream. When but one speck of gold rewarded his washing, he stopped and built a fire of dry twigs. Into this he thrust the gold-pan and burned it till it was blue-black. He held up the pan and examined it critically. Then he nodded approbation. Against such a color-background he could defy the tiniest yellow speck to elude him.

Still moving down the stream, he panned again. A single speck was his reward. A third pan contained no gold at all. Not satisfied with this, he panned three times again, taking his shovels of dirt within a foot of one another. Each pan proved empty of gold, and the fact, instead of discouraging him, seemed to give him satisfaction. His elation increased with each barren washing, until he arose, exclaiming jubilantly:

"If it ain't the real thing, may God knock off my head with sour apples!"

Returning to where he had started operations, he began to pan up the stream. At first his golden herds increased—increased prodigiously. "Fourteen, eighteen, twenty-one, twenty-six," ran his memory tabulations. Just above the pool he struck his richest pan—thirty-five colors.

"Almost enough to save," he remarked regretfully as he allowed the water to sweep them away.

The sun climbed to the top of the sky. The man worked on. Pan by pan, he went up the stream, the tally of results steadily decreasing.

"It's just booful, the way it peters out," he exulted when a shovelful of dirt contained no more than a single speck of gold.

And when no specks at all were found in several pans, he straightened up and favored the hillside with a confident glance.

"Ah, ha! Mr. Pocket!" he cried out, as though to an auditor hidden somewhere above him beneath the surface of the slope. "Ah, ha! Mr. Pocket! I'm a-comin', I'm a-comin', an' I'm shorely gwine to get yer! You heah me, Mr. Pocket? I'm gwine to get yer as shore as punkins ain't cauliflowers!"

He turned and flung a measuring glance at the sun poised above him in the azure of the cloudless sky. Then he went down the canyon, following the line of shovel-holes he had made in filling the pans. He crossed the stream below the pool and disappeared through the green screen. There was little opportunity for the spirit of the place to return with its quietude and repose, for the man's voice, raised in ragtime song, still dominated the canyon with possession.

After a time, with a greater clashing of steel-shod feet on rock, he returned. The green screen was tremendously agitated. It surged back and forth in the throes of a struggle. There was a loud grating and clanging of metal. The man's voice leaped to a higher pitch and was sharp with imperativeness. A large body plunged and panted. There was a snapping and ripping and rending, and amid a shower of falling leaves a horse burst through the screen. On its back was a pack, and from this trailed broken vines and torn creepers. The animal gazed with astonished eyes at the scene into which it had been precipitated, then dropped its head to the grass and began contentedly to graze. A second horse scrambled into view, slipping once on the mossy rocks and regaining equilibrium when its hoofs sank into the yielding surface of the meadow. It was riderless, though on its back was a high-horned Mexican saddle, scarred and discolored by long usage.

The man brought up the rear. He threw off pack and saddle, with an eye to camp location, and gave the animals their freedom to graze. He unpacked his food and got out frying-pan and coffeepot. He gathered an armful of dry wood, and with a few stones made a place for his fire.

"My!" he said, "but I've got an appetite. I could scoff iron-filings an' horseshoe nails an' thank you kindly, ma'am, for a second helpin'."

He straightened up, and, while he reached for matches in the pocket of his overalls, his eyes travelled across the pool to the side-hill. His fingers had clutched the match-box, but they relaxed their hold and the hand came out empty. The man wavered perceptibly. He looked at his preparations for cooking and he looked at the hill.

"Guess I'll take another whack at her," he concluded, starting to cross the stream.

"They ain't no sense in it, I know," he mumbled apologetically. "But keepin' grub back an hour ain't goin' to hurt none, I reckon."

A few feet back from his first line of test-pans he started a second line. The sun dropped down the western sky, the shadows lengthened, but the man worked on. He began a third line of test-pans. He was cross-cutting the hillside, line by line, as he ascended. The centre of each line produced the richest pans, while the ends came where no colors showed in the pan. And as he ascended the hillside the lines grew perceptibly shorter. The regularity with which their length diminished served to indicate that somewhere up the slope the last line would be so short as to have scarcely length at all, and that beyond could come only a point. The design was growing into an inverted "V." The converging sides of this "V" marked the boundaries of the gold-bearing dirt.

The apex of the "V" was evidently the man's goal. Often he ran his eye along the converging sides and on up the hill, trying to divine the apex, the point where the gold-bearing dirt must cease. Here resided "Mr. Pocket"—for so the man familiarly addressed the imaginary point above him on the slope, crying out:

"Come down out o' that, Mr. Pocket! Be right smart an' agreeable, an' come down!"

"All right," he would add later, in a voice resigned to determination. "All right, Mr. Pocket. It's plain to me I got to come right up an' snatch you out bald-headed. An' I'll do it! I'll do it!" he would threaten still later.

Each pan he carried down to the water to wash, and as he went higher up the hill the pans grew richer, until he began to save the gold in an empty baking-powder can which he carried carelessly in his hip-pocket. So engrossed was he in his toil that he did not notice the long twilight of oncoming night. It was not until he tried vainly to see the gold colors in the bottom of the pan that he realized the passage of time. He straightened up abruptly. An expression of whimsical wonderment and awe overspread his face as he drawled:

"Gosh darn my buttons! if I didn't plumb forget dinner!"

He stumbled across the stream in the darkness and lighted his long-delayed fire. Flapjacks and bacon and warmed-over beans constituted his supper. Then he smoked a pipe by the smouldering coals, listening to the night noises and watching the moonlight stream through the canyon. After that he unrolled his bed, took off his heavy shoes, and pulled the blankets up to his chin. His face showed white in the moonlight, like the face of a corpse. But it was a corpse that knew its resurrection, for the man rose suddenly on one elbow and gazed across at his hillside.

"Good night, Mr. Pocket," he called sleepily. "Good night."

He slept through the early gray of morning until the direct rays of the sun smote his closed eyelids, when he awoke with a start and looked about him until he had established the continuity of his existence and identified his present self with the days previously lived.

To dress, he had merely to buckle on his shoes. He glanced at his fireplace and at his hillside, wavered, but fought down the temptation and started the fire.

"Keep yer shirt on, Bill; keep yer shirt on," he admonished himself. "What's the good of rushin'? No use in gettin' all het up an' sweaty. Mr. Pocket 'll wait for you. He ain't a-runnin' away before you can get yer breakfast. Now, what you want, Bill, is something fresh in yer bill o' fare. So it's up to you to go an' get it."

He cut a short pole at the water's edge and drew from one of his pockets a bit of line and a draggled fly that had once been a royal coachman.

"Mebbe they'll bite in the early morning," he muttered, as he made his first cast into the pool. And a moment later he was gleefully crying: "What 'd I tell you, eh? What 'd I tell you?"

He had no reel, nor any inclination to waste time, and by main strength, and swiftly, he drew out of the water a flashing ten-inch trout. Three more, caught in rapid succession, furnished his breakfast. When he came to the stepping-stones on his way to his hillside, he was struck by a sudden thought, and paused.

"I'd just better take a hike down-stream a ways," he said. "There's no tellin' what cuss may be snoopin' around."

But he crossed over on the stones, and with a "I really oughter take that hike," the need of the precaution passed out of his mind and he fell to work.

At nightfall he straightened up. The small of his back was stiff from stooping toil, and as he put his hand behind him to soothe the protesting muscles, he said:

"Now what d'ye think of that, by damn? I clean forgot my dinner again! If I don't watch out, I'll sure be degeneratin' into a two-meal-a-day crank."

"Pockets is the damnedest things I ever see for makin' a man absent-minded," he communed that night, as he crawled into his blankets. Nor did he forget to call up the hillside, "Good night, Mr. Pocket! Good night!"

Rising with the sun, and snatching a hasty breakfast, he was early at work. A fever seemed to be growing in him, nor did the increasing richness of the test-pans allay this fever. There was a flush in his cheek other than that made by the heat of the sun, and he was oblivious to fatigue and the passage of time. When he filled a pan with dirt, he ran down the hill to wash it; nor could he forbear running up the hill again, panting and stumbling profanely, to refill the pan.

He was now a hundred yards from the water, and the inverted "V" was assuming definite proportions. The width of the pay-dirt steadily decreased, and the man extended in his mind's eye the sides of the "V" to their meeting-place far up the hill. This was his goal, the apex of the "V," and he panned many times to locate it.

"Just about two yards above that manzanita bush an' a yard to the right," he finally concluded.

Then the temptation seized him. "As plain as the nose on your face," he said, as he abandoned his laborious cross-cutting and climbed to the indicated apex. He filled a pan and carried it down the hill to wash. It contained no trace of gold. He dug deep, and he dug shallow, filling and washing a dozen pans, and was unrewarded even by the tiniest golden speck. He was enraged at having yielded to the temptation, and cursed himself blasphemously and pridelessly. Then he went down the hill and took up the cross-cutting.

"Slow an' certain, Bill; slow an' certain," he crooned. "Short-cuts to fortune ain't in your line, an' it's about time you know it. Get wise, Bill; get wise. Slow an' certain's the only hand you can play; so go to it, an' keep to it, too."

As the cross-cuts decreased, showing that the sides of the "V" were converging, the depth of the "V" increased. The gold-trace was dipping into the hill. It was only at thirty inches beneath the surface that he could get colors in his pan. The dirt he found at twenty-five inches from the surface, and at thirty-five inches, yielded barren pans.

At the base of the "V," by the water's edge, he had found the gold colors at the grass roots. The higher he went up the hill, the deeper the gold dipped. To dig a hole three feet deep in order to get one test-pan was a task of no mean magnitude; while between the man and the apex intervened an untold number of such holes to be dug. "An' there's no tellin' how much deeper it'll pitch," he sighed, in a moment's pause, while his fingers soothed his aching back.

Feverish with desire, with aching back and stiffening muscles, with pick and shovel gouging and mauling the soft brown earth, the man toiled up the hill. Before him was the smooth slope, spangled with flowers and made sweet with their breath. Behind him was devastation. It looked like some terrible eruption breaking out on the smooth skin of the hill. His slow progress was like that of a slug, befouling beauty with a monstrous trail.

Though the dipping gold-trace increased the man's work, he found consolation in the increasing richness of the pans. Twenty cents, thirty cents, fifty cents, sixty cents, were the values of the gold found in the pans, and at nightfall he washed his banner pan, which gave him a dollar's worth of gold-dust from a shovelful of dirt.

"I'll just bet it's my luck to have some inquisitive cuss come buttin' in here on my pasture," he mumbled sleepily that night as he pulled the blankets up to his chin.

Suddenly he sat upright. "Bill!" he called sharply. "Now, listen to me, Bill; d'ye hear! It's up to you, to-morrow mornin', to mosey round an' see what you can see. Understand? To-morrow morning, an' don't you forget it!"

He yawned and glanced across at his side-hill. "Good night, Mr. Pocket," he called.

In the morning he stole a march on the sun, for he had finished breakfast when its first rays caught him, and he was climbing the wall of the canyon where it crumbled away and gave footing. From the outlook at the top he found himself in the midst of loneliness. As far as he could see, chain after chain of mountains heaved themselves into his vision. To the east his eyes, leaping the miles between range and range and between many ranges, brought up at last against the white-peaked Sierras—the main crest, where the backbone of the Western world reared itself against the sky. To the north and south he could see more distinctly the cross-systems that broke through the main trend of the sea of mountains. To the west the ranges fell away, one behind the other, diminishing and fading into the gentle foothills that, in turn, descended into the great valley which he could not see.

And in all that mighty sweep of earth he saw no sign of man nor of the handiwork of man—save only the torn bosom of the hillside at his feet. The man looked long and carefully. Once, far down his own canyon, he thought he saw in the air a faint hint of smoke. He looked again and decided that it was the purple haze of the hills made dark by a convolution of the canyon wall at its back.

"Hey, you, Mr. Pocket!" he called down into the canyon. "Stand out from under! I'm a-comin', Mr. Pocket! I'm a-comin'!"

The heavy brogans on the man's feet made him appear clumsy-footed, but he swung down from the giddy height as lightly and airily as a mountain goat. A rock, turning under his foot on the edge of the precipice, did not disconcert him. He seemed to know the precise time required for the turn to culminate in disaster, and in the meantime he utilized the false footing itself for the momentary earth-contact necessary to carry him on into safety. Where the earth sloped so steeply that it was impossible to stand for a second upright, the man did not hesitate. His foot pressed the impossible surface for but a fraction of the fatal second and gave him the bound that carried him onward. Again, where even the fraction of a second's footing was out of the question, he would swing his body past by a moment's hand-grip on a jutting knob of rock, a crevice, or a precariously rooted shrub. At last, with a wild leap and yell, he exchanged the face of the wall for an earth-slide and finished the descent in the midst of several tons of sliding earth and gravel.

His first pan of the morning washed out over two dollars in coarse gold. It was from the centre of the "V." To either side the diminution in the values of the pans was swift. His lines of cross-cutting holes were growing very short. The converging sides of the inverted "V" were only a few yards apart. Their meeting-point was only a few yards above him. But the pay-streak was dipping deeper and deeper into the earth. By early afternoon he was sinking the test-holes five feet before the pans could show the gold-trace.

For that matter, the gold-trace had become something more than a trace; it was a placer mine in itself, and the man resolved to come back after he had found the pocket and work over the ground. But the increasing richness of the pans began to worry him. By late afternoon the worth of the pans had grown to three and four dollars. The man scratched his head perplexedly and looked a few feet up the hill at the manzanita bush that marked approximately the apex of the "V." He nodded his head and said oracularly:

"It's one o' two things, Bill; one o' two things. Either Mr. Pocket's spilled himself all out an' down the hill, or else Mr. Pocket's that damned rich you maybe won't be able to carry him all away with you. And that'd be hell, wouldn't it, now?" He chuckled at contemplation of so pleasant a dilemma.

Nightfall found him by the edge of the stream, his eyes wrestling with the gathering darkness over the washing of a five-dollar pan.

"Wisht I had an electric light to go on working," he said.

He found sleep difficult that night. Many times he composed himself and closed his eyes for slumber to overtake him; but his blood pounded with too strong desire, and as many times his eyes opened and he murmured wearily, "Wisht it was sun-up."

Sleep came to him in the end, but his eyes were open with the first paling of the stars, and the gray of dawn caught him with breakfast finished and climbing the hillside in the direction of the secret abiding-place of Mr. Pocket.

The first cross-cut the man made, there was space for only three holes, so narrow had become the pay-streak and so close was he to the fountainhead of the golden stream he had been following for four days.

"Be ca'm, Bill; be ca'm," he admonished himself, as he broke ground for the final hole where the sides of the "V" had at last come together in a point.

"I've got the almighty cinch on you, Mr. Pocket, an' you can't lose me," he said many times as he sank the hole deeper and deeper.

Four feet, five feet, six feet, he dug his way down into the earth. The digging grew harder. His pick grated on broken rock. He examined the rock. "Rotten quartz," was his conclusion as, with the shovel, he cleared the bottom of the hole of loose dirt. He attacked the crumbling quartz with the pick, bursting the disintegrating rock asunder with every stroke.

He thrust his shovel into the loose mass. His eye caught a gleam of yellow. He dropped the shovel and squatted suddenly on his heels. As a farmer rubs the clinging earth from fresh-dug potatoes, so the man, a piece of rotten quartz held in both hands, rubbed the dirt away.

"Sufferin' Sardanopolis!" he cried. "Lumps an' chunks of it! Lumps an' chunks of it!"

It was only half rock he held in his hand. The other half was virgin gold. He dropped it into his pan and examined another piece. Little yellow was to be seen, but with his strong fingers he crumbled the rotten quartz away till both hands were filled with glowing yellow. He rubbed the dirt away from fragment after fragment, tossing them into the gold-pan. It was a treasure-hole. So much had the quartz rotted away that there was less of it than there was of gold. Now and again he found a piece to which no rock clung—a piece that was all gold. A chunk, where the pick had laid open the heart of the gold, glittered like a handful of yellow jewels, and he cocked his head at it and slowly turned it around and over to observe the rich play of the light upon it.

"Talk about yer Too Much Gold diggin's!" the man snorted contemptuously. "Why, this diggin' 'd make it look like thirty cents. This diggin' is All Gold. An' right here an' now I name this yere canyon 'All Gold Canyon,' b' gosh!"

Still squatting on his heels, he continued examining the fragments and tossing them into the pan. Suddenly there came to him a premonition of danger. It seemed a shadow had fallen upon him. But there was no shadow. His heart had given a great jump up into his throat and was choking him. Then his blood slowly chilled and he felt the sweat of his shirt cold against his flesh.

He did not spring up nor look around. He did not move. He was considering the nature of the premonition he had received, trying to locate the source of the mysterious force that had warned him, striving to sense the imperative presence of the unseen thing that threatened him. There is an aura of things hostile, made manifest by messengers too refined for the senses to know; and this aura he felt, but knew not how he felt it. His was the feeling as when a cloud passes over the sun. It seemed that between him and life had passed something dark and smothering and menacing; a gloom, as it were, that swallowed up life and made for death—his death.

Every force of his being impelled him to spring up and confront the unseen danger, but his soul dominated the panic, and he remained squatting on his heels, in his hands a chunk of gold. He did not dare to look around, but he knew by now that there was something behind him and above him. He made believe to be interested in the gold in his hand. He examined it critically, turned it over and over, and rubbed the dirt from it. And all the time he knew that something behind him was looking at the gold over his shoulder.

Still feigning interest in the chunk of gold in his hand, he listened intently and he heard the breathing of the thing behind him. His eyes searched the ground in front of him for a weapon, but they saw only the uprooted gold, worthless to him now in his extremity. There was his pick, a handy weapon on occasion; but this was not such an occasion. The man realized his predicament. He was in a narrow hole that was seven feet deep. His head did not come to the surface of the ground. He was in a trap.

He remained squatting on his heels. He was quite cool and collected; but his mind, considering every factor, showed him only his helplessness. He continued rubbing the dirt from the quartz fragments and throwing the gold into the pan. There was nothing else for him to do. Yet he knew that he would have to rise up, sooner or later, and face the danger that breathed at his back. The minutes passed, and with the passage of each minute he knew that by so much he was nearer the time when he must stand up, or else—and his wet shirt went cold against his flesh again at the thought—or else he might receive death as he stooped there over his treasure.

Still he squatted on his heels, rubbing dirt from gold and debating in just what manner he should rise up. He might rise up with a rush and claw his way out of the hole to meet whatever threatened on the even footing above ground. Or he might rise up slowly and carelessly, and feign casually to discover the thing that breathed at his back. His instinct and every fighting fibre of his body favored the mad, clawing rush to the surface. His intellect, and the craft thereof, favored the slow and cautious meeting with the thing that menaced and which he could not see. And while he debated, a loud, crashing noise burst on his ear. At the same instant he received a stunning blow on the left side of the back, and from the point of impact felt a rush of flame through his flesh. He sprang up in the air, but halfway to his feet collapsed. His body crumpled in like a leaf withered in sudden heat, and he came down, his chest across his pan of gold, his face in the dirt and rock, his legs tangled and twisted because of the restricted space at the bottom of the hole. His legs twitched convulsively several times. His body was shaken as with a mighty ague. There was a slow expansion of the lungs, accompanied by a deep sigh. Then the air was slowly, very slowly, exhaled, and his body as slowly flattened itself down into inertness.

Above, revolver in hand, a man was peering down over the edge of the hole. He peered for a long time at the prone and motionless body beneath him. After a while the stranger sat down on the edge of the hole so that he could see into it, and rested the revolver on his knee. Reaching his hand into a pocket, he drew out a wisp of brown paper. Into this he dropped a few crumbs of tobacco. The combination became a cigarette, brown and squat, with the ends turned in. Not once did he take his eyes from the body at the bottom of the hole. He lighted the cigarette and drew its smoke into his lungs with a caressing intake of the breath. He smoked slowly. Once the cigarette went out and he relighted it. And all the while he studied the body beneath him.

In the end he tossed the cigarette stub away and rose to his feet. He moved to the edge of the hole. Spanning it, a hand resting on each edge, and with the revolver still in the right hand, he muscled his body down into the hole. While his feet were yet a yard from the bottom he released his hands and dropped down.

At the instant his feet struck bottom he saw the pocket-miner's arm leap out, and his own legs knew a swift, jerking grip that overthrew him. In the nature of the jump his revolver-hand was above his head. Swiftly as the grip had flashed about his legs, just as swiftly he brought the revolver down. He was still in the air, his fall in process of completion, when he pulled the trigger. The explosion was deafening in the confined space. The smoke filled the hole so that he could see nothing. He struck the bottom on his back, and like a cat's the pocket-miner's body was on top of him. Even as the miner's body passed on top, the stranger crooked in his right arm to fire; and even in that instant the miner, with a quick thrust of elbow, struck his wrist. The muzzle was thrown up and the bullet thudded into the dirt of the side of the hole.

The next instant the stranger felt the miner's hand grip his wrist. The struggle was now for the revolver. Each man strove to turn it against the other's body. The smoke in the hole was clearing. The stranger, lying on his back, was beginning to see dimly. But suddenly he was blinded by a handful of dirt deliberately flung into his eyes by his antagonist. In that moment of shock his grip on the revolver was broken. In the next moment he felt a smashing darkness descend upon his brain, and in the midst of the darkness even the darkness ceased.

But the pocket-miner fired again and again, until the revolver was empty. Then he tossed it from him and, breathing heavily, sat down on the dead man's legs.

The miner was sobbing and struggling for breath. "Measly skunk!" he panted; "a-campin' on my trail an' lettin' me do the work, an' then shootin' me in the back!"

He was half crying from anger and exhaustion. He peered at the face of the dead man. It was sprinkled with loose dirt and gravel, and it was difficult to distinguish the features.

"Never laid eyes on him before," the miner concluded his scrutiny. "Just a common an' ordinary thief, damn him! An' he shot me in the back! He shot me in the back!"

He opened his shirt and felt himself, front and back, on his left side.

"Went clean through, and no harm done!" he cried jubilantly. "I'll bet he aimed all right all right; but he drew the gun over when he pulled the trigger—the cuss! But I fixed'm! Oh, I fixed'm!"

His fingers were investigating the bullet-hole in his side, and a shade of regret passed over his face. "It's goin' to be stiffer'n hell," he said. "An' it's up to me to get mended an' get out o' here."

He crawled out of the hole and went down the hill to his camp. Half an hour later he returned, leading his pack-horse. His open shirt disclosed the rude bandages with which he had dressed his wound. He was slow and awkward with his left-hand movements, but that did not prevent his using the arm.

The bight of the pack-rope under the dead man's shoulders enabled him to heave the body out of the hole. Then he set to work gathering up his gold. He worked steadily for several hours, pausing often to rest his stiffening shoulder and to exclaim:

"He shot me in the back, the measly skunk! He shot me in the back!"

When his treasure was quite cleaned up and wrapped securely into a number of blanket-covered parcels, he made an estimate of its value.

"Four hundred pounds, or I'm a Hottentot," he concluded. "Say two hundred in quartz an' dirt—that leaves two hundred pounds of gold. Bill! Wake up! Two hundred pounds of gold! Forty thousand dollars! An' it's yourn—all yourn!"

He scratched his head delightedly and his fingers blundered into an unfamiliar groove. They quested along it for several inches. It was a crease through his scalp where the second bullet had ploughed.

He walked angrily over to the dead man.

"You would, would you?" he bullied. "You would, eh? Well, I fixed you good an' plenty, an' I'll give you decent burial, too. That's more'n you'd have done for me."

He dragged the body to the edge of the hole and toppled it in. It struck the bottom with a dull crash, on its side, the face twisted up to the light. The miner peered down at it.

"An' you shot me in the back!" he said accusingly.

With pick and shovel he filled the hole. Then he loaded the gold on his horse. It was too great a load for the animal, and when he had gained his camp he transferred part of it to his saddle-horse. Even so, he was compelled to abandon a portion of his outfit—pick and shovel and gold-pan, extra food and cooking utensils, and divers odds and ends.

The sun was at the zenith when the man forced the horses at the screen of vines and creepers. To climb the huge boulders the animals were compelled to uprear and struggle blindly through the tangled mass of vegetation. Once the saddle-horse fell heavily and the man removed the pack to get the animal on its feet. After it started on its way again the man thrust his head out from among the leaves and peered up at the hillside.

"The measly skunk!" he said, and disappeared.

There was a ripping and tearing of vines and boughs. The trees surged back and forth, marking the passage of the animals through the midst of them. There was a clashing of steel-shod hoofs on stone, and now and again an oath or a sharp cry of command. Then the voice of the man was raised in song:—

> *"Tu'n around an' tu'n yo' face*
> *Untoe them sweet hills of grace*
> *(D' pow'rs of sin yo' am scornin'!).*
> *Look about an' look aroun',*
> *Fling yo' sin-pack on d' groun'*
> *(Yo' will meet wid d' Lord in d' mornin'!)."*

The song grew faint and fainter, and through the silence crept back the spirit of the place. The stream once more drowsed and whispered; the hum of the mountain bees rose sleepily. Down through the perfume-weighted air fluttered the snowy fluffs of the cottonwoods. The butterflies drifted in and out among the trees, and over all blazed the quiet sunshine. Only remained the hoof-marks in the meadow and the torn hillside to mark the boisterous trail of the life that had broken the peace of the place and passed on.

# FRANK NORRIS

*(1870–1902)*

*Born Benjamin Franklin Norris, Jr., son of a Chicago wholesale jew-
eler and a doting mother of New England and Virginia ancestry who,
before marriage, had been a successful actress, Norris at fourteen
moved with his family to California. Since the boy had shown early
artistic ability, his family moved to Europe in 1887 in order to enroll
him in art school. Frank was left in Paris when his parents and
younger brother, Charles (who was also to become a well-known author), returned to California a year later. But in his father's view,
young Norris did not make good use of his time, and after two years
he was called home. He entered the University of California, only to
leave because of a failing grade in mathematics. It was while studying
at Berkeley that Norris discovered the works of Émile Zola, the pioneering French naturalist. Resolving to become the Zola of America,
he enrolled for a year of writing courses at Harvard, where he commenced novels that would not be published until late in the decade.
Norris left Harvard to cover the Boer War for the* San Francisco
Chronicle; *while a prisoner of the Boer forces he contracted African
fever, the effects of which were to be lasting.*

*Released, but still ailing, Norris returned to San Francisco and
associated himself with the* Wave, *a local literary weekly funded by
the Southern Pacific as a promotional device. It was not the last time
that the author would have an equivocal relationship with the railroad. In 1898, Norris moved to New York to work for the muckraking*
McClure's *magazine, for which he covered the Cuban campaigns of
the Spanish-American War (along with Stephen Crane and Frederic
Remington), but, once in Cuba, he suffered a relapse of African fever.
Returning to New York, Norris went to work for his publisher, Dou-
bleday, as an editor, and was instrumental in the publication of Theodore Dreiser's* Sister Carrie, *though the novel was quickly yanked off*

*the market as immoral. Marrying in 1900, Norris returned to Cali-
fornia, where he remained until his early death from the effects of
appendicitis.*

*His death occurred as he was at work on the third volume of a
California trilogy, his* Epic of the Wheat, *which was to follow the three
stages of raising and marketing that essential crop, from the ranches
of California through speculative commodity trading in Chicago to
its distribution as bread to a starving village in Europe. The first two
books of the trilogy,* The Octopus *(1901) and* The Pit *(1903), had already been published; the third,* The Wolf, *remained unfinished at his
death. Though evincing a social consciousness and pledging himself
to the unadorned truth, Norris was also attracted to men of power
and influence, and his attack on the railroad "octopus" in his most
ambitious novel was mitigated by his complex attitude toward the
owner of the exploitive rail line upon which the fortunes of the wheat
farmers in the San Joaquin Valley depended. Less ambiguous toward
the consequences of greed is Norris's early novel, begun while he was
at Harvard,* McTeague *(1899), set in San Francisco with a horrific
finale in Death Valley. Examining the effects of a lottery prize on the
lives of a brutal dentist and his wife, it is undeniably Norris's masterpiece, with a theme intricately related to the idea of California as
a place of succen riches and moral decline. Norris also wrote affir-
mative, even celebratory novels about love and marriage—the autobiographical* Blix *(1899) and* A Man's Woman *(1900)—the latter in a
vein also explored by Jack London, as was an earlier romance,* Moran
of the Lady Letty *(1898), a maritime story with a mannish heroine.
Another, purely coincidental, parallel with London's themes can be
found in* Vandover and the Brute *(written in 1894–95 but published
—from an uncorrected draft—in 1914), a parable of degeneration concerning a derelict artist overcome by the "wolf" within (the "brute" of
the title).*

*Unlike London, Norris is not much known as a writer of short
fiction, and his stories, collected posthumously in* A Deal in Wheat
*(1903) and* The Third Circle *(1909), were clearly crafted to fit the magazine formulas of the day. His few tales of California mining life
follow patterns established by Bret Harte, though Norris studiously
avoided the sentimental endings favored by his predecessor. Norris is
most original in a series of tales about the "Three Black Crows,"
American and British adventurers who extend the California spirit
of exploitation (with highly comic results) into Latin America and
Alaska. Like his novels, Norris's stories often evoke the fiction of Jack
London, and the denouement of "The Passing of Cock-eye Blacklock"
seems to have been borrowed by London for his much more famous*

*tale of revenge, "Moonface." But matters of common styles and themes can be attributed also to the influence of Kipling and Stevenson on both writers, who, despite their mutual espousal of literary natural-ism, were romantics devoted to celebrating deeds of adventure. Nor-ris's literary creed, which reveals the essential romanticism underlying his "realism," can be found in the title essay of* The Re-sponsibilities of the Novelist *(1903).*

# The Passing of
# Cock-eye Blacklock

"Well, m'son," observed Bunt about half an hour after supper, "if your provender has shook down comfortable by now, we might as well jar loose and be moving along out yonder."

We left the fire and moved toward the hobbled ponies, Bunt complaining of the quality of the outfit's meals. "Down in the Panamint country," he growled, "we had a Chink that was a sure frying-pan expert; but *this* Dago—my word! That ain't victuals, that supper. That's just a' ingenious device for removing superfluous appetite. Next time I assimilate nutriment in this camp I'm sure going to take chloroform beforehand. Careful to draw your cinch tight on that pinto bronc' of yours. She always swells up same as a horned toad soon as you begin to saddle up."

We rode from the circle of the camp-fire's light and out upon the desert. It was Bunt's turn to ride the herd that night, and I had volunteered to bear him company.

Bunt was one of a fast-disappearing type. He knew his West as the cockney knows his Piccadilly. He had mined with and for Ralston, had soldiered with Crook, had turned cards in a faro game at Laredo, and had known the Apache Kid. He had fifteen separate and different times driven the herds from Texas to Dodge City, in the good old, rare old, wild old days when Dodge was the headquarters for the cattle trade, and as near to heaven as the cowboy cared to get. He had seen the end of gold and the end of the buffalo, the beginning of cattle, the beginning of wheat, and the spreading of the barbed-wire fence, that, in the end, will take from him his occupation and his revolver, his chaparejos and his usefulness, his lariat and his reason for being. He had seen the rise of a new period, the successive stages of which, singularly enough, tally exactly with the progress of our own world-civilization: first the nomad and hunter, then the herder, next and last the husbandman. He had passed the mid-mark of his life. His mustache was gray. He had four friends—his horse, his pistol, a teamster in the Indian Territory Panhandle named Skinny, and me.

The herd—I suppose all told there were some two thousand head—we found not far from the water-hole. We relieved the other watch and took up our night's vigil. It was about nine o'clock. The night was fine, calm. There was no cloud. Toward the middle watches one could expect a moon. But the stars, the stars! In Idaho, on those lonely reaches of desert and range, where the shadow of the sun by day and the courses of the constellations by night are the only things that move, these stars are a different matter from those bleared pin-points of the city after dark, seen through dust and smoke and the glare of electrics and the hot haze of fire-signs. On such a night as that when I rode the herd with Bunt *anything* might have happened; one could have believed in fairies then, and in the buffalo-ghost, and in all the weirds of the craziest Apache "Messiah" that ever made medicine.

One remembered astronomy and the "measureless distances" and the showy problems, including the rapid moving of a ray of light and the long years of its travel between star and star, and smiled incredulously. Why, the stars were just above our heads, were not much higher than the flat-topped hills that barred the horizons. Venus was a yellow lamp hung in a tree; Mars a red lantern in a clocktower.

One listened instinctively for the tramp of the constellations. Orion, Cassiopeia and Ursa Major marched to and fro on the vault like cohorts of legionaries, seemingly within call of our voices, and all without a sound.

But beneath these quiet heavens the earth disengaged multitudinous sounds—small sounds, minimized as it were by the muffling of the night. Now it was the yap of a coyote leagues away; now the snapping of a twig in the sage-brush; now the mysterious, indefinable stir of the heat-ridden land cooling under the night. But more often it was the confused murmur of the herd itself—the click of a horn, the friction of heavy bodies, the stamp of a hoof, with now and then the low, complaining note of a cow with a calf, or the subdued noise of a steer as it lay down, first lurching to the knees, then rolling clumsily upon the haunch, with a long, stertorous breath of satisfaction.

Slowly at Indian trot we encircle the herd. Earlier in the evening a prairie-wolf had pulled down a calf, and the beasts were still restless.

Little eddies of nervousness at long intervals developed here and there in the mass—eddies that not impossibly might widen at any time with perilous quickness to the maelstrom of a stampede. So as he rode Bunt sang to these great brutes, literally to put them to sleep—sang an old grandmother's song, with all the quaint modulations of sixty, seventy, a hundred years ago:

> *"With her ogling winks*
> *And bobbling blinks,*
> *Her quizzing glass,*
> *Her one eye idle,*
> *Oh, she loved a bold dragoon,*
> *With his broadsword, saddle, bridle.*
> *Whack, fol-de-rol!"*

I remember that song. My grandmother—so they tell me—used to sing it in Carolina, in the thirties, accompanying herself on a harp, if you please:

> *"Oh, she loved a bold dragoon,*
> *With his broadsword, saddle, bridle."*

It was in Charleston, I remembered, and the slave-ships used to discharge there in those days. My grandmother had sung it then to her beaux; officers they were; no wonder she chose it—"Oh, she loved a bold dragoon"—and now I heard it sung on an Idaho cattle-range to quiet two thousand restless steers.

Our talk at first, after the cattle had quieted down, ran upon all manner of subjects. It is astonishing to note what strange things men will talk about at night and in a solitude. That night we covered religion, of course, astronomy, love affairs, horses, travel, history, poker, photography, basket-making, and the Darwinian theory. But at last inevitably we came back to cattle and the pleasures and dangers of riding the herd.

"I rode herd once in Nevada," remarked Bunt, "and I was caught into a blizzard, and I was sure freezing to death. Got to where I couldn't keep my eyes open, I was that sleepy. Tell you what I did. Had some eating-tobacco along, and I'd chew it a spell, then rub the juice into my eyes. Kept it up all night. Blame near blinded me, but I come through. Me and another man named Blacklock—Cock-eye Blacklock we called him, by reason of his having one eye that was some out of line. Cock-eye sure ought to have got it that night, for he went bad afterward, and did a heap of killing before he *did* get it. He was a bad man for sure, and the way he died is a story in itself."

There was a long pause. The ponies jogged on. Rounding on the herd, we turned southward.

"He did 'get it' finally, you say," I prompted.

"He certainly did," said Bunt, "and the story of it is what a man with a' imaginary mind like you ought to make into one of your friction tales."

"Is it about a treasure?" I asked with apprehension. For ever since I once made a tale (of friction) out of one of Bunt's stories of real life, he has been ambitious for me to write another, and is forever suggesting motifs which invariably—I say invariably—imply the discovery of great treasures. With him, fictitious literature must always turn upon the discovery of hidden wealth.

"No," said he, "it ain't about no treasure, but just about the origin, hist'ry and development—and subsequent decease—of as mean a Greaser as ever stole stock, which his name was Cock-eye Blacklock.

"You see, this same Blacklock went bad about two summers after our meet-up with the blizzard. He worked down Yuma way and over into New Mexico, where he picks up with a sure-thing gambler, and the two begin to devastate the population. They do say when he and his running mate got good and through with that part of the Land of the Brave, men used to go round trading guns for commissary, and clothes for ponies, and cigars for whisky and such. There just wasn't any money left *anywhere*. Those sharps had drawed the landscape clean. Some one found a dollar in a floor-crack in a saloon, and the barkeep' gave him a gallon of forty-rod for it, and used to keep it in a box for exhibition, and the crowd would get around it and paw it over and say: 'My! my! Whatever in the world is this extremely curoos coin?'

"Then Blacklock cuts loose from his running mate, and plays a lone hand through Arizona and Nevada, up as far as Reno again, and there he stacks up against a kid—a little tenderfoot kid so new he ain't cracked the green paint off him—and *skins* him. And the kid, being foolish and impulsive-like, pulls out a pea-shooter. It was a *twenty-two*," said Bunt, solemnly. "Yes, the kid was just that pore, pathetic kind to carry a dinky twenty-two, and with the tears runnin' down his cheeks begins to talk tall. Now what does that Cock-eye do? Why, that pore kid that he had skinned couldn't 'a' hurt him with his pore little bric-à-brac. Does Cock-eye take his little parlour ornament away from him, and spank him, and tell him to go home? No, he never. The kid's little tin pop-shooter explodes right in his hand before he can crook his forefinger twice, and while he's a-wondering what-all has happened Cock-eye gets his two guns on him, slow and deliberate like, mind you, and throws forty-eights into him till he ain't worth shooting at no more. Murders him like the mud-eating, horse-thieving snake of a Greaser that he is; but being within the law, the kid drawing on him first, he don't stretch hemp the way he should.

"Well, fin'ly this Blacklock blows into a mining-camp in Placer County, California, where I'm chuck-tending on the night-shift. This here camp is maybe four miles across the divide from Iowa Hill, and it sure is named a cu-roos name, which it is Why-not. They is a barn contiguous, where the mine horses are kep', and, blame me! if there ain't a weathercock on top of that same—a golden trotting-horse—*upside down*. When the stranger an' pilgrim comes in, says he first off: 'Why'n snakes they got that weathercock horse upside down—why?' says he. 'Why-not,' says you, and the drinks is on the pilgrim.

"That all went very lovely till some gesabe opens up a placer drift on the far side the divide, starts a rival camp, an' names her Because. The Boss gets mad at that, and rights up the weathercock, and re-names the camp Ophir, and you don't work no more pilgrims.

"Well, as I was saying, Cock-eye drifts into Why-not and begins diffusing trouble. He skins some of the boys in the hotel over in town, and a big row comes of it, and one of the bed-rock cleaners cuts loose with both guns. Nobody hurt but a quarter-breed, who loses a' eye. But the marshal don't stand for no short-card men, an' closes Cock-eye up some prompt. Him being forced to give the boys back their money is busted an' can't get away from camp. To raise some wind he begins depredating.

"He robs a pore half-breed of a cayuse, and shoots up a Chink who's panning tailings, and generally and variously becomes too pro-nounced, till he's run outen camp. He's sure stony-broke, not being able to turn a card because of the marshal. So he goes to live in a ole cabin up by the mine ditch, and sits there doing a heap o' thinking, and hatching trouble like a' ole he-hen.

"Well, now, with that deporting of Cock-eye comes his turn of bad luck, and it sure winds his clock up with a loud report. I've narrated special of the scope and range of this 'ere Blacklock, so as you'll un-derstand why it was expedient and desirable that he should up an' die. You see, he always managed, with all his killings and robbings and general and sundry flimflamming, to be just within the law. And if anybody took a notion to shoot him up, why, his luck saw him through, and the other man's shooting-iron missed fire, or exploded, or threw wild, or such like, till it seemed as if he sure did bear a charmed life; and so he did till a pore yeller tamale of a fool dog did for him what the law of the land couldn't do. Yes, sir, a fool dog, a pup, a blame yeller pup named Sloppy Weather, did for Cock-eye

Blacklock, sporting character, three-card-monte man, sure-thing sharp, killer, and general bedeviler.

"You see, it was this way. Over in American Cañon, some five miles maybe back of the mine, they was a creek called the American River, and it was sure chock-a-block full of trouts. The Boss used for to go over there with a dinky fish-pole like a buggy-whip about once a week, and scout that stream for fish and bring back a basketful. He was sure keen on it, and had bought some kind of privilege or other, so as he could keep other people off.

"Well, I used to go along with him to pack the truck, and one Saturday, about a month after Cock-eye had been run outen camp, we hiked up over the divide, and went for to round up a bunch o' trouts. When we got to the river there was a mess for your life. Say, that river was full of dead trouts, floating atop the water; and they was some even on the bank. Not a scratch on 'em; just dead. The Boss had the papsy-lals. I never *did* see a man so rip-r'aring, snorting mad. *I* hadn't a guess about what we were up against, but he knew, and he showed down. He said somebody had been shooting the river for fish to sell down Sacramento way to the market. A mean trick; kill more fish in one shoot than you can possibly pack.

"Well, we didn't do much fishing that day—couldn't get a bite, for that matter—and took off home about noon to talk it over. You see, the Boss, in buying the privileges or such for that creek, had made himself responsible to the Fish Commissioners of the State, and 'twasn't a week before they were after him, camping on his trail incessant, and wanting to know how about it. The Boss was some worried, because the fish were being killed right along, and the Commission was making him weary of living. Twicet afterward we prospected along that river and found the same lot of dead fish. We even put a guard there, but it didn't do no manner of good.

"It's the Boss who first suspicions Cock-eye. But it don't take no seventh daughter of no seventh daughter to trace trouble where Blacklock's about. He sudden shows up in town with a bunch of simoleons, buying bacon and tin cows* and such provender, and generally giving it away that he's come into money. The Boss, who's watching his movements sharp, says to me one day:

"'Bunt, the storm-centre of this here low area is a man with a cock-eye, an' I'll back that play with a paint horse against a paper dime.'

"'No takers,' says I. 'Dirty work and a cock-eyed man are two heels of the same mule.'

* Condensed milk.

" 'Which it's a-kicking of me in the stummick frequent and painful,'
he remarks, plenty wrathful.

" 'On general principles,' I said, 'it's a royal flush to a pair of deuces
as how this Blacklock bird ought to stop a heap of lead, and I know
the man to throw it. He's the only brother of my sister, and tends
chuck in a placer mine. How about if I take a day off and drop round
to his cabin and interview him on the fleetin' and unstable nature of
human life?'

"But the Boss wouldn't hear of that.

" 'No,' says he; 'that's not the bluff to back in this game. You an'
me an' Mary-go-round'—that was what we called the marshal, him
being so much all over the country—'you an' me an' Mary-go-round
will have to stock a sure-thing deck against that maverick.'

"So the three of us gets together an' has a talky-talk, an' we lays
it out as how Cock-eye must be watched and caught red-handed.

"Well, let me tell you, keeping case on that Greaser sure did lack
a certain indefinable charm. We tried him at sun-up, an' again at sun-
down, an' nights, too, laying in the chaparral an' tarweed, an' scouting
up an' down that blame river, till we were sore. We built surreptitious
a lot of shooting-boxes up in trees on the far side of the cañon, overlooking certain an' sundry pools in the river where Cock-eye would
be likely to pursue operations, an' we took turns watching. I'll be a
Chink if that bad egg didn't put it on us same as previous, an' we'd
find new-killed fish all the time. I tell you we were *fitchered*; and it
got on the Boss's nerves. The Commission began to talk of withdrawing the privilege, an' it was up to him to make good or pass the deal.
We *knew* Blacklock was shooting the river, y' see, but we didn't have
no evidence. Y' see, being shut off from card-sharping, he was up
against it, and so took to pot-hunting to get along. It was as plain as
red paint.

"Well, things went along sort of catch-as-catch-can like this for
maybe three weeks, the Greaser shooting fish regular, an' the Boss
b'iling with rage, and laying plans to call his hand, and getting bluffed
out every deal.

"And right here I got to interrupt, to talk some about the pup dog,
Sloppy Weather. If he hadn't got caught up into this Blacklock game,
no one'd ever thought enough about him to so much as kick him. But
after it was all over, we began to remember this same Sloppy an' to
recall what he was; no big job. He was just a worthless fool pup, yeller
at that, everybody's dog, that just hung round camp, grinning and
giggling and playing the goat, as half-grown dogs will. He used to go
along with the car-boys when they went swimmin' in the resevoy, an'
dash along in an' yell an' splash round just to show off. He thought it

was a keen stunt to get some gesabe to throw a stick in the resevoy so's he could paddle out after it. They'd trained him always to bring it back an' fetch it to whichever party throwed it. He'd give it up when he'd retrieved it, an' yell to have it throwed again. That was his idea of fun—just like a fool pup.

"Well, one day this Sloppy Weather is off chasing jack-rabbits an' don't come home. Nobody thinks anything about that, nor even notices it. But we afterward finds out that he'd met up with Blacklock that day, an' stopped to visit with him—sorry day for Cock-eye. Now it was the very next day after this that Mary-go-round an' the Boss plans another scout. I'm to go, too. It was a Wednesday, an' we lay it out that the Cock-eye would prob'ly shoot that day so's to get his fish down to the railroad Thursday, so they'd reach Sacramento Friday— fish day, see. It wasn't much to go by, but it was the high card in our hand, an' we allowed to draw to it.

"We left Why-not afore daybreak, an' worked over into the cañon about sun-up. They was one big pool we hadn't covered for some time, an' we made out we'd watch that. So we worked down to it, an' clumb up into our trees, an' set out to keep guard.

"In about an hour we heard a shoot some mile or so up the creek. They's no mistaking dynamite, leastways not to miners, an' we knew that shoot was dynamite an' nothing else. The Cock-eye was at work, an' we shook hands all round. Then pretty soon a fish or so began to go by—big fellows, some of 'em, dead an' floatin', with their eyes popped 'way out same as knobs—sure sign they'd been shot.

"The Boss took and grit his teeth when he see a three-pounder go by, an' made remarks about Blacklock.

" ''Sh!' says Mary-go-round, sudden-like. 'Listen!'

"We turned ear down the wind, an' sure there was the sound of some one scrabbling along the boulders by the riverside. Then we heard a pup yap.

" 'That's our man,' whispers the Boss.

"For a long time we thought Cock-eye had quit for the day an' had coppered us again, but byne-by we heard the manzanita crack on the far side the cañon, an' there at last we see Blacklock working down toward the pool, Sloppy Weather following an' yapping and cayoodling just as a fool dog will.

"Blacklock comes down to the edge of the water quiet-like. He lays his big scoop-net an' his sack—we can see it half full already— down behind a boulder, and takes a good squinting look all round, and listens maybe twenty minutes, he's that cute, same's a coyote stealing sheep. We lies low an' says nothing, fear he might see the leaves move.

"Then byne-by he takes his stick of dynamite out his hip pocket—
he was just that reckless kind to carry it that way—an' ties it careful
to a couple of stones he finds handy. Then he lights the fuse an' heaves
her into the drink, an' just there's where Cock-eye makes the mistake of his life. He ain't tied the rocks tight enough, an' the loop slips
off just as he swings back his arm, the stones drop straight down by
his feet, and the stick of dynamite whirls out right enough into the
pool.

"Then the funny business begins.

"Blacklock ain't made no note of Sloppy Weather, who's been sizing
up the whole game an' watchin' for the stick. Soon as Cock-eye heaves
the dynamite into the water, off goes the pup after it, just as he'd
been taught to do by the car-boys.

" 'Hey, you fool dog!' yells Blacklock.

"A lot that pup cares. He heads out for that stick of dynamite same
as if for a veal cutlet, reaches it, grabs hold of it, an' starts back for
shore, with the fuse sputterin' like hot grease. Blacklock heaves rocks
at him like one possessed, capering an' dancing; but the pup comes
right on. The Cock-eye can't stand it no longer, but lines out. But the
pup's got to shore an' takes after him. Sure; why not? He think's it's
all part of the game. Takes after Cock-eye, running to beat a' express,
while we-all whoops and yells an' nearly falls out the trees for laffing.
Hi! Cock-eye did scratch gravel for sure. But 'tain't no manner of use.
He can't run through that rough ground like Sloppy Weather, an' that
fool pup comes a-cavartin' along, jumpin' up against him, an' him a-
kickin' him away, an' r'arin', an' dancin', an' shakin' his fists, an' the
more he r'ars the more fun the pup thinks it is. But all at once something big happens, an' the whole bank of the cañon opens out like a
big wave, and slops over into the pool, an' the air is full of trees an'
rocks and cart-loads of dirt an' dogs and Blacklocks and rivers an'
smoke an' fire generally. The Boss got a clod o' river-mud spang in
the eye, an' went off his limb like's he was trying to bust a bucking
bronc' an' couldn't; and ol' Mary-go-round was shooting off his gun on
general principles, glarin' round wild-eyed an' like as if he saw a' Injun
devil.

"When the smoke had cleared away an' the trees and rocks quit
falling, we clumb down from our places an' started in to look for Blacklock. We found a good deal of him, but they wasn't hide nor hair left
of Sloppy Weather. We didn't have to dig no grave, either. They was
a big enough hole in the ground to bury a horse an' wagon, let alone
Cock-eye. So we planted him there, an' put up a board, an' wrote
on it:

> Here lies most
> of
> C. BLACKLOCK,
> who died of a'
> entangling alliance with
> a
> stick of dynamite.

> Moral: A hook and line is good enough
> fish-tackle for any honest man.

"That there board lasted for two years, till the freshet of '82, when the American River— Hello, there's the sun!"

All in a minute the night seemed to have closed up like a great book. The East flamed roseate. The air was cold, nimble. Some of the sage-brush bore a thin rim of frost. The herd, aroused, the dew glistening on flank and horn, were chewing the first cud of the day, and in twos and threes moving toward the water-hole for the morning's drink. Far off toward the camp the breakfast fire sent a shaft of blue smoke straight into the moveless air. A jack-rabbit, with erect ears, limped from the sage-brush just out of pistol-shot and regarded us a moment, his nose wrinkling and trembling. By the time that Bunt and I, putting our ponies to a canter, had pulled up by the camp of the Bar-circle-Z outfit, another day had begun in Idaho.

# Two Hearts That Beat As One

"Which I puts it up as how you ain't never heard about that time that Hardenberg and Strokher—the Englisher—had a friendly go with bare knuckles—ten rounds it was—all along o' a feemale woman?"

It is a small world and I had just found out that my friend, Bunt McBride—horse-wrangler, miner, faro-dealer and bone-gatherer—whose world was the plains and ranges of the Great Southwest, was known of the Three Black Crows, Hardenberg, Strokher and Ally Bazan, and had even foregathered with them on more than one of their ventures for Cyrus Ryder's Exploitation Agency—ventures that had nothing of the desert in them, but that involved the sea, and the schooner, and the taste of the great-lunged canorous trades.

"Ye ain't never crossed the trail o' that mournful history?"

I professed my ignorance and said:

"They fought?"

"Mister Man," returned Bunt soberly, as one broaching a subject not to be trifled with, "they sure did. Friendly-like, y'know—like as how two high-steppin', sassy gents figures out to settle any little strained relations—friendly-like but considerable keen."

He took a pinch of tobacco from his pouch and a bit of paper and rolled a cigarette in the twinkling of an eye, using only one hand, in true Mexican style.

"Now," he said, as he drew the first long puff to the very bottom of the leathern valves he calls his lungs. "Now, I'm a-goin' for to relate that same painful proceedin' to you, just so as you kin get a line on the consumin' and devourin' foolishness o' male humans when they's a woman in the wind. Woman," said Bunt, wagging his head thoughtfully at the water, "woman is a weather-breeder. Mister Dixon, they is three things I'm skeered of. The last two I don't just rightly call to mind at this moment, but the first is woman. When I meets up with a feemale woman on my trail, I sheers off some prompt, Mr. Dixon; I sheers off. An' Hardenberg," he added irrelevantly, "would a-took an' married this woman, so he would. Yes, an' Strokher would, too."

"Was there another man?" I asked.

"No," said Bunt. Then he began to chuckle behind his mustaches. "Yes, they was." He smote a thigh. "They sure was another man for fair. Well, now, Mr. Man, lemmee tell you the whole '*how*.'

"It began with me bein' took into a wild-eyed scheme that that maverick, Cy Ryder, had cooked up for the Three Crows. They was a row down Gortamalar way. Some gesabe named Palachi—Barreto Palachi—findin' times dull an' the boys some off their feed, ups an' says to hisself, 'Exercise is wot I needs. I will now take an' overthrow the blame Gover'ment.' Well, this same Palachi rounds up a bunch o' *insurrectos* an' begins pesterin' an' badgerin' an' hectorin' the Gover'ment; an' r'arin' round an' bellerin' an' makin' a procession of hisself, till he sure pervades the landscape; an' before you knows what, lo'n beholt, here's a reel live Revolution-Thing cayoodlin' in the scenery, an' the Gover'ment is plum bothered.

"They rounds up the gesabe at last at a place on the coast, but he escapes as easy as how-do-you-do. He can't, howsomever, git back to his *insurrectos*; the blame Gover'ment being in possession of all the trails leadin' into the hinterland; so says he, 'What for a game would it be for me to hyke up to 'Frisco an' git in touch with my financial backers an' conspirate to smuggle down a load o' arms?' Which the same he does, and there's where the Three Black Crows an' me begin to take a hand.

"Cy Ryder gives us the job o' taking the schooner down to a certain point on the Gortamalar coast and there delivering to the agent o' the gesabe three thousand stand o' forty-eight Winchesters.

"When we gits this far into the game Ryder ups and says:

"'Boys, here's where I cashes right in. You sets right to me for the schooner and the cargo. But you goes to Palachi's agent over 'crost the bay for instructions and directions.'

"'But,' says the Englisher, Strokher, 'this bettin' a blind play don't suit our hand. Why not' says he, 'make right up to Mister Palachi hisself?'

"'No,' says Ryder, 'No, boys. Ye can't. The Signor is lying as low as a toad in a wheel-track these days, because o' the pryin' and meddlin' disposition o' the local authorities. No,' he says, 'ye must have your palaver with the agent which she is a woman,' an' thereon I groans low and despairin'.

"So soon as he mentions 'feemale' I *knowed* trouble was in the atmosphere. An' right there is where I sure loses my presence o' mind.

What I should a-done was to say, 'Mister Ryder, Hardenberg and
gents all: You're good boys an' you drinks and deals fair, an' I loves
you all with a love that can never, never die for the terms o' your
natural lives, an' may God have mercy on your souls; *but* I ain't keepin'
case on this 'ere game no longer. Woman and me is mules an' music.
We ain't never made to ride in the same go-cart. Good-by.' That-all is
wot I should ha' said. But I didn't. I walked right plum into the sloo,
like the mudhead that I was, an' got mired for fair—jes as I might a-
knowed I would.

"Well, Ryder gives us a address over across the bay an' we fair
hykes over there all along o' as crool a rain as ever killed crops. We
finds the place after awhile, a lodgin'-house all lorn and loony, set down
all by itself in the middle o' some real estate extension like a tepee in
a 'barren'—a crazy 'modern' house all gimcrack and woodwork and
frostin', with never another place in so far as you could hear a coyote
yelp.

"Well, we bucks right up an' asks o' the party at the door if the
Sigñorita Esperanza Ulivarri—that was who Ryder had told us to ask
for—might be concealed about the premises, an' we shows Cy Ryder's
note. The party that opened the door was a Greaser, the worst looking
I ever clapped eyes on—looked like the kind wot 'ud steal the coppers
off his dead grandmother's eyes. Anyhow, he says to come in, gruff-
like, an' to wait, *poco tiempo*.

"Well, we waited *mucho tiempo—muy mucho*, all a-settin' on the
edge of the sofy, with our hats on our knees, like philly-loo birds on
a rail, and a-countin' of the patterns in the wall-paper to pass the time
along. An' Hardenberg, who's got to do the talkin', gets the fidgets
byne-by; and because he's only restin' the toes o' his feet on the floor,
his knees begin jiggerin'; an' along o' watchin' him, *my* knees begin
to go, an' then Strokher's and then Ally Bazan's. An' there we sat all
in a row and jiggered an' jiggered. Great snakes, it makes me sick to
the stummick to think o' the idjeets we were.

"Then after a long time we hears a rustle o' silk petticoats, an' we
all grabs holt o' one another an' looks scared-like, out from under our
eyebrows. An' then—then, Mister Man, they walks into that bunkhouse parlour the loveliest-lookin' young feemale woman that ever
wore hair.

"She was lovelier than Mary Anderson; she was lovelier than
Lotta. She was tall, an' black-haired, and had a eye . . . well, I dunno;
when she gave you the littlest flicker o' that same eye, you felt it was
about time to take an' lie right down an' say, 'I would esteem it,
ma'am, a sure smart favour if you was to take an' wipe your boots on

my waistcoat, jus' so's you could hear my heart a-beatin'.' That's the kind o' feemale woman *she* was.

"Well, when Hardenberg had caught his second wind, we begins to talk business.

" 'An' you're to take a passenger back with you,' says Esperanza after awhile.

" 'What for a passenger might it be?' says Hardenberg.

"She fished out her calling-card at that and tore it in two an' gave Hardenberg one-half.

" 'It's the party,' she says, 'that'll come aboard off San Diego on your way down an' who will show up the other half o' the card—the half I have here an' which the same I'm goin' to mail to him. An' you be sure the halves fit before you let him come aboard. An' when that party comes aboard,' she says, 'he's to take over charge.'

" 'Very good,' says Hardenberg, mincing an' silly like a chessy cat lappin' cream. 'Very good, ma'am; your orders shall be obeyed.' He sure said it just like that, as if he spoke out o' a story-book. An' I kicked him under the table for it.

"Then we palavers a whole lot an' settles the way the thing is to be run, an' fin'ly, when we'd got as far as could be that day, the Sigñorita stood up an' says:

" 'Now me good fellows.' 'Twas Spanish she spoke. 'Now, me good fellows, you must drink a drink with me.' She herds us all up into the dining-room and fetches out—not whisky, mind you—but a great, fat, green-and-gold bottle o' champagne, an' when Ally Bazan has fired it off, she fills our glasses—dinky little flat glasses that looked like flower vases. Then she stands up there before us, fine an' tall, all in black silk, an' puts her glass up high an' sings out—

" 'To the Revolution!'

"An' we all solemn-like says, 'To the Revolution,' an' crooks our elbows. When we-all comes to, about half an hour later, we're in the street outside, havin' jus' said good-by to the Sigñorita. We-all are some quiet the first block or so, and then Hardenberg says—stoppin' dead in his tracks:

" 'I pauses to remark that when a certain young feemale party havin' black hair an' a killin' eye gets good an' ready to travel up the centre aisle of a church, I know the gent to show her the way, which he is six feet one in his stocking-feet, some freckled across the nose, an' shoots with both hands.'

" 'Which the same observations,' speaks up Strokher, twirlin' his yeller lady-killer, 'which the same observations,' he says, 'has my hearty indorsement an' coöperation savin' in the particular of the description o' the gent. The gent is five foot eleven high, three feet thick, is the only son of my mother, an' has yeller mustaches and a buck tooth.'

" 'He don't qualify,' puts in Hardenberg. 'First, because he's a Englisher, and second, because he's up again a American—and besides, he has a tooth that's bucked.'

" 'Buck or no buck,' flares out Strokher, 'wot might be the meanin' o' that remark consernin' being a Englisher?'

" 'The fact o' his bein' English,' says Hardenberg, 'is only half the hoe-handle. 'Tother half being the fact that the first-named gent is all American. No Yank ain't never took no dust from aft a Englisher, whether it were war, walkin'-matches, or women.'

" 'But they's a Englisher,' sings out Strokher, 'not forty miles from here as can nick the nose o' a freckled Yank if so be occasion require.'

"Now ain't that plum foolish-like," observed Bunt, philosophically. "Ain't it plum foolish-like o' them two gesabes to go flyin' up in the air like two he-hens on a hot plate—for nothin' in the world but because a neat lookin' feemale woman has looked at 'em some soft?

"Well, naturally, we others—Ally Bazan an' me—we others throws it into 'em pretty strong about bein' more kinds of blame fools than a pup with a bug; an' they simmers down some, but along o' the way home I kin see as how they're a-glarin' at each other, an' a-drawin' theirselves up proud-like an' presumptchoous, an' I groans again, not loud but deep, as the Good Book says.

"We has two or three more palavers with the Signorita Esperanza and stacks the deck to beat the harbor police and the Customs people an' all, an' to nip down the coast with our contraband. An' each time we chins with the Signorita there's them two locoes steppin' and sidle'n' around her, actin' that silly-like that me and Ally Bazan takes an' beats our heads agin' the walls so soon as we're alone just because we're that pizen mortified.

"Fin'ly comes the last talky-talk an' we're to sail away next day an' mebbee snatch the little Joker through or be took an' hung by the *Costa Guardas*.

"An' 'Good-by,' says Hardenberg to Esperanza, in a faintin', die-away voice like a kitten with a cold. 'An' ain't we goin' to meet no more?'

" 'I sure hopes as much,' puts in Strokher, smirkin' so's you'd think he was a he-milliner sellin' a bonnet. 'I hope,' says he, 'our delightful acquaintanceship ain't a-goin' for to end abrupt this-a-way.'

" 'Oh, you nice, big Mister Men,' pipes up the Signorita in English, 'we will meet down there in Gortamalar soon again, yes, because I go down by the vapour carriages to-morrow.'

" 'Unprotected, too,' says Hardenberg, waggin' his fool head. 'An' so young!'

"Holy Geronimo! I don't know what more fool drivelin' they had, but they fin'ly comes away. Ally Bazan and me rounds 'em up and conducts 'em to the boat an' puts 'em to bed like as if they was little —or drunk, an' the next day—or next night, rather—about one o'clock, we slips the heel ropes and hobbles o' the schooner quiet as a mountain-lion stalking a buck, and catches the out-tide through the gate o' the bay. Lord, we was some keyed up, lemmee tell you, an' Ally Bazan and Hardenberg was at the fore end o' the boat with their guns ready in case o' bein' asked impert'nent questions by the patrol-boats.

"Well, how-some-ever, we nips out with the little Jokers (they was writ in the manifest as minin' pumps) an' starts south. This 'ere *pasear* down to Gortamalar is the first time I goes a-gallying about on what the Three Crows calls 'blue water'; and when that schooner hit the bar I begins to remember that my stummick and inside arrangements ain't made o' no chilled steel, nor yet o' rawhide. First I gits plum sad, and shivery, and I feels as mean an' pore as a prairie-dog w'ich 'as eat a horned toad back'ards. I goes to Ally Bazan and gives it out as how I'm going for to die, an' I puts it up that I'm sure sad and depressed-like; an' don't care much about life nohow; an' that present surroundin's lack that certain undescribable charm. I tells him that I *knows* the ship is goin' to sink afore we git over the bar. Waves!—they was higher'n the masts; and I've rode some fair lively sun-fishers in my time, but I ain't never struck anythin' like the r'arin' and buckin' and high-an'-lofty tumblin' that that same boat went through with those first few hours after we had come out.

"But Ally Bazan tells me to go downstairs in the boat an' lie up quiet, an' byne-by I do feel better. By next day I kin sit up and take solid food again. An' then's when I takes special notice o' the ever-lastin' foolishness o' Strokher and Hardenberg.

"You'd a thought each one o' them two mush-heads was tryin' to act the part of a ole cow which has had her calf took. They goes a-moonin' about the boat that mournful it 'ud make you yell jus' out o' sheer nervousness. First one 'ud up an' hold his head on his hand an' lean on the fence-rail that ran around the boat, and sigh till he'd raise his pants clean outa the top o' his boots. An' then the other 'ud go off in another part o' the boat an' *he'd* sigh an' moon an' take on fit to sicken a coyote.

"But byne-by—we're mebbe six days to the good o' 'Frisco— byne-by they two gits kind o' sassy along o' each t'other, an' they has

a heart-to-heart talk and puts it up as how either one o' 'em 'ud stand
to win so only the t'other was out o' the game.

"'It's double or nothing,' says Hardenberg, who is somethin' o' a
card sharp, 'for either you or me, Stroke; an' if you're agreeable I'll
play you a round o' jacks for the chance at the Signõorita—the loser
to pull out o' the running for good an' all.'

"No, Strokher don't come in on no such game, he says. He wins
her, he says, as a man, and not as no poker player. No, nor he won't
throw no dice for the chance o' winnin' Esperanza, nor he won't flip
no coin, nor yet 'rastle. 'But,' says he all of a sudden, 'I'll tell you
which I'll do. You're a big, thick, strappin' hulk o' a two-fisted dray-
horse, Hardie, an' I ain't no effete an' digenerate one-lunger myself.
Here's wot I propose—that we-all takes an' lays out a sixteen-foot
ring on the quarterdeck, an' that the raw-boned Yank and the stodgy
Englisher strips to the waist, an' all-friendly-like, settles the question
by Queensbury rules an' may the best man win.'

"Hardenberg looks him over.

"'An' wot might be your weight?' says he. 'I don't figure on hurtin'
of you, if so be you're below my class.'

"'I fights at a hunder and seventy,' says Strokher.

"'An' me,' says Hardenberg, 'at a hunder an' seventy-five. We're
matched.'

"'Is it a go?' inquires Strokher.

"'You bet your great-gran'mammy's tortis-shell chessy cat it's a
go,' says Hardenberg, prompt as a hop-frog catching flies.

"We don't lose no time trying to reason with 'em, for they is sure
keen on havin' the go. So we lays out a ring by the rear end o' the
deck, an' runs the schooner in till we're in the lee o' the land, an' she
ridin' steady on her pins.

"Then along o' about four o'clock on a fine still day we lays the
boat to, as they say, an' folds up the sail, an' havin' scattered resin in
the ring (which it ain't no ring, but a square o' ropes on posts), we
says all is ready.

"Ally Bazan, he's referee, an' me, I'm the time-keeper which I has
to ring the ship's bell every three minutes to let 'em know to quit an'
that the round is over.

"We gets 'em into the ring, each in his own corner, squattin' on a
bucket, the time-keeper bein' second to Hardenberg an' the referee
being second to Strokher. An' then, after they has shuk hands, I
climbs up on' the chicken-coop an' hollers 'Time' an' they begins.

"Mister Man, I've saw Tim Henan at his best, an' I've saw Sayres
when he was a top-notcher, an' likewise several other irregler boxin'
sharps that were sure tough tarriers. Also I've saw two short-horn

bulls arguin' about a question o' leadership, but so help me Bob—the fight I saw that day made the others look like a young ladies' quadrille. Oh, I ain't goin' to tell o' that mill in detail, nor by rounds. Rounds! After the first five minutes they *wa'n't* no rounds. I rung the blame bell till I rung her loose an' Ally Bazan yells 'break-a-way' an' 'time's up' till he's black in the face, but you could no more separate them two than you could put the brakes on a blame earthquake.

"At about suppertime we pulled 'em apart. We could do it by then, they was both so gone; an' jammed each one o' 'em down in their corners. I rings my bell good an' plenty, an' Ally Bazan stands up on a bucket in the middle o' the ring an' says:

" 'I declare this 'ere glove contest a draw.'

"An' draw it sure was. They fit for two hours stiddy an' never a one got no better o' the other. They give each other lick for lick as fast an' as steady as they could stand to it. 'Rastlin', borin' in, boxin' —all was alike. The one was just as good as t'other. An' both willin' to the very last.

"When Ally Bazan calls it a draw, they gits up and wobbles toward each other an' shakes hands, and Hardenberg he says:

" 'Stroke, I thanks you a whole lot for as neat a go as ever I mixed in.'

"An' Strokher answers up:

" 'Hardie, I loves you better'n ever. You'se the first man I've met up with which I couldn't do for—an' I've met up with some scraggy propositions in my time, too.'

"Well, they two is a sorry-lookin' pair o' birds by the time we runs into San Diego harbour next night. They was fine lookin' objects for fair, all bruises and bumps. You remember now we was to take on a party at San Diego who was to show t'other half o' Esperanza's card, an' thereafterward to boss the job.

"Well, we waits till nightfall an' then slides in an' lays to off a certain pile o' stone, an' shows two green lights and one white every three and a half minutes for half a hour—this being a signal.

"They is a moon, an' we kin see pretty well. After we'd signaled about a hour, mebbee, we gits the answer—a one-minute green flare, and thereafterward we makes out a rowboat putting out and comin' towards us. They is two people in the boat. One is the gesabe at the oars an' the other a party sitting in the hinder end.

"Ally Bazan an' me, an' Strokher an' Hardenberg, we's all leanin' over the fence a-watchin'; when all to once I ups an' groans some sad. The party in the hinder end o' the boat bein' feemale.

" 'Ain't we never goin' to git shut of 'em?' says I; but the words ain't no more'n off my teeth when Strokher pipes up:

" 'It's *she*,' says he, gaspin' as though shot hard.

" 'Wot!' cries Hardenberg, sort of mystified, 'Oh, I'm sure a-dreamin'!" he says, just that silly-like.

" 'An' the mugs we've got!' says Strokher. An' they both sets to swearin' and cussin' to beat all I ever heard.

" 'I can't let her see me so bunged up,' says Hardenberg, doleful-like, 'Oh, whatever is to be done?'

" 'An' *I* look like a real genuine blown-in-the-bottle pug,' whimpers Strokher. 'Never mind,' says he, 'we must face the music. We'll tell her these are sure honourable scars, got because we fit for her.'

"Well, the boat comes up an' the feemale party jumps out and comes up the let-down stairway, onto the deck. Without sayin' a word she hands Hardenberg the half o' the card and he fishes out his half an' matches the two by the light o' a lantern.

"By this time the rowboat has gone a little ways off, an' then at last Hardenberg says:

" 'Welkum aboard, Signorita.'

"And Strokher cuts in with—

" 'We thought it was to be a man that 'ud join us here to take command, but *you*,' he says—an' oh, butter wouldn't a-melted in his mouth—'But *you*' he says, 'is always our mistress.'

" 'Very right, *bueno*. Me good fellows,' says the Signorita, 'but don't you be afraid that they's no man is at the head o' this business.' An' with that the party chucks off hat an' skirts, *and I'll be Mexican if it wa'n't a man after all!*

" 'I'm the Signor Barreto Palachi, gentlemen,' says he. 'The gringo police who wanted for to arrest me made the disguise necessary. Gentlemen, I regret to have been obliged to deceive such gallant *compadres*; but war knows no law.'

"Hardenberg and Strokher gives one look at the Signor and another at their own spiled faces, then:

" 'Come back here with the boat!' roars Hardenberg over the side, and with that—(upon me word you'd a-thought they two both were moved with the same spring)—over they goes into the water and strikes out hands over hands for the boat as hard as ever they kin lay to it. The boat meets 'em—Lord knows what the party at the oars thought—they climbs in an' the last I sees of 'em they was puttin' for shore—each havin' taken a oar from the boatman, an' they sure was makin' that boat *hum*.

"Well, we sails away eventually without 'em; an' a year or more afterward I crosses their trail again in Cy Ryder's office in 'Frisco."

"Did you ask them about it all?" said I.

"Mister Man," observed Bunt. "I'm several kinds of a fool; I know it. But sometimes I'm wise. I wishes for to live as long as I can, an' die when I can't help it. I does *not*, neither there, nor thereafterward, ever make no joke, nor yet no alloosion about, or concerning the Sigñorita Esperanza Palachi in the hearin' o' Hardenberg an' Strokher. I've seen—(ye remember)—both those boys use their fists—an' likewise Hardenberg, as he says hisself, shoots with both hands."

# STEWART EDWARD WHITE

## (1873–1946)

Born in Grand Rapids, Michigan, to wealthy parents, White grew up in a lumber town. Between the ages of eleven and fourteen, he lived and worked on a California ranch, deferring his public education until the age of sixteen. So effective was his tutoring at home that he graduated from high school in two years, and was the president of his senior class. White went on to receive both undergraduate and graduate (M.A.) degrees from the University of Michigan in 1895 and 1903; in between, he spent one year at Columbia Law School and another in a packing house in Chicago, as well as some time prospecting for gold in Dakota. While still an undergraduate, White passed his summers working on a Great Lakes sloop. This complex fabric of formal education and experience in hard physical labor would result in a body of fiction characterized by a sophisticated literary style reinforced by the material of personal encounter.

While studying at Columbia, White came in contact with the influential critic and writer, Brander Matthews, who thought highly of the young man's short fiction, and encouraged him to submit a story for publication. "A Man and His Dog" was quickly accepted, and White soon thereafter was given a contract by Munsey's Magazine for the serial rights to his first novel, The Westerners, published as a book in 1901, and soon followed by a novel of mining life, The Claim-Jumpers (1902). After working for a time in a Chicago bookstore, White headed for the Hudson Bay region, where he isolated himself in order to work on his account of Northwestern life, The Blazed Trail (1902), which was his first real literary success, celebrating the rough heroics of men who had an appeal similar to (if not so lasting as) that of the cowboy. He became a prolific writer of stories and novels celebrating frontier lives; not surprisingly, he was also a successful author of books for boys.

*White married in 1904. His wife shared in his love of wilderness life; she camped with him in Wyoming, Arizona, and California, and they shared a cabin in the High Sierra as he wrote a novel with a Sierra setting—and then an account of building the cabin. In 1911, in search of adventure and material, White traveled on safari in Africa in the wake of his friend Theodore Roosevelt, and during the First World War White served as a major of field artillery. One of his most ambitious projects was a series of novels, published between 1913 and 1920, about the growth of California.*

*As a literary figure, White stands between Owen Wister and Wister's protégé Ernest Hemingway. He lacks the Jamesian manner of the first and the literary genius of the second, but occupies an interesting halfway place nonetheless, in that he helped to create the muscular literary milieu out of which Hemingway's stories emerged. In his use of the vernacular first person and his pervading comic viewpoint, White also provides a vital connection between Mark Twain and Hemingway. He was a close contemporary of Jack London (whom he knew socially), but his adventure writings display none of the other man's radical views, even as they attest to a similar interest in the wilderness life and thus appealed to the same large readership.*

*Of all the authors represented in this collection, White is the one whose reputation is most in decline, with O. Henry running a close second, and his name cannot be found in any comprehensive history of American literature. Like O. Henry, he is best considered as a popular writer; his work is clearly derivative of Wister, Roosevelt, and Mark Twain, but his stories contain considerable narrative power, and are quite readable even today. White is in need of no apology, if only because he treated his Western subjects with so much sympathy and humor. He was rare among fictional chroniclers of the cowboy, in that he actually rode in a work saddle and could render an exact account (as in a sequence of essays in* Arizona Nights*) of what it is that cowboys do on a roundup. He was preceded in this by Andy Adams in* The Log of a Cowboy *(1902), but of the two White is the more imaginative and polished writer. His work, like Adams's, breaks cleanly with all that went before in an avoidance of the condescending, Eastern-made point of view. He is no nostalgist, in the vein of Wister and Remington, but wrote of the immediate, not the distantly heroic, past. And none of the men who wrote of the West before him were capable of such loving particulars in describing the desert landscape. He is second in this only to Mary Austin.*

*Kevin Starr, in his study of California culture, has identified in White a lifelong attempt to "recover something of the frontier experience" by becoming an "outdoorsman"—a phenomenon we can asso-*

*ciate with Boy Scouting and the rise of camping as a recreational activity. Refusing to accept Frederick Jackson Turner's dictum about the closing of the frontier, but not particularly interested in following the tide of empire into the Caribbean or the Pacific (he was old enough to have enlisted in the Spanish-American War, but did not), White pursued an interiorized version of frontier life—the "horizontal" experience described by Starr. His fiction creates an equivalently "horizontal" world, the meaning of which is found in the situation from which the stories emerge in* Arizona Nights *(the title of which alludes to* The Arabian Nights *as well as perhaps to those chivalric horsemen to whom the cowboy was often compared): the book is a series of tales told during a roundup by cowboys, first-person narratives about their experiences in other days. The frame, however, is the narrative told by yet another cowboy, White's representative, who participates in the roundup and passes on the stories to us. It is a complex, even fragmented fabric, and it perfectly captures White's attempt to catch hold of something elusive even as it disappears with the horsemen over the next rise.*

*There is a mysterious quality to his West, a haunting power only hinted at in the coincidences that often trigger his endings. Late in life, following the death of his beloved wife Betty, White claimed to be able to maintain contact with her through a psychic. No one familiar with the mystic undercurrent of his Arizona stories will dismiss this as the vagaries of old age. He was one of those desert dwellers for whom all life is something of a mirage, a shadow cast forward by scenes elsewhere, and in this too he resembles Mary Austin, despite the obvious and defining differences in their works and lives.*

# The Girl
# Who Got Rattled

This is one of the stories of Alfred. There are many of them still floating around the West, for Alfred was in his time very well known. He
was a little man, and he was bashful. That is the most that can be said
against him; but he was very little and very bashful. When on horseback his legs hardly reached the lower body-line of his mount, and
only his extreme agility enabled him to get on successfully. When on
foot, strangers were inclined to call him "sonny." In company he never
advanced an opinion. If things did not go according to his ideas, he
reconstructed the ideas, and made the best of it—only he could make
the most efficient best of the poorest ideas of any man on the plains.
His attitude was a perpetual sidling apology. It has been said that
Alfred killed his men diffidently, without enthusiasm, as though loth
to take the responsibility, and this in the pioneer days on the plains
was either frivolous affectation, or else—Alfred. With women he was
lost. Men would have staked their last ounce of dust at odds that he
had never in his life made a definite assertion of fact to one of the
opposite sex. When it became absolutely necessary to change a woman's preconceived notions as to what she should do—as, for instance,
discouraging her riding through quicksand—he would persuade somebody else to issue the advice. And he would cower in the background
blushing his absurd little blushes at his second-hand temerity. Add to
this narrow, sloping shoulders, a soft voice, and a diminutive pink-
and-white face.

But Alfred could read the prairie like a book. He could ride anything, shoot accurately, was at heart afraid of nothing, and could fight
like a little catamount when occasion for it really arose. Among those
who knew, Alfred was considered one of the best scouts on the plains.
That is why Caldwell, the capitalist, engaged him when he took his
daughter out to Deadwood.

Miss Caldwell was determined to go to Deadwood. A limited experience of the lady's sort, where they have wooden floors to the tents,
towels to the tent-poles, and expert cooks to the delectation of the
campers, had convinced her that "roughing it" was her favorite rec-
reation. So, of course, Caldwell senior had, sooner or later, to take her
across the plains on his annual trip. This was at the time when wagon-
trains went by way of Pierre on the north, and the South Fork on the
south. Incidental Indians, of homicidal tendencies and undeveloped
ideas as to the propriety of doing what they were told, made things
interesting occasionally, but not often. There was really no danger to
a good-sized train.

The daughter had a fiancé named Allen who liked roughing it, too;
so he went along. He and Miss Caldwell rigged themselves out boun-
tifully, and prepared to enjoy the trip.

At Pierre the train of eight wagons was made up, and they were
joined by Alfred and Billy Knapp. These two men were interesting,
but tyrannical on one or two points—such as getting out of sight of
the train, for instance. They were also deficient in reasons for their
tyranny. The young people chafed, and, finding Billy Knapp either
imperturbable or thick-skinned, they turned their attention to Alfred.
Allen annoyed Alfred, and Miss Caldwell thoughtlessly approved of
Allen. Between them they succeeded often in shocking fearfully all
the little man's finer sensibilities. If it had been a question of Allen
alone, the annoyance would soon have ceased. Alfred would simply
have bashfully killed him. But because of his innate courtesy, which
so saturated him that his philosophy of life was thoroughly tinged by
it, he was silent and inactive.

There is a great deal to recommend a plains journey at first. Later,
there is nothing at all to recommend it. It has the same monotony as
a voyage at sea, only there is less living room, and, instead of being
carried, you must progress to a great extent by your own volition.
Also the food is coarse, the water poor, and you cannot bathe. To a
plainsman, or a man who has the instinct, these things are as nothing
in comparison with the charm of the outdoor life, and the pleasing
tingling of adventure. But woman is a creature wedded to comfort.
She also has a strange instinctive desire to be entirely alone every
once in a while, probably because her experiences, while not less numerous than man's, are mainly psychical, and she needs occasionally
time to get "thought up to date." So Miss Caldwell began to get very
impatient.

The afternoon of the sixth day Alfred, Miss Caldwell, and Allen
rode along side by side. Alfred was telling a self-effacing story
of adventure, and Miss Caldwell was listening carelessly because

she had nothing else to do. Allen chaffed lazily when the fancy took him.

"I happened to have a limb broken at the time," Alfred was observing, parenthetically, in his soft tones, "and so—"

"What kind of a limb?" asked the young Easterner, with direct brutality. He glanced with a half-humourous aside at the girl, to whom the little man had been mainly addressing himself.

Alfred hesitated, blushed, lost the thread of his tale, and finally in great confusion reined back his horse by the harsh Spanish bit. He fell to the rear of the little wagon-train, where he hung his head, and went hot and cold by turns in thinking of such an indiscretion before a lady.

The young Easterner spurred up on the right of the girl's mount.

"He's the queerest little fellow *I* ever saw!" he observed, with a laugh. "Sorry to spoil his story. Was it a good one?"

"It might have been if you hadn't spoiled it," answered the girl, flicking her horse's ears mischievously. The animal danced. "What did you do it for?"

"Oh, just to see him squirm. He'll think about that all the rest of the afternoon, and will hardly dare look you in the face next time you meet."

"I know. Isn't he funny? The other morning he came around the corner of the wagon and caught me with my hair down. I *wish* you could have seen him!"

She laughed gayly at the memory.

"Let's get ahead of the dust," she suggested.

They drew aside to the firm turf of the prairie and put their horses to a slow lope. Once well ahead of the canvas-covered schooners they slowed down to a walk again.

"Alfred says we'll see them to-morrow," said the girl.

"See what?"

"Why, the Hills! They'll show like a dark streak, down past that butte there—what's its name?"

"Porcupine Tail."

"Oh, yes. And after that it's only three days. Are you glad?"

"Are you?"

"Yes, I believe I am. This life is fun at first, but there's a certain monotony in making your toilet where you have to duck your head because you haven't room to raise your hands, and this barrelled water palls after a time. I think I'll be glad to see a house again. People like camping about so long—"

"It hasn't gone back on me yet."

"Well, you're a man and can do things."

"Can't you do things?"

"You know I can't. What do you suppose they'd say if I were to ride out just that way for two miles? They'd have a fit."

"Who'd have a fit? Nobody but Alfred, and I didn't know you'd gotten afraid of him yet! I say, just *let's!* We'll have a race, and then come right back." The young man looked boyishly eager.

"It would be nice," she mused. They gazed into each other's eyes like a pair of children, and laughed.

"Why shouldn't we?" urged the young man. "I'm dead sick of staying in the moving circle of these confounded wagons. What's the sense of it all, anyway?"

"Why, Indians, I suppose," said the girl, doubtfully.

"Indians!" he replied, with contempt. "Indians! We haven't seen a sign of one since we left Pierre. I don't believe there's one in the whole blasted country. Besides, you know what Alfred said at our last camp?"

"What did Alfred say?"

"Alfred said he hadn't seen even a teepee-trail, and that they must be all up hunting buffalo. Besides that, you don't imagine for a moment that your father would take you all this way to Deadwood just for a lark, if there was the slightest danger, do you?"

"I don't know; I made him."

She looked out over the long sweeping descent to which they were coming, and the long sweeping ascent that lay beyond. The breeze and the sun played with the prairie grasses, the breeze riffling them over, and the sun silvering their under surfaces thus exposed. It was strangely peaceful, and one almost expected to hear the hum of bees as in a New England orchard. In it all was no sign of life.

"We'd get lost," she said, finally.

"Oh, no, we wouldn't!" he asserted with all the eagerness of the amateur plainsman. "I've got that all figured out. You see, our train is going on a line with that butte behind us and the sun. So if we go ahead and keep our shadows just pointing to the butte, we'll be right in their line of march."

He looked to her for admiration of his cleverness. She seemed convinced. She agreed, and sent him back to her wagon for some article of invented necessity. While he was gone she slipped softly over the little hill to the right, cantered rapidly over two more, and slowed down with a sigh of satisfaction. One alone could watch the directing shadow as well as two. She was free and alone. It was the one thing she had desired for the last six days of the long plains journey, and she enjoyed it now to the full. No one had seen her go. The drivers droned stupidly along, as was their wont; the occupants of the wagons slept, as was their wont; and the diminutive Alfred was hiding his blushes behind clouds of dust in the rear, as was not his wont at all. He had been severely shocked, and he might have brooded over it all the afternoon, if a discovery had not startled him to activity.

On a bare spot of the prairie he discerned the print of a hoof. It was not that of one of the train's animals. Alfred knew this, because just to one side of it, caught under a grass-blade so cunningly that only the little scout's eyes could have discerned it at all, was a single blue bead. Alfred rode out on the prairie to right and left, and found the hoof-prints of about thirty ponies. He pushed his hat back and wrinkled his brow, for the one thing he was looking for he could not find—the two narrow furrows made by the ends of teepee-poles dragging along on either side of the ponies. The absence of these indicated that the band was composed entirely of bucks, and bucks were likely to mean mischief.

He pushed ahead of the whole party, his eyes fixed earnestly on the ground. At the top of the hill he encountered the young Easterner. The latter looked puzzled, in a half-humorous way.

"I left Miss Caldwell here a half-minute ago," he observed to Alfred, "and I guess she's given me the slip. Scold her good for me when she comes in—will you?" He grinned, with good-natured malice at the idea of Alfred's scolding anyone.

Then Alfred surprised him.

The little man straightened suddenly in his saddle and uttered a fervent curse. After a brief circle about the prairie, he returned to the young man.

"You go back to th' wagons, and wake up Billy Knapp, and tell him this—that I've gone scoutin' some, and I want him to *watch out*. Understand? *Watch out!*"

"What?" began the Easterner, bewildered.

"I'm agoin' to find her," said the little man, decidedly.

"You don't think there's any danger, do you?" asked the Easterner, in anxious tones. "Can't I help you?"

"You do as I tell you," replied the little man, shortly, and rode away.

He followed Miss Caldwell's trail quite rapidly, for the trail was fresh. As long as he looked intently for hoof-marks, nothing was to be seen, the prairie was apparently virgin; but by glancing the eye forty or fifty yards ahead, a faint line was discernible through the grasses.

Alfred came upon Miss Caldwell seated quietly on her horse in the very centre of a prairie-dog town, and so, of course, in the midst of an area of comparatively desert character. She was amusing herself by watching the marmots as they barked, or watched, or peeped at her, according to their distance from her. The sight of Alfred was not welcome, for he frightened the marmots.

When he saw Miss Caldwell, Alfred grew bashful again. He sidled his horse up to her and blushed.

"I'll show you th' way back, miss," he said, diffidently.

"Thank you," replied Miss Caldwell, with a slight coldness, "I can find my own way back."

"Yes, of course," hastened Alfred, in an agony. "But don't you think we ought to start back now? I'd like to go with you, miss, if you'd let me. You see the afternoon's quite late."

Miss Caldwell cast a quizzical eye at the sun.

"Why, it's hours yet till dark!" she said, amusedly.

Then Alfred surprised Miss Caldwell.

His diffident manner suddenly left him. He jumped like lightning from his horse, threw the reins over the animal's head so he would stand, and ran around to face Miss Caldwell.

"Here, jump down!" he commanded.

The soft Southern *burr* of his ordinary conversation had given place to a clear incisiveness. Miss Caldwell looked at him amazed.

Seeing that she did not at once obey, Alfred actually began to fumble hastily with the straps that held her riding-skirt in place. This was so unusual in the bashful Alfred that Miss Caldwell roused and slipped lightly to the ground.

"Now what?" she asked.

Alfred, without replying, drew the bit to within a few inches of the animal's hoofs, and tied both fetlocks firmly together with the double-loop. This brought the pony's nose down close to his shackled feet. Then he did the same thing with his own beast. Thus neither animal could so much as hobble one way or the other. They were securely moored.

Alfred stepped a few paces to the eastward. Miss Caldwell followed.

"Sit down," said he.

Miss Caldwell obeyed with some nervousness. She did not understand at all, and that made her afraid. She began to have a dim fear lest Alfred might have gone crazy. His next move strengthened this suspicion. He walked away ten feet and raised his hand over his head, palm forward. She watched him so intently that for a moment she saw nothing else. Then she followed the direction of his gaze, and uttered a little sobbing cry.

Just below the sky-line of the first slope to eastward was silhouetted a figure on horseback. The figure on horseback sat motionless.

"We're in for fight," said Alfred, coming back after a moment. "He won't answer my peace-sign, and he's a Sioux. We can't make a run for it through this dog-town. We've just got to stand 'em off."

He threw down and back the lever of his old .44 Winchester, and softly uncocked the arm. Then he sat down by Miss Caldwell.

From various directions, silently, warriors on horseback sprang into sight and moved dignifiedly toward the first-comer, forming at the last a band of perhaps thirty men. They talked together for a moment, and then one by one, at regular intervals, detached themselves and began circling at full speed to the left, throwing themselves behind their horses, and yelling shrill-voiced, but firing no shot as yet.

"They'll rush us," speculated Alfred. "We're too few to monkey with this way. This is a bluff."

The circle about the two was now complete. After watching the whirl of figures a few minutes, and the motionless landscape beyond, the eye became dizzied and confused.

"They won't have no picnic," went on Alfred, with a little chuckle. "Dog-hole's as bad fer them as fer us. They don't know how to fight. If they was to come in on all sides, I couldn't handle 'em, but they always rush in a bunch, like *damn* fools!" and then Alfred became suffused with blushes, and commenced to apologise abjectly and profusely to a girl who had heard neither the word nor its atonement. The savages and the approaching fight were all she could think of.

Suddenly one of the Sioux threw himself forward under his horse's neck and fired. The bullet went wild, of course, but it shrieked with the rising inflection of a wind-squall through bared boughs, seeming to come ever nearer. Miss Caldwell screamed and covered her face. The savages yelled in chorus.

The one shot seemed to be the signal for a spattering fire all along the line. Indians never clean their rifles, rarely get good ammunition, and are deficient in the philosophy of hind-sights. Besides this, it is not easy to shoot at long range in a constrained position from a running horse. Alfred watched them contemptuously in silence.

"If they keep that up long enough, the wagon-train may hear 'em," he said, finally. "Wisht we weren't so far to nor-rard. There, it's comin'!" he said, more excitedly.

The chief had paused, and, as the warriors came to him, they threw their ponies back on their haunches, and sat motionless. They turned the ponies' heads toward the two.

Alfred arose deliberately for a better look.

"Yes, that's right," he said to himself, "that's old Lone Pine, sure thing. I reckon we-all's got to make a *good* fight!"

The girl had sunk to the ground, and was shaking from head to foot. It is not nice to be shot at in the best of circumstances, but to be shot at by odds of thirty to one, and the thirty of an outlandish and terrifying species, is not nice at all. Miss Caldwell had gone to pieces badly, and Alfred looked grave. He thoughtfully drew from its holster his beautiful Colt's with its ivory handle, and laid it on the grass. Then he blushed hot and cold, and looked at the girl doubtfully. A sudden movement in the group of savages, as the war-chief rode to the front, decided him.

"Miss Caldwell," he said.

The girl shivered and moaned.

Alfred dropped to his knees and shook her shoulder roughly.

"Look up here," he commanded. "We ain't got but a minute."

Composed a little by the firmness of his tone, she sat up. Her face had gone chalky, and her hair had partly fallen over her eyes.

"Now, listen to every word," he said, rapidly. "Those Injins is goin' to rush us in a minute. P'r'aps I can break them, but I don't know. In that pistol there, I'll always save two shots—understand?—it's always loaded. If I see it's all up, I'm a-goin' to shoot you with one of 'em, and myself with the other."

"Oh!" cried the girl, her eyes opening wildly. She was paying close enough attention now.

"And if they kill me first"—he reached forward and seized her wrist impressively—"if they kill me first, you must take that pistol and shoot yourself. Understand? Shoot yourself—in the head—here!"

He tapped his forehead with a stubby forefinger.

The girl shrank back in horror. Alfred snapped his teeth together and went on grimly.

"If they get hold of you," he said, with solemnity, "they'll first take off every stitch of your clothes, and when you're quite naked they'll stretch you out on the ground with a rawhide to each of your arms and legs. And then they'll drive a stake through the middle of your body into the ground—and leave you there—to die—slowly!"

And the girl believed him, because, incongruously enough, even through her terror she noticed that at this, the most immodest speech of his life, Alfred did not blush. She looked at the pistol lying on the turf with horrified fascination.

The group of Indians, which had up to now remained fully a thousand yards away, suddenly screeched and broke into a run directly toward the dog-town.

There is an indescribable rush in a charge of savages. The little ponies make their feet go so fast, the feathers and trappings of the warriors stream behind so frantically, the whole attitude of horse and man is so eager, that one gets an impression of fearful speed and resistless power. The horizon seems full of Indians.

As if this were not sufficiently terrifying, the air is throbbing with sound. Each Indian pops away for general results as he comes jumping along, and yells shrilly to show what a big warrior he is, while underneath it all is the hurried monotone of hoof-beats becoming ever louder, as the roar of an increasing rainstorm on the roof. It does not seem possible that anything can stop them.

Yet there is one thing that can stop them, if skilfully taken advantage of, and that is their lack of discipline. An Indian will fight hard when cornered, or when heated by lively resistance, but he hates to go into it in cold blood. As he nears the opposing rifle, this feeling gets stronger. So often a man with nerve enough to hold his fire, can break a fierce charge merely by waiting until it is within fifty yards or so, and then suddenly raising the muzzle of his gun. If he had gone to shooting at once, the affair would have become a combat, and the Indians would have ridden him down. As it is, each has had time to think. By the time the white man is ready to shoot, the suspense has done its work. Each savage knows that but one will fall, but, cold-blooded, he does not want to be that one; and, since in such disciplined fighters it is each for himself, he promptly ducks behind his mount and circles away to the right or the left. The whole band swoops and divides, like a flock of swift-winged terns on a windy day.

This Alfred relied on in the approaching crisis.

The girl watched the wild sweep of the warriors with strained eyes. She had to grasp her wrist firmly to keep from fainting, and she seemed incapable of thought. Alfred sat motionless on a dog-mound, his rifle across his lap. He did not seem in the least disturbed.

"It's good to fight again," he murmured, gently fondling the stock of his rifle. "Come on, ye devils! Oho!" he cried as a warrior's horse went down in a dog-hole, "I thought so!"

His eyes began to shine.

The ponies came skipping here and there, nimbly dodging in and out between the dog-holes. Their riders shot and yelled wildly, but none of the bullets went lower than ten feet. The circle of their advance looked somehow like the surge shoreward of a great wave, and the similarity was heightened by the nodding glimpses of the light eagles' feathers in their hair.

The run across the honey-combed plain was hazardous—even to Indian ponies—and three went down kicking, one after the other. Two of the riders lay stunned. The third sat up and began to rub his knee. The pony belonging to Miss Caldwell, becoming frightened, threw itself and lay on its side, kicking out frantically with its hind legs.

At the proper moment Alfred cocked his rifle and rose swiftly to his knees. As he did so, the mound on which he had been kneeling caved into the hole beneath it, and threw him forward on his face. With a furious curse, he sprang to his feet and levelled his rifle at the thick of the press. The scheme worked. In a flash every savage disappeared behind his pony, and nothing was to be seen but an arm and a leg. The band divided on either hand as promptly as though the signal for such a drill had been given, and swept gracefully around in two long circles until it reined up motionless at nearly the exact point from which it had started on its imposing charge. Alfred had not fired a shot.

He turned to the girl with a short laugh.

She lay face upward on the ground, staring at the sky with wideopen, horror-stricken eyes. In her brow was a small blackened hole, and under her head, which lay strangely flat against the earth, the grasses had turned red. Near her hand lay the heavy Colt's .44.

Alfred looked at her a minute without winking. Then he nodded his head.

"It was 'cause I fell down that hole—she thought they'd got me!" he said aloud to himself. "Pore little gal! She hadn't ought to have did it!"

He blushed deeply, and, turning his face away, pulled down her skirt until it covered her ankles. Then he picked up his Winchester and fired three shots. The first hit directly back of the ear one of the stunned Indians who had fallen with his horse. The second went through the other stunned Indian's chest. The third caught the Indian with the broken leg between the shoulders just as he tried to get behind his struggling pony.

Shortly after, Billy Knapp and the wagon-train came along.

# The Prospector

In the old mining days out West the law of the survival of the fittest held good, and he who survived had to be very fit indeed. There were a number of ways of not surviving. One of them was to die. And there were a number of ways of being very fit; such as holding an accurate gun or an even temper, being blessed with industry or a vital-tearing ambition, knowing the game thoroughly or understanding the great American expedient of bluff. In any case the man who survived must see his end clearly through that end's means. Whether it were gold, poker, or life, he must cling to his purpose with a bulldog tenacity that no amount of distraction could loosen. Otherwise, as has been said, he died, or begged, or robbed, or became a tramp, or committed the suicide of horse-stealing, or just plain drifted back East broken—a shameful thing.

Why Peter lived on was patent enough to anyone. He was harmless, good-natured, and, in the estimation of hard-hewn men, just "queer" enough to be a little pathetic. Anyone who had once caught a fair look at his narrow, hatchet face with the surprised blue eyes and the loose-falling, sparse light hair; or had enjoyed his sweet, rare smile as he deprecatingly answered a remark before effacing himself; or had chanced on the fortune of asking him for some trifling favour to meet his eager and pleased rendering of it: none of these hypothetical individuals, and that meant about everyone who came in contact with Peter at all, could have imagined anybody, let alone themselves, harming a hair of his head. But how he continued to be a prospector remained a puzzle. The life is hard, full of privations, sown with difficulties, clamant for technical knowledge, exacting of physical strength, dependent on shrewdness and knowledge of the world. Peter had none of these, not even in the smallest degree. There was also, of course, the instinct. This Peter did possess. He could follow his leads of crumbling brown rock with that marvellous intuitive knowledge which is so important an element in the equipment of your true prospector. But it is only an element. By all the rules of the game Peter should have failed long since, should have "cashed in and quit" some five years back; and still he grubbed away cheerfully at divers mountains and many ranges. He had not succeeded; still, he had not failed.

Three times had he made his "strike." On the first of these three occasions he had gone in with two San Francisco men to develop the property. The San Francisco men had persuaded him to form a stock company of certain capitalisation. In two deals they had "frozen out" Peter completely, and reorganised on a basis which is paying them good dividends. Returning overwhelmed with sophistries and "explanations" from his expostulatory interview, Peter decided he knew more about quartz leads than about business and the disgorging of gains, so he went over into Idaho to try again. There he found the famous Antelope Gap lode. This time he determined to sell outright and have nothing more to do with the matter after the transfer of the property. He drew up the deeds, received a small amount down, and took notes for the balance. When the notes came due he could not collect them. The mine had been resold to third parties. Peter had no money to contest the affair; and probably would not have done so if he had. He knew too little—or too much—of law; but the instinct was his, so he moved one State farther east to Montana for his third trial. This resulted in the Eagle Ridge. And for the third time he was swindled by a persuasive man and a lying one-sided contract.

A sordid, silly enough little tale, is it not? but that is why men wondered at Peter's survival, marvelled at the recuperative force that made possible his fourth attempt, speculated with a certain awe over that cheerful disposition which had earned him, even in his adversity, the sobriquet of Happy Peter.

All of these phenomena, had they but known it, resulted from one simple cause. Peter's mental retrospect for a considerable space would have conjured up nothing but a succession of grand sweeps of mountains, singing pines, rare western skies, and the simplicity of a frontiersman's log-cabin; and yet to his inner vision over the border of that space lay a very different scene. It was the scene he saw the oftenest. Oftenest? he saw it always; across the mountains, through the pines, beyond the skies. As time went on, the vision simplified itself to Peter, as visions will. It came to have two phases, two elements, which visited him always together.

One of these was a house; the other a girl. The house was low, white-painted, with green blinds and a broad stoop. Its front yard was fragrant with lilacs, noisy with crickets, fluttering with butterflies of sulphur yellow. About it lay a stony, barren farm, but lovely with the glamour of home. The girl was not pretty, as we know girls; but she had straight steady eyes, a wide brow, smooth matronly bands of hair, and a wholesome, homely New England character, sweet, yet with a tang to give it a flavour, like the apples on the tree near the old-fashioned, long-armed well. Peter could gain no competence from the stony farm, no consent from the girl. It was to win both that he had come West.

In those days, around the western curve of the earth, every outlook borrowed the tints of sunset. Nothing but the length of the journey stood between a man and his fortune.

"I love you dearly, Peter," she had said, both hands on his shoulders, "and I do not care for the money. But I have seen too much of it here—too much of the unhappiness that comes from debt, from poverty. Misery does not love the company of those it loves. Go make your fortune, Peter, bravely, and come back to me."

"I will," replied Peter, soberly. "I will, God help me. But it may be long. I don't know; I have not the knack; I am stupid about people, about men."

She smiled, and leaned over to kiss his eyes. "People love you, Peter," she said, simply. "*I* love you, and I will wait. If it were fifty years, you will find me here ready when you come."

Peter knew this to be true. And so to the unpeopled rooms of the little old Vermont farmhouse Peter's gentle thoughts ever swarmed, like homing bees. In his vision of it the lilac-bush outside the window always smelled of spring; she always sat there beside the open sash, waiting—for him. What wonder that he survived when so many others went down? What wonder that he persevered? What wonder that his patient soul, comparing the eternity of love's happiness with the paltry years of love's waiting, saw nothing in the condition of affairs to ruffle its peaceful serenity? And yet to most the time would have seemed very, very long. Men may blunder against rich pockets or leads and wealthy say farewell to a day which they greeted as the poorest of the poor. So may men win fortunes on a turn of the wheat market. But the one is no more prospecting than the other is business. True prospecting has only the normal percentage of uncertainties, the usual alloy of luck to brighten its toil with the hope of the unexpected. A man must know his business to succeed. A bit of rock, a twist of ledge, a dip of country, an abundance or an absence of dikes—these and many others are the symbols with which the prospector builds the formula that spells gold. And after the formula is made, it must be proved. It is the proving that bends the back, tries the patience, strains to the utmost the man's inborn Instinct of the Metal. For that is the work of the steel and the fire, the water and the power of explosion. Until the proof is done to the Q.E.D., the man must draw for inspiration on his stock of faith. In the morning he sharpens his drills at a forge. In the afternoon he may, by the grace of labour, his Master, have accomplished a little round hole in the rock, which, being filled with powder and fired, will tear loose into a larger hole with débris. The débris must be removed by pick and shovel. After the hole has been sufficiently deepened, the débris must be loaded into a bucket, which must then be hauled to the surface of the ground and emptied. How long do you calculate the man will require to dig in this manner, fifty, a hundred feet? How long to sink one or two such shafts on each and every claim he has staked? How long to excavate the numerous lateral tunnels which the Proof demands?

And besides this, from time to time the shaft must be elaborately timbered in order to prevent its caving in and burying work and workman together—a tedious job, requiring the skill alike of a woodsman, a carpenter, a sailor, and a joiner. The man must make his trips to town for supplies. He must cook his meals. He must meet his fellows occasionally, or lose the power of speech. The years slip by rapidly. He numbers his days by what he has accomplished; and it is little. He measures time by his trips to camp; and they are few. It is no small thing to make three discoveries—and lose them. It is a greater thing to find courage for a fourth attempt.

After the Eagle Ridge fiasco, Peter, as cheerful as ever, journeyed over into Wyoming to try his luck once more. He moved up into the hills, spent a month in looking about him, narrowed his localities to one gulch, and built himself a log cabin in which to live. Then he made his general survey. He went on foot up every gulch, even every little transverse wrinkle that lay tributary to his valley, to the shallow top of it filled with loose stones; he followed the sky-line of every ridge which bordered and limited these gulches; he seized frequent opportunities of making long diagonals down the slopes. Nothing escaped him. In time he knew the general appearance of every bit of drift or outcrop in his district. Then he sat down in his cabin and carefully considered the probabilities. If they had not happened to please him, he would have repeated the whole wearisome process in another valley; but as in this case they did, he proceeded to take the next step. In other words, he went over the same ground again with a sampling-pick and a bundle of canvas bags. Where his theories or experience advised, he broke off quantities of rock from the ledges, which he crushed and mixed in the half of an old blanket; dividing, and recrushing again and again, until an "average" was obtained in small compass. The "average" he took home, where he dumped it into a heavy iron mortar, over which he had suspended a pestle from a springy sapling. By alternately pulling down and letting up on the sapling he crushed the quartz fragments with the pestle into fine red and white sand. The sand he "panned out" for indications of free gold.

The ledges whose averages thus showed the colour, he marked on his map with a cross. Some leads which did not so exhibit gold, but whose other indications he considered promising, he exploited still further, penetrating to a layer below the surface by means of a charge or so of powder. Or perhaps he even spent several weeks in making an irregular hole like a well, from which he carried the broken rock in bags, climbing up a notched tree. Then he selected more samples. This is hard work.

Thus Peter came to know his country, and when he knew it thoroughly, when he had made all his numerous speculations as to horses, blowouts, and slips—then, and not until then, did he stake out his claims; then, and not until then, did he consider himself ready to *begin* work.

He might be quite wrong in his calculations. In that case, it was all to do over again somewhere else. He had had this happen. Every prospector has. The claims which Peter selected were four in number. He started in without delay on the proof. Foot by foot the shafts descended through the red, the white, vein matter. One by one the spider arms of the tunnels felt out into the innermost crevices of the lode. Little by little Peter's table of statistics filled; here a pocket, there a streak, yon a clear ten feet of low-grade ore. The days, the months, even the years slipped by. Summers came and went with a flurry of thunder-showers that gathered about Harney, spread abroad in long bands of blackness, broke in a deluge of rain and hail and passed out to dissipate in the hot air of the prairies. Autumns, clear-eyed and sweet-breathed, faded wanly in the smoke of their forest fires. Winters sidled by with constant threat of arctic weather which somehow never came; powdering the hills with their snow; making bitter cold the shadows, and warm the silver-like sun. Another spring was at hand. Like all the rest, it coquetted with the season as a young girl with her lover; smiling with the brightness of a western sun; frowning with the fierceness of a sudden snow-squall, strangely out of place in contrast to the greenery of the mountain "parks"; creeping slowly up the gullies from the prairie in staccato notes of bursting buds; at last lifting its many voices in the old swelling song of delight over the birth of new loves and new desires among its creatures.

Like all the rest, did I say? No, not quite. To Peter this particular spring was a rare thing of beauty. Its gilding was a little brighter, its colours a little fresher, its skies a little deeper, its songs rang a little truer than ever the gilding or colours or skies or songs of any spring he had ever known. For he was satisfied. Steadily the value of the property had proved itself. One clear, cold day he collected all his drills and picks and sledges and brought them back to camp, where he stacked them behind the door. It was his way of signing Q.E.D. to the proof.

The doubtful spot on the Jim Crow was not a blow-out, but a "horse." He had penetrated below it. The mines were rich beyond his dreams. Yet he sat there at his noon meal as cheerful, as unexcited, as content as ever. When one has waited so long, impatience sleeps soundly, arouses with the sluggishness of unbelief itself. Outside he saw the sun, for the first time in weeks, and heard the pines singing their endless song. Inside, his fire sparkled and crackled; his kettle purred like a fireside cat. Peter was tired; tired, but content. The dream was very near to him.

When he had finished his meal he got up and examined himself in his little square mirror. Then he did so again. Then he walked heavily back to his table and sat down and buried his face in his hands. When he had looked the first time he had seen a gray hair. When he had looked the second time he had discovered that there were many. With a sudden pang Peter realised that he was getting to be an old man. He took a picture from a pocket-case and looked at that. Was she getting to be an old woman?

It was fearful what a difference that little thought suddenly made. A moment ago he had had the eternities before him. Now there was not an instant to be wasted. Every minute, every second even, that he sat there gazing at the faded old picture in his hand was so much lost to him and to its original. Not God himself could bring it and its possibilities back to him. Until now he had looked about him upon Youth; he must henceforth look back to it—back to the things which might have been, but could never be—and each pulse-beat carried him inevitably farther from even the retrospective simulacrum of their joys. He and she could never begin young now. They must take up life cold in the moulds, ready fashioned. The delight of influencing each other's development was denied such as they; instead, they must find each other out, must throw a thousand strands of loving-kindness to span the gap which the patient years had sundered between them, a gap which should never have widened at all. Again that remorseless hurry of the moments! Each one of them made the cast across longer, increased the need for loving-kindness, demanded anew, for the mere pitiful commonplace task of understanding each other—which any mother and her child find so trivially easy—the power of affection which each would have liked to shower on the other undictated except by the desires of their hearts. Peter called up the image of himself as he had been when he had left the East, and set it remorselessly by the side of that present image in the mirror. Then he looked at the portrait. Could the years have changed her as much? If so, he would hardly know her!

Those miserable years of waiting! He had not minded them before, but now they were horrible. In the retrospect the ceaseless drudgery of rock and pick and drill loomed larger than the truth of it; his patience, at the time so spontaneous a result of his disposition, seemed that of a man clinging desperately to a rope, able to hang on only by the concentration of every ounce of his will. Peter felt himself clutching the rope so hard that he could think of nothing, absolutely nothing, else. He proved a great necessity of letting go.

And for her, these years? What had they meant? By the internal combustion which had so suddenly lighted up the dark corners of his being, he saw with almost clairvoyant distinctness how it must have been. He saw her growing older, as he had grown older, but in the dull apathy of monotony. She had none of this great filling Labour wherewith to drug herself into day-dreams of a future. The seasons as they passed showed her the same faces, growing ever a little more jaded, as dancers in the light of dawn. Perhaps she had ceased counting them? No, he knew better than that. But the pity of it! washing, scrubbing, mending; mending, scrubbing, washing to the time of an invalid's complaints. To-day she was doing as she had done yesterday; to-morrow she would do the same. To-morrow?

"No, by God!" cried Peter, starting to his feet. "There shall be no more to-morrow!"

He took from the shelf over the window a number of pieces of quartz, which he stuffed into the pockets of a pair of saddle-bags lying near the door. In the corral was Jenny, a sleek, fat mare. He saddled Jenny and departed with the saddle-bags, leaving the door of his cabin open to the first comer, as is the hospitable Western way.

At Beaver Dam he spread the chunks of rock out on the bar of the principal saloon and invited inspection. He did not think to find a purchaser among the inhabitants of Beaver Dam, but he knew that the tidings of his discoveries would arouse interest and attract other prospectors to the locality of his claims. In this manner his property would come prominently on the market.

The discoveries certainly were accorded attention enough. Peter was well known. Men were perfectly sure of his veracity and his mining instinct. If Peter said there existed a good lode of the stuff he exhibited to them, that settled it.

"Hum," said a man named Squint-eye Dobs, after examining a bit of the transparent crystal through which small kernels of yellow metal shone. Then he laid down the specimen, and walked quietly out the door without further comment. He had gone to get his outfit ready.

To others, not so prompt of action, Peter explained at length, always in that hesitating, diffident voice of his.

"I have my claims all staked," said he; "you boys can come up and hook onto what's left. There's plenty left. I ain't saying it's as good as mine; still, it's pretty good. I think it'll make a camp."

"Make a camp!" shouted Cheyenne Harry. "I should think it would! If there's any more like that up country you can sell a 'tater-patch if it lays anywheres near the district!"

"Well, I must be goin', boys," said Peter, sidling toward the door; "and I 'spect I'll see some of you boys up there?"

The boys did not care to commit themselves as to that before each other, but they were all mentally locating the ingredients of their prospecting outfits.

"Have a drink, Happy, on me," hospitably suggested the proprietor.

Peter slowly returned to the bar.

"Here's luck to the new claim, Happy," said the proprietor; "and here's hoping the sharps doesn't make all there is on her."

The men laughed, but not ill-naturedly. They all knew Peter, as has been said.

Peter turned again to the door.

"You'll have a reg'lar cyclone up thar by to-morrow!" called a joker after him; "look out fer us! There'll be an unholy mob on hand, and they'll try to do you, sure!"

Peter stopped short, looked at the speaker, and went out hurriedly.

The next morning the men came into his gulch. He heard them even before he had left his bunk—the *clink*, creak, creak! of their wagons. By the time he had finished breakfast the side-hills were covered with them. From his window he could catch glimpses of them through the straight pines as patches of red, or flashes of light reflected from polished metal. In the cañon was the gleam of fires; in the air the smell of wood-smoke and of bacon broiling; among the still bare bushes and saplings the shine of white lean-tops; horses fed eagerly on the young grasses and the browse of trees, raising their heads as the creak of wheels farther down the draw told of yet newcomers. The boom was under way.

Peter knew that the tidings of the discovery would spread. To-morrow a new town would deserve a place on the map. Men would come to the town, men with money, men anxious to invest. With them Peter would treat. There was to be no chance of a careless bargain this time. He would take no chances. And yet he had thought that before.

Peter began to forestall difficulties in his mind. The former experience suggested many, but he drew from the same source their remedies. It was the great unknown that terrified him. In spite of his years, in spite of his gray hairs, in spite of his memories of those former failures, he had to confess to himself that he knew nothing, absolutely nothing of sharpers and their methods. They could not fleece him again in precisely the way they had done so before; but how could he guess at the tricks they had in reserve? Eight years out of a man's life ought surely to teach him caution as thoroughly as twelve. Yet he walked into the Eagle Ridge trap as confidently as he had into the Antelope Gap. He had made it twelve years. What was to prevent his making it sixteen? There is no fear like that of the absolutely unknown. You cannot forestall that; you must depend upon your own self-confidence. Self-confidence was just what Peter did not possess.

Then in a flash he saw what he should have done. It was all so ridiculously simple—a mere question of division of labour. He, Peter, knew prospecting, but did not understand business. Back in his old Vermont home were a dozen honest men who knew business, but understood nothing of prospecting. Nothing would have been easier than to have combined these qualities and lacks. If Peter had returned quietly to his people, concealing his discoveries from the men of Beaver Dam, he could have returned in three weeks' time equipped for his negotiations. Now it was too late. The minute his back was turned they would jump his claims. Peter's mind worked slowly. If he had felt himself less driven by the sight of those gray hairs, he might have come in time to another idea—that of wiring or writing East for a partner, pending whose arrival he could merely hold possession of the claims. As it was, the terror and misgiving, having obtained entry, rapidly usurped the dominion of his thoughts. He could see nothing before him but the inevitable and dread bargaining with unknown powers of dishonesty, nothing behind him but the mistake of starting the "boom."

As the morning wore away he went out into the hills to look about him. The men were all busily enough engaged in chipping out the shallow troughs of their "discoveries," piling supporting rocks about their corner and side stakes, or tacking up laboriously composed mining "notices." They paid scant attention to the man who passed them a hundred yards away. Peter visited his own four claims. On one he found a small group anxiously examining the indications of the lead. He did not join it. The parting words flung after him at the saloon came to his mind. "Look out for us! There'll be an unholy mob on hand, and they'll try to do you, sure."

Peter cooked himself a noon meal, but he did not eat much of it. Instead, he sat quite still and stared with wide, blind eyes at the wavering mists of steam that arose from the various hot dishes. From time to time he got up with apparent purpose, which, however, left him before he had taken two steps, so that his movement speedily became aimless, and he sat down again. Late in the afternoon he went the rounds of his claims again, but saw nothing unusual. He did not take the trouble to cook supper. During the evening some men looked in for a moment or so, but went away, because the cabin was empty. Peter was at the moment of their visit walking back and forth, back and forth, away up high there on the top of the ridge, in a little cleared flat space next the stars. When he came to the end, he whirled sharp on his heels. It was six paces one way and five the other. He counted the steps consciously, until the mental process became mechanical. Then the count went on steadily behind his other thoughts—five, six; five, six; five, six; over and over again, like that. About ten o'clock he ceased opening and shutting his hands and began to scream, at first under his breath, then louder in the over tone, then with the full strength of his lungs. A mountain lion on another slope answered him. He stretched his arms up over his head, every muscle tense, and screamed. And then, without appreciable transition, he sank to the rock and hid his face. For the moment the nerve tension had relaxed.

The clear western stars, like fine silver powder, seemed to glimmer in some light stronger than their own, as dust-motes in the sun. A breeze from the prairie rested its light, invisible hands on the man's bent head. Certain homely night-sounds, such as the tree-toads and crickets and the cries of the poor wills, stole here and there through the pine-aisles like living creatures on the wing. A faint, sweet odour of the woods came with them. Peter arose, and drew a deep breath, and went to his cabin. The peace of nature had for the moment become his own.

But then, in the darkness of his low bunk, the old doubts, the old terrors returned. They perched there above him and compelled him to look at them until his eyes were hot and red. "*Do, do, do!*" said they, until Peter arose, and there, in the chill of dawn, he walked the three miles necessary for the inspection of his claims. Everything was as it should be. The men in the gulch were not yet awake. From the Jim Crow a drowsy porcupine trundled away bristling.

This could not go on. It would be weeks before he could hope even to open his negotiations. Peter cooked himself an elaborate breakfast—and drank half a cup of coffee. Then he sat, as he had the day before, staring straight in front of him, seeing nothing. After a time he placed the girl's picture and the square mirror side by side on the table and looked at them intently.

He rose, kicking his chair over backward, and went out to his claims once more.

The men in the gulch had awakened. Most of them had finished the more imperative demands of location the day before, so now they were more at leisure to satisfy their curiosity and their love of comment by inspecting the original discovery to which all this stampede was due. As a consequence Peter found a great gathering on the *Jim Crow*. Some of the men were examining chunks of ore, others were preparing to descend the shafts, still others were engaged idly in reading the location-notice tacked against a stub pine. One of the latter, the same individual who had joked Peter in the saloon, caught sight of the prospector as he approached.

"Hullo, Happy!" he called, pointing at the weather-beaten notice. "What do you call this?" He winked at the rest. The history of Peter's losses was well known.

"What?" asked Peter, strangely.

"You ain't got this readin' right. She says 'fifteen hundred feet'; the law says she ought t' read 'fifteen hundred *linear* feet.' Your claim is n.g. I'm goin' t' jump her on you."

The statement was ridiculous; everybody knew it, and prepared to laugh, loud-mouthed.

Peter, without a word, shot the speaker through the heart. Men said at his trial that it was the most brutal and unprovoked murder they had ever known.

# The Ole Virginia

The ring around the sun had thickened all day long, and the turquoise blue of the Arizona sky had filmed. Storms in the dry countries are infrequent, but heavy; and this surely meant storm. We had ridden since sun-up over broad mesas, down and out of deep cañons, along the base of the mountains in the wildest parts of the territory. The cattle were winding leisurely toward the high country; the jack rabbits had disappeared; the quail lacked; we did not see a single antelope in the open.

"It's a case of hole up," the Cattleman ventured his opinion. "I have a ranch over in the Double R. Charley and Windy Bill hold it down. We'll tackle it. What do you think?"

The four cowboys agreed. We dropped into a low, broad water-course, ascended its bed to big cottonwoods and flowing water, followed it into box cañons between rim-rock carved fantastically and painted like a Moorish façade, until at last in a widening below a rounded hill, we came upon an adobe house, a fruit tree, and a round corral. This was the Double R.

Charley and Windy Bill welcomed us with soda biscuits. We turned our horses out, spread our beds on the floor, filled our pipes, and squatted on our heels. Various dogs of various breeds investigated us. It was very pleasant, and we did not mind the ring around the sun.

"Somebody else coming," announced the Cattleman finally.

"Uncle Jim," said Charley, after a glance.

A hawk-faced old man with a long white beard and long white hair rode out from the cottonwoods. He had on a battered broad hat abnormally high of crown, carried across his saddle a heavy "eight square" rifle, and was followed by a half-dozen lolloping hounds.

The largest and fiercest of the latter, catching sight of our group, launched himself with lightning rapidity at the biggest of the ranch dogs, promptly nailed that canine by the back of the neck, shook him violently a score of times, flung him aside, and pounced on the next. During the ensuing few moments that hound was the busiest thing in the West. He satisfactorily whipped four dogs, pursued two cats up a tree, upset the Dutch oven and the rest of the soda biscuits, stampeded the horses, and raised a cloud of dust adequate to represent the smoke of battle. We others were too paralysed to move. Uncle Jim sat placidly on his white horse, his thin knees bent to the ox-bow stirrups, smoking.

In ten seconds the trouble was over, principally because there was no more trouble to make. The hound returned leisurely, licking from his chops the hair of his victims. Uncle Jim shook his head.

"Trailer," said he sadly, "is a little severe."

We agreed heartily, and turned in to welcome Uncle Jim with a fresh batch of soda biscuits.

The old man was one of the typical "long hairs." He had come to the Galiuro Mountains in '69, and since '69 he had remained in the Galiuro Mountains, spite of man or the devil. At present he possessed some hundreds of cattle, which he was reputed to water, in a dry season, from an ordinary dishpan. In times past he had prospected.

That evening, the severe Trailer having dropped to slumber, he held forth on big-game hunting and dogs, quartz claims and Apaches.

"Did you ever have any very close calls?" I asked.

He ruminated a few moments, refilled his pipe with some awful tobacco, and told the following experience:

In the time of Geronimo I was living just about where I do now; and that was just about in line with the raiding. You see, Geronimo, and Ju,[1] and old Loco used to pile out of the reservation at Camp Apache, raid south to the line, slip over into Mexico when the soldiers got too promiscuous, and raid there until they got ready to come back. Then there was always a big medicine talk. Says Geronimo:

"I am tired of the warpath. I will come back from Mexico with all my warriors, if you will escort me with soldiers and protect my people."

"All right," says the General, being only too glad to get him back at all.

So, then, in ten minutes there wouldn't be a buck in camp, but next morning they shows up again, each with about fifty head of hosses.

"Where'd you get those hosses?" asks the General, suspicious.

[1] Pronounced "Hoo."

"Had 'em pastured in the hills," answers Geronimo.

"I can't take all those hosses with me; I believe they're stolen!" says the General.

"My people cannot go without their hosses," says Geronimo.

So, across the line they goes, and back to the reservation. In about a week there's fifty-two frantic Greasers wanting to know where's their hosses. The army is nothing but an importer of stolen stock, and knows it, and can't help it.

Well, as I says, I'm between Camp Apache and the Mexican line, so that every raiding party goes right on past me. The point is that I'm a thousand feet or so above the valley, and the renegades is in such a devil of a hurry about that time that they never stop to climb up and collect me. Often I've watched them trailing down the valley in a cloud of dust. Then, in a day or two, a squad of soldiers would come up and camp at my spring for a while. They used to send soldiers to guard every water hole in the country so the renegades couldn't get water. After a while, from not being bothered none, I got to thinking I wasn't worth while with them.

Me and Johnny Hooper were pecking away at the Ole Virginia mine then. We'd got down about sixty feet, all timbered, and was thinking of cross-cutting. One day Johnny went to town, and that same day I got in a hurry and left my gun at camp.

I worked all the morning down at the bottom of the shaft, and when I see by the sun it was getting along towards noon, I put in three good shots, tamped 'em down, lit the fusees, and started to climb out.

It ain't noways pleasant to light a fuse in a shaft, and then have to climb out a fifty-foot ladder, with it burning behind you. I never did get used to it. You keep thinking, "Now suppose there's a flaw in that fuse, or something, and she goes off in six seconds instead of two minutes? where'll you be then?" It would give you a good boost towards your home on high, anyway.

So I climbed fast, and stuck my head out the top without looking —and then I froze solid enough. There, about fifty feet away, climbing up the hill on mighty tired hosses, was a dozen of the ugliest Chiricahuas you ever don't want to meet, and in addition a Mexican renegade named Maria, who was worse than any of 'em. I see at once their hosses was tired out, and they had a notion of camping at my water hole, not knowing nothing about the Ole Virginia mine.

For two bits I'd have let go all holts and dropped backwards, trusting to my thick head for easy lighting. Then I heard a little fizz and sputter from below. At that my hair riz right up so I could feel the breeze blow under my hat. For about six seconds I stood there like an imbecile, grinning amiably. Then one of the Chiricahuas made a sort of grunt, and I sabed that they'd seen the original exhibit your Uncle Jim was making of himself.

Then that fuse gave another sputter and one of the Apaches said "Un dah." That means "white man." It was harder to turn my head than if I'd had a stiff neck; but I managed to do it, and I see that my ore dump wasn't more than ten foot away. I mighty near overjumped it; and the next I knew I was on one side of it and those Apaches on the other. Probably I flew; leastways I don't seem to remember jumping.

That didn't seem to do me much good. The renegades were grinning and laughing to think how easy a thing they had; and I couldn't rightly think up any arguments against that notion—at least from their standpoint. They were chattering away to each other in Mexican for the benefit of Maria. Oh, they had me all distributed, down to my suspender buttons! And me squatting behind that ore dump about as formidable as a brush rabbit!

Then, all at once, one of my shots went off down in the shaft.

"Boom!" says she, plenty big; and a slather of rocks and stones come out of the mouth, and began to dump down promiscuous on the scenery. I got one little one in the shoulder-blade, and found time to wish my ore dump had a roof. But those renegades caught it square in the thick of trouble. One got knocked out entirely for a minute, by a nice piece of country rock in the head.

"Otra vez!" yells I, which means "again."

"Boom!" goes the Ole Virginia prompt as an answer.

I put in my time dodging, but when I gets a chance to look, the Apaches has all got to cover, and is looking scared.

"Otra vez!" yells I again.

"Boom!" says the Ole Virginia.

This was the biggest shot of the lot, and she surely cut loose. I ought to have been halfway up the hill watching things from a safe distance, but I wasn't. Lucky for me the shaft was a little on the drift, so she didn't quite shoot my way. But she distributed about a ton over those renegades. They sort of half got to their feet uncertain.

"Otra vez!" yells I once more, as bold as if I could keep her shooting all day.

It was just a cold, raw blazer; and if it didn't go through I could see me as an Apache parlour ornament. But it did. Those Chiricahuas give one yell and skipped. It was surely a funny sight, after they got aboard their war ponies, to see them trying to dig out on horses too tired to trot.

I didn't stop to get all the laughs, though. In fact, I give one jump off that ledge, and I lit a-running. A quarter-hoss couldn't have beat me to that shack. There I grabbed old Meat-in-the-pot and made a climb for the tall country, aiming to wait around until dark, and then to pull out for Benson. Johnny Hooper wasn't expected till next day, which was lucky. From where I lay I could see the Apaches camped out beyond my draw, and I didn't doubt they'd visited the place. Along about sunset they all left their camp, and went into the draw, so there, I thinks, I sees a good chance to make a start before dark. I dropped down from the mesa, skirted the butte, and angled down across the country. After I'd gone a half mile from the cliffs, I ran across Johnny Hooper's fresh trail headed towards camp!

My heart jumped right up into my mouth at that. Here was poor old Johnny, a day too early, with a pack-mule of grub, walking inno-cent as a yearling, right into the hands of those hostiles. The trail looked pretty fresh, and Benson's a good long day with a pack animal, so I thought perhaps I might catch him before he runs into trouble. So I ran back on the trail as fast as I could make it. The sun was down by now, and it was getting dusk.

I didn't overtake him, and when I got to the top of the cañon I crawled along very cautious and took a look. Of course, I expected to see everything up in smoke, but I nearly got up and yelled when I see everything all right, and old Sukey, the pack-mule, and Johnny's hoss hitched up as peaceful as babies to the corral.

"*That's* all right!" thinks I, "they're back in their camp, and haven't discovered Johnny yet. I'll snail him out of there."

So I ran down the hill and into the shack. Johnny sat in his chair —what there was of him. He must have got in about two hours before sundown, for they'd had lots of time to put in on him. That's the reason they'd stayed so long up the draw. Poor old Johnny! I was glad it was night, and he was dead. Apaches are the worst Injuns there is for tortures. They cut off the bottoms of old man Wilkins's feet, and stood him on an ant-hill—

In a minute or so, though, my wits gets to work.

"Why ain't the shack burned?" I asks myself, "and why is the hoss and the mule tied all so peaceful to the corral?"

It didn't take long for a man who knows Injins to answer *those* conundrums. The whole thing was a trap—for me—and I'd walked into it, chuckle-headed as a prairie-dog!

With that I makes a run outside—by now it was dark—and listens. Sure enough, I hears hosses. So I makes a rapid sneak back over the trail.

Everything seemed all right till I got up to the rim-rock. Then I heard more hosses—ahead of me. And when I looked back I could see some Injuns already at the shack, and starting to build a fire outside.

In a tight fix, a man is pretty apt to get scared till all hope is gone. Then he is pretty apt to get cool and calm. That was my case. I couldn't go ahead—there was those hosses coming along the trail. I couldn't go back—there was those Injins building the fire. So I skirmished around till I got a bright star right over the trail ahead, and I trained old Meat-in-the-pot to bear on that star, and I made up my mind that when the star was darkened I'd turn loose. So I lay there a while listening. By and by the star was blotted out, and I cut loose, and old Meat-in-the-pot missed fire—she never did it before nor since—I think that cartridge—

Well, I don't know where the Injins came from, but it seemed as if the hammer had hardly clicked before three or four of them had piled on me. I put up the best fight I could, for I wasn't figuring to be caught alive, and this miss-fire deal had fooled me all along the line. They surely had a lively time. I expected every minute to feel a knife in my back, but when I didn't get it then I knew they wanted to bring me in alive, and that made me fight harder. First and last we rolled and plunged all the way from the rim-rock down to the cañon-bed. Then one of the Injins sung out:

"Maria!"

And I thought of that renegade Mexican, and what I'd heard about him, and that made me fight harder yet.

But after we'd fought down to the cañon-bed, and had lost most of our skin, a half-dozen more fell on me, and in less than no time they had me tied. Then they picked me up and carried me over to where they'd built a big fire by the corral.

Uncle Jim stopped with an air of finality, and began lazily to refill his pipe. From the open mud fireplace he picked a coal. Outside, the rain, faithful to the prophecy of the wide-ringed sun, beat fitfully against the roof.

"That was the closest call I ever had," said he at last.

"But, Uncle Jim," we cried in a confused chorus, "how did you get away? What did the Indians do to you? Who rescued you?"

Uncle Jim chuckled.

"The first man I saw sitting at that fire," said he, "was Lieutenant Price of the United States Army, and by him was Tom Horn.

"'What's this?' he asks, and Horn talks to the Injins in Apache.

"'They say they've caught Maria,' translates Horn back again.

"'Maria nothing!' says Lieutenant Price. 'This is Jim Fox. I know him.'

"So they turned me loose. It seems the troops had driven off the renegades an hour before."

"And the Indians who caught you, Uncle Jim? You said they were Indians."

"Were Tonto Basin Apaches," explained the old man—"government scouts under Tom Horn."

# A Corner in Horses

It was dark night. The stray-herd bellowed frantically from one of the big corrals; the cow-and-calf-herd from a second. Already the remuda, driven in from the open plains, scattered about the thousand acres of pasture. Away from the conveniences of fence and corral, men would have had to patrol all night. Now, however, everyone was gathered about the camp fire.

Probably forty cowboys were in the group, representing all types, from old John, who had been in the business forty years, and had punched from the Rio Grande to the Pacific, to the Kid, who would have given his chance of salvation if he could have been taken for ten years older than he was. At the moment Jed Parker was holding forth to his friend Johnny Stone in reference to another old crony who had that evening joined the round-up.

"Johnny," inquired Jed with elaborate gravity, and entirely ignoring the presence of the subject of conversation, "what is that thing just beyond the fire, and where did it come from?"

Johnny Stone squinted to make sure.

"That?" he replied. "Oh, this evenin' the dogs see something run down a hole, and they dug it out, and that's what they got."

The newcomer grinned.

"The trouble with you fellows," he proffered, "is that you're so plumb alkalied you don't know the real thing when you see it."

"That's right," supplemented Windy Bill drily. "*He* come from New York."

"No!" cried Jed. "You don't say so? Did he come in one box or in two?"

Under cover of the laugh, the newcomer made a raid on the dutch ovens and pails. Having filled his plate, he squatted on his heels and fell to his belated meal. He was a tall, slab-sided individual, with a lean, leathery face, a sweeping white moustache, and a grave and sardonic eye. His leather chaps were plain and worn, and his hat had been fashioned by time and wear into much individuality. I was not surprised to hear him nicknamed Sacatone Bill.

"Just ask him how he got that game foot," suggested Johnny Stone to me in an undertone, so, of course, I did not.

Later someone told me that the lameness resulted from his refusal of an urgent invitation to return across a river. Mr. Sacatone Bill happened not to be riding his own horse at the time.

The Cattleman dropped down beside me a moment later.

"I wish," said he in a low voice, "we could get that fellow talking. He is a queer one. Pretty well educated apparently. Claims to be writing a book of memoirs. Sometimes he will open up in good shape, and sometimes he will not. It does no good to ask him direct, and he is as shy as an old crow when you try to lead him up to a subject. We must just lie low and trust to Providence."

A man was playing on the mouth organ. He played excellently well, with all sorts of variations and frills. We smoked in silence. The deep rumble of the cattle filled the air with its diapason. Always the shrill coyotes raved out in the mesquite. Sacatone Bill had finished his meal, and had gone to sit by Jed Parker, his old friend. They talked together low-voiced. The evening grew, and the eastern sky silvered over the mountains in anticipation of the moon.

Sacatone Bill suddenly threw back his head and laughed.

"Reminds me of the time I went to Colorado!" he cried.

"He's off!" whispered the Cattleman.

A dead silence fell on the circle. Everybody shifted position the better to listen to the story of Sacatone Bill.


About ten year ago I got plumb sick of punchin' cows around my part of the country. She hadn't rained since Noah, and I'd forgot what water outside a pail or a trough looked like. So I scouted around inside of me to see what part of the world I'd jump to, and as I seemed to know as little of Colorado and minin' as anything else, I made up the pint of bean soup I call my brains to go there. So I catches me a buyer at Benson and turns over my pore little bunch of cattle and prepared to fly. The last day I hauled up about twenty good buckets of water and threw her up against the cabin. My buyer was settin' his hoss waitin' for me to get ready. He didn't say nothin' until we'd got down about ten mile or so.

"Mr. Hicks," says he, hesitatin' like, "I find it a good rule in this country not to overlook other folks' plays, but I'd take it mighty kind if you'd explain those actions of yours with the pails of water."

"Mr. Jones," says I, "it's very simple. I built that shack five year ago, and it's never rained since. I just wanted to settle in my mind whether or not that damn roof leaked."

So I quit Arizona, and in about a week I see my reflection in the winders of a little place called Cyanide in the Colorado mountains.

Fellows, she was a bird. They wasn't a pony in sight, nor a squar' foot of land that wasn't either street or straight up. It made me plumb lonesome for a country where you could see a long ways even if you didn't see much. And this early in the evenin' they wasn't hardly any-body in the streets at all.

I took a look at them dark, gloomy, old mountains, and a sniff at a breeze that would have frozen the whiskers of hope, and I made a dive for the nearest lit winder. They was a sign over it that just said:

## THIS IS A SALOON

I was glad they labelled her. I'd never have known it. They had a fifteen-year-old kid tendin' bar, no games goin', and not a soul in the place.

"Sorry to disturb your repose, bub," says I, "but see if you can sort out any rye among them collections of sassapariller of yours."

I took a drink, and then another to keep it company—I was be-ginnin' to sympathise with anythin' lonesome. Then I kind of saun-tered out to the back room where the hurdy-gurdy ought to be. Sure enough, there was a girl settin' on the pianner stool, another in a chair, and a nice shiny Jew drummer danglin' his feet from a table. They looked up when they see me come in, and went right on talkin'.

"Hello, girls!" says I.

At that they stopped talkin' complete.

"How's tricks?" says I.

"Who's your woolly friend?" the shiny Jew asks of the girls.

I looked at him a minute, but I see he'd been raised a pet, and then, too, I was so hungry for sassiety I was willin' to pass a bet or two.

"Don't you *admire* these cow gents?" snickers one of the girls.

"Play somethin', sister," says I to the one at the pianner.

She just grinned at me.

"Interdooce me," says the drummer in a kind of a way that made them all laugh a heap.

"Give us a tune," I begs, tryin' to be jolly, too.

"She don't know any pieces," says the Jew.

"Don't you?" I asks pretty sharp.

"No," says she.

"Well, I do," says I.

I walked up to her, jerked out my guns, and reached around both sides of her to the pianner. I run the muzzles up and down the keyboard two or three times, and then shot out half a dozen keys.

"That's the piece I know," says I.

But the other girl and the Jew drummer had punched the breeze.

The girl at the pianner just grinned, and pointed to the winder where they was some ragged glass hangin'. She was dead game.

"Say, Susie," says I, "you're all right, but your friends is tur'ble. I may be rough, and I ain't never been curried below the knees, but I'm better to tie to than them sons of guns."

"I believe it," says she.

So we had a drink at the bar, and started out to investigate the wonders of Cyanide.

Say, that night *was* a wonder. Susie faded after about three drinks, but I didn't seem to mind that. I hooked up to another saloon kept by a thin Dutchman. A fat Dutchman is stupid, but a thin one is all right.

In ten minutes I had more friends in Cyanide than they is fiddlers in hell. I begun to conclude Cyanide wasn't so lonesome. About four o'clock in comes a little Irishman about four foot high, with more upper lip than a muley cow, and enough red hair to make an artificial aurorer borealis. He had big red hands with freckles pasted onto them, and stiff red hairs standin' up separate and lonesome like signal stations. Also his legs was bowed.

He gets a drink at the bar, and stands back and yells:

"God bless the Irish and let the Dutch rustle!"

Now, this was none of my town, so I just stepped back of the end of the bar quick where I wouldn't stop no lead. The shootin' didn't begin.

"Probably Dutchy didn't take no note of what the locoed little dogie *did* say," thinks I to myself.

The Irishman bellied up to the bar again, and pounded on it with his fist.

"Look here!" he yells. "Listen to what I'm tellin' ye! God bless the Irish and let the Dutch rustle! Do ye hear me?"

"Sure, I hear ye," says Dutchy, and goes on swabbin' his bar with a towel.

At that my soul just grew sick. I asked the man next to me why Dutchy didn't kill the little fellow.

"Kill him!" says this man. "What for?"

"For insultin' of him, of course."

"Oh, he's drunk," says the man, as if that explained anythin'.

That settled it with me. I left that place, and went home, and it wasn't more than four o'clock, neither. No, I don't call four o'clock late. It may be a little late for night before last, but it's just the shank of the evenin' for to-night.

Well, it took me six weeks and two days to go broke. I didn't know sic 'em about minin'; and before long I *knew* that I didn't know sic 'em. Most all day I poked around them mountains—not like our'n— too much timber to be comfortable. At night I got to droppin' in at Dutchy's. He had a couple of quiet games goin', and they was one fellow among that lot of grubbin' prairie dogs that had heerd tell that cows had horns. He was the wisest of the bunch on the cattle business. So I stowed away my consolation, and made out to forget comparing Colorado with God's country.

About three times a week this Irishman I told you of—name O'Toole—comes bulgin' in. When he was sober he talked minin' high, wide, and handsome. When he was drunk he pounded both fists on the bar and yelled for action, tryin' to get Dutchy on the peck.

"God bless the Irish and let the Dutch rustle!" he yells about six times. "Say, do you hear?"

"Sure," says Dutchy, calm as a milk cow, "sure, I hears ye!"

I was plumb sorry for O'Toole. I'd like to have given him a run; but, of course, I couldn't take it up without makin' myself out a friend of this Dutchy party, and I couldn't stand for that. But I did tackle Dutchy about it one night when they wasn't nobody else there.

"Dutchy," says I, "what makes you let that bow-legged cross between a bulldog and a flamin' red sunset tromp on you so? It looks to me like you're plumb spiritless."

Dutchy stopped wipin' glasses for a minute.

"Just you hold on," says he. "I ain't ready yet. Bimeby I make him sick; also those others who laugh with him."

He had a little grey flicker in his eye, and I thinks to myself that maybe they'd get Dutchy on the peck yet.

As I said, I went broke in just six weeks and two days. And I was broke a plenty. No hold-outs anywhere. It was a heap long ways to cows; and I'd be teetotally chawed up and spit out if I was goin' to join these minin' terrapins defacin' the bosom of nature. It sure looked to me like hard work.

While I was figurin' what next, Dutchy came in. Which I was tur'-ble surprised at that, but I said good-mornin' and would he rest his poor feet.

"You like to make some money?" he asks.

"That depends," says I, "on how easy it is."

"It is easy," says he. "I want you to buy hosses for me."

"Hosses! Sure!" I yells, jumpin' up. "You bet you! Why, hosses is where I live! What hosses do you want?"

"All hosses," says he, calm as a faro dealer.

"What?" says I. "Elucidate, my bucko. I don't take no such blanket order. Spread your cards."

"I mean just that," says he. "I want you to buy all the hosses in this camp, and in the mountains. Every one."

"Whew!" I whistles. "That's a large order. But I'm your meat."

"Come with me, then," says he. I hadn't but just got up, but I went with him to his little old poison factory. Of course, I hadn't had no breakfast; but he staked me to a Kentucky breakfast. What's a Kentucky breakfast? Why, a Kentucky breakfast is a three-pound steak, a bottle of whisky, and a setter dog. What's the dog for? Why, to eat the steak, of course.

We come to an agreement. I was to get two-fifty a head commission. So I started out. There wasn't many hosses in that country, and what there was the owners hadn't much use for unless it was to work a whim. I picked up about a hundred head quick enough, and reported to Dutchy.

"How about burros and mules?" I asks Dutchy.

"They goes," says he. "Mules same as hosses; burros four bits a head to you."

At the end of a week I had a remuda of probably two hundred animals. We kept them over the hills in some "parks," as these sots call meadows in that country. I rode into town and told Dutchy.

"Got them all?" he asks.

"All but a cross-eyed buckskin that's mean, and the bay mare that Noah bred to."

"Get them," says he.

"The bandits want too much," I explains.

"Get them anyway," says he.

I went away and got them. It was scand'lous; such prices.

When I hit Cyanide again I ran into scenes of wild excitement. The whole passel of them was on that one street of their'n, talkin' sixteen ounces to the pound. In the middle was Dutchy, drunk as a soldier— just plain foolish drunk.

"Good Lord!" thinks I to myself, "he ain't celebratin' gettin' that bunch of buzzards, is he?"

But I found he wasn't that bad. When he caught sight of me, he fell on me drivellin'.

"Look there!" he weeps, showin' me a letter.

I was the last to come in; so I kept that letter—here she is. I'll read her.

DEAR DUTCHY:—I suppose you thought I'd flew the coop, but I haven't and this is to prove it. Pack up your outfit and hit the trail. I've made the biggest free gold strike you ever see. I'm sending you specimens. There's tons just like it, tons and tons. I got all the claims I can hold myself; but there's heaps more. I've writ to Johnny and Ed at Denver to come on. Don't give this away. Make tracks. Come in to Buck Cañon in the Whetstones and oblige.

Yours truly,
Henry Smith.

Somebody showed me a handful of white rock with yeller streaks in it. His eyes was bulgin' until you could have hung your hat on them. That O'Toole party was walkin' around, wettin' his lips with his tongue and swearin' soft.

"God bless the Irish and let the Dutch rustle!" says he. "And the fool had to get drunk and give it away!"

The excitement was just started, but it didn't last long. The crowd got the same notion at the same time, and it just melted. Me and Dutchy was left alone.

I went home. Pretty soon a fellow named Jimmy Tack come around a little out of breath.

"Say, you know that buckskin you bought off'n me?" says he, "I want to buy him back."

"Oh, you do," says I.

"Yes," says he. "I've got to leave town for a couple of days, and I got to have somethin' to pack."

"Wait and I'll see," says I.

Outside the door I met another fellow.

"Look here," he stops me with. "How about that bay mare I sold you? Can you call that sale off? I got to leave town for a day or two and—"

"Wait," says I. "I'll see."

By the gate was another hurryin' up.

"Oh, yes," says I when he opens his mouth. "I know all your troubles. You have to leave town for a couple of days, and you want back that lizard you sold me. Well, wait."

After that I had to quit the main street and dodge back of the hog ranch. They was all headed my way. I was as popular as a snake in a prohibition town.

I hit Dutchy's by the back door.

"Do you want to sell hosses?" I asks. "Everyone in town wants to buy."

Dutchy looked hurt.

"I wanted to keep them for the valley market," says he, "but— How much did you give Jimmy Tack for his buckskin?"

"Twenty," says I.

"Well, let him have it for eighty," says Dutchy; "and the others in proportion."

I lay back and breathed hard.

"Sell them all, but the one best hoss," says he—"no, the *two* best."

"Holy smoke!" says I, gettin' my breath. "If you mean that, Dutchy, you lend me another gun and give me a drink."

He done so, and I went back home to where the whole camp of Cyanide was waitin'.

I got up and made them a speech and told them I'd sell them hosses all right, and to come back. Then I got an Injin boy to help, and we rustled over the remuda and held them in a blind cañon. Then I called up these miners one at a time, and made bargains with them. Roar! Well, you could hear them at Denver, they tell me, and the weather reports said, "Thunder in the mountains." But it was cash on delivery, and they all paid up. They had seen that white quartz with the gold stickin' into it, and that's the same as a dose of loco to miner gents.

Why didn't I take a hoss and start first? I did think of it—for about one second. I wouldn't stay in that country then for a million dollars a minute. I was plumb sick and loathin' it, and just waitin' to make high jumps back to Arizona. So I wasn't aimin' to join this stampede, and didn't have no vivid emotions.

They got to fightin' on which should get the first hoss; so I bent my gun on them and made them draw lots. They roared some more, but done so; and as fast as each one handed over his dust or dinero he made a rush for his cabin, piled on his saddle and pack, and pulled his freight in a cloud of dust. It was sure a grand stampede, and I enjoyed it no limit.

So by sundown I was alone with the Injin. Those two hundred head brought in about twenty thousand dollars. It was heavy, but I could carry it. I was about alone in the landscape; and there were the two best hosses I had saved out for Dutchy. I was sure some tempted. But I had enough to get home on anyway; and I never yet drank behind the bar, even if I might hold up the saloon from the floor. So I grieved some inside that I was so tur'ble conscientious, shouldered the sacks, and went down to find Dutchy.

I met him headed his way, and carryin' of a sheet of paper.

"Here's your dinero," says I, dumpin' the four big sacks on the ground.

He stooped over and hefted them. Then he passed one over to me.

"What's that for?" I asks.

"For you," says he.

"My commission ain't that much," I objects.

"You've earned it," says he, "and you might have skipped with the whole wad."

"How did you know I wouldn't?" I asks.

"Well," says he, and I noted that jag of his had flew. "You see, I was behind that rock up there, and I had you covered."

I saw; and I began to feel better about bein' so tur'ble conscientious.

We walked a little ways without sayin' nothin'.

"But ain't you goin' to join the game?" I asks.

"Guess not," says he, jinglin' of his gold. "I'm satisfied."

"But if you don't get a wiggle on you, you are sure goin' to get left on those gold claims," says I.

"There ain't no gold claims," says he.

"But Henry Smith—" I cries.

"There ain't no Henry Smith," says he.

I let that soak in about six inches.

"But there's a Buck Cañon," I pleads. "Please say there's a Buck Cañon."

"Oh, yes, there's a Buck Cañon," he allows. "Nice limestone formation—make good hard water."

"Well, you're a marvel," says I.

We walked on together down to Dutchy's saloon. We stopped outside.

"Now," says he, "I'm goin' to take one of those hosses and go somewheres else. Maybe you'd better do likewise on the other."

"You bet I will," says I.

He turned around and tacked up the paper he was carryin'. It was a sign. It read:

## THE DUTCH HAS RUSTLED

"Nice sentiment," says I. "It will be appreciated when the crowd comes back from that little *pasear* into Buck Cañon. But why not tack her up where the trail hits the camp? Why on this particular door?"

"Well," said Dutchy, squintin' at the sign sideways, "you see I sold this place day before yesterday—to Mike O'Toole."

# The Two-Gun Man

## I

### The Cattle Rustlers

Buck Johnson was American born, but with a black beard and a dignity of manner that had earned him the title of Señor. He had drifted into southeastern Arizona in the days of Cochise and Victorio and Geronimo. He had persisted, and so in time had come to control the water—and hence the grazing—of nearly all the Soda Springs Valley. His troubles were many, and his difficulties great. There were the ordinary problems of lean and dry years. There were also the extraordinary problems of devastating Apaches; rivals for early and ill-defined range rights—and cattle rustlers.

Señor Buck Johnson was a man of capacity, courage, directness of method, and perseverance. Especially the latter. Therefore he had survived to see the Apaches subdued, the range rights adjusted, his cattle increased to thousands, grazing the area of a principality. Now, all the energy and fire of his frontiersman's nature he had turned to wiping out the third uncertainty of an uncertain business. He found it a task of some magnitude.

For Señor Buck Johnson lived just north of that terra incognita filled with the mystery of a double chance of death from man or the flaming desert known as the Mexican border. There, by natural gravitation, gathered all the desperate characters of three States and two republics. He who rode into it took good care that no one should ride behind him, lived warily, slept light, and breathed deep when once he had again sighted the familiar peaks of Cochise's Stronghold. No one professed knowledge of those who dwelt therein. They moved, mysterious as the desert illusions that compassed them about. As you rode, the ranges of mountains visibly changed form, the monstrous, snaky, sea-like growths of the cactus clutched at your stirrup, mock lakes sparkled and dissolved in the middle distance, the sun beat hot and merciless, the powdered dry alkali beat hotly and mercilessly back—and strange, grim men, swarthy, bearded, heavily armed, with red-rimmed unshifting eyes, rode silently out of the mists of illusion to look on you steadily, and then to ride silently back into the desert haze. They might be only the herders of the gaunt cattle, or again they might belong to the Lost Legion that peopled the country. All you could know was that of the men who entered in, but few returned.

Directly north of this unknown land you encountered parallel fences running across the country. They enclosed nothing, but offered a check to the cattle drifting toward the clutch of the renegades, and an obstacle to swift, dashing forays.

Of cattle-rustling there are various forms. The boldest consists quite simply of running off a bunch of stock, hustling it over the Mexican line, and there selling it to some of the big Sonora ranch owners. Generally this sort means war. Also are there subtler means, grading in skill from the re-branding through a wet blanket, through the crafty refashioning of a brand to the various methods of separating the cow from her unbranded calf. In the course of his task Señor Buck Johnson would have to do with them all, but at present he existed in a state of warfare, fighting an enemy who stole as the Indians used to steal.

Already he had fought two pitched battles, and had won them both. His cattle increased, and he became rich. Nevertheless he knew that constantly his resources were being drained. Time and again he and his new Texas foreman, Jed Parker, had followed the trail of a stampeded bunch of twenty or thirty, followed them on down through the Soda Springs Valley to the cut drift fences, there to abandon them. For, as yet, an armed force would be needed to penetrate the borderland. Once he and his men had experienced the glory of a night pursuit. Then, at the drift fences, he had fought one of his battles. But it was impossible adequately to patrol all parts of a range bigger than some Eastern States.

Buck Johnson did his best, but it was like stopping with sand the innumerable little leaks of a dam. Did his riders watch toward the Chiricahuas, then a score of beef steers disappeared from Grant's Pass forty miles away. Pursuit here meant leaving cattle unguarded there. It was useless, and the Señor soon perceived that sooner or later he must strike in offence.

For this purpose he began slowly to strengthen the forces of his riders. Men were coming in from Texas. They were good men, addicted to the grass-rope, the double cinch, and the ox-bow stirrup. Señor Johnson wanted men who could shoot, and he got them.

"Jed," said Señor Johnson to his foreman, "the next son of a gun that rustles any of our cows is sure loading himself full of trouble.

We'll hit his trail and will stay with it, and we'll reach his cattle-rustling conscience with a rope."

So it came about that a little army crossed the drift fences and entered the border country. Two days later it came out, and mighty pleased to be able to do so. The rope had not been used.

The reason for the defeat was quite simple. The thief had run his cattle through the lava beds where the trail at once became difficult to follow. This delayed the pursuing party; they ran out of water, and, as there was among them not one man well enough acquainted with the country to know where to find more, they had to return.

"No use, Buck," said Jed. "We'd any of us come in on a gun play, but we can't buck the desert. We'll have to get someone who knows the country."

"That's all right—but where?" queried Johnson.

"There's Pereza," suggested Parker. "It's the only town down near that country."

"Might get someone there," agreed the Señor.

Next day he rode away in search of a guide. The third evening he was back again, much discouraged.

"The country's no good," he explained. "The regular inhabitants're a set of Mexican bums and old soaks. The cowmen's all from north and don't know nothing more than we do. I found lots who claimed to know that country, but when I told 'em what I wanted they shied like a colt. I couldn't hire 'em, for no money, to go down in that country. They ain't got the nerve. I took two days to her, too, and rode out to a ranch where they said a man lived who knew all about it down there. Nary riffle. Man looked all right, but his tail went down like the rest when I told him what we wanted. Seemed plumb scairt to death. Says he lives too close to the gang. Says they'd wipe him out sure if he done it. Seemed plumb *scairt*." Buck Johnson grinned. "I told him so and he got hosstyle right off. Didn't seem no ways scairt of me. I don't know what's the matter with that outfit down there. They're plumb terrorised."

That night a bunch of steers was stolen from the very corrals of the home ranch. The home ranch was far north, near Fort Sherman itself, and so had always been considered immune from attack. Consequently these steers were very fine ones.

For the first time Buck Johnson lost his head and his dignity. He ordered the horses.

"I'm going to follow that —— —— into Sonora," he shouted to Jed Parker. "This thing's got to stop!"

"You can't make her, Buck," objected the foreman. "You'll get held up by the desert, and, if that don't finish you, they'll tangle you up in all those little mountains down there, and ambush you, and massacre you. You know it damn well."

"I don't give a ———," exploded Señor Johnson, "if they do. No man can slap my face and not get a run for it."

Jed Parker communed with himself.

"Señor," said he, at last, "it's no good; you can't do it. You got to have a guide. You wait three days and I'll get you one."

"You can't do it," insisted the Señor. "I tried every man in the district."

"Will you wait three days?" repeated the foreman.

Johnson pulled loose his latigo. His first anger had cooled.

"All right," he agreed, "and you can say for me that I'll pay five thousand dollars in gold and give all the men and horses he needs to the man who has the nerve to get back that bunch of cattle, and bring in the man who rustled them. I'll sure make this a test case."

So Jed Parker set out to discover his man with nerve.

## II

### The Man with Nerve

At about ten o'clock of the Fourth of July a rider topped the summit of the last swell of land, and loped his animal down into the single street of Pereza. The buildings on either side were flat-roofed and coated with plaster. Over the sidewalks extended wooden awnings, beneath which opened very wide doors into the coolness of saloons. Each of these places ran a bar, and also games of roulette, faro, craps, and stud poker. Even this early in the morning every game was patronised.

The day was already hot with the dry, breathless, but exhilarating, heat of the desert. A throng of men idling at the edge of the sidewalks, jostling up and down their centre, or eddying into the places of amusement, acknowledged the power of summer by loosening their collars, carrying their coats on their arms. They were as yet busily engaged in recognising acquaintances. Later they would drink freely and gamble, and perhaps fight. Toward all but those whom they recognised they preserved an attitude of potential suspicion, for here were gathered the "bad men" of the border countries. A certain jealousy or touchy egotism lest the other man be considered quicker on the trigger, bolder, more aggressive than himself, kept each strung to tension. An occasional shot attracted little notice. Men in the cow-countries shoot as casually as we strike matches, and some subtle instinct told them that the reports were harmless.

As the rider entered the one street, however, a more definite cause of excitement drew the loose population toward the centre of the road. Immediately their mass blotted out what had interested them. Curiosity attracted the saunterers; then in turn the frequenters of the bars and gambling games. In a very few moments the barkeepers, gamblers, and look-out men, held aloof only by the necessities of their calling, alone of all the population of Pereza were not included in the newly-formed ring.

The stranger pushed his horse resolutely to the outer edge of the crowd where, from his point of vantage, he could easily overlook their heads. He was a quiet-appearing young fellow, rather neatly dressed in the border costume, rode a "centre fire," or single-cinch, saddle, and wore no chaps. He was what is known as a "two-gun man": that is to say, he wore a heavy Colt's revolver on either hip. The fact that the lower ends of his holsters were tied down, in order to facilitate the easy withdrawal of the revolvers, seemed to indicate that he expected to use them. He had furthermore a quiet grey eye, with the glint of steel that bore out the inference of the tied holsters.

The newcomer dropped his reins on his pony's neck, eased himself to an attitude of attention, and looked down gravely on what was taking place.

He saw over the heads of the bystanders a tall, muscular, wild-eyed man, hatless, his hair rumpled into staring confusion, his right sleeve rolled to his shoulder, a wicked-looking nine-inch knife in his hand, and a red bandana handkerchief hanging by one corner from his teeth.

"What's biting the locoed stranger?" the young man inquired of his neighbour.

The other frowned at him darkly.

"Dares anyone to take the other end of that handkerchief in his teeth, and fight it out without letting go."

"Nice joyful proposition," commented the young man.

He settled himself to closer attention. The wild-eyed man was talking rapidly. What he said cannot be printed here. Mainly was it derogatory of the southern countries. Shortly it became boastful of the northern, and then of the man who uttered it. He swaggered up and down, becoming always the more insolent as his challenge remained untaken.

"Why don't you take him up?" inquired the young man, after a moment.

"Not me!" negatived the other vigorously. "I'll go yore little old gunfight to a finish, but I don't want any cold steel in mine. Ugh! it gives me the shivers. It's a reg'lar Mexican trick! With a gun it's down and out, but this knife work is too slow and searchin'."

The newcomer said nothing, but fixed his eye again on the raging man with the knife.

"Don't you reckon he's bluffing?" he inquired.

"Not any!" denied the other with emphasis. "He's jest drunk enough to be crazy mad."

The newcomer shrugged his shoulders and cast his glance searchingly over the fringe of the crowd. It rested on a Mexican.

"Hi, Tony! come here," he called.

The Mexican approached, flashing his white teeth.

"Here," said the stranger, "lend me your knife a minute."

The Mexican, anticipating sport of his own peculiar kind, obeyed with alacrity.

"You fellows make me tired," observed the stranger, dismounting. "He's got the whole townful of you bluffed to a standstill. Damn if I don't try his little game."

He hung his coat on his saddle, shouldered his way through the press, which parted for him readily, and picked up the other corner of the handkerchief.

"Now, you mangy son of a gun," said he.

### III

### The Agreement

Jed Parker straightened his back, rolled up the bandana handkerchief, and thrust it into his pocket, hit flat with his hand the touselled mass of his hair, and thrust the long hunting knife into its sheath.

"You're the man I want," said he.

Instantly the two-gun man had jerked loose his weapons and was covering the foreman.

"*Am* I!" he snarled.

"Not jest that way," explained Parker. "My gun is on my hoss, and you can have this old toad-sticker if you want it. I been looking for you, and took this way of finding you. Now, let's go talk."

The stranger looked him in the eye for nearly a half minute without lowering his revolvers.

"I go you," said he briefly, at last.

But the crowd, missing the purport, and in fact the very occurrence of this colloquy, did not understand. It thought the bluff had been called, and naturally, finding harmless what had intimidated it, gave way to an exasperated impulse to get even.

"You ———bluffer!" shouted a voice, "don't you think you can run any such ranikaboo here!"

Jed Parker turned humorously to his companion.

"Do we get that talk?" he inquired gently.

For answer the two-gun man turned and walked steadily in the direction of the man who had shouted. The latter's hand strayed uncertainly toward his own weapon, but the movement paused when the stranger's clear, steel eye rested on it.

"This gentleman," pointed out the two-gun man softly, "is an old friend of mine. Don't you get to calling of him names."

His eye swept the bystanders calmly.

"Come on, Jack," said he, addressing Parker.

On the outskirts he encountered the Mexican from whom he had borrowed the knife.

"Here, Tony," said he with a slight laugh, "here's a *peso*. You'll find your knife back there where I had to drop her."

He entered a saloon, nodded to the proprietor, and led the way through it to a box-like room containing a board table and two chairs.

"Make good," he commanded briefly.

"I'm looking for a man with nerve," explained Parker, with equal succinctness. "You're the man."

"Well?"

"Do you know the country south of here?"

The stranger's eyes narrowed.

"Proceed," said he.

"I'm foreman of the Lazy Y of Soda Springs Valley range," explained Parker. "I'm looking for a man with sand enough and *sabe* of the country enough to lead a posse after cattle-rustlers into the border country."

"I live in this country," admitted the stranger.

"So do plenty of others, but their eyes stick out like two raw oysters when you mention the border country. Will you tackle it?"

"What's the proposition?"

"Come and see the old man. He'll put it to you."

They mounted their horses and rode the rest of the day. The desert compassed them about, marvellously changing shape and colour, and every character, with all the noiselessness of phantasmagoria. At evening the desert stars shone steady and unwinking, like the flames of candles. By moonrise they came to the home ranch.

The buildings and corrals lay dark and silent against the moonlight that made of the plain a sea of mist. The two men unsaddled their horses and turned them loose in the wire-fenced "pasture," the necessary noises of their movements sounding sharp and clear against the velvet hush of the night. After a moment they walked stiffly past the sheds and cook shanty, past the men's bunk houses, and the tall windmill silhouetted against the sky, to the main building of the home ranch under its great cottonwoods. There a light still burned, for this was the third day, and Buck Johnson awaited his foreman.

Jed Parker pushed in without ceremony.

"Here's your man, Buck," said he.

The stranger had stepped inside and carefully closed the door behind him. The lamplight threw into relief the bold, free lines of his face, the details of his costume powdered thick with alkali, the shiny butts of the two guns in their open holsters tied at the bottom. Equally it defined the resolute countenance of Buck Johnson turned up in inquiry. The two men examined each other—and liked each other at once.

"How are you," greeted the cattleman.

"Good-evening," responded the stranger.

"Sit down," invited Buck Johnson.

The stranger perched gingerly on the edge of a chair, with an appearance less of embarrassment than of habitual alertness.

"You'll take the job?" inquired the Señor.

"I haven't heard what it is," replied the stranger.

"Parker here—?"

"Said you'd explain."

"Very well," said Buck Johnson. He paused a moment, collecting his thoughts. "There's too much cattle-rustling here. I'm going to stop it. I've got good men here ready to take the job, but no one who knows the country south. Three days ago I had a bunch of cattle stolen right here from the home-ranch corrals, and by one man, at that. It wasn't much of a bunch—about twenty head—but I'm going to make a starter right here, and now. I'm going to get that bunch back, and the man who stole them, if I have to go to hell to do it. And I'm going to do the same with every case of rustling that comes up from now on. I don't care if it's only one cow, I'm going to get it back—every trip. Now, I want to know if you'll lead a posse down into the south country and bring out that last bunch, and the man who rustled them?"

"I don't know—" hesitated the stranger.

"I offer you five thousand dollars in gold if you'll bring back those cows and the man who stole 'em," repeated Buck Johnson. "And I'll give you all the horses and men you think you need."

"I'll do it," replied the two-gun man promptly.

"Good!" cried Buck Johnson, "and you better start to-morrow."

"I shall start to-night—right now."

"Better yet. How many men do you want, and grub for how long?"

"I'll play her a lone hand."

"Alone!" exclaimed Johnson, his confidence visibly cooling. "Alone! Do you think you can make her?"

"I'll be back with those cattle in not more than ten days."

"And the man," supplemented the Señor.

"And the man. What's more, I want that money here when I come in. I don't aim to stay in this country over night."

A grin overspread Buck Johnson's countenance. He understood.

"Climate not healthy for you?" he hazarded. "I guess you'd be safe enough all right with us. But suit yourself. The money will be here."

"That's agreed?" insisted the two-gun man.

"Sure."

"I want a fresh horse—I'll leave mine—he's a good one. I want a little grub."

"All right. Parker'll fit you out."

The stranger rose.

"I'll see you in about ten days."

"Good luck," Señor Buck Johnson wished him.

## IV

### The Accomplishment

The next morning Buck Johnson took a trip down into the "pasture" of five hundred wire-fenced acres.

"He means business," he confided to Jed Parker, on his return. "That cavallo of his is a heap sight better than the Shorty horse we let him take. Jed, you found your man with nerve, all right. How did you do it?"

The two settled down to wait, if not with confidence, at least with interest. Sometimes, remembering the desperate character of the outlaws, their fierce distrust of any intruder, the wildness of the country, Buck Johnson and his foreman inclined to the belief that the stranger had undertaken a task beyond the powers of any one man. Again, remembering the stranger's cool grey eye, the poise of his demeanour, the quickness of his movements, and the two guns with tied holsters to permit of easy withdrawal, they were almost persuaded that he might win.

"He's one of those long-chance fellows," surmised Jed. "He likes excitement. I see that by the way he takes up with my knife play. He'd rather leave his hide on the fence than stay in the corral."

"Well, he's all right," replied Señor Buck Johnson, "and if he ever gets back, which same I'm some doubtful of, his dinero'll be here for him."

In pursuance of this he rode in to Willets, where shortly the overland train brought him from Tucson the five thousand dollars in double eagles.

In the meantime the regular life of the ranch went on. Each morning Sang, the Chinese cook, rang the great bell, summoning the men. They ate, and then caught up the saddle horses for the day, turning those not wanted from the corral into the pasture. Shortly they jingled away in different directions, two by two, on the slow Spanish trot of the cow-puncher. All day long thus they would ride, without food or water for man or beast, looking the range, identifying the stock, branding the young calves, examining generally into the state of affairs, gazing always with grave eyes on the magnificent, flaming, changing, beautiful, dreadful desert of the Arizona plains. At evening, when the coloured atmosphere, catching the last glow, threw across the Chiricahuas its veil of mystery, they jingled in again, two by two, untired, unhasting, the glory of the desert in their deep-set, steady eyes.

And all the day long, while they were absent, the cattle, too, made their pilgrimage, straggling in singly, in pairs, in bunches, in long files, leisurely, ruminantly, without haste. There, at the long troughs filled by the windmill or the blindfolded pump mule, they drank, then filed away again into the mists of the desert. And Señor Buck Johnson, or his foreman, Parker, examined them for their condition, noting the increase, remarking the strays from another range. Later, perhaps, they, too, rode abroad. The same thing happened at nine other ranches from five to ten miles apart, where dwelt other fierce, silent men all under the authority of Buck Johnson.

And when night fell, and the topaz and violet and saffron and amethyst and mauve and lilac had faded suddenly from the Chiricahuas, like a veil that has been rent, and the ramparts had become slate-grey and then black—the soft-breathed night wandered here and there over the desert, and the land fell under an enchantment even stranger than the day's.

So the days went by, wonderful, fashioning the ways and the characters of men. Seven passed. Buck Johnson and his foreman began to look for the stranger. Eight, they began to speculate. Nine, they doubted. On the tenth they gave him up—and he came.

They knew him first by the soft lowing of cattle. Jed Parker, dazzled by the lamp, peered out from the door, and made him out dimly turning the animals into the corral. A moment later his pony's hoofs impacted softly on the baked earth, he dropped from the saddle and entered the room.

"I'm late," said he briefly, glancing at the clock, which indicated ten; "but I'm here."

His manner was quick and sharp, almost breathless, as though he had been running.

"Your cattle are in the corral: all of them. Have you the money?"

"I have the money here," replied Buck Johnson, laying his hand against a drawer, "and it's ready for you when you've earned it. I don't care so much for the cattle. What I wanted is the man who stole them. Did you bring him?"

"Yes, I brought him," said the stranger. "Let's see that money."

Buck Johnson threw open the drawer, and drew from it the heavy canvas sack.

"It's here. Now bring in your prisoner."

The two-gun man seemed suddenly to loom large in the doorway. The muzzles of his revolvers covered the two before him. His speech came short and sharp.

"I told you I'd bring back the cows and the one who rustled them," he snapped. "I've never lied to a man yet. Your stock is in the corral. I'll trouble you for that five thousand. I'm the man who stole your cattle!"

# O. HENRY

## (William Sydney Porter)

### (1862–1910)

Porter was born in Greensboro, North Carolina, son of a peripatetic physician and a mother who died when he was three. He attended a school kept by an aunt, but dropped out at fifteen to work in his uncle's pharmacy. Illness sent him to Texas in 1882, where he spent some time recuperating on a ranch. There he benefited not only from enforced leisure, but also from the multicultural environs by learning a smattering of French and German and something more of Spanish. His health restored, Porter moved to Austin, where he worked as a bookkeeper, land-office draftsman, and (most critically) as a bank teller. In 1887, he married. Having had some sketches published in the Detroit Free Press, Porter in 1894 bought out The Iconoclast, a violently original periodical founded by William Cowper Brann, a freethinker whose outspoken opinions about organized religion led to his murder in 1898. Brann insisted on retaining the title to his periodical (styling himself Brann, the Iconoclast) so Porter renamed the paper The Rolling Stone, but gave it up a year later, and moved to Houston, where he compiled a column of anecdotes and sketches for the Daily Post.

In 1898, Porter was indicted for embezzlement in Austin. His "crime" was apparently a matter of loose accounting practices then (as even now) customary in Texas banking circles, and he probably would not have been convicted—but suddenly, on his way to the trial, he lost his nerve and switched trains. He headed for New Orleans, and from there to Honduras, where, among other refugees, he met two American outlaws, the Jennings brothers. Porter spent the next year knocking about Central America and Mexico, brushing up on his Spanish and helping the Jenningses spend the proceeds of their most recent robbery.

News of the fatal illness of his wife brought Porter back to Texas

*in 1897, and he was sentenced to five years in the Ohio State Peniten-*
*tiary. The conditions of his incarceration were mild; he worked in the*
*prison pharmacy and was given considerable freedom. His compan-*
*ions included one of the Jennings boys and a number of other engag-*
*ing felons, from whom he heard tales that would provide the basis for*
*some of his subsequent stories. Where "Mark Twain" had found his*
*sobriquet on the river, "O. Henry" found his up the river—though*
*whether the name originally belonged to the author of a medical ref-*
*erence book, a prison guard, or someone else remains unresolved.*

*Let off after three years for good behavior, Porter in 1901 headed*
*for New York City at the behest of the editor of* Ainslee's *Magazine,*
*on the strength of stories written in prison under his new pseudonym.*
*This product of small Southern and Southwestern towns suddenly*
*found himself in the largest city in the United States—and find him-*
*self he did. Reacting to the stimulus of urban life, Porter began to*
*turn out the stories that would make "O. Henry" not only a popular*
*but a beloved name. His output was prodigious despite his increasing*
*dependency on whiskey (he reportedly averaged two quarts a day),*
*and in the few years of life remaining to him he wrote six hundred*
*stories and sketches. Despite the crowded scenes of his fiction, with its*
*Dickensian emphasis on the goodness of humanity even in the worst*
*of circumstances, Porter was something of a loner, who socialized*
*chiefly with his editors. In 1907, he married for a second time. As in*
*the case of Stephen Crane, Porter's productivity may have been ac-*
*celerated by the effects of tuberculosis, which, along with the ravages*
*of alcohol, killed him at the age of forty-eight. By the time he died, he*
*had published—in addition to a highly episodic novel,* Cabbages and
Kings *(1905), based on his Honduras adventures—a dozen collections*
*of his short stories:* The Four Million *(1906),* Heart of the West *(1907),*
*and* The Gentle Grafter *(1908) were among the chief of these; along*
*with a couple of posthumous volumes, they were republished in a col-*
*lected works edition in 1913, greatly increasing his readership.*

*Never more popular than in the years following his death,*
*O. Henry was honored posthumously by an annual award given in*
*his name for the best short story of the year. It was an association*
*that became increasingly ironic as the writer's reputation began to*
*decline, his fame eclipsed by the younger talents whose stories were*
*associated with his name but who disavowed the mechanical tricks*
*that first made him famous. O. Henry's own stories continued to be*
*anthologized in high school readers but seldom elsewhere, and when*
*in the 1950s a motion picture based on three of his best-known tales*
*was made it had little effect on his literary reputation. In a recent*

history of American literature, he was merely listed as one of many writers who used city life for material.

In a time such as ours, when the short story is struggling to survive in the few venues allowed it outside the sanctuary of little magazines, a time moreover distinguished by the minimalist fiction associated with The New Yorker, not much of a case can be made for O. Henry's formulaic and repetitive tales. And yet, to return to them is to find an impressive vitality beyond the tricks of plot and the easy sentimentality of his endings, an intense outpouring of words that at times energizes the page. Long recognized as having set the vernacular fashion for writers like Ring Lardner and Damon Runyon, O. Henry's display of slang is so versatile as to be often incomprehensible. It is, finally, a kind of music, best allowed to flow without interruption, for it carries its own sense. Like the busy, eclectic architecture of Porter's heyday, which for so long suffered obloquy and demolition, O. Henry's stories are a veritable Baghdad of exuberance, bristling with minarets of pure luxuriant style.

He is also very funny. Readers raised on the tearful version of O. Henry found in "The Last Leaf" and "The Gift of the Magi" will be surprised by the hilarity of his other stories, most especially those set in the Southwest. Never mentioned as a Western writer or as a contributor to the "myth" of the cowboy, O. Henry is essential to an absurdist conception of the Far West, with his often loony cowpokes and ineffectual outlaws. His Westerners are obsessive, setting goals that are the essence of comedy, incongruous to the core. If Stephen Crane wrote to disabuse us of the Western myth of heroic cowboys, he had a vital ally in O. Henry, who presupposes a level of heroism hardly conducive to the kinds of inflation of which Wister was at times guilty. At the end of a story like "The Last of the Troubadours," the reader is left without a boot to stand in or a ten-gallon hat in which to . . . put his head. A study in the decline of the cattle-ranching West that so moved Wister and Remington, one that centers on the traditional and often bloody rivalry between cattlemen and sheep herders, O. Henry's story does not belong to the chronicles of the Johnson County War—though at one point it does threaten to provide a Texas annex. With bittersweet irony, the story celebrates the illusoriness of all human affairs, in which the best of intentions like the plans of a mouse can go awry.

O. Henry's New York has gone the way of automats and nickel subway fares, and his city settings now add an unintentional element of quaintness to his sentimental fables; here, one can stroll about at night without fearing harm, and a homeless bum can spend a com-

*fortable winter in jail. Today's urban landscape bears not even the remotest resemblance to O. Henry's fairyland, in which wishes can come true for those who deserve the gift. But, oddly enough, we can still accept his Western settings, for the paradoxical reason that for the vast majority of readers Texas is still a large territory of the mind. The movies have given an extra century of life to the West about which O. Henry wrote. The stories have a quality of perpetual rejuvenation for which any snake-oil doctor would give the remnants of his soul. It is a quality shared with the otherwise different stories of Owen Wister, Frederic Remington, and Stewart E. White—stories which inspired the conventions, and occasionally the scripts, which turned the West into a vast continuum of Saturday matinees and flickering television screens. By such a process of mesmerism and galvanic action, the stories of O. Henry's West are still very much alive.*

# The Ransom of Mack

Me and old Mack Lonsbury, we got out of that Little Hide-and-Seek gold mine affair with about $40,000 apiece. I say "old" Mack; but he wasn't old. Forty-one, I should say; but he always seemed old.

"Andy," he says to me, "I'm tired of hustling. You and me have been working hard together for three years. Say we knock off for a while, and spend some of this idle money we've coaxed our way."

"The proposition hits me just right," says I. "Let's be nabobs a while and see how it feels. What'll we do—take in the Niagara Falls, or buck at faro?"

"For a good many years," says Mack, "I've thought that if I ever had extravagant money I'd rent a two-room cabin somewhere, hire a Chinaman to cook, and sit in my stocking feet and read Buckle's History of Civilization."

"That sounds self-indulgent and gratifying without vulgar ostentation," says I; "and I don't see how money could be better invested. Give me a cuckoo clock and a Sep Winner's Self-Instructor for the Banjo, and I'll join you."

A week afterward me and Mack hits this small town of Piña, about thirty miles out from Denver, and finds an elegant two-room house that just suits us. We deposited half-a-peck of money in the Piña bank and shook hands with every one of the 340 citizens in the town. We brought along the Chinaman and the cuckoo clock and Buckle and the Instructor with us from Denver; and they made the cabin seem like home at once.

Never believe it when they tell you riches don't bring happiness. If you could have seen old Mack sitting in his rocking-chair with his blue-yarn sock feet up in the window and absorbing in that Buckle stuff through his specs you'd have seen a picture of content that would have made Rockefeller jealous. And I was learning to pick out "Old Zip Coon" on the banjo, and the cuckoo was on time with his remarks, and Ah Sing was messing up the atmosphere with the handsomest smell of ham and eggs that ever laid the honeysuckle in the shade. When it got too dark to make out Buckle's nonsense and the notes in the Instructor, me and Mack would light our pipes and talk about science and pearl diving and sciatica and Egypt and spelling and fish and trade-winds and leather and gratitude and eagles, and a lot of subjects that we'd never had time to explain our sentiments about before.

One evening Mack spoke up and asked me if I was much apprised in the habits and policies of women folks.

"Why, yes," says I, in a tone of voice; "I know 'em from Alfred to Omaha. The feminine nature and similitude," says I, "is as plain to my sight as the Rocky Mountains is to a blue-eyed burro. I'm onto all their little sidesteps and punctual discrepancies."

"I tell you, Andy," says Mack, with a kind of sigh. "I never had the least amount of intersection with their predispositions. Maybe I might have had a proneness in respect to their vicinity, but I never took the time. I made my own living since I was fourteen; and I never seemed to get my ratiocinations equipped with the sentiments usually depicted toward the sect. I sometimes wish I had," says old Mack.

"They're an adverse study," says I, "and adapted to points of view. Although they vary in rationale, I have found 'em quite often obviously differing from each other in divergences of contrast."

"It seems to me," goes on Mack, "that a man had better take 'em in and secure his inspirations of the sect when he's young and so preordained. I let my chance go by; and I guess I'm too old now to go hopping into the curriculum."

"Oh, I don't know," I tells him. "Maybe you better credit yourself with a barrel of money and a lot of emancipation from a quantity of uncontent. Still, I don't regret my knowledge of 'em," I says. "It takes a man who understands the symptoms and by-plays of women-folks to take care of himself in this world."

We stayed on in Piña because we liked the place. Some folks might enjoy their money with noise and rapture and locomotion; but me and Mack we had had plenty of turmoils and hotel towels. The people were friendly; Ah Sing got the swing of the grub we liked; Mack and Buckle were as thick as two body-snatchers, and I was hitting out a cordial resemblance to "Buffalo Gals, Can't You Come Out To-night," on the banjo.

One day I got a telegram from Speight, the man that was working a mine I had an interest in out in New Mexico. I had to go out there; and I was gone two months. I was anxious to get back to Piña and enjoy life once more.

When I struck the cabin I nearly fainted. Mack was standing in the door; and if angels ever wept, I saw no reason why they should be smiling then.

That man was a spectacle. Yes; he was worse; he was a spyglass; he was the great telescope in the Lick Observatory. He had on a coat and shiny shoes and a white vest and a high silk hat; and a geranium as big as an order of spinach was spiked onto his front. And he was smirking and warping his face like an infernal storekeeper or a kid with colic.

"Hello, Andy," says Mack, out of his face. "Glad to see you back. Things have happened since you went away."

"I know it," says I, "and a sacrilegious sight it is. God never made you that way, Mack Lonsbury. Why do you scarify His works with this presumptious kind of ribaldry?"

"Why, Andy," said he, "they've elected me justice of the peace since you left."

I looked at Mack close. He was restless and inspired. A justice of the peace ought to be disconsolate and assuaged.

Just then a young woman passed on the sidewalk; and I saw Mack kind of half snicker and blush, and then he raised up his hat and smiled and bowed, and she smiled and bowed, and went on by.

"No hope for you," says I, "if you've got the Mary-Jane infirmity at your age. I thought it wasn't going to take on you. And patent leather shoes! All this in two little short months!"

"I'm going to marry the young lady who just passed to-night," says Mack, in a kind of a flutter.

"I forgot something at the post-office," says I, and walked away quick.

I overtook that young woman a hundred yards away. I raised my hat and told her my name. She was about nineteen; and young for her age. She blushed, and then looked at me cool, like I was the snow scene from the "Two Orphans."

"I understand you are to be married to-night," I said.

"Correct," says she. "You got any objections?"

"Listen, sissy," I begins.

"My name is Miss Rebosa Reed," says she in a pained way.

"I know it," says I. "Now, Rebosa, I'm old enough to have owed money to your father. And that old, specious, dressed-up, garbled, seasick ptomaine prancing around avidiously like an irremediable turkey gobbler with patent leather shoes on is my best friend. Why did you go and get him invested in this marriage business?"

"Why, he was the only chance there was," answered Miss Rebosa.

"Nay," says I, giving a sickening look of admiration at her complexion and style of features; "with your beauty you might pick any kind of a man. Listen, Rebosa. Old Mack ain't the man you want. He was twenty-two when you was *née* Reed, as the papers say. This bursting into bloom won't last with him. He's all ventilated with old-ness and rectitude and decay. Old Mack's down with a case of Indian summer. He overlooked his bet when he was young; and now he's suing Nature for the interest on the promissory note he took from Cupid instead of the cash. Rebosa, are you bent on having this mar-riage occur?"

"Why, sure I am," says she, oscillating the pansies on her hat, "and so is somebody else, I reckon."

"What time is it to take place?" I asks.

"At six o'clock," says she.

I made up my mind right away what to do. I'd save old Mack if I could. To have a good, seasoned, ineligible man like that turn chicken for a girl that hadn't quit eating slate pencils and buttoning in the back was more than I could look on with easiness.

"Rebosa," says I, earnest, drawing upon my display of knowledge concerning the feminine intuitions of reason—"ain't there a young man in Piña—a nice young man that you think a heap of?"

"Yep," says Rebosa, nodding her pansies—"Sure there is! What do you think! Gracious!"

"Does he like you?" I asks. "How does he stand in the matter?"

"Crazy," says Rebosa. "Ma has to wet down the front steps to keep him from sitting there all the time. But I guess that'll be all over after to-night," she winds up with a sigh.

"Rebosa," says I, "you don't really experience any of this adoration called love for old Mack, do you?"

"Lord! no," says the girl, shaking her head. "I think he's as dry as a lava bed. The idea!"

"Who is this young man that you like, Rebosa?" I inquires.

"It's Eddie Bayles," says she. "He clerks in Crosby's grocery. But he don't make but thirty-five a month. Ella Noakes was wild about him once."

"Old Mack tells me," I says, "that he's going to marry you at six o'clock this evening."

"That's the time," says she. "It's to be at our house."

"Rebosa," says I, "listen to me. If Eddie Bayles had a thousand dollars cash—a thousand dollars, mind you, would buy him a store of his own—if you and Eddie had that much to excuse matrimony on, would you consent to marry him this evening at five o'clock?"

The girl looks at me a minute; and I can see these inaudible cogi-tations going on inside of her, as women will.

"A thousand dollars?" says she. "Of course I would."

"Come on," says I. "We'll go and see Eddie."

We went up to Crosby's store and called Eddie outside. He looked to be estimable and freckled; and he had chills and fever when I made my proposition.

"At five o'clock?" says he, "for a thousand dollars? Please don't wake me up! Well, you *are* the rich uncle retired from the spice business in India. I'll buy out old Crosby and run the store myself."

We went inside and got old man Crosby apart and explained it. I wrote my check for a thousand dollars and handed it to him. If Eddie and Rebosa married each other at five he was to turn the money over to them.

And then I gave 'em my blessing, and went to wander in the wildwood for a season. I sat on a log and made cogitations on life and old age and the zodiac and the ways of women and all the disorder that goes with a lifetime. I passed myself congratulations that I had probably saved my old friend Mack from his attack of Indian summer. I knew when he got well of it and shed his infatuation and his patent leather shoes, he would feel grateful. "To keep old Mack disinvolved," thinks I, "from relapses like this, is worth more than a thousand dollars." And most of all I was glad that I'd made a study of women, and wasn't to be deceived any by their means of conceit and evolution.

It must have been half-past five when I got back home. I stepped in; and there sat old Mack on the back of his neck in his old clothes with his blue socks on the window and the History of Civilization propped up on his knees.

"This don't look like getting ready for a wedding at six," I says, to seem innocent.

"Oh," says Mack, reaching for his tobacco, "that was postponed back to five o'clock. They sent me a note saying the hour had been changed. It's all over now. What made you stay away so long, Andy?"

"You heard about the wedding?" I asks.

"I operated it," says he. "I told you I was justice of the peace. The preacher is off East to visit his folks, and I'm the only one in town that can perform the dispensations of marriage. I promised Eddie and Rebosa a month ago I'd marry 'em. He's a busy lad; and he'll have a grocery of his own some day."

"He will," says I.

"There was lots of women at the wedding," says Mack, smoking up. "But I didn't seem to get any ideas from 'em. I wish I was informed in the structure of their attainments like you said you was."

"That was two months ago," says I, reaching up for the banjo.

# A Call Loan

In those days the cattlemen were the anointed. They were the grandees of the grass, kings of the kine, lords of the lea, barons of beef and bone. They might have ridden in golden chariots had their tastes so inclined. The cattleman was caught in a stampede of dollars. It seemed to him that he had more money than was decent. But when he had bought a watch with precious stones set in the case so large that they hurt his ribs, and a California saddle with silver nails and Angora skin *suaderos*, and ordered everybody up to the bar for whisky—what else was there for him to spend money for?

Not so circumscribed in expedient for the reduction of surplus wealth were those lairds of the lariat who had womenfolk to their name. In the breast of the rib-sprung sex the genius of purse lightening may slumber through years of inopportunity, but never, my brothers, does it become extinct.

So, out of the chaparral came Long Bill Longley from the Bar Circle Branch on the Frio—a wife-driven man—to taste the urban joys of success. Something like half a million dollars he had, with an income steadily increasing.

Long Bill was a graduate of the camp and trail. Luck and thrift, a cool head, and a telescopic eye for mavericks had raised him from cowboy to be a cowman. Then came the boom in cattle, and Fortune, stepping gingerly among the cactus thorns, came and emptied her cornucopia at the doorstep of the ranch.

In the little frontier city of Chaparosa, Longley built a costly residence. Here he became a captive, bound to the chariot of social existence. He was doomed to become a leading citizen. He struggled for a time like a mustang in his first corral, and then he hung up his quirt and spurs. Time hung heavily on his hands. He organized the First National Bank of Chaparosa, and was elected its president.

One day a dyspeptic man, wearing double-magnifying glasses, inserted an official-looking card between the bars of the cashier's window of the First National Bank. Five minutes later the bank force was dancing at the beck and call of a national bank examiner.

This examiner, Mr. J. Edgar Todd, proved to be a thorough one.

At the end of it all the examiner put on his hat, and called the president, Mr. William R. Longley, into the private office.

"Well, how do you find things?" asked Longley, in his slow, deep tones. "Any brands in the round-up you didn't like the looks of?"

"The bank checks up all right, Mr. Longley," said Todd; "and I find your loans in very good shape—with one exception. You are carrying one very bad bit of paper—one that is so bad that I have been thinking that you surely do not realize the serious position it places you in. I refer to a call loan of $10,000 made to Thomas Merwin. Not only is the amount in excess of the maximum sum the bank can loan any individual legally, but it is absolutely without endorsement or security. Thus you have doubly violated the national banking laws, and have laid yourself open to criminal prosecution by the Government. A report of the matter to the Comptroller of the Currency—which I am bound to make—would, I am sure, result in the matter being turned over to the Department of Justice for action. You see what a serious thing it is."

Bill Longley was leaning his lengthy, slowly moving frame back in his swivel chair. His hands were clasped behind his head, and he turned a little to look the examiner in the face. The examiner was surprised to see a smile creep about the rugged mouth of the banker, and a kindly twinkle in his light-blue eyes. If he saw the seriousness of the affair, it did not show in his countenance.

"Of course, you don't know Tom Merwin," said Longley, almost genially. "Yes, I know about that loan. It hasn't any security except Tom Merwin's word. Somehow, I've always found that when a man's word is good, it's the best security there is. Oh, yes, I know the Government doesn't think so. I guess I'll see Tom about that note."

Mr. Todd's dyspepsia seemed to grow suddenly worse. He looked at the chaparral banker through his double-magnifying glasses in amazement.

"You see," said Longley, easily explaining the thing away, "Tom heard of 2,000 head of two-year-olds down near Rocky Ford on the Rio Grande that could be had for $8 a head. I reckon 'twas one of old Laendro Garcia's outfits that he had smuggled over, and he wanted to make a quick turn on 'em. Those cattle are worth $15 on the hoof in Kansas City. Tom knew it and I knew it. He had $6,000, and I let him have the $10,000 to make the deal with. His brother Ed took 'em on to market three weeks ago. He ought to be back 'most any day now with the money. When he comes Tom'll pay that note."

The bank examiner was shocked. It was, perhaps, his duty to step out to the telegraph office and wire the situation to the Comptroller. But he did not. He talked pointedly and effectively to Longley for three minutes. He succeeded in making the banker understand that he stood upon the border of a catastrophe. And then he offered a tiny loophole of escape.

"I am going to Hilldale's to-night," he told Longley, "to examine a bank there. I will pass through Chaparosa on my way back. At twelve to-morrow I shall call at this bank. If this loan has been cleared out of the way by that time it will not be mentioned in my report. If not —I will have to do my duty."

With that the examiner bowed and departed.

The President of the First National lounged in his chair half an hour longer, and then he lit a mild cigar, and went over to Tom Merwin's house. Merwin, a ranchman in brown duck, with a contemplative eye, sat with his feet upon a table, plaiting a rawhide quirt.

"Tom," said Longley, leaning against the table, "you heard anything from Ed yet?"

"Not yet," said Merwin, continuing his plaiting. "I guess Ed'll be along back now in a few days."

"There was a bank examiner," said Longley, "nosing around our place to-day, and he bucked a sight about that note of yours. You know I know it's all right, but the thing *is* against the banking laws. I was pretty sure you'd have paid it off before the bank was examined again, but the son-of-a-gun slipped in on us, Tom. Now, I'm short of cash myself just now, or I'd let you have the money to take it up with. I've got till twelve o'clock to-morrow, and then I've got to show the cash in place of that note or—"

"Or what, Bill?" asked Merwin, as Longley hesitated.

"Well, I suppose it means be jumped on with both of Uncle Sam's feet."

"I'll try to raise the money for you on time," said Merwin, interested in his plaiting.

"All right, Tom," concluded Longley, as he turned toward the door; "I knew you would if you could."

Merwin threw down his whip and went to the only other bank in town, a private one, run by Cooper & Craig.

"Cooper," he said, to the partner by that name, "I've got to have $10,000 to-day or to-morrow. I've got a house and lot here that's worth about $6,000 and that's all the actual collateral. But I've got a cattle deal on that's sure to bring me in more than that much profit within a few days."

Cooper began to cough.

"Now, for God's sake don't say no," said Merwin. "I owe that much money on a call loan. It's been called, and the man that called it is a man I've laid on the same blanket with in cow-camps and ranger-camps for ten years. He can call anything I've got. He can call the blood out of my veins and it'll come. He's got to have the money. He's in a devil of a— Well, he needs the money, and I've got to get it for him. You know my word's good, Cooper."

"No doubt of it," assented Cooper, urbanely, "but I've a partner, you know. I'm not free in making loans. And even if you had the best security in your hands, Merwin, we couldn't accommodate you in less than a week. We're just making a shipment of $15,000 to Myer Brothers in Rockdell, to buy cotton with. It goes down on the narrow gauge to-night. That leaves our cash quite short at present. Sorry we can't arrange it for you."

Merwin went back to his little bar office and plaited at his quirt again. About four o'clock in the afternoon he went to the First National and leaned over the railing of Longley's desk.

"I'll try to get that money for you to-night—I mean to-morrow, Bill."

"All right, Tom," said Longley, quietly.

At nine o'clock that night Tom Merwin stepped cautiously out of the small frame house in which he lived. It was near the edge of the little town, and few citizens were in the neighborhood at that hour. Merwin wore two six-shooters in a belt and a slouch hat. He moved swiftly down a lonely street, and then followed the sandy road that ran parallel to the narrow-gauge track until he reached the water-tank, two miles below the town. There Tom Merwin stopped, tied a black silk handkerchief about the lower part of his face, and pulled his hat down low.

In ten minutes the night train for Rockdell pulled up at the tank, having come from Chaparosa.

With a gun in each hand Merwin raised himself from behind a clump of chaparral and started for the engine. But before he had taken three steps, two long, strong arms clasped him from behind, and he was lifted from his feet and thrown, face downward, upon the grass. There was a heavy knee pressing against his back, and an iron hand grasping each of his wrists. He was held thus, like a child, until the engine had taken water, and until the train had moved, with accelerating speed, out of sight. Then he was released, and rose to his feet to face Bill Longley.

"The case never needed to be fixed up this way, Tom," said Longley. "I saw Cooper this evening, and he told me what you and him talked about. Then I went down to your house to-night and saw you come out with your guns on, and I followed you. Let's go back, Tom."

They walked away together, side by side.

" 'Twas the only chance I saw," said Merwin, presently. "You called your loan, and I tried to answer you. Now, what'll you do, Bill, if they sock it to you?"

"What would you have done if they'd socked it to you?" was the answer Longley made.

"I never thought I'd lay in a bush to stick up a train," remarked Merwin; "but a call loan's different. A call's a call with me. We've got twelve hours yet, Bill, before this spy jumps onto you. We've got to raise them spondulicks somehow. Maybe we can— Great Sam Houston! do you hear that?"

Merwin broke into a run, and Longley kept with him, hearing only a rather pleasing whistle somewhere in the night rendering the lugubrious air of "The Cowboy's Lament."

"It's the only tune he knows," shouted Merwin, as he ran. "I'll bet—"

They were at the door of Merwin's house. He kicked it open and fell over an old valise lying in the middle of the floor. A sunburned, firm-jawed youth, stained by travel, lay upon the bed puffing at a brown cigarette.

"What's the word, Ed?" gasped Merwin.

"So, so," drawled that capable youngster. "Just got in on the 9:30. Sold the bunch for fifteen, straight. Now, buddy, you want to quit kickin' a valise around that's got $29,000 in greenbacks in its in'ards."

# The Princess
# and the Puma

There had to be a king and queen, of course. The king was a terrible old man who wore six-shooters and spurs, and shouted in such a tremendous voice that the rattlers on the prairie would run into their holes under the prickly pear. Before there was a royal family they called the man "Whispering Ben." When he came to own 50,000 acres of land and more cattle than he could count, they called him O'Donnell "the Cattle King."

The queen had been a Mexican girl from Laredo. She made a good, mild, Coloradoclaro wife, and even succeeded in teaching Ben to modify his voice sufficiently while in the house to keep the dishes from being broken. When Ben got to be king she would sit on the gallery of Espinosa Ranch and weave rush mats. When wealth became so irresistible and oppressive that upholstered chairs and a centre table were brought down from San Antone in the wagons, she bowed her smooth, dark head, and shared the fate of the Danaë.

To avoid *lèse-majesté* you have been presented first to the king and queen. They do not enter the story, which might be called "The Chronicle of the Princess, the Happy Thought, and the Lion that Bungled his Job."

Josefa O'Donnell was the surviving daughter, the princess. From her mother she inherited warmth of nature and a dusky, semi-tropic beauty. From Ben O'Donnell the royal she acquired a store in intrepidity, common sense, and the faculty of ruling. The combination was worth going miles to see. Josefa while riding her pony at a gallop could put five out of six bullets through a tomato-can swinging at the end of a string. She could play for hours with a white kitten she owned, dressing it in all manner of absurd clothes. Scorning a pencil, she could tell you out of her head what 1545 two-year-olds would bring on the hoof, at $8.50 per head. Roughly speaking, the Espinosa Ranch is forty

miles long and thirty broad—but mostly leased land. Josefa, on her
pony, had prospected over every mile of it. Every cow-puncher on the
range knew her by sight and was a loyal vassal. Ripley Givens, foreman of one of the Espinoso outfits, saw her one day, and made up his
mind to form a royal matrimonial alliance. Presumptuous? No. In
those days in the Nueces country a man was a man. And, after all,
the title of cattle king does not presuppose blood royal. Often it only
signifies that its owner wears the crown in token of his magnificent
qualities in the art of cattle stealing.

One day Ripley Givens rode over to the Double Elm Ranch to
inquire about a bunch of strayed yearlings. He was late in setting out
on his return trip, and it was sundown when he struck the White
Horse Crossing of the Nueces. From there to his own camp it was
sixteen miles. To the Espinosa ranch-house it was twelve. Givens was
tired. He decided to pass the night at the Crossing.

There was a fine water hole in the river-bed. The banks were
thickly covered with great trees, undergrown with brush. Back from
the water hole fifty yards was a stretch of curly mesquite grass—
supper for his horse and bed for himself. Givens staked his horse, and
spread out his saddle blankets to dry. He sat down with his back
against a tree and rolled a cigarette. From somewhere in the dense
timber along the river came a sudden, rageful, shivering wail. The
pony danced at the end of his rope and blew a whistling snort of
comprehending fear. Givens puffed at his cigarette, but he reached
leisurely for his pistol-belt, which lay on the grass, and twirled the
cylinder of his weapon tentatively. A great gar plunged with a loud
splash into the water hole. A little brown rabbit skipped around a
bunch of catclaw and sat twitching his whiskers and looking humorously at Givens. The pony went on eating grass.

It is well to be reasonably watchful when a Mexican lion sings
soprano along the arroyos at sundown. The burden of his song may
be that young calves and fat lambs are scarce, and that he has a car-
nivorous desire for your acquaintance.

In the grass lay an empty fruit can, cast there by some former
sojourner. Givens caught sight of it with a grunt of satisfaction. In his
coat pocket tied behind his saddle was a handful or two of ground
coffee. Black coffee and cigarettes! What ranchero could desire more?

In two minutes he had a little fire going clearly. He started, with
his can, for the water hole. When within fifteen yards of its edge he
saw, between the bushes, a side-saddled pony with down-dropped
reins cropping grass a little distance to his left. Just rising from her
hands and knees on the brink of the water hole was Josefa O'Donnell.
She had been drinking water, and she brushed the sand from the

palms of her hands. Ten yards away, to her right, half concealed by a clump of sacuista, Givens saw the crouching form of the Mexican lion. His amber eyelids glared hungrily; six feet from them was the tip of the tail stretched straight, like a pointer's. His hind-quarters rocked with the motion of the cat tribe preliminary to leaping.

Givens did what he could. His six-shooter was thirty-five yards away lying on the grass. He gave a loud yell, and dashed between the lion and the princess.

The "rucus," as Givens called it afterward, was brief and somewhat confused. When he arrived on the line of attack he saw a dim streak in the air, and heard a couple of faint cracks. Then a hundred pounds of Mexican lion plumped down upon his head and flattened him, with a heavy jar, to the ground. He remembered calling out: "Let up, now—no fair gouging!" and then he crawled from under the lion like a worm, with his mouth full of grass and dirt, and a big lump on the back of his head where it had struck the root of a water-elm. The lion lay motionless. Givens, feeling aggrieved, and suspicious of fouls, shook his fist at the lion, and shouted: "I'll rastle you again for twenty—" and then he got back to himself.

Josefa was standing in her tracks, quietly reloading her silver-mounted .38. It had not been a difficult shot. The lion's head made an easier mark than a tomato-can swinging at the end of a string. There was a provoking, teasing, maddening smile upon her mouth and in her dark eyes. The would-be-rescuing knight felt the fire of his fiasco burn down to his soul. Here had been his chance, the chance that he had dreamed of; and Momus, and not Cupid, had presided over it. The satyrs in the wood were, no doubt, holding their sides in hilarious, silent laughter. There had been something like vaudeville—say Signor Givens and his funny knockabout act with the stuffed lion.

"Is that you, Mr. Givens?" said Josefa, in her deliberate, saccharine contralto. "You nearly spoiled my shot when you yelled. Did you hurt your head when you fell?"

"Oh, no," said Givens, quietly; "that didn't hurt." He stooped ig-nominiously and dragged his best Stetson hat from under the beast. It was crushed and wrinkled to a fine comedy effect. Then he knelt down and softly stroked the fierce, open-jawed head of the dead lion.

"Poor old Bill!" he exclaimed, mournfully.

"What's that?" asked Josefa, sharply.

"Of course you didn't know, Miss Josefa," said Givens, with an air of one allowing magnanimity to triumph over grief. "Nobody can blame you. I tried to save him, but I couldn't let you know in time."

"Save who?"

"Why, Bill. I've been looking for him all day. You see, he's been

our camp pet for two years. Poor old fellow, he wouldn't have hurt a
cottontail rabbit. It'll break the boys all up when they hear about it.
But you couldn't tell, of course, that Bill was just trying to play
with you."

Josefa's black eyes burned steadily upon him. Ripley Givens met
the test successfully. He stood rumpling the yellow-brown curls on his
head pensively. In his eyes was regret, not unmingled with a gentle
reproach. His smooth features were set to a pattern of indisputable
sorrow. Josefa wavered.

"What was your pet doing here?" she asked, making a last stand.
"There's no camp near the White Horse Crossing."

"The old rascal ran away from camp yesterday," answered Givens,
readily. "It's a wonder the coyotes didn't scare him to death. You see,
Jim Webster, our horse wrangler, brought a little terrier pup into
camp last week. The pup made life miserable for Bill—he used to
chase him around and chew his hind legs for hours at a time. Every
night when bedtime came Bill would sneak under one of the boys'
blankets and sleep to keep the pup from finding him. I reckon he must
have been worried pretty desperate or he wouldn't have run away.
He was always afraid to get out of sight of camp."

Josefa looked at the body of the fierce animal. Givens gently patted
one of the formidable paws that could have killed a yearling calf with
one blow. Slowly a red flush widened upon the dark olive face of the
girl. Was it the signal of shame of the true sportsman who has brought
down ignoble quarry? Her eyes grew softer, and the lowered lids
drove away all their bright mockery.

"I'm very sorry," she said, humbly; "but he looked so big, and
jumped so high that—"

"Poor old Bill was hungry," interrupted Givens, in quick defence
of the deceased. "We always made him jump for his supper in camp.
He would lie down and roll over for a piece of meat. When he saw
you he thought he was going to get something to eat from you."

Suddenly Josefa's eyes opened wide.

"I might have shot you!" she exclaimed. "You ran right in between.
You risked your life to save your pet! That was fine, Mr. Givens. I
like a man who is kind to animals."

Yes; there was even admiration in her gaze now. After all, there
was a hero rising out of the ruins of the anti-climax. The look on
Givens's face would have secured him a high position in the S.P.C.A.

"I always loved 'em," said he; "horses, dogs, Mexican lions, cows,
alligators—"

"I hate alligators," instantly demurred Josefa; "crawly, muddy
things!"

"Did I say alligators?" said Givens. "I meant antelopes, of course."

Josefa's conscience drove her to make further amends. She held out her hand penitently. There was a bright, unshed drop in each of her eyes.

"Please forgive me, Mr. Givens, won't you? I'm only a girl, you know, and I was frightened at first. I'm very, very sorry I shot Bill. You don't know how ashamed I feel. I wouldn't have done it for anything."

Givens took the proffered hand. He held it for a time while he allowed the generosity of his nature to overcome his grief at the loss of Bill. At last it was clear that he had forgiven her.

"Please don't speak of it any more, Miss Josefa. 'Twas enough to frighten any young lady the way Bill looked. I'll explain it all right to the boys."

"Are you really sure you don't hate me?" Josefa came closer to him impulsively. Her eyes were sweet—oh, sweet and pleading with gracious penitence. "I would hate any one who would kill my kitten. And how daring and kind of you to risk being shot when you tried to save him! How very few men would have done that!" Victory wrested from defeat! Vaudeville turned into drama! Bravo, Ripley Givens!

It was now twilight. Of course Miss Josefa could not be allowed to ride on to the ranch-house alone. Givens resaddled his pony in spite of that animal's reproachful glances, and rode with her. Side by side they galloped across the smooth grass, the princess and the man who was kind to animals. The prairie odors of fruitful earth and delicate bloom were thick and sweet around them. Coyotes yelping over there on the hill! No fear. And yet—

Josefa rode closer. A little hand seemed to grope. Givens found it with his own. The ponies kept an even gait. The hands lingered together, and the owner of one explained.

"I never was frightened before, but just think! How terrible it would be to meet a really wild lion! Poor Bill! I'm so glad you came with me!"

O'Donnell was sitting on the ranch gallery.

"Hello, Rip!" he shouted—"that you?"

"He rode in with me," said Josefa. "I lost my way and was late."

"Much obliged," called the cattle king. "Stop over, Rip, and ride to camp in the morning."

But Givens would not. He would push on to camp. There was a bunch of steers to start off on the trail at daybreak. He said good-night, and trotted away.

An hour later, when the lights were out, Josefa, in her night-robe,

came to her door and called to the king in his own room across the
brick-paved hallway:

"Say, Pop, you know that old Mexican lion they call the 'Gotch-
eared Devil'—the one that killed Gonzales, Mr. Martin's sheep herder,
and about fifty calves on the Salada range? Well, I settled his hash
this afternoon over at the White Horse Crossing. Put two balls in his
head with my .38 while he was on the jump. I knew him by the slice
gone from his left ear that old Gonzales cut off with his machete. You
couldn't have made a better shot yourself, Daddy."

"Bully for you!" thundered Whispering Ben from the darkness of
the royal chamber.

# The Passing of Black Eagle

For some months of a certain year a grim bandit infested the Texas border along the Rio Grande. Peculiarly striking to the optic nerve was this notorious marauder. His personality secured him the title of "Black Eagle, the Terror of the Border." Many fearsome tales are on record concerning the doings of him and his followers. Suddenly, in the space of a single minute, Black Eagle vanished from earth. He was never heard of again. His own band never even guessed the mystery of his disappearance. The border ranches and settlements feared he would come again to ride and ravage the mesquite flats. He never will. It is to disclose the fate of Black Eagle that this narrative is written.

The initial movement of the story is furnished by the foot of a bartender in St. Louis. His discerning eye fell upon the form of Chicken Ruggles as he pecked with avidity at the free lunch. Chicken was a "hobo." He had a long nose like the bill of a fowl, an inordinate appetite for poultry, and a habit of gratifying it without expense, which accounts for the name given him by his fellow vagrants.

Physicians agree that the partaking of liquids at meal times is not a healthy practice. The hygiene of the saloon promulgates the opposite. Chicken had neglected to purchase a drink to accompany his meal. The bartender rounded the counter, caught the injudicious diner by the ear with a lemon squeezer, led him to the door and kicked him into the street.

Thus the mind of Chicken was brought to realize the signs of coming winter. The night was cold; the stars shone with unkindly brilliancy; people were hurrying along the streets in two egotistic, jostling streams. Men had donned their overcoats, and Chicken knew to an exact percentage the increased difficulty of coaxing dimes from those buttoned-in vest pockets. The time had come for his annual exodus to the South.

A little boy, five or six years old, stood looking with covetous eyes in a confectioner's window. In one small hand he held an empty two-ounce vial; in the other he grasped tightly something flat and round, with a shining milled edge. The scene presented a field of operations commensurate to Chicken's talents and daring. After sweeping the horizon to make sure that no official tug was cruising near, he insidiously accosted his prey. The boy, having been early taught by his household to regard altruistic advances with extreme suspicion, received the overtures coldly.

Then Chicken knew that he must make one of those desperate, nerve-shattering plunges into speculation that fortune sometimes requires of those who would win her favor. Five cents was his capital, and this he must risk against the chance of winning what lay within the close grasp of the youngster's chubby hand. It was a fearful lottery, Chicken knew. But he must accomplish his end by strategy, since he had a wholesome terror of plundering infants by force. Once, in a park, driven by hunger, he had committed an onslaught upon a bottle of peptonized infant's food in the possession of an occupant of a baby carriage. The outraged infant had so promptly opened its mouth and pressed the button that communicated with the welkin that help arrived, and Chicken did his thirty days in a snug coop. Wherefore he was, as he said, "leary of kids."

Beginning artfully to question the boy concerning his choice of sweets, he gradually drew out the information he wanted. Mamma said he was to ask the drug-store man for ten cents' worth of paregoric in the bottle; he was to keep his hand shut tight over the dollar; he must not stop to talk to any one in the street; he must ask the drug-store man to wrap up the change and put it in the pocket of his trousers. Indeed, they had pockets—two of them! And he liked chocolate creams best.

Chicken went into the store and turned plunger. He invested his entire capital in C.A.N.D.Y. stocks, simply to pave the way to the greater risk following.

He gave the sweets to the youngster, and had the satisfaction of perceiving that confidence was established. After that it was easy to obtain leadership of the expedition, to take the investment by the hand and lead it to a nice drug store he knew of in the same block. There Chicken, with a parental air, passed over the dollar and called for the medicine, while the boy crunched his candy, glad to be relieved of the responsibility of the purchase. And then the successful investor searching his pockets, found an overcoat button—the extent of his winter trousseau—and, wrapping it carefully, placed the ostensible change in the pocket of confiding juvenility. Setting the youngster's face homeward, and patting him benevolently on the back—for Chicken's heart was as soft as those of his feathered namesakes—the speculator quit the market with a profit of 1,700 per cent on his invested capital.

Two hours later an Iron Mountain freight engine pulled out of the railroad yards, Texas bound, with a string of empties. In one of the cattle cars, half buried in excelsior, Chicken lay at ease. Beside him in his nest was a quart bottle of very poor whisky and a paper bag of bread and cheese. Mr. Ruggles, in his private car, was on his trip south for the winter season.

For a week that car was trundled southward, shifted, laid over, and manipulated after the manner of rolling stock, but Chicken stuck to it, leaving it only at necessary times to satisfy his hunger and thirst. He knew it must go down to the cattle country, and San Antonio, in the heart of it, was his goal. There the air was salubrious and mild; the people indulgent and long-suffering. The bartenders there would not kick him. If he should eat too long or too often at one place they would swear at him as if by rote and without heat. They swore so drawlingly, and they rarely paused short of their full vocabulary, which was copious, so that Chicken had often gulped a good meal during the process of the vituperative prohibition. The season there was always spring-like; the plazas were pleasant at night, with music and gayety: except during the slight and infrequent cold snaps one could sleep comfortably out of doors in case the interiors should develop inhospitality.

At Texarkana his car was switched to the I. and G.N. Then still southward it trailed until, at length, it crawled across the Colorado bridge at Austin, and lined out, straight as an arrow, for the run to San Antonio.

When the freight halted at that town Chicken was fast asleep. In ten minutes the train was off again for Laredo, the end of the road. Those empty cattle cars were for distribution along the line at points from which the ranches shipped their stock.

When Chicken awoke his car was stationary. Looking out between the slats he saw it was a bright, moonlit night. Scrambling out, he saw his car with three others abandoned on a little siding in a wild and lonesome country. A cattle pen and chute stood on one side of the track. The railroad bisected a vast, dim ocean of prairie, in the midst of which Chicken, with his futile rolling stock, was as completely stranded as was Robinson with his land-locked boat.

A white post stood near the rails. Going up to it, Chicken read the letters at the top, S. A. 90. Laredo was nearly as far to the south. He was almost a hundred miles from any town. Coyotes began to yelp in the mysterious sea around him. Chicken felt lonesome. He had lived in Boston without an education, in Chicago without nerve, in Philadelphia without a sleeping place, in New York without a pull, and in Pittsburg sober, and yet he had never felt so lonely as now.

Suddenly through the intense silence, he heard the whicker of a horse. The sound came from the side of the track toward the east, and Chicken began to explore timorously in that direction. He stepped high along the mat of curly mesquite grass, for he was afraid of everything there might be in this wilderness—snakes, rats, brigands, centipedes, mirages, cowboys, fandangoes, tarantulas, tamales—he had read of them in the story papers. Rounding a clump of prickly pear that reared high its fantastic and menacing array of rounded heads, he was struck to shivering terror by a snort and a thunderous plunge, as the horse, himself startled, bounded away some fifty yards, and then resumed his grazing. But here was the one thing in the desert that Chicken did not fear. He had been reared on a farm; he had handled horses, understood them, and could ride.

Approaching slowly and speaking soothingly, he followed the animal, which, after its first flight, seemed gentle enough, and secured the end of the twenty-foot lariat that dragged after him in the grass. It required him but a few moments to contrive the rope into an ingenious nose-bridle, after the style of the Mexican *borsal*. In another he was upon the horse's back and off at a splendid lope, giving the animal free choice of direction. "He will take me some where," said Chicken to himself.

It would have been a thing of joy, that untrammelled gallop over the moonlit prairie, even to Chicken, who loathed exertion, but that his mood was not for it. His head ached; a growing thirst was upon him; the "somewhere" whither his lucky mount might convey him was full of dismal peradventure.

And now he noted that the horse moved to a definite goal. Where the prairie lay smooth he kept his course straight as an arrow's toward the east. Deflected by hill or arroyo or impracticable spinous brakes, he quickly flowed again into the current, charted by his unerring instinct. At last, upon the side of a gentle rise, he suddenly subsided to a complacent walk. A stone's cast away stood a little mott of coma trees; beneath it a *jacal* such as the Mexicans erect—a one-room house of upright poles daubed with clay and roofed with grass or tule reeds. An experienced eye would have estimated the spot as the headquarters of a small sheep ranch. In the moonlight the ground in the nearby corral showed pulverized to a level smoothness by the hoofs

of the sheep. Everywhere was carelessly distributed the parapher-
nalia of the place—ropes, bridles, saddles, sheep pelts, wool sacks,
feed troughs, and camp litter. The barrel of drinking water stood in
the end of the two-horse wagon near the door. The harness was piled,
promiscuous, upon the wagon tongue, soaking up the dew.

Chicken slipped to earth, and tied the horse to a tree. He hallooed
again and again, but the house remained quiet. The door stood open,
and he entered cautiously. The light was sufficient for him to see that
no one was at home. He struck a match and lighted a lamp that stood
on a table. The room was that of a bachelor ranchman who was content
with the necessaries of life. Chicken rummaged intelligently until he
found what he had hardly dared hope for—a small brown jug that still
contained something near a quart of his desire.

Half an hour later, Chicken—now a gamecock of hostile aspect—
emerged from the house with unsteady steps. He had drawn upon the
absent ranchman's equipment to replace his own ragged attire. He
wore a suit of coarse brown ducking, the coat being a sort of rakish
bolero, jaunty to a degree. Boots he had donned, and spurs that
whirred with every lurching step. Buckled around him was a belt full
of cartridges with a big six-shooter in each of its two holsters.

Prowling about, he found blankets, a saddle and bridle with which
he caparisoned his steed. Again mounting, he rode swiftly away, singing a loud and tuneless song.

Bud King's band of desperadoes, outlaws and horse and cattle
thieves were in camp at a secluded spot on the bank of the Frio. Their
depredations in the Rio Grande country, while no bolder than usual,
had been advertised more extensively, and Captain Kinney's company
of rangers had been ordered down to look after them. Consequently,
Bud King, who was a wise general, instead of cutting out a hot trail
for the upholders of the law, as his men wished to do, retired for the
time to the prickly fastnesses of the Frio valley.

Though the move was a prudent one, and not incompatible with
Bud's well-known courage, it raised dissension among the members of
the band. In fact, while they thus lay ingloriously *perdu* in the brush,
the question of Bud King's fitness for the leadership was argued, with
closed doors, as it were, by his followers. Never before had Bud's skill
or efficiency been brought to criticism; but his glory was waning (and
such is glory's fate) in the light of a newer star. The sentiment of the
band was crystallizing into the opinion that Black Eagle could lead
them with more luster, profit, and distinction.

This Black Eagle—sub-titled the "Terror of the Border"—had
been a member of the gang about three months.

One night while they were in camp on the San Miguel water-hole a solitary horseman on the regulation fiery steed dashed in among them. The newcomer was of portentous and devastating aspect. A beak-like nose with a predatory curve projected above a mass of bristling, blue-black whiskers. His eye was cavernous and fierce. He was spurred, sombreroed, booted, garnished with revolvers, abundantly drunk, and very much unafraid. Few people in the country drained by the Rio Bravo would have cared thus to invade alone the camp of Bud King. But this fell bird swooped fearlessly upon them and demanded to be fed.

Hospitality in the prairie country is not limited. Even if your enemy pass your way you must feed him before you shoot him. You must empty your larder into him before you empty your lead. So the stranger of undeclared intentions was set down to a mighty feast.

A talkative bird he was, full of most marvellous loud tales and exploits, and speaking a language at times obscure but never colorless. He was a new sensation to Bud King's men, who rarely encountered new types. They hung, delighted, upon his vainglorious boasting, the spicy strangeness of his lingo, his contemptuous familiarity with life, the world, and remote places, and the extravagant frankness with which he conveyed his sentiments.

To their guest the band of outlaws seemed to be nothing more than a congregation of country bumpkins whom he was "stringing for grub" just as he would have told his stories at the back door of a farmhouse to wheedle a meal. And, indeed, his ignorance was not without excuse, for the "bad man" of the Southwest does not run to extremes. Those brigands might justly have been taken for a little party of peaceable rustics assembled for a fish-fry or pecan gathering. Gentle of manner, slouching of gait, soft-voiced, unpicturesquely clothed; not one of them presented to the eye any witness of the desperate records they had earned.

For two days the glittering stranger within the camp was feasted. Then, by common consent, he was invited to become a member of the band. He consented, presenting for enrollment the prodigious name of "Captain Montressor." This was immediately overruled by the band, and "Piggy" substituted as a compliment to the awful and insatiate appetite of its owner.

Thus did the Texas border receive the most spectacular brigand that ever rode its chaparral.

For the next three months Bud King conducted business as usual, escaping encounters with law officers and being content with reasonable profits. The band ran off some very good companies of horses from the ranges, and a few bunches of fine cattle which they got safely across the Rio Grande and disposed of to fair advantage. Often the band would ride into the little villages and Mexican settlements, terrorizing the inhabitants and plundering for the provisions and ammunition they needed. It was during these bloodless raids that Piggy's ferocious aspect and frightful voice gained him a renown more widespread and glorious than those other gentle-voiced and sad-faced desperadoes could have acquired in a lifetime.

The Mexicans, most apt in nomenclature, first called him The Black Eagle, and used to frighten the babes by threatening them with tales of the dreadful robber who carried off little children in his great beak. Soon the name extended, and Black Eagle, the Terror of the Border, became a recognized factor in exaggerated newspaper reports and ranch gossip.

The country from the Nueces to the Rio Grande was a wild but fertile stretch, given over to the sheep and cattle ranches. Range was free; the inhabitants were few; the law was mainly a letter, and the pirates met with little opposition until the flaunting and garish Piggy gave the band undue advertisement. Then Kinney's ranger company headed for those precincts, and Bud King knew that it meant grim and sudden war or else temporary retirement. Regarding the risk to be unnecessary, he drew off his band to an almost inaccessible spot on the bank of the Frio. Wherefore, as has been said, dissatisfaction arose among the members, and impeachment proceedings against Bud were premeditated, with Black Eagle in high favor for the succession. Bud King was not unaware of the sentiment, and he called aside Cactus Taylor, his trusted lieutenant, to discuss it.

"If the boys," said Bud, "ain't satisfied with me, I'm willin' to step out. They're buckin' against my way of handlin' 'em. And 'specially because I concludes to hit the brush while Sam Kinney is ridin' the line. I saves 'em from bein' shot or sent up on a state contract, and they up and says I'm no good."

"It ain't so much that," explained Cactus, "as it is they're plum locoed about Piggy. They want them whiskers and that nose of his to split the wind at the head of the column."

"There's somethin' mighty seldom about Piggy," declared Bud, musingly. "I never yet see anything on the hoof that he exactly grades up with. He can shore holler a plenty, and he straddles a hoss from where you laid the chunk. But he ain't never been smoked yet. You know, Cactus, we ain't had a row since he's been with us. Piggy's all right for skearin' the greaser kids and layin' waste a cross-roads store. I reckon he's the finest canned oyster buccaneer and cheese pirate that ever was, but how's his appetite for fightin'? I've knowed some citizens you'd think was starvin' for trouble get a bad case of dyspepsy the first dose of lead they had to take."

"He talks all spraddled out," said Cactus, " 'bout the rookuses he's been in. He claims to have saw the elephant and hearn the owl."

"I know," replied Bud, using the cow-puncher's expressive phrase of skepticism, "but it sounds to me!"

This conversation was held one night in camp while the other members of the band—eight in number—were sprawling around the fire, lingering over their supper. When Bud and Cactus ceased talking they heard Piggy's formidable voice holding forth to the others as usual while he was engaged in checking, though never satisfying, his ravening appetite.

"Wat's de use," he was saying, "of chasin' little red cowses and hosses 'round for t'ousands of miles? Dere ain't nuttin' in it. Gallopin' t'rough dese bushes and briers, and gettin' a t'irst dat a brewery couldn't put out, and missin' meals! Say! You know what I'd do if I was main finger of dis bunch? I'd stick up a train. I'd blow de express car and make hard dollars where you guys get wind. Youse makes me tired. Dis sook-cow kind of cheap sport gives me a pain."

Later on, a deputation waited on Bud. They stood on one leg, chewed mesquite twigs and circumlocuted, for they hated to hurt his feelings. Bud foresaw their business, and made it easy for them. Bigger risks and larger profits was what they wanted.

The suggestion of Piggy's about holding up a train had fired their imagination and increased their admiration for the dash and boldness of the instigator. They were such simple, artless, and custom-bound bush-rangers that they had never before thought of extending their habits beyond the running off of live-stock and the shooting of such of their acquaintances as ventured to interfere.

Bud acted "on the level," agreeing to take a subordinate place in the gang until Black Eagle should have been given a trial as leader.

After a great deal of consultation, studying of time-tables and discussion of the country's topography, the time and place for carrying out their new enterprise was decided upon. At that time there was a feedstuff famine in Mexico and a cattle famine in certain parts of the United States, and there was a brisk international trade. Much money was being shipped along the railroads that connected the two republics. It was agreed that the most promising place for the contemplated robbery was at Espina, a little station on the I. and G.N., about forty miles north of Laredo. The train stopped there one minute; the country around was wild and unsettled; the station consisted of but one house in which the agent lived.

Black Eagle's band set out, riding by night. Arriving in the vicinity of Espina they rested their horses all day in a thicket a few miles distant.

The train was due at Espina at 10:30 P.M. They could rob the train and be well over the Mexican border with their booty by daylight the next morning.

To do Black Eagle justice, he exhibited no signs of flinching from the responsible honors that had been conferred upon him.

He assigned his men to their respective posts with discretion, and coached them carefully as to their duties. On each side of the track four of the band were to lie concealed in the chaparral. Gotch-Ear Rodgers was to stick up the station agent. Bronco Charlie was to remain with the horses, holding them in readiness. At a spot where it was calculated the engine would be when the train stopped, Bud King was to lie hidden on one side, and Black Eagle himself on the other. The two would get the drop on the engineer and fireman, force them to descend and proceed to the rear. Then the express car would be looted, and the escape made. No one was to move until Black Eagle gave the signal by firing his revolver. The plan was perfect.

At ten minutes to train time every man was at his post, effectually concealed by the thick chaparral that grew almost to the rails. The night was dark and lowering, with a fine drizzle falling from the flying gulf clouds. Black Eagle crouched behind a bush within five yards of the track. Two six-shooters were belted around him. Occasionally he drew a large black bottle from his pocket and raised it to his mouth.

A star appeared far down the track which soon waxed into the headlight of the approaching train. It came on with an increasing roar; the engine bore down upon the ambushing desperadoes with a glare and a shriek like some avenging monster come to deliver them to justice. Black Eagle flattened himself upon the ground. The engine, contrary to their calculations, instead of stopping between him and Bud King's place of concealment, passed fully forty yards farther before it came to a stand.

The bandit leader rose to his feet and peered around the bush. His men all lay quiet, awaiting the signal. Immediately opposite Black Eagle was a thing that drew his attention. Instead of being a regular passenger train it was a mixed one. Before him stood a box car, the door of which, by some means, had been left slightly open. Black Eagle went up to it and pushed the door farther open. An odor came forth —a damp, rancid, familiar, musty, intoxicating, beloved odor stirring strongly at old memories of happy days and travels. Black Eagle sniffed at the witching smell as the returned wanderer smells of the rose that twines his boyhood's cottage home. Nostalgia seized him. He put his hand inside. Excelsior—dry, springy, curly, soft, enticing, covered the floor. Outside the drizzle had turned to a chilling rain.

The train bell clanged. The bandit chief unbuckled his belt and cast it, with its revolvers, upon the ground. His spurs followed quickly, and his broad sombrero. Black Eagle was moulting. The train started with a rattling jerk. The ex-Terror of the Border scrambled into the box car and closed the door. Stretched luxuriously upon the excelsior, with the black bottle clasped closely to his breast, his eyes closed, and a foolish, happy smile upon his terrible features Chicken Ruggles started upon his return trip.

Undisturbed, with the band of desperate bandits lying motionless, awaiting the signal to attack, the train pulled out from Espina. As its speed increased, and the black masses of chaparral went whizzing past on either side, the express messenger, lighting his pipe, looked through his window and remarked, feelingly:

"What a jim-dandy place for a hold-up!"

# A Departmental Case

In Texas you may travel a thousand miles in a straight line. If your course is a crooked one, it is likely that both the distance and your rate of speed may be vastly increased. Clouds there sail serenely against the wind. The whippoorwill delivers its disconsolate cry with the notes exactly reversed from those of the Northern brother. Given a drought and a subsequently lively rain, and lo! from a glazed and stony soil will spring in a single night blossomed lilies, miraculously fair. Tom Green County was once the standard of measurement. I have forgotten how many New Jerseys and Rhode Islands it was that could have been stowed away and lost in its chaparral. But the legislative axe has slashed Tom Green into a handful of counties hardly larger than European kingdoms. The legislature convenes at Austin, near the centre of the state; and, while the representative from Rio Grande country is gathering his palm leaf fan and his linen duster to set out for the capital, the Pan-handle solon winds his muffler above his well-buttoned overcoat and kicks the snow from his well-greased boots ready for the same journey. All this merely to hint that the big ex-republic of the Southwest forms a sizable star on the flag, and to prepare for the corollary that things sometimes happen there uncut to pattern and unfettered by metes and bounds.

The Commissioner of Insurance, Statistics, and History of the State of Texas was an official of no very great or very small importance. The past tense is used, for now he is Commissioner of Insurance alone. Statistics and history are no longer proper nouns in the government records.

In the year 188–, the governor appointed Luke Coonrod Standifer to be the head of this department. Standifer was then fifty-five years of age, and a Texan to the core. His father had been one of the state's earliest settlers and pioneers. Standifer himself had served the commonwealth as Indian fighter, soldier, ranger, and legislator. Much learning he did not claim, but he had drunk pretty deep of the spring of experience.

If other grounds were less abundant, Texas should be well up in the lists of glory as the grateful republic. For both as republic and state, it has busily heaped honors and solid rewards upon its sons who rescued it from the wilderness.

Wherefore and therefore, Luke Coonrod Standifer, son of Ezra Standifer, ex-Terry ranger, simon-pure democrat, and lucky dweller in an unrepresented portion of the politico-geographical map, was appointed Commissioner of Insurance, Statistics, and History.

Standifer accepted the honor with some doubt as to the nature of the office he was to fill and his capacity for filling it—but he accepted, and by wire. He immediately set out from the little country town where he maintained (and was scarcely maintained by) a somnolent and unfruitful office of surveying and map-drawing. Before departing, he had looked up under the I's, S's, and H's in the "Encyclopædia Britannica" what information and preparation toward his official duties that those weighty volumes afforded.

A few weeks of incumbency diminished the new commissioner's awe of the great and important office he had been called upon to conduct. An increasing familiarity with its workings soon restored him to his accustomed placid course of life. In his office was an old spectacled clerk—a consecrated, informed, able machine, who held his desk regardless of changes of administrative heads. Old Kauffman instructed his new chief gradually in the knowledge of the department without seeming to do so, and kept the wheels revolving without the slip of a cog.

Indeed, the Department of Insurance, Statistics, and History carried no great heft of the burden of state. Its main work was the regulating of the business done in the state by foreign insurance companies, and the letter of the law was its guide. As for statistics—well, you wrote letters to county officers, and scissored other people's reports, and each year you got out a report of your own about the corn crop and the cotton crop and pecans and pigs and black and white population, and a great many columns of figures headed "bushels" and "acres" and "square miles," etc.—and there you were. History? The branch was purely a receptive one. Old ladies interested in the science bothered you some with long reports of proceedings of their historical societies. Some twenty or thirty people would write you each year that they had secured Sam Houston's pocket-knife or Santa Ana's whisky-flask or Davy Crockett's rifle—all absolutely authenticated—

and demanded legislative appropriation to purchase. Most of the work in the history branch went into pigeonholes.

One sizzling August afternoon the commissioner reclined in his office chair, with his feet upon the long, official table covered with green billiard cloth. The commissioner was smoking a cigar, and dreamily regarding the quivering landscape framed by the window that looked upon the treeless capitol grounds. Perhaps he was thinking of the rough and ready life he had led, of the old days of breathless adventure and movement, of the comrades who now trod other paths or had ceased to tread any, of the changes civilization and peace had brought, and, maybe, complacently, of the snug and comfortable camp pitched for him under the dome of the capitol of the state that had not forgotten his services.

The business of the department was lax. Insurance was easy. Statistics were not in demand. History was dead. Old Kauffman, the efficient and perpetual clerk, had requested an infrequent half-holiday, incited to the unusual dissipation by the joy of having successfully twisted the tail of a Connecticut insurance company that was trying to do business contrary to the edicts of the great Lone Star State.

The office was very still. A few subdued noises trickled in through the open door from the other departments—a dull tinkling crash from the treasurer's office adjoining, as a clerk tossed a bag of silver to the floor of the vault—the vague, intermittent clatter of a dilatory typewriter—a dull tapping from the state geologist's quarters as if some woodpecker had flown in to bore for his prey in the cool of the massive building—and then a faint rustle, and the light shuffling of the well-worn shoes along the hall, the sounds ceasing at the door toward which the commissioner's lethargic back was presented. Following this, the sound of a gentle voice speaking words unintelligible to the commissioner's somewhat dormant comprehension, but giving evidence of bewilderment and hesitation.

The voice was feminine; the commissioner was of the race of cavaliers who make salaam before the trail of a skirt without considering the quality of its cloth.

There stood in the door a faded woman, one of the numerous sisterhood of the unhappy. She was dressed all in black—poverty's perpetual mourning for lost joys. Her face had the contours of twenty and the lines of forty. She may have lived that intervening score of years in a twelve-month. There was about her yet an aurum of indignant, unappeased, protesting youth that shone faintly through the premature veil of unearned decline.

"I beg your pardon, ma'am," said the commissioner, gaining his feet to the accompaniment of a great creaking and sliding of his chair.

"Are you the governor, sir?" asked the vision of melancholy.

The commissioner hesitated at the end of his best bow, with his hand in the bosom of his double-breasted "frock." Truth at last conquered.

"Well, no, ma'am. I am not the governor. I have the honor to be Commissioner of Insurance, Statistics, and History. Is there anything, ma'am, I can do for you? Won't you have a chair, ma'am?"

The lady subsided into the chair handed her, probably from purely physical reasons. She wielded a cheap fan—last token of gentility to be abandoned. Her clothing seemed to indicate a reduction almost to extreme poverty. She looked at the man who was not the governor, and saw kindliness and simplicity and a rugged, unadorned courtliness emanating from a countenance tanned, and toughened by forty years of outdoor life. Also, she saw that his eyes were clear and strong and blue. Just as they had been when he used them to skim the horizon for raiding Kiowas and Sioux. His mouth was as set and firm as it had been on that day when he bearded the old Lion Sam Houston himself, and defied him during that season when secession was the theme. Now, in bearing and dress, Luke Coonrod Standifer endeavored to do credit to the important arts and sciences of Insurance, Statistics, and History. He had abandoned the careless dress of his country home. Now, his broad-brimmed black slouch hat, and his long-tailed "frock" made him not the least imposing of the official family, even if his office was reckoned to stand at the tail of the list.

"You wanted to see the governor, ma'am?" asked the commissioner, with a deferential manner he always used toward the fair sex.

"I hardly know," said the lady, hesitatingly. "I suppose so." And then, suddenly drawn by the sympathetic look of the other, she poured forth the story of her need.

It was a story so common that the public has come to look at its monotony instead of its pity. The old tale of an unhappy married life —made so by a brutal, conscienceless husband, a robber, a spendthrift, a moral coward, and a bully, who failed to provide even the means of the barest existence. Yes, he had come down in the scale so low as to strike her. It happened only the day before—there was the bruise on one temple—she had offended his highness by asking for a little money to live on. And yet she must needs, womanlike, append a plea for her tyrant—he was drinking; he had rarely abused her thus when sober.

"I thought," mourned this pale sister of sorrow, "that maybe the state might be willing to give me some relief. I've heard of such things being done for the families of old settlers. I've heard tell that the state used to give land to the men who fought for it against Mexico, and settled up the country, and helped drive out the Indians. My father did all of that, and he never received anything. He never would take it. I thought the governor would be the one to see, and that's why I came. If Father was entitled to anything, they might let it come to me."

"It's possible, ma'am," said Standifer, "that such might be the case. But 'most all the veterans and settlers got their land certificates issued and located long ago. Still, we can look that up in the land office and be sure. Your father's name, now, was—"

"Amos Colvin, sir."

"Good Lord!" exclaimed Standifer, rising and unbuttoning his tight coat, excitedly. "Are you Amos Colvin's daughter? Why, ma'am, Amos Colvin and me were thicker than two hoss thieves for more than ten years! We fought Kiowas, drove cattle, and rangered side by side nearly all over Texas. I remember seeing you once before, now. You were a kid, about seven, a-riding a little yellow pony up and down. Amos and me stopped at your home for a little grub when we were trailing that band of Mexican cattle thieves down through Karnes and Bee. Great tarantulas! and you're Amos Colvin's little girl! Did you ever hear your father mention Luke Standifer—just kind of casually —as if he'd met me once or twice?"

A little pale smile flitted across the lady's white face.

"It seems to me," she said, "that I don't remember hearing him talk about much else. Every day there was some story he had to tell about what he and you had done. Mighty near the last thing I heard him tell was about the time when the Indians wounded him, and you crawled out to him through the grass, with a canteen of water while they—"

"Yes, yes—well—oh, that wasn't anything," said Standifer, "hemming" loudly and buttoning his coat again briskly. "And now, ma'am, who was the infernal skunk—I beg your pardon, ma'am—who was the gentleman you married?"

"Benton Sharp."

The commissioner plumped down again into his chair with a groan. This gentle, sad little woman in the rusty black gown the daughter of his oldest friend, the wife of Benton Sharp! Benton Sharp, one of the most noted "bad" men in that part of the state—a man who had been a cattle thief, an outlaw, a desperado, and was now a gambler, a swaggering bully, who plied his trade in the larger frontier towns, relying upon his record and the quickness of his gun play to maintain his supremacy. Seldom did anyone take the risk of going "up against" Benton Sharp. Even the law officers were content to let him make his own terms of peace. Sharp was a ready and an accurate shot, and as lucky as a brand-new penny at coming clear of scrapes. Standifer wondered how this pillaging eagle ever came to be mated with Amos Colvin's little dove, and expressed his wonder.

Mrs. Sharp sighed.

"You see, Mr. Standifer, we didn't know anything about him, and he can be very pleasant and kind when he wants to. We lived down in the little town of Goliad. Benton came riding down that way and stopped there a while. I reckon I was some better looking then than I am now. He was good to me for a whole year after we were married. He insured his life for me for five thousand dollars. But for the last six months he has done everything but kill me. I often wish he had done that, too. He got out of money for a while, and abused me shamefully for not having anything he could spend. Then Father died and left me the little home in Goliad. My husband made me sell that and turned me out into the world. I've barely been able to live, for I'm not strong enough to work. Lately, I heard he was making money in San Antonio, so I went there, and found him, and asked for a little help. This," touching the livid bruise on her temple, "is what he gave me. So I came on to Austin to see the governor. I once heard Father say that there was some land or a pension coming to him from the state that he never would ask for."

Luke Standifer rose to his feet, and pushed his chair back. He looked rather perplexedly around the big office with its handsome furniture.

"It's a long trail to follow," he said, slowly, "trying to get back dues from the government. There's red tape and lawyers and rulings and evidences and courts to keep you waiting. I'm not certain," continued the commissioner, with a profoundly meditative frown, "whether this department that I'm the boss of has any jurisdiction or not. It's only Insurance, Statistics, and History, ma'am, and it don't sound as if it would cover the case. But sometimes a saddle blanket can be made to stretch. You keep your seat, just for a few minutes, ma'am, till I step into the next room and see about it."

The state treasurer was seated within his massive, complicated railings, reading a newspaper. Business for the day was about over. The clerks lolled at their desks, awaiting the closing hour. The Commissioner of Insurance, Statistics, and History entered, and leaned in at the window.

The treasurer, a little, brisk old man, with snow-white moustache and beard, jumped up youthfully and came forward to greet Standifer. They were friends of old.

"Uncle Frank," said the commissioner, using the familiar name by which the historic treasurer was addressed by every Texan, "how much money have you got on hand?"

The treasurer named the sum of the last balance down to the odd cents—something more than a million dollars.

The commissioner whistled lowly, and his eyes grew hopefully bright.

"You know, or else you've heard of, Amos Colvin, Uncle Frank?"

"Knew him well," said the treasurer, promptly. "A good man. A valuable citizen. One of the first settlers in the Southwest."

"His daughter," said Standifer, "is sitting in my office. She's penniless. She's married to Benton Sharp, a coyote and a murderer. He's reduced her to want and broken her heart. Her father helped build up this state, and it's the state's turn to help his child. A couple of thousand dollars will buy back her home and let her live in peace. The State of Texas can't afford to refuse it. Give me the money, Uncle Frank, and I'll give it to her right away. We'll fix up the red-tape business afterward."

The treasurer looked a little bewildered.

"Why, Standifer," he said, "you know I can't pay a cent out of the treasury without a warrant from the comptroller. I can't disburse a dollar without a voucher to show for it."

The commissioner betrayed a slight impatience.

"I'll give you a voucher," he declared. "What's this job they've given me for? Am I just a knot on a mesquite stump? Can't my office stand for it? Charge it up to Insurance and the other two sideshows. Don't Statistics show that Amos Colvin came to this state when it was in the hands of Greasers and rattlesnakes and Comanches, and fought day and night to make a white man's country of it? Don't they show that Amos Colvin's daughter is brought to ruin by a villain who's trying to pull down what you and I and old Texans shed our blood to build up? Don't History show that the Lone Star State never yet failed to grant relief to the suffering and oppressed children of the men who made her the grandest commonwealth in the Union? If Statistics and History don't bear out the claim of Amos Colvin's child I'll ask the next legislature to abolish my office. Come, now, Uncle Frank, let her have the money. I'll sign the papers officially, if you say so; and then if the governor or the comptroller or the janitor or anybody else makes a kick, by the Lord I'll refer the matter to the people, and see if they won't indorse the act."

The treasurer looked sympathetic but shocked. The commissioner's voice had grown louder as he rounded off the sentences that, however praiseworthy they might be in sentiment, reflected somewhat upon the capacity of the head of a more or less important department of state. The clerks were beginning to listen.

"Now, Standifer," said the treasurer, soothingly, "you know I'd like to help in this matter, but stop and think a moment, please. Every cent in the treasury is expended only by appropriation made by the legislature, and drawn out by checks issued by the comptroller. I can't control the use of a cent of it. Neither can you. Your department isn't disbursive—it isn't even administrative—it's purely clerical. The only way for the lady to obtain relief is to petition the legislature, and—"

"To the devil with the legislature," said Standifer, turning away.

The treasurer called him back.

"I'd be glad, Standifer, to contribute a hundred dollars personally toward the immediate expenses of Colvin's daughter." He reached for his pocketbook.

"Never mind, Uncle Frank," said the commissioner, in a softer tone. "There's no need of that. She hasn't asked for anything of that sort yet. Besides, her case is in my hands. I see now what a little rag-tag, bob-tail, gotch-eared department I've been put in charge of. It seems to be about as important as an almanac or a hotel register. But while I'm running it, it won't turn away any daughters of Amos Colvin without stretching its jurisdiction to cover, if possible. You want to keep your eye on the Department of Insurance, Statistics, and History."

The commissioner returned to his office, looking thoughtful. He opened and closed an inkstand on his desk many times with extreme and undue attention before he spoke. "Why don't you get a divorce?" he asked, suddenly.

"I haven't the money to pay for it," answered the lady.

"Just at present," announced the commissioner, in a formal tone, "the powers of my department appear to be considerably stringhalted. Statistics seem to be overdrawn at the bank, and History isn't good for a square meal. But you've come to the right place, ma'am. The department will see you through. Where did you say your husband is, ma'am?"

"He was in San Antonio yesterday. He is living there now."

Suddenly the commissioner abandoned his official air. He took the faded little woman's hands in his, and spoke in the old voice he used on the trail and around campfires.

"Your name's Amanda, isn't it?"

"Yes, sir."

"I thought so. I've heard your dad say it often enough. Well, Amanda, here's your father's best friend, the head of a big office in the state government, that's going to help you out of your troubles. And here's the old bush-whacker and cowpuncher that your father has helped out of scrapes time and time again wants to ask you a question. Amanda, have you got enough money to run you for the next two or three days?"

Mrs. Sharp's white face flushed the least bit.

"Plenty, sir—for a few days."

"All right, then, ma'am. Now you go back where you are stopping here, and you come to the office again the day after to-morrow at four o'clock in the afternoon. Very likely by that time there will be something definite to report to you." The commissioner hesitated, and looked a trifle embarrassed. "You said your husband had insured his life for $5,000. Do you know whether the premiums have been kept paid upon it or not?"

"He paid for a whole year in advance about five months ago," said Mrs. Sharp. "I have the policy and receipts in my trunk."

"Oh, that's all right, then," said Standifer. "It's best to look after things of that sort. Some day they may come in handy."

Mrs. Sharp departed, and soon afterward Luke Standifer went down to the little hotel where he boarded and looked up the railroad time-table in the daily paper. Half an hour later he removed his coat and vest, and strapped a peculiarly constructed pistol holster across his shoulders, leaving the receptacle close under his left armpit. Into the holster he shoved a short-barreled .44-calibre revolver. Putting on his clothes again, he strolled down to the station and caught the five-twenty afternoon train for San Antonio.

The San Antonio *Express* of the following morning contained this sensational piece of news:

## BENTON SHARP MEETS HIS MATCH

### The Most Noted Desperado in Southwest Texas Shot to Death in the Gold Front Restaurant— Prominent State Official Successfully Defends Himself Against the Noted Bully—Magnificent Exhibition of Quick Gun Play.

Last night about eleven o'clock Benton Sharp, with two other men, entered the Gold Front Restaurant and seated themselves at a table. Sharp had been drinking, and was loud and boisterous, as he always was when under the influence of liquor. Five minutes after the party was seated a tall, well-dressed, elderly gentleman entered the restaurant. Few present recognized the Honorable Luke Standifer, the recently appointed Commissioner of Insurance, Statistics, and History.

Going over to the same side where Sharp was, Mr. Standifer prepared to take a seat at the next table. In hanging his hat upon one of the hooks along the wall he let it fall upon Sharp's head. Sharp turned, being in an especially ugly humor, and cursed the other roundly. Mr. Standifer apologized calmly for the accident, but Sharp continued his vituperations. Mr. Standifer was observed to draw near and speak a few sentences to the desperado in so low a tone that no one else caught the words. Sharp sprang up, wild with rage. In the meantime Mr. Standifer had stepped some yards away, and was standing quietly with his arms folded across the breast of his loosely hanging coat.

With that impetuous and deadly rapidity that made Sharp so dreaded, he reached for the gun he always carried in his hip pocket—a movement that has preceded the death of at least a dozen men at his hands. Quick as the motion was, the bystanders assert that it was met by the most beautiful exhibition of lightning gun-pulling ever witnessed in the Southwest. As Sharp's pistol was being raised—and the act was really quicker than the eye could follow—a glittering .44 appeared as if by some conjuring trick in the right hand of Mr. Standifer, who, without a perceptible movement of his arm, shot Benton Sharp through the heart. It seems that the new Commissioner of Insurance, Statistics, and History has been an old-time Indian fighter and ranger for many years, which accounts for the happy knack he has of handling a .44.

It is not believed that Mr. Standifer will be put to any inconvenience beyond a necessary formal hearing to-day, as all the witnesses who were present unite in declaring that the deed was done in self-defense.

When Mrs. Sharp appeared at the office of the commissioner, according to appointment, she found that gentleman calmly eating a golden russet apple. He greeted her without embarrassment and without hesitation at approaching the subject that was the topic of the day.

"I had to do it, ma'am," he said, simply, "or get it myself. Mr. Kauffman," he added, turning to the old clerk, "please look up the records of the Security Life Insurance Company and see if they are all right."

"No need to look," grunted Kauffman, who had everything in his head. "It's all O.K. They pay all losses within ten days."

Mrs. Sharp soon rose to depart. She had arranged to remain in town until the policy was paid. The commissioner did not detain her. She was a woman, and he did not know just what to say to her at present. Rest and time would bring her what she needed.

But, as she was leaving, Luke Standifer indulged himself in an official remark:

"The Department of Insurance, Statistics, and History, ma'am, has done the best it could with your case. 'Twas a case hard to cover according to red tape. Statistics failed, and History missed fire, but, if I may be permitted to say it, we came out particularly strong on Insurance."

# The Last of
# the Troubadours

Inexorably Sam Galloway saddled his pony. He was going away from the Rancho Altito at the end of a three months' visit. It is not to be expected that a guest should put up with wheat coffee and biscuits yellow-streaked with saleratus for longer than that. Nick Napoleon, the big Negro man cook, had never been able to make good biscuits. Once before, when Nick was cooking at the Willow Ranch, Sam had been forced to fly from his *cuisine*, after only a six weeks' sojourn.

On Sam's face was an expression of sorrow, deepened with regret and slightly tempered by the patient forgiveness of a connoisseur who cannot be understood. But very firmly and inexorably he buckled his saddle-cinches, looped his take-rope and hung it to his saddle-horn, tied his slicker and coat on the cantle, and looped his quirt on his right wrist. The Merrydews (householders of the Rancho Altito), men, women, children, and servants, vassals, visitors, employés, dogs, and casual callers, were grouped in the "gallery" of the ranch house, all with face set to the tune of melancholy and grief. For, as the coming of Sam Galloway to any ranch, camp, or cabin between the rivers Frio or Bravo del Norte aroused joy, so his departure caused mourning and distress.

And then, during absolute silence, except for the bumping of a hind elbow of a hound dog as he pursued a wicked flea, Sam tenderly and carefully tied his guitar across his saddle on top of his slicker and coat. The guitar was in a green duck bag; and if you catch the significance of it, it explains Sam.

Sam Galloway was the Last of the Troubadours. Of course you know about the troubadours. The encyclopaedia says they flourished between the eleventh and the thirteenth centuries. What they flourished doesn't seem clear—you may be pretty sure it wasn't a sword:

maybe it was a fiddle-bow, or a forkful of spaghetti, or a lady's scarf. Anyhow, Sam Galloway was one of 'em.

Sam put on a martyred expression as he mounted his pony. But the expression on his face was hilarious compared with the one on his pony's. You see, a pony gets to know his rider mighty well, and it is not unlikely that cow ponies in pastures and at hitching racks had often guyed Sam's pony for being ridden by a guitar player instead of by a rollicking, cussing, all-wool cowboy. No man is a hero to his saddle-horse. And even an escalator in a department store might be excused for tripping up a troubadour.

Oh, I know I'm one; and so are you. You remember the stories you memorize and the card tricks you study and that little piece on the piano—how does it go—ti-tum-te-tum-ti-tum—those little Arabian Ten-Minute Entertainments that you furnish when you go up to call on your rich Aunt Jane. You should know that *omnae personae in tres partes divisae sunt*. Namely: Barons, Troubadours, and Workers. Barons have no inclination to read such folderol as this; and Workers have no time: so I know you must be a Troubadour, and that you will understand Sam Galloway. Whether we sing, act, dance, write, lecture, or paint, we are only troubadours; so let us make the worst of it.

The pony with the Dante Alighieri face, guided by the pressure of Sam's knees, bore that wandering minstrel sixteen miles southeastward. Nature was in her most benignant mood. League after league of delicate, sweet flowerets made fragrant the gently undulating prairie. The east wind tempered the spring warmth; wool-white clouds flying in from the Mexican Gulf hindered the direct rays of the April sun. Sam sang songs as he rode. Under his pony's bridle he had tucked some sprigs of chaparral to keep away the deer flies. Thus crowned, the long-faced quadruped looked more Dantesque than before, and, judging by his countenance, seemed to think of Beatrice.

Straight as topography permitted, Sam rode to the sheep ranch of old man Ellison. A visit to a sheep ranch seemed to him desirable just then. There had been too many people, too much noise, argument, competition, confusion, at Rancho Altito. He had never conferred upon old man Ellison the favour of sojourning at his ranch; but he knew he would be welcome. The troubadour is his own passport everywhere. The Workers in the castle let down the drawbridge to him, and the Baron sets him at his left hand at table in the banquet hall. There ladies smile upon him and applaud his songs and stories, while the Workers bring boars' heads and flagons. If the Baron nods once or twice in his carved oaken chair, he does not do it maliciously.

Old man Ellison welcomed the troubadour flatteringly. He had often heard praises of Sam Galloway from other ranchmen who had been complimented by his visits, but had never aspired to such an honor for his own humble barony. I say barony because old man Ellison was the Last of the Barons. Of course, Mr. Bulwer-Lytton lived too early to know him or he wouldn't have conferred that sobriquet upon Warwick. In life it is the duty and the function of the Baron to provide work for the Workers and lodging and shelter for the Troubadours.

Old man Ellison was a shrunken old man, with a short, yellow-white beard and a face lined and seamed by past-and-gone smiles. His ranch was a little two-room box house in a grove of hackberry trees in the lonesomest part of the sheep country. His household consisted of a Kiowa Indian man cook, four hounds, a pet sheep, and a half-tamed coyote chained to a fence-post. He owned 3,000 sheep, which he ran on two sections of leased land and many thousands of acres neither leased nor owned. Three or four times a year some one who spoke his language would ride up to his gate and exchange a few bald ideas with him. Those were red-letter days to old man Ellison. Then in what illuminated, embossed, and gorgeously decorated capitals must have been written the day on which a troubadour—a troubadour who, according to the encyclopaedia, should have flourished between the eleventh and the thirteenth centuries—drew rein at the gates of his baronial castle!

Old man Ellison's smiles came back and filled his wrinkles when he saw Sam. He hurried out of the house in his shuffling, limping way to greet him.

"Hello, Mr. Ellison," called Sam, cheerfully. "Thought I'd drop over and see you a while. Notice you've had fine rains on your range. They ought to make good grazing for your spring lambs."

"Well, well, well," said old man Ellison. "I'm mighty glad to see you, Sam. I never thought you'd take the trouble to ride over to as out-of-the-way an old ranch as this. But you're mighty welcome. 'Light. I've got a sack of new oats in the kitchen—shall I bring out a feed for your hoss?"

"Oats for him?" said Sam, derisively. "No, sir-ee. He's as fat as a pig now on grass. He don't get rode enough to keep him in condition. I'll just turn him in the horse pasture with a drag rope on if you don't mind."

I am positive that never during the eleventh and thirteenth centuries did Baron, Troubadour, and Worker amalgamate as harmoniously as their parallels did that evening at old man Ellison's sheep ranch. The Kiowa's biscuits were light and tasty and his coffee strong. Ineradicable hospitality and appreciation glowed on old man Ellison's weather-tanned face. As for the troubadour, he said to himself that he had stumbled upon pleasant places indeed. A well-cooked, abundant meal, a host whom his lightest attempt to entertain seemed to delight far beyond the merits of the exertion, and the reposeful atmosphere that his sensitive soul at that time craved united to confer upon him a satisfaction and luxurious ease that he had seldom found on his tours of the ranches.

After the delectable supper, Sam untied the green duck bag and took out his guitar. Not by way of payment, mind you—neither Sam Galloway nor any other of the true troubadours are lineal descendants of the late Tommy Tucker. You have read of Tommy Tucker in the works of the esteemed but often obscure Mother Goose. Tommy Tucker sang for his supper. No true troubadour would do that. He would have his supper, and then sing for Art's sake.

Sam Galloway's repertoire comprised about fifty funny stories and between thirty and forty songs. He by no means stopped there. He could talk through twenty cigarettes on any topic that you brought up. And he never sat up when he could lie down; and never stood when he could sit. I am strongly disposed to linger with him, for I am drawing a portrait as well as a blunt pencil and a tattered thesaurus will allow.

I wish you could have seen him: he was small and tough and inactive beyond the power of imagination to conceive. He wore an ultramarine-blue woollen shirt laced down the front with a pearl-gray, exaggerated sort of shoestring, indestructible brown duck clothes, inevitable high-heeled boots with Mexican spurs, and a Mexican straw sombrero.

That evening Sam and old man Ellison dragged their chairs out under the hackberry trees. They lighted cigarettes; and the troubadour gaily touched his guitar. Many of the songs he sang were the weird, melancholy, minor-keyed *canciones* that he had learned from the Mexican sheep herders and *vaqueros*. One, in particular, charmed and soothed the soul of the lonely baron. It was a favourite song of the sheep herders, beginning: "*Huile, huile, palomita,*" which being translated means, "Fly, fly, little dove." Sam sang it for old man Ellison many times that evening.

The troubadour stayed on at the old man's ranch. There was peace and quiet and appreciation there, such as he had not found in the noisy camps of the cattle kings. No audience in the world could have crowned the work of poet, musician, or artist with more worshipful and unflagging approval than that bestowed upon his efforts by old man Ellison. No visit by a royal personage to a humble woodchopper or peasant could have been received with more flattering thankfulness and joy.

On a cool, canvas-covered cot in the shade of the hackberry trees Sam Galloway passed the greater part of his time. There he rolled his brown paper cigarettes, read such tedious literature as the ranch afforded, and added to his repertoire of improvisations that he played so expertly on his guitar. To him, as a slave ministering to a great lord, the Kiowa brought cool water from the red jar hanging under the brush shelter, and food when he called for it. The prairie zephyrs fanned him mildly; mockingbirds at morn and eve competed with but scarce equalled the sweet melodies of his lyre; a perfumed stillness seemed to fill all his world. While old man Ellison was pottering among his flocks of sheep on his mile-an-hour pony, and while the Kiowa took his siesta in the burning sunshine at the end of the kitchen, Sam would lie on his cot thinking what a happy world he lived in, and how kind it is to the ones whose mission in life it is to give entertainment and pleasure. Here he had food and lodging as good as he had ever longed for; absolute immunity from care or exertion or strife; an endless welcome, and a host whose delight at the sixteenth repetition of a song or a story was as keen as at its initial giving. Was there ever a troubadour of old who struck upon as royal a castle in his wanderings? While he lay thus, meditating upon his blessings, little brown cottontails would shyly frolic through the yard; a covey of white-topknotted blue quail would run past, in single file, twenty yards away; a *paisano* bird, out hunting for tarantulas, would hop upon the fence and salute him with sweeping flourishes of its long tail. In the eighty-acre horse pasture the pony with the Dantesque face grew fat and almost smiling. The troubadour was at the end of his wanderings.

Old man Ellison was his own *vaciero*. That means that he supplied his sheep camps with wood, water, and rations by his own labors instead of hiring a *vaciero*. On small ranches it is often done.

One morning he started for the camp of Encarnación Felipe de la Cruz y Monto Piedras (one of his sheep herders) with the week's usual rations of brown beans, coffee, meal, and sugar. Two miles away on the trail from old Fort Ewing he met, face to face, a terrible being called King James, mounted on a fiery, prancing, Kentucky-bred horse.

King James's real name was James King; but people reversed it because it seemed to fit him better, and also because it seemed to please his majesty. King James was the biggest cattleman between the Alamo plaza in San Antone and Bill Hopper's saloon in Brownsville. Also he was the loudest and most offensive bully and braggart and bad man in southwest Texas. And he always made good whenever he bragged; and the more noise he made the more dangerous he was. In the story papers it is always the quiet, mild-mannered man with light blue eyes and a low voice who turns out to be really dangerous; but in real life and in this story such is not the case. Give me my choice between assaulting a large, loud-mouthed rough-houser and an inoffensive stranger with blue eyes sitting quietly in a corner, and you will see something doing in the corner every time.

King James, as I intended to say earlier, was a fierce, two-hundred-pound, sunburned, blond man, as pink as an October strawberry, and with two horizontal slits under shaggy red eyebrows for eyes. On that day he wore a flannel shirt that was tan-colored, with the exception of certain large areas which were darkened by transudations due to the summer sun. There seemed to be other clothing and garnishings about him, such as brown duck trousers stuffed into immense boots, and red handkerchiefs and revolvers; and a shotgun laid across his saddle and a leather belt with millions of cartridges shining in it—but your mind skidded off such accessories; what held your gaze was just the two little horizontal slits that he used for eyes.

This was the man that old man Ellison met on the trail; and when you count up in the baron's favor that he was sixty-five and weighed ninety-eight pounds and had heard of King James's record and that he (the baron) had a hankering for the *vita simplex* and had no gun with him and wouldn't have used it if he had, you can't censure him if I tell you that the smiles with which the troubadour had filled his wrinkles went out of them and left them plain wrinkles again. But he was not the kind of baron that flies from danger. He reined in the mile-an-hour pony (no difficult feat), and saluted the formidable monarch.

King James expressed himself with royal directness.

"You're that old snoozer that's running sheep on this range, ain't you? What right have you got to do it? Do you own the land, or lease any?"

"I have two sections leased from the state," said old man Ellison, mildly.

"Not by no means, you haven't," said King James. "Your lease expired yesterday; and I had a man at the land office on the minute to take it up. You don't control a foot of grass in Texas. You sheep men have got to git. Your time's up. It's a cattle country, and there ain't any room in it for snoozers. This range you've got your sheep on is mine. I'm putting up a wire fence, forty by sixty miles; and if there's a sheep inside of it when it's done it'll be a dead one. I'll give you a week to move yours away. If they ain't gone by then, I'll send six men over here with Winchesters to make mutton out of the whole lot. And if I find you here at the same time this is what you'll get."

King James patted the breech of his shotgun warningly.

Old man Ellison rode on to the camp of Encarnación. He sighed many times, and the wrinkles in his face grew deeper. Rumors that the old order was about to change had reached him before. The end of Free Grass was in sight. Other troubles, too, had been accumulating upon his shoulders. His flocks were decreasing instead of growing; the price of wool was declining at every clip; even Bradshaw, the store-keeper at Frio City, at whose store he bought his ranch supplies, was dunning him for his last six months' bill and threatening to cut him off. And so this last greatest calamity suddenly dealt out to him by the terrible King James was a crusher.

When the old man got back to the ranch at sunset he found Sam Galloway lying on his cot, propped against a roll of blankets and wool sacks, fingering his guitar.

"Hello, Uncle Ben," the troubadour called, cheerfully. "You rolled in early this evening. I been trying a new twist on the Spanish Fan-dango to-day. I just about got it. Here's how she goes—listen."

"That's fine, that's mighty fine," said old man Ellison, sitting on the kitchen step and rubbing his white, Scotch-terrier whiskers. "I reckon you've got all the musicians beat east and west, Sam, as far as the roads are cut out."

"Oh, I don't know," said Sam reflectively. "But I certainly do get there on variations. I guess I can handle anything in five flats about as well as any of 'em. But you look kind of fagged out, Uncle Ben—ain't you feeling right well this evening?"

"Little tired; that's all, Sam. If you ain't played yourself out, let's have that Mexican piece that starts off with: '*Huile, huile, palomita.*' It seems that that song always kind of soothes and comforts me after I've been riding far or anything bothers me."

"Why, *seguramente, señor*," said Sam. "I'll hit her up for you as often as you like. And before I forget about it, Uncle Ben, you want to jerk Bradshaw up about them last hams he sent us. They're just a little bit strong."

A man sixty-five years old, living on a sheep ranch and beset by a complication of disasters, cannot successfully and continuously dissem-ble. Moreover, a troubadour has eyes quick to see unhappiness in oth-ers around him—because it disturbs his own ease. So, on the next day, Sam again questioned the old man about his air of sadness and abstraction. Then old man Ellison told him the story of King James's threats and orders and that pale melancholy and red ruin appeared to have marked him for their own. The troubadour took the news thoughtfully. He had heard much about King James.

On the third day of the seven days of grace allowed him by the autocrat of the range, old man Ellison drove his buckboard to Frio

City to fetch some necessary supplies for the ranch. Bradshaw was hard but not implacable. He divided the old man's order by two, and let him have a little more time. One article secured was a new, fine ham for the pleasure of the troubadour.

Five miles out of Frio City on his way home the old man met King James riding into town. His majesty could never look anything but fierce and menacing, but to-day his slits of eyes appeared to be a little wider than they usually were.

"Good day," said the king, gruffly. "I've been wanting to see you. I hear it said by a cowman from Sandy yesterday that you was from Jackson County, Mississippi, originally. I want to know if that's a fact."

"Born there," said old man Ellison, "and raised there till I was twenty-one."

"This man says," went on King James, "that he thinks you was related to the Jackson County Reeveses. Was he right?"

"Aunt Caroline Reeves," said the old man, "was my half-sister."

"She was my aunt," said King James. "I run away from home when I was sixteen. Now, let's re-talk over some things that we discussed a few days ago. They call me a bad man; and they're only half right. There's plenty of room in my pasture for your bunch of sheep and their increase for a long time to come. Aunt Caroline used to cut out sheep in cake dough and bake 'em for me. You keep your sheep where they are, and use all the range you want. How's your finances?"

The old man related his woes in detail, dignifiedly, with restraint and candor.

"She used to smuggle extra grub into my school basket—I'm speaking of Aunt Caroline," said King James. "I'm going over to Frio City to-day, and I'll ride back by your ranch tomorrow. I'll draw $2,000 out of the bank there and bring it over to you; and I'll tell Bradshaw to let you have anything you want on credit. You are bound to have heard the old saying at home, that the Jackson County Reeveses and Kings would stick closer by each other than chestnut burs. Well, I'm a King yet whenever I run across a Reeves. So you look out for me along about sundown to-morrow, and don't you worry about nothing. Shouldn't wonder if the dry spell don't kill out the young grass."

Old man Ellison drove happily ranchward. Once more the smiles filled out his wrinkles. Very suddenly, by the magic of kinship and the good that lies somewhere in all hearts, his troubles had been removed.

On reaching the ranch he found that Sam Galloway was not there. His guitar hung by its buckskin string to a hackberry limb, moaning as the gulf breeze blew across its masterless strings.

The Kiowa endeavored to explain.

"Sam, he catch pony," said he, "and say he ride to Frio City. What for no can damn sabe. Say he come back to-night. Maybe so. That all."

As the first stars came out the troubadour rode back to his haven. He pastured his pony and went into the house, his spurs jingling martially.

Old man Ellison sat at the kitchen table, having a tin cup of before-supper coffee. He looked contented and pleased.

"Hello, Sam," said he, "I'm darned glad to see ye back. I don't know how I managed to get along on this ranch, anyhow, before ye dropped in to cheer things up. I'll bet ye've been skylarking around with some of them Frio City gals, now, that's kept ye so late."

And then old man Ellison took another look at Sam's face and saw that the minstrel had changed to the man of action.

And while Sam is unbuckling from his waist old man Ellison's six-shooter, that the latter had left behind when he drove to town, we may well pause to remark that anywhere and whenever a troubadour lays down the guitar and takes up the sword trouble is sure to follow. It is not the expert thrust of Athos nor the cold skill of Aramis nor the iron wrist of Porthos that we have to fear—it is the Gascon's fury—the wild and unacademic attack of the troubadour—the sword of D'Artagnan.

"I done it," said Sam. "I went over to Frio City to do it. I couldn't let him put the skibunk on you, Uncle Ben. I met him in Summer's saloon. I knowed what to do. I said a few things to him that nobody else heard. He reached for his gun first—half a dozen fellows saw him do it—but I got mine unlimbered first. Three doses I gave him—right around the lungs, and a saucer could have covered up all of 'em. He won't bother you no more."

"This—is—King—James—you speak—of?" asked old man Ellison, while he sipped his coffee.

"You bet it was. And they took me before the county judge; and the witnesses what saw him draw his gun first was all there. Well, of course, they put me under $300 bond to appear before the court, but there was four or five boys on the spot ready to sign the bail. He won't bother you no more, Uncle Ben. You ought to have seen how close them bullet holes was together. I reckon playing a guitar as much as I do must kind of limber a fellow's trigger finger a little, don't you think, Uncle Ben?"

Then there was a little silence in the castle except for the spluttering of a venison steak that the Kiowa was cooking.

"Sam," said old man Ellison, stroking his white whiskers with a tremulous hand, "would you mind getting the guitar and playing that 'Huile, huile, palomita' piece once or twice? It always seems to be kind of soothing and comforting when a man's tired and fagged out."

There is no more to be said, except that the title of the story is wrong. It should have been called "The Last of the Barons." There never will be an end to the troubadours; and now and then it does seem that the jingle of their guitars will drown the sound of the muffled blows of the pickaxes and trip hammers of all the Workers in the world.

# MARY AUSTIN

## (1868–1934)

Born in Carlinville, Illinois, to a veteran of the Civil War turned farmer and a puritanical Methodist mother with feminist convictions, Mary Hunter grew up with a distinct sense of her own unworth. She graduated from Blackburn College in 1868, the year that her father died and her mother and oldest brother, James, inspired by stories of quick wealth from farming, moved the family to the desert regions of California, settling finally on a Bakersfield ranch. Mary was married in 1891 to Wallace Austin, a civil engineer whose attempts to wrest a living from a farm in the Inyo County region, on the promise of an irrigation scheme that never materialized, kept the couple in a perpetual state of unrealized expectations. In 1892 Mary Austin gave birth to a child, Ruth, who suffered from such severe retardation that, after more than a decade of trying to care for the girl herself, Austin had her committed to an institution at the age of thirteen. The source of the "tainted blood" that caused Ruth's condition was a cause of contention between husband and wife, and Mary Austin spent much of the rest of her life assigning blame for her feelings of guilt. Ruth died during the flu epidemic of 1918, by which time her parents had divorced.

Austin had early demonstrated literary promise, and the difficulties of raising a retarded child as well as living in relative isolation on a California ranch were exacerbated by her attempts to develop as a writer. Another burden was the need to supplement her husband's income by teaching. Shortly after her marriage, Austin met Ina Coolbrith, the doyenne of polite letters in San Francisco, who recognized her talents. The year that Ruth was born, Austin had a story published in the Overland Monthly. Early on she had evinced a mystical streak, and her contact with the Indians of the Owens Valley desert awakened her interest in the psychic powers associated with primitiv-

*ism. In 1898, she met William James, whose psychological theories meshed with her own notions of primal creativity, a deeply religious but hardly institutionalized faith that had long since put her at odds with her mother's strict Methodism. Still suffering from a deep sense of parental disapproval and neglect, Austin took strength from the encouragement of James as she had earlier from Coolbrith's interest, and when in 1899 she moved with her daughter to Los Angeles, in the first tentative break with her husband, Austin drew further self-esteem from the praise of Charles Lummis, the wealthy mentor of the close-knit cultural circle in that still small city.*

*Wallace Austin eventually gave up serious hopes for ranching and filled a number of teaching and bureaucratic positions with considerable success. In 1899, he was appointed registrar of the Land Office in Independence, California, where Mary and Ruth joined him in 1900. There she wrote the book that would bring her literary fame,* The Land of Little Rain *(1903), much of which had been previously published as sketches and stories in such Eastern magazines as the* Atlantic Monthly, *but the cumulative effect was to announce the arrival of a distinct and original talent. Austin soon began to visit San Francisco regularly, where she associated with other local literary people. Among these were Jack London and George Sterling, who introduced her to the arts colony at Carmel—where in 1906 she bought land and built a house. In 1904, her study of Indian life,* The Basket Woman, *was published, an early synthesis of her feminist and primitivist beliefs. In 1907, she was diagnosed as having breast cancer, but the symptoms eventually disappeared, in a "cure" she attributed to the powers of creative inner strength. In the meantime, told that she had less than a year to live, Austin headed for Europe, and in the next two years traveled through England, Italy, and France. In her absence, her novel based on the hothouse society of literary Carmel,* Santa Lucia, *was published (1908), as well as a collection of short stories,* Lost Borders *(1909), essentially a sequel to* Land of Little Rain.

*In 1910, Austin moved to New York City, where she remained for only a year, overseeing the production of her play* The Arrow Maker. *Like* Basket Woman, *the drama gave indirect expression to her increasing commitment to feminism by championing Indian culture, an equivalent and powerful marginal zone, centered in the dominant figure of a sorceress, in whom artistry and religion are combined. In 1911, Austin moved back to Carmel, and for the next few years would travel back and forth between the two places, retreating to write and then entering the larger world in order to promote her career and push for feminist reform. Her feminist novel,* A Woman of Genius, *appeared in 1912, and thereafter she produced a stream of books, all promoting her favorite themes, centered about the theme of the empowerment derived from a mystical conception of art. Although she perceived herself as lonely and suffering neglect in the erotic zones of Carmel because of her short, even stumpy, stature and homely features, Austin was a personal powerhouse, a living example of her teachings.*

*Finding New York a much too competitive arena, Austin, after a number of tentative visits, decided to settle in Santa Fe, which like Carmel was an intensely literary and artistic milieu, but which also had intimate connections with the prevailing Native American culture, thanks to the efforts of Mabel Dodge Luhan, a wealthy enthusiast for Indian life, who had relocated to Taos from New York in 1917. Luhan invited a number of leading artistic and literary lights to Taos, and she was responsible for Austin's move. In 1924, Austin published* The Land of Journey's Endings, *a wide-ranging study of the human geography of the Southwest, and in that year she settled permanently in New Mexico. Leaving Taos to Luhan, Austin set up her own sphere of influence in Santa Fe, where she exerted a considerable authority, in effect becoming a local dictator of the arts; she became as well a mover in the cause of Indian rights, drawing upon the "deep self" of which she had for so long been a celebrant.*

*For the next twenty years Austin lived and worked in Santa Fe, spending much of her creative energies compiling her autobiography,* Earth Horizon *(1932), a lengthy and detailed account of her mystical experience and the painful circumstances of her married and literary life. Her companion during much of this time was her niece, Mary Hunter, over whom she exercised as much control as possible; this proved stressful for both women, and may have been the long-range result of Austin's guilt over the abandonment of her daughter. Austin was a powerfully neurotic person, perhaps more feared than loved, but too much attention has been paid to her mental problems by recent students of her work, presumably the dubious fruit of Freud's association of art and neuroses. As much blame can be put on the social and cultural circumstances of her times, which disenfranchised women in every possible way, blocking creative and political ambitions and pushing persons such as Mary Austin forever back into the home.*

*Fortunately, she persisted, and something more than endured. Like Frederic Remington, Austin was a celebrant of the primitive, and though her creative energies were chiefly channeled into novels and autobiographical prose, in* Lost Borders *she gave concentered power to a number of short stories that deserve more attention than they have received. A high-voltage version of John Muir (whose Pu-*

*ritan background she shared, along with a mystical apperception of
the California wilderness), she derived terrific psychic strength from
a region far less likely than the forested high Sierra, with its para-
disiac Yosemite Valley; and unlike Muir, she was vitally interested
in the Indian dwellers of the desert, with whose marginal lives she
was quick to identify.*

*Most important for our considerations, Mary Austin created from
her experience in the Owens Valley a literary region that serves as a
corrective to much of the previous writing that had characterized the
American West—even as she evinced an indebtedness to Bret Harte,
who was chiefly responsible for setting the male mythos of the West
in motion. Chronology suggests that Stewart Edward White's rhap-
sodic sympathy with the Arizona desert was similarly indebted to*
Land of Little Rain, *a book of which he could hardly have been unaware; and the resemblances to (and differences from) Jack London's
Yukon, portrayed as an environment of relentless, unrelieved adversity and death, is an important antidote to the male version of
Theodore Roosevelt's "strenuous life." Where the celebration of the
American natural scene is concerned, Austin is undoubtedly the most
important woman writer of her generation, against whose accomplishment even the work of Willa Cather pales, in its emphasis less on the
land than on the struggles and triumphs of immigrant farmers.*

*Cather of course belongs to the "great tradition," a line stretching
from Hamlin Garland to Frank Norris to John Steinbeck, in which
the West is an extension of the old, perpetually betrayed American
pastoral dream, the very trap in which Austin's family and husband
were caught. But Austin, like the male authors with whom she was
surrounded during the first emergence of her talents, celebrated a different West, that region dominated by the kinds of mirage that could
result in the deaths of the uninitiated, the unprepared. It was a primitive zone, in which men and women struggled to survive not by farming but by mining and ranching—pursuits which are essentially
hostile to the land, primal forms of exploitation without due return.
It was Austin's virtue that she, like Thoreau, understood the syncre-
tistic relationship possible between humans and the nature of which
they were finally a part, a Way that could be discovered by following
Indian trails, those barely discernible tracks that covered the desert
with weblike graffiti, a kind of writing visible only to practiced and
sympathetic eyes.*

# The Land

When the Paiute nations broke westward through the Sierra wall they cut off a remnant of the Shoshones, and forced them south as far as Death Valley and the borders of the Mojaves, they penned the Washoes in and around Tahoe, and passing between these two, established themselves along the snow-fed Sierra creeks. And this it was proper they should do, for the root of their name-word is Pah, meaning water, to distinguish them from their brothers the Utes of the Great Basin.

In time they passed quite through the sawcut cañons by Kern and Kings rivers and possessed all the east slope of the San Joaquin, but chiefly they settled by small clans and family groups where the pines leave off and the sage begins and the desert abuts on the great Sierra fault. On the northeast they touched the extreme flanks of the Utes, and with them and the southerly tribes swept a wide arc about that region of mysterious desertness of which you shall presently hear more particularly.

The boundaries between the tribes and between the clans within the tribe were plainly established by natural landmarks—peaks, hillcrests, creeks, and chains of water-holes—beginning at the foot of the Sierra and continuing eastward past the limit of endurable existence. Out there, a week's journey from everywhere, the land was not worth parcelling off, and the boundaries which should logically have been continued until they met the cañon of the Colorado ran out in foolish wastes of sand and Duke o' Wild Rose. Young Woodin brought me a potsherd once from a kitchen-midden in Shoshone Land. It might have been, for antiquity, one of those Job scraped himself withal, but it was dotted all over with colors and specks of pure gold from the riverbed from which the sand and clay were scooped. Said he:

"You ought to find a story about this somewhere."

I was sore then about not getting myself believed in some ele-

mentary matters, such as that horned toads are not poisonous, and
that Indians really have the bowels of compassion. Said I:

"I will do better than that, I will *make* a story."

We sat out a whole afternoon under the mulberry-tree, with the
landscape disappearing in shimmering heat-waves around us, testing
our story for likelihood and proving it. There was an Indian woman
in the tale, not pretty, for they are mostly not that in life, and the
earthenware pot, of course, and a lost river bedded with precious sand.
Afterward my friend went to hold down some claims in the Coso country, and I north to the lake region where the red firs are, and we told
the pot-of-gold story as often as we were permitted. One night when
I had done with it, a stranger by our camp-fire said the thing was well
known in his country. I said, "Where was that?"

"Coso," said he, and that was the first I had heard of my friend.

Next winter, at Lone Pine, a prospector from Panamint-way
wanted to know if I had ever heard of the Indian-pot Mine which was
lost out toward Pharump. I said I had a piece of the pot, which I
showed him. Then I wrote the tale for a magazine of the sort that
gets taken in camps and at miners' boarding-houses, and several men
were at great pains to explain to me where my version varied from
the accepted one of the hills. By this time, you understand, I had
begun to believe the story myself. I had a spasm of conscience, though,
when Tennessee told me that he thought he knew the very squaw of
the story, and when the back of the winter was broken he meant to
make a little "pasear" in search of the lost river. But Tennessee died
before spring, and spared my confessing. Now it only needs that some
one should find another shard of the gold-besprinkled pot to fix the
tale in the body of desert myths. Well—it had as much fact behind it
as the Gunsight, and is more interesting than the Bryfogle, which
began with the finding of a dead man, clothless as the desert dead
mostly are, with a bag of nuggets clutched in his mummied hands.

First and last, accept no man's statement that he knows this Country of Lost Borders well. A great number having lost their lives in
the process of proving where it is not safe to go, it is now possible to
pass through much of the district by guide-posts and well-known
water-holes, but the best part of it remains locked, inviolate, or at
best known only to some far-straying Indian, sheepherder, or pocket
hunter, whose account of it does not get into the reports of the Geo-
logical Survey. But a boast of knowledge is likely to prove as hollow
as the little yellow gourds called apples of Death Valley.

Pure desertness clings along the pits of the long valleys and the
formless beds of vanished lakes. Every hill that lifts as high as the
cloud-line has some trees upon it, and deer and bighorn to feed on

the tall, tufted, bunch grass between the boulders. In the year when Tonopah, turning upon itself like a swarm, trickled prospectors all over that country from Hot Creek to the Armagosa, Indians brought me word that the men had camped so close about the water-holes that the bighorn died of thirst on the headlands, turned always in the last agony toward the man-infested springs.

That is as good a pointer as any if you go waterless in the country of Lost Borders: where you find cattle dropped, skeleton or skin dried, the heads almost invariably will be turned toward the places where water-holes should be. But no such reminders will fend men from its trails. This is chiefly, I am persuaded, because there is something incomprehensible to the man-mind in the concurrence of death and beauty. Shall the tender opal mist betray you? the airy depth of mountain blueness, the blazonry of painted wind-scoured buttes, the far peaks molten with the alpen glow, cooled by the rising of the velvet violet twilight tide, and the leagues and leagues of stars? As easy for a man to believe that a beautiful woman can be cruel. Mind you, it is men who go mostly into the desert, who love it past all reasonableness, slack their ambitions, cast off old usages, neglect their families because of the pulse and beat of a life laid bare to its thews and sinews. Their women hate with implicitness the life like the land, stretching interminably whity-brown, dim and shadowy blue hills that hem it, glimmering pale waters of mirage that creep and crawl about its edges. There was a woman once at Agua Hedionda—but you wouldn't believe that either.

If the desert were a woman, I know well what like she would be: deep-breasted, broad in the hips, tawny, with tawny hair, great masses of it lying smooth along her perfect curves, full lipped like a sphinx, but not heavy-lidded like one, eyes sane and steady as the polished jewel of her skies, such a countenance as should make men serve without desiring her, such a largeness to her mind as should make their sins of no account, passionate, but not necessitious, patient—and you could not move her, no, not if you had all the earth to give, so much as one tawny hair's-breadth beyond her own desires. If you cut very deeply into any soul that has the mark of the land upon it, you find such qualities as these—as I shall presently prove to you.

# A Case of Conscience

Saunders was an average Englishman with a lung complaint. He tried Ashfork, Arizona, and Indio, and Catalina. Then he drifted north through the San Jacinta mountains and found what he was looking for. Back in England he had left so many of the things a man wishes to go on with, that he bent himself with great seriousness to his cure. He bought a couple of pack-burros, a pair of cayaques, and a camp kit. With these, a Shakespeare, a prayer-book, and a copy of *Ingoldsby Legends*, he set out on foot to explore the coast of Lost Borders. The prayer-book he had from his mother; I believe he read it regularly night and morning, and the copy of *Ingoldsby Legends* he gave me in the second year of his exile. It happened about that time I was wanting the *Ingoldsby Legends*, three hundred miles from a library, and book money hard to come by. Now there is nearly always a copy of *Ingoldsby Legends* in the vicinity of an Englishman. Englishmen think them amusing, though I do not know why. So I asked my friend, the barkeeper at the Last Chance, to inquire for it of the next Englishman who hit the town. I had to write the name out plainly so the barkeeper could remember it. The first who came was an agent for a London mining syndicate, and he left an address of a book-shop where it could be bought. The next was a remittance man, and of course he hadn't anything. If he had he would have put it in soak. That means he would have put the book up for its value in bad drink, and I write it as a part of our legitimate speech, because it says so exactly what had occurred: that particular Englishman had put everything, including his honor and his immortal soul, in soak. And the third was Saunders. He was so delighted to find an appreciator of the *Ingoldsby Legends* in the wilderness, that he offered to come to the house and render the obscure passages, and that was the beginning of my knowing about what went on later at Ubehebe.

Saunders had drifted about from water-hole to water-hole, living hardily, breathing the driest, cleanest air, sleeping and waking with the ebb and flow of light that sets in a mighty current around the world. He went up in summer to the mountain heads under the foxtail pines, and back in winter to watch the wild almond bloom by Resting Springs. He saw the Medicine dance of the Shoshones, and hunted the bighorn on Funeral Mountains, and dropped a great many things out of his life without making himself unhappy. But he kept the conscience he had brought with him. Of course it was a man's conscience that allowed him to do a great many things that by the code and the commandments are as wrong as any others, but in the end the wilderness was too big for him, and forced him to a violation of what he called his sense of duty.

In the course of time, Saunders came to a range of purplish hills lying west from Lost Valley, because of its rounded, swelling, fair twin peaks called Ubehebe (Maiden's Breast). It is a good name. Saunders came there in the spring, when the land is lovely and alluring, soft with promise and austerely virgin. He lingered in and about its pleasant places until the month of the Deer-Star, and it was then, when he would come up a week's journey to Lone Pine, for supplies, he began to tell me about Turwhasé, the gray-eyed Shoshone. He thought I would be interested, and I was, though for more reasons than Saunders at first supposed. There is a story current and confirmed, I believe, by proper evidence, that a man of one of the emigrant trains that suffered so much, and went so far astray in the hell trap of Death Valley, wandering from his party in search of water, for want of which he was partly crazed, returned to them no more and was accounted dead. But wandering in the witless condition of great thirst, he was found by the Shoshones, and by them carried to their campody in the secret places of the hills. There, though he never rightly knew himself, he showed some skill and excellences of the white men, and for that, and for his loose wit, which was fearful to them, he was kept and reverenced as a Coyote-man and a Medicine-maker of strange and fitful powers. And at the end of fifteen years his friends found him and took him away. As witness of his sojourning, there is now and then born to the descendants of that campody a Shoshone with gray eyes.

When Saunders began to tell me about Turwhasé, I knew to what it must come, though it was not until his mother wrote me that I could take any notice of it. Some too solicitous person had written her that Saunders had become a squaw-man. She thought he had married Turwhasé, and would bring home a handful of little half-breeds to inherit the estate.

She never knew how near Saunders came to doing that very thing, nor to say truth did I when I wrote her that her son was not married, and that she had nothing to fear; but with the letter I was able to get out of Saunders as much as I did not already know of the story.

I suppose at bottom the things a man loves a woman for are pretty much the same, though it is only when he talks to you of a woman not of his own class that he is willing to tell you what those things are. Saunders loved Turwhasé: first, because he was lonely and had to love somebody; then because of the way the oval of her cheek melted into the chin, and for the lovely line that runs from the waist to the knee, and for her soft, bubbling laughter; and kept on loving her because she made him comfortable.

I suppose the white strain that persisted in her quickened her aptitude for white ways. Saunders taught her to cook. She was never weary nor afraid. She was never out of temper, except when she was jealous, and that was rather amusing. Saunders told me himself how she glowed and blossomed under his caress, and wept when he neglected her. He told me everything I had the courage to know. When a man has gone about the big wilderness with slow death and sure camping on his trail, there is not much worth talking about except the things that are. Turwhasé had the art to provoke tenderness and the wish to protect, and the primitive woman's capacity for making no demands upon it. And this, in fine, is how these women take our men from us, and why, at the last, they lose them.

If you ask whether we discussed the ethics of Saunders' situation —at first there didn't appear to be any. Turwhasé was as much married as if Church and State had witnessed it; as for Saunders, society, life itself, had cast him off. He was unfit for work or marrying; being right-minded in regard to his lung complaint, he drank from no man's cup nor slept in any bed but his own. And if society had no use for him, how had it a right to say what he should do out there in the bloomy violet spaces at Maiden's Breast? Yet, at the last, the Englishman found, or thought he found, a moral issue.

Maiden's Breast—virgin land, clear sun, unsullied airs, Turwhasé. Isn't there a hint all through of the myth of the renewal of life in a virgin embrace? A great many myths come true in the big wilderness. Saunders went down to Los Angeles once in the year to a consulting physician to please his mother, not because he hoped for anything. He came back from one such journey looking like a sleepwalker newly awakened. He had been told that the diseased portion of his lung was all sloughed away, and if nothing happened to him in six months more of Ubehebe, he might go home! It was then Saunders' conscience began to trouble him, for by this time, you understand, Turwhasé had a

child—a daughter, small and gold-colored and gray-eyed. By a trick
of inheritance the eyes were like Saunders' mother's, and in the long
idle summer she had become a plaything of which he was extremely
fond. The mother, of course, was hopeless. She had never left off her
blanket, and like all Indian women when they mature, had begun to
grow fat. Oh, I *said* he had a man's conscience! Turwhasé must be left
behind, but what to do about the daughter lay heavily on Saunders'
mind.

It made an obstinate ripple in his complacency like a snag in the
current of his thought, which set toward England. Out there by the
water-holes, where he had expected to leave his bones, life had been
of a simplicity that did not concern itself beyond the happy day. Now
the old needs and desires awoke and cried in him, and along with them
the old, obstinate Anglo-Saxon prejudice that makes a man responsible for his offspring. Saunders must have had a bad time of it with
himself before he came to a decision that he must take the child to
England. It would be hard on Turwhasé; if it came to that, it would
be hard on him—there would be explanations. As matters stood he
looked to make a very good marriage at home, and the half-breed child
would be against him. All his life she would be against him. But then
it was a question of duty. Duty is a potent fetish of Englishmen, but
the wilderness has a word bigger than that. Just how Turwhasé took
his decision about the child I never heard, but as I know Indian
women, I suppose she must have taken it quietly at first, said no, and
considered it done with; then, as she saw his purpose clear, sat wordless in her blanket, all its folds drawn forward as a sign of sullenness,
her thick hair falling on either side to screen her grief; neither moved
to attend him, nor ate nor slept; and at last broke under it and seemed
to accept, put the child from her as though it was already not hers,
and made no more of it.

If there was in this acquiescence a gleam in her gray eye that
witnessed she had found the word, Saunders was not aware of it.

As to what he felt himself in regard to Turwhasé I am equally
uninformed. I've a notion, though, that men do not give themselves
time to feel in such instances; they just get it over with. All I was
told was, that when at last he felt himself strong for it, Saunders put
the child before him on the horse—she was then about two years
old—and set out from Ubehebe. He went all of one day down a long
box cañon, where at times his knees scraped the walls on either side,
and over the tortuous roots of the mountain blown bare of the sand.
The evening of the next day saw the contour of the Maiden's Breast
purpling in the east, fading at last in the blurred horizon. He rode all
day on glittering pale sands and down steep and utterly barren

barrancas. All through that riding something pricked between his shoulders, troubled his sleep with expectancy, haunted him with a suggestion of impossible espionage. The child babbled at first, or slept in his arm; he hugged it to him and forgot that its mother was a Shoshone. It cried in the night and began to refuse its food. Great tears of fatigue stood upon its cheeks; it shook with long, quivering sobs, crying silently as Indian children do when they are frightened. Saunders' arm ached with the weight of it; his heart with the perplexity. The little face looked up at him, hard with inscrutable savagery. When he came to the Inyo range and the beaten trail, he distrusted his judgment; his notion of rearing the child in England began to look ridiculous. By the time he had cleared the crest and saw the fields and orchards far below him, it appeared preposterous. And the hint of following hung like some pestiferous insect about his trail.

In all the wide, uninterrupted glare no speck as of a moving body swam within his gaze. By what locked and secret ways the presence kept pace with him, only the vultures hung high under the flaring heaven could have known.

At the hotel at Keeler that night he began to taste the bitterness he had chosen. Men, white men, mining men, mill superintendents, well-dressed, competent, looked at the brat which had Shoshone written plainly all over it, and looked away unsmiling; being gentlemen, they did not so much as look at one another. Saunders gave money to the women at the hotel to keep his daughter all night out of his sight. Riding next day toward Lone Pine between the fenced lands, farms and farmhouses, schools, a church, he began to understand that there was something more than mere irresponsibility in the way of desert-faring men who formed relations such as this and left them off with the land, as they left the clothes they wore there and its tricks of speech.

He was now four days from Ubehebe. The child slept little that night; sat up in bed, listened; would whisper its mother's name over and over, questioning, expectant; left off, still as a young quail, if Saunders moved or noticed it. It occurred to him that the child might die, which would be the best thing for it.

Coming out of his room in the early morning he stumbled over something soft in a blanket. It unrolled of itself and stood up—Turwhasé! The child gave a little leap in his arms and was still, pitifully, breathlessly still. The woman stretched out her own arms, her eyes were red and devouring.

"My baby!" she said. "Give it to me!" Without a word Saunders held it out to her. The little dark arms went around her neck, prehensile and clinging; the whole little body clung, the lines of the small face softened with a sigh of unutterable content. Turwhasé drew up her blanket and held it close.

"Mine!" she said, fiercely. "Mine, not yours!"

Saunders did not gainsay her; he drew out all the money he had and poured it in her bosom. Turwhasé laughed. With a flirt of her blanket she scattered the coins on the ground; she turned with dignity and began to walk desertward. You could see by the slope of the shoulders under the blanket and the swing of her hips, as she went, that she was all Indian.

Saunders reached down to me from the platform of the train that morning for a last good-bye. He was looking very English, smug and freshly shaven.

"I am convinced," he said, "that it really wouldn't have done, you know." I believe he thought he had come to that conclusion by himself.

What I like most about the speech of the campody is that there are no confidences. When they talk there of the essential performances of life, it is because they are essential and therefore worth talking about. Only Heaven, who made my heart, knows why it should have become a pit, bottomless and insatiable for the husks of other people's experiences, as if it were not, as I declare it, filled to the brim with the entertainment of its own affairs; as if its mere proximity were an advertisement for it, there must be always some one letting fall confidences as boys drop stones in wells, to listen afterward in some tale of mine for the faint, reverberating sound. But this is the mark of sophistication, that they always appear *as* confidences, always with that wistful back-stroke of the ego toward a personal distinction. "I don't know why I am telling you this—I shouldn't like to have you repeat it"—and then the heart loosening intimacy of speech and its conscious easement.

But in a campody it is possible to speak of the important operations of life without shamefacedness. Mid-afternoons of late fall and winter weather—for though you may speak to your brother man without curtailment, it is not well to do so in summer when the snakes are about, for the snakes are two-tongued and carry word to the gods, who, if they are to be of use to you, must not know too much of your affairs—in mid-afternoon then, when the women weave baskets and grind at the metate, and the men make nets and snares, there is good talk and much to be learned by it. Such times the sky is hard like polished turquoise set in the tawny matrix of the earth, the creek goes thinly over the stones, and the very waters of mirage are rolled back to some shut fountain in the skies; the *plump, plump!* of the metate beats on under the talk of the women like the comfortable pulse of not too insistent toil.

When Indian women talk together, and they are great gossips, three things will surely come to the surface in the course of the afternoon—children, marriage, and the ways of the whites. This last appears as a sort of pageant, which, though it is much of it sheer foolishness, is yet charged with a mysterious and compelling portent. They could never, for example, though they could give you any number of fascinating instances, get any rational explanation of the effect of their familiar clear space and desertness upon the white man adventuring in it. It was as if you had discovered in your parlor-furniture an inexplicable power of inciting your guest to strange behavior. And what in the conduct of men most interests women of the campody, or women anywhere for that matter, is their relation to women. If this, which appears to have rooted about the time the foundations of the earth were laid, is proved amenable to the lack of shade, scarcity of vegetation, and great spaces disinterested of men—not these of course, but the Power moving nakedly in the room of these things— it only goes to show that the relation is more incidental than we are disposed to think it. There is nothing in the weather and the distance between water-holes to affect a man's feeling for his children, as I have already explained to you in the case of Saunders and Mr. Wills.* But there where the Borders run out, through all the talk of the women, white women, too, who get no better understanding of the thing they witness to, through the thin web of their lives moves the vast impersonal rivalry of desertness. But because of what I said in the beginning I can tell you no more of that than I had from Tiawa in the campody of Sacabuete, where there are no confidences.

---

* The story of Mr. Wills, chapter 5 in the original text, does not precede but follows this remark, and may be found below, beginning on page 440.

# The Ploughed Lands

Tiawa came from a Shoshone camp of three wickiups somewhere between Toquina and Fish Lake Valley. When she was young and comely she had come out of that country at the heels of a white man, and wrestled with the wilderness for the love of Curly Gavin. Gavin had been swamper for Ike Mallory's eighteen-mule team, and when the news of rich strikes in the Ringold district made red flares like rockets on Mallory's horizon, he grub-staked Curly to go with Burke and Estes to prospect the Toquina. Gavin had a lot of reddish curls and a lot of good-nature and small vices; the rest of him was sheer grit. The party was out three weeks, made some fair prospects, and had a disagreement. As to that, there was never any clear account, only it became immensely important to Gavin's own mind that he should get back to Maverick and record the location of some claims before Burke and Estes had a chance at them. Accordingly he left the others at Mud Springs, and, with one day's ration of water, set out by what he believed to be a short cut for home; and he had never been loose in the wilderness before! It was spring of the year after a winter of strong rains, and a bloom on the world, all the air soft as shed petals. Every inch of the moon-white soil had a flower in it, purple or golden; mornings the light made a luminous mist about the long wands of the creosote, at noon it slid and shimmered on the slopes as the hills breathed evenly in sleep. It is as easy, I say, to believe that such a land could neglect men to their death, as for man to believe that a lovely woman can be unkind. Gavin, for one, did not believe it.

By noon of the second day he began to suspect he had missed the trail—by night he was sure of it, and thinking to behave very sensibly walked back by the stars to recover the lost landmarks. By that time his water was quite gone. There came a time soon after that when the one consuming desire of the man was to get shut of the whole

affair, the swimming earth that swung and tilted about the pivot of
his feet, the hell-bent sun, the tormenting thirst, the glare of the sand
that ate into his eyes. He was horribly bored; he wanted the thing to
quit, to let him rest.

"Have done, curse you!" he shouted to it. As if the land had heard
him, it reeled and sank; a grateful blackness swallowed all his sense.
It was about that time Tiawa's father, hunting chuckwallas, found him
and led him to his camp.

In the interval before Gavin was quite himself again, Tiawa tended
him. When he rose in his delirium to go to record those claims, she
dropped her strong arms about him and eased him to the ground,
rocking him in her bosom. So long as he did not know her, her tenderness had scope and power. But Gavin was annoyed when, as soon
as he was able to travel, though not properly fit for it, he asked for a
guide and got Tiawa. By the usage of her people it was Tiawa's right,
because she loved him. She could do that—these gentle savages who
will not be seen walking abreast with their women grant them the
right to love unasked and unashamed. *They* have no place, let me tell
you, in the acceptance or rejection of a proffered love, for the snigger
of the sophisticated male. Tiawa was pretty—so slim and round of
limb, so smoothly brown and lustrous eyed! Gavin had no scruples,
you may be sure; he was merely in the grip of another mistress who
might or might not loose his bonds.

Well do I know the way of that tawny-throated one. If she but
turns toward our valley with her hot breath to blow back the winter's
rains, you hear the prophecy of that usurpation in the flat trumpeting
of the bucks that bell the does; there will be few young that season
in the lairs along Salt Creek, the quail will not mate; and this, mind
you, if she no more than turns toward us her fulgent, splendid smiling
for the three months between the piñon harvest and the time of ta-
boose. Judge, then, what she would do to man.

Said Tiawa's father, who knew something of white men, and had
looked between Gavin's eyes where the mark of the desert was set:
"My daughter, when you have brought him as far as the ploughed
lands, best you come home again."

Tiawa had put on her best bead necklace for the journey, and her
cheeks were smooth with vermilion earth. She did not mean to come
back. Tiawa told me this at Sacabuete, middle aged and fat, smiling
above the metate as she paused in her grinding, for she had married
a Paiute after Gavin left her, and made him very comfortable.

"But I did not know then," she said, "that a white man could take
service from such as we and not requite it. If I had done the half of
that for a Shoshone he would have loved me, for there were not two

sticks laid together on that journey that I had not the doing of it."

They made a dry camp the first night, and when Gavin from sheer weakness lay down along the sand, and Tiawa had brought him food, before the glow was gone from the top of Toquina, when the evening star was lit and the heaven was clear and tender, he turned his back on Tiawa and stretched himself to sleep. On her side of the fire, Tiawa, dry-eyed and hot with shame, lay and pondered the reasons for these things. He was white, therefore he could accept her service without regarding the love that prompted it, and sleep upon it compunctionless. In the morning he spoke to her kindly, and she hoped again, for her desire was toward him and the spring was in her blood; but the obsession of his errand was on Gavin's mind, and he did not know. The morning wind blew out the strands of her thick hair, and shaped her garments to her loveliest curves as she brushed against him in the trail; every turn of her soft throat and the glint of her lustrous eyes was of love, but the sun-glare was heavy in his eyes, and he did not see. At the end of the third day, being at the end of her woman's devices, Tiawa bethought her of the gods. When it was full dark, before the moon was up, she went a little aside from the camp and made a medicine of songs. She swung and swayed to the postures of desire, beat upon the full, young, aching breast, and sang to the gods for the satisfaction of her love. Her voice reached him heavy with world-old anguish of women.

"Aw, shut up, can't you!" said Gavin. "I want to go to sleep!"

The desert had him. He had come into it fearlessly and unguarded, and it struck home; but Tiawa, who did not know any better, thought only that she had lost. She took off her bead collar because it had failed her, and wiped the vermilion from her cheeks. Only service remained, and that flowed from her as naturally as the long wands of the creosote flowed upon the wind. By day she went before him in the trails, by night at nameless water-holes she cooked his food. She did not know the places on the map where Gavin wished to go. She had set out by her father's direction for the shortest cut to the Ploughed Lands, and as they neared her heart sank inwardly as she remembered her father's word. For the Ploughed Lands meant the end of her Indian world. It meant white people, towns, farms at least— things, the desire of which had hurried Gavin mindlessly along the trail, the comfortable, long-turned furrow in which his life ran wontedly, the Ploughed Lands where he had no need of her.

Out here toward Toquina in the stark cañons, in the thin-sown pastures, she knew the way of subsistence; there in the fat, well-watered fields, unless Gavin accepted her when they came to the Ploughed Lands, she must go back. It is only our pitiful civilization, you understand, that attempts to magnify the love of man by shaming its end. In her own country Tiawa could venture much, as she pitted herself against the wilderness, but in the end she lay all night with her face between her arms weeping tearlessly. About noon of the last day they sighted the planted fields. From a hill-crest looking down they saw the dark smears of green on the golden valley, and out beyond these the line of willows, the thin gleam of the irrigating ditch like a blade from which the foiled desert started back. The rest of that day's trudging was down and down. Tiawa went before, and Gavin, breathing more evenly in the cooled air, felt the grip of the desert loosen on him with the tension of a spring released. He perceived suddenly that the woman was lovely and young. She was not so round by now, for they had come a long way with scant rations; but by the mark of her service upon her, he was suddenly aware that she loved him.

"Give me that pack," said Gavin, "you've carried it long enough."

The intent was kind, but to the girl it was the intimation of dismissal; he had refused her love, and now he would not even have her service. His tongue was freed of the spell of the silent places, and he talked as they went, pointing out this ranch and that as they went down.

About sunset they came to the out-curve of the canal and the farthest corner of an alfalfa field, and made their camp there. For the last time Tiawa laid the sticks together under the cooking-pot. For the last time; so it seemed to Tiawa. Lights began to come out in the ranch houses, faint and far. Tiawa thought of the little fires by the huts in Toquina; tears in her heart welled and brimmed about her eyes. Just then Gavin called her. She turned, and by the faint stars, by the dying flicker of their fire, she saw incredibly that he smiled. And to such as Tiawa, you understand, the smile of a white man—a man with ruddy curls, broad in the shoulders and young—is as the favor of the gods.

"Tiawa?"

"Great One!" she whispered.

Still smiling, he stretched out his arm to her and hollowed it in invitation . . . for he had come to the Ploughed Lands. He was his own man again.

In the end—as I have already explained to you—Gavin went back to his own kind, and Tiawa married a Paiute and grew fat, for mostly in encounter with the primal forces woman gets the worst of it except now and then, when there are children in question, she becomes a primal force herself.

Great souls that go into the desert come out mystics—saints and prophets—declaring unutterable things: Buddha, Mahomet, and the Gallilean, convincing of the casual nature of human relations, because the desert itself has no use for the formal side of man's affairs. What need, then, of so much pawing over precedent and discoursing upon it, when the open country lies there, a sort of chemist's cup for resolving obligations? Say whether, when all decoration is eaten away, there remains any bond, and what you shall do about it.

# The Return
# of Mr. Wills

Mrs. Wills had lived seventeen years with Mr. Wills, and when he left her for three, those three were so much the best of her married life that she wished he had never come back. And the only real trouble with Mr. Wills was that he should never have moved West. Back East I suppose they breed such men because they need them, but they ought really to keep them there.

I am quite certain that when Mr. Wills was courting Mrs. Wills he parted his hair in the middle, and the breast-pocket of his best suit had a bright silk lining which Mr. Wills pulled up to simulate a silk handkerchief. Mrs. Wills had a certain draggled prettiness, and a way of tossing her head which came back to her after Mr. Wills left, which made you think she might have been the prettiest girl of her town. They were happy enough at first, when Mr. Wills was a grocery clerk, assistant Sunday-school superintendent, and they owned a cabinet organ and four little Willses. It might have been that Mr. Wills thought he could go right on being the same sort of a man in the West—he was clerk at the Bed Rock Emporium, and had brought the organ and the children; or it might have been at bottom he thought himself a very different sort of man, and meant to be it if he got a chance.

There is a sort of man bred up in close communities, like a cask, to whom the church, public opinion, the social note, are a sort of hoop to hold him in serviceable shape. Without these there are a good many ways of going to pieces. Mr. Wills' way was Lost Mines.

Being clerk at the Emporium, where miners and prospectors bought their supplies, he heard a lot of talk about mines, and was too new to it to understand that the man who has the most time to stop and talk about it has the least to do with mining. And of all he heard, the most fascinating to Mr. Wills, who was troubled with an imagination, was of the lost mines: incredibly rich ledges, touched and not found again. To go out into the unmapped hills on the mere chance of coming across something was, on the face of it, a risky business; but to look for a mine once located, sampled and proved, definitely situated in a particular mountain range or a certain cañon, had a smack of plausibility. Besides that, an ordinary prospect might or might not prove workable, but the lost mines were always amazingly rich. Of all the ways in the West for a man to go to pieces this is the most insidious. Out there beyond the towns the long Wilderness lies brooding, imperturbable; she puts out to adventurous minds glittering fragments of fortune or romance, like the lures men use to catch antelopes—clip! then she has them. If Mr. Wills had gambled or drank, his wife could have gone to the minister about it, his friends could have done something. There was a church in Maverick of twenty-seven members, and the Willses had brought letters to it, but except for the effect it had on Mrs. Wills, it would not be worth mentioning. Though he might never have found it out in the East, Mr. Wills belonged to the church, not because of what it meant to himself, but for what it meant to other people. Back East it had meant social standing, repute, moral impeccability. To other people in Maverick it meant a weakness which was excused in you so long as you did not talk about it. Mr. Wills did not, because there was so much else to talk about in connection with lost mines.

He began by grub-staking Pedro Ruiz to look for the Lost Ledge of Fisherman's Peak, and that was not so bad, for it had not been lost more than thirty years, the peak was not a hundred miles from Maverick, and, besides, I have a piece of the ore myself. Then he was bitten by the myth of the Gunsight, of which there was never anything more tangible than a dime's worth of virgin silver, picked up by a Jayhawker, hammered into a sight for a gun; and you had to take the gun on faith at that, for it and the man who owned it had quite disappeared; and afterward it was the Duke o' Wild Rose, which was never a mine at all, merely an arrow-mark on a map left by a penniless lodger found dead in a San Francisco hotel. Grub-staking is expensive, even to a clerk at the Bed Rock Emporium getting discounts on the grub, and grub-staked prospectors are about as dependable as the dreams they chase, often pure fakes, lying up at seldom-visited waterholes while the stake lasts, returning with wilder tales and clews more alluring. It was a late conviction that led Mr. Wills, when he put the last remnant of his means into the search for the White Cement mines, to resign his clerkship and go in charge of the expedition himself. There is no doubt whatever that there is a deposit of cement on Bald Mountain, with lumps of gold sticking out of it like plums in a pudding. It lies at the bottom of a small gulch near the middle fork of Owens

River, and is overlaid by pumice. There is a camp kit buried somewhere near, and two skeletons. There is also an Indian in that vicinity
who is thought to be able to point out the exact location—if he would.
It is quite the sort of thing to appeal to the imagination of Mr. Wills,
and he spent two years proving that he could not find it. After that
he drifted out toward the Lee district to look for Lost Cabin mine,
because a man who had immediate need of twenty dollars, had, for
that amount, offered Wills some exact and unpublished information as
to its location. By that time Wills' movements had ceased to interest
anybody in Maverick. He could be got to believe anything about any
sort of a prospect, providing it was lost.

The only visible mark left by all this was on Mrs. Wills. Everybody
in a mining-town, except the minister and professional gamblers who
wear frock-coats, dresses pretty much alike, and Wills very soon got
to wear in his face the guileless, trustful fixity of the confirmed prospector. It seemed as if the desert had overshot him and struck at Mrs.
Wills, and Richard Wills, Esther Wills, Benjy Wills, and the youngest
Wills, who was called Mugsey. Desertness attacked the door-yard and
the house; even the cabinet organ had a weathered look. During the
time of the White Cement obsession the Wills family appeared to be
in need of a grub-stake themselves. Mrs. Wills' eyes were like the
eyes of trail-weary cattle; her hands grew to have that pitiful way of
catching the front of her dress of the woman not so much a slattern
as hopeless. It was when her husband went out after Lost Cabin she
fell into the habit of sitting down to a cheap novel with the dishes
unwashed, a sort of drugging of despair common among women of the
camps. All this time Mr. Wills was drifting about from camp to camp
of the desert borders, working when it could not be avoided, but
mostly on long, fruitless trudges among the unmindful ranges. I do
not know if the man was honest with himself; if he knew by this time
that the clew of a lost mine was the baldest of excuses merely to be
out and away from everything that savored of definiteness and responsibility. The fact was, the desert had got him. All the hoops were
off the cask. The mind of Mr. Wills faded out at the edges like the
desert horizon that melts in mists and mirages, and finally he went on
an expedition from which he did not come back.

He had been gone nearly a year when Mrs. Wills gave up expecting
him. She had grown so used to the bedraggled crawl of life that she
might never have taken any notice of the disappearance of Mr. Wills
had not the Emporium refused to make any more charges in his name.
There had been a great many dry water-holes on the desert that year,
and more than the usual complement of sun-dried corpses. In a general
way this accounted for Mr. Wills, though nothing transpired of suffi-

cient definiteness to justify Mrs. Wills in putting on a widow's dress, and, anyway, she could not have afforded it.

Mrs. Wills and the children went to work, and work was about the only thing in Maverick of which there was more than enough. It was a matter of a very few months when Mrs. Wills made the remarkable discovery that after the family bills were paid at the end of the month, there was a little over. A very little. Mrs. Wills had lived so long with the tradition that a husband is a natural provider that it took some months longer to realize that she not only did not need Mr. Wills, but got on better without him. This was about the time she was able to have the sitting-room repapered and put up lace curtains. And the next spring the children planted roses in the front yard. All up and down the wash of Salt Creek there were lean coyote mothers, and wild folk of every sort could have taught her that nature never makes the mistake of neglecting to make the child-bearer competent to provide. But Mrs. Wills had not been studying life in the lairs. She had most of her notions of it from the church and her parents, and all under the new sense of independence and power she had an ache of forlornness and neglect. As a matter of fact she filled out, grew stronger, had a spring in her walk. She was not pining for Mr. Wills; the desert had him—for whatever conceivable use, it was more than Mrs. Wills could put him to—let the desert keep what it had got.

It was in the third summer that she regained a certain air that made me think she must have been pretty when Mr. Wills married her. And no woman in a mining-town can so much as hint at prettiness without its being found out. Mrs. Wills had a good many prejudices left over from the time when Mr. Wills had been superintendent of the Sunday-school, and would not hear of divorce. Yet, as the slovenliness of despair fell away from her, as she held up her head and began to have company to tea, it is certain somebody would have broached it to her before the summer was over; but by that time Mr. Wills came back.

It happened that Benjy Wills, who was fourteen and driving the Bed Rock delivery wagon, had a runaway accident in which he had behaved very handsomely and gotten a fractured skull. News of it went by way of the local paper to Tonopah, and from there drifted south to the Funeral Mountains and the particular prospect that Mr. Wills was working on a grub-stake. He had come to that. Perhaps as much because he had found there was nothing in it, as from paternal anxiety, he came home the evening of the day the doctor had declared the boy out of danger.

It was my turn to sit up that night, I remember, and Mrs. Meyer, who had the turn before, was telling me about the medicines. There was a neighbor woman who had come in by the back door with a bowl of custard, and the doctor standing in the sitting-room with Mrs. Wills, when Mr. Wills came in through the black block of the doorway with his hand before his face to ward off the light—and perhaps some shamefacedness—who knows?

I saw Mrs. Wills quiver, and her hand went up to her bosom as if some one had struck her. I have seen horses start and check like that as they came over the Pass and the hot blast of the desert took them fairly. It was the stroke of desolation. I remember turning quickly at the doctor's curt signal to shut the door between the sitting-room and Benjy.

"Don't let the boy see you to-night, Wills," said the doctor, with no hint of a greeting, "he's not to be excited." With that he got himself off as quickly as possible, and the neighbor woman and I went out and sat on the back steps a long time, and tried to talk about everything but Mr. Wills. When I went in, at last, he was sitting in the Morris chair, which had come with soap-wrappers, explaining to Mrs. Meyer about the rich prospect he had left to come to his darling boy. But he did not get so much as a glimpse of his darling boy while I was in charge.

Mr. Wills settled on his family like a blight. For a man who has prospected lost mines to that extent is positively not good for anything else. It was not only as if the desert had sucked the life out of him and cast him back, but as if it would have Mrs. Wills in his room. As the weeks went on you could see a sort of dinginess creeping up from her dress to her hair and her face, and it spread to the house and the doorway. Mr. Wills had enjoyed the improved condition of his home, though he missed the point of it; his wife's cooking tasted good to him after miner's fare, and he was proud of his boys. He didn't want any more of the desert. Not he. "There's no place like home," said Mr. Wills, or something to that effect.

But he had brought the desert with him on his back. If it had been at any other time than when her mind was torn with anxiety for Benjy, Mrs. Wills might have made a fight against it. But the only practical way to separate the family from the blight was to divorce Mr. Wills, and the church to which Mrs. Wills belonged admitted divorce only in the event of there being another woman.

Mrs. Wills rose to the pitch of threatening, I believe, about the time Mr. Wills insisted on his right to control the earnings of his sons. But the minister called; the church put out its hand upon her poor, staggered soul that sunk aback. The minister himself was newly from the East, and did not understand that the desert is to be dealt with as a woman and a wanton; he was thinking of it as a place on the map.

Therefore, he was not of the slightest use to Mrs. Wills, which did not prevent him from commanding her behavior. And the power of the wilderness lay like a wasting sickness on the home.

About that time Mrs. Wills took to novel-reading again; the eldest son drifted off up Tonopah way; and Benjy began to keep back a part of the wages he brought home. And Mr. Wills is beginning to collect misinformation about the exact locality where Peg-leg Smith is supposed to have found the sunburnt nuggets. He does not mention the matter often, being, as he says, done with mines; but whenever the Peg-leg comes up in talk I can see Mrs. Wills chirk up a little, her gaze wandering to the inscrutable grim spaces, not with the hate you might suppose, but with something like hope in her eye, as if she had guessed what I am certain of—that in time its insatiable spirit will reach out and take Mr. Wills again.

And this time, if I know Mrs. Wills, he will not come back.

# The Fakir

Whenever I come up to judgment, and am hard pushed to make good on my own account (as I expect to be), I shall mention the case of Netta Saybrick, for on the face of it, and by all the traditions in which I was bred, I behaved rather handsomely. I say on the face of it, for except in the matter of keeping my mouth shut afterward, I am not so sure I had anything to do with the affair. It was one of those incidents that from some crest of sheer inexplicableness seems about to direct the imagination over vast tracts of human experience, only to fall away into a pit of its own digging, all fouled with weed and sand. But, by keeping memory and attention fixed on its pellucid instant as it mounted against the sun, I can still see the Figure shining through it as I saw it that day at Posada, with the glimmering rails of the P. and S. running out behind it, thin lines of light toward the bar of Heaven.

Up till that time Netta Saybrick had never liked me, though I never laid it to any other account than Netta's being naturally a little fool; afterward she explained to me that it was because she thought I gave myself airs. The Saybricks lived in the third house from mine, around the corner, so that our back doors overlooked each other, and up till the coming of Doctor Challoner there had never been anything in Netta's conduct that the most censorious of the villagers could remark upon. Nor afterward, for that matter. The Saybricks had been married four years, and the baby was about two. He was not an interesting child to anybody but his mother, and even Netta was sometimes thought to be not quite absorbed in him.

Saybrick was a miner, one of the best drillers in our district, and consequently away from home much of the time. Their house was rather larger than their needs, and Netta, to avoid loneliness more than for profit, let out a room or two. That was the way she happened to fall into the hands of the Fakir.

Franklin Challoner had begun by being a brilliant and promising student of medicine. I had known him when his natural gifts prophesied the unusual, but I had known him rather better than most, and I was not surprised to have him turn up five years later at Maverick as a Fakir.

It had begun in his being poor, and having to work his way through the Medical College at the cost of endless pains and mortification to himself. Like most brilliant people, Challoner was sensitive and had an enormous egotism, and, what nearly always goes with it, the faculty of being horribly fascinating to women. It was thought very creditable of him to have put himself through college at his own charge, though in reality it proved a great social waste. I have a notion that the courage, endurance, and steadfastness which should have done Frank Challoner a lifetime was squeezed out of him by the stress of those overworked, starved, mortifying years. His egotism made it important to his happiness to keep the centre of any stage, and this he could do in school by sheer brilliance of scholarship and the distinction of his struggles. But afterward, when he had to establish himself without capital among strangers, he found himself impoverished of manliness. Always there was the compelling need of his temperament to stand well with people, and almost the only means of accomplishing it his poverty allowed was the dreadful facility with which he made himself master of women. I suppose this got his real ability discredited among his professional fellows. Between that and the sharp need of money, and the incredible appetite which people have for being fooled, somewhere in the Plateau of Fatigue between promise and accomplishment, Frank Challoner lost himself. Therefore, I was not surprised when he turned up finally at Maverick, lecturing on phrenology, and from the shape of their craniums advising country people of their proper careers at three dollars a sitting. He advertised to do various things in the way of medical practice that had a dubious sound.

It was court week when he came, and the only possible lodging to be found at Netta Saybrick's. Doctor Challoner took the two front rooms as being best suited to his clients and himself, and I believe he did very well. I was not particularly pleased to see him, on account of having known him before, not wishing to prosecute the acquaintance; and about that time Indian George brought me word that a variety of redivivus long sought was blooming that year on a certain clayey tract over toward Waban. It was not supposed to flower oftener than once in seven years, and I was five days finding it. That was why I never knew what went on at Mrs. Saybrick's. Nobody else did, apparently, for I never heard a breath of gossip, and *that* must have been Doctor Challoner's concern, for I am sure Netta would never have known how to avoid it.

Netta was pretty, and Saybrick had been gone five months. Challoner had a thin, romantic face, and eyes—even I had to admit the compelling attraction of his eyes; and his hands were fine and white. Saybrick's hands were cracked, broken-nailed, a driller's hands, and one of them was twisted from the time he was leaded, working on the Lucky Jim. If it came to that, though, Netta's husband might have been anything he pleased, and Challoner would still have had his way with her. He always did with women, as if to make up for not having it with the world. And the life at Maverick was deadly, appallingly dull. The stark houses, the rubbishy streets, the women who went about in them in calico wrappers, the draggling speech of the men, the wide, shadowless table-lands, the hard, bright skies, and the days all of one pattern, that went so stilly by that you only knew it was afternoon when you smelled the fried cabbage Mrs. Mulligan was cooking for supper.

At this distance I cannot say that I blamed Netta, am not sure of not being glad that she had her hour of the rose-red glow—*if* she had it. You are to bear in mind that all this time I was camping out in the creosote belt on the slope of Waban, and as to what had really happened neither Netta nor Challoner ever said a word. I keep saying things like this about Netta's being pretty and all, just as if I thought they had anything to do with it; truth is, the man had just a gift of taking souls, and I, even I, judicious and disapproving—but you shall hear.

At that time the stage from Maverick was a local affair going down to Posada, where passengers from the P. and S. booked for the Mojave line, returning after a wait of hours on the same day.

It happened that the morning I came back from Waban, Doctor Challoner left Maverick. Being saddle weary, I had planned to send on the horses by Indian George, and take the stage where it crossed my trail an hour out from Posada, going home on it in the afternoon. I remember poking the botany-case under the front seat and turning round to be hit straight between the eyes, as it were, by Netta Saybrick and Doctor Challoner. The doctor was wearing his usual air of romantic mystery; wearing it a little awry—or perhaps it was only knowing the man that made me read the perturbation under it. But it was plain to see what Netta was about. Her hat was tilted by the jolting of the stage, while alkali dust lay heavy on the folds of her dress, and she never *would* wear hair-pins enough; but there was that in every turn and posture, in every note of her flat, childish voice, that acknowledged the man beside her. Her excitement was almost febrile. It was part of Netta's unsophistication that she seemed not to know that she gave herself away, and the witness of it was that she had brought the baby.

You would not have believed that any woman would plan to run away with a man like Frank Challoner and take that great, heavy-headed, drooling child. But that is what Netta had done. I am not sure it was maternal instinct, either; she probably did not know what else to do with him. He had pale, protruding eyes and reddish hair, and every time he clawed at the doctor's sleeve I could see the man withhold a shudder.

I suppose it was my being in a manner confounded by this extraordinary situation that made it possible for Doctor Challoner to renew his acquaintance with more warmth than the facts allowed. He fairly pitched himself into an intimacy of reminiscence, and it was partly to pay him for this, I suppose, and partly to gratify a natural curiosity, that made me so abrupt with him afterward. I remember looking around, when we got down, at the little station where I must wait two hours for the return stage, at the seven unpainted pine cabins, at the eating-house, and the store, and the two saloons, in the instant hope of refuge, and then out across the alkali flat fringed with sparse, unwholesome pickle-weed, and deciding that that would not do, and then turning round to take the situation by the throat, as it were. There was Netta, with that great child dragging on her arm and her hat still on one side, with a silly consciousness of Doctor Challoner's movements, and he still trying for the jovial note of old acquaintances met by chance. In a moment more I had him around the corner of the station-house and out with my question.

"Doctor Challoner, are you running away with Netta Saybrick?"

"Well, no," trying to carry it jauntily; "I think she is running away with me." Then, all his pretension suddenly sagging on him like an empty cayaque: "On my soul, I don't know what's got into the woman. I was as surprised as you were when she got on the stage with me" —on my continuing to look steadily at him—"she was a pretty little thing . . . and the life is devilish dull there. . . . I suppose I flirted a little"—blowing himself out, as it were, with an assumption of honesty—"on my word, there was nothing more than that."

Flirted! He called it that; but women do not take their babies and run away from home for the sake of a little flirting. The life was devilish dull—did he need to tell me that! And she was pretty—well, whatever had happened he was bound to tell me that it was nothing, and I was bound to behave as if I believed him.

"She will go back," he began to say, looking bleak and drawn in the searching light. "She must go back! She must!"

"Well, maybe you can persuade her," said I; but I relented after that enough to take care of the baby while he and Netta went for a walk.

The whole mesa and the flat crawled with heat, and the steel rails ran on either side of them like thin tires, as if the slagged track were the appointed way that Netta had chosen to walk. They went out as far as the section-house and back toward the deserted station till I could almost read their faces clear, and turned again, back and forth through the heat-fogged atmosphere like the figures in a dream. I could see this much from their postures, that Challoner was trying to hold to some consistent attitude which he had adopted, and Netta wasn't understanding it. I could see her throw out her hands in a gesture of abandonment, and then I saw her stand as if the Pit yawned under her feet. The baby slept on a station bench, and I kept the flies from him with a branch of pickle-weed. I was out of it, smitten anew with the utter inutility of all the standards which were not bred of experience, but merely came down to me with the family teaspoons. Seen by the fierce desert light they looked like the spoons, thin and worn at the edges. I should have been ashamed to offer them to Netta Saybrick. It was this sense of detached helplessness toward the life at Maverick that Netta afterward explained she and the other women sensed but misread in me. They couldn't account for it on any grounds except that I felt myself above them. And all the time I was sick with the strained, meticulous inadequacy of my own soul. I understood well enough, then, that the sense of personal virtue comes to most women through an intervening medium of sedulous social guardianship. It is only when they love that it reaches directly to the centre of consciousness, as if it were ultimately nothing more than the instinctive movement of right love to preserve itself by a voluntary seclusion. It was not her faithlessness to Saybrick that tormented Netta out there between the burning rails; it was going back to him that was the intolerable offence. Passion had come upon her like a flame-burst, heaven-sent; she justified it on the grounds of its completeness, and lacked the sophistication for any other interpretation.

Challoner was a bad man, but he was not bad enough to reveal to Netta Saybrick the vulgar cheapness of his own relation to the incident. Besides, he hadn't time. In two hours the return stage for Maverick left the station, and he could never in that time get Netta Saybrick to realize the gulf between his situation and hers.

He came back to the station after a while on some pretext, and said, with his back to Netta, moving his lips with hardly any sound: "She must go back on the stage. She must!" Then with a sudden setting of his jaws, "You've got to help me." He sat down beside me, and began to devote himself to the baby and the flies.

Netta stood out for a while expecting him, and then came and sat provisionally on the edge of the station platform, ready at the slightest hint of an opportunity to carry him away into the glimmering heat out toward the station-house, and resume the supremacy of her poor charms.

She was resenting my presence as an interference, and I believe always cherished a thought that but for the accident of my being there the incident might have turned out differently. I could see that Challoner's attitude, whatever it was, was beginning to make itself felt. She was looking years older, and yet somehow pitifully puzzled and young, as if the self of her had had a wound which her intelligence had failed to grasp. I could see, too, that Challoner had made up his mind to be quit of her, quietly if he could, but at any risk of a scene, still to be quit. And it was forty minutes till stage-time.

Challoner sat on the bare station bench with his arm out above the baby protectingly—it was a manner always effective—and began to talk about "goodness," of all things in the world. Don't ask me what he said. It was the sort of talk many women would have called beautiful, and though it was mostly addressed to me, it was every word of it directed to Netta Saybrick's soul. Much of it went high and wide, but I could catch the pale reflection of it in her face like a miner guessing the sort of day it is from the glimmer of it on a puddle at the bottom of a shaft. In it Netta saw a pair of heroic figures renouncing a treasure they had found for the sake of the bitter goodness by which the world is saved. They had had the courage to take it while they could, but were much too exemplary to enjoy it at the cost of pain to any other heart. He started with the assumption that she meant to go back to Maverick, and recurred to it with a skilful and hypnotic insistence, painting upon her mind by large and general inference the picture of himself, helped greatly in his career by her noble renunciation of him. As a matter of fact, Saybrick, if his wife really had gone away with Doctor Challoner, would have followed him up and shot him, I suppose, and no end of vulgar and disagreeable things might have come from the affair; but Challoner managed to keep it on so high a plane that even I never thought of them until long afterward. And right here is where the uncertainty as to the part I really played begins. I can never make up my mind whether Challoner, from long practice in such affairs, had hit upon just the right

note of extrication, or whether, cornered, he fell back desperately on
the eternal rightness. And what was he, to know rightness at his
need?

He was terribly in earnest, holding Netta's eyes with his own; his
forehead sweated, hollows showed about his eyes, and the dreadful
slackness of the corner of the mouth that comes of the whole mind
being drawn away upon the object of attack to the neglect of its de-
fences. He was so bent on getting Netta fixed in the idea that she
must go back to Maverick that if she had not been a good deal of a
fool she must have seen that he had given away the whole situation
into my hands. I believed—I hope—I did the right thing, but I am
not sure I could have helped taking the cue which was pressed upon
me; he was as bad as they made them, but there I was lending my
whole soul to the accomplishment of his purpose, which was, briefly,
to get comfortably off from an occasion in which he had behaved very
badly.

All this time Challoner kept a conscious attention on the stage
stables far at the other end of the shadeless street. The moment he
saw the driver come out of it with the horses, the man's soul fairly
creaked with the release of tension. It released, too, an accession of
that power of personal fascination for which he was remarkable.

Netta sat with her back to the street, and the beautiful solicitude
with which he took up the baby at that moment, smoothed its dress
and tied on its little cap, had no significance for her. It was not until
she heard the rattle of the stage turning into the road that she stood
up suddenly, alarmed. Challoner put the baby into my arms.

Did I tell you that all this time between me and this man there
ran the inexplicable sense of being bonded together; the same suggestion of a superior and exclusive intimacy which ensnared poor
Netta Saybrick no doubt, the absolute call of self and sex by which a
man, past all reasonableness and belief, ranges a woman on his side.
He was a Fakir, a common quack, a scoundrel if you will, but there
was the call. I had answered it. I was under the impression, though
not remembering what he said, when he had handed me that great
lump of a child, that I had received a command to hold on to it, to get
into the stage with it, and not to give it up on any consideration; and
without saying anything, I had promised.

I do not know if it was the look that must have passed between
us at that, or the squeal of the running-gear that shattered her dream,
but I perceived on the instant that Netta had had a glimpse of where
she stood. She saw herself for the moment a fallen woman, forsaken,
despised. There was the Pit before her which Challoner's desertion
and my knowledge of it had digged. She clutched once at her bosom

and at her skirts as if already she heard the hiss of crawling shame. Then it was that Challoner turned toward her with the Look.

It rose in his face and streamed to her from his eyes as though it were the one thing in the world of a completeness equal to the anguish in her breast, as though, before it rested there, it had been through all the troubled intricacies of sin, and come upon the root of a superior fineness that every soul feels piteously to lie at the back of all its own affronting vagaries, brooding over it in a large, gentle way. It was the forgiveness—nay, the obliteration of offence—and the most Challoner could have known of forgiveness was his own great need of it. Out of that Look I could see the woman's soul rising rehabilitated, astonished, and on the instant, out there beyond the man and the woman, between the thin fiery lines of the rails, leading back to the horizon, the tall, robed Figure writing in the sand.

Oh, it was a hallucination, if you like, of the hour, the place, the perturbed mind, the dazzling glimmer of the alkali flat, of the incident of a sinful woman and a common fakir, faking an absolution that he might the more easily avoid an inconvenience, and I the tool made to see incredibly by some trick of suggestion how impossible it should be that any but the chief of sinners should understand forgiveness. But the Look continued to hold the moment in solution, while the woman climbed out of the Pit. I saw her put out her hand with the instinctive gesture of the sinking, and Challoner take it with the formality of farewell; and as the dust of the arriving stage billowed up between them, the Figure turned, fading, dissolving . . . but with the Look, consoling, obliterating. . . . He too . . . !

"It was very good of you, Mrs. Saybrick, to give me so much of a good-bye . . ." Challoner was saying as he put Netta into the stage; and then to me, "You must take good care of her . . . good-bye."

"Good-bye, Frank"—I had never called Doctor Challoner by his name before. I did not like him well enough to call him by it at any time, but there was the Look; it had reached out and enwrapped me in a kind of rarefied intimacy of extenuation and understanding. He stood on the station platform staring steadily after us, and as long as we had sight of him in the thick, bitter dust, the Look held.

If this were a story merely, or a story of Franklin Challoner, it would end there. He never thought of us again, you may depend, except to thank his stars for getting so lightly off, and to go on in the security of his success to other episodes from which he returned as scatheless.

But I found out in a very few days that whether it was to take rank as an incident or an event in Netta Saybrick's life depended on whether or not I said anything about it. Nobody had taken any notice of her day's ride to Posada. Saybrick came home in about ten days, and Netta seemed uncommonly glad to see him, as if in the preoccupation of his presence she found a solace for her fears.

But from the day of our return she had evinced an extraordinary liking for my company. She would be running in and out of the house at all hours, offering to help me with my sewing or to stir up a cake, kindly offices that had to be paid in kind; and if I slipped into the neighbors' on an errand, there a moment after would come Netta. Very soon it became clear to me that she was afraid of what I might tell. So long as she had me under her immediate eye she could be sure I was not taking away her character, but when I was not, she must have suffered horribly. I might have told, too, by the woman's code; she was really not respectable, and we made a great deal of that in Maverick. I might refuse to have anything to do with her and justified myself explaining why.

But Netta was not sure how much I knew, and could not risk betrayal by a plea. She had, too, the natural reticence of the villager, and though she must have been aching for news of Doctor Challoner, touch of him, the very sound of his name, she rarely ever mentioned it, but grew strained and thinner; watching, watching.

If that incident was known, Netta would have been ostracized and Saybrick might have divorced her. And I was going dumb with amazement to discover that nothing had come of it, nothing *could* come of it so long as I kept still. It was a deadly sin, as I had been taught, as I believed—of damnable potentiality; and as long as nobody told it was as if it had never been, as if that look of Challoner's had really the power as it had the seeming of absolving her from all soil and stain.

I cannot now remember if I was ever tempted to tell on Netta Saybrick, but I know with the obsession of that look upon my soul I never did. And in the mean time, from being so much in each other's company, Netta and I became very good friends. That was why, a little more than a year afterward, she chose to have me with her when her second child was born. In Maverick we did things for one another that in more sophisticated communities go to the service of paid attendants. That was the time when the suspicion that had lain at the bottom of Netta's shallow eyes whenever she looked at me went out of them forever.

It was along about midnight and the worst yet to come. I sat holding Netta's hands, and beyond in the room where the lamp was, the doctor lifted Saybrick through his stressful hour with cribbage and toddy. I could see the gleam of the light on Saybrick's red, hairy hands, a driller's hands, and whenever a sound came from the inner room, the uneasy lift of his shoulders and the twitching of his lip; then the doctor pushed the whiskey over toward him and jovially dealt the cards anew.

Netta, tossing on her pillow, came into range with Saybrick's blunt profile outlined against the cheaply papered wall, and I suppose her husband's distress was good to her to see. She looked at him a long time quietly.

"Henry's a good man," she said at last.

"Yes," I said; and then she turned to me narrowly with the expiring spark of anxious cunning in her eyes.

"And I've been a good wife to him," said she. It was half a challenge. And I, trapped by the hour, became a fakir in my turn, called instantly on all my soul and answered—with the Look—"Everybody knows that, Netta"—held on steadily until the spark went out. However I had done it I could not tell, but I saw the trouble go out of the woman's soul as the lids drooped, and with it out of my own heart the last of the virtuous resentment of the untempted. I had really forgiven her; how then was it possible for the sin to rise up and trouble her; more? Mind you, I grew up in a church that makes a great deal of the forgiveness of sins and signifies it by a tremendous particularity about behavior, and the most I had learned of the efficient exercise of forgiveness was from the worst man I had ever known.

About an hour before dawn, when a wind began to stir, and out on the mesa the coyotes howled returning from the hunt, stooping to tuck the baby in her arms, I felt Netta's lips brush against my hand.

"You've been mighty good to me," she said. Well—if I were pushed for it, I should think it worth mentioning—but I am not so sure.

# The Readjustment

Emma Jeffries had been dead and buried three days. The sister who had come to the funeral had taken Emma's child away with her, and the house was swept and aired; then, when it seemed there was least occasion for it, Emma came back. The neighbor woman who had nursed her was the first to know it. It was about seven of the evening in a mellow gloom: the neighbor woman was sitting on her own stoop with her arms wrapped in her apron, and all at once she found herself going along the street under an urgent sense that Emma needed her. She was half-way down the block before she recollected that this was impossible, for Mrs. Jeffries was dead and buried; but as soon as she came opposite the house she was aware of what had happened. It was all open to the summer air; except that it was a little neater, not otherwise than the rest of the street. It was quite dark; but the presence of Emma Jeffries streamed from it and betrayed it more than a candle. It streamed out steadily across the garden, and even as it reached her, mixed with the smell of the damp mignonette, the neighbor woman owned to herself that she had always known Emma would come back.

"A sight stranger if she wouldn't," thought the woman who had nursed her. "She wasn't ever one to throw off things easily."

Emma Jeffries had taken death as she had taken everything in life, hard. She had met it with the same bright, surface competency that she had presented to the squalor of the encompassing desertness, to the insuperable commonness of Sim Jeffries, to the affliction of her crippled child; and the intensity of her wordless struggle against it had caught the attention of the townspeople and held it in a shocked curious awe. She was so long a-dying, lying there in that little low house, hearing the abhorred footsteps going about her rooms and the vulgar procedure of the community encroach upon her like the advances of the sand wastes on an unwatered field. For Emma had always wanted things different, wanted them with a fury of intentness that implied offensiveness in things as they were. And the townspeople had taken offence, the more so because she was not to be surprised in any inaptitude for their own kind of success. Do what you could, you could never catch Emma Jeffries in a wrapper after three o'clock in the afternoon. And she would never talk about the child—in a country where so little ever happened that even trouble was a godsend if it gave you something to talk about. It was reported that she did not even talk to Sim. But there the common resentment got back at her. If she had thought to effect anything with Sim Jeffries against the benumbing spirit of the place, the evasive hopefulness, the large sense of leisure that ungirt the loins, if she still hoped somehow to get away with him to some place for which by her dress, by her manner, she seemed forever and unassailably fit, it was foregone that nothing would come of it. They knew Sim Jeffries better than that. Yet so vivid had been the force of her wordless dissatisfaction that when the fever took her and she went down like a pasteboard figure in the damp, the wonder was that nothing toppled with her. And, as if she too had felt herself indispensable, Emma Jeffries had come back.

The neighbor woman crossed the street, and as she passed the far corner of the garden, Jeffries spoke to her. He had been standing, she did not know how long a time, behind the syringa-bush, and moved even with her along the fence until they came to the gate. She could see in the dusk that before speaking he wet his lips with his tongue.

"She's in there," he said, at last.

"Emma?"

He nodded. "I been sleeping at the store since—but I thought I'd be more comfortable—as soon as I opened the door there she was."

"Did you see her?"

"No."

"How do you know, then?"

"Don't you know?"

The neighbor felt there was nothing to say to that.

"Come in," he whispered, huskily. They slipped by the rose-tree and the wistaria, and sat down on the porch at the side. A door swung inward behind them. They felt the Presence in the dusk beating like a pulse.

"What do you think she wants?" said Jeffries. "Do you reckon it's the boy?"

"Like enough."

"He's better off with his aunt. There was no one here to take care of him like his mother wanted." He raised his voice unconsciously with a note of justification, addressing the room behind.

"I am sending fifty dollars a month," he said; "he can go with the best of them."

He went on at length to explain all the advantage that was to come to the boy from living at Pasadena, and the neighbor woman bore him out in it.

"He was glad to do," urged Jeffries to the room. "He said it was what his mother would have wanted."

They were silent then a long time, while the Presence seemed to swell upon them and encroached upon the garden.

Finally, "I gave Ziegler the order for the monument yesterday," Jeffries threw out, appeasingly. "It's to cost three hundred and fifty."

The Presence stirred. The neighbor thought she could fairly see the controlled tolerance with which Emma Jeffries endured the evidence of Sim's ineptitudes.

They sat on helplessly without talking after that until the woman's husband came to the fence and called her.

"Don't go," begged Sim.

"Hush," she said. "Do you want all the town to know? You had naught but good from Emma living, and no call to expect harm from her now. It's natural she should come back—if—if she was lonesome like—in—the place where she's gone to."

"Emma wouldn't come back to this place," Jeffries protested, "without she wanted something."

"Well, then, you've got to find out," said the neighbor woman.

All the next day she saw, whenever she passed the house, that Emma was still there. It was shut and barred, but the Presence lurked behind the folded blinds and fumbled at the doors. When it was night and the moths began in the columbine under the windows, it went out and walked in the garden.

Jeffries was waiting at the gate when the neighbor woman came. He sweated with helplessness in the warm dusk, and the Presence brooded upon them like an apprehension that grows by being entertained.

"She wants something," he appealed, "but I can't make out what. Emma knows she is welcome to everything I've got. Everybody knows I've been a good provider."

The neighbor woman remembered suddenly the only time she had ever drawn close to Emma Jeffries touching the boy. They had sat up with it together all one night in some childish ailment, and she had ventured a question. "What does his father think?" And Emma had turned her a white, hard face of surpassing dreariness.

"I don't know," she admitted, "he never says."

"There's more than providing," suggested the neighbor woman.

"Yes. There's feeling . . . but she had enough to do to put up with me. I had no call to be troubling her with such." He left off to mop his forehead, and began again.

"Feelings!" he said, "there's times a man gets so wore out with feelings he doesn't have them any more."

He talked, and presently it grew clear to the woman that he was voiding all the stuff of his life, as if he had sickened on it and was now done. It was a little soul knowing itself and not good to see. What was singular was that the Presence left off walking in the garden, came and caught like a gossamer on the ivy-tree, swayed by the breath of his broken sentences. He talked, and the neighbor woman saw him for once as he saw himself and Emma, snared and floundering in an inexplicable unhappiness. He had been disappointed, too. She had never relished the man he was, and it made him ashamed. That was why he had never gone away, lest he should make her ashamed among her own kind. He was her husband, he could not help that though he was sorry for it. But he could keep the offence where least was made of it. And there was a child—she had wanted a child; but even then he had blundered—begotten a cripple upon her. He blamed himself utterly, searched out the roots of his youth for the answer to that, until the neighbor woman flinched to hear him. But the Presence stayed.

He had never talked to his wife about the child. How should he? There was the fact—the advertisement of his incompetence. And she had never talked to him. That was the one blessed and unassailable memory; that she had spread silence like a balm over his hurt. In return for it he had never gone away. He had resisted her that he might save her from showing among her own kind how poor a man he was. With every word of this ran the fact of his love for her—as he had loved her, with all the stripes of clean and uncleanness. He bared himself as a child without knowing; and the Presence stayed. The talk trailed off at last to the common places of consolation between the retchings of his spirit. The Presence lessened and streamed toward them on the wind of the garden. When it touched them like the warm air of noon that lies sometimes in hollow places after nightfall, the neighbor woman rose and went away.

The next night she did not wait for him. When a rod outside the town—it was a very little one—the burrowing owls *whoo-whooed*, she hung up her apron and went to talk with Emma Jeffries. The Presence was there, drawn in, lying close. She found the key between the wistaria and the first pillar of the porch, but as soon as she opened the door she felt the chill that might be expected by one intruding on Emma Jeffries in her own house.

" 'The Lord is my shepherd,' " said the neighbor woman; it was the first religious phrase that occurred to her; then she said the whole of the psalm and after that a hymn. She had come in through the door and stood with her back to it and her hand upon the knob. Everything was just as Mrs. Jeffries had left it, with the waiting air of a room kept for company.

"Em," she said, boldly, when the chill had abated a little before the sacred words. "Em Jeffries, I've got something to say to you. And you've got to hear," she added with firmness, as the white curtains stirred duskily at the window. "You wouldn't be talked to about your troubles when . . . you were here before; and we humored you. But now there is Sim to be thought of. I guess you heard what you came for last night, and got good of it. Maybe it would have been better if Sim had said things all along instead of hoarding them in his heart, but any way he has said them now. And what I want to say is, if you was staying on with the hope of hearing it again, you'd be making a mistake. You was an uncommon woman, Emma Jeffries, and there didn't none of us understand you very well, nor do you justice maybe; but Sim is only a common man, and I understand him because I'm that way myself. And if you think he'll be opening his heart to you every night, or be any different from what he's always been on account of what's happened, that's a mistake too . . . and in a little while, if you stay, it will be as bad as it always was . . . Men are like that. . . . You'd better go now while there's understanding between you." She stood staring into the darkling room that seemed suddenly full of turbulence and denial. It seemed to beat upon her and take her breath, but she held on.

"You've got to go . . . Em . . . and I'm going to stay until you do." She said this with finality, and then began again.

" 'The Lord is nigh unto them that are of a broken heart,' " and repeated the passage to the end. Then as the Presence sank before it, "You better go, Emma," persuasively, and again after an interval:

" 'He shall deliver thee in six troubles, yea, in seven shall no evil touch thee.' "

. . . The Presence gathered itself and was still. She could make out that it stood over against the opposite corner by the gilt easel with the crayon portrait of the child.

. . . " 'For thou shalt forget thy misery. Thou shalt remember it as waters that are past,' " concluded the neighbor woman, as she heard

Jeffries on the gravel outside. What the Presence had wrought upon him in the night was visible in his altered mien. He looked more than anything else to be in need of sleep. He had eaten his sorrow, and that was the end of it—as it is with men.

"I came to see if there was anything I could do for you," said the woman, neighborly, with her hand upon the door.

"I don't know as there is," said he; "I'm much obliged, but I don't know as there is."

"You see," whispered the woman over her shoulder, "not even to me." She felt the tug of her heart as the Presence swept past her.

The neighbor went out after that and walked in the ragged street, past the school-house, across the creek below the town, out by the fields, over the headgate, and back by the town again. It was full nine of the clock when she passed the Jeffries house. It looked, except for being a little neater, not other than the rest of the street. The door was open and the lamp was lit; she saw Jeffries, black against it. He sat reading in a book, like a man at ease in his own house.

# The House of Offence

It began to be called the House when it was the only frame building in the camp, and wore its offence upon its front—long and low, little rooms, each with its own door opening upon the shallow veranda. Such a house in a mining country is the dial finger of prosperity. All the ores thereabout were argent, and as the lords of far market-places made silver to go up a few points, you were aware of it in the silken rustle and the heel-click of satin slippers in the House. When the Jews got their heads together and whispered in the Bourse, the gay skirts would flit and the lights go out in the little rooms behind the two cottonwood-trees that should have screened their entrances, but clacking their leaves as if forever fluttered and aghast at what went on in them, betrayed it all the more.

Inmates came and went; sometimes they had names and personalities, but mostly they were simply the women of the House. It was always spoken of in that way, as if but to pass the door-sill were to be seized of its full inheritance of turbulence and shame; and as the town poised and hung upon the turn of the appointed fortune of mining-camps, the House passed from being an outburst, an excess, to a backwater pool of enticement, wherein men swam or sunk themselves, and at last, as the quality of its attractions fell off with the grade of ores, it became merely the overt sign of an admitted and ineradicable baseness.

Always it served to keep alive in the camp the consciousness of style and the allurement of finery; for when the House was at its best, the conditions in desert camps, the price freight was, scrub-water to be bought by the gallon, the prohibitive cost of service, ground terribly the faces of good women. But they could always tell what kind of sleeves were being worn in San Francisco by watching the House. They all watched it; women whose lean breasts sagged from the lips of many children, virtuous slattern in calico, petted wives secure in a traditional honor; and their comment kept a stir about it like the pattering trail of the wind in the cottonwoods. In time, as the spring of mining interest drew away from that district to flash and rise again in some unguessed other side of the world, even that fell off before the dead weight of stable interests and a respectability too stale to be curious; the ground about it was parcelled off; all the accustomed activities of small towns went on around it screened from its contamination by no more than a high board fence, from which in time the palings rotted away. Good women exercised themselves no more against it than to prevent their children from playing under the shade of the two cottonwoods that broadened before it, like the shadow of professional impropriety, behind which the House had shrunk, and, in its condition of unregarded sordidness, pointed the last turn of the dial.

About this time it came into the sole possession of Hard Mag, who was handsome enough to have done much better by herself, and concerning whom nothing worth recording might have transpired had it not been for Mrs. Henby.

The Henbys had taken the place which faced the adjacent street and abutted on the back yard of the House. Henby was blast foreman at the Eclipse, and came home every other Sunday; and his wife, who was very fond of him, found a consolation for the lack of his company in the ordered life of the town. To wash on Monday, iron on Tuesday, bake on Wednesday, and keep the front room always looking as if nobody lived in it, gave Mrs. Henby a virtuous sense of well-being that she had not known in twenty years of scrambled existence at the mines. The trouble with Mrs. Henby was that she had no children. If there had been small footsteps going about the rooms and small finger-clutchings at her dress she would have been perfectly happy, and consequently had no time to trouble about the doing of the House. There had been hopes—but at forty, though her cheeks were smooth and bright, her hair still black, and her figure looking as if it had been melted and poured into her neat print wrapper, Mrs. Henby did not hope any more. She made a silk crazy-quilt for the bed-lounge in the parlor, and began to take an interest in Hard Mag and the draggled birds of passage that preened themselves occasionally in the dismantled rooms of the House, though being the most virtuous of women she would never have admitted the faintest distraction in the affairs of "such like."

It began by Mrs. Henby discovering, through the cracks of the fence, that Mag, in the intervals of sinning, was largely occupied with the tasks of widowed and neglected women. Mrs. Henby cut kindlings

for herself sometimes if Henby was detained at the mine beyond his
week-end visits, but to see Mag of the hard, red lips, the bright, unglinting hair, and the burnt-out blackness of her eyes under the pale,
long lids, so employed made it of an amazing opprobriousness. For, as
Mrs. Henby understood it, the root of sin lay in self-indulgence, and
might be fostered by such small matters as sitting too much in rocking-chairs and wearing too becoming hats; she saw it now as the sign
of an essential incompetency in the offices of creditable living. Mag,
she perceived, did not even know how to pin up her skirts properly
when she swept the back stoop. To see her thus fumbling at the mech-
anism of existence was to put her forever beyond the reach of resentment into the region of pitiable humanness. In time it grew upon
Mrs. Henby that the poor creatures, who took the air of late after-
noons in the yard behind the House, might have possibilities even of
being interested in the crazy-quilt and the garden, and being prevented by some mysterious law of their profession from doing so. She
went so far upon this supposition as to offer Mag a bunch of radishes
out of her minute vegetable plot, which Mag, to her relief, refused.
Mrs. Henby could no more refrain from neighborliness than she could
help being large at the waist, but she really would not like to be seen
handing things through the fence to the inmates of the House. She
came to that in time, though.

Some wretched consort of Mag's fell sick at the House of the lead
poisoning common in the mines when the doctor was away at Maverick, and nobody in the neighborhood so skilled in the remedies
proper to the occasion as Mrs. Henby. This led to several conferences,
and the passage between the palings of sundry preparations of hot
milk and soups and custards. Mrs. Henby would hand them out after
nightfall, and find the dishes on her side of the fence in the morning.
She was so ashamed of it that she never told even her husband, and
the man having gone away to his own place and died there, Mag had
nobody to tell it to in any case. But Mrs. Henby always entertained
a subconscious sureness that something unpleasant was likely to come
of her condonings of iniquity, and one morning, when she came out of
the kitchen door to find Mag furtively waiting at the fence, she
roughed forward all the quills of her respectability at once. Mag leaned
her breast upon the point of a broken paling, as though the sharpness
of it stayed her. She had no right to the desultory courtesies of back-
fence neighborliness, and did not attempt them.

"I've had a letter," she said, abruptly, showing it clinched against
her side; the knuckles of her hand were strained and white.

"A letter?"

"From Kansas. My daughter's coming." She lowered her voice

and looked back cautiously at the shut House, as if the thing could overhear.

So she had a daughter—this painted piece; and God-fearing women might long and long! Twenty years' resentment began to burn in Mrs. Henby's cushiony bosom.

"What are you doin' with a daughter?" she said.

"Oh," cried Mag, impatiently. "I had her years ago—ten—eleven years! She has been living with my aunt in Kansas: and now my aunt is dead, and they are sending her."

"Who is sending her?"

"I don't know—the neighbors. I've nobody belonging to me back there. They have to do something with her, so they are sending her to me. Here!" She struck upon the paling wickedly with her hand.

"Where's her father?" Mrs. Henby's interest rose superior to her resentment.

"How should I know? I tell you it was a long time ago. I came away when she was a little, little baby. My aunt was religious and couldn't have anything to do with me, but she took care of—her! I sent money."

Mrs. Henby recalled herself to the aloofness of entire respectability. "If your aunt wouldn't have you, I don't see how she could feel to abide your money?"

"I told her I was married," said Mag, "and respectable." She leaned upon the paling and laughed a hard, sharp laugh.

Mrs. Henby gathered up her apron full of kindlings.

"Well, you've made your bed," she said. "I guess you will lie in it."

But she sat down trembling as soon as she had shut the door. A daughter—to that woman—and she—Mrs. Henby went about shaking her head and talking to herself with indignation. All day the House remained shut and slumbering, its patched and unwashed windows staring blankly on the yard; but if ever Mrs. Henby came out of her kitchen door, as if she were the cuckoo on the striking of the hour, Mag appeared from the House. It was evident she had ordered a clear field for herself, for no one came out in draggled finery to take the air that day. It was dusk before Mrs. Henby's humanness got the better of her. She went out to the woodpile and whispered to the stirring of Mag's dress:

"When's she coming?"

"Wednesday. She will be started before I can get a letter to her."

"Well, I reckon you'll have to take her," said Mrs. Henby, unconsolingly. A flash of Mag's insuperable hardness broke from her.

"She'll spoil trade," she said.

Mrs. Henby looked up the dusky bulk of the House beyond her, lines of light at the windows like the red lids of distempered eyes. All at once, and, as she said afterward, without for the moment any consciousness relativity, she recalled the quagmires of unwarned water-holes where cattle sink and flounder, and the choking call of warning that sounds to the last above the stifling slime. When Mag said that about the child and her way of making a living, Mrs. Henby jumped. She thought she heard the smothering suck of the mire. Somebody in the House laughed and cried out coarsely, and then she heard Mag's voice going on hurriedly behind the palings:

"Mrs. Henby! Mrs. Henby! you've got to help me—I must find some place for her to board— She has been well brought up, I tell you. My aunt is religious— She would be a comfort to some good person."

"Meaning me, I suppose," sniffed Mrs. Henby. Mag had not meant anybody in particular, but she swept it up urgently.

"Oh, if you would—she'd be a comfort to you! She's real sweet-looking—they sent me her picture once." She felt for phrases to touch the other woman, but they rang insincerely. "You'd be the saving of her—if you would."

"Well, I won't!" snapped Mrs. Henby; and as soon as she was inside she locked the door against even the suggestion. "Me to take anything off that painted piece!" she quivered, angrily.

It was five days until Wednesday, and Mag struck to her trail insistently.

"You been thinking of what I said last night?" she questioned in the morning interval at the woodpile.

Mrs. Henby denied it, but she had. She had thought of what Henby would say to it, and wondered if Mag's daughter had hard eyes, and bright, unglinting, canary-colored hair. She thought of what explanation she might make to the neighbors in case she decided suddenly to adopt the daughter of—of an old friend in Kansas; then she thought of the faces of the women who went in and out of the House, and resolved not to think any more.

She kept away from the woodpile as much as possible during Saturday and Sunday, but Monday evening she heard Mag calling her from the back of the yard. This was the worst yet, for there was no telling who might overhear.

"Mrs. Henby," demanded the painted piece, "are you going to see that innocent child brought to this place and never lift a hand to it?"

"I don't know as I got any call to interfere," said Mrs. Henby.

"And you with a good home, and calling yourself Christian, and all," went on the hard one. "Besides, I'd pay you."

"I don't feel to need any of your money," thrust in Mrs. Henby, resentfully. "I guess I could take care of one child without—but I ain't going to." She broke off, and moved rapidly toward the house.

"Mrs. Henby, listen to me!" cried Mag, shaking at the palings as though they had been the bars of a cage and she trapped in it. "For Gods' sake, Mrs. Henby, you must! Mrs. Henby, if you won't listen to me here, I shall come to your house."

Mrs. Henby heard the crack of the rotten palings as she shut the door.

"Mrs. Henby! Mrs. Henby!" threatened the voice, "I'm coming in!"

Then the crash of splintering wood, and Mag's hand on the knob. The vehemence of her mood, her tragic movements, the bright vividness of her lips and hair seemed to force Mrs. Henby into the attitude of the offender. She sat limply in a chair twisting her hands in her fat lap while the other assailed her. Behind her on the wall Mag's shadow shook and threatened like the shape of an uncouth destiny.

"I know what you are thinking, Mrs. Henby. You think there's bad blood, and she will turn out like me maybe, but I tell you it's no such thing. Look here—if it's any satisfaction to you to know—I was good when I had her, and her father was good—only we were young and didn't know any better—we hadn't any feelings except what we'd have had if we had been married—only we didn't happen to— It's the truth, Mrs. Henby, if I die for it. Bad blood!" she said, hardness augmenting upon her. "How many a man comes to the House and goes away to raise a family, and not a word said about bad blood! You don't reckon—"

But Mrs. Henby had her apron over her face, and was crying into it. Mag floundered back to the other woman's point of view.

"If it is a question what she'll come to, you know well enough if I have to take her with me. *Me!*" she said. She threw round herself an indescribable air of lascivious deviltry, as though she had been blown upon by the blast of an unseen furnace, and the shadow upon the wall shook and confirmed it. "That's what she will come to unless you save her from it. It's up to you, Mrs. Henby."

"I—I don't know what Henby will say," whimpered Mrs. Henby, afresh.

"Say?" urged Mag, with the scorn of her kind for the well-regulated husband. "He'll say anything he thinks you want him to say. He'll be as fond as anything of her—and you can bring her up to be a comfort to him." The poverty of Mag's experience furnished her with no phrases to express what a child might become.

"A nice time I'd have," burst out the other woman, in a last throb of resentment, "bringing her up to be a comfort to anybody, with her own mother living a sinful life right under her eyes."

"Oh," said Mag, with enlightenment, "so that's what is troubling you! Well—if you say the word—I'll clear out. The girls will kick—but they have to do what I say. Look here, then! If you'll take the kid—I'll go."

"And never come back—nor let her know?"

"Cross my heart to die," said Mag.

"Well, then"—Mrs. Henby let her apron fall tremulously—"I'll take her."

"For keeps?"

"For keeps," vowed Mrs. Henby, solemnly.

They were silent, regarding each other for a time, neither knowing how to terminate the interview without offence.

"What's her name?" asked Mrs. Henby, timidly, at last.

"Marietta."

Mag searched her scant remembrances and brought up this: "She's got dark hair."

Mrs. Henby was visibly comforted.

Mrs. Henby found, after all, that she was not put to any great strain of inventiveness to account for the little girl she had decided to adopt, the event being overshadowed, in the estimation of the townspeople, by the more memorable one which occurred on the very night of Marietta's arrival. This was no less than the departure of Hard Mag and the women of the House. They went out of it as they came, with scant warning, helped by coarse laughter of the creatures they had preyed upon, and with so much of careless haste that about two hours after their flitting—caught, it was supposed, from their neglected fires—the whole shell of the House burst into flame. It made a red flare in the windows in the middle of the night, but, as none of the townspeople had any interest in it and no property was endangered, it was allowed to burn quite out, which it did as quickly as the passions it had thrived upon, to an inconsiderable heap of cinders. The next year the Henbys took over the place where it had stood for a garden, and Henby made a swing under the cottonwood-trees for his adopted daughter.

# The Walking Woman

The first time of my hearing of her was at Temblor. We had come all one day between blunt, whitish bluffs rising from mirage water, with a thick, pale wake of dust billowing from the wheels, all the dead wall of the foothills sliding and shimmering with heat, to learn that the Walking Woman had passed us somewhere in the dizzying dimness, going down to the Tulares on her own feet. We heard of her again in the Carrisal, and again at Adobe Station, where she had passed a week before the shearing, and at last I had a glimpse of her at the Eighteen-Mile House as I went hurriedly northward on the Mojave stage; and afterward sheepherders at whose camps she slept, and cowboys at rodeos, told me as much of her way of life as they could understand. Like enough they told her as much of mine. That was very little. She was the Walking Woman, and no one knew her name, but because she was a sort of whom men speak respectfully, they called her to her face Mrs. Walker, and she answered to it if she was so inclined. She came and went about our western world on no discoverable errand, and whether she had some place of refuge where she lay by in the interim, or whether between her seldom, unaccountable appearances in our quarter she went on steadily walking, was never learned. She came and went, oftenest in a kind of muse of travel which the un-trammelled space begets, or at rare intervals flooding wondrously with talk, never of herself, but of things she had known and seen. She must have seen some rare happenings, too—by report. She was at Maverick the time of the Big Snow, and at Tres Piños when they brought home the body of Morena; and if anybody could have told whether De Borba killed Mariana for spite or defence, it would have been she, only she could not be found when most wanted. She was at Tunawai at the time of the cloud-burst, and if she had cared for it could have known most desirable things of the ways of trail-making, burrow-habiting small things.

All of which should have made her worth meeting, though it was not, in fact, for such things I was wishful to meet her; and as it turned out, it was not of these things we talked when at last we came together. For one thing, she was a woman, not old, who had gone about alone in a country where the number of women is as one in fifteen. She had eaten and slept at the herder's camps, and laid by for days at one-man stations whose masters had no other touch of human kind than the passing of chance prospectors, or the halting of the tri-weekly stage. She had been set on her way by teamsters who lifted her out of white, hot desertness and put her down at the crossing of unnamed ways, days distant from anywhere. And through all this she passed unarmed and unoffended. I had the best testimony to this, the witness of the men themselves. I think they talked of it because they were so much surprised at it. It was not, on the whole, what they expected of themselves.

Well I understand that nature which wastes its borders with too eager burning, beyond which rim of desolation it flares forever quick and white, and have had some inkling of the isolating calm of a desire too high to stoop to satisfaction. But you could not think of these things pertaining to the Walking Woman; and if there were ever any truth in the exemption from offence residing in a frame of behavior called ladylike, it should have been inoperative here. What this really means is that you get no affront so long as your behavior in the estimate of the particular audience invites none. In the estimate of the immediate audience—conduct which affords protection in Mayfair gets you no consideration in Maverick. And by no canon could it be considered ladylike to go about on your own feet, with a blanket and a black bag and almost no money in your purse, in and about the haunts of rude and solitary men.

There were other things that pointed the wish for a personal encounter with the Walking Woman. One of them was the contradiction of reports of her—as to whether she was comely, for example. Report said yes, and again, plain to the point of deformity. She had a twist to her face, some said; a hitch to one shoulder; they averred she limped as she walked. But by the distance she covered she should have been straight and young. As to sanity, equal incertitude. On the mere evidence of her way of life she was cracked; not quite broken, but unserviceable. Yet in her talk there was both wisdom and information, and the word she brought about trails and water-holes was as reliable as an Indian's.

By her own account she had begun by walking off an illness. There had been an invalid to be taken care of for years, leaving her at last broken in body, and with no recourse but her own feet to carry her out of that predicament. It seemed there had been, besides the death of her invalid, some other worrying affairs, upon which, and the nature of her illness, she was never quite clear, so that it might very well have been an unsoundness of mind which drove her to the open, sobered and healed at last by the large soundness of nature. It must have been about that time that she lost her name. I am convinced that she never told it because she did not know it herself. She was the Walking Woman, and the country people called her Mrs. Walker. At the time I knew her, though she wore short hair and a man's boots, and had a fine down over all her face from exposure to the weather, she was perfectly sweet and sane.

I had met her occasionally at ranch-houses and road-stations, and had got as much acquaintance as the place allowed; but for the things I wished to know there wanted a time of leisure and isolation. And when the occasion came we talked altogether of other things.

It was at Warm Spring in the Little Antelope I came upon her in the heart of a clear forenoon. The spring lies off a mile from the main trail, and has the only trees about it known in that country. First you come upon a pool of waste full of weeds of a poisonous dark green, every reed ringed about the water-level with a muddy white incrustation. Then the three oaks appear staggering on the slope, and the spring sobs and blubbers below them in ashy-colored mud. All the hills of that country have the down plunge toward the desert and back abruptly toward the Sierra. The grass is thick and brittle and bleached straw-color toward the end of the season. As I rode up the swale of the spring I saw the Walking Woman sitting where the grass was deepest, with her black bag and blanket, which she carried on a stick, beside her. It was one of those days when the genius of talk flows as smoothly as the rivers of mirage through the blue hot desert morning.

You are not to suppose that in my report of a Borderer I give you the words only, but the full meaning of the speech. Very often the words are merely the punctuation of thought; rather, the crests of the long waves of inter-communicative silences. Yet the speech of the Walking Woman was fuller than most.

The best of our talk that day began in some dropped word of hers from which I inferred that she had had a child. I was surprised at that, and then wondered why I should have been surprised, for it is the most natural of all experiences to have children. I said something of that purport, and also that it was one of the perquisites of living I should be least willing to do without. And that led to the Walking Woman saying that there were three things which if you had known you could cut out all the rest, and they were good any way you got them, but best if, as in her case, they were related to and grew each one out of the others. It was while she talked that I decided that she really did have a twist to her face, a sort of natural warp or skew into which it fell when it was worn merely as a countenance, but which disappeared the moment it became the vehicle of thought or feeling.

The first of the experiences the Walking Woman had found most worth while had come to her in a sand-storm on the south slope of Techachapi in a dateless spring. I judged it should have been about the time she began to find herself, after the period of worry and loss in which her wandering began. She had come, in a day pricked full of intimations of a storm, to the camp of Filon Geraud, whose companion shepherd had gone a three days' *pasear* to Mojave for supplies. Geraud was of great hardihood, red-blooded, of a full laughing eye, and an indubitable spark for women. It was the season of the year when there is a soft bloom on the days, but the nights are cowering cold and the lambs tender, not yet flockwise. At such times a sand-storm works incalculable disaster. The lift of the wind is so great that the whole surface of the ground appears to travel upon it slantwise, thinning out miles high in air. In the intolerable smother the lambs are lost from the ewes; neither dogs nor man make headway against it.

The morning flared through a horizon of yellow smudge, and by mid-forenoon the flock broke.

"There were but the two of us to deal with the trouble," said the Walking Woman. "Until that time I had not known how strong I was, nor how good it is to run when running is worth while. The flock travelled down the wind, the sand bit our faces; we called, and after a time heard the words broken and beaten small by the wind. But after a little we had not to call. All the time of our running in the yellow dusk of day and the black dark of night, I knew where Filon was. A flock-length away, I knew him. Feel? What should I feel? I knew. I ran with the flock and turned it this way and that as Filon would have.

"Such was the force of the wind that when we came together we held by one another and talked a little between pantings. We snatched and ate what we could as we ran. All that day and night until the next afternoon the camp kit was not out of the cayaques. But we held the flock. We herded them under a butte when the wind fell off a little, and the lambs sucked; when the storm rose they broke, but we kept upon their track and brought them together again. At night the wind quieted, and we slept by turns; at least Filon slept. I lay on the ground when my turn was and beat with the storm. I was no more tired than the earth was. The sand filled in the creases of the blanket, and where

I turned, dripped back upon the ground. But we saved the sheep. Some ewes there were that would not give down their milk because of the worry of the storm, and the lambs died. But we kept the flock together. And I was not tired."

The Walking Woman stretched out her arms and clasped herself, rocking in them as if she would have hugged the recollection to her breast.

"For you see," said she, "I worked with a man, without excusing, without any burden on me of looking or seeming. Not fiddling or fumbling as women work, and hoping it will all turn out for the best. It was not for Filon to ask, Can you, or Will you. He said, Do, and I did. And my work was good. We held the flock. And that," said the Walking Woman, the twist coming in her face again, "is one of the things that make you able to do without the others."

"Yes," I said; and then, "What others?"

"Oh," she said, as if it pricked her, "the looking and the seeming."

And I had not thought until that time that one who had the courage to be the Walking Woman would have cared! We sat and looked at the pattern of the thick crushed grass on the slope, wavering in the fierce noon like the waterings in the coat of a tranquil beast; the ache of a world-old bitterness sobbed and whispered in the spring. At last—

"It is by the looking and the seeming," said I, "that the opportunity finds you out."

"Filon found out," said the Walking Woman. She smiled; and went on from that to tell me how, when the wind went down about four o'clock and left the afternoon clear and tender, the flock began to feed, and they had out the kit from the cayaques, and cooked a meal. When it was over, and Filon had his pipe between his teeth, he came over from his side of the fire, of his own notion, and stretched himself on the ground beside her. Of his own notion. There was that in the way she said it that made it seem as if nothing of the sort had happened before to the Walking Woman, and for a moment I thought she was about to tell me one of the things I wished to know; but she went on to say what Filon had said to her of her work with the flock. Obvious, kindly things, such as any man in sheer decency would have said, so that there must have something more gone with the words to make them so treasured of the Walking Woman.

"We were very comfortable," said she, "and not so tired as we expected to be. Filon leaned up on his elbow. I had not noticed until then how broad he was in the shoulders, and how strong in the arms. And we had saved the flock together. We felt that. There was something that said together, in the slope of his shoulders toward me. It was around his mouth and on the cheek high up under the shine of his eyes. And under the shine the look—the look that said, 'We are of one sort and one mind'—his eyes that were the color of the flat water in the toulares—do you know the look?"

"I know it."

"The wind was stopped and all the earth smelled of dust, and Filon understood very well that what I had done with him I could not have done so well with another. And the look—the look in the eyes—"

"Ah-ah—!"

I have always said, I will say again, I do not know why at this point the Walking Woman touched me. If it were merely a response to my unconscious throb of sympathy, or the unpremeditated way of her heart to declare that this, after all, was the best of all indispensable experiences; or if in some flash of forward vision, encompassing the unimpassioned years, the stir, the movement of tenderness were for *me*—but no; as often as I have thought of it, I have thought of a different reason, but no conclusive one, why the Walking Woman should have put out her hand and laid it on my arm.

"To work together, to love together," said the Walking Woman, withdrawing her hand again; "there you have two of the things; the other you know."

"The mouth at the breast," said I.

"The lips and the hands," said the Walking Woman. "The little, pushing hands and the small cry." There ensued a pause of fullest understanding, while the land before us swam in the noon, and a dove in the oaks behind the spring began to call. A little red fox came out of the hills and lapped delicately at the pool.

"I stayed with Filon until the fall," said she. "All that summer in the Sierras, until it was time to turn south on the trail. It was a good time, and longer than he could be expected to have loved one like me. And besides, I was no longer able to keep the trail. My baby was born in October."

Whatever more there was to say to this, the Walking Woman's hand said it, straying with remembering gesture to her breast. There are so many ways of loving and working, but only one way of the first-born. She added after an interval, that she did not know if she would have given up her walking to keep at home and tend him, or whether the thought of her son's small feet running beside her in the trails would have driven her to the open again. The baby had not stayed long enough for that. "And whenever the wind blows in the night," said the Walking Woman, "I wake and wonder if he is well covered."

She took up her black bag and her blanket; there was the ranch-house of Dos Palos to be made before night, and she went as outliers do, without a hope expressed of another meeting and no word of good-bye. She was the Walking Woman. That was it. She had walked off all sense of society-made values, and, knowing the best when the best came to her, was able to take it. Work—as I believed; love—as the Walking Woman had proved it; a child—as you subscribe to it. But look you: it was the naked thing the Walking Woman grasped, not dressed and tricked out, for instance, by prejudices in favor of certain occupations; and love, man love, taken as it came, not picked over and rejected if it carried no obligation of permanency; and a child; *any* way you get it, a child is good to have, say nature and the Walking Woman; to have it and not to wait upon a proper concurrence of so many decorations that the event may not come at all.

At least one of us is wrong. To work and to love and to bear children. *That* sounds easy enough. But the way we live establishes so many things of much more importance.

Far down the dim, hot valley I could see the Walking Woman with her blanket and black bag over her shoulder. She had a queer, sidelong gait, as if in fact she had a twist all through her.

Recollecting suddenly that people called her lame, I ran down to the open place below the spring where she had passed. There in the bare, hot sand the track of her two feet bore evenly and white.